THE LOST VA

Algernon Blackwood s̖
around Switzerland. When he returned to England, he produced around twenty stories, most of which formed the basis for his next collection, *The Lost Valley*, published by Eveleigh Nash in June, 1910. Here are supernatural nature mysteries, ghost stories and visions galore—tales of loss and redemption, and the horror of the unknown—taking the reader from the stark terror of "The Wendigo" and "Old Clothes" to the light of hope in "Carlton's Drive" and the spiritual finale, "The Eccentricity of Simon Parnacute."

THE WOLVES OF GOD

By 1920, Blackwood had recovered from the depression of the First World War, and began writing again with a renewed zest, inspired to some degree by his explorer friend, Wilfrid Wilson, to whom he gave co-credit for the 1921 collection, *The Wolves of God*, though all the stories were by Blackwood. Many of these tales are wilderness stories, like the title story, "Running Wolf," "First Hate" and "The Valley of the Beasts."

But *The Wolves of God* also features some fine supernatural romance like "The Call" and "The Lane That Ran East and West;" ghostly retribution in "The Decoy;" mystery and murder in "Confession;" and the strange call of the past in "The Tarn of Sacrifice." These are strange stories of retribution and mystical intervention, of horror and hope—of the magic and mystery of life. In all, twenty-four stories by the master supernatural writer of the 20th century—Algernon Blackwood!

Algernon Blackwood List of Titles

NOVELS

Jimbo: A Fantasy (1909)
The Education of Uncle Paul (1909)
The Human Chord (1910)
The Centaur (1911)
A Prisoner in Fairyland (1913)
The Extra Day (1916)
Julius Le Vallon: An Episode (1916)
The Wave: An Egyptian Aftermath (1916)
The Promise of Air (1918)
The Garden of Survival (1918)
The Bright Messenger (1921)

ORIGINAL SHORT STORY COLLECTIONS

The Empty House and Other Ghost Stories (1906)
The Listener and Other Stories (1907)
John Silence — Physician Extraordinary (1908)
The Lost Valley and Other Stories (1910)
Pan's Garden: A Volume of Nature Stories (1912)
Incredible Adventures (1914)
Ten Minute Stories (1914)
Day and Night Stories (1917)
The Wolves of God and Other Fey Stories w/Wildred Wilson (1921)
Tongues of Fire and Other Sketches (1924)
Full Circle (1929) [single story]

Shocks (1935)
The Doll and One Other (1946)
The Mysterious House (1987) [single story]
The Magic Mirror: Lost Supernatural and Mystery Stories (1989)

CHILDREN'S BOOKS

Sambo and Snitch (1927)
Mr. Cupboard (1928)
Dudley and Gilderoy: A Nonsense (1929)
By Underground (1930)
The Parrot and the - Cat (1931)
The Italian Conjuror (1932)
Maria (of England) in the Rain (1933)
Sergeant Poppett and Policeman James (1934)
The Fruit Stoners (1934)
How the Circus Came to Tea (1936)
The Adventures of Dudley and Gilderoy (1941)

PLAYS

Karma: A Reincarnation Play w/Violet Pearn (1918)
Through the Crack w/Violet Pearn (1925)

AUTOBIOGRAPHY

Episodes Before Thirty (1923)

ALGERNON BLACKWOOD
THE LOST VALLEY
THE WOLVES OF GOD

**TWO STORY COLLECTIONS IN ONE
COMPLETE VOLUME BY THE MASTER
OF MAGIC AND MYSTERY**

INTRODUCTION BY SIMON CLARK

STARK HOUSE

Stark House Press • Eureka California

THE LOST VALLEY AND OTHER STORIES /
THE WOLVES OF GOD AND OTHER FEY STORIES

Published by Stark House Press
1315 H Street
Eureka, CA 95501, USA
griffinskye3@sbcglobal.net
www.starkhousepress.com

THE LOST VALLEY AND OTHER STORIES
Originally published in 1910 by Eveleigh Nash, London; and in 1914 by Vaughn &
Gomme, New York; copyright © 1910, 1914 by Algernon Blackwood

THE WOLVES OF GOD AND OTHER FEY STORIES
Originally published in 1921 by Cassell, London; and by Dutton, New York;
copyright © 1921 by Algernon Blackwood & Wilfred Wilson

"Algernon Blackwood, An Introduction to a Man of Starlight and Mystery"
copyright © 2003 by Simon Clark

ISBN: 1-933586-04-4
ISBN 13: 978-1-933586-04-5

Cover design and layout by Mark Shepard, www.SHEPGRAPHICS.COM
Cover art by Cynthia Bryn Williams
Proofread by Joanne Applen

Note: Rather than tamper with Blackwood's prose, we have kept in all cases to the
spelling from the original hardback edition.

First Stark House Press Edition: February 2006

REPRINT EDITION

CONTENTS

Algernon Blackwood

An Introduction to a Man of Starlight and Mystery

By Simon Clark

Good evening. My name is Simon Clark. Ever since the final decade of the last century I have earned my living writing novels of supernatural horror. Whether that makes me the prime candidate to introduce a collection of short stories by one of the undisputed masters of horror fiction I cannot say. But I can say this. I love Blackwood's work. It has the power to not only frighten me but mesmerize me.

Firstly, I think we have to make one single fact clear. And it's this: Algernon Blackwood believed his stories and novels were vehicles of a great Truth. He embedded his spiritual beliefs in tales of fantastic fiction in a way that not only entertained readers of popular literature but also educated them, too. And to take this a little further, he was a man on a mission: he intended to 'reconfigure' his reader's mind. He wouldn't have employed the same terminology, yet in many a Blackwood work, whether it's *The Centaur* or *The Lost Valley,* this extraordinary writer was downloading new software into his reader via the printed word. This isn't especially extraordinary these days. The makers of TV commercials and propagandists do it all the time. Jung understood the power of symbols, too. Only Blackwood was one of the best exponents. And the message he strove to impart was one of staggering power.

I don't know whether you're familiar with Algernon Blackwood? Whether you've seen any photographs of this enigmatic and gifted author? But just to sketch out my mental image of him: In adult life he was a great outdoors man, lean and tall, who loved canoeing remote rivers, climbing mountains, skiing, trekking through wilderness forests. A man of action. In my mind's eye, an archetypal gentleman with all the dash and poise of a James Bond. He was born March 14, 1869 into a prosperous family with blood links to nobility. The Blackwoods were strict in morals and religion. Certainly not the kind of family to nurture a dreamy visionary or endorse the counter-culture, proto-hippy life-style that Algernon Blackwood was going to pursue in adulthood.

However, his infant years may have sown some important seeds. The Blackwood home was the typical residence of a rich nineteenth century Englishman. Wood Lodge stood on the outskirts of London in thirty acres of land. Here was plenty of space for a young boy to roam freely in huge gardens, and space for his imagination to grow—'imagination of the winged sort' he might have added. As the son of a gentleman he was inevitably bound for the kind of school inhabited by the children of England's privileged elite. Only Blackwood's heart, it seems, pumped the blood of a rock and roll rebel. Expelled from at least one school, he moved through a succession of what he describes later as 'horrible private schools.' While his elder brothers followed the usual route to Cambridge University, his despairing parents sent their dreamy son, Algernon, to something spectacularly known as the School of the Moravian Brotherhood in Germany's Black Forest. This was an unusual step. The school was run by—some might add policed by—a strict evangelical sect of Protestants. It was a strange place with a regime of iron. Its pupils were forced to abandon their native tongue in favor of German. Bedtime was eight-thirty with an early morning start at five-thirty. Misdemeanors of a minor nature were punishable by reducing the pupil's food ration. This must be as obvious as the ribs sticking out of the young Algernon's chest that his father was determined to erase every trace of dreaminess and every suggestion of free-thought from his son's head.

If anything, this strict religious education in prison-like surroundings stimulated an in interest in Blackwood in the spiritual world, opening up the possibility in his mind that there might be spheres beyond this one. Although to the horror of his masters this would range far beyond the traditional Christian worldview. Blackwood became fascinated by ghosts and other supernatural beings, such as fairies. Rather than cute elfin forms he regarded fairies as emissaries of some all-pervading Cosmic Spirit. A 'spirit' that would manifest itself in many different forms in his future works.

OK. So Algernon Blackwood's in his late teens. He returns home to his parents from a school that appears part monastery, part prison. His father expects his son to stride through the door 'rid of all those fairy stories, and supernatural hocus pocus.' Young Blackwood, the daydreamer will have been crushed out of existence, to be replaced by a young man eager for a no-nonsense career in the military or civil service. Ahm, no.

You're wrong Blackwood senior. If anything, Algernon Blackwood is even more fired up by a sense of wonder; the natural world fills him with amazement; he devours books on folklore and legend. He's discovered the work, *Yoga Aphorisms*, by the Eastern Mystic, Patanjali. The book instructs: 'Mind attains peace when meditation produces extra ordinary sense perceptions... Thus mind masters everything from the smallest to the greatest.' This is the same vibe that prompted Jimi Hendrix to sing, 'Excuse me while I kiss the sky.' Words that transcend our perception of reality. Blackwood was hooked on Eastern philosophy, saying of his experience when reading the book, 'A deeper feeling than I had yet known woke in me.' The man had kissed the sky—and seen our world by the light of a different sun. There was nothing that Blackwood senior could do to halt his son's journey of discovery through those previously hidden doors of perception.

What Algernon's father did not long after could be seen as moving this burgeoning visionary (perhaps potential social embarrassment in the eyes of the family?) out of the country yet again. First to a little school run by a pastor in Switzerland to learn French, then onto Canada for a long vacation. In October 1888 Algernon was travelling again; this time to Edinburgh University to study Agriculture. This addition to Blackwood's education proved a failure. Eventually Blackwood senior would pay his son, still the esoteric dreamer, an allowance of £100 a year to start his adult life in Canada. This episode of Blackwood's life is vividly described in his autobiography *Adventures Before Thirty*. In short, however, a naïve Blackwood in his early twenties bought a dairy farm complete with cattle, quickly lost (or was defrauded) of all the money his father had given him, then fled to New York (possibly leaving many unpaid debts). Readers of *Adventures Before Thirty* might start to form the impression, that as well as recalling the man's early life, it also reads like an elaborate alibi. In the hurly-burly of nineteenth century New York the young Blackwood experiences many scrapes with the law, while 'naively' he makes the acquaintance of several criminals and winds up 'innocently' on the periphery of fraud, petty theft and insurance scams.

Vibrant, gritty, bustling New York, however, gives Algernon a first-rate education in reality. In 1899 he returns to Britain (or should that be, flees to Britain when the heat from the law gets too uncomfortable? You decide). With the adrenaline powered days of youth behind him he at last settles down to begin working seriously on fiction.

With the publication of his first collection *The Empty House and other Ghost Stories* in 1906 Blackwood appears to have decided to become a career writer. What's more, he intends to infuse his stories with his own beliefs developed on his travels and from reading a huge body of esoteric work. Space is limited here, so I'm taking the path that will lead to discussing his work rather than his life story. But what a life! Even though his writings earned him a healthy income he led a nomadic existence. Without a permanent address, and very little in the way of possessions, he traveled Europe and Egypt, with only a trunk containing a change or two of clothes, a portable typewriter and the manuscript of the current work in progress. He stayed at friends' houses, hotels or lodging houses. In those first decades of the twentieth century he also became a member of the Order of the Golden Dawn, created the psychic detective John Silence (that would lead some individuals to plead with Blackwood to rid their haunted houses of ghosts). He wrote a successful play, *The Starlight Express* that featured music by Elgar. During World War One he became a spy for Britain. Later he broadcast his stories live on both BBC Radio and the fledgling BBC TV service. These television appearances were universally popular and he became one of the most famous writers in the country. For more on the man, treat yourself to *Starlight Man: the extraordinary life of Algernon Blackwood* by Mike Ashley.

But what about the stories? Why are they so fascinating? Why do they endure? What makes publishers risk hard dollars to reprint ninety-year-old stories for a modern, sophisticated readership?

It's because the stories work on two levels. On the first, they can be read for pure entertainment. They are the work of a master of his craft who knows how to construct a story where character, plot and vivid descriptions of place carry the reader on a ride that is by turns uncanny, suspenseful, enchanting and sometimes downright frightening. Like Shirley Jackson, Algernon Blackwood employed subliminal techniques to turn an account of something as unthreatening as a visit to a country house, for example, into a dark, dark tale of suspense and foreboding, leaving the reader downright scared without knowing what scared them in the first place. On the second level, Blackwood's fiction enshrines his own belief in the existence of a cosmic 'spirit,' and hints to his readership that they, too, should seek keys that access the power of supernature. A power that manifests itself in the world of nature and deep in the mind of humankind. In these stories collected here, plus others of Blackwood's, you will encounter such phrases as the 'subliminal self' and 'higher ego'. At the same time as Blackwood began his own writing career Freud and Jung were developing their own theories about the unconscious mind. And if you wish to compare Blackwood's fiction with Jung's writings its easy to spot similarities. Even though the pair probably wouldn't have been familiar with each other's work—certainly not in the early days—they were basically in the same ballpark. Both men believed that beneath the conscious mind dwelt an eternal and wise personality, or personalities, in the human unconscious. Whereas Jung, however, identified what some might argue is God in the unconscious mind, Blackwood saw the signature of an omnipresent 'intelligence' in the entire world. A quotation he makes in *The Man Whom the Trees Loved* (not included here—but that's no excuse: seek it out!) neatly sums up much of his philosophy. In this story a man becomes fascinated by the trees near his house, suspecting they are far more significant than merely large plants or a source of timber. At one point he quotes Darwin's son, Francis, then president of the Royal Society, a body of distinguished scholars and scientists. The quotation runs: 'It is impossible to know whether or not plants are conscious; but it is consistent with the doctrine of continuity that in all living things there is something psychic, and if we accept this point of view *we must believe that in plants there exists a faint copy of what we know as consciousness in ourselves.*' Are the plants intelligent in Blackwood's view, or are they a conduit for a higher intelligence? Probably the latter. For near-perfect examples of supernature enshrined in nature check out *The Willows* together with the classic tale of horror included here, *The Wendigo:* a warning to those who disrespect the 'spirit' manifested in wilderness.

In many of these stories he deals with innocent people naively stumbling on a supernatural force that has invaded their world. Rarely, with the exception of John Silence, do Blackwood's characters go looking for psychical trouble. Moreover, many of his characters, though they might become victims of the supernatural, only suffer due to 'collateral damage' inflicted by the manifestation. That is, they were in the wrong place at the wrong time. If anything, Blackwood is at pains to emphasize the beneficial effect of understanding the relationship between the natural and supernatural—or should that be preternatural? Blackwood's personal quest was to introduce the public at large to the world beyond this one, and the 'spirit' that inhabits it and that from time to time manifests itself in ours. He's encouraging us to understand the 'spirit,' and to learn to interact with it. Do this and our lives will be enriched; we will no longer fear death, because a vital part of our *selves* is immortal. A philosophy I'm sure Jung would have agreed with, at least in part.

So, here I'm reaching the end of this introduction, convinced that you will enjoy Blackwood's artistry as a writer, and even though you might not embrace his deeply held beliefs, you can't but fail to appreciate the numinous power—that glint of something 'extra'—that gives this body of work an aura all of its own.

Ah, but did Blackwood's Faith enhance his own life? Well, he gained financial wealth, though he assiduously avoided owning property. He became famous. He enjoyed a life of adventure; of robust health and great physical fitness—he still enjoyed skiing and hill walking in old age. Mortality only caught up with him at the age of eighty-two, when he died, satisfied with his lot I believe, in 1951.

This volume, *The Lost Valley & Other Stories,* is a faithful reprint of the 1910 collection first published by Eveleigh Nash. As such, the stories are in the order that the publisher and Algernon Blackwood intended. My introduction has run its course now and there is little more than I can add. But if this is your first reading of Blackwood you are in for something closer to a revelation than a treat, although every page will be a joy to read. If you are re-visiting Blackwood you know the pleasure that lies ahead. So, as I draw this introduction to an end, I'm going to move onto the next page and enjoy, once more, *The Lost Valley.* Won't you join me?

Doncaster
England
June 19, 2003

The Lost Valley
and Other Stories
by Algernon Blackwood

TO
D–M–J
AND
THE OLD FRIENDS AT BÔLE
1887-1910

THE LOST VALLEY

I

M ARK and Stephen, twins, were remarkable even of their kind: they were not so much one soul split in twain, as two souls fashioned in precisely the same mould. Their characters were almost identical—tastes, hopes, fears, desires, everything. They even liked the same food, wore the same kind of hats, ties, suits; and, strongest link of all, of course disliked the same things too. At the age of thirty-five neither had married, for they invariably liked the same woman; and when a certain type of girl appeared upon their horizon they talked it over frankly, agreed it was impossible to separate, and together turned their backs upon her for a change of scene before she could endanger their peace.

For their love for one another was unbounded—irresistible as a force of nature, tender beyond words—and their one keen terror was that they might one day be separated.

To look at, even for twins, they were uncommonly alike. Even their eyes were similar: that grey-green of the sea that sometimes changes to blue, and at night becomes charged with shadows. And both faces were of the same strong type with aquiline noses, stern-lipped mouths, and jaws well marked. They possessed imagination, real imagination of the winged kind, and at the same time the fine controlling will without which such a gift is apt to prove a source of weakness. Their emotions, too, were real and living: not the sort that merely tickle the surface of the heart, but the sort that plough.

Both had private means, yet both had studied medicine because it interested them, Mark specializing in diseases of eye and ear, Stephen in mental and nervous cases; and they carried on a select, even distinguished, practice in the same house in Wimpole Street with their names on the brass plate thus Dr. Mark Winters, Dr. Stephen Winters.

In the summer of 1900 they went abroad together as usual for the months of July and August. It was their custom to explore successive ranges of mountains, collecting the folklore and natural history of the region into small volumes, neatly illustrated with Stephen's photographs. And this particular year they chose the Jura, that portion of it, rather, that lies between the Lac de Joux, Baulmes and Fleurier. For, obviously, they could not exhaust a whole range in a single brief holiday. They explored it in sections, year by year. And they invariably chose for their head-quarters quiet, unfashionable places where there was less danger of meeting attractive people who might break in upon the happiness of their profound brotherly devotion—the incalculable, mystical devotion of twins.

"For abroad, you know," Mark would say, "people have an insinuating way with them that is often hard to withstand. The chilly English reserve disappears. Acquaintanceship becomes intimacy before one has time to weigh it."

"Exactly," Stephen added. "The conventions that protect one at home suddenly wear thin, don't they? And one becomes soft and open to attack—unexpected attack."

They looked up and laughed, reading each other's thoughts like trained telepathists. What each meant was the dread that one should, after all, be taken and the other left—by a woman.

"Though at our age, you know, one is almost immune," Mark observed; while Stephen smiling agreed philosophically—

"Or *ought* to be."

"*Is*," quoth Mark decisively. For by common consent Mark played the *rôle* of the elder brother. His character, if anything, was a shade more practical. He was slightly more critical of life, perhaps, Stephen being ever more apt to accept without analysis, even without reflection. But Stephen had that richer heritage of dreams which comes from an imagination loved for its own sake.

II

In the peasant's châlet, where they had a sitting-room and two bedrooms, they were very comfortable. It stood on the edge of the forests that run along the slopes of Chasseront, on the side of Les Rasses farthest from Ste Croix. Marie Petavel provided them with the simple cooking they liked; and they spent their days walking, climbing, exploring, Mark collecting legend and folklore, Stephen making his natural history studies, with the little maps and surveys he drew so cleverly. Even this was only a division of labour, for each was equally interested in the occupation of the other; and they shared results in the long evenings, when expeditions brought them back in time, smoking in the rickety wooden balcony, comparing notes, shaping chapters, happy as two children. They brought the enthusiasm of boys to all they did, and they enjoyed the days apart almost as much as those they spent together. After separate expeditions each invariably returned with surprises which awakened the other's interest—even amazement.

Thus, the life of the foreign element in the hotels—unpicturesque in the daytime, noisy and overdressed at night—passed them by. The glimpses they caught as they passed these caravansarais, when gaieties were the order of the evening, made them value their peaceful retreat among the skirts of the forest. They brought no evening dress with them, not even "le smoking."

"The atmosphere of these huge hotels simply poisons the mountains," quoth Stephen. "All that 'haunted' feeling goes."

"Those people," agreed Mark, with scorn in his eyes, "would be far happier at Trouville or Dieppe, gambling, flirting, and the rest."

Feeling, thus, secure from that jealousy which lies so terribly close to the surface of all giant devotions where the entire life depends upon exclusive possession, the brothers regarded with indifference the signs of this gayer world about them. In that throng there was no one who could introduce an element of danger into their lives-no woman, at least, either of them could like would be found *there!*

For this thought must be emphasized, though not exaggerated. Certain incidents in the past, from which only their strength of will had made escape possible, proved the danger to be a real one. (Usually, too, it was some un-English woman: to wit, the Budapesth adventure, or the incident in London with the Greek girl who was first Mark's patient and then Stephen's.) Neither of them made definite reference to the danger, though undoubtedly it was present in their minds more or less vividly whenever they came to a new place: this singular dream that one day a woman would carry off one, and leave the other lonely. It was instinctive, probably, just as the dread of the wolf is instinctive in the deer. The curious fact, though natural enough, was that each brother feared for the other and not for himself. Had any one told Mark that some day he would marry, Mark would have shrugged his shoulders with a smile, and replied, "No; but I'm awfully afraid Stephen may!" And *vice versâ.*

III

Then, out of a clear sky, the bolt fell—upon Stephen. Catching him utterly unawares, it sent him fairly reeling. For Stephen, even more than his brother, possessed that glorious yet fatal gift, common to poets and children, by which out of a few insignificant details the soul builds for itself a whole sweet heaven to dwell in.

It was at the end of their first month, a month of unclouded happiness together. Since their exploration of the Abruzzi, two years before, they had never enjoyed anything so much. And not a soul had come to disturb their privacy. Plans were being mooted for moving their head-quarters some miles farther towards the Val de Travers and the Creux du Van;

only the day of departure, indeed, remained to be fixed, when Stephen, coming home from an afternoon of photography alone, saw, with bewildering and arresting suddenness—a Face. And with the effect of a blow full upon the heart it literally struck him.

How such a thing can come upon a strong man, a man of balanced mind, healthy in nerves and spirit, and in a single moment change his serenity into a state of feverish and passionate desire for possession, is a mystery that lies too deep for philosophy or science to explain. It turned him dizzy with a sudden and tempestuous delight—a veritable sickness of the soul, wondrous sweet as it was deadly. Rare enough, of course, such instances may be, but that they happen is undeniable.

He was making his way home in the dusk somewhat wearily. The sun had already dipped below the horizon of France behind him. Across the open country that stretched away to the distant mountains of the Rhone Valley, the moonlight climbed with wings of ghostly radiance that fanned their way into the clefts and pine-woods of the Jura all about him. Cool airs of night stirred and whispered; lights twinkled through the openings among the trees, and all was scented like a garden.

He must have strayed considerably from the right trail—path there was none—for instead of striking the mountain road that led straight to his châlet, he suddenly emerged into a pool of electric light that shone round one of the smaller wooden hotels by the borders of the forest. He recognized it at once, because he and his brother always avoided it deliberately. Not so gay or crowded as the larger caravansarais, it was nevertheless full of people of the kind they did not care about. Stephen was a good half-mile out of his way.

When the mind is empty and the body tired it would seem that the system is sensitive to impressions with an acuteness impossible when these are vigorously employed. The face of this girl, framed against the glass of the hotel verandah, rushed out towards him with a sudden invading glory, and took the most complete imaginable possession of this temporary unemployment of his spirit. Before he could think or act, accept or reject, it had lodged itself eternally at the very centre of his being. He stopped, as before an unexpected flash of lightning, caught his breath—and stared.

A little apart from the throng of "dressy" folk who sat there in the glitter of the electric light, this face of melancholy dark splendour rose close before his eyes, all soft and wondrous as though the beauty of the night—of forest, stars and moon-rise—had dropped down and focussed itself within the compass of a single human countenance. Framed within a corner pane of the big windows, peering sideways into the darkness, the vision of this girl, not twenty feet from where he stood, produced upon him a shock of the most convincing delight he had ever known. It was almost as though he saw someone who had dropped down among all these hotel people from another world. And from another world, in a sense, she undoubtedly was; for her face held in it nothing that belonged to the European countries he knew. She was of the East. The magic of other suns swept into his soul with the vision; the pageantry of other skies flashed brilliantly and was gone. Torches flamed in recesses of his being hitherto dark.

The incongruous surroundings unquestionably deepened the contrast to her advantage, but what made this first sight of her so extraordinarily arresting was the curious chance that where she sat the glare of the electric light did not touch her. She was in shadow from the shoulders downwards. Only, as she leaned backwards against the window, the face and neck turned slightly, there fell upon her exquisite Eastern features the soft glory of the rising moon. And comely she was in Stephen's eyes as nothing in his life had hitherto seemed comely. Apart from the vulgar throng as an exotic is apart from the weeds that choke its growth, this face seemed to swim towards him along the pathway of the slanting moonbeams. And, with it, came literally herself. Some released projection of his consciousness flew forth to meet her. The sense of nearness took his breath away with the faintness of too great happiness. She was in his arms, and his lips were buried in her scented hair. The sensation was vivid with pain and joy, as an ecstasy. And of the nature of true ecstasy, perhaps, it was: for he stood, it seemed, *outside himself.*

He remained there riveted in the patch of moonlight at the forest edge, for perhaps a whole minute, perhaps two, before he realized what had happened. Then came a second shock that was even more conquering than the first, for the girl, he saw, was not only gazing into his very face, she was also rising, as with an incipient gesture of recognition. As though she knew him, the little head bent itself forward gently, gracefully, and the dear eyes positively smiled.

The impetuous yearning that leaped full-fledged into his blood taught him in that instant the spiritual secret that pain and pleasure are fundamentally the same force. His attempt at self-control, made instinctively, was utterly overwhelmed. Something flashed to him from her eyes that melted the very roots of resolve; he staggered backwards, catching at the nearest tree for support, and in so doing left the patch of moonlight and stood concealed from view within the deep shadows behind.

Incredible as it must seem in these days of starved romance, this man of strength and firm character, who had hitherto known of such attacks only vicariously from the description of others, now reeled back against the trunk of a pine-tree, knowing all the sweet faintness of an overpowering love at first sight.

"For that, by God, I'd let myself waste utterly to death! To bring her an instant's happiness I'd suffer torture for a century—!"

For the words, with their clumsy, concentrated passion, were out before he realized what he was saying, what he was doing; but, once out, he knew how pitifully inadequate they were to express a tithe of what was in him like a rising storm. All words dropped away from him; the breath that came and went so quickly clothed no further speech.

With his retreat into the shadows the girl had sat down again, but she still gazed steadily at the place where he had stood. Stephen, who had lost the power of further movement, also stood and stared. The picture, meanwhile, was being traced with hot iron upon plastic deeps in his soul of which he had never before divined the existence. And, again, with the magic of this master-yearning, it seemed that he drew her out from that horde of hotel guests till she stood close before his eyes, warm, perfumed, caressing. The delicate, sharp splendour of her face, already dear beyond all else in life, flamed there within actual touch of his lips. He turned giddy with the joy, wonder and mystery of it all. The frontiers of his being melted—then extended to include her.

From the words a lover fights among to describe the face he worships one divines only a little of the picture; these dimly-coloured symbols conceal more beauty than they reveal. And of this dark, young oval face, first seen sideways in the moonlight, with drooping lids over the almond-shaped eyes, soft cloudy hair, all enwrapped with the haunting and penetrating mystery of love, Stephen never attempted to analyze the ineffable secret. He just accepted it with a plunge of utter self-abandonment. He only realized vaguely by way of detail that the little nose, without being Jewish, curved singularly down towards a chin daintily chiselled in firmness; that the mouth held in its lips the invitation of all womankind as expressed in another race, a race alien to his own-an Eastern race; and that something untamed, almost savage, in the face was corrected by the exquisite tenderness of the large dreamy, brown eyes. The mighty revolution of love spread its soft tide into every corner of his being.

Moreover, that gesture of welcome, so utterly unexpected yet so spontaneous (so natural, it seemed to him now!), the smile of recognition that had so deliciously perplexed him, he accepted in the same way. The girl had felt what he had felt, and had betrayed herself even as he had done by a sudden, uncontrollable movement of revelation and delight; and to explain it otherwise by any vulgar standard of worldly wisdom, would be to rob it of all its dear modesty, truth and wonder. She yearned to know him, even as he yearned to know her.

And all this in the little space, as men count time, of two minutes, even less.

How he was able at the moment to restrain all precipitate and impulsive action, Stephen has never properly understood. There was a fight, and it was short, painful and confused. But it ended on a note of triumphant joy—the rapture of happiness to come...

With a great effort he remembers that he found the use of his feet and continued his journey homewards, passing out once more into the moonlight. The girl in the verandah followed his disappearing figure with her turning head; she craned her neck to watch till he disappeared beyond the angle of vision; she even waved her little dark hand.

"I shall be late," ran the thought sharply through Stephen's mind. It was cold; vivid with keen pain. "Mark will wonder what in the world has become of me—!"

For, with swift and terrible reaction, the meaning of it all—the possible consequences of The Face—swept over his heart and drowned it in a flood of icy water. In estimating his brotherly love, even the love of the twin, he had never conceived such a thing as this-had never reckoned with the possibility of a force that could make all else in the world seem so trivial...

Mark, had he been there, with his more critical attitude to life, might have analyzed something of it away. But Mark was not there. And Stephen had—*seen*.

Those mighty strings of life upon which, as upon an instrument, the heart of man lies stretched had been set powerfully a-quiver. The new vibrations poured and beat through him. Something within him swiftly disintegrated; in its place something else grew marvellously. The Face had established dominion over the secret places of his soul; thence-forward the process was automatic and inevitable.

IV

Then, spectre-like and cold, the image of his brother rose before his inner vision. The profound brotherly love of the twin confronted him in the path.

He .tumbled among the roots and stones, searching for the means of self-control, but finding them with difficulty. Windows had opened everywhere in his soul; he looked out through them upon a new world, immense and gloriously coloured. Behind him in the shadows, as his vision searched and his heart sang, reared the single thought that hitherto had dominated his life: his love for Mark. It had already grown indisputably dim.

For both passions were genuine and commanding, the one built up through thirty-five years of devotion cemented by ten thousand associations and sacrifices, the other dropping out of heaven upon him with a suddenness simply appalling. And from the very first instant he understood that both could not live. One must die to feed the other...

On the staircase was the perfume of a strange tobacco, and, to his surprise and intense relief, when he entered the châlet he found that his brother for the first time was not alone. A small, dark man stood talking earnestly with him by the open window-the window where Mark had obviously been watching with anxiety for his arrival. Before introducing him to the stranger, Mark at once gave expression to his relief.

"I was beginning to be afraid something had happened to you," he said quietly enough, but in a way that the other understood. And after a moment's pause, in which he searched Stephen's face keenly, he added, "but we didn't wait supper as you see, and old Petavel has kept yours all hot and ready for you in the kitchen."

"I—er—lost my way," Stephen said quickly, glancing from Mark to the stranger, wondering vaguely who he was. "I got confused somehow in the dusk—"

Mark, remembering his manners now that his anxiety was set at rest, hastened to introduce him—a Professor in a Russian University, interested in folklore and legend, who had read their book on the Abruzzi and discovered quite by chance that they were neighbours here in the forest. He was staying in a little hotel at Les Rasses, and had ventured to come up and introduce himself. Stephen was far too occupied trying to conceal his new battling emotions to notice that Mark and the stranger seemed on quite familiar terms. He was so fearful lest the perturbations of his own heart should betray him that he had no power to detect anything subtle or unusual in anybody else.

"Professor Samarianz comes originally from Tiflis," Mark was explaining, "and has been telling me the most fascinating things about the legends and folklore of the Caucasus. We really must go there another year, Stephen... Mr. Samarianz most kindly has promised me letters to helpful people... He tells me, too, of a charming and exquisite legend of a 'Lost Valley' that exists hereabouts, where the spirits of all who die by their own hands, or otherwise suffer violent deaths, find perpetual peace—the peace denied them by all the religions, that is..."

Mark went on talking for some minutes while Stephen took off his knapsack and exchanged a few words with their visitor, who spoke excellent English. He was not quite sure what he said, but hoped he talked quietly and sensibly enough, in spite of the passions that waged war so terrifically in his breast. He noticed, however, that the man's face held an unusual charm, though he could not detect wherein its secret specifically lay. Presently, with excuses of hunger, he went into the kitchen for his supper, hugely relieved to find the opportunity to collect his thoughts a little; and when he returned twenty minutes later he found that his brother was alone. Professor Samarianz had taken his leave. In the room still lingered the perfume of his peculiarly flavoured cigarettes.

Mark, after listening with half an ear to his brother's description of the day, began pouring out his new interest; he was full of the Caucasus, and its folklore, and of the fortunate chance that had brought the stranger their way. The legend of the "Lost Valley" in the Jura, too, particularly interested him, and he spoke of his astonishment that he had hitherto come across no trace anywhere of the story.

"And fancy," he exclaimed, after a recital that lasted half-an-hour, "the man came up from one of those little hotels on the edge of the forest— that noisy one we have always been so careful to avoid. You never know where your luck hides, do you?" he added, with a laugh.

"You never do, indeed," replied Stephen quietly, now wholly master of himself, or, at least, of his voice and eyes.

And, to his secret satisfaction and delight, it was Mark who provided the excuses for staying on in the châlet, instead of moving further down the valley as they had intended. Besides, it would have been unnatural and absurd to leave without investigating so picturesque a legend as the "Lost Valley."

"We're uncommonly happy here," Mark added quietly; "why not stay on a bit?"

"Why not, indeed?" answered Stephen, trusting that the fearful inner storm instantly roused again by the prospect did not betray itself.

"You're not very keen, perhaps, old fellow?" suggested Mark gently.

"On the contrary—I am, *very,*" was the reply.

"Good. Then we'll stay."

The words were spoken after a pause of some seconds. Stephen, who was down at the end of the room sorting his specimens by the lamp, looked up sharply. Mark's face, where he sat on the window-ledge in the dusk, was hardly visible. It must have been something in his voice that had shot into Stephen's heart with a flash of sudden warning.

A sensation of cold passed swiftly over him and was gone. Had he already betrayed himself? Was the subtle, almost telepathic sympathy between the twins developed to such a point that emotions could be thus transferred with the minimum of word or gesture, within the very shades of their silence even? And another thought: Was there something different in Mark too—something in him also that had changed? Or was it merely his own raging, heaving passion, though so sternly repressed, that distorted his judgment and made him imaginative?

What stood so darkly in the room—between them?

A sudden and fearful pain seared him inwardly as he realized, practically, and with cruelly acute comprehension, that one of these two loves in his heart must inevitably die to feed the other; and that it might have to be—Mark. The complete meaning of it came home to him. And at the thought all his deep love of thirty years rose in a tide within him, flooding through the gates of life, seeking to overwhelm and merge in itself all obstacles that threatened to turn it aside. Unshed tears burned behind his eyes. He ached with a degree of actual, physical pain.

After a moment of savage self-control he turned and crossed the room; but before he had covered half the distance that separated him from the window where his brother sat smoking, the rush of burning words— were they to have been of confession, of self-reproach, or of renewed devotion?—swept away from him, so that he wholly forgot them. In their place came the ordinary dead phrases of convention. He hardly heard them himself, though his lips uttered them.

"Come along, Mark, old chap," he said, conscious that his voice trembled, and that another face slipped imperiously in front of the one his eyes looked upon; "it's time to go to bed. I'm dead tired like yourself."

"You are right," Mark replied, looking at him steadily as he turned towards the lamplight. "Besides, the night air's getting chilly—and we've been sitting in a draught, you know, all along."

For the first time in their lives the eyes of the two brothers could not quite find each other. Neither gaze hit precisely the middle of the other. It was as though a veil hung down between them and a deliberate act of focus was necessary. They looked one another straight in the face as usual, but with an effort—with momentary difficulty. The room, too, as Mark had said, was cold, and the lamp, exhausted of its oil, was beginning to smell. Both light and heat were going. It was certainly time for bed.

The brothers went out together, arm in arm, and the long shadows of the pines, thrown by the rising moon through the window, fell across the floor like arms that waved. And from the black branches outside, the wind caught up a shower of sighs and dropped them about the roofs and walls as they made their way to their bedrooms on opposite sides of the little corridor.

V

Four hours later, when the moon was high overhead and the room held but a single big shadow, the door opened softly and in came— Stephen. He was dressed. He crossed the floor stealthily, unfastened the windows, and let himself out upon the balcony. A minute afterwards he had disappeared into the forest beyond the strip of vegetable garden at the back of the châlet.

It was two o'clock in the morning, and no sleep had touched his eyes. For his heart burned, ached, and fought within him, and he felt the need of open spaces and the great forces of the night and mountains. No such battle had lie ever known before. He remembered his brother saying years ago, with a laugh half serious, half playful, "...for if ever one of us comes a cropper in love, old fellow, it will be time for the other to—go!" And by "go" they both understood the ultimate meaning of the word.

Through the glades of forest, sweet-scented by the night, he made his way till he reached the spot where that Face of soft splendour had first blessed his soul with its mysterious glory. There he sat down and, with his back against the very tree that had supported him a few hours ago, he drove his thoughts forward into battle with the whole strength of his will and character behind him. Very quietly, and with all the care, precision and steadiness of mind that he would have brought to bear upon a difficult "case" at Wimpole Street, he faced the situation and wrestled with it. The emotions during four hours' tossing upon a sleepless bed had worn themselves out a little. He was, in one sense of the word, calm, master of himself. The facts, with the huge issue that lay in their hands, he saw naked. And, as he thus saw them, he discerned how very, very far he had already travelled down the sweet path that led him towards the girl—and away from his brother.

Details about her, of course, he knew none; whether she was free even; for he only knew that he loved, and that his entire life was already breaking with the yearning to sacrifice itself for that love. That was the naked fact. The problem bludgeoned him. Could he do anything to hold back the flood still rising, to arrest its terrific flow? Could he divert its torrent, and take it, girl and all, to offer upon the altar of that other love—the devotion of the twin for its twin, the mysterious affinity that hitherto had ruled and directed all the currents of his soul?

There was no question of undoing what had already been done. Even if he never saw that face again, or heard the accents of those beloved lips; if he never was to know the magic of touch, the perfume of close thought, or the strange blessedness of telling her his burning message and hearing the murmur of her own—the fact of love was already accomplished between them. That was ineradicable. He had seen. The sensitive plate had received its undying picture.

For this was no foolish passion arising from the mere propinquity that causes so many of the world's misfit marriages. It was a profound and mystical union already accomplished, psychical in the utter sense, inevitable as the marriage of wind and fire. He almost heard his soul laugh as he thought of the revolution effected in an instant of time by the message of a single glance. What had science, or his own special department of science, to say to this tempest of force that invaded him, and swept with its beautiful terrors of wind and lightning the furthest recesses of his being? This whirlwind that so shook him, that so deliciously wounded him, that already made the thought of sacrificing his brother seem sweet—what was there to say to it, or do with it, or think of it?

Nothing, nothing, nothing!... He could only lie in its arms and rest, with that peace, deeper than all else in life, which the mystic knows when he is conscious that the everlasting arms are about him and that his union with the greatest force of the world is accomplished.

Yet Stephen struggled like a lion. His will rose up and opposed itself to the whole invasion...and in the end his will of steel, trained as all men of character train their wills against the difficulties of life, did actually produce a certain, definite result. This result was almost a *tour de force*, perhaps, yet it seemed valid. By its aid Stephen forced himself into a position he felt intuitively was an impossible one, but in which nevertheless he determined, by a deliberate act of almost incredible volition, that he would remain fixed. He decided to conquer his obsession, and to remain true to Mark...

The distant ridges of the dim blue Jura were tipped with the splendours of the coming dawn when at length he rose, chilly and exhausted, to retrace his steps to the châlet.

He realized fully the meaning of the resolve he had come to. And the knowledge of it froze something within him into a stiffness that was like the stiffness of death. The pain in his heart battling against the resolution was atrocious. He had estimated, or thought so, at least, the meaning of his sacrifice. As a matter of fact his decision was entirely artificial, of course, and his resolve dictated by a moral code rather than by the living forces that direct life and can alone make its changes permanent. Stephen had in him the stuff of the hero; and, having said that, one has said all that language can say.

On the way home in the cool white dawn, as he crossed the open spaces of meadow where the mist rose and the dew lay like rain, he suddenly thought of her lying dead—dead, that is, as he had thus decided she was to be dead—for him. And instantly, as by a word of command, the entire light went out of the landscape and out of the world. His soul turned wintry, and all the sweetness of his life went bleak. For it was the ancient soul in him that loved, and to deny it was to deny life itself. He had pronounced upon himself a sentence of death by starvation—a lingering and prolonged death accompanied by tortures of the most exquisite description. And along this path he really believed at the moment his little human will could hold him firm.

He made his way through the dew-drenched grass with the elation caused by so vast a sacrifice singing curiously in his blood. The splendour of the mountain sunrise and all the vital freshness of the dawn was in his heart. He was upon the châlet almost before he knew it, and there on the balcony, waiting to receive him, his grey dressing-gown wrapped about his ears in the sharp air, stood—Mark!

And, somehow or other, at the sight, all this false elation passed and dropped. Stephen looked up at him, standing suddenly still there in his tracks, as he might have looked up at his executioner. The picture had restored him most abruptly, with sharpest pain, to reality again.

"Like me, you couldn't sleep, eh?" Mark called softly, so as not to waken the peasants who slept on the ground floor.

"Have *you* been lying awake, too?" Stephen replied.

"All night. I haven't closed an eye." Then Mark added, as his brother came up the wooden steps towards him, "I knew you were awake; I felt it. I knew, too—you had gone out."

A silence passed between them. Both had spoken quietly, naturally, neither expressing surprise.

"Yes," Stephen said slowly at length; "we always reflect each other's pai—each other's moods—" He stopped abruptly, leaving the sentence unfinished.

Their eyes met as of old. Stephen knew an instant of quite freezing terror in which he felt that his brother had divined the truth. Then Mark took his arm and led the way indoors on tiptoe.

"Look here, Stevie, old fellow," he said, with extraordinary tenderness, "there's no good saying anything, but I know perfectly well that you're unhappy about something; and so, of course, I am unhappy too." He paused, as though searching for words. Under ordinary circumstances Stephen would have caught his precise thought, but now the tumult of suppressed emotion in him clouded his divining power. He felt his arm clutched in a sudden vice. They drew closer to one another. Neither spoke. Then Mark, low and hurriedly, said—he almost mumbled it—"It's all my fault *really*, all my fault—dear old boy!"

Stephen turned in amazement and stared. What in the world did his brother mean? What was he talking about? Before he could find speech, however, Mark continued, speaking distinctly now, and with evidences of strong emotion in his voice—

"I'll tell you what we'll do," he exclaimed, with sudden decision; "we'll go away; we'll leave! We've stayed here a bit too long, perhaps. Eh? What d'you say to that?"

Stephen did not notice how sharply Mark searched his face. At the thought of separation all his mighty resolution dropped like a house of cards. His entire life seemed to melt away and run in a stream of impetuous yearning towards the Face.

But he answered quietly, sustaining his purpose artificially by a force of will that seemed to break and twist his life at the source with extraordinary pain. He could not have endured the strain for more than a few seconds. His voice sounded strange and distant.

"All right; at the end of the week," he said—the faintness in him was dreadful, filling him with cold—"and that'll give us just three days to make our plans, won't it?"

Mark nodded his head. Both faces were lined and drawn like the faces of old men; only there was no one there to remark upon it—nor upon the fixed sternness that had dropped so suddenly upon their eyes and lips.

Arm in arm they entered the châlet and went to their bedrooms without another word. The sun, as they went, rose close over the tree-tops and dropped its first rays upon the spot where they had just stood.

VI

They came down in dressing-gowns to a very late breakfast. They were quiet, grave and slightly preoccupied. Neither made the least reference to their meeting at sunrise. New lines had graved themselves upon their faces, identical lines it seemed, drawing the mouth down at the corners with a touch of grimness where hitherto had been merely firmness.

And the eyes of both saw new things, new distances, new terrors. Something, feared till now only as a possibility, had come close, and stood at their elbows for the first time as an actuality. Sleep, in which changes offered to the soul during the day are confirmed and ratified, had established this new element in their personal equation. They had changed-if not towards one another, then towards something else.

But Stephen saw the matter only from his own point of view. For the first time in his memory he seemed to have lost the intuitive sympathy which enabled him to see things from his brother's point of view as well. The change, he felt positive, was in himself, not in Mark.

"He knows—he feels—something in me has altered dreadfully, but he doesn't yet understand what," his thoughts ran. "Pray to God he need never know—at least until I have utterly conquered it!"

For he still held with all the native tenacity of his strong will to the course he had so heroically chosen. The degree of self-deception his imagination brought into the contest seemed incredible when his mind looked back upon it all from the calmness of the end. But at the time he genuinely hoped, wished, intended to conquer, even *believed* that he would conquer.

Mark, he noticed, reacted in little ways that curiously betrayed his mental perturbation, and at any other time might have roused his brother's suspicions. He put sugar in Stephen's coffee, for instance; he forgot to bring him a cigarette when he went to the cupboard to get one for himself; he said and did numerous little things that were contrary to his habits, or to the habits of his twin.

In all of which, however, Stephen saw only the brotherly reaction to the change he was conscious of in himself. Nothing happened to convince him that anything in Mark had suffered revolution. With the mystical devotion peculiar to the twin he was too keenly aware of his own falling away to imagine the falling away of the other. He, Stephen, was the guilty one, and he suffered atrociously. Moreover, the pain of his renunciation was heightened by the sense that his ideal love for Mark had undergone a change—that he was making this fatal sacrifice, therefore, for something that perhaps no longer existed. This, however, he did not realize yet as an accomplished fact. Even if it were true, the resolution he had come to, acted by way of hypnotic suggestion to conceal it. At the same time it added enormously to the confusion and perplexity of his mind.

That day for the brothers was practically a *dies non*. They spent what was left of the morning over many aimless and unnecessary little duties, somewhat after the way of women. Although neither referred to the decision to leave at the end of the week, both acted upon it in desultory fashion, almost as though they wished to make a point of proving to one another that it was *not* forgotten—not wholly forgotten, at any rate. They made a brave pretence of collecting various things with a view to ultimate packing. No word was spoken, however, that bore more closely upon it than occasional phrases such as, "When the time comes to go"— "when we leave"—"better put *that* out, or it will be forgotten, you know."

The sentences dropped from their mouths alternately at long intervals, the only one deceived being the utterer. It was not unlike the pretence of schoolboys, only more elaborate and infinitely more clumsy and ill-done. Stephen, at any other time, would probably have laughed aloud. Yet the curious thing was that he noticed the pretence only in his own case. Mark, he thought, was genuine, though perhaps not too eager. "He's agreed to leave, the dear old chap, because he thinks I want it, and not for himself," he said. And the idea of the small brotherly sacrifice pleased, yet pained him horribly at the same time. For it tended to rehabilitate the old love which stood in the way of the new one.

He began, however, to take less trouble to sort and find his things for packing; he wrote letters, put out photographs to print in the sun, even studied his maps for expeditions, making occasional remarks thereon aloud which Mark did not negative. Presently, he forgot altogether about packing. Mark said nothing. Mark followed his example, however.

During the afternoon both lay down and slept, meeting again for tea at five. It was rare that they found themselves in for tea. Mark today made a special little ritual of it; he made it over their own spirit-lamp—almost tenderly, looking after his brother's wants like a woman. And the little meal was hardly over when a boy in hotel livery arrived with a note—an invitation from Professor Samarianz.

"He has looked up a lot of his papers," observed Mark carelessly as he tossed the note down, "and suggests my coming in for dinner, so that he can show me everything afterwards without hurry."

"I should accept," said Stephen. "It might be valuable for us if we go to the Caucasus later."

Mark hesitated a minute or two, telling the boy to wait in the kitchen. "I think I'll go in *after* dinner instead," he decided presently. There was a trace of eagerness in his manner which Stephen, however, did not notice.

"Take your note-book and pump the old boy dry," Stephen added, with a slight laugh. "I shall go to bed early myself probably." And Mark, stuffing the note into his pocket, laughed back and consented, to the other's great relief.

It was very late when Mark returned from the visit, but his brother did not hear him come, having taken a draught to ensure sleeping. And next morning Mark was so full of the interesting information, he had collected, and would continue to collect, that the question of leaving at the end of the week dropped of its own accord without further ado. Neither of the brothers made the least pretence of packing. Both wished and intended to stay on where they were.

"I shall look up Samarianz again this afternoon," Mark said casually during the morning, "and—if you've no objection—I might bring him back to supper. He's the most obliging fellow I've ever met, and crammed with information."

Stephen, signifying his agreement, took his camera, his specimen-tin and his geological hammer and went out with bread and chocolate in his knapsack for the rest of the afternoon by himself.

VII

Moreover, he not only set out bravely, but for many hours held true, keeping so rigid a control over his feelings that it seemed literally to cost him blood. All the time, however, a passionate yearning most craftily attacked him, and the very memory he strove to smother rose with a persistence that ridiculed repression. Like snowflakes, whose individual weight is inappreciable but their cumulative burden irresistible, the thoughts of *her* gathered behind his spirit, ready at a given moment to overwhelm; and it was on the way home again in the evening that the temptation came upon him like a tidal wave that made the mere idea of resistance seem utterly absurd.

He remembered wondering with a kind of wild delight whether it could be possible for any human will to withstand such a tempest of pressure as that which took him by the shoulders and literally pushed him out of his course towards the little hotel on the edge of the forest.

It was utterly inconsistent, of course, and he made no pretence of argument or excuse. He hardly knew, indeed, what he expected to see or do; his mind, at least, framed no definite idea. But far within him that deep heart which refused to be stifled cried out for a drop of the living water that was now its very life. And, chiefly, he wanted to *see*. If only he could see her once again-even from a distance—the merest glimpse—! With one more sight of her that should charge his memory to the brim for life he might face the future with more courage perhaps. Ah! that *perhaps!*... For she was drawing him with those million invisible cords of love that persuade a man he is acting of his own volition when actually he is but obeying the inevitable forces that bind the planets and the suns.

And this time there was no hurry; there was a good hour before Mark would expect him home for supper; he could sit among the shadows of the wood, and wait.

In his pocket were the field-glasses, and he realized with a sudden secret shame that it was not by accident that they were there. He stumbled, even before he got within a quarter of a mile of the place, for the idea that perhaps he would see her again made him ridiculously happy, and like a school-boy he positively trembled, tripping over roots and misjudging the distance of his steps. It was all part of a great whirling dream in which his soul sang and shouted the first delirious nonsense that came into his head. The possibility of his eyes again meeting hers produced a sensation of triumph and exultation that only one word describes—intoxication.

As he approached the opening in the trees whence the hotel was so easily visible, he went more slowly, moving even on tiptoe. It was instinctive; for he was nearing a place made holy by his love. Picking his way almost stealthily, he found the very tree; then leaned against it while his eyes searched eagerly for a sign of her in the glass verandah. The swiftness and accuracy of sight at such a time may be cause for wonder, but it is beyond question that in less than a single second he knew that the throng of moving figures did not contain the one he sought. She was not among them.

And he was just preparing to make himself comfortable for an extended watch when a sound or movement, perhaps both, somewhere among the trees on his right attracted his attention. There was a faint rustling; a twig snapped.

Stephen turned sharply. Under a big spruce, not half-a-dozen yards away, something moved—then rose up. At first, owing to the gloom, he took it for an animal of some kind, but the same second he saw that it was a human figure. It was *two* human figures, standing close together. Then one moved apart from the other; he saw the outline of a man against a space of sky between the trees. And a voice spoke—a voice charged with great tenderness, yet driven by high passion—

"But it's nothing, nothing! I shall not be gone two minutes. And to save you an instant's discomfort you know that I would run the whole circle of the earth! Wait here for me—!"

That was all; but the voice and figure caused Stephen's heart to stop beating as though it had been suddenly plunged into ice, for they were the voice and the figure of his brother Mark.

Quickly running down the slope towards the hotel, Mark disappeared.

The other figure, leaning against the tree, was the figure of a girl; and Stephen, even in that first instant of fearful bewilderment, understood why it was that the face of the man Samarianz had so charmed him. For this, of course, was his daughter. And then the whole thing flashed mercilessly clear upon his inner vision, and he knew that Mark, too, had been swept from his feet, and was undergoing the same fierce tortures, and fighting the same dread battle, as himself…

There seemed to be no conscious act of recognition. The fire that flamed through him and set his frozen heart so fearfully beating again, hammering against his ribs, left him apparently without volition or any power of cerebral action at all. *She* stood there, not half-a-dozen yards away from where he sat all huddled upon the ground, stood there in all her beauty, her mystery, her wonder, near enough for him to have taken her almost with a single leap into his arms;—stood there, veiled a little by the shadows of the dusk—waiting for the return of—Mark!

He remembers what happened with the blurred indistinctness common to moments of overwhelming passion. For in the next few seconds, that mocked all scale of time, he lived through a series of concentrated emotions that burned his brain too vividly for precise recollection. He rose to his feet unsteadily, his hand upon the rough bark of the tree. Absurd details only seem to remain of these few moments: that a foot was "asleep" with pins and needles up to the knee, and that his slouch hat fell from his head, filling him with fury because it hid her from him for the fraction of a second. These odd details he remembers.

And then, as though the driving-power of the universe had deliberately pushed him from behind, he was advancing slowly, with short, broken steps, towards the tree where the girl stood with her back half turned against him.

He did not know her name, had never heard her voice, had never even stood close enough to "feel" her atmosphere; yet, so deeply had his love and imagination already prepared the little paths of intimacy within him, that he felt he was moving towards someone whom he had known ever since he could remember, and who belonged to him as utterly as if from the beginning of time his possession of her had been absolute. Had they shared together a whole series of previous lives, the sensation could not have been more convincing and complete.

And out of all this whirlwind and tumult two small actions, he remembers, were delivered: a confused cry that was no definite word came from his lips, and—he opened his arms to take her to his heart. Whereupon, of course, she turned with a quick start, and became for the first time aware of his near presence.

"Oh, oh! But how so softly quick you return!" she cried falteringly, looking into his eyes with a smile both of welcome and alarm. "You a little frightened me, I tell you."

It was just the voice he had known would come, with the curiously slow, dragging tone of its broken English, the words lingering against the lips as if loath to leave, the soft warmth of their sound in the throat like a caress. The next instant he held her smothered in his arms, his face buried in the scented hair about her neck.

There was an unbelievable time of forgetfulness in which touch, perfume, and a healing power that emanated from her blessed the depths of his soul with a peace that calmed all pain, stilled all tumult—a moment in which Time itself for once stopped its remorseless journey, and the very processes of life stood still to watch. Then there was a frightened cry, and she had pushed him from her. She stood there, her soft eyes puzzled and surprised, looking hard at him; panting a little, her breast heaving.

And Stephen understood then, if he had not already understood before. The gesture of recognition in the hotel verandah two days ago, and this glorious realization of it that now seemed to have happened a century ago, shared a common origin. They were intended for another, and on both occasions the girl had taken him for his brother Mark.

And, turning sharply, almost falling with the abruptness of it all, as the girl's lips uttered that sudden cry, he saw close beside them the very person for whom they were intended. Mark had come up the slope behind them unobserved, carrying upon his arm the little red cloak he had been to fetch.

It was as though a wind of ice had struck him in the face. The revulsion of feeling with which Stephen saw the return of his brother passed rapidly into a state of numbness where all emotion whatsoever ebbed like the tides of death. He lost momentarily the power of realization. He forgot who he was, what he was doing there. He was dazed by the fact that Mark had so completely forestalled him. His life shook and tottered upon its foundations...

Then the face and figure of his brother swayed before his eyes like the branch of a tree, as an attack of passing dizziness seized him. It may have been a mere hazard that led his fingers to close, moist and clammy, upon the geological hammer at his belt. Certainly, he let it go again almost at once... And, when the tide of emotion returned upon him with the dreadful momentum it had gathered during the interval, the possibility of his yielding to wild impulse and doing something mad or criminal, was obviated by the swift enactment of an exceedingly poignant little drama that made both brothers forget themselves in their desire to save the girl.

In sweetest bewilderment, like a frightened little child or animal, the girl looked from one brother to the other. Her eyes shone in the dusk. Strangely appealing her loveliness was in that moment of seeking some explanation of the double vision. She made a movement first towards Mark—turned halfway in her steps and ran, startled, upon Stephen—then, with a sharp scream of fear, dropped in a heap to the ground midway between the two.

Her indecision of half-a-second, however, seemed to Stephen to have lasted many minutes. Had she fallen finally into the arms of his brother, he felt nothing on earth could have prevented his leaping upon him with the hands of a murderer. As it was—mercifully—the singular beauty of her little Eastern face, touched as it was by the white terror of her soul, momentarily arrested all other feeling in him. A shudder of fearful admiration passed through him as he saw her sway and fall. Thus might have dropped some soft angel from the skies...

It was Mark, however, with his usual decision, who brought some possibility of focus back to his mind; and he did it with an action and a sentence so utterly unexpected, so incongruous amid this whirlwind of passion, that had he seen it on the stage or read it in a novel, he must surely have burst out laughing. For, in that very second after the dear form swayed and fell, while the eyes of the brothers met across her in one swift look that held the possibilities of the direst results, Mark, his face abruptly clearing to calmness, stooped down beside the prostrate girl, and, looking up at Stephen steadily, said in a gentle voice, but with his most deliberate professional manner—

"Stephen, old fellow, this is—*my* patient. One of us, perhaps, had better—go."

He bent down to loosen the dress at the throat and chafe the cold hands, and Stephen, uncertain exactly what he did, and trembling like a child, turned and disappeared among the thick trees in the direction of their little house. For he understood only one thing clearly in that awful moment: that he must either kill—or not see. And his will, well-nigh breaking beneath the pressure, was just able to take the latter course.

"*Go!*" it said peremptorily.

And the little word sounded through the depths of his soul like the tolling of a last bell.

VIII

"*This is my patient!*" The dreadful comedy of the phrase, the grim mockery of the professional manner, the contrast between the words that someone *ought* to have uttered and the words Mark actually *had* uttered—all this had the effect of restoring Stephen to some measure of sanity. No one but his brother, he felt, could have said the thing so exactly calculated to relieve the choking passion of the situation. It was an inspiration—yet horrible in its bizarre mingling of true and false.

"But it's all like a thing in a dream," he heard an inner voice murmur as he stumbled homewards without once looking back; "the kind of thing people say and do in the rooms of strange sleep-houses. We are all surely in a dream, and presently I shall wake up—!"

The voice continued talking, but he did not listen. A web of confusion began to spin itself about his thoughts, and there stole over him an odd sensation of remoteness from the actual things of life. It was surely one of those vivid, haunting dreams he sometimes had when his spirit seemed to take part in real scenes, with real people, only far, far away, and on quite another scale of time and values.

"I shall find myself in my bed at Wimpole Street!" he exclaimed. He even tried to escape from the pain closing about him like a vice—tried to escape by waking up, only to find, of course, that the effort drove him more closely to the reality of his position.

Yet the texture of a dream certainly ran through the whole thing; the outlandish proportions of dream-events showed themselves everywhere; the tiny causes and prodigious effects: the terrific power of the Face upon his soul; the uncanny semi-quenching of his love for Mark; the ridiculous way he had come upon these two in the forest, with the nightmare discovery that they had known one another for days; and then the sight of that dear, magical face dropping through the dusky forest air between the two of them. Moreover-just when the dream ought to have ended with his sudden awakening, it had taken this abrupt and inconsequent turn, and Mark had uttered the language of-well, the impossible and rather horrible language of the nightmare world—

"This is my patient..."

Moreover, his face of ice as he said it; yet, at the same time, the wisdom, the gentleness of the decision that lay behind the words: the desire to relieve an impossibly painful situation. And then-the other words, meant kindly, even meant nobly, but charged for all that with the naked cruelty of life—

"One of us, perhaps, had better—go."

And he had gone—fortunately, he had gone...

Yet an hour later, after lying motionless upon his bed seeking with all his power for a course of action his will could follow and his mind approve, it was no dream-voice that called softly to him through the keyhole—

"Stevie, old fellow...she is well...she is all right now. She leaves in the morning with her father...the first thing...very early..."

And then, after a pause in which Stephen said nothing lest he should at the same time say all—

"...and it is best, perhaps...we should not see one another...you and I...for a bit. Let us go our ways...till tomorrow night. Then we shall be...alone together again...you and I...as of old..."

The voice of Mark did not tremble; but it sounded far away and unreal, almost like wind in the keyhole, thin, reedy, sighing; oddly broken and interrupted.

"...I'm yours, Stevie, old fellow, always yours," it added far down the corridor, more like the voice of dream again than ever.

But, though he made no reply at the moment, Stephen welcomed and approved both the proposal and the spirit in which it was made; and next day, soon after sunrise, he left the châlet very quietly and went off alone into the mountains with his thoughts, and with the pain that all night long had simply been eating him alive.

IX

It is impossible to know precisely what he felt all that morning in the mountains. His emotions charged like wild bulls to and fro. He seemed conscious only of two master-feelings: first, that his life now belonged beyond possibility of change or control—to another; yet, secondly, that his will, tried and tempered weapon of steel that it was, held firm.

Thus his powerful feelings flung him from one wall of his dreadful prison to another without possible means of escape. For his position involved a fundamental contradiction: the new love owned him, yet his will cried, "I love Mark; I hold true to that; in the end I shall conquer!" He refused, that is, to capitulate, or rather to acknowledge that he had capitulated. And meanwhile, even while he cried, his inmost soul listened, watched, and laughed, well content to abide the issue.

But if his feelings were in too great commotion for clear analysis, his thoughts, on the other hand, were painfully definite—some of them, at least; and, as the physical exercise lessened the assaults of emotion, these stood forth in sharp relief against the confusion of his inner world. It was now clear as the day, for instance, that Mark had been through a battle similar to his own. The chance meeting with the .Professor had led to the acquaintance with his daughter. Then, swiftly and inevitably, just as it would have happened to Stephen in his place, love had accomplished its full magic. And Mark had been afraid to tell him. The twins had travelled the same path, only personal feeling having clouded their usual intuition, neither had divined the truth.

Stephen saw it now with pitiless clarity: his brother's frequent visits to the hotel, omitting to mention that the notes of invitation probably also included himself; the desire, nay, the intention to stay on; the delay in packing—and a dozen other details stood out clearly. He remembered, too, with a pang how Mark had not slept that memorable night; he recalled their enigmatical conversation on the balcony as the sun rose...and all the rest of the miserable puzzle.

And, as he realized from his own torments what Mark must also have suffered—be suffering now—he was conscious of a strengthening of his will to conquer. The thought linked him fiercely again to his twin; for nothing in their lives had yet been separate, and the chain of their spiritual intimacy was of incalculably vast strength. They would win-win back to one another's side again. Mark would conquer her. He, Stephen, would also in the end conquer...her...!

But with the thought of her lying thus dead to him, and his life cold and empty without her, came the inevitable revulsion of feeling. It was the anarchy of love. The Face, the perfume, the rushing power of her melancholy dear eyes, with their singular touch of proud languor-in a word, all the amazing magic that had swept himself and Mark from their feet, tore back upon him with such an invasion of entreaty and command, that he sat down upon the very rocks where he was and buried his face in his hands, literally groaning with the pain of it. For the thought lacerated within. To give her up was a sheer impossibility;...to give up his brother was equally inconceivable. The weight of thirty-five years' love and associations thus gave battle against the telling blow of a single moment. Behind the first lay all that life had built into the woof of his personality hitherto, but *beyond* the second lay the potent magic, the huge seductive invitation of what he might become in the future—with her.

The contest, in the nature of the forces engaged, was an unequal one. Yet all that morning as he wandered aimlessly over ridge and summit, and across the high Jura pastures above the forests, meeting no single human being, he fought with himself as only men with innate energy of soul know how to fight—bitterly, savagely, blindly. He did not stop to realize that he was somewhat in the position of a fly that strives to push from its appointed course the planet on which it rides through space. For the tides of life itself bore him upon their crest, and at thirty-five these tides are at the full.

Thus, gradually it was, then, as the hopelessness of the struggle became more and more apparent, that the door of the only alternative opened slightly and let him peer through. Once ajar, however, it seemed the same second wide open; he was through; and it was closed—behind him.

For a different nature the alternative might have taken a different form. As has been seen, he was too strong a man to drift merely; a definite way out that could commend itself to a man of action had to be found; and, though the raw material of heroism may have been in him, he made no claim to a martyrdom that should last as long as life itself. And this alternative dawned upon him now as the grey light of a last morning must dawn upon the condemned prisoner: given Stephen, and given this particular problem, it was the only way out.

He envisaged it thus suddenly with a kind of ultimate calmness and determination that was characteristic of the man. And in every way it *was* characteristic of the man, for it involved the precise combination of courage and cowardice, weakness and strength, selfishness and sacrifice, that expressed the true resultant of all the forces at work in his soul. To him, at the moment of his rapid decision, however, it seemed that the dominant motive was the sacrifice to be offered upon the altar of his love for Mark. The twisted notion possessed him that in this way he might atone in some measure for the waning of his brotherly devotion. His love for the girl, her possible love for him—both were to be sacrificed to obtain the happiness—the eventual happiness—of these other two. Long, long ago Mark had himself said that under such circumstances one or other of them would have to—*go*. And the decision Stephen had come to was that the one to "go" was—himself.

This day among the woods and mountains should be his last on earth. By the evening of the following day Mark should be free.

"I'll give my life for him."

His face was grey and set as he said it. He stood on the high ridge, bathed by sun and wind. He looked over the fair world of wooded vales and mountains at his feet, but his eyes, turned inwards, saw only his brother-and that sweet Eastern face-then darkness.

"He will understand—and perforce accept it-and with time, yes, with time, the new happiness shall fill his soul utterly—and hers. It is for her, too, that I give it. It must-under these unparalleled circumstances be right...!"

And although there was no single cloud in the sky, the landscape at his feet suddenly went dark and sunless from one horizon to the other.

X

Then, having come into the gloom of this terrible decision, his imaginative nature at once bounded to the opposite extreme, and a kind of exaltation possessed him. The stereotyped verdict of a coroner's jury might in this instance have been true. The prolonged stress of emotion under which he had so long been labouring had at last produced a condition of mind that could only be considered—unsound.

A cool wind swept his face as he let his tired eyes wander over the leagues of silent forest below. The blue Jura with its myriad folded valleys lay about him like the waves of a giant sea ready to swallow up the little atom of his life within its deep heart of forgetfulness. Clear away into France he saw on the one side where, beyond the fortress of Pontarlier, white clouds sailed the horizon before a westerly wind; and, on the other, towards the white-robed Alps rising mistily through the haze of the autumn sunshine. Between these extreme distances lay all that world of a hundred intricate valleys, curiously winding, deeply wooded, little inhabited—a region of soft, confusing loveliness where a traveller might well lose himself for days together before he discovered a way out of so vast a maze.

And, as he gazed, there passed across his mind, like the dim memory of something heard in childhood, that legend of the "Lost Valley" in which the souls of the unhappy dead find the deep peace that is denied to them by all the religions—and to which hundreds, who have not yet the sad right of entry, seek to find the mournful forest gates. The memory was vivid, but swiftly engulfed by others and forgotten. They chased each other in rapid succession across his mind, as clouds at sunset pass before a high wind, merging on the horizon in a common mass.

Then, slowly, at length, he turned and made his way down the mountain-side in the direction of the French frontier for a last journey upon the sweet surface of the world he loved. In his soul was the one dominant feeling: this singular exaltation arising from the knowledge that in the long run his great sacrifice must ensure the happiness of the two beings he loved more than all else in life.

At the solitary farm where an hour later he had his lunch of bread and cheese and milk, he learned that he had wandered many miles out of the routes with which he was more or less familiar. He had been walking faster than he knew all these hours of battle. A physical weariness came upon him that made him conscious of every muscle in his body as he realized what a long road over mountain and valley he had to retrace. But, with the heaviness of fatigue, ran still that sense of interior spiritual exaltation. Something in him walked on air with springs of steel—something that was independent of the dragging limbs and the aching back. For the rest, his sensations seemed numb. His great Decision stood black before him, blocking the way. Thoughts and feelings forsook him as rats leave a sinking ship. The time for these was past. Two overmastering desires, however, clung fast: one, to see Mark again, and be with him; the other, to be once more—with her. These two desires left no room for others. With the former, indeed, it was almost as though Mark had called aloud to him by name.

He stood a moment where the depth of the valley he had to thread lay like a twisting shadow at his feet; it, ran, soft and dim, through the slanting sunshine. From the whole surface of the woods rose a single murmur; like the whirring of voices heard in a dream, he thought. The individual purring of separate trees was merged. Peace, most ancient and profound, lay in it, and its hushed whisper soothed his spirit.

He hurried his pace a little. The cool wind that had swept his face on the heights earlier in the afternoon followed him down, urging him forwards with deliberate pressure, as though a thousand soft hands were laid upon his back. And there were spirits in the wind that day. He heard their voices; and far below he traced by the motion of the tree-tops where they coiled upwards to him through miles of forest. His way, meanwhile, dived down through dense growths of spruce and pine into

a region unfamiliar. There was an aspect of the scenery that almost suggested it was unknown—an undiscovered corner of the world. The
countless signs that mark the passage of humanity were absent, or at
least did not obtrude themselves upon him. Something remote from life,
alien, at any rate, to the normal life he had hitherto known, began to
steal gently over his burdened soul...

In this way, perhaps, the effect of his dreadful Decision already showed
its influence upon his mind and senses. So very soon now he would
be—*going!*

The sadness of autumn lay all about him, and the loneliness of this
secluded vale spoke to him of the melancholy of things that die-of vanished springs, of summers unfulfilled, of things for ever incomplete and
unsatisfying. Human effort, he felt, this valley had never known. No
hoofs had ever pressed the mossy turf of these forest clearings; no traffic
of peasants or woodsmen won echoes from these limestone cliffs. All
was hushed, lonely, deserted.

And yet—? The depths to which it apparently plunged astonished him
more and more. Nowhere more than a half-mile across, each turn of the
shadowy trail revealed new distances below. With spots of a haunting,
fairy loveliness too: for here and there, on isolated patches of lawn-like
grass, stood wild lilac bushes, rounded by the wind; willows from the
swampy banks of the stream waved pale hands; firs, dark and erect,
guarded their eternal secrets on the heights. In one little opening, standing all by itself, he found a lime-tree; while beyond it, shining among the
pines, was a group of shimmering beeches. And, although there was no
wild life, there were flowers; he saw clumps of them—tall, graceful, blue
flowers whose name he did not know, nodding in dream across the
foaming water of the little torrent.

And his thoughts ran incessantly to Mark. Never before had he been
conscious of so imperious a desire to see him, to hear his voice, to stand
at his side. At moments it almost obliterated that other great desire...
Again he increased his pace. And the path plunged more and more deeply
into the heart of the mountains, sinking ever into deeper silence, ever
into an atmosphere of deeper peace. For no sound could reach him here
without first passing along great distances that were cushioned with soft
wind, and padded, as it were, with a million feathery pine-tops. A sense
of peace that was beyond reach of all possible disturbance began to cover
his breaking life with a garment as of softest shadows. Never before had
he experienced anything approaching the wonder and completeness of
it. It was a peace, still as the depths of the sea which are motionless
because they *cannot* move—cannot even tremble. It was a peace
unchangeable—what some have called, perhaps, the Peace of God...

"Soon the turn *must* come," he thought, yet without a trace of impatience or alarm, "and the road wind upwards again to cross the last ridge!" But he cared little enough; for this enveloping peace drowned him, hiding even the fear of death.

And still the road sank downwards into the sleep-laden atmosphere of the crowding trees, and with it his thoughts, oddly enough, sank deeper and deeper into dim recesses of his own being. As though a secret sympathy lay between the path that dived and the thoughts that plunged. Only, from time to time, the thought of his brother Mark brought him back to the surface with a violent rush. Dreadfully, in those moments, he wanted him-to feel his warm, strong hand within his own—to ask his forgiveness—perhaps, too, to grant his own...he hardly knew.

"But is there no end to this delicious valley?" he wondered, with something between vagueness and confusion in his mind. "Does it never stop, and the path climb again to the mountains beyond?" Drowsily, divorced from any positive interest, the question passed through his thoughts. Underfoot the grass already grew thickly enough to muffle the sound of his footsteps. The trail even had vanished, swallowed by moss. His feet sank in.

"I wish Mark were with me now—to see and feel all this—"

He stopped short and looked keenly about him for a moment, leaving the thought incomplete. A deep sighing, instantly caught by the wind and merged in the soughing of the trees, had sounded close beside him. Was it perhaps himself that sighed—unconsciously? His heart was surely charged enough!...

A faint smile played over his lips—instantly frozen, however, as another sigh, more distinct than the first, and quite obviously external to himself, passed him closely in the darkening air. More like deep breathing, though, it was, than sighing... It was nothing but the wind, of course. Stephen hurried on again, not surprised that he had been so easily deceived, for this valley was full of sighings and breathings—of trees and wind. It ventured upon no louder noise. Noise of any kind, indeed, seemed impossible and forbidden in this muted vale. And so deeply had he descended now, that the sunshine, silver rather than golden, already streamed past far over his head along the ridges, and no gleam found its way to where he was. The shadows, too, no longer blue and purple, had changed to black, as though woven of some delicate substance that had definite thickness, like a veil. Across the opposite slope, one of the mountain summits in the western sky already dropped its monstrous shadow fringed with pines. The day was rapidly drawing in.

XI

And here, very gradually, there began to dawn upon his overwrought mind certain curious things. They pierced clean through the mingled gloom and exaltation that characterized his mood. And they made the skin upon his back a little to—stir and crawl.

For he now became distinctly aware that the emptiness of this lonely valley was only apparent. It is impossible to say through what sense, or combination of senses, this singular certainty was brought to him that the valley was not really as forsaken and deserted as it seemed—that, on the contrary, it was the very reverse. It came to him suddenly—as a certainty. The valley as a matter of fact was—full. Packed, thronged and crowded it was to the very brim of its mighty wooded walls—with life. It was now borne in upon him, with an inner conviction that left no room for doubt, that on all sides living things—persons—were jostling him, rubbing elbows, watching all his movements, and only waiting till the darkness came to reveal themselves.

Moreover, with this eerie discovery came also the further knowledge that a vast multitude of others, again, with pallid faces and yearning eyes, with arms outstretched and groping feet, were searching everywhere for the way of entrance that he himself had found so easily. All about him, he felt, were people by the hundred, by the thousand, seeking with a kind of restless fever for the narrow trail that led down into the valley, longing with an intensity that beat upon his soul in a million waves, for the rest, the calm silence of the place—but most of all for its strange, deep, and unalterable peace.

He, alone of all these, had found the Entrance; he, *and one other.*

For out of this singular conviction grew another even more singular: his brother Mark was also somewhere in this valley with him. Mark, too, was wandering like himself in and out among its intricate dim turns. He had said but a short time ago, "I wish Mark were here!" Mark *was* here. And it was precisely then—while he stood still a moment, trying to face these overwhelming obsessions and deal with them—that the figure of a man, moving swiftly through the trees, passed him with a great gliding stride, and with averted face. Stephen started horribly, catching his breath. In an instant the man was gone again, swallowed up by the crowding pines.

With a quick movement of pursuit and a cry that should make the man turn, he sprang forward—but stopped again almost the same moment, realizing that the extraordinary speed at which the man had shot past him rendered pursuit out of the question. He had been going downhill into the valley; by this time he was already far, far ahead. But in that momentary glimpse of him he had seen enough to know. The face was turned away, and the shadows under the trees were heavy, but the figure was beyond question the figure of—his brother Mark.

It was his brother, yet not his brother. It was Mark—but Mark altered. And the alteration was in some way—awful; just as the silent speed at which he had moved—the impossible speed in so dense a forest—was likewise awful. Then, still shaking inwardly with the suddenness of it all, Stephen realized that when he called aloud he had uttered certain definite words. And these words now came back to him—

"Mark, Mark! Don't go yet! Don't go—without me!"

Before, however, he could act, a most curious and unaccountable sensation of deadly faintness and pain came upon him, without cause, without explanation, so that he dropped backwards in momentary collapse, and but for the closeness of the tree stems would have fallen full length to the ground. From the centre of the heart it came, spreading thence throughout his whole being like a swift and dreadful fever. All the muscles of his body relaxed; icy perspiration burst forth upon his skin; the pulses of life seemed suddenly reduced to the threshold beyond which they stop. There was a thick, rushing sound in his ears and his mind went utterly blank.

These were the sensations of death by suffocation. He knew this as certainly as though another doctor stood by his side and labelled each spasm, explained each successive sinking of the vital flame. He was passing through the last throes of a dying man. And then into his mind, thus deliberately left blank, rushed at lightning speed a whole series of the pictures of his past life. Even while his breath failed, he saw his thirty-five years pictorially, successively, yet in some queer fashion *at once,* pass through the lighted chambers of his brain. In this way, it is said, they pass through the brain of a drowning man during the last seconds before death.

Childhood rose about him with its scenes, figures, voices; the Kentish lawns where he had played with Mark in stained overalls; the summer-house where they had tea, the hay-fields where they romped. The scent of lime and walnut, of garden pinks, and roses by the tumbled rockery came back to his nostrils... He heard the voices of grown-ups in the distance...faint barking of dogs...the carriage wheels upon the gravel drive...and then the sharp summons from the opened window—"Time to come in now! Time to come in!"...

Time to come in now. It all drove before him as of yesterday on the scented winds of childhood's summer days... He heard his brother's voice—dreadfully faint and far away-calling him by name in the shrill accents of the boy: "Stevie—I say, you *might* shut up...and play properly..."

And then followed the panorama of the thirty years, all the chief events drawn in steel-like lines of white and black, vivid in sunshine, alive—right down to the present moment with the portentous dark shadow of his terrible Decision closing the series like a cloud.

Yes, like a smothering black cloud that blocked the way. There was nothing visible beyond it. There, for him, life ceased—

Only, as he gazed with inward-turned eyes that could not close even if they would, he saw to his amazement that the black cloud suddenly opened, and into a space of clear light there swam the vision, radiant as morning, of that dark young Eastern face—the face that held for him all the beauty in the world. The eyes instantly found his own, and smiled. Behind her, moreover, and beyond, before the moving vapours closed upon it, he saw a long vista of brilliance, crowded with pictures he could but half discern-as though, in spite of himself and his Decision, life continued—as though, too, it *continued with her.*

And instantly, with the sight and thought of her, the consuming faintness passed; strength returned to his body with the glow of life; the pain went; the pictures vanished; the cloud was no more. In his blood the pulses of life once again beat strong, and the blackness left his soul. The smile of those beloved eyes had been charged with the invitation to live. Although his determination remained unshaken, there shone behind it the joy of this potent magic: life with her...

With a strong effort, at length he recovered himself and continued on his way. More or less familiar, of course, with the psychology of vision, he dimly understood that his experiences had been in some measure subjective—within himself. To find the line of demarcation, however, was beyond him. That Mark had wandered out to fight his own battle upon the mountains, and so come into this same valley, was well within the bounds of coincidence. But the nameless and dreadful alteration discerned in that swift moment of his passing—that remained inexplicable. Only he no longer thought about it. The glory of that sweet vision had bewildered him beyond any possibility of reason or analysis.

His watch told him that the hour was past five o'clock—ten minutes past, to be exact. He still had several hours before reaching the country he was familiar with nearer home. Following the trail at an increased pace, he presently saw patches of meadow glimmering between the thinning trees, and knew that the bottom of the valley was at last in sight.

"And Mark, God bless him, is down there too—somewhere!" he exclaimed aloud. "I shall surely find him." For, strange to say, nothing could have persuaded him that his twin was not wandering among the shadows of this peaceful and haunted valley with himself, and—that he would shortly find him.

XII

And a few minutes later he passed from the forest as through an open door and found himself before a farmhouse standing in a patch of bright green meadow against the mountain-side. He was in need both of food and information.

The châlet, less lumbering and picturesque than those found in the Alps, had, nevertheless, the appearance of being exceedingly ancient. It was not toy-like—as the Jura châlets sometimes are. Solidly built, its balcony and overhanging roof supported by immense beams of deeply stained wood, it stood so that the back walls merged into the mountain slope behind, and the arms of pine, spruce and fir seemed stretched out to include it among their shadows. A last ray of sunshine, dipping between two far summits overhead, touched it with pale gold, bringing out the rich beauty of the heavily-dyed beams. Though no one was visible at the moment, and no smoke rose from the shingled chimney, it had the appearance of being occupied, and Stephen approached it with the caution due to the first evidence of humanity he had come across since he entered the valley.

Under the shadow of the broad balcony roof he noticed that the door, like that of a stable, was in two parts, and, wondering rather to find it closed, he knocked firmly upon the upper half. Under the pressure of a second knock this upper half yielded slightly, though without opening. The lower half, however, evidently barred and bolted, remained unmoved.

The third time he knocked with more force than he intended, and the knock sounded loud and clamorous as a summons. From within, as though great spaces stretched beyond, came a murmur of voices, faint and muffled, and then almost immediately—the footsteps of someone coming softly up to open.

But, instead of the heavy brown door opening, there came a voice. He heard it, petrified with amazement. For it was a voice he knew—hushed, soft, lingering. His heart, hammering atrociously, seemed to leave its place, and cut his breath away.

"Stephen!" it murmured, calling him by name, "what are *you* doing here so soon? And what is it that you want?"

The knowledge that only this dark door separated him from her, at first bereft him of all power of speech or movement; and the possible significance of her words escaped him. Through the sweet confusion that turned his spirit faint he only remembered, flash-like, that she and her father were indeed to have left the hotel that very morning. After that his thought stopped dead.

Then, also flash-like, swept back upon him the memory of the figure that had passed him with averted face—and, with it, the clear conviction that at this moment Mark, too, was somewhere in this very valley, even close beside him. More: Mark was in this chalet—with her.

The torrent of speech that instantly crowded to his lips was almost too thick for utterance.

"Open, open, open!" was all he heard intelligibly from the throng of words that poured out. He raised his hands to push and force; but her reply again stopped him.

"Even if I open—*you* may not enter yet," came the whisper through the door. And this time he could almost have sworn that it sounded within himself rather than without.

"I must enter," he cried. "Open to me, I say!"

"But you are trembling—"

"Open to me, O my life! Open to me!"

"But your heart—it is shaking."

"Because you—you are so near," came in passionate, stammering tones. "Because you stand there beside me!" And then, before she could answer, or his will control the words, he had added: "And because Mark—my brother—is in there—with you—"

"Hush, hush!" came the soft, astonishing reply. "He is in here, true; but he is not with me. And it is for my sake that he has come—for my sake and for yours. My soul, alas! has led him to the gates..."

But Stephen's emotions had reached the breaking-point, and the necessity for action was upon him like a storm. He drew back a pace so as to fling himself better against the closed door, when to his utter surprise, it moved. The upper half swung slowly outwards, and he—saw.

He was aware of a vast room, with closely shuttered windows, that seemed to stretch beyond the walls into the wooded mountain-side, thronged with moving figures, like forms of life gently gliding to and fro in some huge darkened tank; and there, framed against this opening— the girl herself. She stood, visible to the waist, radiant in the solitary beam of sunshine that reached the châlet, smiling down wondrously into his face with the same exquisite beauty in her eyes that he had seen before in the vision of the cloud: with, too, that supreme invitation in them—the invitation to live.

The loveliness blinded him. He could see the down upon her little dark cheeks where the sunlight kissed them; there was the cloud of hair upon her neck where his lips had lain; there, too, the dear, slight breast that not twenty-four hours ago had known the pressure of his arms. And, once again, driven forward by the love that triumphed over all obstacles, real or artificial, he advanced headlong with outstretched arms to take her.

"Katya!" he cried, never thinking how passing strange it was that he knew her name at all, much more the endearing and shortened form of it. "Katya!"

But the young girl held up her little brown hand against him with a gesture that was more strong to restrain than any number of bolted doors.

"Not here," she murmured, with her grave smile, while behind the words he caught in that darkened room the alternate hush and sighing as of a thousand sleepers. "Not here! You cannot see him now; for these are the Reception Halls of Death and here I stand in the Vestibule of the Beyond. Our way...your way and mine...lies farther yet...traced there since the beginning of the world...together..."

In quaintly broken English it was spoken, but his mind remembers the singular words in their more perfect form. Even this, however, came later. At the moment he only felt the twofold wave of love surge through him with a tide of power that threatened to break him asunder: he *must* hold her to his heart; he *must* come instantly to his brother's side, meet his eyes, have speech with him. The desire to enter that great darkened room and force a path through the dimly gliding forms to his brother became irresistible, while tearing upon its heels came like a fever of joy the meaning of the words she had just uttered, and especially of that last word "*Together!*"

Then, for an instant, all the forces in his being turned negative so that his will refused to act. The excess of feeling numbed him. A flying interval of knowledge, calm and certain, came to him. The exaltation of spirit which produced the pictures of all this spiritual clairvoyance moved a stage higher, and he realized that he witnessed an order of things pertaining to the world of eternal causes rather than of temporary effects. Someone had lifted the Veil.

With a feeling that he could only wait and let things take their extraordinary course, he stood still. For an instant, even less, he must have hidden his eyes in his hand, for when, a moment later, he again looked up, he saw that the half of the swinging door which had been open, was now closed. He stood alone upon the balcony. And the sunshine had faded entirely from the scene.

It was here, it seems, that the last vestige of self-control disappeared. He flung himself against the door; and the door met his assault like a wall of solid rock. Crying aloud alternately the names of his two loved ones, he turned, scarcely knowing what he did, and ran into the meadow. Dusk was about the châlet, drawing the encircling forests closer.

Soon the true darkness would stalk down the slopes. The walls of the valley reared, it seemed, up to heaven.

Still calling, he ran about the walls, searching wildly for a way of entrance, his mind charged with bewildering fragments of what he had heard: "The Reception Halls of Death"—"The Vestibule of the Beyond"—"You cannot see him now"—"Our way lies farther—and *together!*"...

And, on the far side of the châlet, by the corner that touched the trees, he suddenly stopped, feeling his gaze drawn upwards, and there, pressed close against the window-pane of an upper room, saw that someone was peering down upon him.

With a sensation of freezing terror he realized that he was staring straight into the eyes of his brother Mark. Bent a little forward with the effort to look down, the face, pale and motionless, gazed into his own, but without the least sign of recognition. Not a feature moved: and although but a few feet separated the brothers, the face wore the dim, misty appearance of great distance. It was like the face of a man called suddenly from deep sleep—dazed, perplexed; nay, more—frightened and horribly distraught.

What Stephen read upon it, however, in that first moment of sight, was the signature of the great, eternal question men have asked since the beginning of time, yet never heard the answer. And into the heart of the twin the pain of it plunged like a sword.

Mark!" he stammered, in that low voice the valley seemed to exact; "Mark! Is that really *you?*" Tears swam already in his eyes, and yearning in a flood choked his utterance.

And Mark, with a dreadful, steady stare that still held no touch of recognition, gazed down upon him from the closed window of that upper chamber, motionless, unblinking as an image of stone. It was almost like an imitation figure of himself—only with the effect of some added alteration. For alteration certainly there was—awful and unknown alteration—though Stephen was utterly unable to detect wherein it lay. And he remembered how the figure had passed him in the woods with averted face.

He made then, it seems, some violent sign or other, in response to which his brother at last moved-slowly opening the window. He leaned forward, stooping with lowered head and shoulders over the sill, while Stephen ran up against the wall beneath and craned up towards him. The two faces drew close; their eyes met clean and straight. Then the lips of Mark moved, and the distraught look half vanished within the borders of a little smile of puzzled and affectionate wonder.

"Stevie, old fellow," issued a tiny, far-away voice; "but where are you? I see you—so dimly?"

It was like a voice crying faintly down half-a-mile of distance. He shuddered to hear it.

"I'm here, Mark—close to you," he whispered.

"I hear your voice, I feel your presence," came the reply like a man talking in his sleep, "but I see you—as through a glass darkly. And I want to see you all clear, and close—"

"But *you!* Where *are* you?" interrupted Stephen, with anguish.

"Alone; quite alone—over here. And it's cold, oh, so cold!" The words came gently, half veiling a complaint. The wind caught them and ran round the walls towards the forest, wailing as it went.

"But how did you come, how did you come?" Stephen raised himself on tiptoe to catch the answer. But there was no answer. The face receded a little, and as it did so the wind, passing up the walls again, stirred the hair on the forehead. Stephen saw it move. He thought, too, the head moved with it, shaking slightly to and fro.

"Oh, but tell me, my dear, dear brother I Tell me—!" he cried, sweating horribly, his limbs shaking.

Mark made a curious gesture, withdrawing at the same time a little farther into the room behind, so that he now stood upright, half in shadow by the window. The alteration in him proclaimed itself more plainly, though still without betraying its exact nature. There was something about him that was terrible. And the air that came from the open window upon Stephen was so freezing that it seemed to turn the perspiration on his face into ice.

"I do not know; I do not remember," he heard the tiny voice inside the room, ever withdrawing. "Besides—I may not speak with you—yet; it is so difficult—and it hurts."

Stephen stretched out his body, the arms scraping the wooden walls above his head, trying to climb the smooth and slippery surface.

"For the love of God!" he cried with passion, "tell me what it all means and what you are doing here—you and—and—oh, and *all three of us?*" The words rang out through the silent valley.

But the other stood there motionless again by the window, his face distraught and dazed as though the effort of speech had already been too much for him. His image had begun to fade a little. He seemed, without moving, yet to be retreating into some sort of interior distance. Presently, it seemed, he would disappear altogether.

"I don't know," came the voice at length, fainter than before, half muffled. "I have been asleep, I think. I have just waked up, and come across from somewhere else—where we were all together, you and I and—and—"

Like his brother, he was unable to speak the name. He ended the sentence a moment later in a whisper that was only just audible. "But I cannot tell you *how* I came," he said, "for I do not know the words."

Stephen, then, with a violent leap tried to reach the window-sill and pull himself up. The distance was too great, however, and he fell back upon the grass, only just keeping his feet.

"I'm coming in to you," he cried out very loud. "Wait there for me! For the love of heaven, wait till I come to you. I'll break the doors in—!"

Once again Mark made that singular gesture; again he seemed to recede a little farther into a kind of veiled perspective that caused his appearance to fade still more; and, from an incredible distance—a distance that somehow conveyed an idea of appalling height—his thin, tiny voice floated down upon his brother from the fading lips of shadow.

"Old fellow, don't you come! You are not ready—and it is too cold here. I shall wait, Stevie, I shall wait for you. Later—I mean farther from here—we shall one day all three be together... Only you cannot understand now. I am here for your sake, old fellow, and for hers. She loves us both, but...it is...you...she loves...the best..."

The whispering voice rose suddenly on these last words into a long high cry that the wind instantly caught away and buried far in the smothering silences of the woods. For, at the same moment, Mark had come with a swift rush back to the window, had leaned out and stretched both hands towards his brother underneath. And his face had cleared and smiled. Caught within that smile, the awful change in him had vanished.

Stephen turned and made a mad rush round the châlet to find the door he would batter in with his hands and feet and body. He searched in vain, however, for in the shadows the supporting beams of the building were indistinguishable from the stems of the trees behind; the roof sank away, blotted out by the gloom of the branches, and the darkness now wove forest, sky and mountain into a uniform black sheet against which no item was separately visible.

There was no châlet any longer. He was simply battering with bruised hands and feet upon the solid trunks of pines and spruces in his path; which he continued to do, calling ever aloud for Mark, until finally he grew dizzy with exhaustion and fell to the ground in a state of semi-consciousness.

And for the best part of half-an-hour he lay there motionless upon the moss, while the vast hands of Night drew the cloak of her softest darkness over valley and mountain, covering his small body with as much care as she covered the sky, the hemisphere, and all those leagues of velvet forest.

XIII

It was not long before he came to himself again—shivering with cold, for the perspiration had dried upon him where he lay. He got up and ran. The night was now fairly down, and the keen air stung his cheeks. But, with a sure instinct not to be denied, he took the direction of home.

He travelled at an extraordinary pace, considering the thickness of the trees and the darkness. How he got out of the valley he does not remember; nor how he found his way over the intervening ridges that lay between him and the country he knew. At the back of his mind crashed and tumbled the loose fragments of all he had seen and heard, forming as yet no coherent pattern. For himself, indeed, the details were of small interest. He was a man under sentence of death. His determination, in spite of everything, remained unshaken. In a few short hours he would be gone.

Yet, with the habit of the professional mind, he tried a little to sort out things. During that state of singular exaltation, for instance, he understood vaguely that his deep longings had somehow translated themselves into act and scene. For these longings were life; his decision negatived them; hence, they dramatized themselves pictorially with what vividness his imagination allowed.

They were dramatized inventions, singularly elaborate, of the emotions that burned so fiercely within. All were projections of his consciousness, maimed and incomplete, masquerading as persons before his inner vision. It began with the singular sensations of death by drowning he had experienced. From that moment the other forces at work in the problem had taken their cue and played their part more or less convincingly, according to their strength...

He thought and argued a great deal as he hurried homewards through the night. But all the time he knew that it was untrue. He had no real explanation at all!

From the high ridges, cold and bleak under the stars, swept by the free wind of night, he ran almost the entire way. It was downhill. And during that violent descent of nearly an hour the details of his "going" shaped themselves. Until then he had formed no definite plans. Now he settled everything. He chose the very pool where the water coiled and bubbled as in a cauldron just where the little torrent made a turn above their house; he decided upon the very terms of the letter he would leave behind. He would put it on the kitchen table so that they should know where to find him.

He urged his pace tremendously, for the idea that his brother would have left—that he would find him gone—haunted him. It grew, doubt-less, out of that singular, detailed vision that had come upon him in his great weakness in the valley. He was terrified that he would not see his brother again—that he had already gone deliberately—after her...

"I *must* see Mark once more. I *must* get home before he leaves!" flashed the strong thought continually in his mind, making him run like a deer down the winding trail.

It was after ten o'clock when he reached the little clearing behind the châlet, panting with exhaustion, blinded with perspiration. There was no light visible; all the windows were dark; but presently he made out a figure moving to and fro below the balcony. It was *not* Mark—he saw that in a flash. It moved oddly. A sound of moaning reached him at the same time. And then he saw that it was the figure of the peasant woman who cooked for them, Marie Petavel.

And the instant he saw who it was, and heard her moaning, he knew what had happened. Mark had left a letter to explain-and gone: gone after the girl. His heart sank into death.

The woman came forward heavily through the darkness, the dew-drenched grass swishing audibly against her skirts. And the words he heard were precisely what he had expected to hear, though patois and excitement rendered them difficult—

"Your brother—oh, your poor brother, Monsieur le Docteur—he—has gone!"

And then he saw the piece of white paper glimmering in her hands as she stood quite close. He took it mechanically from her. It was the letter Mark had left behind to explain.

But before Stephen had time to read it, a man with a lantern came out of the barn that stood behind the house. It was her husband. He came slowly towards them.

"We searched for you, oh, we searched," he said in a thick voice, "my son went as far as Buttes even, and hasn't come back yet. You've been long, too long away—"

He stopped short and glanced down at his wife, telling her roughly to cease her stupid weeping. Stephen, shaking inwardly, with an icy terror in his blood, began to feel that things were not precisely as he had antic-ipated. Something else was the matter. The expression in the face of the peasant as the lantern's glare fell upon it came to him suddenly with the shock of a revelation.

"You have told monsieur—all?" the man whispered, stooping to his wife. She shook her head; and her husband led the way without anoth-er word. The interval of a few seconds seemed endless to Stephen; he was trembling all over like a man with the ague. Behind them the old woman floundered through the wet grass, moaning to herself.

"No one would have believed it could have happened—anything of *that* sort," the man mumbled. The lantern was unsteady in his hand. The next minute the barn, like some monstrous animal, rose against the stars, and the huge wooden doors gaped wide before them.

The peasant, uncovering his head, went first, and Stephen, following with stumbling footsteps, saw the shadows of the beams and posts shift across the boarded floor. Against the wall, whither the man led, was a small littered heap of hay, and upon this, covered by a white sheet, was stretched a human body. The peasant drew back the sheet gently with his heavy brown hand, stooping close over it so that the lantern threw its light full upon the act.

And Stephen, tumbling forward, scarcely knowing what he did, without further warning or preparation, looked down upon the face of his brother Mark. The eyes stared fixedly into—nothing; the features wore the distraught expression he had seen upon them a few hours before through the window-pane of that upper chamber.

"We found him in that deep pool just where the stream makes the quick turn above the house," the peasant whispered. "He left a bit of paper on the kitchen table to say where he would be. It was after dark when we got there. His watch had stopped, though, long before—" He muttered on unintelligibly.

Stephen looked up at the man, unable to utter a word, and the man replied to the unspoken question—

"At ten minutes past five the watch had stopped," he said. "That was when the water reached it."

By the flicker of the lantern, then, sitting beside that still figure covered with the sheet, Stephen read the letter Mark had left for him—

"Stevie, old fellow, one of us, you know, has got to—go; and it is better, I think, that it should not be you. I know all you have been through, for I have fought and suffered every step with you. I have been along the same path, loving her too much for you, and you too much for her. And I leave her to you, boy, because I am convinced she now loves you even as she first believed she loved me. But all that evening she cried incessantly for you. More I cannot explain to you now; she will do that. And she need never know more than that I have withdrawn in your favour: she need never know *how*. Perhaps, one day, when there is no marriage or giving in marriage, we may all three be together, and happy. I have often wondered, as you know..."

The remainder of the sentence was scratched out and illegible.

"...And, if it be possible, old fellow, of course *I shall wait.*"
Then came more words blackened out.

"...I am now going, within a few minutes of writing this last word
to you of blessing and forgiveness (for I know you will want that,
although there is nothing, *nothing* to forgive!)—going down into
that Lost Valley her father told us about—the Valley hidden
among these mountains we love—the Lost Valley where even the
unhappy dead find peace. There I shall wait for you both.—
MARK."

Several weeks later, before he took the train eastwards, Stephen
retraced his steps to the farmhouse where he had bought milk and asked
for directions. Thence for some distance he followed the path he well
remembered. At a point, however, the confusion of the woods grew
strangely upon him. The mountains, true to the map, were not true to
his recollections. The trail stopped; high, unknown ridges intervened;
and no such deep and winding valley as he had travelled that afternoon
for so many hours was anywhere to be found. The map, the peasants, the
very configuration of the landscape even, denied its existence.

THE WENDIGO

I

A CONSIDERABLE number of hunting parties were out that year without finding so much as a fresh trail; for the moose were uncommonly shy, and the various Nimrods returned to the bosoms of their respective families with the best excuses the facts or their imaginations could suggest. Dr. Cathcart, among others, came back without a trophy; but he brought instead the memory of an experience which he declares was worth all the bull-moose that had ever been shot. But then Cathcart, of Aberdeen, was interested in other things besides moose—amongst them the vagaries of the human mind. This particular story, however, found no mention in his book on *Collective Hallucination* for the simple reason (so he confided once to a fellow colleague) that he himself played too intimate a part in it to form a competent judgment of the affair as a whole...

Besides himself and his guide, Hank Davis, there was young Simpson, his nephew, a divinity student destined for the "Wee Kirk" (then on his first visit to Canadian backwoods), and the latter's guide, Défago. Joseph Défago was a French "Canuck," who had strayed from his native Province of Quebec years before, and had got caught in Rat Portage when the Canadian Pacific Railway was a-building; a man who, in addition to his unparalleled knowledge of woodcraft and bush-lore, could also sing the old *voyageur* songs and tell a capital hunting yarn into the bargain. He was deeply susceptible, moreover, to that singular spell which the wilderness lays upon certain lonely natures, and he loved the wild solitudes with a kind of romantic passion that amounted almost to an obsession. The life of the backwoods fascinated him—whence, doubtless, his surpassing efficiency in dealing with their mysteries.

On this particular expedition he was Hank's choice. Hank knew him and swore by him. He also swore at him, "jest as a pal might," and since he had a vocabulary of picturesque, if utterly meaningless, oaths, the conversation between the two stalwart and hardy woodsmen was often of a rather lively description. This river of expletives, however, Hank agreed to dam a little out of respect for his old "hunting boss," Dr. Cathcart, whom of course he addressed after the fashion of the country as "Doc"; and also because he understood that young Simpson was already a "bit of a parson." He had, however, one objection to Défago, and one only—which was, that the French Canadian sometimes exhibited what Hank described as "the output of a cursed and dismal mind," meaning apparently that he sometimes was true to type, Latin type, and suffered fits of a kind of silent moroseness when nothing could induce him to utter speech. Défago, that is to say, was imaginative and melancholy. And, as a rule, it was too long a spell of "civilization" that induced the attacks, for a few days of the wilderness invariably cured them.

This, then, was the party of four that found themselves in camp the last week in October of that "shy moose year" 'way up in the wilderness north of Rat Portage—a forsaken and desolate country. There was also Punk, an Indian, who had accompanied Dr. Cathcart and Hank on their hunting trips in previous years, and who acted as cook. His duty was merely to stay in camp, catch fish, and prepare venison steaks and coffee at a few minutes' notice. He dressed in the worn-out clothes bequeathed to him by former patrons, and, except for his coarse black hair and dark skin, he looked in these city garments no more like a real redskin than a stage negro looks like a real African. For all that, however, Punk had in him still the instincts of his dying race; his taciturn silence and his endurance survived; also his superstition.

The party round the blazing fire that night were despondent, for a week had passed without a single sign of recent moose discovering itself. Défago had sung his song and plunged into a story, but Hank, in bad humour, reminded him so often that "he kep' mussing-up the fac's so, that it was 'most all nothin' but a petred-out lie," that the Frenchman had finally subsided into a sulky silence which nothing seemed likely to break. Dr. Cathcart and his nephew were fairly done after an exhausting day. Punk was washing up the dishes, grunting to himself under the lean-to of branches, where he later also slept. No one troubled to stir the slowly dying fire. Overhead the stars were brilliant in a sky quite wintry, and there was so little wind that ice was already forming stealthily along the shores of the still lake behind them. The silence of the vast listening forest stole forward and enveloped them.

Hank broke in suddenly with his nasal voice.

"I'm in favour of breaking new ground tomorrow, Doc," he observed with energy, looking across at his employer. "We don't stand a dead Dago's chance about here."

"Agreed," said Cathcart, always a man of few words. "Think the idea's good."

"Sure pop, it's good," Hank resumed with confidence. "S'pose, now, you and I strike west, up Garden Lake way for a change! None of us ain't touched that quiet bit o' land yet—"

"I'm with you."

"And you, Défago, take Mr. Simpson along in the small canoe, skip across the lake, portage over into Fifty Island Water, and take a good squint down that thar southern shore. The moose 'yarded' there like hell last year, and for all we know they may be doin' it agin this year jest to spite us."

Défago, keeping his eyes on the fire, said nothing by way of reply. He was still offended, possibly, about his interrupted story.

"No one's been up that way this year, an' I'll lay my bottom dollar on *that!*" Hank added with emphasis, as though he had a reason for knowing. He looked over at his partner sharply. "Better take the little silk tent and stay away a couple o' nights," he concluded, as though the matter were definitely settled. For Hank was recognized as general organizer of the hunt, and in charge of the party.

It was obvious to any one that Défago did not jump at the plan, but his silence seemed to convey something more than ordinary disapproval, and across his sensitive dark face there passed a curious expression like a flash of firelight—not so quickly, however, that the three men had not time to catch it. "He funked for some reason, I thought," Simpson said afterwards in the tent he shared with his uncle. Dr. Cathcart made no immediate reply, although the look had interested him enough at the time for him to make a mental note of it. The expression had caused him a passing uneasiness he could not quite account for at the moment.

But Hank, of course, had been the first to notice it, and the odd thing was that instead of becoming explosive or angry over the other's reluctance, he at once began to humour him a bit.

"But there ain't no *speshul* reason why no one's been up there this year," he said, with a perceptible hush in his tone; "not the reason *you* mean, anyway! Las' year it was the fires that kep' folks out, and this year I guess-I guess it jest happened so, that's all!" His manner was clearly meant to be encouraging.

Joseph Défago raised his eyes a moment, then dropped them again. A breath of wind stole out of the forest and stirred the embers into a passing blaze. Dr. Cathcart again noticed the expression in the guide's face, and again he did not like it. But this time the nature of the look betrayed itself. In those eyes, for an instant, he caught the gleam of a man scared in his very soul. It disquieted him more than he cared to admit.

"Bad Indians up that way?" he asked, with a laugh to ease matters a little, while Simpson, too sleepy to notice this subtle by-play, moved off to bed with a prodigious yawn; "or—or anything wrong with the country?" he added, when his nephew was out of hearing.

Hank met his eye with something less than his usual frankness.

"He's jest skeered," he replied good-humouredly, "skeered stiff about some ole feery tale! That's all, ain't it, ole pard?" And he gave Défago a friendly kick on the moccasined foot that lay nearest the fire.

Défago looked up quickly, as from an interrupted reverie, a reverie, however, that had not prevented his seeing all that went on about him. "Skeered—*nuthin'!*" he answered, with a flush of defiance. "There's nuthin' in the Bush that can skeer Joseph Défago, and don't you forget it!" And the natural energy with which he spoke made it impossible to know whether he told the whole truth or only a part of it.

Hank turned towards the doctor. He was just going to add something when he stopped abruptly and looked round. A sound close behind them in the darkness made all three start. It was old Punk, who had moved up from his lean-to while they talked and now stood there just beyond the circle of firelight—listening.

"'Nother time, Doc!" Hank whispered, with a wink, "when the gallery ain't stepped down into the stalls!" And, springing to his feet, he slapped the Indian on the back and cried noisily, "Come up t' the fire an' warm yer dirty red skin a bit." He dragged him towards the blaze and threw more wood on. "That was a mighty good feed you give us an hour or two back," he continued heartily, as though to set the man's thoughts on another scent, "and it ain't Christian to let you stand out there freezin' yer ole soul to hell while we're gettin' all good an' toasted!" Punk moved in and warmed his feet, smiling darkly at the other's volubility which he only half understood, but saying nothing. And presently Dr. Cathcart, seeing that further conversation was impossible, followed his nephew's example and moved off to the tent, leaving the three men smoking over the now blazing fire.

It is not easy to undress in a small tent without waking one's companion, and Cathcart, hardened and warm-blooded as he was in spite of his fifty odd years, did what Hank would have described as "considerable of his twilight" in the open. He noticed, during the process, that Punk had meanwhile gone back to his lean-to, and that Hank and Défago were at it hammer and tongs, or, rather, hammer and anvil, the little French Canadian being the anvil. It was all very like the conventional stage picture of Western melodrama: the fire lighting up their faces with patches of alternate red and black; Défago, in slouch hat and moccasins in the part of the "badlands'" villain; Hank, open-faced and hatless, with that reckless fling of his shoulders, the honest and deceived hero; and old Punk, eavesdropping in the background, supplying the atmosphere of mystery. The doctor smiled as he noticed the details; but at the same time something deep within him—he hardly knew what—shrank a little, as though an almost imperceptible breath of warning had touched the surface of his soul and was gone again before he could seize it. Probably it was traceable to that "scared expression" he had seen in the eyes of Défago; "probably"—for this hint of fugitive emotion otherwise escaped his usually so keen analysis. Défago, he was vaguely aware, might cause trouble somehow... He was not as steady a guide as Hank, for instance... Further than that he could not get...

He watched the men a moment longer before diving into the stuffy tent where Simpson already slept soundly. Hank, he saw, was swearing like a mad African in a New York nigger saloon; but it was the swearing of "affection." The ridiculous oaths flew freely now that the cause of their obstruction was asleep. Presently he put his arm almost tenderly upon his comrade's shoulder, and they moved off together into the shadows where their tent stood faintly glimmering. Punk, too, a moment later followed their example and disappeared between his odorous blankets in the opposite direction.

Dr. Cathcart then likewise turned in, weariness and sleep still fighting in his mind with an obscure curiosity to know what it was had scared Défago about the country up Fifty Island Water way,—wondering, too, why Punk's presence had prevented the completion of what Hank had to say. Then sleep overtook him. He would know tomorrow. Hank would tell him the story while they trudged after the elusive moose.

Deep silence fell about the little camp, planted there so audaciously in the jaws of the wilderness. The lake gleamed like a sheet of black glass beneath the stars. The cold air pricked. In the draughts of night that poured their silent tide from the depths of the forest, with messages from distant ridges and from lakes just beginning to freeze, there lay already the faint, bleak odours of coming winter. White men, with their dull scent, might never have divined them; the fragrance of the wood-fire would have concealed from them these almost electrical hints of moss and bark and hardening swamp a hundred miles away. Even Hank and Défago, subtly in league with the soul of the woods as they were, would probably have spread their delicate nostrils in vain...

But an hour later, when all slept like the dead, old Punk crept from his blankets and went down to the shore of the lake like a shadow—silently, as only Indian blood can move. He raised his head and looked about him. The thick darkness rendered sight of small avail, but, like the animals, he possessed other senses that darkness could not mute. He listened—then sniffed the air. Motionless as a hemlock-stem he stood there. After five minutes again he lifted his head and sniffed, and yet once again. A tingling of the wonderful nerves that betrayed itself by no outer sign, ran through him as he tasted the keen air. Then, merging his figure into the surrounding blackness in a way that only wild men and animals understand, he turned, still moving like a shadow, and went stealthily back to his lean-to and his bed.

And soon after he slept, the change of wind he had divined stirred gently the reflection of the stars within the lake. Rising among the far ridges of the country beyond Fifty Island Water, it came from the direction in which he had stared, and it passed over the sleeping camp with a faint and sighing murmur through the tops of the big trees that was almost too delicate to be audible. With it, down the desert paths of night, though too faint, too high even for the Indian's hair-like nerves, there passed a curious, thin odour, strangely disquieting, an odour of something that seemed unfamiliar—utterly unknown.

The French Canadian and the man of Indian blood each stirred uneasily in his sleep just about this time, though neither of them woke. Then the ghost of that unforgettably strange odour passed away and was lost among the leagues of tenantless forest beyond.

II

In the morning the camp was astir before the sun. There had been a light fall of snow during the night and the air was sharp. Punk had done his duty betimes, for the odours of coffee and fried bacon reached every tent. All were in good spirits.

"Wind's shifted!" cried Hank vigorously, watching Simpson and his guide already loading the small canoe. "It's across the lake—dead right for you fellers. And the snow'll make bully trails! If there's any moose mussing around up thar, they'll not get so much as a tail-end scent of you with the wind as it is. Good luck, Monsieur Défago!" he added, facetiously giving the name its French pronunciation for once, "bonne chance!"

Défago returned the good wishes, apparently in the best of spirits, the silent mood gone. Before eight o'clock old Punk had the camp to himself, Cathcart and Hank were far along the trail that led westwards, while the canoe that carried Défago and Simpson, with silk tent and grub for two days, was already a dark speck bobbing on the bosom of the lake, going due east.

The wintry sharpness of the air was tempered now by a sun that topped the wooded ridges and blazed with a luxurious warmth upon the world of lake and forest below; loons flew skimming through the sparkling spray that the wind lifted; divers shook their dripping heads to the sun and popped smartly out of sight again; and as far as eye could reach rose the leagues of endless, crowding Bush, desolate in its lonely sweep and grandeur, untrodden by foot of man, and stretching its mighty and unbroken carpet right up to the frozen shores of Hudson Bay.

Simpson, who saw it all for the first time as he paddled hard in the bows of the dancing canoe, was enchanted by its austere beauty. His heart drank in the sense of freedom and great spaces just as his lungs drank in the cool and perfumed wind. Behind him in the stern seat, singing fragments of his native chanties, Défago steered the craft of birchbark like a thing of life, answering cheerfully all his companion's questions. Both were gay and light-hearted. On such occasions men lose the superficial, worldly distinctions; they become human beings working together for a common end. Simpson, the employer, and Défago the employed, among these primitive forces, were simply—two men, the "guider" and the "guided." Superior knowledge, of course, assumed control, and the younger man fell without a second thought into the quasi-subordinate position. He never dreamed of objecting when Défago dropped the "Mr.," and addressed him as "Say, Simpson," or "Simpson, boss," which was invariably the case before they reached the farther shore after a stiff paddle of twelve miles against a head wind. He only laughed, and liked it; then ceased to notice it at all.

For this "divinity student" was a young man of parts and character, though as yet, of course, untravelled; and on this trip—the first time he had seen any country but his own and little Switzerland—the huge scale of things somewhat bewildered him. It was one thing, he realized, to hear about primeval forests, but quite another to see them. While to dwell in them and seek acquaintance with their wild life was, again, an initiation that no intelligent man could undergo without a certain shifting of personal values hitherto held for permanent and sacred.

Simpson knew the first faint indication of this emotion when he held the new .303 rifle in his hands and looked along its pair of faultless, gleaming barrels. The three days' journey to their headquarters, by lake and portage, had carried the process a stage farther. And now that he was about to plunge beyond even the fringe of wilderness where they were camped into the virgin heart of uninhabited regions as vast as Europe itself, the true nature of the situation stole upon him with an effect of delight and awe that his imagination was fully capable of appreciating. It was himself and Défago against a multitude—at least, against a Titan!

The bleak splendours of these remote and lonely forests rather overwhelmed him with the sense of his own littleness. That stern quality of the tangled backwoods which can only be described as merciless and terrible, rose out of these far blue woods swimming upon the horizon, and revealed itself. He understood the silent warning. He realized his own utter helplessness. Only Défago, as a symbol of a distant civilization where man was master, stood between him and a pitiless death by exhaustion and starvation.

It was thrilling to him, therefore, to watch Défago turn over the canoe upon the shore, pack the paddles carefully underneath, and then proceed to "blaze" the spruce stems for some distance on either side of an almost invisible trail, with the careless remark thrown in, "Say, Simpson, if anything happens to me, you'll find the canoe all correc' by these marks;— then strike doo west into the sun to hit the home camp agin, see?"

It was the most natural thing in the world to say, and he said it without any noticeable inflexion of the voice, only it happened to express the youth's emotions at the moment with an utterance that was symbolic of the situation and of his own helplessness as a factor in it. He was alone with Défago in a primitive world: that was all. The canoe, another symbol of man's ascendancy, was now to be left behind. Those small yellow patches, made on the trees by the axe, were the only indications of its hiding-place.

Meanwhile, shouldering the packs between them, each man carrying his own rifle, they followed the slender trail over rocks and fallen trunks and across half-frozen swamps; skirting numerous lakes that fairly gemmed the forest, their borders fringed with mist; and towards five o'clock found themselves suddenly on the edge of the woods, looking out across a large sheet of water in front of them, dotted with pine-clad islands of all describable shapes and sizes.

"Fifty Island Water," announced Défago wearily, "and the sun jest goin' to dip his bald old head into it!" he added, with unconscious poetry; and immediately they set about pitching camp for the night.

In a very few minutes, under those skilful hands that never made a movement too much or a movement too little, the silk tent stood taut and cosy, the beds of balsam boughs ready laid, and a brisk cooking-fire burned with the minimum of smoke. While the young Scotchman cleaned the fish they had caught trolling behind the canoe, Défago "guessed" he would "jest as soon" take a turn through the Bush for indications of moose. "May come across a trunk where they bin and rubbed horns," he said, as he moved off, "or feedin' on the last of the maple leaves,"—and he was gone.

His small figure melted away like a shadow in the dusk, while Simpson noted with a kind of admiration how easily the forest absorbed him into herself. A few steps, it seemed, and he was no longer visible.

Yet there was little underbrush hereabouts; the trees stood somewhat apart, well spaced; and in the clearings grew silver-birch and maple, spear-like and slender, against the immense stems of spruce and hemlock. But for occasional prostrate monsters, and the boulders of grey rock that thrust uncouth shoulders here and there out of the ground, it might well have been a bit of park in the Old Country. Almost, one might have seen in it the hand of man. A little to the right, however, began the great burnt section, miles in extent, proclaiming its real character—*brulé,* as it is called, where the fires of the previous year had raged for weeks, and the blackened stumps now rose gaunt and ugly, bereft of branches, like gigantic match-heads stuck into the ground, savage and desolate beyond words. The perfume of charcoal and rain-soaked ashes still hung faintly about it.

The dusk rapidly deepened; the glades grew dark; the crackling of the fire and the wash of little waves along the rocky lake shore were the only sounds audible. The wind had dropped with the sun, and in all that vast world of branches nothing stirred. Any moment, it seemed, the woodland gods, who are to be worshipped in silence and loneliness, might sketch their mighty and terrific outlines among the trees. In front, through doorways pillared by huge straight stems, lay the stretch of Fifty Island Water, a crescent-shaped lake some fifteen miles from tip to tip, and perhaps five miles across where they were camped. A sky of rose and saffron, more clear than any atmosphere Simpson had ever known, still dropped its pale streaming fires across the waves, where the islands—a hundred, surely, rather than fifty —floated like the fairy barques of some enchanted fleet. Fringed with pines, whose crests fingered most delicately the sky, they almost seemed to move upwards as the light faded— about to weigh anchor and navigate the pathways of the heavens instead of the currents of their native and desolate lake.

And strips of coloured cloud, like flaunting pennons, signalled their departure to the stars...

The beauty of the scene was strangely uplifting. Simpson smoked the fish and burnt his fingers into the bargain in his efforts to enjoy it and at the same time tend the frying-pan and the fire. Yet, ever at the back of his thoughts, lay that other aspect of the wilderness: the indifference to human life, the merciless spirit of desolation which took no note of man. The sense of his utter loneliness, now that even Défago had gone, came close as he looked about him and listened for the sound of his companion's returning footsteps.

There was pleasure in the sensation, yet with it a perfectly comprehensible alarm. And instinctively the thought stirred in him: "What should I—*could* I, do—if anything happened and he did not come back—?"

They enjoyed their well-earned supper, eating untold quantities of fish, and drinking unmilked tea strong enough to hill men who had not covered thirty miles of hard "going," eating little on the way. And when it was over, they smoked and told stories round the blazing fire, laughing, stretching weary limbs, and discussing plans for the morrow. Défago was in excellent spirits, though disappointed at having no signs of moose to report. But it was dark and he had not gone far. The *brulé*, too, was bad. His clothes and hands were smeared with charcoal. Simpson, watching him, realized with renewed vividness their position—alone together in the wilderness.

"Défago," he said presently, "these woods, you know, are a bit too big to feel quite at home in—to feel comfortable in, I mean!...Eh?" He merely gave expression to the mood of the moment; he was hardly prepared for the earnestness, the solemnity even, with which the guide took him up.

"You've hit it right, Simpson, boss," he replied, fixing his searching brown eyes on his face, "and that's the truth, sure. There's no end to 'em—no end at all." Then he added in a lowered tone as if to himself, "There's lots found out *that*, and gone plumb to pieces!"

But the man's gravity of manner was not quite to the other's liking; it was a little too suggestive for this scenery and setting; he was sorry he had broached the subject. He remembered suddenly how his uncle had told him that men were sometimes stricken with a strange fever of the wilderness, when the seduction of the uninhabited wastes caught them so fiercely that they went forth, half fascinated, half deluded, to their death. And he had a shrewd idea that his companion held something in sympathy with that queer type. He led the conversation on to other topics, on to Hank and the doctor, for instance, and the natural rivalry as to who should get the first sight of moose.

"If they went doo west," observed Défago carelessly, "there's sixty miles between us now—with ole Punk at halfway house eatin' himself full to bustin' with fish and corfee." They laughed together over the picture. But the casual mention of those sixty miles again made Simpson realize the prodigious scale of this land where they hunted; sixty miles was a mere step; two hundred little more than a step. Stories of lost hunters rose persistently before his memory. The passion and mystery of homeless and wandering men, seduced by the beauty of great forests, swept his soul in a way too vivid to be quite pleasant. He wondered vaguely whether it was the mood of his companion that invited the unwelcome suggestion with such persistence.

"Sing us a song, Défago, if you're not too tired," he asked; "one of those old *voyageur* songs you sang the other night." He handed his tobacco pouch to the guide and then filled his own pipe, while the Canadian, nothing loth, sent his light voice across the lake in one of those plaintive, almost melancholy chanties with which lumbermen and trappers lessen the burden of their labour. There was an appealing and romantic flavour about it, something that recalled the atmosphere of the old pioneer days when Indians and wilderness were leagued together, battles frequent, and the Old Country farther off than it is today. The sound travelled pleasantly over the water, but the forest at their backs seemed to swallow it down with a single gulp that permitted neither echo nor resonance.

It was in the middle of the third verse that Simpson noticed something unusual—something that brought his thoughts back with a rush from far-away scenes. A curious change had come into the man's voice. Even before he knew what it was, uneasiness caught him, and looking up quickly, he saw that Défago, though still singing, was peering about him into the Bush, as though he heard or saw something. His voice grew fainter—dropped to a hush—then ceased altogether. The same instant, with a movement amazingly alert, he started to his feet and stood upright—*sniffing the air*. Like a dog scenting game, he drew the air into his nostrils in short, sharp breaths, turning quickly as he did so in all directions, and finally "pointing" down the lake shore, eastwards. It was a performance unpleasantly suggestive and at the same time singularly dramatic. Simpson's heart fluttered disagreeably as he watched it.

"Lord, man! How you made me jump!" he exclaimed, on his feet beside him the same instant, and peering over his shoulder into the sea of darkness. "What's up? Are you frightened—?"

Even before the question was out of his mouth he knew it was foolish, for any man with a pair of eyes in his head could see that the Canadian had turned white down to his very gills. Not even sunburn and the glare of the fire could hide that.

The student felt himself trembling a little, weakish in the knees. "What's up?" he repeated quickly. "D'you smell moose? Or anything queer, anything—wrong?" He lowered his voice instinctively.

The forest pressed round them with its encircling wall; the nearer tree-stems gleamed like bronze in the firelight; beyond that—blackness, and, so far as he could tell, a silence of death. Just behind them a passing puff of wind lifted a single leaf, looked at it, then laid it softly down again without disturbing the rest of the covey. It seemed as if a million invisible causes had combined just to produce that single visible effect. *Other* life pulsed about them—and was gone.

Défago turned abruptly; the livid hue of his face had turned to a dirty grey.

"I never said I heered—or smelt—nuthin'," he said slowly and emphatically, in an oddly altered voice that conveyed somehow a touch of defiance. "I was only—takin' a look round—so to speak. It's always a mistake to be too previous with yer questions." Then he added suddenly with obvious effort, in his more natural voice, "Have you got the matches, Boss Simpson?" and proceeded to fight the pipe he had half filled just before he began to sing.

Without speaking another word they sat down again by the fire, Défa-go changing his side so that he could face the direction the wind came from. For even a tenderfoot could tell that. Défago changed his position in order to hear and smell—all there was to be heard and smelt. And, since he now faced the lake with his back to the trees it was evidently nothing in the forest that had sent so strange and sudden a warning to his marvellously trained nerves.

"Guess now I don't feel like singing any," he explained presently of his own accord. "That song kinder brings back memories that's troublesome to me; I never oughter've begun it. It sets me on t' imagining things, see?"

Clearly the man was still fighting with some profoundly moving emo-tion. He wished to excuse himself in the eyes of the other. But the expla-nation, in that it was only a part of the truth, was a lie, and he knew per-fectly well that Simpson was not deceived by it. For nothing could explain away the livid terror that had dropped over his face while he stood there sniffing the air. And nothing—no amount of blazing fire, or chatting on ordinary subjects—could make that camp exactly as it had been before. The shadow of an unknown horror, naked if unguessed, that had flashed for an instant in the face and gestures of the guide, had also communicated itself, vaguely and therefore more potently, to his companion. The guide's visible efforts to dissemble the truth only made things worse. Moreover, to add to the younger man's uneasiness, was the difficulty, nay, the impossibility he felt of asking questions, and also his complete ignorance as to the cause... Indians, wild animals, forest fires— all these, he knew, were wholly out of the question. His imagination searched vigorously, but in vain...

Yet, somehow or other, after another long spell of smoking, talking and roasting themselves before the great fire, the shadow that had so sud-denly invaded their peaceful camp began to lift. Perhaps Défago's efforts, or the return of his quiet and normal attitude accomplished this; perhaps Simpson himself had exaggerated the affair out of all proportion to the truth; or possibly the vigorous air of the wilderness brought its own powers of healing. Whatever the cause, the feeling of immediate horror seemed to have passed away as mysteriously as it had come, for nothing occurred to feed it. Simpson began to feel that he had permitted himself the unreasoning terror of a child. He put it down partly to a certain sub-conscious excitement that this wild and immense scenery generated in his blood, partly to the spell of solitude, and partly to over fatigue. That pallor in the guide's face was, of course, uncommonly hard to explain, yet it *might* have been due in some way to an effect of firelight, or his own imagination... He gave it the benefit of the doubt; he was Scotch. When a somewhat unordinary emotion has disappeared, the mind always finds a dozen ways of explaining away its causes... Simpson lit a last pipe and tried to laugh to himself. On getting home to Scotland it would make quite a good story. He did not realize that this laughter was a sign that terror still lurked in the recesses of his soul—that, in fact, it was merely one of the conventional signs by which a man, seriously alarmed, tries to persuade himself that he is *not* so.

Défago, however, heard that low laughter and looked up with surprise on his face. The two men stood, side by side, kicking the embers about before going to bed. It was ten o'clock—a late hour for hunters to be still awake.

"What's ticklin' yer?" he asked in his ordinary tone, yet gravely.

"I—I was thinking of our little toy woods at home, just at that moment," stammered Simpson, coming back to what really dominated his mind, and startled by the question, "and comparing them to—to all this," and he swept his arm round to indicate the Bush.

A pause followed in which neither of them said anything.

"All the same I wouldn't laugh about it, if I was you," Défago added, looking over Simpson's shoulder into the shadows. "There's places in there nobody won't never see into—nobody knows what lives in there either."

"Too big—too far off?" The suggestion in the guide's manner was immense and horrible.

Défago nodded. The expression on his face was dark. He, too, felt uneasy. The younger man understood that in a *hinterland* of this size there might well be depths of wood that would never in the life of the world be known or trodden. The thought was not exactly the sort he welcomed. In a loud voice, cheerfully, he suggested that it was time for bed. But the guide lingered, tinkering with the fire, arranging the stones needlessly, doing a dozen things that did not really need doing. Evidently there was something he wanted to say, yet found it difficult to "get at."

"Say, you, Boss Simpson," he began suddenly, as the last shower of sparks went up into the air, "you don't-smell nothing, do you—nothing pertickler, I mean?" The commonplace question, Simpson realized, veiled a dreadfully serious thought in his mind. A shiver ran down his back.

"Nothing but this burning wood," he replied firmly, kicking again at the embers. The sound of his own foot made him start.

"And all the evenin' you ain't smelt—nothing?" persisted the guide, peering at him through the gloom; "nothing extrordiny, and different to anything else you ever smelt before?"

"No, no, man; nothing at all!" he replied aggressively, half angrily. Défago's face cleared. "That's good!" he exclaimed, with evident relief. "That's good to hear."

"Have *you?*" asked Simpson sharply, and the same instant regretted the question.

The Canadian came closer in the darkness. He shook his head. "I guess not," he said, though without overwhelming conviction. "It must've been jest that song of mine that did it. It's the song they sing in lumber-camps and god-forsaken places like that, when they're skeered the Wendigo's somewheres around, doin' a bit of swift travellin'—"

"And what's the Wendigo, pray?" Simpson asked quickly, irritated because again he could not prevent that sudden shiver of the nerves. He knew that he was close upon the man's terror and the cause of it. Yet a rushing passionate curiosity overcame his better judgment, *and* his fear.

Défago turned swiftly and looked at him as though he were suddenly about to shriek. His eyes shone, his mouth was wide open. Yet all he said, or whispered rather, for his voice sank very low, was—

"It's nuthin'—nuthin' but what those lousy fellers believe when they've bin hittin' the bottle too long—a sort of great animal that lives up yonder," he jerked his head northwards, "quick as lightning in its tracks, an' bigger'n anything else in the Bush, an' ain't supposed to be very good to look at—*that's all!*"

"A backwoods' superstition—" began Simpson, moving hastily towards the tent in order to shake off the hand of the guide that clutched his arm. "Come, come, hurry up for God's sake, and get the lantern going! It's time we were in bed and asleep if we're to be up with the sun tomorrow..."

The guide was close on his heels. "I'm coming," he answered out of the darkness, "I'm coming." And after a slight delay he appeared with the lantern and hung it from a nail in the front pole of the tent. The shadows of a hundred trees shifted their places quickly as he did so, and when he stumbled over the rope, diving swiftly inside, the whole tent trembled as though a gust of wind struck it.

The two men lay down, without undressing, upon their beds of soft balsam boughs, cunningly arranged. Inside, all was warm and cosy, but outside the world of crowding trees pressed close about them, marshalling their million shadows, and smothering the little tent that stood there like a wee white shell facing the ocean of tremendous forest.

Between the two lonely figures within, however, there pressed another shadow that was *not* a shadow from the night. It was the Shadow cast by the strange Fear, never wholly exorcised, that had leaped suddenly upon Défago in the middle of his singing. And Simpson, as he lay there, watching the darkness through the open flap of the tent, ready to plunge into the fragrant abyss of sleep, knew first that unique and profound stillness of a primeval forest when no wind stirs...and when the night has weight and substance that enters into the soul to bind a veil about it... Then sleep took him...

III

Thus it seemed to him, at least. Yet it was true that the lap of the water, just beyond the tent door, still beat time with his lessening pulses when he realized that he was lying with his eyes open and that another sound had recently introduced itself with cunning softness between the splash and murmur of the little waves.

And, long before he understood what this sound was, it had stirred in him the centres of pity and alarm. He listened intently, though at first in vain, for the running blood beat all its drums too noisily in his ears. Did it come, he wondered, from the lake, or from the woods?...

Then, suddenly, with a rush and a flutter of the heart, he knew that it was close beside him in the tent; and, when he turned over for a better hearing, it focussed itself unmistakably not two feet away. It was a sound of weeping: Défago upon his bed of branches was sobbing in the darkness as though his heart would break, the blankets evidently stuffed against his mouth to stifle it.

And his first feeling, before he could think or reflect, was the rush of a poignant and searching tenderness. This intimate, human sound, heard amid the desolation about them, woke pity. It was so incongruous, so pitifully incongruous—and so vain! Tears—in this vast and cruel wilderness: of what avail? He thought of a little child crying in mid-Atlantic... Then, of course, with fuller realization, and the memory of what had gone before, came the descent of the terror upon him, and his blood ran cold.

"Défago," he whispered quickly, "what's the matter?" He tried to make his voice very gentle. "Are you in pain—unhappy—?" There was no reply, but the sounds ceased abruptly. He stretched his hand out and touched him. The body did not stir.

"Are you awake?" for it occurred to him that the man was crying in his sleep. "Are you cold?" He noticed that his feet, which were uncovered, projected beyond the mouth of the tent. He spread an extra fold of his own blankets over them. The guide had slipped down in his bed, and the branches seemed to have been dragged with him. He was afraid to pull the body back again, for fear of waking him.

One or two tentative questions he ventured softly, but though he waited for several minutes there came no reply, nor any sign of movement. Presently he heard his regular and quiet breathing, and putting his hand again gently on the breast, felt the steady rise and fall beneath.

"Let me know if anything's wrong," he whispered, "or if I can do anything. Wake me at once if you feel—queer."

He hardly knew quite what to say. He lay down again, thinking and wondering what it all meant. Défago, of course, had been crying in his sleep. Some dream or other had afflicted him. Yet never in his life would he forget that pitiful sound of sobbing, and the feeling that the whole awful wilderness of woods listened...

His own mind busied itself for a long time with the recent events, of which *this* took its mysterious place as one, and though his reason successfully argued away all unwelcome suggestions, a sensation of uneasiness remained, resisting ejection, very deep-seated—peculiar beyond ordinary.

IV

But sleep, in the long run, proves greater than all emotions. His thoughts soon wandered again; he lay there, warm as a toast, exceedingly weary; the night soothed and comforted, blunting the edges of memory and alarm. Half-an-hour later he was oblivious of everything in the outer world about him.

Yet sleep, in this case, was his great enemy, concealing all approaches, smothering the warning of his nerves.

As, sometimes, in a nightmare events crowd upon each others' heels with a conviction of dreadfullest reality, yet some inconsistent detail accuses the whole display of incompleteness and disguise, so the events that now followed, though they actually happened, persuaded the mind somehow that the detail which could explain them had been overlooked in the confusion, and that therefore they were but partly true, the rest delusion. At the back of the sleeper's mind something remains awake, ready to let slip the judgment, "All this is not *quite* real; when you wake up you'll understand."

And thus, in a way, it was with Simpson. The events, not wholly inexplicable or incredible in themselves, yet remain for the man who saw and heard them a sequence of separate acts of cold horror, because the little piece that might have made the puzzle clear lay concealed or overlooked.

So far as he can recall, it was a violent movement, running downwards through the tent towards the door, that first woke him and made him aware that his companion was sitting bolt upright beside him—quivering. Hours must have passed, for it was the pale gleam of the dawn that revealed his outline against the canvas. This time the man was not crying; he was quaking like a leaf; the trembling he felt plainly through the blankets down the entire length of his own body. Défago had huddled down against him for protection, shrinking away from something that apparently concealed itself near the doorflaps of the little tent.

Simpson thereupon called out in a loud voice some question or other—in the first bewilderment of waking he does not remember exactly what—and the man made no reply. The atmosphere and feeling of true nightmare lay horribly about him, making movement and speech both difficult. At first, indeed, he was not sure where he was—whether in one of the earlier camps, or at home in his bed at Aberdeen. The sense of confusion was very troubling.

And next—almost simultaneous with his waking, it seemed—the profound stillness of the dawn outside was shattered by a most uncommon sound. It came without warning, or audible approach; and it was unspeakably dreadful. It was a voice, Simpson declares, possibly a human voice; hoarse yet plaintive—a soft, roaring voice close outside the tent, overhead rather than upon the ground, of immense volume, while in some strange way most penetratingly and seductively sweet. It rang out, too, in three separate and distinct notes, or cries, that bore in some odd fashion a resemblance, far-fetched yet recognizable, to the name of the guide: "Dé—fa—go!"

The student admits he is unable to describe it quite intelligently, for it was unlike any sound he had ever heard in his life, and combined a blending of such contrary qualities. "A sort of windy, crying voice," he calls it, "as of something lonely and untamed, wild and of abominable power..."

And, even before it ceased, dropping back into the great gulfs of silence, the guide beside him had sprung to his feet with an answering though unintelligible cry. He blundered against the tent-pole with violence, shaking the whole structure, spreading his arms out frantically for more room, and kicking his legs impetuously free of the clinging blankets. For a second, perhaps two, he stood upright by the door, his outline dark against the pallor of the dawn; then, with a furious, rushing speed, before his companion could move a hand to stop him, he shot with a plunge through the flaps of canvas—and was gone. And as he went—so astonishingly fast that the voice could actually be heard dying in the distance—he called aloud in tones of anguished terror that at the same time held something strangely like the frenzied exultation of delight—

"Oh! Oh! My feet of fire! My burning feet of fire! Oh! Oh! This height and fiery speed!"

And then the distance quickly buried it, and the deep silence of very early morning descended upon the forest as before.

It had all come about with such rapidity that, but for the evidence of the empty bed beside him, Simpson could almost have believed it to have been the memory of a nightmare carried over from sleep. He still felt the warm pressure of that vanished body against his side; there lay the twisted blankets in a heap; the very tent yet trembled with the vehemence of the impetuous departure. The strange words rang in his ears, as though he still heard them in the distance—wild language of a suddenly stricken mind. Moreover, it was not only the senses of sight and hearing that reported uncommon things to his brain, for even while the man cried and ran, he had become aware that a strange perfume, faint yet pungent, pervaded the interior of the tent. And it was at this point, it seems, brought to himself by the consciousness that his nostrils were taking this distressing odour down into his throat, that lie found his courage, sprang quickly to his feet—and went out.

The grey light of dawn that dropped, cold and glimmering, between the trees revealed the scene tolerably well. There stood the tent behind him, soaked with dew; the dark ashes of the fire, still warm; the lake, white beneath a coating of mist, the islands rising darkly out of it like objects packed in wool; and patches of snow beyond among the clearer spaces of the Bush—everything cold, still, waiting for the sun. But nowhere a sign of the vanished guide—still, doubtless, flying at frantic speed through the frozen woods. There was not even the sound of disappearing footsteps, nor the echoes of the dying voice. He had gone—utterly.

There was nothing; nothing but the sense of his recent presence, so strongly left behind about the camp; and—this penetrating, all-pervading odour.

And even this was now rapidly disappearing in its turn. In spite of his exceeding mental perturbation, Simpson struggled hard to detect its nature, and define it, but the ascertaining of an elusive scent, not recognized subconsciously and at once, is a very subtle operation of the mind. And he failed. It was gone before he could properly seize or name it. Approximate description, even, seems to have been difficult, for it was unlike any smell he knew. Acrid rather, not unlike the odour of a lion, he thinks, yet softer and not wholly unpleasing, with something almost sweet in it that reminded him of the scent of decaying garden leaves, earth, and the myriad, nameless perfumes that make up the odour of a big forest. Yet the "odour of lions" is the phrase with which he usually sums it all up.

Then—it was wholly gone, and he found himself standing by the ashes of the fire in a state of amazement and stupid terror that left him the helpless prey of anything that chose to happen. Had a musk-rat poked its pointed muzzle over a rock, or a squirrel scuttled in that instant down the bark of a tree, he would most likely have collapsed without more ado and fainted. For he felt about the whole affair the touch somewhere of a great Outer Horror...and his scattered powers had not as yet had time to collect themselves into a definite attitude of fighting self-control.

Nothing did happen, however. A great kiss of wind ran softly through the awakening forest, and a few maple leaves here and there rustled tremblingly to earth. The sky seemed to grow suddenly much lighter. Simpson felt the cool air upon his cheek and uncovered head; realized that he was shivering with the cold; and, making a great effort, realized next that he was alone in the Bush—*and* that he was called upon to take immediate steps to find and succour his vanished companion.

Make an effort, accordingly, he did, though an ill-calculated and futile one. With that wilderness of trees about him, the sheet of water cutting him off behind, and the horror of that wild cry in his blood, he did what any other inexperienced man would have done in similar bewilderment: he ran about, without any sense of direction, like a frantic child, and called loudly without ceasing the name of the guide—

"Défago! Défago! Défago!" he yelled, and the trees gave him back the name as often as he shouted, only a little softened—"Défago! Défago! Défago!"

He followed the trail that lay for a short distance across the patches of snow, and then lost it again where the trees grew too thickly for snow to lie. He shouted till he was hoarse, and till the sound of his own voice in all that unanswering and listening world began to frighten him. His confusion increased in direct ratio to the violence of his efforts. His distress became formidably acute, till at length his exertions defeated their own object, and from sheer exhaustion he headed back to the camp again. It remains a wonder that he ever found his way. It was with great difficulty, and only after numberless false clues, that he at last saw the white tent between the trees, and so reached safety.

Exhaustion then applied its own remedy, and he grew calmer. He made the fire and breakfasted. Hot coffee and bacon put a little sense and judgment into him again, and he realized that he had been behaving like a boy. He now made another, and more successful attempt to face the situation collectedly, and, a nature naturally plucky coming to his assistance, he decided that he must first make as thorough a search as possible, failing success in which, he must find his way to the home camp as best he could and bring help.

And this was what he did. Taking food, matches and rifle with him, and a small axe to blaze the trees against his return journey, he set forth. It was eight o'clock when he started, the sun shining over the tops of the trees in a sky without clouds. Pinned to a stake by the fire he left a note in case Défago returned while he was away.

This time, according to a careful plan, he took a new direction, intending to make a wide sweep that must sooner or later cut into indications of the guide's trail; and, before he had gone a quarter of a mile he came across the tracks of a large animal in the snow, and beside it the light and smaller tracks of what were beyond question human feet—the feet of Défago. The relief he at once experienced was natural, though brief; for at first sight he saw in these tracks a simple explanation of the whole matter: these big marks had surely been left by a bull moose that, wind against it, had blundered upon the camp, and uttered its singular cry of warning and alarm the moment its mistake was apparent. Défago, in whom the hunting instinct was developed to the point of uncanny perfection, had scented the brute coming down the wind hours before. His excitement and disappearance were due, of course, to—to his—

Then the impossible explanation at which he grasped faded, as common sense showed him mercilessly that none of this was true. No guide, much less a guide like Défago, could have acted in so irrational a way, going off even without his rifle…! The whole affair demanded a far more complicated elucidation, when he remembered the details of it all—the cry of terror, the amazing language, the grey face of horror when his nostrils first caught the new odour; that muffled sobbing in the darkness, and—for this, too, now came back to him dimly—the man's original aversion for this particular bit of country...

Besides, now that he examined them closer, these were not the tracks of a moose at all! Hank had explained to him the outline of a bull's hoofs, of a cow's or calf's, too, for that matter; he had drawn them clearly on a strip of birch bark. And these were wholly different. They were big, round, ample, and with no pointed outline as of sharp hoofs. He wondered for a moment whether bear-tracks were like that. There was no other animal he could think of, for caribou did not come so far south at this season, and, even if they did, would leave hoof-marks.

They were ominous signs—these mysterious writings left in the snow by the unknown creature that had lured a human being away from safety—and when he coupled them in his imagination with that haunting sound that broke the stillness of the dawn, a momentary dizziness shook his mind, distressing him again beyond belief. He felt the *threatening* aspect of it all. And, stooping down to examine the marks more closely, he caught a faint whiff of that sweet yet pungent odour that made him instantly straighten up again, fighting a sensation almost of nausea.

Then his memory played him another evil trick. He suddenly recalled those uncovered feet projecting beyond the edge of the tent, and the body's appearance of having been dragged towards the opening; the man's shrinking from something by the door when he woke later. The details now beat against his trembling mind with concerted attack. They seemed to gather in those deep spaces of the silent forest about him, where the host of trees stood waiting, listening, watching to see what he would do. The woods were closing round him.

With the persistence of true pluck, however, Simpson went forward, following the tracks as best he could, smothering these ugly emotions that sought to weaken his will. He blazed innumerable trees as he went, ever fearful of being unable to find the way back, and calling aloud at intervals of a few seconds the name of the guide. The dull tapping of the axe upon the massive trunks, and the unnatural accents of his own voice became at length sounds that he even dreaded to make, dreaded to hear. For they drew attention without ceasing to his presence and exact whereabouts, and if it were really the case that something was hunting himself down in the same way that he was hunting down another—

With a strong effort, he crushed the thought out the instant it rose. It was the beginning, he realized, of a bewilderment utterly diabolical in kind that would speedily destroy him.

Although the snow was not continuous, lying merely in shallow flurries over the more open spaces, he found no difficulty in following the tracks for the first few miles. They went straight as a ruled line wherever the trees permitted. The stride soon began to increase in length, till it finally assumed proportions that seemed absolutely impossible for any ordinary animal to have made. Like huge flying leaps they became. One of these he measured, and though he knew that "stretch" of eighteen feet must be somehow wrong, he was at a complete loss to understand why he found no signs on the snow between the extreme points. But what perplexed him even more, making him feel his vision had gone utterly awry, was that Défago's stride increased in the same manner, and finally covered the same incredible distances. It looked as if the great beast had lifted him with it and carried him across these astonishing intervals. Simpson, who was much longer in the limb, found that he could not compass even half the stretch by taking a running jump.

And the sight of these huge tracks, running side by side, silent evidence of a dreadful journey in which terror or madness had urged to impossible results, was profoundly moving. It shocked him in the secret depths of his soul. It was the most horrible thing his eyes had ever looked upon. He began to follow them mechanically, absent-mindedly almost, ever peering over his shoulder to see if *he, too, were being followed by something with a gigantic tread... And soon it came about that he no longer quite realized what it was they signified-these impressions left upon the snow by something nameless and untamed, always accompanied by the footmarks of the little French Canadian, his guide, his comrade, the man who had shared his tent a few hours before, chatting, laughing, even singing by his side...

V

For a man of his years and inexperience, only a canny Scot, perhaps, grounded in common sense and established in logic, could have preserved even that measure of balance that this youth somehow or other did manage to preserve through the whole adventure. Otherwise, two things he presently noticed, while forging pluckily ahead, must have sent him headlong back to the comparative safety of his tent, instead of only making his hands close more tightly upon the rifle-stock, while his heart, trained for the Wee Kirk, sent a wordless prayer winging its way to heaven. Both tracks, he saw, had undergone a change, and this change, so far as it concerned the footsteps of the man, was in some undecipherable manner—appalling.

It was in the bigger tracks he first noticed this, and for a long time he could not quite believe his eyes. Was it the blown leaves that produced odd effects of light and shade, or that the dry snow, drifting like finely-ground rice about the edges, cast shadows and high lights? Or was it actually the fact that the great marks had become faintly coloured? For round about the deep, plunging holes of the animal there now appeared a mysterious, reddish tinge that was more like an effect of light than of anything that dyed the substance of the snow itself. Every mark had it, and had it increasingly—this indistinct fiery tinge that painted a new touch of ghastliness into the picture.

But when, wholly unable to explain or credit it, he turned his attention to the other tracks to discover if they, too, bore similar witness, he noticed that these had meanwhile undergone a change that was infinitely worse, and charged with far more horrible suggestion. For, in the last hundred yards or so, he saw that they had grown gradually into the semblance of the parent tread. Imperceptibly the change had come about, yet unmistakably. It was hard to see where the change first began. The result, however, was beyond question. Smaller, neater, more cleanly modelled, they formed now an exact and careful duplicate of the larger tracks beside them. The feet that produced them had, therefore, also changed. And something in his mind reared up with loathing and with terror as he saw it.

Simpson, for the first time, hesitated; then, ashamed of his alarm and indecision, took a few hurried steps ahead; the next instant stopped dead in his tracks. Immediately in front of him all signs of the trail ceased; both tracks came to an abrupt end. On all sides, for a hundred yards and more, he searched in vain for the least indication of their continuance. There was—nothing.

The trees were very thick just there, big trees all of them, spruce, cedar, hemlock; there was no underbrush. He stood, looking about him, all distraught; bereft of any power of judgment. Then he set to work to search again, and again, and yet again, but always with the same result: *nothing.* The feet that printed the surface of the snow thus far had now, apparently, left the ground!

And it was in that moment of distress and confusion that the whip of terror laid its most nicely calculated lash about his heart. It dropped with deadly effect upon the sorest spot of all, completely unnerving him. He had been secretly dreading all the time that it would come—and come it did.

Far overhead, muted by great height and distance, strangely thinned and wailing, he heard the crying voice of Défago, the guide.

The sound dropped upon him out of that still, wintry sky with an effect of dismay and terror unsurpassed. The rifle fell to his feet. He stood motionless an instant, listening as it were with his whole body, then staggered back against the nearest tree for support, disorganized hopelessly in mind and spirit. To him, in that moment, it seemed the most shattering and dislocating experience he had ever known, so that his heart emptied itself of all feeling whatsoever as by a sudden draught.

"Oh! Oh! This fiery height! Oh, my feet of fire! My burning feet of fire...!" ran in far, beseeching accents of indescribable appeal this voice of anguish down the sky. Once it called—then silence through all the listening wilderness of trees.

And Simpson, scarcely knowing what he did, presently found himself running wildly to and fro, searching, calling, tripping over roots and boulders, and flinging himself in a frenzy of undirected pursuit after the Caller. Behind the screen of memory and emotion with which experience veils events, he plunged, distracted and half-deranged, picking up false lights like a ship at sea, terror in his eyes and heart and soul. For the Panic of the Wilderness had called to him in that far voice—the Power of untamed Distance—the Enticement of the Desolation that destroys. He knew in that moment all the pains of someone hopelessly and irretrievably lost, suffering the lust and travail of a soul in the final Loneliness. A vision of Défago, eternally hunted, driven and pursued across the skiey vastness of those ancient forests, fled like a flame across the dark ruin of his thoughts...

It seemed ages before he could find anything in the chaos of his disorganized sensations to which he could anchor himself steady for a moment, and think....

The cry was not repeated; his own hoarse calling brought no response; the inscrutable forces of the Wild had summoned their victim beyond recall—and held him fast.

Yet he searched and called, it seems, for hours afterwards, for it was late in the afternoon when at length he decided to abandon a useless pursuit and return to his camp on the shores of Fifty Island Water. Even then he went with reluctance, that crying voice still echoing in his ears. With difficulty he found his rifle and the homeward trail. The concentration necessary to follow the badly blazed trees, and a biting hunger that gnawed, helped to keep his mind steady. Otherwise, he admits, the temporary aberration he had suffered might have been prolonged to the point of positive disaster. Gradually the ballast shifted back again, and he regained something that approached his normal equilibrium.

But for all that the journey through the gathering dusk was miserably haunted. He heard innumerable following footsteps; voices that laughed and whispered; and saw figures crouching behind trees and boulders, making signs to one another for a concerted attack the moment he had passed. The creeping murmur of the wind made him start and listen. He went stealthily, trying to hide where possible, and making as little sound as he could. The shadows of the woods, hitherto protective or covering merely, had now become menacing, challenging; and the pageantry in his frightened mind masked a host of possibilities that were all the more ominous for being obscure. The presentiment of a nameless doom lurked ill-concealed behind every detail of what had happened.

It was really admirable how he emerged victor in the end; men of riper powers and experience might have come through the ordeal with less success. He had himself tolerably well in hand, all things considered, and his plan of action proves it. Sleep being absolutely out of the question, and travelling an unknown trail in the darkness equally impracticable, he sat up the whole of that night, rifle in hand, before a fire he never for a single moment allowed to die down. The severity of the haunted vigil marked his soul for life; but it was successfully accomplished; and with the very first signs of dawn he set forth upon the long return journey to the home-camp to get help. As before, he left a written note to explain his absence, and to indicate where he had left a plentiful *cache* of food and matches—though he had no expectation that any human hands would find them!

How Simpson found his way alone by lake and forest might well make a story in itself, for to hear him tell it is to *know* the passionate loneliness of soul that a man can feel when the Wilderness holds him in the hollow of its illimitable hand—and laughs. It is also to admire his indomitable pluck.

He claims no skill, declaring that he followed the almost invisible trail mechanically, and without thinking. And this, doubtless, is the truth. He relied upon the guiding of the unconscious mind, which is instinct. Perhaps, too, some sense of orientation, known to animals and primitive men, may have helped as well, for through all that tangled region he succeeded in reaching the exact spot where Défago had hidden the canoe nearly three days before with the remark, "Strike doo west across the lake into the sun to find the camp."

There was not much sun left to guide him, but he used his compass to the best of his ability, embarking in the frail craft for the last twelve miles of his journey with a sensation of immense relief that the forest was at last behind him. And, fortunately, the water was calm; he took his line across the centre of the lake instead of coasting round the shores for another twenty miles. Fortunately, too, the other hunters were back. The light of their fires furnished a steering-point without which he might have searched all night long for the actual position of the camp.

It was close upon midnight all the same when his canoe grated on the sandy cove, and Hank, Punk and his uncle, disturbed in their sleep by his cries, ran quickly down and helped a very exhausted and broken specimen of Scotch humanity over the rocks towards a dying fire.

VI

The sudden entrance of his prosaic uncle into this world of wizardry and horror that had haunted him without interruption now for two days and two nights, had the immediate effect of giving to the affair an entirely new aspect. The sound of that crisp "Hulloa, my boy! And what's up *now?*" and the grasp of that dry and vigorous hand introduced another standard of judgment. A revulsion of feeling washed through him. He realized that he had let himself "go" rather badly. He even felt vaguely ashamed of himself. The native hard-headedness of his race reclaimed him.

And this doubtless explains why he found it so hard to tell that group round the fire—everything. He told enough, however, for the immediate decision to be arrived at that a relief party must start at the earliest possible moment, and that Simpson, in order to guide it capably, must first have food and, above all, sleep. Dr. Cathcart observing the lad's condition more shrewdly than his patient knew, gave him a very slight injection of morphine. For six hours he slept like the dead.

From the description carefully written out after. wards by this student of divinity, it appears that the account he gave to the astonished group omitted sundry vital and important details. He declares that, with his uncle's wholesome, matter-of-fact countenance staring him in the face, he simply had not the courage to mention them. Thus, all the search-party gathered, it would seem, was that Défago had suffered in the night an acute and inexplicable attack of mania, had imagined himself "called" by someone or something, and had plunged into the bush after it without food or rifle, where he must die a horrible and lingering death by cold and starvation unless he could be found and rescued in time. "In time," moreover, meant "at once."

In the course of the following day, however—they were off by seven, leaving Punk in charge with instructions to have food and fire always ready—Simpson found it possible to tell his uncle a good deal more of the story's true inwardness, without divining that it was drawn out of him as a matter of fact by a very subtle form of cross-examination. By the time they reached the beginning of the trail, where the canoe was laid up against the return journey, he had mentioned how Défago spoke vaguely of "something he called a 'Wendigo'"; how he cried in his sleep; how he imagined an unusual scent about the camp; and had betrayed other symptoms of mental excitement. He also admitted the bewildering effect of "that extraordinary odour" upon himself, "pungent and acrid like the odour of lions." And by the time they were within an easy hour of Fifty Island Water he had let slip the further fact—a foolish avowal of his own hysterical condition, as he felt afterwards—that he had heard the vanished guide call "for help." He omitted the singular phrases used, for he simply could not bring himself to repeat the preposterous language. Also, while describing how the man's footsteps in the snow had gradually assumed an exact miniature likeness of the animal's plunging tracks, he left out the fact that they measured a *wholly* incredible distance. It seemed a question, nicely balanced between individual pride and honesty, what he should reveal and what suppress. He mentioned the fiery tinge in the snow, for instance, yet shrank from telling that body and bed had been partly dragged out of the tent...

With the net result that Dr. Cathcart, adroit psychologist that he fancied himself to be, had assured him clearly enough exactly where his mind, influenced by loneliness, bewilderment and terror, had yielded to the strain and invited delusion. While praising his conduct, he managed at the same time to point out where, when, and how his mind had gone astray. He made his nephew think himself finer than he was by judicious praise, yet more foolish than he was by minimizing the value of his evidence. Like many another materialist, that is, he lied cleverly on the basis of insufficient knowledge, *because* the knowledge supplied seemed to his own particular intelligence inadmissible.

"The spell of these terrible solitudes," he said, "cannot leave any mind untouched, any mind, that is, possessed of the higher imaginative qualities. It has worked upon yours exactly as it worked upon my own when I was your age. The animal that haunted your little camp was undoubtedly a moose, for the 'belling' of a moose may have, sometimes, a very peculiar quality of sound. The coloured appearance of the big tracks was obviously a defect of vision in your own eyes produced by excitement. The size and stretch of the tracks we shall prove when we come to them. But the hallucination of an audible voice, of course, is one of the commonest forms of delusion due to mental excitement—an excitement, my dear boy, perfectly excusable, and, let me add, wonderfully controlled by you under the circumstances. For the rest, I am bound to say, you have acted with a splendid courage, for the terror of feeling oneself lost in this wilderness is nothing short of awful, and, had I been in your place, I don't for a moment believe I could have behaved with one quarter of your wisdom and decision. The only thing I find it uncommonly difficult to explain is—that—damned odour."

"It made me feel sick, I assure you," declared his nephew, "positively dizzy!" His uncle's attitude of calm omniscience, merely because he knew more psychological formulae, made him slightly defiant. It was so easy to be wise in the explanation of an experience one has not personally witnessed. "A kind of desolate and terrible odour is the only way I can describe it," he concluded, glancing at the features of the quiet, unemotional man beside him.

"I can only marvel," was the reply, "that under the circumstances it did not seem to you even worse." The dry words, Simpson knew, hovered between the truth, and his uncle's interpretation of "the truth."

And so at last they came to the little camp and found the tent still standing, the remains of the fire, and the piece of paper pinned to a stake beside it—untouched. The *cache*, poorly contrived by inexperienced hands, however, had been discovered and opened—by musk rats, mink and squirrel. The matches lay scattered about the opening, but the food had been taken to the last crumb.

"Well, fellers, he ain't here," exclaimed Hank loudly after his fashion, "and that's as sartain as the coal supply down below! But whar he's got to by this time is 'bout as onsartain as the trade in crowns in t'other place." The presence of a divinity student was no barrier to his language at such a time, though for the reader's sake it may be severely edited. "I propose," he added, "that we start out at once an' hunt for'm like hell!"

The gloom of Défago's probable fate oppressed the whole party with a sense of dreadful gravity the moment they saw the familiar signs of recent occupancy. Especially the tent, with the bed of balsam branches still smoothed and flattened by the pressure of his body, seemed to bring his presence near to them. Simpson, feeling vaguely as if his word were somehow at stake, went about explaining particulars in a hushed tone. He was much calmer now, though overwearied with the strain of his many journeys. His uncle's method of explaining—"explaining away," rather—the details still fresh in his haunted memory helped, too, to put ice upon his emotions.

"And that's the direction he ran off in," he said to his two companions, pointing in the direction where the guide had vanished that morning in the grey dawn. "Straight down there he ran like a deer, in between the birch and the hemlock..."

Hank and Dr. Cathcart exchanged glances.

"And it was about two miles down there, in a straight line," continued the other, speaking with something of the former terror in his voice, "that I followed his trail to the place where—it stopped—dead!"

"And where you heered him callin' an' caught the stench, an' all the rest of the wicked entertainment," cried Hank, with a volubility that betrayed his keen distress.

"And where your excitement overcame you to the point of producing illusions," added Dr. Cathcart under his breath, yet not so low that his nephew did not hear it.

It was early in the afternoon, for they had travelled quickly, and there were still a good two hours of daylight left. Dr. Cathcart and Hank lost no time in beginning the search, but Simpson was too exhausted to accompany them. They would follow the blazed marks on the trees, and where possible, his footsteps. Meanwhile the best thing he could do was to keep a good fire going, and rest.

But after something like three hours' search, the darkness already down, the two men returned to camp with nothing to report. Fresh snow had covered all signs, and though they had followed the blazed trees to the spot where Simpson had turned back, they had not discovered the smallest indications of a human being—or, for that matter, of an animal. There were no fresh tracks of any kind; the snow lay undisturbed.

It was difficult to know what was best to do, though in reality there was nothing more they *could* do. They might stay and search for weeks without much chance of success. The fresh snow destroyed their only hope, and they gathered round the fire for supper, a gloomy and despondent party. The facts, indeed, were sad enough, for Défago had a wife at Rat Portage, and his earnings were the family's sole means of support.

Now that the whole truth in all its ugliness was out, it seemed useless to deal in further disguise or pretence. They talked openly of the facts and probabilities. It was not the first time, even in the experience of Dr. Cathcart, that a man had yielded to the singular seduction of the Solitudes and gone out of his mind; Défago, moreover, was predisposed to something of the sort, for he already had the touch of melancholia in his blood, and his fibre was weakened by bouts of drinking that often lasted for weeks at a time. Something on this trip—one might never know precisely what—had sufficed to push him over the line, that was all. And he had gone, gone off into the great wilderness of trees and lakes to die by starvation and exhaustion. The chances against his finding camp again were overwhelming; the delirium that was upon him would also doubtless have increased, and it was quite likely he might do violence to himself and so hasten his cruel fate. Even while they talked, indeed, the end had probably come. On the suggestion of Hank, his old pal, however, they proposed to wait a little longer and devote the whole of the following day, from dawn to darkness, to the most systematic search they could devise. They would divide the territory between them. They discussed their plan in great detail. All that men could do they would do.

And, meanwhile, they talked about the particular form in which the singular Panic of the Wilderness had made its attack upon the mind of the unfortunate guide. Hank, though familiar with the legend in its general outline, obviously did not welcome the turn the conversation had taken. He contributed little, though that little was illuminating. For he admitted that a story ran over all this section of country to the effect that several Indians had "seen the Wendigo" along the shores of Fifty Island Water in the "fall" of last year, and that this was the true reason of Défago's disinclination to hunt there. Hank doubtless felt that he had in a sense helped his old pal to death by over-persuading him. "When an Indian goes crazy," he explained, talking to himself more than to the others, it seemed, "it's always put that he's 'seen the Wendigo.' An' pore old Défago was superstitious down to his very heels...!"

And then Simpson, feeling the atmosphere more sympathetic, told over again the full story of his astonishing tale; he left out no details this time; he mentioned his own sensations and gripping fears. He only omitted the strange language used.

"But Défago surely had already told you all these details of the Wendigo legend, my dear fellow," insisted the doctor. "I mean, he had talked about it, and thus put into your mind the ideas which your own excitement afterwards developed?"

Whereupon Simpson again repeated the facts. Défago, he declared, had barely mentioned the beast. He, Simpson, knew nothing of the story, and, so far as he remembered, had never even read about it. Even the word was unfamiliar.

Of course he was telling the truth, and Dr. Cathcart was reluctantly compelled to admit the singular character of the whole affair. He did not do this in words so much as in manner, however. He kept his back against a good, stout tree; he poked the fire into a blaze the moment it showed signs of dying down; he was quicker than any of them to notice the least sound in the night about them—a fish jumping in the lake, a twig snapping in the bush, the dropping of occasional fragments of frozen snow from the branches overhead where the heat loosened them. His voice, too, changed a little in quality, becoming a shade less confident, lower also in tone. Fear, to put it plainly, hovered close about that little camp, and though all three would have been glad to speak of other matters, the only thing they seemed able to discuss was this—the source of their fear. They tried other subjects in vain; there was nothing to say about them. Hank was the most honest of the group; he said next to nothing. He never once, however, turned his back to the darkness. His face was always to the forest, and when wood was needed he didn't go farther than was necessary to get it.

VII

A wall of silence wrapped them in, for the snow, though not thick, was sufficient to deaden any noise, and the frost held things pretty tight besides. No sound but their voices and the soft roar of the flames made itself heard. Only, from time to time, something soft as the flutter of a pine-moth's wings went past them through the air. No one seemed anxious to go to bed. The hours slipped towards midnight.

"The legend is picturesque enough," observed the doctor after one of the longer pauses, speaking to break it rather than because he had anything to say, "for the Wendigo is simply the Call of the Wild personified, which some natures hear to their own destruction."

"That's about it," Hank said presently. "An' there's no misunderstandin' when you hear it. It calls you by name right 'nough."

Another pause followed. Then Dr. Cathcart came back to the forbidden subject with a rush that made the others jump.

"The allegory *is* significant," he remarked, looking about him into the darkness, "for the Voice, they say, resembles all the minor sounds of the Bush—wind, falling water, cries of animals, and so forth. And, once the victim hears *that*—he's off for good, of course! His most vulnerable points, moreover, are said to be the feet and the eyes; the feet, you see, for the lust of wandering, and the eyes for the lust of beauty. The poor beggar goes at such a dreadful speed that he bleeds beneath the eyes, and his feet burn."

Dr. Cathcart, as he spoke, continued to peer uneasily into the surrounding gloom. His voice sank to a hushed tone.

"The Wendigo," he added, "is said to burn his feet-owing to the friction, apparently caused by its tremendous velocity—till they drop off, and new ones form exactly like its own."

Simpson listened in horrified amazement; but it was the pallor on Hank's face that fascinated him most. He would willingly have stopped his ears and closed his eyes, had he dared.

"It don't always keep to the ground neither," came in Hank's slow, heavy drawl, "for it goes so high that he thinks the stars have set him all a-fire. An' it'll take great thumpin' jumps sometimes, an' run along the tops of the trees, carrying its partner with it, an' then droppin' him jest as a fish-hawk'll drop a pickerel to kill it before eatin'. An' its food, of all the muck in the whole Bush is—moss!" And he laughed a short, unnatural laugh. "It's a moss-eater, is the Wendigo," he added, looking up excitedly into the faces of his companions, "moss-eater," he repeated, with a string of the most outlandish oaths he could invent.

But Simpson now understood the true purpose of all this talk. What these two men, each strong and "experienced "in his own way, dreaded more than anything else was—silence. They were talking against time. They were also talking against darkness, against the invasion of panic, against the admission reflection might bring that they were in an enemy's country—against anything, in fact, rather than allow their inmost thoughts to assume control. He himself, already initiated by the awful vigil with terror, was beyond both of them in this respect. He had reached the stage where he was immune. But these two, the scoffing, analytical doctor, and the honest, dogged backwoodsman, each sat trembling in the depths of his being.

Thus the hours passed; and thus, with lowered voices and a kind of taut inner resistance of spirit, this little group of humanity sat in the jaws of the wilderness and talked foolishly of the terrible and haunting legend. It was an unequal contest, all things considered, for the wilderness had already the advantage of first attack—and of a hostage. The fate of their comrade hung over them with a steadily increasing weight of oppression that finally became insupportable.

It was Hank, after a pause longer than the preceding ones that no one seemed able to break, who first let loose all this pent-up emotion in very unexpected fashion, by springing suddenly to his feet and letting out the most ear-shattering yell imaginable into the night. He could not contain himself any longer, it seemed. To make it carry even beyond an ordinary cry he interrupted its rhythm by shaking the palm of his hand before his mouth.

"That's for Défago," he said, looking down at the other two with a queer, defiant laugh, "for it's my belief"—the sandwiched oaths may be omitted—"that my ole partner's not far from us at this very minute."

There was a vehemence and recklessness about his performance that made Simpson, too, start to his feet in amazement, and betrayed even the doctor into letting the pipe slip from between his lips. Hank's face was ghastly, but Cathcart's showed a sudden weakness —a loosening of all his faculties, as it were. Then a momentary anger blazed into his eyes, and he too, though with deliberation born of habitual self-control, got upon his feet and faced the excited guide. For this was unpermissible, foolish, dangerous, and he meant to stop it in the bud.

What might have happened in the next minute or two one may speculate about, yet never definitely know, for in the instant of profound silence that followed Hank's roaring voice, and as though in answer to it, something went past through the darkness of the sky overhead at terrific speed—something of necessity very large, for it displaced much air, while down between the trees there fell a faint and windy cry of a human voice, calling in tones of indescribable anguish and appeal—

"Oh, oh! This fiery height! Oh, oh! My feet of fire! My burning feet of fire!"

White to the very edge of his shirt, Hank looked stupidly about him like a child. Dr. Cathcart uttered some kind of unintelligible cry, turning as he did so with an instinctive movement of blind terror towards the protection of the tent, then halting in the act as though frozen. Simpson, alone of the three, retained his presence of mind a little. His own horror was too deep to allow of any immediate reaction. He had heard that cry before.

Turning to his stricken companions, he said almost calmly—

"That's exactly the cry I heard—the very words he used!"

Then, lifting his face to the sky, he cried aloud, "Défago, Défago! Come down here to us! Come down—!"

And before there was time for anybody to take definite action one way or another, there came the sound of something dropping heavily between the trees, striking the branches on the way down, and landing with a dreadful thud upon the frozen earth below. The crash and thunder of it was really terrific.

"That's him, s'help me the good Gawd!" came from Hank in a whispering cry half choked, his hand going automatically towards the hunting-knife in his belt. "And he's coming! He's coming!" he added, with an irrational laugh of terror, as the sounds of heavy footsteps crunching over the snow became distinctly audible, approaching through the blackness towards the circle of light.

And while the steps, with their stumbling motion, moved nearer and nearer upon them, the three men stood round that fire, motionless and dumb. Dr. Cathcart had the appearance as of a man suddenly withered; even his eyes did not move. Hank, suffering shockingly, seemed on the verge again of violent action; yet did nothing. He, too, was hewn of stone. Like stricken children they seemed. The picture was hideous. And, meanwhile, their owner still invisible, the footsteps came closer, crunching the frozen snow. It was endless—too prolonged to be quite real—this measured and pitiless approach. It was accursed.

VIII

Then at length the darkness, having this laboriously conceived, brought forth—a figure. It drew forward into the zone of uncertain light where fire and shadows mingled, not ten feet away; then halted, staring at them fixedly. The same instant it started forward again with the spasmodic motion as of a thing moved by wires, and coming up closer to them, full into the glare of the fire, they perceived then that—it was a man; and apparently that this man was—Défago.

Something like a skin of horror almost perceptibly drew down in that moment over every face, and three pairs of eyes shone through it as though they saw across the frontiers of normal vision into the Unknown.

Défago advanced, his tread faltering and uncertain; he made his way straight up to them as a group first, then turned sharply and peered close into the face of Simpson. The sound of a voice issued from his lips—

"Here I am, Boss Simpson. I heered someone calling me." It was a faint, dried-up voice, made wheezy and breathless as by immense exertion. "I'm havin' a reg'lar hell-fire kind of a trip, I am." And he laughed, thrusting his head forward into the other's face.

But that laugh started the machinery of the group of wax-work figures with the wax-white skins. Hank immediately sprang forward with a stream of oaths so far-fetched that Simpson did not recognize them as English at all, but thought he had lapsed into Indian or some other lingo. He only realized that Hank's presence, thrust thus between them, was welcome—uncommonly welcome. Dr. Cathcart, though more calmly and leisurely, advanced behind him, heavily stumbling.

Simpson seems hazy as to what was actually said and done in those next few seconds, for the eyes of that detestable and blasted visage peering at such close quarters into his own utterly bewildered his senses at first. He merely stood still. He said nothing. He had not the trained will of the older men that forced them into action in defiance of all emotional stress. He watched them moving as behind a glass, that half destroyed their reality: it was dream-like, perverted. Yet, through the torrent of Hank's meaningless phrases, he remembers hearing his uncle's tone of authority—hard and forced—saying several things about food and warmth, blankets, whisky and the rest;...and, further, that whiffs of that penetrating, unaccustomed odour, vile, yet sweetly bewildering, assailed his nostrils during all that followed.

It was no less a person than himself, however—less experienced and adroit than the others though he was—who gave instinctive utterance to the sentence that brought a measure of relief into the ghastly situation by expressing the doubt and thought in each one's heart.

"It is—YOU, isn't it, Défago?" he asked under his breath, horror breaking his speech.

And at once Cathcart burst out with the loud answer before the other had time to move his lips. "Of course it is! Of course it is! Only—can't you see—he's nearly dead with exhaustion, cold and terror? Isn't that enough to change a man beyond all recognition?" It was said in order to convince himself as much as to convince the others. The overemphasis alone proved that. And continually, while he spoke and acted, he held a handkerchief to his nose. That odour pervaded the whole camp.

For the "Défago" who sat huddled by the big fire, wrapped in blankets, drinking hot whisky and holding food in wasted hands, was no more like the guide they had last seen alive than the picture of a man of sixty is like the daguerreotype of his early youth in the costume of another generation. Nothing really can describe that ghastly caricature, that parody, masquerading there in the firelight as Défago. From the ruins of the dark and awful memories he still retains, Simpson declares that the face was more animal than human, the features drawn about into wrong proportions, the skin loose and hanging, as though he had been subjected to extraordinary pressures and tensions. It made him think vaguely of those bladder-faces blown up by the hawkers on Ludgate Hill, that change their expression as they swell, and as they collapse emit a faint and wailing imitation of a voice. Both face and voice suggested some such abominable resemblance: But Cathcart long afterwards, seeking to describe the indescribable, asserts that thus might have looked a face and body that had been in air so rarified that, the weight of atmosphere being removed, the entire structure threatened to fly asunder and become—*incoherent*...

It was Hank, though all distraught and shaking with a tearing volume of emotion he could neither handle nor understand, who brought things to a head without more ado. He went off to a little distance from the fire, apparently so that the light should not dazzle him too much, and shading his eyes for a moment with both hands, shouted in a loud voice that held anger and affection dreadfully mingled—

"You ain't Défaygo! You ain't Défaygo at all! I don't give a—damn, but that ain't you, my ole pal of twenty years!" He glared upon the huddled figure as though he would destroy him with his eyes. "An' if it is I'll swab the floor of hell with a wad of cotton-wool on a toothpick, s'help me the good Gawd!" he added, with a violent fling of horror and disgust.

It was impossible to silence him. He stood there shouting like one possessed, horrible to see, horrible to hear—*because it was the truth*. He repeated himself in fifty different ways, each more outlandish than the last. The woods rang with echoes. At one time it looked as if he meant to fling himself upon "the intruder," for his hand continually jerked towards the long hunting-knife in his belt.

But in the end he did nothing, and the whole tempest completed itself very nearly with tears. Hank's voice suddenly broke, he collapsed on the ground, and Cathcart somehow or other persuaded him at last to go into the tent and lie quiet. The remainder of the affair, indeed, was witnessed by him from behind the canvas, his white and terrified face peeping through the crack of the tent door-flap.

Then Dr. Cathcart, closely followed by his nephew who so far had kept his courage better than all of them, went up with a determined air and stood opposite to the figure of Défago huddled over the fire. He looked him squarely in the face and spoke. At first his voice was firm.

"Défago, tell us what's happened—just a little, so that we can know how best to help you?" he asked in a tone of authority, almost of command. And at that point, it was command. At once afterwards, however, it changed in quality, for the figure turned up to him a face so piteous, so terrible and so little like humanity, that the doctor shrank back from him as from something spiritually unclean. Simpson, watching close behind him, says he got the impression of a mask that was on the verge of dropping off, and that underneath they would discover something black and diabolical, revealed in utter nakedness. "Out with it, man, out with it!" Cathcart cried, terror running neck and neck with entreaty. "None of us can stand this much longer...!" It was the cry of instinct over reason.

And then "Défago," smiling *whitely*, answered in that thin and fading voice that already seemed passing over into a sound of quite another character—

"I seen that great Wendigo thing," he whispered, sniffing the air about him exactly like an animal. "I been with it too—"

Whether the poor devil would have said more, or whether Dr. Cathcart would have continued the impossible cross-examination cannot be known, for at that moment the voice of Hank was heard yelling at the top of his shout from behind the canvas that concealed all but his terrified eyes. Such a howling was never heard.

"His feet! Oh, Gawd, his feet! Look at his great changed—feet!"

Défago, shuffling where he sat, had moved in such a way that for the first time his legs were in full light and his feet were visible. Yet Simpson had no time, himself, to see properly what Hank had seen. And Hank has never seen fit to tell. That same instant, with a leap like that of a frightened tiger, Cathcart was upon him, bundling the folds of blanket about his legs with such speed that the young student caught little more than a passing glimpse of something dark and oddly massed where moccasined feet ought to have been, and saw even that but with uncertain vision.

Then, before the doctor had time to do more, or Simpson time to even think a question, much less ask it, Défago was standing upright in front of them, balancing with pain and difficulty, and upon his shapeless and twisted visage an expression so dark and so malicious that it was, in the true sense, monstrous.

"Now *you* seen it too," he wheezed, "you seen my fiery, burning feet! And now—that is, unless you kin save me an' prevent—it's 'bout time for—"

His piteous and beseeching voice was interrupted by a sound that was like the roar of wind coming across the lake. The trees overhead shook their tangled branches. The blazing fire bent its flames as before a blast. And something swept with a terrific, rushing noise about the little camp and seemed to surround it entirely in a single moment of time. Défago shook the clinging blankets from his body, turned towards the woods behind, and with the same stumbling motion that had brought him—was gone: gone, before any one could move muscle to prevent him, gone with an amazing, blundering swiftness that left no time to act. The darkness positively swallowed him; and less than a dozen seconds later, above the roar of the swaying trees and the shout of the sudden wind, all three men, watching and listening with stricken hearts, heard a cry that seemed to drop down upon them from a great height of sky and distance—

"Oh, oh! This fiery height! Oh, oh! My feet of fire! My burning feet of fire...!" then died away, into untold space and silence.

Dr. Cathcart—suddenly master of himself, and therefore of the others—was just able to seize Hank violently by the arm as he tried to dash headlong into the Bush.

"But I want ter know,—you!" shrieked the guide. "I want ter see! That ain't him at all, but some—devil that's shunted into his place...!"

Somehow or other—he admits he never quite knew how he accomplished it—he managed to keep him in the tent and pacify him. The doctor, apparently, had reached the stage where reaction had set in and allowed his own innate force to conquer. Certainly he "managed" Hank admirably. It was his nephew, however, hitherto so wonderfully controlled, who gave him most cause for anxiety, for the cumulative strain had now produced a condition of lachrymose hysteria which made it necessary to isolate him upon a bed of boughs and blankets as far removed from Hank as was possible under the circumstances.

And there he lay, as the watches of that haunted night passed over the lonely camp, crying startled sentences, and fragments of sentences, into the folds of his blankets. A quantity of gibberish about speed and height and fire mingled oddly with biblical memories of the class-room. "People with broken faces all on fire are coming at a most awful, awful, pace towards the camp!" he would moan one minute; and the next would sit up and stare into the woods, intently listening, and whisper, "How terrible in the wilderness are-are the feet of them that—" until his uncle came across to change the direction of his thoughts and comfort him.

The hysteria, fortunately, proved but temporary. Sleep cured him, just as it cured Hank.

Till the first signs of daylight came, soon after five o'clock, Dr. Cathcart kept his vigil. His face was the colour of chalk, and there were strange flushes beneath the eyes. An appalling terror of the soul battled with his will all through those silent hours. These were some of the outer signs...

At dawn he lit the fire himself, made breakfast, and woke the others, and by seven they were well on their way back to the home camp—three perplexed and afflicted men, but each in his own way having reduced his inner turmoil to a condition of more or less systematized order again.

IX

They talked little, and then only of the most wholesome and common things, for their minds were charged with painful thoughts that clamoured for explanation, though no one dared refer to them. Hank, being nearest to primitive conditions, was the first to find himself, for he was also less complex. In Dr. Cathcart "civilization" championed his forces against an attack singular enough. To this day, perhaps, he is not *quite* sure of certain things. Anyhow, he took longer to "find himself."

Simpson, the student of divinity, it was who arranged his conclusions probably with the best, though not most scientific, appearance of order. Out there, in the heart of unreclaimed wilderness, they had surely witnessed something crudely and essentially primitive. Something that had survived somehow the advance of humanity had emerged terrifically, betraying a scale of life still monstrous and immature. He envisaged it rather as a glimpse into prehistoric ages, when superstitions, gigantic and uncouth, still oppressed the hearts of men; when the forces of nature were still untamed, the Powers that may have haunted a primeval universe not yet withdrawn. To this day he thinks of what he termed years later in a sermon "savage and formidable Potencies lurking behind the souls of men, not evil perhaps in themselves, yet instinctively hostile to humanity as it exists."

With his uncle he never discussed the matter in detail, for the barrier between the two types of mind made it difficult. Only once, years later, something led them to the frontier of the subject—of a single detail of the subject, rather—

"Can't you even tell me what—*they* were like?" he asked; and the reply, though conceived in wisdom, was not encouraging, "It is far better you should not try to know, or to find out."

"Well—that odour...?" persisted the nephew. "What do you make of that?"

Dr. Cathcart looked at him and raised his eyebrows.

"Odours," he replied, "are not so easy as sounds and sights of telepathic communication. I make as much, or as little, probably, as you do yourself."

He was not quite so glib as usual with his explanations. That was all.

At the fall of day, cold, exhausted, famished, the party came to the end of the long portage and dragged themselves into a camp that at first glimpse seemed empty. Fire there was none, and no Punk came forward to welcome them. The emotional capacity of all three was too overspent to recognize either surprise or annoyance; but the cry of spontaneous affection that burst from the lips of Hank, as he rushed ahead of them towards the fireplace, came probably as a warning that the end of the amazing affair was not quite yet. And both Cathcart and his nephew confessed afterwards that when they saw him kneel down in his excitement and embrace something that reclined, gently moving, beside the extinguished ashes, they felt in their very bones that this "something" would prove to be Défago—the true Défago, returned.

And so, indeed, it was.

It is soon told. Exhausted to the point of emaciation, the French Canadian—what was left of him, that is—fumbled among the ashes, trying to make a fire. His body crouched there, the weak fingers obeying feebly the instinctive habit of a lifetime with twigs and matches. But there was no longer any mind to direct the simple operation. The mind had fled beyond recall. And with it, too, had fled memory. Not only recent events, but all previous life was a blank.

This time it was the real man, though incredibly and horribly shrunken. On his face was no expression of any kind whatever—fear, welcome, or recognition. He did not seem to know who it was that embraced him, or who it was that fed, warmed and spoke to him the words of comfort and relief. Forlorn and broken beyond all reach of human aid, the little man did meekly as he was bidden. The "something" that had constituted him "individual" had vanished for ever.

In some ways it was more terribly moving than anything they had yet seen—that idiot smile as he drew wads of coarse moss from his swollen cheeks and told them that he was "a damned moss eater"; the continued vomiting of even the simplest food; and, worst of all, the piteous and childish voice of complaint in which he told them that his feet pained him—"burn like fire"—which was natural enough when Dr. Cathcart examined them and found that both were dreadfully frozen. Beneath the eyes there were faint indications of recent bleeding.

The details of how he survived the prolonged exposure, of where he had been, or of how he covered the great distance from one camp to the other, including an immense detour of the lake on foot since he had no canoe—all this remains unknown. His memory had vanished completely. And before the end of the winter whose beginning witnessed this strange occurrence, Défago, bereft of mind, memory and soul, had gone with it. He lingered only a few weeks.

And what Punk was able to contribute to the story throws no further light upon it. He was cleaning fish by the lake shore about five o'clock in the evening—an hour, that is, before the search party returned—when he saw this shadow of the guide picking its way weakly into camp. In advance of him, he declares, came the faint whiff of a certain singular odour.

That same instant old Punk started for home. He covered the entire journey of three days as only Indian blood could have covered it. The terror of a whole race drove him. He knew what it all meant. Défago had "seen the Wendigo."

OLD CLOTHES

I

IMAGINATIVE children with their odd questionings of life and their delicate nervous systems must be often a source of greater anxiety than delight to their parents, and Aileen, the child of my widowed cousin, impressed me from the beginning as being a strangely vivid specimen of her class. Moreover, the way she took to me from the first placed quasi-avuncular responsibilities upon my shoulders (in her mother's eyes), that I had no right, even as I had no inclination, to shirk. Indeed, I loved the queer, wayward, mysterious little being. Only it was not always easy to advise; and her somewhat marked peculiarities certainly called for advice of a skilled and special order.

It was not merely that her make-believe was unusually sincere and haunting, and that she would talk by the hour with invisible playmates (touching them, putting up her lips to be kissed, opening doors for them to pass in and out, and setting chairs, footstools and even flowers for them), for many children in my experience have done as much and done it with a vast sincerity; but that she also accepted what *they told her* with so steady a degree of conviction that their words influenced her life and, accordingly, her health.

They told her stories, apparently, in which she herself played a central part, stories, moreover, that were neither comforting nor wise. She would sit in a corner of the room, as both her mother and myself can vouch, face to face with some make-believe Occupant of the chair so carefully arranged; the footstool had been placed with precision, and sometimes she would move it a little this way or that; the table whereon rested the invisible elbows was beside her with a jar of flowers that changed according to the particular visitor. And there she would wait motionless, perhaps an hour at a time, staring up into the viewless features of the person who was talking with her—who was telling her a story in which she played an exceedingly poignant part. Her face altered with the run of emotions, her eyes grew large and moist, and sometimes frightened; rarely she laughed, and rarely asked a whispered question, but more often sat there, tense and eager, uncannily absorbed in the inaudible tale falling from invisible lips—the tale of her own adventures.

But it was the terror inspired by these singular recitals that affected her delicate health as early as the age of eight, and when, owing to her mother's well-meant but ill-advised ridicule, she indulged them with more secrecy, the effect upon her nerves and character became so acute that I was summoned down upon a special advisory visit I scarcely appreciated.

"Now, George, what *do* you think I had better do? Dr. Hale insists upon more exercise and more companionship, sea air and all the rest of it, but none of these things seem to do any good."

"Have you taken her into your confidence, or rather has *she* taken you into hers?" I ventured mildly.

The question seemed to give offence a little.

"Of course," was the emphatic answer. "The child has no secrets from her mother. She is perfectly devoted to me."

"But you *have* tried to laugh her out of it, haven't you now?"

"Yes. But with such success that she holds these conversations far less than she used to—"

"Or more secretly?" was my comment, that was met with a superior shrug of the shoulders.

Then, after a further pause, in which my cousin's distress and my own affectionate interest in the whimsical imagination of my little niece combined to move me, I tried again—

"Make-believe," I observed, "is always a hit puzzling to us older folk, because, though we indulge in it all our lives, we no longer believe in it; whereas children like Aileen—"

She interrupted me quickly—

"You know what I feel anxious about," she said, lowering her voice. "I think there may be cause for serious alarm." Then she added frankly, looking up with grave eyes into my face, "George, I want your help—your best help, please. You've always been a true friend."

I gave it her in calculated words.

"Theresa," I said with grave emphasis, "there is no trace of insanity on either side of the family, and my own opinion is that Aileen is perfectly well-balanced in spite of this too highly developed imagination. But, above all things, you must not drive it inwards by making fun of it. Lead it out. E—ducate it. Guide it by intelligent sympathy. Get her to tell you all about it, and so on. I think Aileen wants careful observing, perhaps—but nothing more."

For some minutes she watched my face in silence, her eyes intent, her features slightly twitching. I knew at once from her manner what she was driving at. She approached the subject with awkwardness and cir-cumlocution, for it was something she dreaded, not feeling sure whether it was of heaven or of hell.

"You are very wonderful, George," she said at length, "and you have theories about almost everything—"

"Speculations," I admitted.

"And your hypnotic power is helpful, you know. Now—if—if you thought it safe, and that Providence would not be offended—"

"Theresa," I stopped her firmly before she had committed herself to the point where she would feel hurt by a refusal, "let me say at once that I do *not* consider a child a fit subject for hypnotic experiment, and I feel quite sure that an intelligent person like yourself will agree with me that it's unpermissible."

"I was only thinking of a little 'suggestion,'" she murmured.

"Which would come far better from the mother."

"If the mother had not already lost her power by using ridicule," she confessed meekly.

"Yes, you never should have laughed. Why did you, I wonder?"

An expression came into her eyes that I knew to be invariably with hysterical temperaments the precursor of tears. She looked round to make sure no one was listening.

"George," she whispered, and into the dusk of that September evening passed some shadow between us that left behind an atmosphere of sudden and inexplicable chill, "George, I wish—I wish it was *quite* clear to me that it really is all make-believe, I mean—"

"What do you mean?" I said, with a severity that was assumed to hide my own uneasiness. But the tears came the same instant in a flood that made any intelligent explanation out of the question. The terror of the mother for her own blood burst forth.

"I'm frightened—horribly frightened," she said between the sobs.

"I'll go up and see the child myself," I said comfortingly at length when the storm had subsided. "I'll run up to the nursery. You mustn't be alarmed. Aileen's all right. I think I can help you in the matter a good deal."

II

In the nursery as usual Aileen was alone. I found her sitting by the open window, an empty chair opposite to her. She was staring at it—into it, but it is not easy to describe the certainty she managed to convey that there was someone sitting in that chair, talking with her. It was her manner that did it. She rose quickly, with a start as I came in, and made a half gesture in the direction of the empty chair as though to shake hands, then corrected herself quickly, and gave a friendly little nod of farewell or dismissal—then turned towards me. Incredible as it must sound, that chair looked at once slightly otherwise. It was empty.

"Aileen, what in the world are you up to?"

"*You* know, uncle," she replied, without hesitation.

"Oh, rather! *I* know!" I said, trying to get into her mood so as later to get her out of it, "because I do the same thing with the people in my own stories. I talk to them too—"

She came up to my side, as though it were a matter of life and death.

"But do they *answer?*"

I realized the overwhelming sincerity, even the seriousness, of the question to her mind. The shadow evoked down-stairs by my cousin had followed me up here. It touched me on the shoulder.

"Unless they answer," I told her, "they are not really alive, and the story hangs fire when people read it."

She watched me very closely a moment as we leaned out of the open window where the rich perfume of the Portuguese laurels came up from the lawns below. The proximity of the child brought a distinct atmosphere of its own, an atmosphere charged with suggestions, almost with faint pictures, as of things I had once known. I had often felt this before, and did not altogether welcome it, for the pictures seemed framed in some emotional setting that invariably escaped my analysis. I understood in a vague way what it was about the child that made her mother afraid. There flashed across me a fugitive sensation, utterly elusive yet painfully real, that she knew moments of suffering by rights she ought not to have known. Bizarre and unreasonable as the conception was, it was convincing. And it touched a profound sympathy in me.

Aileen undoubtedly was aware of this sympathy.

"It's Philip that talks to me *most* of the time," she volunteered, "and he's always, always explaining—but never quite finishes."

"Explaining what, dear little Child of the Moon?" I urged gently, giving her a name she used to love when she was smaller.

"Why he couldn't come in time to save me, of course," she said. "You see, they cut off both his hands."

I shall never forget the sensation these words of a child's mental adventure caused me, nor the kind of bitter reality they forced into me that they were true, and not merely a detail of some attempted rescue of a "Princess in a Tower." A vivid rush of thought seemed to focus my consciousness upon my own two wrists, as though I felt the pain of the operation she mentioned, and with a swift instinct that slipped into action before I could control it, I had hidden both hands from her sight in my coat pockets.

"And what else does 'Philip' tell you?" I asked gently.

Her face flushed. Tears came into her eyes, then fled away again lest they should fall from their softly-coloured nests.

"That he loved me so *awfully*," she replied; "and that he loved me to the very end, and that all his life after I was gone, and after they cut his hands off, he did nothing but pray for me—from the end of the world where he went to hide—"

I shook myself free with an effort from the enveloping atmosphere of tragedy, realizing that her imagination must be driven along brighter channels and that my duty must precede my interest.

"But you must get Philip to tell you all his funny and jolly adventures, too," I said, "the ones he had, you know, when his hands grew again—"

The expression that came into her face literally froze my blood.

"That's only making-up stories," she said icily. "They never did grow again. There *were* no happy or funny adventures."

I cast about in my mind for an inspiration how to help her mind into more wholesome ways of invention. I realized more than ever before the profundity of my affection for this strange, fatherless child, and how I would give my whole soul if I could help her and teach her joy. It was a real love that swept me, rooted in things deeper than I realized.

But, before the right word was given me to speak, I felt her nestle up against my side, and heard her utter the very phrase that for some time I had been dreading in the secret places of my soul she *would* utter. The sentence seemed to shake me within. I knew a hurried, passing moment of unspeakable pain that is utterly beyond me to reason about.

"*You* know," was what she said, "because it's *you* who are Philip!"

And the way she said it—so quietly, the words touched somehow with a gentle though compassionate scorn, yet made golden by a burning love that filled her little person to the brim—robbed me momentarily of all power of speech. I could only bend down and put my arm about her and kiss her head that came up barely to the level of my chin. I swear I loved that child as I never loved any other human being.

"Then Philip is going to teach you all sorts of jolly adventures with his new hands," I remember saying, with blundering good intention, "because he's no longer sad, and is full of fun, and loves you twice as much as ever!"

And I caught her up and carried her down the long stairs of the house out into the garden, where we joined the dogs and romped together until the face of the motherly Kempster at an upper window shouted down something stupid about bed-time, supper, or the rest of it, and Aileen, flushed yet with brighter eyes, ran into the house and, turning at the door, showed me her odd little face wreathed in smiles and laughter.

For a long time I paced to and fro with a cigar between the box hedges of the old-time garden, thinking of the child and her queer imaginings, and of the profoundly moving and disquieting sensations she stirred in me at the same time. Her face flitted by my side through the shadows. She was not pretty, properly speaking, but her appearance possessed an original charm that appealed to me strongly. Her head was big and in some way old-fashioned; her eyes, dark but not large, were placed close together, and she had a wide mouth that was certainly not beautiful. But the look of distressed and yearning passion that sometimes swept over these features, not otherwise prepossessing, changed her look into sudden beauty, a beauty of the soul, a soul that knew suffering and was acquainted with grief. This, at least, is the way my own mind saw the child, and therefore the only way I can hope to make others see her. Were I a painter I might put her upon canvas in some imaginary portrait and call it, perhaps, "Reincarnation"—for I have never seen anything in child-life that impressed me so vividly with that odd idea of an old soul come back to the world in a new young body—a new Suit of Clothes.

But when I talked with my cousin after dinner, and consoled her with the assurance that Aileen was gifted with an unusually vivid imagination which time and ourselves must train to some more practical end—while I said all this, and more besides, two sentences the child had made use of kept ringing in my head. One—when she told me with merciless perception that I was only "making-up" stories; and the other, when she had informed me with that quiet rush of certainty and conviction that "Philip" was—myself.

III

A big-game expedition of some months put an end temporarily to my avuncular responsibilities; at least so far as action was concerned, for there were certain memories that held curiously vivid among all the absorbing turmoil of our camp life. Often, lying awake in my tent at night, or even following the tracks of our prey through the jungle, these pictures would jump out upon me and claim attention. Aileen's little face of suffering would come between me and the sight of my rifle; or her assurance that I was the "Philip" of her imagination would attack me with an accent of reality that seemed queer enough until I analyzed it away. And more than once I found myself thinking of her dark and serious countenance when she told how "Philip" had loved her to the end, and would have saved her if they had not cut off his hands. My own imagination, it seemed, was weaving the details of her child's invention into a story, for I never could think of this latter detail without positively experiencing a sensation of smarting pain in my wrists...!

When I returned to England in the spring they had moved, I found, into a house by the sea, a tumbled-down old rookery of a building my cousin's father had rarely occupied during his lifetime, nor had she been able to let since it had passed into her possession. An urgent letter summoned me thither, and I travelled down the very day after my arrival to the bleak Norfolk coast with a sense of foreboding in my heart that increased almost to a presentiment when the cab entered the long drive and I recognized the grey and gloomy walls of the old mansion. The sea air swept the gardens with its salt wash, and the moan of the surf was audible even up to the windows.

"I wonder what possessed her to come here?" was the first thought in my mind. "Surely the last place in the world to bring a morbid or too-sensitive child to!" My further dread that something had happened to the little child I loved so tenderly was partly dispelled, however, when my cousin met me at the door with open arms and smiling face, though the welcome I soon found, was chiefly due to the relief she gained from my presence. Something *had* happened to little Aileen, though not the final disaster that I dreaded. She had suffered from nervous attacks of so serious a character during my absence that the doctor had insisted upon sea air, and my cousin, not with the best judgment, had seized upon the idea of making the old house serve the purpose. She had made a wing habitable for a few weeks; she hoped the entire change of scene would fill the little girl's mind with new and happier ideas. Instead—the result had been exactly the reverse. The child had wept copiously and hysterically the moment she set eyes on the old walls and smelt the odour of the sea.

But before we had been talking ten minutes there was a cry and a sound of rushing footsteps, and a scampering figure, with dark, flying hair, had dived headlong into my arms, and Aileen was sobbing—

"Oh, you've come, you've come at last! I *am* so awfully glad. I thought it would be the same as before, and you'd get caught." She ran from me next and kissed her mother, laughing with pleasure through her tears, and was gone from the room as quickly as she had come.

I caught my cousin's glance of frightened amazement.

"Now isn't *that* odd?" she exclaimed in a hushed voice. "Isn't *that* odd? Those are the tears of happiness,—the first time I've seen her smile since we came here last week."

But it rather nettled me, I think. "Why odd?" I asked. "Aileen loves me, it's delightful to—!"

"Not that, not that!" she said quickly. "It's odd, I meant, she should have found you out so soon. She didn't even know you were back in England, and I'd sent her off to play on the sands with Kempster and the dogs so as to be sure of an opportunity of telling you everything before you saw her."

Our eyes met squarely, yet not with complete sympathy or comprehension.

"You see, she knew perfectly well you were here—the instant you
came."

"But there's nothing in that," I asserted. "Children know things just as
animals do. She scented her favourite uncle from the shore like a dog!"
And I laughed in her face.

That laugh perhaps was a mistake on my part. Its well-meant cheerfulness was possibly overdone. Even to myself it did not ring quite true.

"I do believe you are in league with her—against me," was the remark
that greeted it, accompanied by an increase of that expression of fear in
the eyes I had divined the moment we met upon the doorstep. Finding
nothing genuine to say in reply, I kissed the top of her head.

In due course, after the tea things had been removed, I learned the exact
state of affairs, and even making due allowance for my cousin's excited
exaggerations, there were things that seemed to me inexplicable enough
on any ground of normal explanation. Slight as the details may seem
when set down seriatim, their cumulative effect upon my own mind
touched an impressive and disagreeable climax that I did my best to conceal from outward betrayal. As I sat in the great shadowy room, listening
to my cousin's jerky description of "childish" things, it was borne in upon
me that they might well have the profoundest possible significance. I
watched her eager, frightened face, lit only by the flickering flames the
sharp spring evening made necessary, and thought of the subject of our
conversation flitting about the dreary halls and corridors of the huge old
building, a little figure of tragedy, laughing, crying and dreaming in a
world entirely her own—and there stirred in me an unwelcome recognition of those mutinous and dishevelled forces that lie but thinly
screened behind the common-place details of life and that now seemed
ready to burst forth and play their mysterious *rôle* before our very eyes.

"Tell me *exactly* what has happened," I urged, with decision but sympathy.

"There's so little, when it's put into words, George; but—well, the
thing that first upset me was that she—knew the whole place, though
she's never been here before. She knew every passage and staircase,
many of them that I did not know myself; she showed us an underground passage to the sea, that father himself didn't know; and she actually drew a scrawl of the house as it used to be three hundred years ago
when the other wing was standing where the copper beeches grow now.
It's accurate, too."

It seemed impossible to explain to a person of my cousin's temperament the theories of pre-natal memory and the like, or the possibility of

her own knowledge being communicated telepathically to the brain of her own daughter. I said therefore very little, but listened with an uneasiness that grew horribly.

"She found her way about the gardens instantly, as if she had played in them all her life; and she keeps drawing figures of people—men and women—in old costumes, the sort of thing our ancestors wore, you know—"

"Well, well, well!" I interrupted impatiently; "what can be more natural? She is old enough to have seen pictures she can remember enough to copy—?"

"Of course," she resumed calmly, but with a calmness due to the terror that ate her very soul and swallowed up all minor emotions; "of course, but one of the faces she gets is—*a portrait.*"

She rose suddenly and came closer to me across the big stone hearth, lowering her voice to a whisper, "George," she whispered, "it's the very image of that awful—de Lorne!"

The announcement, I admit, gave me a thrill, for that particular ancestor on my father's side had largely influenced my boyish imagination by the accounts of his cruelty and wickedness in days gone by. But I think now the shiver that ran down my back was due to the thought of my little Aileen practising her memory and pencil upon so vile an object. That, and my cousin's pale visage of alarm, combined to shake me. I said, however, what seemed wise and reasonable at the moment.

"You'll be claiming next, Theresa, that the house is haunted," I suggested.

She shrugged her shoulders with an indifference that was very eloquent of the strength of this other more substantial terror.

"That would be so easy to deal with," she said, without even looking up. "A ghost stays in one place. Aileen could hardly take it about with her."

I think we both enjoyed the pause that followed. It gave *me* time to collect my forces for what I knew was coming. It gave *her* time to get her further facts into some pretence of coherence.

"I told you about the belt?" she asked at length, weakly, and as though unutterable things she longed to disown forced the question to her unwilling lips.

The sentence shot into me like the thrust of a naked sword... I shook my head.

"Well, even a year or two ago she had that strange dislike of wearing a belt with her frocks. We thought it was a whim, and did not humour her. Belts are necessary, you know, George," she tried to smile feebly. "But now it has come to such a point that I've had to give in."

"She dislikes a belt round her waist, you mean?" I asked, fighting a sudden inexplicable spasm in my heart.

"It makes her scream. The moment anything encloses her waist she sets up such a hubbub, and struggles so, and hides away, and I've been obliged to yield."

"But really, Theresa—!"

"She declares it fastens her in, and she will never get free again, and all kinds of other things. Oh, her fear is dreadful, poor child. Her face gets that sort of awful grey, don't you know? Even Kempster, who if anything is too firm, had to give in."

"And what else, pray?" I disliked hearing these details intensely. It made me ache with a kind of anger that I could not at once relieve the child's pain.

"The way she spoke to me after Dr. Hale had left—you know how awfully kind and gentle he is, and how Aileen likes him and even plays with him and sits on his knee? Well, he was talking about her diet, regulating it and so forth, teasing her that she mustn't eat this and that, and the rest of it, when she turned that horrid grey again and jumped off his knee with her scream—that thin wailing scream she has that goes through me like a knife, George—and flew to the nursery and locked herself in with—what do you think?—with all the bread, apples, cold meat and other eatables she could find!"

"Eatables!" I exclaimed, aware of another spasm of vivid pain.

"When I coaxed her out, hours later, she was trembling like a leaf and fell into my arms utterly exhausted, and all I could get her to tell me was this—which she repeated again and again with a sort of beseeching, appealing tone that made my heart bleed—"

She hesitated an instant.

"Tell me at once."

"'I shall starve again, I shall starve again,' were the words she used. She kept repeating it over and over between her sobs. 'I shall be without anything to eat. I shall starve!' And, would you believe it, while she hid in that nursery cupboard she had crammed so much cake and stuff into her little self that she was violently sick for a couple of days. Moreover, she now hates the sight of Dr. Hale so much, poor man, that it's useless for him to see her. It does more harm than good."

I had risen and begun to walk up and down the hall while she told me this. I said very little. In my mind strange thoughts tore and raced, standing erect before me out of unbelievably immense depths of shadow. There was nothing very pregnant I found to say, however, for theories and speculations are of small avail as practical help—unless two minds see eye to eye in them.

"And the rest?" I asked gently, coming behind the chair and resting both hands upon her shoulders. She got up at once and faced me. I was afraid to show too much sympathy lest the tears should come.

"Oh, George," she exclaimed, "I *am* relieved you have come. You are really strong and comforting. To feel your great hands on my shoulders gives me courage. But, you know, truly and honestly I am frightened out of my very wits by the child—"

"You won't stay here, of course?"

"We leave at the end of this week," she replied. "You will not desert me till then, I know. And Aileen will be all right as long as you are here, for you have the most extraordinary effect on her for good."

"Bless her little suffering imagination," I said. "You can count on me. I'll send to town to-night for my things."

And then she told me about the room. It was simple enough, but it conveyed a more horrible certainty of something true than all the other details put together. For there was a room on the ground floor, intended to be used on wet days when the nursery was too far for muddy boots— and into this room Aileen could not go. Why? No one could tell. The facts were that the first moment the child ran in, her mother close behind, she stopped, swayed, and nearly fell. Then, with shrieks that were even heard outside by the gardeners sweeping the gravel path, she flung herself headlong against the wall, against a particular corner of it that is to say, and beat it with her little fists until the skin broke and left stains upon the paper. It all happened in less than a minute. The words she cried so frantically her mother was too shocked and flabbergasted to remember, or even to hear properly. Aileen nearly upset her in her bewildered efforts next to find the door and escape. And the first thing she did when escape was accomplished, was to drop in a dead faint upon the stone floor of the passage outside.

"Now, is *that* all make-believe?" whispered Theresa, unable to keep the shudder from her lips. "Is that all merely part of a story she has make up and plays a part in?"

We looked one another straight in the eyes for a space of some seconds. The dread in the mother's heart leaped out to swell a terror in my own— a terror of another kind, but greater.

"It is too late to-night," I said at length, "for it would only excite her unnecessarily; but tomorrow I will talk with Aileen. And-if it seems wise—I might—I might be able to help in other ways too," I added.

So I did talk to her—next day.

IV

I always had her confidence, this little dark-eyed maid, and there was an intimacy between us that made play and talk very delightful. Yet as a rule, without giving myself a satisfactory reason, I preferred talking with her in the sunlight. She was not eerie, bless her little heart of queerness and mystery, but she had a way of suggesting other ways of life and existence shouldering about us that made me look round in the dark and wonder what the shadows concealed or what waited round the next corner.

We were on the lawn, where the bushy yews drop thick shade, the soft air making tea possible out of doors, my cousin out driving to distant calls; and Aileen had invited herself and was messing about with my manuscripts in a way that vexed me, for I had been reading my fairy tales to her and she kept asking me questions that shamed my limited powers. I remember, too, that I was glad the collie ran to and fro past us, scampering and barking after the swallows on the lawn.

"Only *some* of your stories are true, aren't they?" she asked abruptly.

"How do you know that, young critic?" I had been waiting for an opening supplied by herself. Anything forced on my part she would have suspected.

"Oh, I can tell."

Then she came up and whispered without any hint of invitation on my part, "Uncle, it is true, isn't it, that I've been in other places with you? And isn't it only the things we did *there* that make the true stories?"

The opening was delivered all perfect and complete into my hands. I cannot conceive how it was I availed myself of it so queerly—I mean, how it was that the words and the name slipped out of their own accord as though I was saying something in a dream.

"Of course, my little Lady Aileen, because in imagination, you see, we—"

But before I had time to finish the sentence with which I hoped to coax out the true inwardness of her own distress, she was upon me in a heap.

"Oh," she cried, with a sudden passionate outburst, "then you *do* know my name? You know all the story—*our* story!"

She was very excited, face flushed, eyes dancing, all the emotions of a life charged to the brim with experience playing through her little person.

"Of course, Miss Inventor, I know your name," I said quickly, puzzled, and with a sudden dismay that was hideous, clutching at my throat.

"And all that we did in this place?" she went on, pointing with increased excitement to the thick, ivy-grown walls of the old house.

My own emotion grew extraordinarily, a swift, rushing uneasiness upsetting all my calculations. For it suddenly came back to me that in calling her "Lady Aileen "I had not pronounced the name quite as usual. My tongue had played a trick with the consonants and vowels, though at the moment of utterance I had somehow failed to notice the change. "Aileen" and "Helen" are almost interchangeable sounds...! And it was "Lady Helen" that I had actually said.

The discovery took my breath away for an instant—and the way she had leaped upon the name to claim it.

"No one else, you see, knows me as 'Lady Helen,'" she continued whispering, "because that's only in our story, isn't it? And now I'm just Aileen Langton. But as long as you know, it's all right. Oh, I am so awf'ly glad you knew, most awf'ly, *awf'ly* glad."

I was momentarily at a loss for words. Keenly desirous to guide the child's "pain-stories" into wiser channels, and thus help her to relief, I hesitated a moment for the right clue. I murmured something soothing about "our story," while in my mind I searched vigorously for the best way of leading her on to explain all her terror of the belt, the fear of starvation, the room that made her scream, and all the rest. All *that* I was most anxious to get out of her little tortured mind and then replace it by some brighter dream.

But the insidious experience had shaken my confidence a little, and these explicable emotions destroyed my elder wisdom. The little Inventor had caught me away into the reality of her own "story" with a sense of conviction that was even beyond witchery. And the next sentence she almost instantly let loose upon me completed my discomfiture—

"With you," she said, still half whispering, "with you I could even go into the room. I never could—alone—!"

The spring wind whispering in the yews behind us brought in that moment something upon me from vanished childhood days that made me tremble. Some wave of lost passion—lost because I guessed not its origin or nature—surged through the depths of me, sending faint messages to the surface of my consciousness. Aileen, little mischief-maker, changed before my very eyes as she stood there close-changed into a tall sad figure that beckoned to me across seas of time and distance, with the haze of ages in her eyes and gestures,... I was obliged to focus my gaze upon her with a deliberate effort to see her again as the tumble-haired girl I was accustomed to...

Then, sitting in the creaky garden chair, I drew her down upon my knee, determined to win the whole story from her mind. My back was to the house; she was perched at an angle, however, that enabled her to command the doors and windows. I mention this because, scarcely had I begun my attack, when I saw that her attention wandered, and that she seemed curiously uneasy. Once or twice, as she shifted her position to get a view of something that was going on over my shoulder, I was aware that a slight shiver passed from her small person down to my knees. She seemed to be expecting something—with dread.

"We'll make a special expedition, armed to the teeth," I said, with a laugh, referring to her singular words about the room. "We'll send Pat in first to bark at the cobwebs, and we'll take lots of provisions and-and water in case of a siege—and a file—"

I cannot pretend to understand why I chose those precise words—or why it was as though other thoughts than those I had intended rose up, clamouring for expression. It seemed all I could manage not to say a lot of other things about the room that could only have frightened instead of relieving her.

"Will you talk *into the wall* too?" she asked, turning her eyes down suddenly upon me with a little, rush and flame of passion. And though I had not the faintest conception what she meant, the question sent an agony of yearning pain through me. "Talking into the wall," I instantly grasped, referred to the core of her trouble, the very central idea that frightened her and provided the suffering and terror of all her imaginings.

But I had no time to follow up the clue thus mysteriously offered to me, for almost at the same moment her eyes fixed themselves upon something behind me with an expression of tense horror, as though she saw the approach of a danger that might—*kill.*

"Oh, oh!" she cried under her breath, "he's coming! He's coming to take me! Uncle George—Philip—!"

The same impulse operated upon us simultaneously, it seems, for I sprang up with my fists clenched at the very instant she shot off my knee and stood with all her muscles rigid as though to resist attack. She was shaking dreadfully. Her face went the colour of linen.

"*Who's* coming—?" I began sharply, then stopped as I saw the figure of a man moving towards us from the house. It was the butler—the new butler who had arrived only that very afternoon. It is impossible to say what there was in his swift and silent approach that was—abominable. The man was upon us, it seemed, almost as soon as I caught sight of him, and the same moment Aileen, with a bursting cry, looking wildly about her for a place to hide in, plunged headlong into my arms and buried her face in my coat.

Horribly perplexed, yet mortified that the servant should see my little friend in such a state, I did my best to pretend that it was all part of some mad game or other, and catching her up in my arms, I ran, calling the collie to follow with, "Come on, Pat! She's our prisoner!"—and only set her down when we were under the limes at the far end of the lawn. She was all white and ghostly from her terror, still looking frantically about her, trembling in such a way that I thought any minute she must collapse in a dead faint. She clung to me with very tight fingers. How I hated that man. Judging by the sudden violence of my loathing he might have been some monster who wanted to torture her...

"Let's go away, oh, much farther, ever so far away!" she whispered, and I took her by the hand, comforting her as best I could with words, while realizing that the thing she wanted was my big arm about her to protect. My heart ached, oh, so fiercely, for her, but the odd thing about it was that I could not find anything of real comfort to say that I felt would be *true*. If I "made up" soothing rubbish, it would not deceive either of us and would only shake her confidence in me, so that I should lose any power I had to help. Had a tiger come upon her out of the wood I might as well have assured her it would not bite!

I did stammer something, however—

"It's only the new butler. He startled me, too; lie came so softly, didn't he?" Oh! How eagerly I searched for a word that might make the thing seem as ordinary as possible-yet how vainly.

"But you know who he *is—really!*" she said in a crying whisper, running down the path and dragging me after her; "and if he gets me again...oh! oh!" and she shrieked aloud in the anguish of her fear.

That fear chased both of us down the winding path between the bushes.

"Aileen, darling," I cried, surrounding her with both arms and holding her very tight, "you need not be afraid. I'll always save you. I'll always be with you, dear child."

"Keep me in your big arms, always, always, won't you, Uncle—Philip?" She mixed both names. The choking stress of her voice wrung me dreadfully. "Always, always, like in our story," she pleaded, hiding her little face again in my coat.

I really was at a complete loss to know what best to do; I hardly dared to bring her back to the house; the sight of the man, I felt, might be fatal to her already too delicately balanced reason, for I dreaded a fit or seizure if she chanced to run across him when I was not with her. My mind was easily made up on one point, however.

"I'll send him away at once, Aileen," I told her. "When you wake up tomorrow he'll be gone. Of course mother won't keep him."

This assurance seemed to bring her some measure of comfort, and at last, without having dared to win the whole story from her as I had first hoped, I got her back to the house by covert ways, and saw her myself up-stairs to her own quarters. Also I took it upon myself to give the necessary orders. She must set no eye upon the man. Only, why was it that in my heart of hearts I longed for him to do something outrageous that should make it possible for me to break his very life at its source and kill him...?

But my cousin, alarmed to the point of taking even frantic measures, finally had a sound suggestion to offer, namely that I should take the afflicted little child away with me the very next day, run down to Harwich and carry her off for a week of absolute change across the North Sea. And I, meanwhile, had reached the point where I had persuaded myself that the experiment I had hitherto felt unable to consent to had now become a permissible, even a necessary one. Hypnotism should win the story from that haunted mind without her being aware of it, and provided I could drive her deep enough into the trance state, I could then further wipe the memory from her outer consciousness so completely that she might know at last some happiness of childhood.

V

It was after ten o'clock, and I was still sitting in the big hall before the, fire of logs, talking with lowered voice. My cousin sat opposite to me in a deep arm-chair. We had discussed the matter pretty fully, and the deep uneasiness we felt clothed not alone our minds but the very building with gloom. The fact that, instinctively, neither of us referred to the possible assistance of doctors is eloquent, I think, of the emotion that troubled us both so profoundly, the emotion, I mean, that sprang from the vivid sense of the reality of it all. No child's make-believe merely could have thus caught us away, or spread a net that entangled our minds to such a point of confusion and dismay. It was perfectly comprehensible to me now that my cousin should have cried in very helplessness before the convincing effects of the little girl's calamitous distress. Aileen was living through a Reality, not an Invention. This was the fact that haunted the shadowy halls and corridors behind us. Already I hated the very building. It seemed charged to the roof with the memories of melancholy and ancient pain that swept my heart with shivering, cold winds.

Purposely, however, I affected some degree of cheerfulness, and concealed from my cousin any mention of the attacks that certain emotions and alarms had made upon myself; I said nothing of my replacing "Lady Aileen" with "Lady Helen," nothing of my passing for "Philip," or of my sudden dashes of quasi-memory arising from the child's inclusion of myself in her "story," and my own singular acceptance of the *rôle*. I did not consider it wise to mention *all* that the sight of the new servant with his sinister dark face and his method of stealthy approach had awakened in my thoughts. None the less these things started constantly to the surface of my mind and doubtless betrayed themselves somewhere in my "atmosphere," sufficiently at least for a woman's intuition to divine them. I spoke passingly of the "room," and of Aileen's singular aversion for it, and of her remark about "talking to the wall." Yet strange thoughts pricked their way horribly into both our minds. In the hall the stuffed heads of deer and fox and badger stared upon us like masks of things still alive beneath their fur and dead skin.

"But what disturbs me more than all the rest of her delusions put together," said my cousin, peering at me with eyes that made no pretence of hiding dark things, "is her extraordinary knowledge of this place. I assure you, George, it was the most uncanny thing I've ever known when she showed me over and asked questions as if she had actually lived here." Her voice sank to a whisper, and she looked up startled. It seemed to me for a moment that someone was coming near to listen, moving stealthily upon us along the dark approaches to the hall.

"I can understand you found it strange," I began quickly. But she interrupted me at once. Clearly it gave her a certain relief to say the things and get them out of her mind where they hid, breeding new growths of abhorrence.

"George," she cried aloud, "there's a limit to imagination. Aileen *knows*. That's the awful thing—"

Something sprang into my throat. My eyes moistened.

"The horror of the belt—" she whispered, loathing her own words.

"Leave that thought alone," I said with decision. The detail pained me inexpressibly—beyond belief.

"I wish I could," she answered, "but if you had seen the look on her face when she struggled—and the—the frenzy she got into about the food and starving—I mean when Dr. Hale spoke—oh, if you had seen all that, you would understand that I—"

She broke off with a start. Someone had entered the hall behind us and was standing in the doorway at the far end. The listener had moved upon us from the dark. Theresa, though her back was turned, had felt the presence and was instantly upon her feet.

"You need not sit up, Porter," she said, in a tone that only thinly veiled the fever of apprehension behind, "we will put the lights out," and the man withdrew like a shadow. She exchanged a quick glance with me. A sensation of darkness that seemed to have come with the servant's presence was gone. It is wholly beyond me to explain why neither myself nor my cousin found anything to say for some minutes. But it was still more a mystery, I think, why the muscles of my two hands should have contracted involuntarily with a force that drove the nails into my palms, and why the violent impulse should have leaped into my blood to fling myself upon the man and strangle the life out of his neck before he could take another breath. I have never before or since experienced this apparently causeless desire to throttle anybody. I hope I never may again.

"He hangs about rather," was all my cousin said presently. "He's always watching us—" But my own thoughts were horribly busy, and I was marvelling how it was this ugly and sinister creature had ever come to be accepted in the story that Aileen lived, and that I was slowly coming to *believe* in.

It was a relief to me when, towards midnight, Theresa rose to go to bed. We had skirted through the horrors of the child's possessing misery without ever quite facing it, and as we stood there lighting the candles, our voices whispering, our minds charged with the strain of thoughts neither of us had felt it wise to utter, my cousin started back against the wall and stared up into the darkness above where the staircase climbed the well of the house. She uttered a cry. At first I thought she was going to collapse. I was only just in time to catch the candle.

All the emotions of fearfulness she had repressed during our long talk came out in that brief cry, and when I looked up to discover the cause I saw a small white figure come slowly down the wide staircase and just about to step into the hall. It was Aileen, with bare feet, her dark hair tumbling down over her nightgown, her eyes wide open, an expression in them of anguished expectancy that her tender years could never possibly have known. She was walking steadily, yet somehow not quite as a child walks.

"Stop!" I whispered peremptorily to my cousin, putting my hand quickly over her mouth, and holding her back from the first movement of rescue, "don't wake her. She's walking in her sleep."

Aileen passed us like a white shadow, scarcely audible, and went straight across the hall. She was utterly unaware of our presence. Avoiding all obstructions of chairs and tables, moving with decision and purpose, the little figure dipped into the shadows at the far end and disappeared from view in the mouth of the corridor that had once—three hundred years ago—led into the wing where now the copper beeches grew upon open lawns. It was clearly a way familiar to her. And the instant I recovered from my surprise and moved after her to act, Theresa found her voice and cried aloud—a voice that broke the midnight silence with shrill discordance—

"George, oh, George! She's going to that awful room...!"

"Bring the candle and come after me," I replied from halfway down the hall, "but do not interrupt unless I call for you," and was after the child at a pace to which the most singular medley of emotions I have ever known urged me imperiously. A sense of tragic disaster gripped my very vitals. All that I did seemed to rise out of some subconscious region of the mind where the haunting passions of a deeply buried past stirred in their sleep and woke.

"Helen!" I cried, "Lady Helen!" I was close upon the gliding figure. Aileen turned and for the first time saw me with eyes that seemed to waver between sleep and waking. They gazed straight at me over the flickering candle flame, then hesitated. In similar fashion the gesture of her little hands towards me was arrested before it had completed itself. She saw me, knew my presence, yet was uncertain who I was. It was astonishing the way I actually surprised this momentary indecision between the two personalities in her—caught the two phases of her consciousness at grips—discerned the Aileen of To-day in the act of waking to know me as her "Uncle George," and that other Aileen of her great dark story, the "Helen" of some far Yesterday, that drew her in this condition of somnambulism to the scene in the past where our two lives were linked in her imagination. For it was quite clear to me that the child was dreaming in her sleep the action of the story she lived through in the vivid moments of her waking terror.

But the choice was swift. I just had time to signal Theresa to set the candle upon a shelf and wait, when she came up, stretched her hands out in completion of the original gesture, and fell into my arms with a smothered cry of love and anguish that, coming from those childish lips, I think is the most thrilling human sound I have ever known. She knew and saw me, but not as "Uncle" George of this present life.

"Oh, Philip!" she cried, "then you have come after all—"

"Of course, dear heart," I whispered. "Of course I have come. Did I not give my promise that I would?"

Her eyes searched my face, and then settled upon my hands that held her little cold wrists so tightly. "But—but," she stammered in comment, "they are not cut! They have made you whole again! You will save me and get me out, and we—we—"

The expressions of her face ran together into a queer confusion of perplexity, and she seemed to totter on her feet. In another instant she would probably have wakened; again she felt the touch of uncertainty and doubt as to my identity. Her hands resisted the pressure of my own; she drew back half a step; into her eyes rose the shallower consciousness of the present. Once awake it would drive out the profoundly strange passion and mystery that haunted the corridors of thought and memory and plunged so obscurely into the inmost recesses of her being. For, once awake, I realized that I should lose her, lose the opportunity of getting the complete story. The chance was unique. I heard my cousin's footsteps approaching behind us down the passage on tiptoe—and I came to an immediate decision.

In the state of deep sleep, of course, the trance condition is very close, and many experiments had taught me that the human spirit can be subjected to the influence of hypnotism far more speedily when asleep than when awake; for if hypnotism means chiefly—as I then held it to mean—the merging of the little ineffectual surface-consciousness with the deep sea of the greater subliminal consciousness below, then the process has already been partially begun in normal slumber and its completion need be no very long or difficult matter. It was Aileen's very active subconsciousness that "invented" or "remembered" the dark story which haunted her life, her subconscious region too readily within tap... By deepening her sleep state I could learn the whole story...

Stopping her mother's approach with a sign that I intended she should clearly understand, and which accordingly she did understand, I took immediate steps to plunge the spirit of this little sleep-walking child down again into the subconscious region that had driven her thus far, and wherein lay the potentialities of all her powers, of memory, knowledge and belief. Only the simplest passes were necessary, for she yielded quickly and easily; that first look came back into her eyes; she no longer wavered or hesitated, but drew close against me, with the name of "Philip" upon her lips, and together we moved down the long passage till we reached the door of her horrid room of terror.

And there, whether it was that Theresa's following with the candle disturbed the child—for the subconscious tie with the mother is of such unalterable power—or whether anxiety weakened my authority over her fluctuating mental state, I noticed that she again wavered and hesitated, looking up with eyes that saw partly "Uncle George," partly the "Philip" she remembered.

"We'll go in," I said firmly, "and you shall see that there is nothing to be afraid of." I opened the door, and the candle from behind threw a triangle of light into the darkness. It fell upon a bare floor, pictureless walls, and just tipped the high white ceiling overhead. I pushed the door still wider open and we went in hand in hand, Aileen shaking like a leaf in the wind.

How the scene lives in my mind, even as I write it today so many years after it took place: the little child in her nightgown facing me in that empty room of the ancient building, all the passionate emotions of a tragic history in the small young eyes, her mother like a ghost in the passage, afraid to come in, the tossing shadows thrown by the candle and the soft moan of the night wind against the outside walls.

I made further passes over the small flushed face and pressed my thumbs gently along the temples. "Sleep!" I commanded; "sleep—and remember!" My will poured over her being to control and protect. She passed still deeper into the trance condition in which the somnambulistic lucidity manifests itself and the deeper self gives up its dead. Her eyes grew wider, rounder, charged with memories as they fastened themselves upon my own. The present, which a few minutes before had threatened to claim her consciousness by waking her, faded. She saw me no longer as her familiar Uncle George, but as the faithful friend and lover of her great story, Philip, the man who had come to save her. There she stood in the atmosphere of bygone days, in the very room where she had known great suffering—this room that three centuries ago had led by a corridor into the wing of the house where now the beeches grew upon the lawns.

She came up close and put her thin bare arms about my neck and stared with peering, searching eyes into mine.

"Remember what happened here," I said resolutely. "Remember, and tell me."

Her brows contracted slightly as with the effort, and she whispered, glancing over her shoulder towards the farther end where the corridor once began, "It hurts a little, but I—I'm in your arms, Philip dear, and you will get me out, I know—"

"I hold you safe and you are in no danger, little one," I answered. "You can remember and speak without it hurting you. Tell me."

The suggestion, of course, operated instantly, for her face cleared, and she dropped a great sigh of relief. From time to time I continued the passes that held the trance condition firm.

Then she spoke in a low, silvery little tone that cut into me like a sword and searched my inmost parts. I seemed to bleed internally. I could have sworn that she spoke of things I knew as though I had lived through them.

"This was when I last saw you," she said, "this was the room where you were to fetch me and carry me away into happiness and safety from—him," and it was the voice and words of no mere child that said it; "and this was where you did come on that night of snow and wind. Through that window you entered;" she pointed to the deep, embrasured window behind us. "Can't you hear the storm? How it howls and screams! And the boom of the surf on the beach below... You left the horses outside, the swift horses that were to carry us to the sea and away from all his cruelties, and then—"

She hesitated and searched for words or memories; her face darkened with pain and loathing.

"Tell me the rest," I ordered, "but forget all your own pain." And she smiled up at me with an expression of unbelievable tenderness and confidence while I drew the frail form closer.

"*You* remember, Philip," she went on, "you know just what it was, and how he and his men seized you the moment you stepped inside, and how you struggled and called for me, and heard me answer—"

"Far away—outside—" I interrupted quickly, helping her out of some flashing memory in my own deep heart that seemed to burn and leave a scar. "You answered from the lawn!"

"*You* thought it was the lawn, but really, you see, it was there—in there," and she pointed to the side of the room on my right. She shook dreadfully, and her voice dwindled most oddly in volume, as though coming from a distance—almost muffled.

"In there?" I asked it with a shudder that put ice and fire mingled in my blood.

"In the wall," she whispered. "You see, someone had betrayed us, and he knew you were coming. He walled me up alive in there, and only left two little holes for my eyes so that I could see. You heard my voice calling through those holes, but you never knew where I was. And then—"

Her knees gave way, and I had to hold her. She looked suddenly with torture in her eyes down the length of the room—towards the old wing of the house.

"You won't let him come," she pleaded beseechingly, and in her voice was the agony of death. "I thought I heard him. Isn't that his footsteps in the corridor?" She listened fearfully, her eyes trying to pierce the wall and see out on to the lawn.

"No one is coming, dear heart," I said, with conviction and authority. "Tell it all. Tell me everything."

"I saw the whole of it because I could not close my eyes," she continued. "There was an iron band round my waist fastening me in—an iron belt I never could escape from. The dust got into my mouth—I bit the bricks. My tongue was scraped and bleeding, but before they put in the last stones to smother me I saw them—cut both your hands off so that you could never save me—never let me out."

She dashed without warning from my side and flew up to the wall, beating it with her hands and crying aloud—

"Oh, you poor, poor thing. I know how awful it was. I remember—when I was in you and you wore and carried me, poor, poor body! That thunder of the last brick as they drove it in against the mouth, and the iron clamp that cut into the waist, and the suffocation and hunger and thirst!"

"What are you talking to in there?" I asked sternly, crushing down the tears.

"The body I was in—the one he walled up—my body—my own body!"

She flew back to my side. But even before my cousin had uttered that "mother-cry" that broke in upon the child's deeper consciousness, disturbing the memories, I had given the command with all the force of my being to "forget" the pain. And only those few who are familiar with the instantaneous changes of emotion that can be produced by suggestion under hypnosis will understand that Aileen came back to me from that moment of "talking to the wall" with laughter on her lips and in her eyes.

The small white figure with the cascade of dark hair tumbling over the nightgown ran up and jumped into my arms.

"But I saved you," I cried, "you were never properly walled-up; I got you out and took you away from him over the sea, and we were happy ever afterwards, like the people in the fairy tales." I drove the words into her with my utmost force, and inevitably she accepted them as the truth, for she clung to me with love and laughter all over her child's face of mystery, the horror fading out, the pain swept clean away. With kaleidoscopic suddenness the change came.

"So they never really cut your poor dead hands off at all," she said hesitatingly.

"Look! How could they? There they are!" And I first showed them to her and then pressed them against her little cheeks, drawing her mouth up to be kissed. "They're big enough still and strong enough to carry you off to bed and stroke you into so deep a sleep that when you wake in the morning you will have forgotten everything about your dark story, about Philip, Lady Helen, the iron belt, the starvation, your cruel old husband, and all the rest of it. You'll wake up happy and jolly just like any other child—"

"If you say so, of course I shall," she answered, smiling into my eyes.

And it was just then there came in that touch of abomination that so nearly made my experiment a failure, for it came with a black force that threatened at first to discount all my "suggestion" and make it of no account. My new command that she should forget had apparently not yet fully registered itself in her being; the tract of deeper consciousness that constructed the "Story" had not sunk quite below the threshold. Thus she was still open to any detail of her former suffering that might obtrude itself with sufficient force. And such a detail *did* obtrude itself. This touch of abomination was calculated with a really superhuman ingenuity.

"Hark!" she cried—and it was that *scream in a whisper* that only utter terror can produce—"Hark! I hear his steps! He's coming! Oh, I told you he was coming! He's in *that* passage!" pointing down the room. And she first sprang from my arms as though something burned her, and then almost instantly again flew back to my protection. In that interval of a few seconds she tore into the middle of the room, put her hand to her ear to listen, and then shaded her eyes in the act of peering down through the, wall at the far end. She stared at the very place where in olden days the corridor had led into the vanished wing. The window my great-uncle had built into the wall now occupied the exact spot where the opening had been.

Theresa then for the first time came forward with a rush into the room, dropping the candle-grease over the floor. She clutched me by the arm. The three of us stood there—listening—listening apparently to nought but the sighing of the sea-wind about the walls, Aileen with her eyes buried in my coat. I was standing erect trying in vain to catch the new sound. I remember my cousin's face of chalk with the fluttering eyes and the candle held aslant.

Then suddenly she raised her hand and pointed over my shoulder. I thought her jaw would drop from her face. And she and the child both spoke in the same breath the two sharp phrases that brought the climax of the vile adventure upon us in that silent room of night.

They were like two pistol-shots.

"My God! There's a face watching us...!" I heard her voice, all choked and dry.

And at the same second, Aileen—

"Oh, oh! He's seen us!... He's *here!* Look.... He'll get me...hide your hands, hide your poor hands...!"

And, turning to the place my cousin stared at, I saw sure enough that a face—apparently a living human face—was pressed against the window-pane, framed between two hands as it tried to peer upon us into the semi-obscurity of the room. I saw the swift momentary rolling of the two eyes as the candle glare fell upon them, and caught a glimpse even of the hunched-up shoulders behind, as their owner, standing outside upon the lawn, stooped down a little to see better. And though the apparition instantly withdrew, I recognized it beyond question as the dark and evil countenance of the butler. His breath still stained the window.

Yet the strange thing was that Aileen, struggling violently to bury herself amid the scanty folds of my coat, could not possibly have seen what we saw, for her face was turned from the window the entire time, and from the way I held her she could never for a single instant have been in a position to know. It all took place behind her back... A moment later, with her eyes still hidden against me, I was carrying her swiftly in my arms across the hall and up the main staircase to the night nursery.

My difficulty with her was, of course, while she hovered between the two states of sleep and waking, for once I got her into bed and plunged her deeply again into the trance condition, I was easily able to control her slightest thought or emotion. Within ten minutes she was sleeping peacefully, her little face smoothed of all anxiety or terror, and my imperious command ringing from end to end of her consciousness that when she woke next morning all should be forgotten. She was finally to forget...utterly and completely.

And, meanwhile, of course, the man, when I went with loathing and anger in my heart to his room in the servants' quarters, had a perfectly plausible explanation. He was in the act of getting ready for bed, he declared, when the noise had aroused his suspicions, and, as in duty bound, he had made a tour of the house outside, thinking to discover burglars...

With a month's wages in his pocket, and a considerable degree of wonder in his soul, probably—for the man was guilty of nothing worse than innocently terrifying a child's imagination!—he went back to London the following day; and a few hours later I myself was travelling with Aileen and old Kempster over the blue waves of the North Sea, carrying her off, curiously enough, to freedom and happiness in the very way her "imagination" had pictured her escape in the "story" of long ago, when she was Lady Helen, held in bondage by a cruel husband, and I was Philip, her devoted lover.

Only this time her happiness was lasting and complete. Hypnotic suggestion had wiped from her mind the last vestige of her dreadful memories; her face was wreathed in jolly smiles; her enjoyment of the journey and our week in Antwerp was absolutely unclouded; she played and laughed with all the radiance of an unhaunted childhood, and her imagination was purged and healed.

And when we got back her mother had again moved her household gods to the original family mansion where she had first lived. Thither it was I took the restored child, and there it was my cousin and I looked up the old family records and verified certain details of the history of De Lorne, that wicked and semi-fabulous ancestor whose portrait hung in the dark corner of the stairs. That his life was evil to the brim I had always understood, but neither myself nor Theresa had known—at least had not consciously remembered—that he had married twice, and that his first wife, Lady Helen, had mysteriously disappeared, and Sir Philip

Lansing, a neighbouring knight, supposed to be her lover, had soon afterwards emigrated to France and left his lands and property to go to ruin. But another discovery I made, and kept to myself, had to do with that "room of terror" in the old Norfolk house where, on the plea of necessary renovation, I had the stones removed, and in the very spot where Aileen used to beat her hands against the bricks and "talk to the wall," the workmen under my own eyes laid bare the skeleton of a woman, fastened to the granite by means of a narrow iron band that encircled the waist—the skeleton of some unfortunate who had been walled-up alive and had come to her dreadful death by the pangs of hunger, thirst and suffocation centuries ago.

PERSPECTIVE

I

THE amount of duty and pleasure combined in Alpine summer chaplaincies of a month each just suited the Rev. Phillip Ambleside. He was still young enough to climb—carefully; and genuine enough to enjoy seeing the crowd of holiday-makers having a good time. As a rule he was on the Entertainment Committee that organized the tennis, dances, and gymkhanas. During the week one would hardly have guessed his calling. On Sundays he appeared a bronzed, lean, vigorous figure in the pulpit of the hot little wooden church, and people liked to see him. His sermons, never over ten minutes, were the same four every year: one for each Sunday of the month; and when he passed on to another month's duty in the next place he repeated them. The surroundings suggested them obviously: Beauty, Rest, Power, Majesty; and they were more like little confidential talks than sermons. Moreover, incidents from the life of the place—the escape of a tourist, the accident to a guide, and what not, usually came ready to hand to point a moral. One summer, however, there occurred a singular adventure that he has never yet been able to introduce into a sermon. Only in private conversation with souls as full of faith as himself does he ever mention it. And the short recital always begins with a sentence more or less as follows—

"...Talking of the wondrous ways of God, and the little understanding of the children of men, I am always struck by the huge machinery He sometimes adopts to accomplish such delicate and apparently insignificant ends. I remember once when I was doing summer 'duty' in a Swiss resort high up among the mountains of the Valais..."

And then follows the curious occurrence I was once privileged to hear, and have obtained permission to re-tell, duly disguised.

In the particular mountain village where he was taking a month's duty at the time, his church was full every Sunday, so full indeed that twice a week he held afternoon services for those who cared to worship more quietly. And to these little ceremonies, beloved of his own heart, came two persons regularly who attracted his attention in spite of himself. They sat together at the back; shared the same books, although there was no necessity to do so; courted the shadowy corners of the pews: in a word, they came to worship one another, not to worship God.

But the clergyman took a broad view. Courtships fostered in the holy atmosphere of the sacred building were more likely to be true than those fanned to flame in the feverish surroundings of the dance-room. And true love is ever an offering to God. He knew the couple, too. The man, quiet, earnest, well over forty; the girl, young, dashing, spirited, leader in mischief, hard to believe sincere, flirting with more than one. In spite of the careful concealment with which she covered their proceedings, choosing the deserted afternoon service rather than the glare of the garden or ball-room for their talks, the couple were marked. The difference in their ages, characters, and appearance singled them out, as much as the general knowledge that she was rich, vain, flighty, while he was poor, strenuous, living a life of practical charity in London, that precluded gaiety or pleasure, so called.

"What *can* she see in that dull man twice her age?" the elder women said to one another—the answer generally being that it probably amused the girl to turn him so easily round her little finger.

"What a chance for her fortune to be well spent," reflected one or two. While the men, when they said anything at all, contented themselves with "Pretty hard hit, isn't he? A fine fellow though! Hope he gets her!"

It is always somewhat pathetic to see a man of real value fall before the conquering beauty of an ordinary young girl of the world. The clergyman, however, with an eye for spiritual values, even deeply hidden, divined that beneath her lightness and love for conquest's sake there lay the desire for something more real. And he guessed, though at first the wish may have been father to the thought only, that it was the elder man's fine zeal and power that attracted the butterfly in spite of herself towards a life that was more worth living. Hers, after all, he felt, was a soul worth "saving"; and this middle-aged man, perhaps, was the force God brought into her life to provide her with the opportunity of escape—could she but seize it.

So far Ambleside's story runs along ordinary lines enough. One sees his man and girl without further detail. From this point, however, it slips into a stride where the sense of proportion seems somehow lost, or else "man's little understanding" is too close to the thing to obtain the proper perspective. If any one but this devout and clear-headed clergyman told the tale, one might say "Fancy," "Delusion," or any other description that seemed suitable. But to hear him tell it, with that air of conviction and truth, in those short, abrupt, even jerky sentences, that left so much to the imagination, and with that pallor of the skin that threw into such vivid contrast the fire burning in his far-seeing blue eyes—to sit close to him and hear the story grow in that tense low voice, was to know beyond all question that he spoke of something real and actual, in the same sense that a train or St. Paul's Cathedral are real and actual.

What he saw, he really saw: though the sight may have been of a kind unfamiliar to the majority. He was used as a real pawn in a real game. The girl's life and soul were rescued, so to speak, by the marriage brought about, and her forces of mind and spirit lifted bodily for what they were worth into the scheme that God had ordained for them from the beginning of the world. Only—the machinery brought to bear upon the end in view seemed so prodigious, so extraordinary, so unnecessary... One thinks of the sentence with which Ambleside always began his tale. One wonders. But no one who heard the tale ever asked questions at its close. There was absolutely nothing to say.

Even to the smallest details the affair seemed thought out and planned, for that particular Tuesday Ambleside started without the guide-porter who usually carried his telescope, camera, and lunch. He went off at six a.m., with merely an ice-axe and a small knapsack containing food and Shetland vest for the summit.

It was one of those days towards the end of August when some quality in the atmosphere—usually sign of approaching rain—brings the mountains uncannily close, yet, at the same time, sets out every detail of pinnacle, precipice, and ridge with a terror of size and grandeur that makes one realize their true and gigantic scale. They press up close, yet at the same time stand away in the depths of the sky like unattainable masses in some dream world. This mingling of proximity and distance has a confusing effect upon the eye. When Ambleside toiled up the zigzags without actually looking beyond, he felt that the towering *massif* of the Valais Alps all about him loomed very close; but when he stopped for breath and raised his eyes steadily into their detail, he felt that their distance was too great to be conquered by any little two-legged being like himself merely taking steps. And as he rose out of the valley into the clearer strata of air this effect increased. The whole scale of the chain of Alps about him seemed raised to an immeasurably higher power than he had ever known. He felt like an insect crawling over the craters of the moon. The prodigious splendours of the scenery all round oppressed him more than ever before with his own futile littleness, yet at the same time made him conscious of the grandeur of his soul before the God who had set him and his kind above all this chaos of tumbled planet.

He thought of the mountains as part of the "garment of God," and of nature as expressing some portion of the Deity not intended to be expressed by man—all part of His purpose, alive with His informing will. This glory of the inanimate Alps linked on to some stranger glory in himself that interpreted for him, as in a mystical revelation, God's thundering message and purpose known in the great forms and moods of nature. Closely in touch with the spirit of the mountains he was; glad to be alone.

This, in a sentence, expresses his mood: that the mountains accepted him. Forces in his deepest being that were akin to the life of the planet on which he made his tiny track rose up and triumphed. Over the treacherous Pas d'Iliez, where he usually felt giddy and unsafe, he felt this morning only exhilaration. The gulf yawning at his feet touched him with its splendour, not its terror.

Thus, feeling inclined to shout and run, he eventually reached the desolate valley of rock and shale that lies, unrelieved by a single blade of grass, between the glacier-covered slopes that shut it in impassably on three sides. The bed of this valley lies some 7,000 feet above the sea. The peaks and ridges that rear about it reach 12,000 feet. Here, being a good climber, he rested for the first time at the end of two hours' steady ascent. The air nipped. The loneliness and desolation were very impressive. Beyond him hung the glaciers like immense thick blankets of blue-white upon the steep slopes, dropping from time to time lumps of ice into the shale-strewn valley below. For the sun shining in a cloudless sky was fierce. The clergyman, before attacking the long snow-field that began at his very feet, took out his blue spectacles and disentangled the cord. He ate some chocolate, and took the dried prunes from his knapsack, knowing that thirst would soon be upon him, and that ice-water was not for drinking.

"What a mite I am, to be sure, amid all this appalling wilderness!" he exclaimed; "and how splendid to be able to hold my own!"

And then it was, just as he stood up to arrange the glasses on his forehead, ready to pull down at a moment's notice, that he became aware of something that was strange-unaccustomed. Through the giant splendours of the scorching August day, across all this stupendous scenery of desolation and loneliness, something fine as a needle, delicate as a hair, had begun picking at his mind. The idea came to him that he was no longer alone. Like a man who hears his name called out of darkness he turned instinctively to find the speaker; almost as though someone had been calling to him for a considerable time, and he had only just had his attention drawn to it. He looked keenly up and down the immense, deserted valley.

In every direction, however, he saw nothing but miles of rock, dazzling snow-fields, dark precipices, and endless peaks cutting the blue sky overhead with teeth that gleamed like burnished steel. It was desolation everywhere. The gentle wind that fanned his cheek made no sound against the stones. There was neither tree nor grass for it to rustle through. No bird's wing whirred the air; and the far-off falling of a hundred cascades was of too regular and monotonous a character to have taken on the quality of a voice or the rhythm of uttered words. He examined, so far as he could, the enormous sides of mountain about him, and the great soaring ridges. It was just possible some climber in distress had spied him out, and shouted down upon him from the heights. But he searched in vain. There was no moving human figure. The sound, if sound it had been, was not repeated; only he was no longer alone, as before. That, at least, was certain... He nibbled more chocolate, put a couple of sour prunes into his mouth to suck, arranged the blue snow-glass over his eyes, and started on again for a steady pull up to the next ridge.

And as he rose the scale of the surrounding mountains rose appallingly with him. The true distance of the peaks proclaimed itself; the tremendous reaches that from below appeared telescoped up into a little space opened up and stretched themselves. The hour grew into two. It was considerably after twelve before he reached the *arête* where he had promised himself lunch. And all the way, without ceasing, the idea that he was being accompanied remained insistent in his mind. It troubled and perplexed him. Perhaps it frightened him a little, too. More than once it came close enough to make him pause and consider whether he should continue or turn back.

For the curious part of it was that this idea exercised a direct and deliberate effect upon him. By a hundred little details that seemed to be spontaneous until he examined them, it kept suggesting somehow that he should change his route. Something in his consciousness grew that had not been there before. He thought of a bird bringing tiny morsels of grass and twig until a nest formed. In this way the steady stream of thoughts from somewhere outside himself came nesting in his brain until at length they acquired the consistency of an impression, next of a distinct desire, lastly, the momentum of a definite intention. They acted upon his volition, stirring softly among; the roots of his will. Before he realized how it had quite come about he had *changed his mind*.

"Instead of going on to the top as I intended," he said to himself, as he sat on the dizzy ledge munching hard-boiled eggs and sugar sandwiches, "I shall strike off to the left and find my way back into the valley again. That, I think, would be—nicer!"

He had no real reason; he invented none.

And the moment he said it there was a sense of pressure removed, a consciousness of relief, the knowledge, in a word, that he was following a route that it was desired he should follow.

To a man, of course, whose habit it was to seek often the will of a personal Deity he worshipped, there was nothing very out of the way in all this, although he never remembered to have felt any guidance so distinctly and forcibly indicated before. The feeling that he was being "guided" now became a certainty, and in order to follow instructions as well as possible he made his will of no account and opened himself to receive the slightest token this other Directing Agency might care to vouchsafe.

After lunch, therefore, he struck out a diagonal course across a steep snow-slope that would eventually bring him down again to the valley a little nearer its head. And before he had gone a hundred yards he ran into the track of another climber. The marks were a couple of days old, perhaps, for in their hollows lay little heaps of fine snow-dust, freshly blown. Judging by the size there had been two men. He noted the trace of the ice-axe and the occasional streak of the trailing rope. The men had made straight for the valley far below. Here and there they had glissaded. Here and there, too, they had also tumbled gloriously, for the snow was tossed about by their floundering. Yet there was no danger; no precipices intervened; the snow sloped without a break right down into the shale below.

"I'll follow their example," said the Rev. Phillip Ambleside. He strapped on the extra leather seat lie carried for sliding and sat down. A moment later he was rushing at high speed over the hard surface. There were hollows of softer snow, however, which stopped him from time to time, drifts as it were into which he plunged, and from which he emerged, wet and shivering. Then he stood up and leaned on his axe, trying to glissade on his feet. For this, however, the surface was not smooth enough. The result was he tumbled, rolled, slid, sat down, and took immense gliding strides. It was very exhilarating. He revelled in it.

But all the while he kept his eyes sharply about him, for in his heart he felt that he was obeying that guiding Influence so strongly impressed upon him—the Power that had persuaded him to change his route, and was now leading him to some particular point with some particular purpose. Now, too, for the first time a vague sense of calamity touched him. Once introduced, it grew. Soon it amounted to a positive foreboding, a presentiment of disaster almost. He could not avoid the idea that he was being led by supernatural means to the scene of some catastrophe where he was to prove of use—a rescue, an arrival in the nick of time to save someone. He actually looked about him already for—yes, for the body. And through his sub-conscious mind, with the force of habit, ran the magnificent use he could make of it all in a future sermon.

Yet nothing came. The tracks of the other men stretched clear and unbroken into the valley of rocks below. He traced the wavering thin line the whole way down.

"It's nothing to do with *these* men, at any rate," he said to himself, as he sat down for the final slide that should take him to the bottom of the slope. "No accident could possibly have happened here. The snow's too soft, and there are no rocks to fall over or—"

The sentence, or the thought, remained unfinished, for the mouth of the Rev. Phillip was stopped temporarily with wet snow as he lost his balance and rushed sideways with an undignified plunge into a drifted hollow. His eyes were blinded, his feet twisted, the skin of his back drenched and *icy*. He rose spluttering and gasping. Luckily his axe had a leather loop, or he would have lost it; as it was, his slouch hat was already a hundred feet below, sliding and turning like a top on its way to the bottom, followed by the snow-goggles.

And in the act of brushing himself free of snow the truth came to him. It was as though a hand had struck him on the back and pointed—as though a voice had uttered the five words: *"This is the place. Look!"*

Swiftly, searchingly, keenly he looked, and saw—nothing; nothing, at least, that explained the impression of disaster that had possessed him. There was no body certainly, nor any sign of an accident; no place, indeed, where an accident could possibly have come about. He dug quickly in the loose snow with his axe, but the snow was barely two feet deep in this particular hollow, and all round it was a hard surface of smoothly and tightly-packed stuff that was almost ice. Nothing bigger than a cat could have lain buried there!

"This is the place! Look well!" the words seemed to ring in his ears.

Yet the more he looked and saw nothing, the more strongly beat this message upon his brain. This was the place where he was to come, where he was to fulfill some purpose, to find something, do something, accomplish the end intended by the Will that had so carefully guided him all day. The feeling was positive; not to be denied. It was, at the same time, distressingly vast—mighty.

Fixing himself securely against his axe, he stood and stared. The sun beat back into his face from the glittering snow on all sides. Tremendous black precipices towered not far behind him; to his left rolled the frozen mass of the huge glacier, its pinnacles of tottering ice catching the afternoon sun; to his right stretched into bewildering distance the interminable and desolate reaches of shale and moraine till the eye rested upon summits of a dozen peaks that literally swam in the sky where white clouds streamed westwards. There was no sound but falling water, no sign of humanity except the single track of those other climbers, no indication of any disturbance upon the vast face of nature that spread all about him, immense, still, terrific.

Then, piercing the monotony of the falling water, a faint sound of fluttering, heard for the first time, reached his ear. He turned as at the sound of a pistol-shot in the direction whence it came—but again saw nothing. The sound ceased. From the slope below came a breath of icy wind that made him shiver, and with it, he fancied, came the faint hissing noise of his sliding hat and spectacles. This, perhaps, was the sound he had heard as "fluttering."

At length after prolonged and vain searching, the clergyman decided there was nothing for him to do but continue his journey, for the sun was getting low, and he had a long way to go before dusk could be regarded with equanimity. He felt exhausted, wearied, impatient too if the truth were told, yet ashamed of his impatience.

"If this is all *real*," he argued under his breath, "why isn't it made clear what I'm to do?"

And immediately upon the heels of the thought came again that faint and curious sound of something fluttering.

Now, there can be no question that he understood perfectly well that this sound of fluttering had a direct connection with the whole purpose of the day—that it was the clue to his presence in this particular spot, and that he had been forced to halt here by means of his fall in order that he might investigate something or other on this very spot. He knew it; he felt it. But he was too impatient, too cold, too weary to spend any further time over it all. Alarm, too, was plucking uneasily at his reins.

So this time he affected to ignore the sound. Leaning back on his axe he threw his body into position for sliding down to the bottom of the slope. In another second he would have started—when something that froze him into the immobility of a terror worse than death arrested him with a power beyond anything he had ever known before in his life—a Power that seemed to carry behind it the pressure of the entire universe.

There, close beside him in this mountain wilderness, had risen up suddenly a Face—close as the handle of the ice-axe he so tightly grasped, yet at the same time so far away, so immense, so stupendous in scale that he has never understood to this day how it was he could have perceived that it was—a Face. Yet a face it undoubtedly was, a living face; and its eyes—its regard, at any rate, for eyes he divined rather than saw—were focussed upon some object that lay at his very feet.

Clammy with fear, his heart thumping dreadfully, he dropped back upon the snow. Without looking at any particular detail he became aware that the entire world of giant scenery about him was involved in the building up of this appalling Countenance, whose gaze was directed upon a tiny point immediately before him—the point, he now perceived, whence proceeded that familiar little sound of fluttering.

Words obviously fail him when he attempts to describe the terror of this Visage that rose about him through the day. Pallid and immense, it seemed to stretch itself against the wastes of grey rock, with entire slopes of snow upon the cheeks, ridged and furrowed by precipice and cliff, with torn clouds of flying hair that streaked the blue, and the expanse of glaciers for the splendid brows. Across it the dark line of two moraines tilted for eyebrows, and the massive columns of compressed strata embedded in the whole structure of the mountain chain bulged for the muscles of the awful neck... Moreover, the shoulders upon which it all rested—the vast framework of body that he divined below—the dizzy drop in space where such fearful limbs must seek their resting-place—!

His mind went reeling. The titanic proportions of this Countenance of splendour threatened in some horrible way to overwhelm his life. Its calmness, its iron immobility, its remorseless fixity of mien petrified him. The thought that he had dared to question it, to put himself in opposition to its purpose, even to be impatient with it—this turned all his soul within him soft and dead with a kind of ultimate terror that bereft him of any clear memory, perhaps momentarily, too, of consciousness.

The clergyman *thinks* he fainted. Exactly what happened, probably, he never knew nor realized. All that he can say in attempting to describe it is that he found his own eyes caught up and carried away in the gigantic stream of vision that this Face of Mountains poured upon the ground—caught up and directed upon a tiny little white object that fluttered in the wind at his very feet.

He saw what the Face was looking at and wished him to look at. It made him see what it saw.

For there, in front of him, unnoticed hitherto, lay a scrap of paper half embedded in the snow. Automatically he stooped and picked it up. It was an envelope bearing the printed inscription of an hotel in the village. It was sealed. On the outside in a fine handwriting, he read the Christian name of a man. Opening the corner he saw inside a small lock of dark-coloured hair. And this was all...!

Then it was just at this moment that the snow where his feet rested gave way, and he started off at full speed to slide to the bottom of the slope, where he only just stopped himself in time to prevent shooting with a violent collision into a mass of shale and loose stones.

In less than thirty seconds it had all happened...and the swift descent and tumble had shaken him back as it were into a normal state of mind. But the oppression that had burdened him all day was gone. The mountains looked as usual. An indescribable sense of relief came over him. He felt a free agent once more—no longer guided, pushed, directed. He had fulfilled the purpose.

Putting the little envelope in his inside pocket he picked up his slouch hat and snow-goggles, ate some chocolate and dried prunes, and started off at a brisk pace for his return journey of three hours to the village and—dinner. And the whole way home the grandeur of that face, with its splendid pallor, and its expression of majesty, haunted him with indescribable sensations. With it, however, all the time ran the accompanying thought: "What a tremendous business for so small a result! All that vast manoeuvring, all that terror of the imagination, and all that complex pressure upon my insignificant spirit merely in the end to find a wisp of girl's hair in an envelope evidently fallen from the pocket of some careless climber!"

The more the Rev. Phillip Ambleside thought about it, the more bewildered he felt. He was uncommonly glad, however, to get in before dark. The memory of that Mountain Countenance was no agreeable companion for the forest paths and lonely slopes through which his way led in the dusk.

II

That same night it so happened, before he was able to take any steps to trace the owner of the little envelope, there was a Bal de Têtes at the principal hotel. Although the clergyman was on the Entertainment Committee which organized the simple gaieties of the place, he held that honorary position only as a personal compliment to himself; he did not at a rule take an active part in the detail, nor did he as a general rule attend the balls.

This particular night, however, he strolled down to the hotel, and after a little conversation with one or two friends in the hall he made his way to a secluded corner of the glass gallery where the dancers sat out between times, and lit his pipe for a quiet smoke. From behind the shelter of a large sham palm he was able to see all he wanted of the ballroom, to hear the music, and to take in the pleasant sight of all the people enjoying themselves. And the sight did him good. He liked to see it. A number were in costume, which added to the picturesqueness of the scene. Perhaps he sat more in the shadows than he knew, or perhaps the dancers who came to "sit out" near him in the gallery did not realize how their voices carried. Several couples, as the evening advanced, came so close to him that, had he wished, he could have overheard easily every word they uttered. He did not wish, however. His mind was busy with thoughts of its own. That haunting scene of desolation in the mountains obsessed him still; and about ten o'clock, his pipe being finished, he was on the point of getting up to leave, when two dancers came and sat down immediately behind him and began to talk in such very distinct tones that it was impossible to avoid hearing every single word they uttered.

The clergyman pushed his chair aside to make room to go, when, in doing so, he threw a passing glance at the couple—and instantly recognized them. The girl, a Carmen, and a very becoming Carmen, was the one who frequented his afternoon services, and the man, who wore simple evening dress and was not in costume at all, was the middle-aged Englishman who had been at her heels like a slave all the summer. They were absorbed in one another, and evidently unaware of his presence.

To say that he hesitated would not be true. Some force beyond himself simply took him by the shoulders and pushed him back into the chair. Against his own will—for Mr. Ambleside was no eavesdropper—he remained there deliberately to listen.

In telling the story he tells it just like this, making no excuses for conduct that was certainly dishonourable. He declares he could not help himself; the instinct was too imperious to be disobeyed. Again, as in the afternoon, he understood that he was merely being used as a pawn in the game, a game of great importance to some Intelligence that saw through to the distant end.

The man was quiet, but tremendously in earnest, with the kind of steady manner that no woman likes unless she finds it in her to respond with a similar sincerity. Under the bronze his skin showed pale a little. He began to speak the instant they sat down; and in his voice was passion.

"I want you, and I want your money, and I want your life and soul—everything," he said, evidently continuing a conversation; "your youth and energy, your talents, your will, all that is you and yours—*all*." His voice was pitched very low, yet without tremor. He was playing the whole stake, as a strong man of middle age plays it when he is utterly in earnest. "For my scheme, for *our* scheme, for God's scheme I want you; and no one else but you will do. I want you to awake, and change your life, and be your true, fine self. We can make a success, you and I, a success for ourselves and for others. I shall never give you up until—until you give yourself to the world, or"—his voice dropped very low—"to another."

The clergyman waited breathlessly for the answer. The man's words vibrated with such suppressed fire that only a serious reply could be forthcoming. But for a space Carmen merely toyed with her fan, the little red spangled fan that swung from a single finger. Behind the black domino her eyes sparkled, but the expression of her face was hidden.

"The difference in age is nothing," he continued almost sternly. "For me, you are *the* woman, and for you I will prove that I am *the* man. I see clean through to the great soul hidden in you. I can bring it out. I can make you *real*—a soul of value in the big order of God's purposes. What can these boys ever be, or do, for you? I've got a big, useful, practical scheme that can use you, just as it can use me. And my great unselfish love has picked you out of the whole world as the one woman necessary. Will you come to me?"

Still the girl was silent. She tapped him on the knee two or three times, would-be playfully, with the tip of her fan. Her head was bent down a little.

"And I'm strong," he went on earnestly; "I'm a man. The power in me recognizes and calls to the power in you. Let me hold you and mould you, and let's take the fine, high life together. Drop this life of child's play you've been leading. Come to me; my arms are hungry for you! But I want you for a higher purpose than my own happiness—though I swear I can make you happy as no woman in this world has ever before been happy. And without you," he added more softly after a slight pause, "this splendid scheme of mine, of ours, can come to nothing. For I cannot do it alone—and there is only one *You* in the world. Answer me now. It was to-night, remember, you promised. I leave tomorrow, and London days lie far ahead. Give me your answer to go back with."

It was a curious way to make love. The reverend gentleman thought he had never heard anything quite like it. An ordinarily frivolous girl, of course, would have been impatient long ago. But the fine passion of the man broke everywhere through his rather lame words, and set something in the air about them aflame. The violins sounded thin and trashy compared to the rhythm of this earnest voice; all the glitter of the ball-room seemed cheap—the costume of Carmen absurdly incongruous. Mr. Ambleside slipped back somehow into the key of the afternoon when Cosmic Powers had held direct communion with his soul. He understood that he was meant to listen. Something big was in progress, something important in a high sense. He did listen—to every word. It was Carmen speaking now; but her voice marred the picture. It was thin, trifling, even affected.

"It's very flattering," she simpered, "but—don't you see—it means the end of all my fun and enjoyment in life. You're so fearfully in earnest. You'd exhaust me in the first week!" She cocked her pretty head on one side, holding the fan against her cheek. Something, nevertheless, belied the lightness of her words, the listener felt.

"But I'll teach you a different kind of happiness," replied the man eagerly, "so that you'll never again want this passing excitement, this 'unrest which men miscall delight.' Give me your answer—now. I see it in your eyes. Let me go away tomorrow with this great new happiness in my heart." He leaned forward. "Let your real self speak out once for all!" He took her fan away and she made no resistance. She clasped her hands in her lap, still looking at him mischievously through her mask.

"Let's wait till we meet later in town," she sighed at length prettily, coaxingly. "I shall be able to enjoy myself here then. for the rest of the summer first—I feel so young for such a programme."

But the man cut her short.

"Now," he said, holding her steadily with his eyes. "You said that to me a year ago, remember. I have waited ever since. It is your youth I want."

The girl played with him for another ten minutes, while the clergyman listened, wondering greatly at the other's patience. Clearly, she delighted to feel his great love beating up against the citadel she meant in the end to yield. The lighter side of her was vastly interested and amused by it; but all the time the deeper part was ready with its answer. It was only that the "child" in her wanted to enjoy itself a little longer before it capitulated for ever to the strength that should take her captive, and lead her by sharp ways of sacrifice to the high *rôle* she was meant to fill.

It would all have vexed and wearied Mr. Ambleside exceedingly, but for this singular feeling that it was part of some much larger scheme of which he might never know the whole perhaps, but in which he was playing his little part with a secret thrill. Through the tawdry glitter of that scented ball-room he saw again that terrible white-lipped Face, and felt the measure of this great purpose rolling past him—immense, remorseless—which, for all its splendour, could include even so small a thing as this vain and silly girl. The tide of it rose about him with a flood of power. He glanced at the small black domino of the Carmen opposite him...he saw the little flashing eyes, the pert lips and mouth—thinking with something like a shudder of that other Countenance in the hollow of whose eyes hid tempests, yet which could look down upon a tiny fluttering paper, because that paper was an item of importance in its great scheme of which both beginning and end were nevertheless veiled...

His thoughts must have wandered for a time. The conversation, at any rate, had meanwhile taken a singular turn. The girl was on her feet, the man facing her.

"Then what is this test of yours?" he was saying, half serious, half laughing—"this test which you say will prove how much I care?"

The girl put back between her lips the small red rose that was part of the Carmen costume. Either it was that the stalk made her lisp a little, or else that a sudden rush of the violins in the waltz drowned her words. The Reverend Phillip, standing there trembling—he never quite understood why he should have awaited her answer so nervously—only caught the second half of her phrase.

"...that I gave you in this very room six weeks ago, and that you promised to carry about with you always?" he heard the end of her sentence, in a voice that for the first time that evening was serious; "because, if you've kept your word in a small thing like that I can trust you to keep it in bigger things. It was a part of myself, you know, that little bit of hair!" She laughed deliciously in his face, raising herself on tiptoe with her hands behind her back. "You said so yourself, didn't you? You promised it should never, *never* leave you."

The man made a curiously sudden gesture as though a pain beyond his control passed through him. His hands were on the back of a chair. The chair squeaked audibly along the polished floor beneath a violent momentary pressure. He looked straight into his companion's eyes, but made no immediate reply.

Carmen's gaze behind the black mask became hard. With a truly feminine idiocy she was obviously playing this whim as a serious move in the game.

"For if you have lost *that*," she continued, her face flushing beneath the paint, "how can you expect to keep the rest of me, the important part of me?" She spoke as though she believed that he, too, was half-playing— that the next minute he would put his hand into his pocket and produce it. His delay, his awkwardness, above all his silence, angered her. For the surface of her self-contradictory character was obviously—minx.

After a pause that seemed interminable the man spoke, and for the first time his deep voice shook a little.

"This time tomorrow night you shall have it," he said.

"But you're leaving, you said, in the morning!" The tone was piqued and shrill.

"I shall stay another day—on purpose." A pause followed.

"Then you really have lost it—envelope and all—with your name in *my* writing on the outside, and *my* hair for all to recognize who find it— and to sneer."

Her eyes flashed as she said it. The girl was disappointed, incensed, furious. It was all silly enough, of course, and utterly out of proportion. But how silly and childish real life is apt to be at such moments, only those who have reached middle age and have observed closely can know. At the time, to the clergyman who stood there listening and observing, it seemed genuinely poignant, even tragic.

"Until the day before yesterday it had never left me for a single instant," he said at length. "I was in the mountains-glissading with your brother. It fell out of my pocket with a lot of other papers. I lost it on the upper snow slopes of the Dents Blenches—"

The rest of his words were drowned by an inrush of people, for the band was beginning a two-step and couples were sorting themselves and seeking their partners. A Frenchman, dressed as Napoleon, came up to claim his dance. Carmen was swept away. Scornfully, angrily, with concentrated resentment in her voice and manner, she turned upon her heel and from the lips that bit the stalk of the small red rose came the significant words—

"And with it you have also lost—*me!*"

She was gone. Perhaps the Reverend Phillip Ambleside only imagined the tears in her voice. He never knew, and had no time to think, for he found himself looking straight into the eyes of the lover, thus absurdly rejected, and who now became aware of his close presence for the first time. Even then the absurdity of the whole situation did not wholly reveal itself. It came later with reflection. At the moment he felt that it was all like a vivid and singular dream in which the values and proportions were oddly exaggerated, yet in which the sense of tragedy was distressingly real. His heart went out to the faithful and patient man who was being so trifled with, yet who might be in danger of losing by virtue of his very simplicity what was to be of real value in his life—and scheme.

"It's my move now," was the thought in his mind as he took a step forward.

The other, embarrassed and annoyed to discover that the whole scene had probably been overheard, made an awkward movement to withdraw, but before he could do so, the clergyman approached him. Only one step was necessary. He moved up from behind a palm, and drawing his hand from an inner pocket, he handed across to him a white envelope bearing the printed name of the hotel and a neat inscription in feminine writing just below it.

"I found this on the snow slopes of the Dents Blanches this afternoon," he said courteously. The other stared him steadily in the face—his colour coming and going quickly. "Take it to her and say that after all it was you—you, who were applying the test—that you wished to see if for so small a thing she was ready to reject so true a love. And, pray, pardon this interference which—er—chance has placed in my power. The matter, I need hardly say, is entirely between yourself and me."

The man took the paper awkwardly, a soft smile of gratitude and comprehension dawning in his eyes. He began to stammer a few words, but the clergyman did not stay to listen. He bowed politely and left him.

He went out of the hotel into the night, and a wind from the surrounding snow slopes brushed his face with its touch of great spaces. He looked up and saw the crowding stars, brilliant as in winter. The mountains in this faint light seemed incredibly close. Slowly he walked up the village street to his rooms in the châlet by the church.

And suddenly the true proportion of normal things in this little life returned to him, and with it a sharp realization of the triviality of the scene he had been forced to witness—and of the horrible grandeur of the means by which he had been dragged, by the scruff of his priestly neck as it were, so awkwardly into the middle of it all: merely to provide a scrap of evidence the loss of which threatened to bring about a foolish estrangement, and might conceivably have prevented a marriage of apparently insignificant importance.

He felt as though the machinery of the entire solar system had been employed to help a pair of ants carry a pine-needle too heavy for them to the top of the nest.

And then a moment's reflection brought to him another thought. For who could say what the result of this marriage might be? Who could say that from just the exact combination of those two forces—the earnest man, and the lighter girl—a son might not be born who should shake the world and lead some cherished purpose of Deity to completion? For, truly, of the threads which weave into the pattern of life and out again, men see but the tiny section immediately beneath their eyes. The majority focus their gaze upon some detail—thus losing the view of the whole. The beginning and the end are for ever hidden; and what appears insignificant and out of proportion when caught alone at close quarters, may reveal all the splendour of the Eternal Purpose when surveyed with the proper perspective—of the Infinite. The Reverend Phillip Ambleside felt as if for a moment he had been lifted to a height whence he had caught perhaps a glimpse of these larger horizons.

With his faith vastly strengthened, but his nerves considerably shaken, the clergyman went to bed and slept the sleep of a just man who has done his duty by chance as it were. He had helped forward a purpose of which he really understood nothing, but which, he somehow felt, was bigger than anything with which he had so far been connected in his life. Some day—his faith whispered it next morning while he was preparing his sermon—he would see the matter with proper perspective, and would understand.

THE TERROR
OF THE TWINS

THAT the man's hopes had built upon a son to inherit his name and estates—a single son, that is—was to be expected; but no one could have foreseen the depth and bitterness of his disappointment, the cold, implacable fury, when there arrived instead twins. For, though the elder legally must inherit, that other ran him so deadly close. A daughter would have been a more reasonable defeat. But twins—! To miss his dream by so feeble a device—!

The complete frustration of a hope deeply cherished for years may easily result in strange fevers of the soul, but the violence of the father's hatred, existing as it did side by side with a love he could not deny, was something to set psychologists thinking. More than unnatural, it was positively uncanny. Being a man of rigid self-control, however, it operated inwardly, and doubtless along some morbid line of weakness little suspected even by those nearest to him, preying upon his thought to such dreadful extent that finally the mind gave way. The suppressed rage and bitterness deprived him, so the family decided, of his reason, and he spent the last years of his life under restraint. He was possessed naturally of immense forces—of will, feeling, desire; his dynamic value truly tremendous, driving through life like a great engine; and the intensity of this concentrated and buried hatred was guessed by few. The twins themselves, however, knew it. They divined it, at least, for it operated ceaselessly against them side by side with the genuine soft love that occasionally sweetened it, to their great perplexity. They spoke of it only to each other, though.

"At twenty-one," Edward, the elder, would remark sometimes, unhappily, "we shall know more." "Too much," Ernest would reply, with a rush of unreasoning terror the thought never failed to evoke—*in him.* "Things father said always happened—in life." And they paled perceptibly. For the hatred, thus compressed into a veritable bomb of psychic energy, had found at the last a singular expression in the cry of the father's distraught mind. On the occasion of their final visit to the asylum, preceding his death by a few hours only, very calmly, but with an intensity that drove the words into their hearts like points of burning metal, he had spoken. In the presence of the attendant, at the door of the dreadful padded cell, he said it: "You are not two, but *one*. I still regard you as one. And at the coming of age, by h—, you shall find it out!"

The lads perhaps had never fully divined that icy hatred which lay so well concealed against them, but that this final sentence was a curse, backed by all the man's terrific force, they quite well realized; and accordingly, almost unknown to each other, they had come to dread the day inexpressibly. On the morning of that twenty-first birthday—their father gone these five years into the Unknown, yet still sometimes so strangely close to them—they shared the same biting, inner terror, just as they shared all other emotions of their life—intimately, without speech. During the daytime they managed to keep it at a distance, but when the dusk fell about the old house they knew the stealthy approach of a kind of panic sense. Their self-respect weakened swiftly...and they persuaded their old friend, and once tutor, the vicar, to sit up with them till midnight... He had humoured them to that extent, willing to forgo his sleep, and at the same time more than a little interested in their singular belief-that before the day was out, before midnight struck, that is, the curse of that terrible man would somehow come into operation against them.

Festivities over and the guests departed, they sat up in the library, the room usually occupied by their father, and little used since. Mr. Curtice, a robust man of fifty-five, and a firm believer in spiritual principalities and powers, dark as well as good, affected (for their own good) to regard the youths' obsession with a kindly cynicism. "I do not think it likely for one moment," he said gravely, "that such a thing would be permitted. All spirits are in the hands of God, and the violent ones more especially." To which Edward made the extraordinary reply: "Even if father does not come himself he will—*send!*" And Ernest agreed: "All this time he's been making preparations for this very day. We've both known it for a long time—by odd things that have happened, by our dreams, by nasty little dark hints of various kinds, and by these persistent attacks of terror that come from nowhere, especially of late. Haven't we, Edward?" Edward assenting with a shudder: "Father has been *at us* of late with renewed violence. To-night it will be a regular assault upon our lives, or minds, or souls!"

"Strong personalities *may* possibly leave behind them forces that continue to act," observed Mr. Curtice with caution, while the brothers replied almost in the same breath: "That's exactly what we feel so curiously. Though—nothing has actually happened yet, you know, and it's a good many years now since—"

This was the way the twins spoke of it all. And it was their profound conviction that had touched their old friend's sense of duty. The experiment should justify itself—and cure them. Meanwhile none of the family knew. Everything was planned secretly.

The library was the quietest room in the house. It had shuttered bow-windows, thick carpets, heavy doors. Books lined the walls, and there was a capacious open fireplace of brick in which the wood-logs blazed and roared, for the autumn night was chilly. Round this the three of them were grouped, the clergyman reading aloud from the Book of Job in low tones; Edward and Ernest, in dinner-jackets, occupying deep leather arm-chairs, listening. They looked exactly what they were—Cambridge "undergrads," their faces pale against their dark hair, and alike as two peas. A shaded lamp behind the clergyman threw the rest of the room into shadow. The reading voice was steady, even monotonous, but something in it betrayed an underlying anxiety, and although the eyes rarely left the printed page, they took in every movement of the young men opposite, and noted every change upon their faces. It was his aim to produce an unexciting atmosphere, yet to miss nothing; if anything did occur to see it from the very beginning. Not to be taken by surprise was his main idea... And thus, upon this falsely peaceful scene, the minutes passed the hour of eleven and slipped rapidly along towards midnight.

The novel element in his account of this distressing and dreadful occurrence seems to be that what happened—happened without the slightest warning or preparation. There was no gradual presentment of any horror; no strange blast of cold air; no dwindling of heat or light; no shaking of windows or mysterious tapping upon furniture. Without preliminaries it fell with its black trappings of terror upon the scene.

The clergyman had been reading aloud for some considerable time, one or other of the twins—Ernest usually—making occasional remarks, which proved that his sense of dread was disappearing. As the time grew short and nothing happened they grew more at their ease. Edward, indeed, actually nodded, dozed, and finally fell asleep. It was a few minutes before midnight. Ernest, slightly yawning, was stretching himself in the big chair. "Nothing's going to happen," he said aloud, in a pause. "Your good influence has prevented it." He even laughed now. "What superstitious asses we've been, sir; haven't we—?"

Curtice, then, dropping his Bible, looked hard at him under the lamp. For in that second, even while the words sounded, there had come about a most abrupt and dreadful change; and so swiftly that the clergyman, in spite of himself, was taken utterly by surprise and had no time to think. There had swooped down upon the quiet library—so he puts it—an immense hushing silence, so profound that the peace already reigning there seemed clamour by comparison; and out of this enveloping stillness there rose through the space about them a living and abominable

Invasion-soft, motionless, terrific. It was as though vast engines, working at full speed and pressure, yet too swift and delicate to be appreciable to any definite sense, had suddenly dropped down upon them—from nowhere. "It made me think," the vicar used to say afterwards, "of the *Mauretania* machinery compressed into a nutshell, yet losing none of its awful power."

"...haven't we?" repeated Ernest, still laughing. And Curtice, making no audible reply, heard the true answer in his heart: "Because everything has *already happened*—even as you feared."

Yet, to the vicar's supreme astonishment, Ernest still noticed—nothing!

"Look," the boy added, "Eddy's sound asleep—sleeping like a pig. Doesn't say much for your reading, you know, sir!" And he laughed again—lightly, even foolishly. But that laughter jarred, for the clergyman understood now that the sleep of the elder twin was either feigned—or *unnatural*.

And while the easy words fell so lightly from his lips, the monstrous engines worked and pulsed against him and against his sleeping brother, all their huge energy concentrated down into points fine as Suggestion, delicate as Thought. The Invasion affected everything. The very objects in the room altered incredibly, revealing suddenly behind their normal exteriors horrid little hearts of darkness. It was truly amazing, this vile metamorphosis. Books, chairs, pictures, all yielded up their pleasant aspect, and betrayed, as with silent mocking laughter, their inner soul of blackness—their *decay*. This is how Curtice tries to body forth in words what he actually witnessed... And Ernest, yawning, talking lightly, half foolishly-still noticed nothing!

For all this, as described, came about in something like ten seconds; and with it swept into the clergyman's mind, like a blow, the memory of that sinister phrase used more than once by Edward: "If father doesn't come, he will certainly—send." And Curtice understood that he had done both—both sent and come himself... That violent mind, released from its spell of madness in the body, yet still retaining the old implacable hatred, was now directing the terrible, unseen assault. This silent room, so hushed and still, was charged to the brim. The horror of it, as he said later, "seemed to peel the very skin from my back."...And, while Ernest noticed nothing, Edward slept!... The soul of the clergyman, strong with the desire to help or save, yet realizing that he was alone against a Legion, poured out in wordless prayer to his Deity. The clock just then, whirring before it struck, made itself audible.

"By Jove! It's all right, you see!" exclaimed Ernest, his voice oddly fainter and lower than before. "There's midnight—and nothing's happened. Bally nonsense, all of it!" His voice had dwindled curiously in volume. "I'll get the whisky and soda from the hall." His relief was great and his manner showed it. But in him somewhere was a singular change. His voice, manner, gestures, his very tread as he moved over the thick carpet towards the door, all showed it. He seemed less *real*, less alive, reduced somehow to littleness, the voice without timbre or quality, the appearance of him diminished in some fashion quite ghastly. His presence, if not actually shrivelled, was at least impaired. Ernest had suffered a singular and horrible *decrease...*

The clock was still whirring before the strike. One heard the chain running up softly. Then the hammer fell upon the first stroke of midnight.

"I'm off," he laughed faintly from the door; "it's all been pure funk— on my part, at least...!" He passed out of sight into the hall. *The Power that throbbed* so *mightily about the room followed him out.* Almost at the same moment Edward woke up. But he woke with a tearing and indescribable cry of pain and anguish on his lips: "Oh, oh, oh! But it hurts! It hurts! I can't hold you; leave me. It's breaking me asunder—"

The clergyman had sprung to his feet, but in the same instant everything had become normal once more—the room as it was before, the horror gone. There was nothing he could do or say, for there was no longer anything to put right, to defend, or to attack. Edward was speaking; his voice, deep and full as it never had been before: "By Jove, how that sleep has refreshed me! I feel twice the chap I was before—twice the chap. I feel quite splendid. Your voice, sir, must have hypnotized me to sleep..." He crossed the room with great vigour. "Where's—er— where's—Ernie, by the bye?" he asked casually, hesitating—almost searching—for the name. And a shadow as of a vanished memory crossed his face and was gone. The tone conveyed the most complete indifference where once the least word or movement of his twin had wakened solicitude, love. "Gone away, I suppose—gone to bed, I mean, of course."

Curtice has never been able to describe the dreadful conviction that overwhelmed him as he stood there staring, his heart in his mouth—the conviction, the positive certainty, that Edward had changed interiorly, had suffered an incredible accession to his existing personality. But he *knew* it as he watched. His mind, spirit, soul had most wonderfully increased. Something that hitherto the lad had known from the outside only, or by the magic of loving sympathy, had now passed, to be incorporated with his own being. And, being himself, it required no expression. Yet this visible increase was somehow terrible. Curtice shrank back from him. The instinct—he has never grasped the profound psychology of *that,* nor why it turned his soul dizzy with a kind of nausea—the instinct to strike him where he stood, passed, and a plaintive sound from the hall, stealing softly into the room between them, sent all that was left to him of self-possession into his feet. He turned and ran. Edward followed him—very leisurely.

They found Ernest, or what had been Ernest, crouching behind the table in the hall, weeping foolishly to himself. On his face lay blackness. The mouth was open, the jaw dropped; he dribbled hopelessly; and from the face had passed all signs of intelligence—of spirit.

For a few weeks he lingered on, regaining no sign of spiritual or mental life before the poor body, hopelessly disorganized, released what was left of him, from pure inertia—from complete and utter loss of vitality.

And the horrible thing—so the distressed family thought, at least—was that all those weeks Edward showed an indifference that was singularly brutal and complete. He rarely even went to visit him. I believe, too, it is true that he only once spoke of him by name; and that was when he said—

"Ernie? Oh, but Ernie is much better and happier where he is—!"

THE MAN
FROM THE 'GODS'

THAT there was something wrong with all his work Le Maistre well knew. Words and music, as the critics never failed to remind him, "just missed" that nameless "something" which would have made them good—perhaps great. Moreover, he was sane enough to realize that the blame lay not with an uncomprehending public, but simply with himself. The spark of inspiration that was beyond question in all his work never gathered to the flame stage. Thus his productions warmed people, but did not light them. He understood well enough what was lacking— and that no amount of mere painstaking "work" could put it right.

But on one occasion Le Maistre achieved a singular and startling success. As a sober record of fact, concealed by initials, it was reported in the Proceedings of the French Psychological Society for that year; and people who believed in the Subliminal Self, the Higher Ego, and all that consoling teaching about an attainable God within, made great havoc with the facts.

The way it came about, moreover, probably has a profound psychical significance. In any case, the result remains as the very best kind of tangible proof; for it was the only great thing he ever really achieved—this Fairy Play (so called); and its beauty was absolutely arresting.

He was something over fifty when he wrote it in its original form. The central idea came to him with the quick flash of a genuine inspiration; so did most of the music; but, in the working out of both, the fire had become smothered. The spark had never .gathered into flame. The result was mediocrity. Yet, like so many artists, he confused what was in his mind and imagination with what he had actually set down upon paper; for, when he went over the score to himself, he heard the original beauty in his thoughts and believed he had transferred into his work his own memory of that beauty. The music and words themselves, however, had *not* caught it. Thus, those who heard the preliminary recital in his rooms were more or less bored according to their powers of divination.

"It's fine; it's original," they remarked, shaking their heads as they went home after the performance; "but just misses it!"

The transformation that changed the common lead into gold as by some mysterious process of spiritual alchemy came about as follows:—

The little play was finished, and Le Maistre, having his eye upon a certain manager, went to that particular theatre one night in order to study the "feel" of it—to catch the flavour of the house, the size of the stage, and any other details he could. The management had given him a dress circle box, and he saw admirably. It was characteristic of the man, rather, that he put himself to this far-fetched kind of trouble. During the performance his mind was keenly at work. Yet he saw nothing of what was going on before his eyes; he had come with a definite purpose; he saw his own play all the time, heard his own music; watched his own creatures come on and go off among his own scenery.

At the same time the music, light and colour provided a stimulus that acted upon his own imagination, and set all the finer machinery of his own creative genius working. Sub-consciously he revised his own work, with the illuminating result that a white light shone through his mind and showed up all the flaws, all the places where he had "missed it"; all the passages where he had trailed off into banality. And a tremendous desire went crashing through his being to revise his work in the light of this knowledge. "I felt," he said, "as though a great prayer had gone out of me—a cry, as it were, to my higher self to come to my assistance. Never in my life have I wished anything so intensely before."

Then, in that curious fashion with which many artists must be familiar, it all faded again, and the reaction set in. The effort had no doubt exhausted him. He turned his attention to the actual performances on the stage before him, and lost the power to visualize his own piece. But the play—trivial, vulgar and untrue to life—wearied him; and he withdrew into the back of the box, and incontinently—fell asleep upon the little plush sofa!

When a considerable time later he woke up, the entire theatre was dark and empty; the piece was over; the audience had gone home to a man; and the building was deserted.

Le Maistre at once realized what had happened, though he could not understand why the final applause had not waked him, and hurried into his overcoat. A faint glimmer pervaded the vast auditorium, for as he leaned over the edge he could just make out the rows of empty stalls, the scattered white patches where the discarded programmes lay, the music-stands of the orchestra, and the exit doors of glass where the pit began. The air still smelt unpleasantly of a crowd—wraps, furs, stale scent and cigarettes.

Then he struck a match and saw by his watch that it was two o'clock in the morning. He had slept three hours!

He pushed open the door and passed out into the passage, his one idea being how he could get out into the street, or how he would spend the time if he did not get out. He felt hungry, stiff and a trifle chilly. Feeling his way along by the backs of the upper circle seats, he advanced slowly and carefully, his footsteps making no sound upon the soft carpet, and so came at last to the first exit door. It was locked and barred. He tried the next door with the same result. There was no other exit—nothing but that narrow semi-circular gangway between the wall and the seats, a box at either end, and pillars at intervals to mark the distance. "Like the exercise-walk in a prison-yard," he thought to himself, laughing. No single light was left burning anywhere in the building. Even the hall was in darkness. He saw the gilt-framed pictures of actors and actresses on the walls; a faint rumble from the streets reached him too—voices, traffic, footsteps, wind. Then he turned back into the theatre and carefully made his way down the aisle to the front, feeling the steps first with his toe, and peered over into the body of the house. A sea of shadows swam to and fro below him. Here and there certain stalls picked themselves out of the general gloom almost as though they were occupied; he could easily imagine he saw figures still sitting in them...

And it was here, just at this point, he said, that he began for the first time to feel a little uneasy. A slight tremor of the nerves passed over him, and sitting down in one of the front-row seats he considered the situation carefully and deliberately. There was not much to consider. He was shut in for the rest of the night; the dress circle seemed to be the limits of his prison; he could get neither up nor down; there was no escape till the morning. The prospect was not pleasant; still, it was not very terrible, and his sense of humour would easily have carried him through with credit, but for one thing—this curiously disturbing sense of something he could not quite define: of something that was *going to happen*, it seemed...

It was too vague, too remote for him to deal with squarely. His mind, always keenly imaginative and pictorial, preferred to see it in the terms of a picture. He thought of the Thames as he had sometimes seen it from the Chelsea Embankment in the dusk when dark barges, too far for their outline to be defined, come looming up through the mist. In this way thoughts lie in the depths of the mind; in this way they rise gradually before the consciousness; in this way the cause of his present discomfort would presently reach the point where he would recognize it and understand. In similar fashion, he felt this "something" that moved at the back of his mind, coming slowly forward.

A sudden idea came to him—

"If I could climb down to the auditorium floor I might find a door open somewhere, or escape by way of the orchestra, perhaps!"

And the idea of action was pleasant; though how he climbed over the edge of the box in the dark and swarmed down the slippery pillar, landing with a crash upon the rim of the stage box below, he never quite understood. With a plunge he dropped backwards into the dark space, kicking over as he did so a couple of chairs, which fell with a loud clatter and woke resounding echoes all through the empty building. That clatter seemed prodigious. He held his breath for several seconds to listen, standing motionless against the wall with the distinct idea that all this noise would attract attention to himself, and that if, after all, there was any one watching him—that if among those shadows someone—

"Ah!" he exclaimed quickly. "Now I've got it! There *is* someone watching me in another part of the building. That's why I felt uneasy—"

That tumble into the box had shaken the thought up to the surface of his mind. The picture had emerged from the mist, and he recognized the cause of his uneasiness. All this time, though none of his senses had yet proved it to him, the mind of another person, perhaps the eyes too, had been focused upon him. He was not alone.

Le Maistre felt no alarm, he said, but rather a definite thrill of exhilaration, as though the idea of this other person came to him with a sense of pleasurable excitement. His first instinct to sit concealed in the corner of the box and await events he dismissed almost at once in favour of some kind of prompt action. Stumbling in the gloom, he made his way down to the orchestra, and while groping cautiously among the crowded easels, his hand touched a tiny knob, and a dozen lights that bent over the music folios, like little heads screened under black bonnets, sprang into brilliance. The first thing he noticed was that the fire curtain was down, closing the cavernous mouth of the stage.

The shaded lights, however, were so carefully arranged that they fell only upon the music, and the main body of the theatre still yawned in comparative darkness behind him. Vast and unfriendly it seemed; charged to the brim with faint shufflings and whispers as though an audience sat there stealthily turning over programmes. The stalls faced him like fixed but living beings; the balconies frowned down upon him; the boxes—especially the upper ones—had an air of concealing people behind their curtains. Far overhead, glimmered a huge skylight; he heard the wind sighing across it like wind in the rigging of a ship. And, more than once, he fancied he caught the faint tread of footsteps moving about among the stalls and gangways.

Regretting that he had turned the lights up (they made himself so conspicuous, so easily visible!), he made an instinctive movement to turn them out again; but he touched the wrong knob, so that a row of lights flashed out up under the roof. In that top-most gallery of all, known as "the gods," a little line of starry lights leaped into being, and the first thing he noticed as he looked up was the figure of a man leaning over the edge of the railing—watching him.

The same moment he saw that this figure was making a movement of some kind—a gesture. It beckoned to him. So his feeling that someone was in the theatre with him was justified. There had been a man in the gods all the time.

Le Maistre admitted frankly that, in his first surprise, he collapsed backwards upon the stool usually occupied by the second 'cello. But his alarm passed with a strange swiftness, and gave place almost immediately to a peculiar and deep-seated thrill. The instant he perceived this dim figure of a man up there under the roof his heart leaped with an emotion that was partly delight, partly pleasurable anticipation, and partly—most curious of all—*awe*. And in a voice that was unlike his own, and that carried across the intervening space, for all its faintness, with perfect ease, he heard the words driven out of him as if by command of some deeper instinct than he understood—yet the very last words that he could have imagined as appropriate—

"You're up there in the gods!" he called out. "Won't you come down to me here?"

And then the figure withdrew, and he heard the sound of the footsteps descending the winding passages and stairs behind, as their owner obeyed him and came.

Alarmed, yet curiously exultant, Le Maistre stood up among the music-easels to await his coming. He was extraordinarily alert, prepared. He fumbled again with the little switch-board under the conductor's desk, for he wished to see the man face to face in full light—not to be gradually approached in darkness. But the only thing that came of the button he pressed was a creaking noise behind him, and when he turned quickly to examine, lo and behold, he saw the huge fire-curtain rising slowly and majestically into the air. And, as it rose, revealing the stage beyond, he got the distinct impression that this very stage, now empty, had a moment before been crowded with a throng of living people, and that even now they were there concealed among the wings within a few feet of where he stood, waiting the summons to appear.

Moreover, this discovery, far from causing him the kind of amazement that might have been expected, only communicated, for the second time within the space of a few minutes, another thrill of delight. Again this lightning sense of exhilaration swept him from head to foot.

The footsteps, meanwhile, came nearer; sometimes disappearing behind a thickness of walls that rendered them inaudible, and at other times starting suddenly into greater clearness as they came down from floor to floor. Le Maistre, unable to endure the suspense any longer, felt

impelled to go forward and meet them half-way. An intense desire to see
this stranger face to face came upon him. He climbed awkwardly over
the orchestra railing and made his way past the first rows of the stalls.
Already the steps sounded upon the same floor as himself. Hardly a
dozen yards, to judge by the fall of these oddly cushioned footsteps, could
now separate them. He moved more slowly, and the stranger moved
more slowly too—entering at last the gangway in which he stood.

"And it is from this point," to use the words of the report he afterwards
wrote for the society, "that my memory begins to fade somewhat, or
rather, that the sense of bewilderment grew so astonishingly disturbing
that I find it difficult to look back and recall with accuracy the true
sequence of what followed. My normal measurement of the passage of
time changed too, I think; all went so swiftly, almost as in a dream,
though at the time it did not appear to me to be short or hurried. But—
describe the sense of glory, wonder and happiness that enveloped me as
in a cloud, I simply cannot. As well might a hashish-eater attempt during the dulness of next morning to reconstruct the phantasmal wonder
of all he experienced the night before. Only, this was no phantasy; it was
real and actual, and more palpitatingly vivid than any other experience
of my life.

"I stood waiting in the gangway while this other person—the
stranger—came towards me along the narrow space between the wall
and the main body of seats. The footsteps were unhurried and regular. It
was very dark; all I could see were two faint patches of light where the
exit doors of the pit glimmered beyond. First one patch of light, then the
other, was temporarily obscured as he passed in front of these doors.
Down he moved steadily towards me through the gloom, and at the barrier of velvet rope that separated the stalls from the pit, he stopped—just
near enough for me to distinguish the head and shoulders of a man
about my own height and about my own size. He stood facing me there,
some ten or twelve feet away.

"For a few seconds there was complete silence—like the silence in a
mine, I remember thinking—and I instinctively clenched my fists,
almost expecting something violent to happen. But the next instant the
man spoke; and the moment I heard his voice all traces of fear left me,
and I felt nothing but this peculiarly delightful sense of exhilaration I
have already mentioned. It ran through me like the flush of a generous
wine, rousing all my faculties, critical and imaginative, to their highest
possible power, yet at the same time so bewildering me for the moment
that I scarcely realized what I was saying, doing, or thinking. From this
point I went through the whole scene without hesitation or dismay—
certainly without a thought of disobeying. I mean, it was a pleasure to

me to help it all forward, rather than to seek to prevent.

"'Here I am,' said the man in a voice wholly wonderful. 'You called me down, and I have come!'

"'You have come from up there—from the gods,' I heard myself reply.

"'I have come from up there—from the gods,' he answered; and his sentence seemed to mean so much more than mine did, although we used identical words.

"I held on to the back of the stall nearest to me. I could think for the moment of nothing further to say. The idea of what was coming thrilled me inexpressibly, though I could only hazard wild guesses as to its character.

"'Are you ready then?' he asked.

"'Ready! Ready for what?'

"'For the rehearsal,' he said, 'the secret rehearsal.'

"'The secret rehearsal—?' I stammered, pretending, as a child pretends in order to heighten its joy, that I did not understand.

"'—of your play, you know; your fairy play,' he finished the sentence.

"Then he moved towards me a few steps, and, hardly knowing why, I retreated. It was still impossible to see his face. The curious idea came to me that there was something odd about the man that prevented, and that would always prevent, me getting closer to him, and that perhaps I should never see his face completely at all. I cannot point to anything definite that caused this impression; I can merely report that it was so.

"'Look!' he went on, 'every one is ready and waiting. The moment the music starts we can begin. You will find a violin down there; the rehearsal can go on at once.'

"And although it struck me at the time as most curious he should be aware of the fact, it seemed quite natural, because I do play the violin, and in fact compose all my melodies first on that instrument before I put a pen to paper. At the same time I can remember faintly protesting—

"'I?' I remember asking; 'I'm to play?'

"'Certainly,' replied this soft-spoken figure among the shadows. 'You're to play. Who else, pray? And see! Every one is ready and waiting.'

"I was far too happily bewildered to object further; there seemed, indeed, no time for reflection at all; I felt impelled, driven forward as it were, to go through with the adventure and to ask no questions. Besides, I wanted to go through with it. I felt the old power of the first inspiration upon me—only heightened; I felt in me the supreme and splendid confidence that I could do it all better than I had ever dreamed—do it perfectly as it should he done. I was borne forwards upon a wave of inspiration that nothing in the whole world could interfere with.

"And, as I turned to obey, I saw for the first time that the stage was brilliantly lighted; that the scenery was the scenery already chosen by my mind; that the performers thronged the wings, and the opening characters were actually standing in their places waiting for the signal of the music to begin. The performers, moreover, I perceived, were identical in figure, feature and bearing with those ideal performers who had already enacted the play upon the inner stage of my imagination. It was all, in fact, precisely as the original inspiration had come to me weeks ago before the fires of beauty had faded during the wearisome toil of working it all out in limited terms upon the paper.

"The power that drove me forward, and at the same time filled me with this splendour of untrammelled creation, refused me, however, the least moment for consideration. I could only make my way into the orchestra and pick up the first violin-case that came to hand, belonging, doubtless, to some member of the band I had listened to earlier in the evening; and all eyes were fixed upon me from the stage as I clambered into the conductor's seat and drew the bow across the strings to tune the instrument. At the first sound I realized that my fingers, accustomed to the harsh tones of my own cheaper fiddle, were now feeling their way over the exquisite nervous system of a genuine Guarnierius that responded instantly to the lightest touch; and that the bow in my right hand was so perfectly balanced that even the best Tourte ever made could only seem like a strip of raw, unfinished wood by comparison. For the bow 'swam' over the strings, the sound streamed, smooth as honey, past my ears, and my fingers found the new intervals as easily as if they had never known any other key-board. Harmonics, double-stopping and arpeggios issued from my efforts as perfectly as trills from the throat of a bird.

"In that moment I *lived;* I understood much; I heard my soul singing within me... I finished tuning, and tapped sharply on the back of the violin to indicate that I was ready, and in the slight pause that ensued before I actually played the opening bars, I became aware that the stalls behind me, the boxes, the dress circle, and the whole house in fact right up to the 'gods,' were crowded with eager listeners; and, further, that the stranger—that man among the shadows in the background— standing ever beyond the reach of the light, still remained in some mysterious and potent fashion intimately in touch with my inner self, directing, helping, inspiring the performance from beginning to end.

"And, in front of me, upon the conductor's desk, lay the score of my own music in clearest manuscript, no longer crossed out and corrected as it lay in my rooms after all the first passion of beauty had been ground out of it, but lovely and perfect as the original inspiration had rushed flame-like into my soul months before.

"The whole performance from that moment—'rehearsal' seems no adequate word to describe it—went with the smoothness of a dream from beginning to end. Just as the music was my own music made perfect, so the words and songs were the mature expression of the original conception before my blundering efforts had confined them, stammering and incomplete, in broken form. Moreover—more wonderful still—I noticed the very places in my score where I had floundered, and where, in the laborious process of composition, the first inspiration had failed me and I had filled in with what was mediocre and banal. It was as if a master pointed out to me with the simplicity of true power the passages where the commonplace might pass—could—*did* pass—by deft, inspired touches into what was fine, moving, noble... The lesson was a sublime one; at the time, however, it all seemed so ridiculously simple and easy that I felt I could never again write anything that was not great and splendid.

"Moreover, the acting, speaking and dancing provided the perfect medium for my ideas; and the whole performance was the consummate representation of my first conception; even the scenery shifted swiftly and noiselessly, and the intervals between the acts were hardly noticeable...

"And the end came with a curious abruptness, bringing me to myself—my limited, stammering, caged little self, as, it seemed, after these moments of intoxicating expression—with a sharp sense of pain that all was over; and I became aware that, without hurry, without noise, the entire audience that filled the huge building had risen to their feet like one man, and that thousands of hands were clapping *silently* the measure of their intense appreciation. From floor to ceiling, and from wall to wall, flew a great wave of emotion that swept their praise into me, gathered and focused into a single mighty draught of applause. It was, I remember thinking, all their thoughts of joy, their feelings of gratitude, beating in upon my soul in that form of praise which is the artist's only adequate reward; and it reminded me of nothing so much as the whirring of innumerable soft wings all rising through the air at the same moment. Pictorially, in this fashion, it came before my mind.

"Violin in hand, I rose too, and turned to face the auditorium, for I realized that they were calling for the author—for him who had ministered so adequately to their pleasure-and that I must be prepared to say something in reply. I had, indeed, made my first bow, and was already casting about in my mind for suitable words, when, for the first time during the whole adventure—something in me *hesitated*. Either it was that the sea of glimmering faces frightened me, or that I was obeying instinctively some faint warning that it was not myself, but some other, who was the true author of the play, and that it was for him these thousands before me clamoured and called.

"But when, still hesitating in confusion, I turned again towards the stage, I saw that the great fire curtain had meanwhile descended and that a footstep, regular and unhurried, was at that very moment coming forward towards the footlights. I heard the tread. I knew at once who it was. The stranger from the shadows behind me who had directed the entire performance was now moving to the front. It was he for whom the audience clamoured; it was he who was the true author of the play!

"And instantly I clamoured with them, forgetting my own small pain in a kind of delightful exultation that I, too, owed this man everything, and that I should at last see him face to face and join my thanks and gratitude to theirs.

"Almost that same instant he appeared and stood before the centre of the curtains, the glare of the footlights casting upwards into his face. And he looked, not at the great throng behind and beyond me, but down into *my own* face, into *my own* eyes, smiling, approving, his expression radiant with a glory I have never seen before or since upon any human countenance.

"And the stranger, I then realized—was *myself!*

"What happened next is so difficult to describe—though I scarcely know why it should be so—that I cannot hope to convey the reality of it properly, or paint the instantaneous manner in which he vanished and was gone. He neither faded nor moved. But in a second that seemed to have no perceptible duration he was beside me—with me—*in* me; and this swift way he became suddenly merged into myself has always seemed to me the most amazing thing I have ever witnessed. The wave of delight and exultation swept into me anew. I felt for one brief moment that I was as a god—with a god's power of perfect expression.

"But for one second only; for, at once, a new sound, terrible and overwhelming, rose in a flood and tore me away from all that I had ever known. And the sound was ugly and distressing…and darkness followed it…

"It was real clapping this time, the clapping of human hands…and an indifferent orchestra was playing a noisy march just below me with a great blare of brass out of tune. The lights were up all over the theatre; the audience, busy with wraps and overcoats and applause, were hurrying out. I saw the actors and actresses of the play bowing and scraping before the curtain; and the sight of the perspiration trickling down over the grease-paint of the leading man directly beneath my box struck me like a blow in the face. Then came the frantic whistling for broughams and taxicabs and the hoarse shouting from the street where men cried the evening papers in the roar of the outer world. I picked up my opera-hat, which had rolled into the middle of the floor while I had slept upon the sofa, scrambled into my overcoat, rushed out into the street, and told the driver of the first taxicab I found to drive for his life at double rates...

"And all that night, before the memory of the wonder and the glory faded, I worked upon my score of words and music, striving to get down on the paper something at least of what had been shown to me. How much, or how little I succeeded it is now impossible to say. As I have already explained in this report, the memory faded with distressing swiftness. But I did my best. I hope—I believe—I am told, at least—that there is something in the work that people like..."

THE MAN WHO PLAYED UPON THE LEAF

W HERE the Jura pine-woods push the fringe of their purple cloak down the slopes till the vineyards stop them lest they should troop into the lake of Neuchâtel, you may find the village where lived the Man Who Played upon the Leaf.

My first sight of him was genuinely prophetic—that spring evening in the garden *café* of the little mountain auberge. But before I saw him I heard him, and ever afterwards the sound and the sight have remained inseparable in my mind.

Jean Grospierre and Louis Favre were giving me confused instructions—the *vin rouge* of Neuchâtel is heady, you know—as to the best route up the Tête-de-Rang, when a thin, wailing music, that at first I took to be rising wind, made itself heard suddenly among the apple trees at the end of the garden, and riveted my attention with a thrill of I know not what.

Favre's description of the bridle path over Mont Racine died away; then Grospierre's eyes wandered as he, too, stopped to listen; and at the same moment a mongrel dog of indescribably forlorn appearance came whining about our table under the walnut tree.

"It's Perret 'Comment-va,' the man who plays on the leaf," said Favre.

"And his cursed dog," added Grospierre, with a shrug of disgust. And, after a pause, they fell again to quarrelling about my complicated path up the Tête-de-Rang.

I turned from them in the direction of the sound.

The dusk was falling. Through the trees I saw the vineyards sloping down a mile or two to the dark blue lake with its distant-shadowed shore and the white line of misty Alps in the sky beyond. Behind us the forests rose in folded purple ridges to the heights of Boudry and La Tourne, soft and thick like carpets of cloud. There was no one about in the cabaret. I heard a horse's hoofs in the village street, a rattle of pans from the kitchen, and the soft roar of a train climbing the mountain railway through gathering darkness towards France—and, singing through it all, like a thread of silver through a dream, this sweet and windy music.

But at first there was nothing to be seen. The Man Who Played on the Leaf was not visible, though I stared hard at the place whence the sound apparently proceeded. The effect, for a moment, was almost ghostly.

Then, down there among the shadows of fruit trees and small pines, something moved, and I became aware with a start that the little *sapin* I had been looking at all the time was really not a tree, but a man—hatless, with dark face, loose hair, and wearing a *pélerine* over his shoulders. How he had produced this singularly vivid impression and taken upon himself the outline and image of a tree is utterly beyond me to describe. It was, doubtless, some swift suggestion in my own imagination that deceived me... Yet he was thin, small, straight, and his flying hair and spreading *pélerine* somehow pictured themselves in the network of dusk and background into the semblance, I suppose, of branches.

I merely record my impression with the truest available words—also my instant persuasion that this first view of the man was, after all, significant and prophetic: his dominant characteristics presented themselves to me symbolically. I saw the man first as a tree; I heard his music first as wind.

Then, as he came slowly towards us, it was clear that he produced the sound by blowing upon a leaf held to his lips between tightly closed hands. And at his heel followed the mongrel dog.

"The inseparables!" sneered Grospierre, who did not appreciate the interruption. He glanced contemptuously at the man and the dog, his face and manner, it seemed to me, conveying a merest trace, however, of superstitious fear. "The tune your father taught you, *hein?*" he added, with a cruel allusion I did not at the moment understand.

"Hush!" Favre said; "he plays thunderingly well all the same!" His glass had not been emptied quite so often, and in his eyes as he listened there was a touch of something that was between respect and wonder.

"The music of the devil," Grospierre muttered as he turned with the gesture of surly impatience to the wine and the rye bread. "It makes me dream at night. Ooua!"

The man, paying no attention to the gibes, came closer, continuing his leaf-music, and as I watched and listened the thrill that had first stirred in me grew curiously. To look at, he was perhaps forty, perhaps fifty; worn, thin, broken; and something seizingly pathetic in his appearance told its little wordless story into the air. The stamp of the outcast was mercilessly upon him. But the eyes were dark and fine. They proclaimed the possession of something that was neither worn nor broken, something that was proud to be outcast, and welcomed it.

"He's cracky, you know," explained Favre, "and half blind. He lives in that hut on the edge of the forest"—pointing with his thumb toward Côtendard—"and plays on the leaf for what he can earn."

We listened for five minutes perhaps while this singular being stood there in the dusk and piped his weird tunes; and if imagination had influenced my first sight of him it certainly had nothing to do with what I now heard. For it was unmistakable; the man played, not mere tunes and melodies, but the clean, strong, elemental sounds of Nature—especially the crying voices of wind. It was the raw material, if you like, of what the masters have used here and there—Wagner, and so forth—but by him heard closely and wonderfully, and produced with marvellous accuracy. It was now the notes of birds or the tinkle and rustle of sounds heard in groves and copses, and now the murmur of those airs that lose their way on summer noons among the tree tops; and then, quite incredibly, just as the man came closer and the volume increased, it grew to the crying of bigger winds and the whispering rush of rain among tossed branches...

How he produced it passed my comprehension, but I think he somehow mingled his own voice with the actual notes of the vibrating edge of the leaf; perhaps, too, that the strange passion shaking behind it all in the depths of the bewildered spirit poured out and reached my mind by ways unknown and incalculable.

I must have momentarily lost myself in the soft magic of it, for I remember coming back with a start to notice that the man had stopped, and that his melancholy face was turned to me with a smile of comprehension and sympathy that passed again almost before I had time to recognize it, and certainly before I had time to reply. And this time I am ready to admit that it was my own imagination, singularly stirred, that translated his smile into the words that no one else heard—

"I was playing for you—because you understand."

Favre was standing up and I saw him give the man the half loaf of coarse bread that was on the table, offering also his own partly-emptied wine-glass. "I haven't the sou today," he was saying, "but if you're hungry, mon brave—" And the man, refusing the wine, took the bread with an air of dignity that precluded all suggestion of patronage or favour, and ought to have made Favre feel proud that he had offered it.

"And that for his son!" laughed the stupid Grospierre, tossing a cheeserind to the dog, "or for his forest god!"

The music was about me like a net that still held my words and thoughts in a delicate bondage—which is my only explanation for not silencing the coarse guide in the way he deserved; but a few minutes later, when the men had gone into the inn, I crossed to the end of the garden, and there, where the perfumes of orchard and forest deliciously mingled, I came upon the man sitting on the grass beneath an appletree. The dog, wagging its tail, was at his feet, as he fed it with the best and largest portions of the bread. For himself, it seemed, he kept nothing but the crust, and—what I could hardly believe, had I not actually witnessed it—the cur, though clearly hungry, had to be coaxed with smiles and kind words to eat what it realized in some dear dog-fashion was needed even more by its master. A pair of outcasts they looked indeed, sharing dry bread in the back garden of the village inn; but in the soft, discerning eyes of that mangy creature there was an expression that raised it, for me at least, far beyond the ranks of common curdom; and in the eyes of the man, half-witted and pariah as he undoubtedly was, a look that set him somewhere in a lonely place where he heard the still, small voices of the world and moved with the elemental tides of life that are never outcast and that include the farthest suns.

He took the franc I offered; and, closer, I perceived that his eyes, for all their moments of fugitive brilliance, were indeed half sightless, and that perhaps he saw only well enough to know men as trees walking. In the village some said he saw better than most, that he saw in the dark, possibly even into the peopled regions beyond this world, and there were reasons—uncanny reasons—to explain the belief. I only know, at any rate, that from this first moment of our meeting he never failed to recognize me at a considerable distance, and to be aware of my whereabouts even in the woods at night; and the best explanation I ever heard, though of course unscientific, was Louis Favre's whispered communication that "he sees with the whole surface of his skin!"

He took the franc with the same air of grandeur that he took the bread, as though he conferred a favour, yet was grateful. The beauty of that gesture has often come back to me since with a sense of wonder for the sweet nobility that I afterwards understood inspired it. At the time, however, he merely looked up at me with the remark, "C'est pour le Dieu—merci!"

He did not say "le bon Dieu," as every one else did.

And though I had meant to get into conversation with him, I found no words quickly enough, for he at once stood up and began to play again on his leaf; and while he played his thanks and gratitude, or the thanks and gratitude of his God, that shaggy mongrel dog stopped eating and sat up beside him to listen. Both fixed their eyes upon me as the sounds of wind and birds and forest poured softly and wonderfully about my ears...so that, when it was over and I went down the quiet street to my pension, I was aware that some tiny sense of bewilderment had crept into the profounder regions of my consciousness and faintly disturbed my normal conviction that I belonged to the common world of men as of old. Some aspect of the village, especially of the human occupants in it, had secretly changed for me.

Those pearly spaces of sky, where the bats flew over the red roofs, seemed more alive, more exquisite than before; the smells of the open stables where the cows stood munching, more fragrant than usual of sweet animal life that included myself delightfully, keenly; the last chatterings of the sparrows under the eaves of my own *pension* more intimate and personal...

Almost as if those strands of elemental music the man played on his leaf had for the moment made me free of the life of the earth, as distinct from the life of men...

I can only suggest this, and leave the rest to the care of the imaginative reader; for it is impossible to say along what inner byways of fancy I reached the conclusion that when the man spoke of "the God," and not "the *good* God," he intended to convey his sense of some great woodland personality—some Spirit of the Forests whom he knew and loved and worshipped, and whom, he was intuitively aware, I also knew and loved and worshipped.

During the next few weeks I came to learn more about this poor, half-witted man. In the village he was known as Perret "Comment-va," the Man Who Plays on the Leaf; but when the people wished to be more explicit they described him as the man "without parents and without God." The origin of "Comment-va" I never discovered, but the other titles were easily explained—he was illegitimate and outcast. The mother had been a wandering Italian girl and the father a loose-living *bûcheron,* who was, it seems, a standing disgrace to the community. I think the villagers were not conscious of their severity; the older generation of farmers and *vignerons* had pity, but the younger ones and those of his own age were certainly guilty, if not of deliberate cruelty, at least of a harsh neglect and the utter withholding of sympathy. It was like the thoughtless cruelty of children, due to small unwisdom, and to that absence of charity which is based on ignorance. They could not in the least understand this crazy, picturesque being who wandered day and night in the forests and spoke openly, though never quite intelligibly, of worshipping another God than their own anthropomorphic deity. People looked askance at him because he was queer; a few feared him; one or two I found later—all women—felt vaguely that there was something in him rather wonderful, they hardly knew what, that lifted him beyond the reach of village taunts and sneers. But from all he was remote, alien, solitary—an outcast and a pariah.

It so happened that I was very busy at the time, seeking the seclusion of the place for my work, and rarely going out until the day was failing; and so it was, I suppose, that my sight of the man was always associated with a gentle dusk, long shadows and slanting rays of sunlight. Every time I saw that thin, straight, yet broken figure, every time the music of the leaf reached me, there came too, the inexplicable thrill of secret wonder and delight that had first accompanied his presence, and with it the subtle new values. To this day I see that sad, dark face moving about the street, touched with melancholy, yet with the singular light of an inner glory that sometimes lit flames in the poor eyes. Perhaps—the fancy entered my thoughts sometimes when I passed him—those who are half out of their minds, as the saying goes, are at the same time half in another region whose penetrating loveliness has so bewildered and amazed them that they no longer can play their dull part in our commonplace world; and certainly for me this man's presence never failed to convey an awareness of some hidden and secret beauty that he knew apart from the ordinary haunts and pursuits of men.

Often I followed him up into the woods—in spite of the menacing growls of the dog, who invariably showed his teeth lest I should approach too close—with a great longing to know what he did there and how he spent his time wandering in the great forests, sometimes, I was assured, staying out entire nights or remaining away for days together. For in these Jura forests that cover the mountains from Neuchâtel to Yverdon, and stretch thickly up to the very frontiers of France, you may walk for days without finding a farm or meeting more than an occasional *bûcheron*. And at length, after weeks of failure, and by some process of sympathy he apparently communicated in turn to the dog, it came about that I was—*accepted*. I was allowed to follow at a distance, to listen and, if I could, to watch.

I make use of the conditional, because once in the forest this man had the power of concealing himself in the same way that certain animals and insects conceal themselves by choosing places instinctively where the colour of their surroundings merge into their outlines and obliterate them. So long as he moved all was well; but the moment he stopped and a chance dell or cluster of trees intervened I lost sight of him, and more than once passed within a foot of his presence without knowing it, though the dog was plainly there at his feet. And the instant I turned at the sound of the leaf, there he was, leaning against some dark tree-stem, part of a shadow perhaps, growing like a forest-thing out of the thick moss that hid his feet, or merging with extraordinary intimacy into the fronds of some drooping pine bough! Moreover, this concealment was never intentional, it seems, but instinctive. The life to which he belonged took him close to its heart, draping about the starved and wasted shoulders the cloak of kindly sympathy which the world of men denied him.

And, while I took my place some little way off upon a fallen stem, and the dog sat looking up into his face with its eyes of yearning and affection, Perret "Comment-va" would take a leaf from the nearest ivy, raise it between tightly pressed palms to his lips and begin that magic sound that seemed to rise out of the forest-voices themselves rather than to be a thing apart.

It was a late evening towards the end of May when I first secured this privilege at close quarters, and the memory of it lives in me still with the fragrance and wonder of some incredible dream. The forest just there was scented with wild lilies of the valley which carpeted the more open spaces with their white bells and big, green leaves; patches of violets and pale anemone twinkled down the mossy stairways of every glade; and through slim openings among the pine-stems I saw the shadowed blues of the lake beyond and the far line of the high Alps, soft and cloud-like in the sky. Already the woods were drawing the dusk out of the earth to cloak themselves for sleep, and in the east a rising moon stared close over the ground between the big trees, dropping trails of faint and yellowish silver along the moss. Distant cow-bells, and an occasional murmur of village voices, reached the ear. But a deep hush lay over all that mighty slope of mountain forest, and even the footsteps of ourselves and the dog had come to rest.

Then, as sounds heard in a dream, a breeze stirred the topmost branches of the pines, filtering down to us as from the wings of birds. It brought new odours of sky and sun-kissed branches with it. A moment later it lost itself in the darkening aisles of forest beyond; and out of the stillness that followed, I heard the strange music of the leaf rising about us with its extraordinary power of suggestion.

And, turning to see the face of the player more closely, I saw that it had marvellously changed, had become young, unlined, soft with joy. The spirit of the immense woods possessed him, and he was at peace...

While he played, too, he swayed a little to and fro, just as a slender *sapin* sways in wind, and a revelation came to me of that strange beauty of combined sound and movement—trees bending while they sing, branches trembling and a-whisper, children that laugh while they dance. And, oh, the crying, plaintive notes of that leaf, and the profound sense of elemental primitive sound that they woke in the penetralia of the imagination, subtly linking simplicity to grandeur! Terribly yet sweetly penetrating, how they searched the heart through, and troubled the very sources of life! Often and often since have I wondered what it was in that singular music that made me *know* the distant Alps listened in their sky-spaces, and that the purple slopes of Boudry and Mont Racine bore it along the spires of their woods as though giant harp-strings stretched to the far summits of Chasseral and the arid wastes of Tête de Rang.

In the music this outcast played upon the leaf there was something of a wild, mad beauty that plunged like a knife to the home of tears, and at the same time sang out beyond them—something coldly elemental, close to the naked heart of life. The truth, doubtless, was that his strains, making articulate the sounds of Nature, touched deep, primitive yearnings that for many are buried beyond recall. And between the airs, even between the bars, there fell deep weeping silences when the sounds merged themselves into the sigh of wind or the murmur of falling water, just as the strange player merged his body into the form and colour of the trees about him.

And when at last he ceased, I went close to him, hardly knowing what it was I wanted so much to ask or say. He straightened up at my approach. The melancholy dropped its veil upon his face instantly.

"But that was beautiful—unearthly!" I faltered. "You never have played like that in the village—"

And for a second his eyes lit up as he pointed to the dark spaces of forest behind us:

"In there," he said softly, "there is light!"

"You hear true music in these woods," I ventured, hoping to draw him out; "this music you play—this exquisite singing of winds and trees—?"

He looked at me with a puzzled expression and I knew, of course, that I had blundered with my banal words. Then, before I could explain or alter, there floated to us through the trees a sound of church bells from villages far away; and instantly, as he heard, his face grew dark, as though he understood in some vague fashion that it was a symbol of the faith of those parents who had wronged him, and of the people who continually made him suffer. Something of this, I feel sure, passed through his tortured mind, for he looked menacingly about him, and the dog, who caught the shadow of all his moods, began to growl angrily.

"My music," he said, with a sudden abruptness that was almost fierce, "is for my God."

"Your God of the Forests?" I said, with a real sympathy that I believe reached him.

"*Pour sûr! Pour sûr!* I play it all over the world"—he looked about him down the slopes of villages and vineyards—"and for those who understand—those who belong—to come."

He was, I felt sure, going to say more, perhaps to unbosom himself to me a little; and I might have learned something of the ritual this self-appointed priest of Pan followed in his forest temples—when, the sound of the bells swelled suddenly on the wind, and he turned with an angry gesture and made to go. Their insolence, penetrating even to the privacy of his secret woods, was too much for him.

"And you find many?" I asked.

Perret "Comment-va" shrugged his shoulders and smiled pityingly.

"Moi. Puis le chien—puis maintenant—*vous!*"

He was gone the same minute, as if the branches stretched out dark arms to draw him away among them,...and on my way back to the village, by the growing light of the moon, I heard far away in that deep world of a million trees the echoes of a weird, sweet music, as this unwitting votary of Pan piped and fluted to his mighty God upon an ivy leaf.

And the last thing I actually saw was the mongrel cur turning back from the edge of the forest to look at me for a moment of hesitation. He thought it was time now that I should join the little band of worshippers and follow them to the haunted spots of worship.

"Moi—puis le chien—puis maintenant—*vous!*"

From that moment of speech a kind of unexpressed intimacy between us came into being, and whenever we passed one another in the street he would give me a swift, happy look, and jerk his head significantly towards the forests. The feeling that, perhaps, in his curious lonely existence I counted for something important made me very careful with him. From time to time I gave him a few francs, and regularly twice a week when I knew he was away, I used to steal unobserved to his hut on the edge of the forest and put parcels of food inside the door—*salamé*, cheese, bread; and on one or two occasions when I had been extravagant with my own tea, pieces of plum-cake—what the Colombier baker called *plume-cak'!*

He never acknowledged these little gifts, and I sometimes wondered to what use he put them, for though the dog remained well favoured, so far as any cur can be so, he himself seemed to waste away more rapidly than ever. I found, too, that he did receive help from the village—official help—but that after the night when he was caught on the church steps with an oil can, kindling-wood and a box of matches, this help was reduced by half, and the threat made to discontinue it altogether. Yet I feel sure there was no inherent maliciousness in the Man who Played upon the Leaf, and that his hatred of an "alien" faith was akin to the mistaken zeal that in other days could send poor sinners to the stake for the ultimate safety of their souls.

Two things, moreover, helped to foster the tender belief I had in his innate goodness: first, that all the children of the village loved him and were unafraid, to the point of playing with him and pulling him about as though he were a big dog; and, secondly, that his devotion for the mongrel hound, his equal and fellow-worshipper, went to the length of genuine self-sacrifice. I could never forget how he fed it with the best of the bread, when his own face was pinched and drawn with hunger; and on other occasions I saw many similar proofs of his unselfish affection. His love for that mongrel, never uttered, in my presence at least, perhaps unrecognized as love even by himself, must surely have risen in some form of music or incense to sweeten the very halls of heaven.

In the woods I came across him anywhere and everywhere, sometimes so unexpectedly that it occurred to me he must have followed me stealthily for long distances. And once, in that very lonely stretch above the mountain railway, towards Montmollin, where the trees are spaced apart with an effect of cathedral aisles and Gothic arches, he caught me suddenly and did something that for a moment caused me a thrill of genuine alarm.

Wild lilies of the valley grow very thickly thereabouts,, and the ground falls into a natural hollow that shuts it off from the rest of the forest with a peculiar and delightful sense of privacy; and when I came across it for the first time I stopped with a sudden feeling of quite bewildering enchantment—with a kind of childish awe that caught my breath as though I had slipped through some fairy door or blundered out of the ordinary world into a place of holy ground where solemn and beautiful things were the order of the day.

I waited a moment and looked about me. It was utterly still. The haze of the day had given place to an evening clarity of atmosphere that gave the world an appearance of having just received its finishing touches of pristine beauty. The scent of the lilies was overpoweringly sweet. But the whole first impression—before I had time to argue it away—was that I stood before some mighty chancel steps on the eve of a secret festival of importance, and that all was prepared and decorated with a view to the coming ceremony. The hush was the most delicate and profound imaginable—almost forbidding. I was a rude disturber.

Then, without any sound of approaching footsteps, my hat was lifted from my head, and when I turned with a sudden start of alarm, there before me stood Perret "Comment-va," the Man Who Played upon the Leaf.

An extraordinary air of dignity hung about him. His face was stern, yet rapt; something in his eyes genuinely impressive; and his whole appearance produced the instant impression—it touched me with a fleeting sense of awe—that here I had come upon him in the very act—had surprised this poor, broken being in some dramatic moment when his soul sought to find its own peculiar region, and to transform itself into loveliness through some process of outward worship.

He handed the hat back to me without a word, and I understood that I had unwittingly blundered into the secret place of his strange cult, some shrine, as it were, haunted doubly by his faith and imagination, perhaps even into his very Holy of Holies. His own head, as usual, was bared. I could no more have covered myself again than I could have put my hat on in Communion service of my own church.

"But—this wonderful place—this peace, this silence!" I murmured, with the best manner of apology for the intrusion I could muster on the instant. "May I stay a little with you, perhaps—and see?"

And his face passed almost immediately, when he realized that I understood, into that soft and happy expression the woods invariably drew out upon it—the look of the soul, complete and healed.

"Hush!" he whispered, his face solemn with the mystery of the listening trees; *"Vous êtes un peu en retard—mais pourtant..."*

And lifting the leaf to his lips he played a soft and whirring music that had for its undercurrent the sounds of running water and singing wind mingled exquisitely together. It was half chant, half song, solemn enough for the dead, yet with a strain of soaring joy in it that made me think of children and a perfect faith. The music *blessed* me, and the leagues of forest, listening, poured about us all their healing forces.

I swear it would not have greatly surprised me to see the shaggy flanks of Pan himself disappearing behind the moss-grown boulders that lay about the hollows, or to have caught the flutter of white limbs as the nymphs stepped to the measure of his tune through the mosaic of slanting sunshine and shadow beyond.

Instead, I saw only that picturesque madman playing upon his ivy leaf, and at his feet the faithful dog staring up without blinking into his face, from time to time turning to make sure that I listened and understood.

But the desolate places drew him most, and no distance seemed too great either for himself or his dog.

In this part of the Jura there is scenery of a sombre and impressive grandeur that, in its way, is quite as majestic as the revelation of far bigger mountains. The general appearance of soft blue pine woods is deceptive. The Boudry cliffs, slashed here and there with inaccessible couloirs, are undeniably grand, and in the sweep of the Creux du Van precipices there is a splendid terror quite as solemn as that of the Matterhorn itself. The shadows of its smooth, circular walls deny the sun all day, and the winds, caught within the 700ft. sides of its huge amphitheatre, as in the hollow of some awful cup, boom and roar with the crying of lost thunders.

I often met him in these lonely fastnesses, wearing that half-bewildered, half-happy look of the wandering child; and one day in particular, when I risked my neck scrambling up the most easterly of the Boudry couloirs, I learned afterwards that he had spent the whole time—four hours and more—on the little Champ de Trémont at the bottom, watching me with his dog till I arrived in safety at the top. His fellow-worshippers were few, he explained, and worth keeping; though it was ever inexplicable to me how his poor damaged eyes performed the marvels of sight they did.

And another time, at night, when, I admit, no sane man should have been abroad, and I had lost my way coming home from a climb along the torn and precipitous ledges of La Tourne, I heard his leaf thinly piercing the storm, always in front of me yet never overtaken, a sure though invisible guide. The cliffs on that descent are sudden and treacherous. The torrent of the Areuse, swollen with the melting snows, thundered ominously far below; and the forests swung their vast wet cloaks about them with torrents of blinding rain and clouds of darkness—yet all fragrant with warm wind as a virgin world answering to its first spring tempest. There he was, the outcast with his leaf, playing to his God amid all these crashings and bellowings...

In the night, too, when skies were quiet and stars a-gleam, or in the still watches before the dawn, I would sometimes wake with the sound of clustered branches combing faint music from the gently-rising wind, and figure to myself that strange, lost creature wandering with his dog and leaf, his *pélerine*, his flying hair, his sweet, rapt expression of an inner glory, out there among the world of swaying trees he loved so well. And then my first soft view of the man would come back to me when I had seen him in the dust: as a tree; as though by some queer optical freak my outer and my inner vision had mingled so that I perceived both his broken body and his soul of magic.

For the mysterious singing of the leaf, heard in such moments from my window while the world slept, expressed absolutely the inmost cry of that lonely and singular spirit, damaged in the eyes of the village beyond repair, but in the sight of the wood-gods he so devoutly worshipped, made whole with their own peculiar loveliness and fashioned after the image of elemental things.

The spring wonder was melting into the peace of the long summer days when the end came. The vineyards had begun to dress themselves in green, and the forest in those soft blues when individual trees lose their outline in the general body of the mountain. The lake was indistinguishable from the sky; the Jura peaks and ridges gone a-soaring into misty distances; the white Alps withdrawn into inaccessible and remote solitudes of heaven. I was making reluctant preparations for leaving—dark London already in my thoughts—when the news came.

I forget who first put it into actual words. It had been about the village all the morning, and something of it was in every face as I went down the street. But the moment I came out and saw the dog on my doorstep, looking up at me with puzzled and beseeching eyes, I knew that something untoward had happened; and when he bit at my boots and caught my trousers in his teeth, pulling me in the direction of the forest, a sudden sense of poignant bereavement shot through my heart that I found it hard to explain, and that must seem incredible to those who have never known how potent may be the conviction of a sudden intuition.

I followed the forlorn creature whither it led, but before a hundred yards lay behind us I had learned the facts from half-a-dozen mouths. That morning, very early, before the countryside was awake, the first mountain train, swiftly descending the steep incline below Chambrelien, had caught Perret "Comment-va" just where the Mont Racine *sentier* crosses the line on the way to his best-beloved woods, and in one swift second had swept him into eternity. The spot was in the direct line he always took to that special woodland shrine—his Holy Place.

And the manner of his death was characteristic of what I had divined in the man from the beginning; for he had given up his life to save his dog—this mongrel and faithful creature that now tugged so piteously at my trousers. Details, too, were not lacking; the engine-driver had not failed to tell the story at the next station, and the news had travelled up the mountain-side in the way that all such news travels—swiftly. Moreover, the woman who lived at the hut beside the crossing, and lowered the wooden barriers at the approach of all trains, had witnessed the whole sad scene from the beginning.

And it is soon told. Neither she nor the engine-driver knew exactly how the dog got caught in the rails, but both saw that it *was* caught, and both saw plainly how the figure of the half-witted wanderer, hatless as usual and with cape flying, moved deliberately across the line to release it. It all happened in a moment. The man could only have saved himself by leaving the dog to its fate. The shrieking whistle had as little effect upon him as the powerful breaks had upon the engine in those few available moments. Yet, in the fraction of a second before the engine caught them, the dog somehow leapt free, and the soul of the Man Who Played upon the Leaf passed into the presence of his God—singing.

As soon as it realized that I followed willingly, the beastie left me and trotted on ahead, turning every few minutes to make sure that I was coming. But I guessed our destination without difficulty. We passed the Pontarlier railway first, then climbed for half-an-hour and crossed the mountain line about a mile above the scene of the disaster, and so eventually entered the region of the forest, still quivering with innumerable flowers, where in the shaded heart of trees we approached the spot of lilies that I knew—the place where a few weeks before the devout worshipper had lifted the hat from my head because the earth whereon I stood was holy ground. We stood in the pillared gateway of his Holy of Holies. The cool airs, perfumed beyond belief, stole out of the forest to meet us on the very threshold, for the trees here grew so thickly that only patches of the summer blaze found an entrance. And this time I did not wait on the outskirts, but followed my four-footed guide to a group of mossy boulders that stood in the very centre of the hollow.

And there, as the dog raised its eyes to mine, soft with the pain of its great unanswerable question, I saw in a cleft of the grey rock the ashes of many hundred fires; and, placed about them in careful array, an assortment of the sacrifices he had offered, doubtless in sharp personal deprivation, to his deity:—bits of mouldy bread, half-loaves, untouched portions of cheese, *salamé* with the skin uncut—most of it exactly as I had left it in his hut; and last of all, wrapped in the original white paper, the piece of Colombier *plume-cak',* and a row of ten silver francs round the edge...

I learned afterwards, too, that among the almost unrecognizable remains on the railway, untouched by the devouring terror of the iron, they had found a hand—tightly clasping in its dead fingers a crumpled ivy leaf...

My efforts to find a home for the dog delayed my departure, I remember, several days; but in the autumn when I returned it was only to hear that the creature had refused to stay with any one, and finally had escaped into the forest and deliberately starved itself to death. They found its skeleton, Louis Favre told me, in a rocky hollow on the lower slopes of Mont Racine in the direction of Montmollin. But Louis Favre did not know, as I knew, that this hollow had received other sacrifices as well, and was consecrated ground.

And somewhere, if you search well the Jura slopes between Champ du Moulin, where Jean-Jacques Rousseau had his temporary house, and Côtendard where he visited Lord Wemyss when "Milord Maréchal Keith" was Governor of the Principality of Neuchâtel under Frederic II, King of Prussia—if you look well these haunted slopes, somewhere between the vineyards and the gleaming limestone heights, you shall find the forest glade where lie the bleached bones of the mongrel dog, and the little village cemetery that holds the remains of the Man Who Played upon the Leaf to the honour of the Great God Pan.

THE PRICE OF
WIGGINS'S ORGY

I

IT happened to be a Saturday when Samuel Wiggins drew the first cash sum on account of his small legacy—some twenty pounds, ten in gold and ten in notes. It felt in his pocket like a bottled-up prolongation of life. Never before had he seen so many dreams within practical reach. It produced in him a kind of high and elusive exaltation of the spirit. From time to time he put his hand down to make the notes crackle and let his fingers play through the running sovereigns as children play through sand.

For twenty years he had been secretary to a philanthropist interested in feeding—feeding the poor. Soup kitchens had been the keynote of those twenty years, the distribution of victuals his sole objective. And now he had his reward—a legacy of £100 a year for the balance of his days.

To him it was riches. He wore a shortish frockcoat, a low, spreading collar, a black made-up tie, and boots with elastic sides. On this particular day he wore also a new pair of rather bright yellow leather gloves. He was unmarried, over forty, bald, plump in the body, and possessed of a simple and emotional heart almost childlike. His brown eyes shone in a face that was wrinkled and dusty—all his dreams driven inwards by the long years of uninspired toil for another.

For the first time in his life, released from the dingy purlieus of soup kitchens and the like, he wandered towards evening among the gay and lighted streets of the "West End"—Piccadilly Circus where the flaming lamps positively hurt the eyes, and Leicester Square. It was bewildering and delightful, this freedom. It went to his head. Yet he ought to have known better.

"I'm going to dine at a restaurant to-night, by Jove," he said to himself, thinking of the gloomy boarding-house where he usually sat between a missionary and a typewriter. He fingered his money. "I'm going to celebrate my legacy. I've earned it." The thought of a motor-car flashed absurdly through his mind; it was followed by another: a holiday in Spain, Italy, Hungary—one of those sunny countries where music was cheap, in the open air, and of the romantic kind he loved. These thoughts show the kind of exaltation that possessed him.

"It's nearly, though not quite, £2 a week," he repeated to himself for the fiftieth time, reflecting upon his legacy. "I simply can't believe it!"

After indecision that threatened to be endless, he turned at length through the swinging glass doors of a big and rather gorgeous restaurant. Only once before in his life had he dined at a big London restaurant—a Railway Hotel! Passing with some hesitation through the gaudy *café* where a number of foreigners sat drinking at little marble tables, he entered the main dining-room, long, lofty, and already thronged. Here the light and noise and movement dazed him considerably, and for the life of him he could not decide upon a table. The people all looked so prosperous and important; the waiters so like gentlemen in evening dress—the kind that came to the philanthropist's table. The roar of voices, eating, knives and forks, rose about him and filled him with a certain dismay. It was all rather overwhelming.

"I should have liked a smaller place better," he murmured, "but still—" And again he fingered his money to gain confidence.

The choice of a table *was* intimidating, for he was absurdly retiring, was Wiggins; more at home with papers and the reports of philanthropic societies; his holidays spent in a boarding-house at Worthing with his sister and her invalid husband. Then relief came in the form of a sub-head waiter who, spying his helplessness, inquired with a bland grandeur of manner if he "looked perhaps for someone?"

"Oh, a table, thanks, only a table—"

The man, washing his hands in mid-air, swept down the crowded aisles and found one without the least difficulty. It emerged from nowhere so easily that Wiggins felt he had been a fool not to discover it alone. He wondered if he ought to tip the man half-a-crown now or later, but, before he could decide, another occupied his place, bland and smiling, with black eyes and plush-like hair, bending low before him and holding out a large pink programme.

He examined it, feeling that he ought to order dishes with outlandish names just to show that he knew his way about. Before he could steady his eye upon a single line, however, a third waiter, very youthful, suggested in broken English that Wiggins should leave his hat, coat and umbrella elsewhere. This he did willingly, though without grace or dispatch, for the yellow gloves stuck ridiculously to his hands. Then he sat down and turned to the menu again.

It was a very ordinary restaurant really, in spite of the vast height of the gilded ceiling, the scale of its sham magnificence and the excessive glitter of its hundred lights. The menu, disguised by various expensive and *recherché* dishes (which when ordered were invariably found to be "off"), was even more ordinary than the hall. But to the dazed Wiggins the words looked like a series of death-sentences printed in different languages, but all meaning the same thing: *order me—or die!* That waiter standing over him was the executioner. Unless he speedily ordered something really worth the proprietor's while to provide, the head waiter would be summoned and he, Wiggins, would be beheaded. Those stars against certain cheap dishes meant that they could only be ordered by privileged persons, and those crosses—

"This is *vairy* nice this sevening, sir," said the waiter, suddenly bending and pointing with a dirty finger to a dish that Wiggins found buried in a list uncommonly like "Voluntary Subscriptions" in his reports. It was entitled "Lancashire Hot-Pot...2/o"—two shillings, not two pounds, as he first imagined! He leaped at it.

"Yes, thanks; that'll do, then—for to-night," he said, and the waiter ambled away indifferently, looking all round the room in search of sympathy.

By degrees, however, the other recovered his self-possession, and realized that to spend his legacy on mere Hot-Pot was to admit he knew not the values of life. He called the plush-headed waiter back and with a rush of words ordered some oysters, soup, a fried sole, and half a partridge to follow.

"Then ze 'Ot-Pot, sir?" queried the man, with respect.

"I'll see about that later."

For he was already wondering what he should drink, knowing nothing of wines and vintages. At luncheon with the philanthropist he sometimes had a glass of sherry; at Worthing with his sister he drank beer. But now he wanted something really good, something generous that would help him to celebrate. He would have ordered champagne as a conciliation to the waiter, now positively obsequious, but someone had told him once that there was not enough champagne in the world to go round, and that hotels and restaurants were supplied with "something rather bad." Burgundy, he felt, would be more the thing—rich, sunny, full-bodied.

He studied the wine-card till his head swam. A waiter, while he was thus engaged, sidled up and watched him from an angle. Wiggins, looking up distractedly at the same moment, caught his eye. Whew! It was the Head Waiter himself, a man of quite infinite presence, who at once bowed himself forward, and with a gentle but commanding manner drew his attention to the wines he could "especially recommend." Something in the man's face struck him momentarily as familiar—vaguely familiar—then passed.

Now Wiggins, as has been said, did not know one wine from another; but the spirit of his foolish pose fairly had him by the throat at last, and each time this condescending individual indicated a new vintage he shook his head knowingly and shrugged his shoulders with the air of a connoisseur. This pantomime continued for several minutes.

"Something *really* good, you know," he mumbled after a while, determined to justify himself in the eyes of this high official who was taking such pains. "A rare wine—er—with body in it." Then he added, with a sudden impulse of confidence, "It's Saturday night, remember!" And he smiled knowingly, making a gesture that a man of the world was meant to understand.

Why he should have said this remains a mystery. Perhaps it was a semi-apologetic reference to the supposed habit of men to indulge themselves on a Saturday because they need not rise early to work next day. Perhaps it was meant in some way to excuse all the trouble he was giving. In any case, there can be no question that the manner of the Head Waiter instantly changed in a subtle way difficult to describe, and from mere official politeness passed into deferential attention. He bowed slightly. He increased his distance by an inch or two. Wiggins, noticing it and slightly bewildered, repeated his remark, for want of something to say more than anything else. "It's Saturday night, of course," he repeated, murmuring, yet putting more meaning into the words than they could reasonably hold.

"As Monsieur says," the man replied, with a marked respect in his tone not there before; "and we—close early."

"Of course," said the other, gaining confidence pleasantly, "you close early."

He had quite forgotten the fact, even if he ever knew it, but he spoke with decision. Glancing up from the wine-list, he caught the man's eye; then instantly lowered his gaze, for the Head Waiter was staring at him in a fixed and curious manner that seemed unnecessary. And once again that passing touch of familiarity appeared upon the features and was gone.

"Monsieur is here for the first time, if I may ask?" came next.

"Er—yes, I am," he replied, thinking all this attention a trifle excessive.

"Ah, *pardon*, of course, I understand," the Head Waiter added softly. "A new—a recent member, then—?"

A little non-plussed, a little puzzled, Wiggins agreed with a nod of the head. He did not know that head waiters referred to customers as "members." For an instant it occurred to him that possibly he was being mistaken for somebody else. It was really—but at that moment the oysters arrived. The Head Waiter said something in rapid Italian to his subordinate-something that obviously increased that plush-headed person's desire to please—bent over with his best manner to murmur, "And I will get monsieur the wine he will like, the right kind of wine!"—and was gone.

It was a new and delightful sensation. Wiggins, feeling proud, pleased and important under the effect of this excellent service and attention, turned to his oysters. The wine would come presently. And, meanwhile, the music had begun...

II

He began to enjoy himself thoroughly, and the wine—still, fragrant, soft—soon ran in his veins and drove out the last vestige of his absurd shyness. Behind the palm trees, somewhere out of sight, the orchestra played soothingly, and if the selections were somewhat bizarre it made no difference to him. He drank in the sound just as he drank in the wine—eagerly. Both fed the consciousness that he was enjoying himself, and the Danse Macabre gave him as much pleasure as did the Bohème, the Strauss Waltz, or Donizetti. Everything—wine, music, food, people—served to intensify his interest *in himself.* He examined his face in the big mirrors and realized what a dog he was and what a good time he was having. He watched the other customers, finding them splendid and distinguished. The whole place was really fine—he would come again and again, always ordering the same wine, for it was certainly an unusual wine, as the Head Waiter had called it, "the right kind." The price of it he never asked, for in his pocket lay the price of a whole case. His hand slipped down to finger the sovereigns—hot and slippery now—and the notes, somewhat moist and crumpled... The needles of the big staring clock meanwhile swung onwards...

Thus, aided by the tactful and occasional superintendence of the Head Waiter from a distance, the evening passed along in a happy rush of pleasurable emotion. The half-partridge had vanished, and Wiggins toyed now with a wonderful-looking "sweet"—the most expensive he could find. He did not eat much of it, but liked to see it on his plate. The wine helped things enormously. He had ordered another half-bottle some time ago, delighted to find that it exhilarated without confusing him. And every one else in the place was enjoying himself in the same way. He was thrilled to discover this.

Only one thing jarred a little. A very big man, with a round, clean-shaven face inclined to fatness, stared at him more than he cared about from a table in the corner diagonally across the room. He had only come in half-an-hour ago. His face was somehow or other dog-like—something between a boarhound and a pup, Wiggins thought. Each time he looked up the fellow's large and rather fierce eyes were fixed upon him, then lingeringly withdrawn. It was unpleasant to be stared at in this way by an offensive physiognomy.

But most of the time he was too full of personal visions conjured up by the wine to trouble long about external matters. His head was simply brimming over with thoughts and ideas—about himself, about soup-kitchens, feeding the poor, the change of life effected by the legacy, and a thousand other details. Once or twice, however, in sharp, clear moments when the tide of alcohol ebbed a little, other questions assailed him: Why should the Head Waiter have become so obsequious and attentive? What was it in his face that seemed familiar? What was there about the remark "It's Saturday evening" to change his manner? And—what was it about the dinner, the restaurant and the music that seemed just a little out of the ordinary?

Or was he merely thinking nonsense? And was it his imagination that this man stared so oddly? The alcohol rushed deliciously in his veins.

The vague uneasiness, however, was a passing matter, for the orchestra was tearing madly through a Csardas, and his thoughts and feelings were swept away in the wild rhythm. He drank his bottle out and ordered another. Was it the second or the third? He could not remember. Counting always made his head ache. He did not care anyhow. "Let 'er go! I'm enjoying myself! I've got a fat legacy—money lying in the bank—money I haven't earned!" The carefulness of years was destroyed in as many minutes. "That music's simply spiffing!"

Then he glanced up and caught the clean-shaven face bearing down upon him across the shimmering room like the muzzle of a moving gun. He tried to meet it, but found he could not focus it properly. The same moment he saw that he was mistaken; the man was merely staring at him. Two faces swam and wobbled into one. This movement, and the appearance of coming towards him, were both illusions produced by the alcohol. He drank another glass quickly to steady his vision—and then another...

"I'll call for my bill. Itshtime to go...!" he murmured aloud later, with a very deep sigh. He looked about him for the waiter, who instantly appeared—with coffee and liqueurs, however.

"Dear me, yes. Qui' forgot I or'ered those," he observed offhand, smiling in the man's face, willing and anxious to say a lot of things, but not quite certain what.

"My bill," was what he said finally, "mush b'off!"

The waiter laughed pleasantly, but very politely, in reply. Wiggins repeated his remark about his bill.

"Oh, that will be all right, sir," returned the man, as though no such thing as payment was ever heard of in *this* restaurant. It was rather confusing. Wiggins laughed to himself, drank his liqueur and forgot about everything except the ballet music of Délibes the strings were sprinkling in a silver shower about the hall. His mind ran after them through the glittering air.

"Just fancy if I could catch 'em and take 'em home in a bunch," he said to himself, immensely pleased. He was enjoying himself hugely by now.

And then, suddenly, he became aware that the place was rapidly thinning, lights being lowered, goodnights being said, and that everybody seemed—drunk.

"P'rapsh they've all got legacies!" he thought, flushing with excitement. He rose unsteadily to his feet and was delighted to find that *he* was not in the least—drunk. He at once respected himself.

"Itsh really 'sgusting that fellows can't stop when they've had 'nough!" he murmured, making his way with steps that required great determination towards the door, and remembering before he got halfway that he had not paid his bill. Turning in a half-circle that brought an unnecessary quantity of the room round with him, he made his way back, lost his way, fumbled about in the increasing gloom, and found himself face to face with the—Head Waiter. The unexpected meeting braced him astonishingly. The dignity of the man had curiously increased.

"I'm looking for my bill," observed Wiggins thickly, wondering for the twentieth time of whom the man's face reminded him; "you haven't seen it about anywhere, I shuppose?" He sat down with more dignity than he could have supposed possible and produced a £5 note from his pocket, the lining of the pocket coming out with it like a dirty glove.

Most of the guests had gone out by this time, and the big hall was very dark. Two lights only remained, and these, reflected from mirror to mirror, made its proportions seem vast and unreal. They flew from place to place, too, distressingly—these lights.

"Half-a-crown will settle that, sir," replied the man, with a respectful bow.

"Nonshense!" replied the other. "Why, I ordered Lancashire hotch-potch, grilled shole, a—a bird or something of the kind, and the wine—"

"I beg your pardon, sir, but—if you will permit me to say so—the others will soon be here now, and—as there will be a specially large attendance, perhaps you would like to make sure of your place." He pocketed the half-crown with a bow, pointed to the far, dim corner of the room, and stepped aside a little to make space for Wiggins to pass.

And Wiggins did pass—though it is not quite clear how he managed to dodge the flying tables. With deep sighs, hot, confused and puzzled, but too obfuscated to understand what it was all about, he obeyed the directions, at the same time wondering uneasily how it was he had forgotten what was a-foot. He wandered towards the end of the hall with the uncertainty of a butterfly that makes many feints before it settles... At a vast distance off the Head Waiter was moving to close the main doors, utterly oblivious now of his existence. He felt glad of that. Something about that fellow was disagreeable—downright nasty. This suddenly came over him with a flood of conviction. The man was more than peculiar: he was sinister... The air smelt horribly of cooked food, tobacco smoke, breathing crowds, scented women and the rest. Whiffs of it, hot and foetid, brought him a little to his senses... Then suddenly he noticed that the big man with the face that was dark and smooth like the muzzle of a cannon, was watching him keenly from a table on the other side where an electric light still burned.

"By George! There he is again, that feller! Wonder whatsh he's smiling at me for. Looking for'sh bill too, p'raps—Now, in a Soup Kishen nothing of the kind—"

He bowed in return, smiling insolently, holding himself steady by a chair to do so. He shoved and stumbled his way on into the shadows, half-mingling with the throng passing out into the street. Then, making a sharp turn back into the room unobserved, he took a few uncertain steps and collapsed silently and helplessly upon a chair that was hidden behind a big palm-tree in a dark corner.

And the last thing he remembered as he sank, boneless, like soft hay, into that corner was that the sham palm-tree bowed towards him, then ran off into the ceiling, and from that elevation, which in no way diminished its size, bowed to him yet again...

It was just after his eyes closed that the door in the gilt panelling at the end of the room softly opened and a woman entered on tiptoe. She was followed by other women and several girls; these, again, from time to time, by men, all dressed in black, all silent, and all ushered by the majestic Head Waiter to their places. The big man with the face like a gunmuzzle superintended. And each individual, on entering, was held there at the secret doorway until a certain sentence had passed his lips. Evidently a password "It is Saturday night," said the one being admitted, "and we close early," replied the Head Waiter and the big man. And then the door was closed until the next soft tapping came.

But Wiggins, plunged in the stupor of the first sleep, knew none of all this. His frock-coat was bunched about his neck, his black tie under his ear, his feet resting higher than his head. He looked like a collapsed airship in a hedge, and he snored heavily.

III

It was about an hour later when he opened his eyes, climbed painfully and heavily to his feet, staggered back against the wall utterly bewildered—and stared. At the far end of the great hall, its loftiness now dim, was a group of people. The big mirrors on all sides reflected them with the effect of increasing their numbers indefinitely. They stood and sat upon an improvised platform. The electric lights, shaded with black, dropped a pale glitter upon their faces. They were systematically grouped, the big man in the centre, the Head Waiter at a small table just behind him. The former was speaking in low, measured tones.

In his dark and distant corner Wiggins first of all seized the carafe and quenched his feverish thirst. Next he advanced slowly and with the utmost caution to a point nearer the group where he could hear what was being said. He was still a good deal confused in mind, and had no idea what the hour was or what he had been doing in the meantime. There were some twenty or thirty people, he saw, of both sexes, well dressed, many of them distinguished in appearance, and all wearing black; even their gloves were black; some of the women, too, wore black veils—very thick. But in all the faces without exception there was something—was it about the lips and mouths?—that was peculiar and-repellent.

Obviously this was a meeting of some kind. Some society had hired the hall for a private gathering. Wiggins, understanding this, began to feel awkward. He did not wish to intrude; he had no right to listen; yet to make himself known was to betray that he was still very considerably intoxicated. The problem presented itself in these simple terms to his dazed intelligence. He was also aware of another fact: about these black-robed people there was something which made him secretly and horribly—afraid.

The big man with the smooth face like a gun-muzzle sat down after a softly-uttered speech, and the group, instead of applauding with their hands, waved black handkerchiefs. The fluttering sound of them trickled along the wastes of hall towards the concealed eavesdropper. Then the Head Waiter rose to introduce the next speaker, and the instant Wiggins saw him he understood what it was in his face that was familiar. For the false beard no longer adorned his lips, the wig that altered the shape of his forehead and the appearance of his eyes had been removed, and the likeness he bore to the philanthropist, Wiggins's late employer, was too remarkable to be ignored. Wiggins just repressed a cry, but a low gasp apparently did escape him, for several members of the group turned their heads in his direction and stared.

The Head Waiter, meanwhile, saved him from immediate discovery by beginning to speak. The words were plainly audible, and the resemblance of the voice to that other voice he knew now to be stopped with dust, was one of the most dreadful experiences he had ever known. Each word, each trick of expression came as a new and separate shock.

"...and the learned Doctor will say a few words upon the *rationale* of our subject," he concluded, turning with a graceful bow to make room for a distinguished-looking old gentleman who advanced shambling from the back of the improvised platform.

What Wiggins then heard—in somewhat disjointed sentences owing to the buzzing in his ears—was at first apparently meaningless. Yet it was freighted, he knew, with a creeping and sensational horror that would fully reveal itself the instant he discovered the clue. The old clever-faced scoundrel was saying vile things. He knew it. But the key to the puzzle being missing, he could not quite guess what it was all about. The Doctor, gravely and with balanced phrases, seemed to be speaking of the fads of the day with regard to food and feeding. He ridiculed vegetarianism, and all the other *isms*. He said that one and all were based upon ignorance and fallacy, declaring that the time had at last come in the history of the race when a rational system of feeding was a paramount necessity. The physical and psychical conditions of the times demanded it, and the soul of man could never be emancipated until it was adopted. He himself was proud to be one of the founders of their audacious and secret Society, revolutionary and pioneer in the best sense, to which so many of the medical fraternity now belonged, and so many of the brave women too, who were in the van of the feminist movements of the times. He said a great deal in this vein. Wiggins, listening in growing amazement and uneasiness, waited for the clue to it all.

In conclusion, the speaker referred solemnly to the fact that there was a stream of force in their Society which laid them open to the melancholy charge of being called "hysterical." "But after all," he cried, with rising enthusiasm and in accents that rang down the hall, "a Society without hysteria is a dull Society, just as a woman without hysteria is a dull woman. Neither the Society nor the woman need yield to the tendency; but that it is present potentially infers the faculty, so delicious in the eyes of all sane men-the faculty of running to extremes. It is a sign of life, and of very vivid life. It is not for nothing, dear friends, that we are named the—" But the buzzing in Wiggins's ears was so loud at this moment that he missed the name. It sounded to him something between "Can-I-believes" and "Camels," but for the life of him he could not overtake the actual word. The Doctor had uttered it, moreover, in a lowered voice—a suddenly lowered voice... When the noise in his ears had passed he heard the speaker bring his address to an end in these words: "...and I will now ask the secretaries to make their reports from their various sections, after which, I understand"—his tone grew suddenly thick and clouded—"we are to be regaled with a collation—a sacramental collation—of the usual kind..." His voice hushed away to nothing. His mouth was working most curiously. A wave of excitement unquestionably ran over the faces of the others. Their mouths also worked oddly. Dark and sombre things were afoot in that hall.

Wiggins crouched a little lower behind the edge of the overhanging table-cloth and listened. He was perspiring now, but there were touches of icy horror fingering about in the neighbourhood of his heart. His mental and physical discomfort were very great, for the conviction that he was about to witness some dreadful scene—black as the garments of the participants in it—grew rapidly within him. He devised endless plans for escape, only to reject them the instant they were formed. There was no escape possible. He had to wait till the end.

A charming young woman was on her feet, addressing the audience in silvery tones; sweet and comely she was, her beauty only marred by that singular leer that visited the lips and mouths of all of them. The flesh of his back began to crawl as he listened. He would have given his whole year's legacy to be out of it, for behind that voice of silver and sweetness there crowded even to her lips the rush of something that was unutterable—loathsome. Wiggins felt it. The uncertainty as to its exact nature only added to his horror and distress.

"...so this question of supply, my friends," she was saying, "is becoming more and more difficult. It resolves itself into a question of ways and means." She looked round upon her audience with a touch of nervous apprehension before she continued. "In my particular sphere of operations—West Kensington—I have regretfully to report that the suspicions and activity of the police, the foolish, old-fashioned police, have now rendered my monthly contributions no longer possible. There have been too many disappearances of late—" She paused, casting her eyes down. Wiggins felt his hair rise, drawn by a shivery wind. The words "contributions" and "disappearances" brought with them something quite freezing.

"...As you know," the girl resumed, "it is to the doctors that we must look chiefly for our steadier supplies, and unfortunately in my sphere of operations we have but one doctor who is a member... I do not like to—to resign my position, but I must ask for lenient consideration of my failure"—her voice sank lower still—"...my failure to furnish to-night the materials—" She began to stammer and hesitate dreadfully; her voice shook; an ashen pallor spread to her very lips. "...the elements for our customary feast—"

A movement of disapproval ran over the audience like a wave; murmurs of dissent and resentment were heard. As the girl paled more perceptibly the singular beauty of her face stood out with an effect of almost shining against that dark background of shadows and black garments. In spite of himself, and forgetting caution for the moment, Wiggins peeped over the edge of the table to see her better. She was a lady, he saw, highbred and spirited. That pallor, and the timidity it bespoke, was but evidence of a highly sensitive nature facing a situation of peculiar difficulty—and danger. He read in her attitude, in the poise of that slim figure standing there before disapproval and possible disaster, the bearing and proud courage of a type that would face execution with calmness and dignity. Wiggins was amazed that this thought should flash through him so vividly—from nowhere. Born of the feverish aftermath of alcohol, perhaps—yet born inevitably, too, of this situation before his eyes.

With a thrill he realized that the girl was speaking again, her voice steady, but faint with the gravity of her awful position.

"...and I ask for that justice in consideration of my failure which—the difficulties of the position demand. I have had to choose between that bold and ill-considered action which might have betrayed us all to the authorities, and-the risk of providing nothing for to-night."

She sat down. Wiggins understood that it was a question of life and death. The air about him turned icy. He felt the perspiration trickling on several different parts of his body at once.

An old lady rose instantly to reply; her face was stern and dreadful, although the signature of breeding and culture was plainly there in the delicate lines about the nostrils and forehead. Her mien held something implacable. She was dressed in black silk that rustled, and she was certainly well over sixty; but what made Wiggins squirm there in his narrow hiding-place was the extraordinary resemblance she bore to Mrs. Sturgis, the superintendent of one of his late employer's soup kitchens. It was all diabolically grotesque. She glanced round upon the group of members, who clearly regarded her as a leader. The machinery of the whole dreadful scene then moved quicker.

"Then are we to understand from the West Kensington secretary," she began in firm, even tones, "that for to-night there is—nothing?" The young girl bowed her head without rising from her chair.

"I beg to move, then, Mr. Chairman," continued the terrible old lady in iron accents, "that the customary procedure be followed, and that a Committee of Three be appointed to carry it into immediate effect." The words fell like bomb-shells into the deserted spaces of the hall.

"I second the motion," was heard in a man's voice.

"Those in favour of the motion will show their hands," announced the big chairman with the clean-shaven face.

Several score of black-gloved hands waved in the air, with the effect of plumes upon a jolting hearse. "And those who oppose it?"

No single hand was raised. An appalling hush fell upon the group.

"I appoint Signor Carnamorte as chairman of the sub-committee, with power to choose his associates," said the big man. And the "Head Waiter" bowed his acceptance of the duty imposed upon him. There was at once then a sign of hurried movement, and the figure of the young girl was lost momentarily to view as several members surged round her. The next instant they fell away and she stood clear, her hands bound. Her voice, soft as before but very faint, was audible through the hush.

"I claim the privilege belonging to the female members of the Society," she said calmly; "the right to find, if possible, a substitute."

"Granted," answered the chairman gravely. "The customary ten minutes will be allowed you in which to do so. Meanwhile, the preparations must proceed in the usual way."

With a dread that ate all other emotions, Wiggins watched keenly from his concealment, and the preparations that he saw in progress, though simple enough in themselves, filled him with a sense of ultimate horror that was freezing. The Committee of Three were very busy with something at the back of the improvised platform, something that was heavy and, on being touched, emitted a metallic and sonorous ring. As in the strangling terror and heat of nightmare the full meaning of events is often kept concealed until the climax, so Wiggins knew that this simple sound portended something that would only be revealed to him later—something appalling as Satan—sinister as the grave. That ring of metal was the Gong of Death. He heard it in his own heart, and the shock was so great that he could not prevent an actual physical movement. His jerking leg drove sharply against a chair. The chair—squeaked.

The sound pierced the deep silence of the big hall with so shrill a note that of course everybody heard it. Wiggins, expecting to have the whole crew of these black-robed people about his ears, held his breath in an agony of suspense. All those pairs of eyes, he felt, were searching the spot where he lay so thinly hidden by the table-cloth. But no steps came towards him. A voice, however, spoke: the voice of the girl: she had heard the sound and had divined its cause.

"Loosen my bonds," she cried, "for there is someone yonder among the shadows. I have found a substitute! And—I swear to Heaven—he is plump!"

The sentence was so extraordinary, that Wiggins felt a spring of secret merriment touched somewhere deep within him, and a gush of uncontrollable laughter came up in his throat so suddenly that before he could get his hand to his mouth, it rang down the long dim hall and betrayed him beyond all question of escape. Behind it lay the strange need of violent expression. He had to do something. The life of this slender and exquisite girl was in danger. And the nightmare strain of the whole scene, the hints and innuendoes of a dark purpose, the implacable nature of the decree that threatened so fair a life—all resulted in a pressure that was too much for him. Had he not laughed, he would certainly have shrieked aloud. And the next minute he did shriek aloud. The screams followed his laughter with a dreadful clamour, and at the same instant he staggered noisily to his feet and rose into full view from behind the table. Everybody then saw him.

Across the length of that dimly-lighted hall he faced the group of people in all their hideous reality, and what he saw cleared from his fuddled brain the last fumes of the alcohol. The white visage of each member seemed already close upon him. He saw the glimmering pallor of their skins against the black clothes, the eyes ashine, the mouths working, fingers pointing at him. There was the Head Waiter, more than ever like the dead philanthropist whose life had been spent in feeding others; there the odious smooth face of the big chairman; there the stern-lipped old lady who demanded the sentence of death. The whole silent crew of them stared darkly at him, and in front of them, like some fair lily growing amid decay, stood the girl with the proud and pallid face, calm and self-controlled. Immediately beyond her, a little to one side, Wiggins next perceived the huge iron cauldron, already swinging from its mighty tripod, waiting to receive her into its capacious jaws. Beneath it gleamed and flickered the flames from a dozen spirit-lamps.

"My substitute!" rang out her clear voice. "My substitute! Unloose my hands! And seize him before he can escape!"

"He cannot escape!" cried a dozen angry voices.

"In darkness!" thundered the chairman, and at the same moment every light was extinguished from the switch-board—every light but one. The bulb immediately behind him in the wall was left burning.

And the crew were upon him, coming swiftly and stealthily down the empty aisles between the tables. He saw their forms advance and shift by the gleam of the lamps beneath the awful cauldron. With the advance came, too, the sound of rushing, eager breathing. He imagined, though he could not see, those evil mouths a-working. And at this moment the subconscious part of him that had kept the secret all this time, suddenly revealed in letters of flame the name of the Society which fifteen minutes before he had failed to catch. The subconscious self, that supreme stage manager, that arch conspirator, rose and struck him in the face as it were out of the darkness, so that he understood, with a shock of nauseous terror, the terrible nature of the net in which he was caught.

For this Secret Society, meeting for their awful rites in a great public restaurant of mid-London, were maniacs of a rare and singular description—vilely mad on one point but sane on all the rest. They were Cannibals!

Never before had he run with such speed, agility and recklessness; never before had he guessed that he could leap tables, clear chairs with the flying manner of a hurdle race, and dodge palms and flower-pots as an athlete of twenty dodges collisions in the football field. But in each dark corner where he sought a temporary refuge, the electric light on the wall above immediately sprang into brilliance, one of the crew having remained by the switchboard to control this diabolically ingenious method of keeping him ever in sight.

For a long time, however, he evaded his crowding and clumsy pursuers. It was a vile and ghastly chase. His flying frock-coat streamed out behind him, and he felt the elastic side of his worn boots split under the unusual strain of the twisting, turning ankles as he leaped and ran. His pursuers, it seemed, sought to prolong the hunt on purpose. The passion' of the chase was in their blood. Round and round that hall, up and down, over tables and under chairs, behind screens, shaking the handles of doors—all immovable, past gleaming dish-covers on the wheeled joint-tables, taking cover by swing doors, curtains, palms, everything and anything, Wiggins flew for his life from the pursuing forces of a horrible death.

And at last they caught him. Breathless and exhausted, he collapsed backwards against the wall in a dark corner. But the light instantly flashed out above him. He lay in full view, and in another second the advancing horde—he saw their eyes and mouths so close—would be upon him, when something utterly unexpected happened: his head in falling struck against a hard projecting substance and—a bell rang sharply out. It was a telephone!

How he ever managed to get the receiver to his lips, or why the answering exchange came so swiftly he does not pretend to know. He had just time to shout, "Help! Help! Send police X...Restaurant! Murder! Cannibals!" when he was seized violently by the collar, his arms and legs grasped by a dozen pairs of hands, and a struggle began that he knew from the start must prove hopeless.

The fact that help might be on the way, however, gave him courage. Wiggins smashed right and left, screamed, kicked, bit and butted. His frock coat was ripped from his back with a whistling tear of cloth and lining, and he found himself free at the edge of a group that clawed and beat everywhere about him. The dim light was now in his favour. He shot down the hall again like a hare, leaping tables on the way, and flinging dish-covers, carafes, menus at the pursuing crowd as fast as he could lay hands upon them.

Then came a veritable pandemonium of smashed glass and crockery, while a grip of iron caught his arms behind and pinioned them beyond all possibility of moving. Turning quickly, he found himself looking straight into the eyes of a big blue policeman, the door into the street open beside him. The crowd became at once inextricably mixed up and jumbled together. The chairman, and the girl who was to have been eaten, melted into a single person. The philanthropist and the old lady slid into each other. It was a horrible bit of confusion. He felt deadly sick and dizzy. Everything dropped away from his sight then, and darkness tore up round him from the carpet. He remembered nothing more for a long time.

Perhaps the most vivid recollection of what occurred afterwards—he remembers it to this day, and his memory may be trusted, for he never touched wine again—was the weary smile of the magistrate, and the still more weary voice as he said in the court two days later—

"Forty shillings, and be bound over to keep the peace in two sureties for six months. And £5 to the proprietor of the restaurant to pay damages for the broken windows and crockery. Next case...!"

CARLTON'S DRIVE

IT is difficult, of course, to estimate the effect of such a thing upon another's temperament. The change seemed bewilderingly sudden; yet spiritual chemistry is a process incalculable, past finding out, and the results in this case were undeniable. Carlton had changed in the course of a brief year or two. And he dates it from that drive. He knows.

He told it to a few intimates only. Those who know his face as it is today, serene and strong, yet recall how it was scored and beaten with the ravages of dissipation a few years before (so that the human seemed almost to have dropped back into the beast), can scarcely credit his identity. *Now*—its calm austerity, softened by the greatest yearning known to men, the yearning to save, proclaim at a glance the splendid revolution; whereas *then*—! The memory is unpleasant; exceedingly wonderful the contrast. His life was inoffensive enough, negatively, at least, till the money came; then, with the inheritance, his innate sensuality broke out. Yet it seemed a prodigious step for a man to make in so brief a time from that life of depravity that stained his face and smothered his soul, to the Brotherhood of Devotion he founded, and himself led full charge against the vice of the world! But not incomprehensible, perhaps. He did nothing by halves. It was the swing of the pendulum.

He was somewhere about thirty, his nerves shattered by the savagery of concentrated fast living, his system too exhausted to respond even to unusual stimulant, when he found himself one early spring morning on the pavement beside St. George's Hospital. He had been up all night, and was making his way homewards on foot, his pockets stuffed with the proceeds of lucky gambling; and how he happened to be standing at that particular spot, watching the traffic, at eight in the morning, is not clear. Probably, seduced by the sweetness of the air, he had wandered, driven by gusts of mood as by gusts of wind. Though he had drunk steadily since midnight he was not so much intoxicated as fuddled—stupid. He was on the south corner, where the 'buses stop in their journey westwards. The sun poured a flood of light down Piccadilly; the street was brisk with pedestrians going to work; the hospital side-entrance behind him already astir. Across the road the trees in the park shimmered in a wave of fluttering green. The pride of life was in the June air. In his own heart, however, was a loathsome satiety—sign of the first death.

In a line with the trees opposite stood a solitary hansom. A faint surprise that it should be there at such an hour jostled in his sodden brain with the idea that he might as well drive home—when, suddenly, he became aware that the man perched on the box was looking at him across the street with a fixity of manner that was both singular and offensive. Carlton felt his own gaze, blear-eyed and troubled, somehow caught and held—uncomfortably. The other's eyes were fastened upon his own-had been fastened for some time—sinisterly, and with a purpose. Just at this moment, however, a sharp spasm of pain and faintness, due to exhaustion and debauch, shot through him, so that he reeled, half staggering, and, before he quite knew what he was doing, he had nodded to the driver, and saw that the horse was already turning with clattering hoofs to cross the slippery street. A minute later he had climbed heavily in, noticing vaguely that the driver wore all black, the horse was black, and on the whip was a strip of crêpe that fluttered in the breeze. As he got in, too, the effort strained him. But, more than that, something that was cold and terrible—"like a hand of ragged steel," he described it afterwards—clutched at his heart. It puzzled him; but he was too "done" to think; and he lurched back wearily on the cushions as the horse started forward with the jerkiness of long habit.

"Same address, sir?" the man called down through the trap. His voice was harsh "like iron"; and Carlton, supposing that he recognized a fare, replied testily, "Of course, you fool! And let her rip—to the devil!" The spasm of strange pain had passed. He only felt tired to brokenness, sick with his corrupt and unsatisfying life, a dull, incomprehensible anger burning in him against the world, the driver—and himself.

The hansom swung forwards over the smooth, uncrowded streets like a ship with a breeze behind her, for the horse was fresh, and the man drove well. He took off his opera hat and let the cool wind fan his face. That drive of a mile to his rooms was the most soothing and restful he had ever known. But, after a while, braced, perhaps, by the morning wind, he began to notice that they were following a strange route through streets he did not recognize. He had been lolling in the corner with half-closed eyes; now he sat up and looked about him. Time had passed. He ought to have reached home long ago. They were going at a tremendous and unholy pace, too. He poked open the trap sharply.

"Hi, hi!" he called out angrily; "are you drunk? Where, in the name of—are you driving to?"

"It's all right, sir; it's the shortest way. The usual roads are closed."

The man's voice—deep, with a curious rumbling note—had such conviction and authority in it that Carlton accepted the explanation with a growl and flung himself back into his soft corner. Again, however, for a single second, that cold thing of steel moved horribly in his heart. He felt as if the "ragged hand" had given it another twist. Then it passed, and he gave himself up to the swinging motion of the drive. The hansom tore along now; it was delightful. Curious, though, that *all* the known streets should be "up"! Positively the houses were getting less, as though he was driving out into the country. Perhaps, too, the feeling of *laisser aller* that came over him was caused by some inhibition of the will due to prolonged excesses. Carlton admits it was unlike his normal self not to *force* the man to drive where he wanted; but he felt lulled, lazy, indifferent. "Let the fool take his own way!" his thought ran; "I shan't pay him any more for it!..."

Somebody was waving to him from the pavement with a coloured parasol—a girl he knew, one of his sort; gay and smiling, tripping along quickly. With a momentary surprise that she should be thus early astir, he smiled through the window and waved his hand. It gave him pleasure to see she was going in the same direction as himself. The instant he passed her the horse leaped forward with increased speed, so that the hansom rattled, shaking him a little as it lurched from side to side.

"Steady on, idiot!" he shouted, "or you'll smash me up before I get to the end!" And he was just going to bang open the trap and swear, when his attention was caught by another salutation from the pavement. It was a man this time—running hard; a man who played, drank, and the rest of it even harder than himself, a man who shared his trips to Paris. He was radiant and gesticulating. "Good journey, old man!" he heard him cry as the hansom shot past; "Hurry up! We're coming, too! We shall be there together!" Carlton did not quite like this greeting. It reminded him for a second that he was a bit uncertain where the mad driver was heading for. It gave him a passing uneasiness—almost immediately forgotten, however. The pace was too delicious to bring to an end just yet. Presently he would call the fellow to order with a vengeance, but meanwhile—"let her rip!" His friends were all going the same way; it must be all right. His thoughts, he admits, were somewhat mixed; for great speed destroys calm judgment; it exhilarated, but it also bewildered. The pace, assuredly, had something to do with his mental confusion, for it was terrific. Yet he saw on the pavement, from time to time, more friends and acquaintances, and somehow at the moment it did not strike him as *too* peculiar that they should be there, all moving hurriedly in the same direction. He had an odd feeling that they all knew of some destination agreed upon; that he, too, knew it; but that it was not "playing the game" to admit that he knew. Yet about some of them—their hurried steps, their gay faces, their waving hands—there was a queer fugitive suggestion of sadness, even of fear. One or two touched the source of horror in him even. It hardly surprised him that the horse, steaming and sweating, should start forward with a frightened leap as each figure in turn was sighted and left behind. Probably he was himself too much a part of the wild, exhilarating rush to realize how singular it was. Certainly, it seemed as though some faculty of his mind was suspended during that drive.

But at last, after passing another friend, the horse gave a leap that really frightened him, flinging him against the boards. It was a man, twice his own age, who more than any other had helped him in his evil living, not by doing likewise, but by smothering his first remorse with a smile and a sentence: "Of course, my boy, sow your wild oats! You'll settle down later. No man is worth his salt who hasn't sown his wild oats!" He was sliding along—a kind of crawl, with something loathsome in his motion that suggested the reptile. Carlton nodded to him. The same second the horse gave its terrible bound. The whip for the first time slashed down across its flanks. He saw the strip of crêpe, black against the green and sunny landscape. For by now all houses were left behind, and they were rushing at a mad pace along a broad country road, growing momentarily steeper, and—downhill.

At the same moment he caught his own face in the glass. To his utter horror he saw that a black veil, crêpe-like, hung over the upper part, already hiding the eyes, and that it was moving downwards, slowly creeping. The hand of steel turned again within him. He knew that it was Death.

Yet, most singular of all, he instantly found in himself the power to believe it was not there. His hand brushed it off. His face was young, clean, and smiling once more... And now the hansom flew. The horse was running away; he heard the driver shouting to it, and the shouting sounded like a song. The man was drunk after all. Mingled with his song, too, came a confused murmur of voices behind—far away. What in the world did it all mean? Dashing aside the little curtain he looked back out of the window, and the first thing he saw was a face pressed close against the glass, staring straight into his eyes with a beseeching, pitiful expression. Good God! It was the face of his mother. He swore; the face melted away—and he then saw that the whole country behind him was black, and through it, down the darkened road, ran the figures he had passed. But how changed! The girl was no longer gay and smiling; her face was old, streaked with evil, and with one hand she clutched her heart as she ran—trying in vain to stop. Behind her were the others—worn and broken, with bloodshot eyes and toothless gums, all grinning dreadfully, all racing down the ever-steepening descent, yet all trying frantically to stop. One or two, however, still ran with a brave show as if they wished to; debonair, holding themselves with a certain appearance of dignity and pleasure. And some—the old man of the "wild oats" sentence at their head—were close upon the hansom, *push-*

ing it... The face of his mother slid once again upon the glass, between their evil, outstretched hands and himself, but less close, less visible than before...

Carlton knew a spasm of pain that was terrible. He sat up. He flung open the doors, and his eyes measured the leap. But the faculty of mind that had all the time been in suspension returned a little, and he saw that to jump was—impossible. He smashed the trap open with his fist and cried out, "Stop! I tell you, stop!"

"Can't stop here, sir," the driver answered, peering down at him out of the square opening that let in—darkness. "It's not allowed. It's not usual, either."

"Stop, I say," thundered Carlton, trying to rise and strike him.

But the driver laughed through that square of blackness.

"Can't be done, sir. You told me 'same address.' There's no stopping now!"

Carlton's clenched fist was close to the man's eyes when the fingers grew limp and opened. He sank back upon the seat again. The face peering down upon him was—his own.

And in this supreme moment it was that some secret reserve of soul, hitherto untainted—stirred into life, he declares, by the sight of his mother's face at the window—rose and offered itself to him. He accepted it. *His will moved in its sleep and woke.*

"But I say you *shall* stop!" he cried, catching the reins in both hands, and, when they snapped, seizing the rims, and even the spokes, of the wheels. His great strength acted like a brake. The hansom reeled, shook, then slackened. It was a most curious thing, but the force that twisted his heart with its hand of "ragged steel" seemed to lend him its power. His will moved and gripped; the machinery groaned, but worked. Carlton did nothing by halves; he put his life into his efforts; the skin was torn like paper from his hands. The hansom stopped with a trembling jerk and flung him out upon his face in the mud. And the same second he saw the horse and driver, both torn from their fastenings, whirled past him overhead to disappear into a gulf that yawned dreadfully under his very eyes, blacker than night, deeper than all things...

And when, at length, he rose to his feet, he found that he was tied with bands of iron to the shafts. Slowly, with vast efforts, groaning and sweating, he turned and began painfully to reclimb the huge and toilsome ascent, dragging the awful weight behind him...towards the Light.

For the glare that suddenly broke through the sky was the sunshine coming through the windows of the hospital room—St. George's Hospital—where they had carried him when he fainted on the pavement half-an-hour before.

THE ECCENTRICITY OF SIMON PARNACUTE

I

IT was one of those mornings in early spring when even the London streets run beauty. The day, passing through the sky with clouds of flying hair, touched every one with the magic of its own irresponsible gaiety, as it alternated between laughter and the tears of sudden showers.

In the parks the trees, faintly clothed with gauze, were busying themselves shyly with the thoughts of coming leaves. The air held a certain sharpness, but the sun swam through the dazzling blue spaces with bursts of almost summer heat; and a wind, straight from the haunted south, laid its soft persuasion upon all, bringing visions too fair to last—long thoughts of youth, of cowslip-meadows, white sails, waves on yellow sand, and other pictures innumerable and enchanting.

So potent, indeed, was this spell of awakening spring that even Simon Parnacute, retired Professor of Political Economy—elderly, thin-faced, and ruminating in his big skull those large questions that concern the polity of nations—formed no exception to the general rule. For, as he slowly made his way down the street that led from his apartment to the Little Park, he was fully aware that this magic of the spring was in his own blood too, and that the dust which had accumulated with the years upon the surface of his soul was being stirred by one of the softest breezes he had ever felt in the whole course of his arduous and tutorial career.

And—it so happened—just as he reached the foot of the street where the houses fell away towards the open park, the sun rushed out into one of the sudden blue spaces of the sky, and drenched him in a wave of delicious heat that for all the world was like the heat of July.

Professor Parnacute, once lecturer, now merely ponderer, was an exact thinker, dealing carefully with the facts of life as he saw them. He was a good man and a true. He dealt in large emotions, becoming for one who studied nations rather than individuals, and of all diplomacies of the heart he was rudely ignorant. He lived always at the centre of the circle—his own circle—and eccentricity was a thing to him utterly abhorrent. Convention ruled him, body, soul and mind. To know a disordered thought, or an unwonted emotion, troubled him as much as to see a picture crooked on a wall, or a man's collar projecting beyond his overcoat. Eccentricity was the symptom of a disease.

Thus, as he reached the foot of the street and felt the sun and wind upon his withered cheeks, this unexpected call of the spring came to him sharply as something altogether out of place and illegitimate—symptom of an irregular condition of mind that must be instantly repressed. And it was just here, while the crowd jostled and delayed him, that there smote upon his ear the song incarnate of the very spring whose spell he was in the act of relegating to its proper place in his personal economy: he heard the entrancing *singing of a bird!*

Transfixed with wonder and delight, he stood for a whole minute and listened. Then, slowly turning, he found himself staring straight into the small beseeching eyes of a—thrush; a thrush in a cage that hung upon the outside wall of a bird-fancier's shop behind him.

Perhaps he would not have lingered more than these few seconds, however, had not the crowd held him momentarily prisoner in a spot immediately opposite the shop, where his head, too, was exactly on a level with the hanging cage. Thus he was perforce obliged to stand, and watch, and listen; and, as he did so, the bird's rapturous and appealing song played upon the feelings already awakened by the spring, urging them upwards and outwards to a point that grew perilously moving.

Both sound and sight caught and held him spellbound.

The bird, once well-favoured perhaps, he perceived was now thin and bedraggled, its feathers disarrayed by continual flitting along its perch, and by endless fluttering of wings and body against the bars of its narrow cage. There was not room to open both wings properly; it frequently dashed itself against the sides of its wooden prison; and all the force of its vain and passionate desire for freedom shone in the two small and glittering eyes which gazed beseechingly through the bars at the passers-by. It looked broken and worn with the ceaseless renewal of the futile struggle. Hopping along the bar, cocking its dainty little head on one side, and looking straight into the Professor's eyes, it managed (by some inarticulate magic known only to the eyes of creatures in prison) to spell out the message of its pain—the poignant longing for the freedom of the open sky, the lift of the great winds, the glory of the sun upon its lustreless feathers.

Now it so chanced that this combined onslaught of sight and sound caught the elderly Professor along the line of least resistance—the line of an untried, and therefore unexhausted, sensation. Here, apparently, was an emotion hitherto unrealized, and so not yet regulated away into atrophy.

For, with an intuition as singular as it was searching, he suddenly understood something of the passion of the wild Caged Things of the world, and realized in a flash of passing vision something of their unutterable pain.

In one swift moment of genuine mystical sympathy he *felt with* their peculiar quality of unsatisfied longing exactly as though it were his own; the longing, not only of captive birds and animals, but of anguished men and women, trapped by circumstance, confined by weakness, cabined by character and temperament, all yearning for a freedom they knew not how to reach—caged by the smallness of their desires, by the impotence of their wills, by the pettiness of their souls—caged in bodies from which death alone could finally bring release.

Something of all this found its way into the elderly Professor's heart as he stood watching the pantomime of the captive thrush—the Caged Thing;—and, after a moment's hesitation that represented a vast amount of condensed feeling, he deliberately entered the low doorway of the shop and inquired the price of the bird.

"The thrush—er—singing in the small cage," he stammered.

"One *and* six only, sir," replied the coarse, red-faced man who owned the shop, looking up from a rabbit that he was pushing with clumsy fingers into a box; "only one shilling *and* sixpence,"—and then went on with copious remarks upon thrushes in general and the superior qualities of this one in particular. "Been 'ere four months and sings just lovely," he added, by way of climax.

"Thank you," said Parnacute quietly, trying to persuade himself that he did not feel mortified by his impulsive and eccentric action; "then I will purchase the bird—at once—er—if you please."

"Couldn't go far wrong, sir," said the man, shoving the rabbit to one side, and going outside to fetch the thrush.

"No, I shall not require the cage, but—er—you may put him in a cardboard box perhaps, so that I can carry him easily."

He referred to the bird as "him," though at any other time he would have said "it," and the change, noted surreptitiously as it were, added to his general sense of confusion. It was too late, however, to alter his mind, and after watching the man force the bird with gross hands into a cardboard box, he gathered up the noose of string with which it was tied and walked with as much dignity and self-respect as he could muster out of the shop.

But the moment he got into the street with this living parcel under his arm—he both heard and felt the scuttling of the bird's feet—the realization that he had been guilty of what he considered an outrageous act of eccentricity almost overwhelmed him. For he had succumbed in most regrettable fashion to a momentary impulse, and had bought the bird in order to release it!

"Dear me!" he thought, "how ever could I have allowed myself to do so eccentric and impulsive a thing!"

And, but for the fact that it would merely have accentuated his eccentricity, he would then and there have returned to the shop and given back the bird. That, however, being now clearly impossible, he crossed the road and entered the Little Park by the first iron gateway he could find. He walked down the gravel path, fumbling with the string. In another minute the bird would have been out, when he chanced to glance round in order to make sure he was unobserved and saw against the shrubbery on his left—a policeman.

This, he felt, was most vexatious, for he had hoped to complete the transaction unseen. Straightening himself up, he nervously fastened the string again, and walked on slowly as though nothing had happened, searching for a more secluded spot where he should be entirely free from observation.

Professor Parnacute now became aware that his vexation—primarily caused by his act of impulse, and increased by the fact that he was observed—had become somewhat acute. It was extraordinary, he reflected, how policemen had this way of suddenly outlining themselves in the least appropriate—the least necessary—places. There was no reason why a policeman should have been standing against that innocent shrubbery, where there was nothing to do, no one to watch. At almost any other point in the Little Park he might have served some possibly useful purpose, and yet, forsooth, he must select the one spot where he was not wanted—where his presence, indeed, was positively objectionable.

The policeman, meanwhile, watched him steadily as he retreated with the obnoxious parcel. He carried it upside down now without knowing it. He felt as though he had been detected in a crime. He watched the policeman, too, out of the corner of his eye, longing to be done with the whole business.

"That policeman is a tremendous fellow," he thought to himself. "I have never seen a constable so large, so stalwart. He must be *the* policeman of the district"—whatever that might mean—"a veritable wall and tower of defence." The helmet made him think of a battering ram, and the buttons on his overcoat of the muzzles of guns.

He moved away round the corner with as much innocence as he could assume, as though he were carrying a package of books or some new article of apparel.

It is, no doubt, the duty of every alert constable to observe as acutely as possible the course of events passing before his eyes, yet this particular Bobby seemed far more interested than the circumstances warranted in Parnacute's cardboard box. He kept his gaze remorselessly upon it. Perhaps, thought the Professor, he heard the scutterings of the frightened bird within. Perhaps he thought it was a cat going to be drowned in the ornamental water. Perhaps—oh, dreadful idea!—he thought it was a baby!

The suspicions of an intelligent policeman, however, being past finding out, Simon Parnacute wisely ignored them, and just then passed round a corner where he was screened from this persistent observer by a dense growth of rhododendron bushes.

Seizing the opportune moment, and acting with a prompt decision born of the dread of the reappearing policeman, he cut the string, opened the lid of the box, and an instant later had the intense satisfaction of seeing the imprisoned thrush hop upon the cardboard edge and then fly with a beautiful curving dip and a whirr of wings off into the open sky. It turned once as it flew, and its bright brown eye looked at him. Then it was gone, lost in the sunshine that blazed over the shrubberies and beckoned it out over their waving tops across the river.

The prisoner was free. For the space of a whole minute, the Professor stood still, conscious of a sense of genuine relief. That sound of wings, that racing sweep of the little quivering body escaping into limitless freedom, that penetrating look of gratitude from the wee brown eyes— these stirred in him again the same prodigious emotion he had experienced for the first time that afternoon outside the bird-fancier's shop. The release of the "caged creature" provided him with a kind of vicarious experience of freedom and delight such as he had never before known in his whole life. It almost seemed as though he had escaped himself—out of his "circle."

Then, as he faced about, with the empty box dangling in his hand, the first thing he saw, coming slowly down the path towards him with measured tread, was—the big policeman.

Something very stern, something very forbidding, hung like an atmosphere of warning about this guardian of the law in a blue uniform. It brought him back sharply to the rigid facts of life, and the soft beauty of the spring day vanished and left him untouched. He accepted the reminder that life is earnest, and that eccentricities are invitations to disaster. Sooner or later the Policeman is bound to make his appearance.

However, this particular constable, of course, passed him without word or gesture, and as soon as he came to one of the little wire baskets provided for the purpose, the Professor dropped his box into it, and then made his way slowly and thoughtfully back to his apartment and his luncheon.

But the eccentricity of which he had been guilty circled and circled in his mind, reminding him with merciless insistence of a foolish act he should not have committed, and plaguing him with remorseless little stabs for having indulged in an impulsive and irregular proceeding.

For, to him, the inevitableness of life came as a fact to which he was resigned, rather than as a force to be appropriated for the ends of his own soul; and the sight of the happy bird escaping into sky and sunshine, with the figure of the inflexible and stern-lipped policeman in the background, made a deep impression upon him that would sooner or later be certain to bear fruit.

"Dear me," thought the Professor of Political Economy, giving mental expression to this sentiment, "I shall pay for this in the long run! Without question I shall pay for it!"

II

If it may be taken that there is no Chance, playing tricksy-wise behind the scenes of existence, but that all events falling into the lives of men are the calculated results of adequate causes, then Mr. Simon Parnacute, late Professor of Political Economy in C— College, certainly did pay for his spring aberration, in the sense that he caught a violent chill which brought him to bed and speedily developed into pneumonia.

It was the evening of the sixth day, and he lay weary and feverish in his bedroom on the top floor of the building which held his little self-contained apartment. The nurse was down-stairs having her tea. A shaded lamp stood beside the bed, and through the window—the blinds being not yet drawn—he saw the sea of roofs and chimney-pots, and the stream of wires, sharply outlined against a sunset sky of gold and pink. High and thin above the dusk floated long strips of coloured cloud, and the first stars twinkled through the April vapours that gathered with the approach of night.

Presently the door opened and someone came in softly half-way across the room, and then stopped. The Professor turned wearily and saw that the maid stood there and was trying to speak. She seemed flustered, he noticed, and her face was rather white.

"What's the matter *now,* Emily?" he asked feebly, yet irritably.

"Please, Professor—there's a gentleman—" and there she stuck.

"Someone to see me? The doctor again already?" queried the patient, wondering in a vague, absent way why the girl should seem so startled.

As he spoke there was a sound of footsteps on the landing outside—heavy footsteps.

"But please, Professor, sir, it's *not* the doctor," the maid faltered, "only I couldn't get his name, and I couldn't stop him, an' he said you expected him—and I think he looks like—"

The approaching footsteps frightened the girl so much that she could not find words to complete her description. They were just outside the door now.

"—like a perliceman!" she finished with a rush, backing towards the door as though she feared the Professor would leap from his bed to demolish her.

"A *policeman!*" gasped Mr. Parnacute, unable to believe his ears. "A policeman, Emily! In my apartment?"

And before the sick man could find words to express his particular annoyance that any stranger (above all a constable) should intrude at such a time, the door was pushed wide open, the girl had vanished with a flutter of skirts, and the tall figure of a man stood in full view upon the threshold, and stared steadily across the room at the occupant of the bed on the other side.

It was indeed a policeman, and a very large policeman. Moreover, it was *the* policeman.

The instant the Professor recognized the familiar form of the man from the park his anger, for some quite unaccountable reason, vanished almost entirely; the sharp vexation he had felt a moment before died away; and, sinking back exhausted among the pillows, he only found breath to ask him to close the door and come in. The fact was, astonishment had used up the small store of energy at his disposal, and for the moment he could think of nothing else to do.

The policeman closed the door quietly and moved forward towards the centre of the room, so that the circle of light from the shaded lamp at the head of the bed reached his figure but fell just short of his face.

The invalid sat up in bed again and stared. As nothing seemed to happen he recovered his scattered wits a little.

"You are the policeman from the park, unless I mistake?" he asked feebly, with mingled pomposity and resentment.

The big man bowed in acknowledgment and removed his helmet, holding it before him in his hand. His face was peculiarly bright, almost as though it reflected the glow of a bull's-eye lantern concealed somewhere about his huge person.

"I thought I recognized you," went on the Professor, exasperated a little by the other's self-possession. "Are you perhaps aware that I am ill— too ill to see strangers, and that to force your way up in this fashion—!" He left the sentence unfinished for lack of suitable expletives.

"You are certainly ill," replied the constable, speaking for the first time; "but then—I am *not* a stranger." His voice was wonderfully pitched and modulated for a policeman.

"Then, by what right, pray, do you dare to intrude upon me at such a time?" snapped the other, ignoring the latter statement.

"My duty, sir," the man replied, with a rather wonderful dignity, "knows nothing of time or place."

Professor Parnacute looked at him a little more closely as he stood there helmet in hand. He was something more, he gathered, than an ordinary constable; an inspector perhaps. He examined him carefully; but he understood nothing about differences in uniform, of bands or stars upon sleeve and collar.

"If you are here in the prosecution of your duty, then," exclaimed the man of careful mind, searching feverishly for some possible delinquency on the part of his small staff of servants, "pray be seated and state your business; but as briefly as possible. My throat pains me, and my strength is low." He spoke with less acerbity. The dignity of the visitor began to impress him in some vague fashion he did not understand.

The big figure in blue bowed again, but made no sign of advance.

"You come from X— Station, I presume?" Parnacute added, mentioning the police station round the corner. He sank deeper into his pillows, conscious that his strength was becoming exhausted.

"From Headquarters—I come," replied the colossus in a deep voice.

The Professor had only the vaguest idea what Headquarters meant, yet the phrase conveyed an importance that somehow was not lost upon him. Meanwhile his impatience grew with his exhaustion.

"I must request you, officer, to state your business with dispatch," he said tartly, "or to come again when I am better able to attend to you. Next week, no doubt—"

"There is no time *but* the present," returned the other, with an odd choice of words that escaped the notice of his perplexed hearer, as he produced from a capacious pocket in the tail of his overcoat a notebook bound with some shining metal like gold.

"Your name is Parnacute?" he asked, consulting the book.

"Yes," answered the other, with the resignation of exhaustion.

"*Simon* Parnacute?"

"Of course, yes."

"And on the third of April last," he went on, looking keenly over the top of the note-book at the sick man, "you, Simon Parnacute, entered the shop of Theodore Spinks in the Lower P— Road, and purchased from him a certain living creature?"

"Yes," answered the Professor, beginning to feel hot at the discovery of his folly.

"A bird?"

"A bird."

"A thrush?"

"A thrush."

"A singing thrush?"

"Oh yes, it was a singing thrush, if you *must* know."

"In money you paid for this thrush the sum of one shilling *and* six pennies?" He emphasized the "and" just as the bird-fancier had done.

"One and six, yes."

"But in true value," said the policeman, speaking with grave emphasis, "it cost you a great deal more?"

"Perhaps." He winced internally at the memory. He was so astonished, too, that the visit had to do with himself and not with some of his servants.

"You paid for it with your heart?" insisted the other.

The Professor made no reply. He started. He almost writhed under the sheets.

"Am I right?" asked the policeman.

"That is the fact, I suppose," he said in a low voice, sorely puzzled by the catechism.

"You carried this bird away in a cardboard box to E— Gardens by the river, and there you gave it freedom and watched it fly away?"

"Your statement is correct, I think, in every particular. But really—this absurd cross-examination, my good man—!"

"And your motive in so doing," continued the policeman, his voice quite drowning the invalid's feeble tones, "was the unselfish one of releasing an imprisoned and tortured creature?"

Simon Parnacute looked up with the greatest possible surprise.

"I think—well, well!—perhaps it was," he murmured apologetically. "The extraordinary singing—it *was* extraordinary, you know, and the sight of the little thing beating its wings pained me."

The big policeman put away his note-book suddenly, and moved closer to the bed so that his face entered the circle of lamplight.

"In that case," he cried, "*you are my man!*"

"I am your man!" exclaimed the Professor, with an uncontrollable start.

"The man I want," repeated the other, smiling.

His voice had suddenly grown soft and wonderful, like the ringing of a silver gong, and into his face had come an expression of wistful tenderness that made it positively beautiful. It shone. Never before, out of a picture, had he seen such a look upon a human countenance, or heard such tones issue from the lips of a human being. He thought, swiftly and confusedly, of a woman, of *the* woman he had never found—of a dream, an enchantment as of music or vision upon the senses.

"Wants me!" he thought with alarm. "What have I done now? What new eccentricity have I been guilty of?"

Strange, bewildering ideas crowded into his mind, blurred in outline, preposterous in character. A sensation of cold caught at his fever and overmastered it, bathing him in perspiration, making him tremble, yet not with fear. A new and curious delight had begun to pluck at his heart-strings.

Then an extravagant suspicion crossed his brain, yet a suspicion not wholly unwarranted.

"Who are you?" he asked sharply, looking up. "Are you really only a policeman?"

The man drew himself up so that he appeared, if possible, even huger than before.

"I am a World-Policeman," he answered, "a guardian, perhaps, rather than a detective."

"Heavens above!" cried the Professor, thinking of madness and the crimes committed in madness.

"Yes," he went on in those calm, musical tones that before long began to have a reassuring effect upon his listener, "and it is my duty, among many others, to keep an eye upon eccentric people; to lock them up when necessary, and when their sentences have expired, to release them. Also," he added impressively, "as in your case, to let them out of their cages without pain—when they've earned it."

"Gracious goodness me!" exclaimed Parnacute, unaccustomed to the use of expletives, but unable to think of anything else to say.

"And sometimes to see that their cages do not destroy them—and that they do not beat themselves to death against the bars," he went on, smiling quite wonderfully. "Our duties are varied *and* numerous. I am one of a large force."

The man learned in political economy felt as though his head were spinning. He thought of calling for help. Indeed, he had already made a motion with his hand towards the bell when a gesture on the part of his strange visitor restrained him.

"Then why do you want *me*, if I may ask?" he faltered instead.

"To mark you down; and when the time comes to let you out of your cage easily, comfortably, without pain. That's one reward for your kindness to the bird."

The Professor's fears had now quite disappeared. The policeman seemed perfectly harmless after all.

"It's *very* kind of you," he said feebly, drawing his arm back beneath the bed-clothes. "Only—er—I was not aware, exactly, that I lived in a cage."

He looked up resignedly into the man's face.

"You only realize that when you get out," he replied. "They're all like
that. The bird didn't quite understand what was wrong; it only knew
that it felt miserable. Same with you. You feel unhappy in that body of
yours, and in that little careful mind you regulate so nicely; but, for the
life of you, you don't quite know what it is that's wrong. You want space,
freedom, a taste of liberty. You want to fly, that's what you want!" he
cried, raising his voice.

"I—want—to—fly?" gasped the invalid.

"Oh," smiling again, "we World-Policemen have thousands of cases just
like yours. Our field is a large one, a very large one indeed."

He stepped into the light more fully and turned sideways.

"Here's my badge, if you care to see it," he said proudly.

He stooped a little so that the Professor's beady eyes could easily focus
themselves upon the collar of his overcoat. There, just like the lettering
upon the collar of an ordinary London policeman, only in bright gold
instead of silver, shone the constellation of the Pleiades. Then he turned
and showed the other side, and Parnacute saw the constellation of Orion
slanting upwards, as he had often seen it tilting across the sky at night.

"Those are my badges," he repeated proudly, straightening himself up
again and moving back into the shadow.

"And very fine they are, too," said the Professor, his increasing exhaustion suggesting no better observation. But with the sight of those starry
figures had come to him a strange whiff of the open skies, space, and
wind—the winds of the world.

"So that when the time comes," the World-Policeman resumed, "you
may have confidence. I will let you out without pain or fear just as you
let out the bird. And, meanwhile, you may as well realize that you live
in a cage just as cramped and shut away from light and freedom as the
thrush did."

"Thank you; I will certainly try," whispered Parnacute, almost fainting
with fatigue.

There followed a pause, during which the policeman put on his helmet, tightened his belt, and then began to search vigorously for something in his coattail pockets.

"And now," ventured the sick man, feeling half fearful, half happy,
though without knowing exactly why, "is there anything more I can do
for you, Mr. World-Policeman?" He was conscious that his words were
peculiar yet he could not help it. They seemed to slip out of their own
accord.

"There's nothing more you can do for *me*, sir, thank you," answered the
man in his most silvery tones. "But there's something more I can do for
you! And that is to give you a preliminary taste of freedom, so that you

may realize you do live in a cage, and be less confused and puzzled when you come to make the final Escape."

Parnacute caught his breath sharply—staring open-mouthed.

With a single stride the policeman covered the space between himself and the bed. Before the withered, fever-stricken little Professor could utter a word or a cry, he had caught up the wasted body out of the bed, shaken the bed-clothes off him like paper from a parcel, and slung him without ceremony across his gigantic shoulders. Then he crossed the room, and producing the key from his coat-tail pocket, he put it straight into the solid wall of the room. He turned it, and the entire side of the house opened like a door.

For one second Simon Parnacute looked back and saw the lamp, and the fire, and the bed. And in the bed he saw his own body lying motionless in profound slumber.

Then, as the policeman balanced, hovering upon the giddy edge, he looked outward and saw the network of street-lamps far below, and heard the deep roar of the city smite upon his ears like the thunder of a sea.

The next moment the man stepped out into space, and he saw that they were rising up swiftly towards the dark vault of sky, where stars twinkled down upon them between streaks of thin flying clouds.

III

Once outside, floating in the night, the policeman gave his shoulder a mighty jerk and tossed his small burden into free space.

"Jump away!" he cried. "You're quite safe!"

The Professor dropped like a bullet towards the pavement; then suddenly began to rise again, like a balloon. All traces of fever or bodily discomfort had left him utterly. He felt light as air, and strong as lightning.

"Now, where shall we go to?" The voice sounded above him.

Simon Parnacute was no flyer. He had never indulged in those strange flying-dreams that form a weird pleasure in the sleep-lives of many people. He was terrified beyond belief until he found that he did not crash against the earth, and that he had within him the power to regulate his movements, to rise or sink at will. Then, of course, the wildest fury of delight and freedom he had ever known flashed all over him and burned in his brain like an intoxication.

"The big cities, or the stars?" asked the World-Policeman.

"No, no," he cried, "the country—the open country! And other lands!"

For Simon Parnacute had never travelled. Incredible as it may seem, the Professor had never in his life been farther out of England than in a sailing-boat at Southend. His body had travelled even less than his imagination. With this suddenly increased capacity for motion, the desire to race about and see became a passion.

"Woods! Mountains! Seas! Deserts! Anything but houses and people!" he shouted, rising upwards to his companion without the smallest effort.

An intense longing to see the desolate, unfrequented regions of the earth seized him and tore its way out into words strangely unlike his normal and measured mode of speech. All his life he had paced to and fro in a formal little garden with the most precise paths imaginable. Now he wanted a trackless world. The reaction was terrific. The desire of the Arab for the desert, of the gipsy for the open heaths, the "desire of the snipe for the wilderness"—the longing of the eternal wanderer—possessed his soul and found vent in words.

It was just as though the passion of the released thrush were reproducing itself in him and becoming articulate.

"I am haunted by the faces of the world's forgotten places," he cried aloud impetuously. "Beaches lying in the moonlight, all forsaken in the moonlight—"

His utterance, like the bird's, had become lyrical.

"Can this be what the thrush felt?" he wondered.

"Let's be off then," the policeman called back. "There's no time *but the present*, remember." He rushed through space like a huge projectile. He made a faint whistling noise as he went. Parnacute followed suit. The lightest desire, he found, gave him instantly the ease and speed of thought.

The policeman had taken off his helmet, overcoat and belt, and dropped them down somewhere into a London street. He now appeared as a mere blue outline of a man, scarcely discernible against the dark sky—an outline filled with air. The Professor glanced down at himself and saw that he, too, was a mere outline of a man—a pallid outline filled with the purple air of night.

"Now then," sang out this "Bobby-of-the-World."

Side by side they shot up with a wild rush, and the lights of London, town and suburbs, flashed away beneath them in streaming lines and patches. In a second darkness filled the huge gap, pouring behind them like a mighty wave. Other streams and patches of light succeeded quickly, blurred and faint, like lamps of railway stations from a night express, as other towns dropped past them in a series and were swallowed up in the gulf behind.

A cool salt air smote their faces, and Parnacute heard the soft crashing of waves as they crossed the Channel, and swept on over the fields and forests of France, glimmering below like the squares of a mighty chessboard. Like toys, village after village shot by, smelling of peat-smoke, cattle, and the faint windiness of coming spring.

Sometimes they passed below the clouds and lost the stars, sometimes above them and lost the world; sometimes over forests roaring like the sea, sometimes above vast plains still and silent as the grave; but always Parnacute saw the constellations of Orion and Pleiades shining on the coat-collar of the soaring policeman, their little patterns picked out as with tiny electric lamps.

Below them lay the huge map of the earth, raised, scarred, darkly coloured, and breathing—a map *alive*.

Then came the Jura, soft and purple, carpeted with forests, rolling below them like a dream, and they looked down into slumbering valleys and heard far below the tumbling of water and the singing of countless streams.

"Glory, glory!" cried the Professor. "And do the birds know *this?*"

"Not the imprisoned ones," was the reply. And presently they whipped across large gleaming bodies of water as the lakes of Switzerland approached. Then, entering the zones of icy atmosphere, they looked down and saw white towers and pinnacles of silver, and the forms of scarred and mighty glaciers that rose and fell among the fields of eternal snow, folding upon the mountains in vast procession.

"I think—I'm frightened!" gasped Parnacute, clutching at his companion, but seizing only the frigid air.

The policeman shouted with laughter.

"This is nothing—compared to Mars or the moon," he cried, soaring till the Alps looked like a patch of snowdrops shining in a Surrey garden. "You'll soon get accustomed to it."

The Professor of Political Economy rose after him. But presently they sank again in an immense curving sweep and touched the tops of the highest mountains with their toes. This sent them instantly aloft again, bounding with the impetus of rockets, and so they careered on through the perfumed, pathless night till they came to Italy and left the Alps behind them like the shadowy wall of another world that had silently moved up close to them through space.

"Mother of Mountains!" shouted the delighted man of colleges. "And did the thrush know this too?"

"It has you to thank, if so," the policeman answered.

"And I have you to thank."

"No—yourself," replied his flying guide.

And then the desert! They had crossed the scented Mediterranean and reached the zones of sand. It rose in clouds and sheets as a mighty wind stirred across the leagues of loneliness that stretched below them into blue distance. It whirled about them and stung their faces.

"Thin ropes of sand which crumble ere they bind!" cried the Professor with a peal of laughter, not knowing what he said in the delirium of his pleasure.

The hot smell of the sand excited him; the knowledge that for hundreds of miles he could not see a house or a human being thrilled him dizzily with the incalculable delight of freedom. The splendour of the night, mystical and incommunicable, overcame him. He rose, laughing wildly, shaking the sand from his hair, and taking gigantic curves into the starry space about him. He remembered vividly the sight of those bedraggled wings in the little cramped cage—and then looked down and realized that here the winds sank exhausted from the very weariness of too much space. Oh, that he could tear away the bars of every cage the world had ever known—set free all captive creatures—restore to all wild, winged life the liberty of open spaces that is theirs by right!

He cried again to the stars and winds and deserts, but his words found no intelligible expression, for their passion was too great to be confined in any known medium. The World-Policeman alone understood, perhaps, for he flew down in circles round the little Professor and laughed and laughed and laughed.

And it seemed as if tremendous figures formed themselves out of the sky to listen, and bent down to lift him with a single sweep of their immense arms from the earth to the heavens. Such was the torrential power and delight of escape in him, that he almost felt as if he could skim the icy abysses of Death itself—without being ever caught...

The colossal shapes of Egypt, terrible and monstrous, passed far below in huge and shadowy procession, and the desolate Lybian Mountains drew him hovering over their wastes of stone... And this was only a beginning! Asia, India, and the Southern Seas all lay within reach! All could be visited in turn. The interstellar spaces, the far planets, and the white moon were yet to know!

"We must be thinking of turning soon," he heard the voice of his companion, and then remembered how his own body, hot and feverish, lay in that stuffy little room at the other end of Europe. It was indeed caged—the withered body in the room, and himself in the withered body—doubly caged. He laughed and shuddered. The wind swept through him, licking him clean. He rose again in the ecstasy of free flight, following the lead of the policeman on the homeward journey, and the mountains below became a purple line on the map. In a series of great sweeps they rested on the top of the Pyramid, and then upon the forehead of the Sphinx, and so onwards, touching the earth at intervals, till they heard once more the waves upon the coast-line, and soared aloft again across the sea, racing through Spain and over the Pyrenees. The thin blue outline of the policeman kept ever at his side.

"From all the far blue hills of heaven these winds of freedom blow!" he shouted into space, following it with a peal of laughter that made his guide circle round and round him, chuckling as he flew. A curious, silvery chuckle it was—yet it sounded as though it came to him through a much greater distance than before. It came, as it were, through barriers...

The picture of the bird-fancier's shop came again vividly before him. He saw the beseeching and frightened little eyes; heard the ceaseless pattering of the imprisoned feet, wings beating against the bars, and soft furry bodies pushing vainly to get out. He saw the red face of Theodore Spinks, the proprietor, gloating over the scene of captive life that gave him the means to live—the means to enjoy his own little measure of freedom. He saw the sea-gull drooping in its corner, and the owl, its eyes filled with the dust of the street, its feathered ears twitching;—and then he thought again of the caged human beings of the world—men, women and children, and a pain, like the pain of a whole universe, burned in his soul and set his heart aflame with yearning…to set them all instantly free.

And, unable to find words to give expression to what he felt, he found relief again in his strange, impetuous singing.

Simon Parnacute, Professor of Political Economy, sang in mid-heaven! But this was the last vivid memory he knew. It all began to fade a little after that. It changed swiftly like a dream when the body nears the point of waking. He tried to seize and hold it, to delay the moment when it must end; but the power was beyond him. He felt heavy and tired, and flew closer to the ground; the intervals between the curves of flight grew smaller and smaller, the impetus weaker and weaker as he became every moment more dense and stupid. His progress across the fields of the south of England, as he made his way almost laboriously homewards, became rather a series of long, low leaps than actual flight. More and more often he found himself obliged to touch the earth to acquire the necessary momentum. The big policeman seemed suddenly to have quite melted away into the blue of night.

Then he heard a door open in the sky over his head. A star came down rather too close and half blinded his eyes. Instinctively he called for help to his friend, the world-policeman.

"It's time for your soup now," was the only answer he got. And it did not seem the right answer, or the right voice either. A terror of being permanently lost came over him, and he cried out again louder than before.

"And the medicine first," dropped the thin, shrill voice out of endless space.

It was not the policeman's voice at all. He knew now, and understood.

A sensation of weariness, of sickening disgust and boredom came over him. He looked up. The sky had turned white; he saw curtains and walls and a bright lamp with a red shade. This was the star that had nearly blinded him—a lamp merely, in a sick-room!

And, standing at the farther end of the room, he saw the figure of the nurse in cap and apron. Below him lay his body in the bed. His sensation of disgust and boredom became a positive horror. But he sank down exhausted into it—into his cage.

"Take this soup, sir, after the medicine, and then perhaps you'll get another bit of sleep," the nurse was saying with gentle authority, bending over him.

IV

The progress of Professor Parnacute towards recovery was slow and tedious, for the illness had been severe and it left him with a dangerously weak heart. And at night he still had the delights of the flying dreams. Only, by this time, he had learned to fly alone. His phantom friend, the big World-Policeman, no longer accompanied him.

And his chief occupation during these weary hours of convalescence was curious and, the nurse considered, not very suitable for an invalid: for he spent the time with endless calculations, poring over the list of his few investments, and adding up times without number the total of his savings of nearly forty years. The bed was strewn with papers and documents; pencils were always getting lost among the clothes; and each time the nurse collected the paraphernalia and put them aside, he would wait till she was out of the room, and then crawl over to the table and carry them all back into bed with him.

Then, finally, she gave up fighting with him, and acquiesced, for his restlessness increased and he could not sleep unless his beloved half-sheets and pencils lay strewn upon the counterpane within instant reach.

Even to the least observant it was clear that the Professor was hatching the preliminary details of a profound plot.

And his very first visitor, as soon as he was permitted to see anybody, was a gentleman with parchment skin and hard, dry, peeping eyes who came by special request—a solicitor, from the firm of Messrs. Costa & Delay.

"I will ascertain the price of the shop and stock-in-trade and inform you of the result at the earliest opportunity, Professor Parnacute," said the man of law in his gritty, professional voice, as he at length took his departure and left the sick-room with the expressionless face of one to whom the eccentricities of human nature could never be new or surprising.

"Thank you; I shall be *most* anxious to hear," replied the other, turning in his long easy-chair to save his papers, and at the same time to defend himself against the chiding of the good-natured nurse.

"I knew I should have to pay for it," he murmured, thinking of his original sin; "but I hope,"—here he again consulted his pencilled figures— "I think I can manage it—just. Though with Consols so low—" He fell to musing again. "Still, I can always sub-let the shop, of course, as they suggest," he concluded with a sigh, turning to appeal to the bewildered nurse and finding for the first time that she had gone out of the room.

He fell to pondering deeply. Presently the "list enclosed" by the solicitors caught his eye among the pillows, and he began listlessly to examine it. It was type-written and covered several sheets of foolscap. It was split up into divisions headed as "Lot 1, Lot 2, Lot 3," and so on. He began to read slowly half aloud to himself; then with increasing excitement—

"50 Linnets, guaranteed not straight from the fields; *all caged.*"
"10 fierce singing Linnets."
"10 grand cock Throstles, *just on song.*"
"5 Pear-Tree Goldfinches, with deep, square blazes, well buttoned and mooned."
"4 Devonshire Woodlarks, guaranteed full song; *caged three months.*"

The Professor sat up and gripped the paper tightly. His face wore a pained, intent expression. A convulsive movement of his fingers, automatic perhaps, crumpled the sheet and nearly tore it across. He went on reading, shedding rugs and pillows as though they oppressed him. His breath came a little faster.

"5 cock Blackbirds, full plumage, *lovely songsters.*"
"1 Song-Thrush, show-cage and hamper; *splendid whistler,* picked bird."
"1 beautiful, large upstanding singing Skylark; *sings all day; been caged positively five months.*"

Simon Parnacute uttered a curious little cry. It was deep down in his throat. He was conscious of a burning desire to be rich—a millionaire; powerful—an autocratic monarch. After a pause he brought back his attention with an effort to the type-written page and the consideration of further "Lots"—

"3 cock Skylarks; can hear them 200 yards off when singing."

"*Two hundred yards off when singing,*" muttered the Professor into his one remaining pillow. He read on, kicking his feet, somewhat viciously for a sick man, against the wicker rest at the end of the lounge chair.

"1 special, select, singing cock Skylark; guaranteed caged three months; *sings his wild note.*"

He suddenly dashed the list aside. The whole chair creaked and groaned with the violence of his movement. He kicked three times running at the wicker foot-rest, and evidently rejoiced that it was still stiff enough to make it worth while to kick again—harder.

"Oh, that I had all the money in the world!" he cried to himself, letting his eyes wander to the window and the clear blue spaces between the clouds; "all the money in the world!" he repeated with growing excitement. He saw one of London's sea-gulls circling high, high up. He watched it for some minutes, till it sailed against a dazzling bit of white cloud and was lost to view.

"'*Sings his wild note*'—'*guaranteed caged three months*'—'*can be heard two hundred yards off.*'" The phrases burned in his brain like consuming flames.

And so the list went on. He was glancing over the last page when his eye fell suddenly upon an item that described a lot of—

"8 Linnets caged four months; *raving with song.*"

He dropped the list, rose with difficulty from his chair and paced the room, muttering to himself "raving with song, raving with song, raving with song." His hollow cheeks were flushed, his eyes aglow.

"*Caged, caged, caged,*" he repeated under his breath, while his thoughts travelled to that racing flight across Europe, over seas and mountains.

"*Sings his wild note!*" He heard again the whistling wind about his ears as he flew through the zones of heated air above the desert sands.

"*Raving with song!*" He remembered the passion of his own cry—that strange lyrical outburst of his heart when the magic of freedom caught him, and he had soared at will through the unchartered regions of the night.

And then he saw once more the blinking owl, its eyes blinded by the dust of the London street, its feathery ears twitching as it heard the wind sighing past the open doorway of the dingy shop. And again the thrush looked into his face and poured out the rapture of its spring song.

And half-an-hour later he was so exhausted by the unwonted emotion and exercise that the nurse herself was obliged to write at his dictation the letter he sent in reply to the solicitors, Messrs. Costa & Delay in Southampton Row.

But the letter was posted that night and the Professor, still mumbling to himself about "having to pay for it," went to bed with the first hour of the darkness, and plunged straight into another of his delightful flying dreams almost the very moment his eyes had closed.

V

"...Thus, all the animals have been disposed of according to your instructions," ran the final letter from the solicitors, "and we beg to append list of items so allotted, together with country addresses to which they have been sent. We think you may feel assured that they are now in homes where they will be well cared for.

"We still retain the following animals against your further instructions—

2 Zonure Lizards,
1 Angulated Tortoise,
2 Mealy Rosellas,
2 Scaly-breasted Lorikeets.

"With regard to these we should advise...

"The caged birds, meanwhile, which you intend the children shall release, are being cared for satisfactorily; and the premises will be ready for taking over as from June 1..."

And, with the assistance of the nurse, he then began to issue a steady stream of letters to the parents of children he knew in the country, carefully noting and tabulating the replies, and making out little white labels inscribed in plain lettering with the words "Lot 1," "Lot 2," and so on, precisely as though he were in the animal business himself, and were getting ready for a sale.

But the sale which took place a fortnight later on June 1 was no ordinary sale.

It was a brilliant hot day when Simon Parnacute, still worn and shaky from his recent illness, made his way towards the shop of the "retired" bird-fancier. The sale of the premises and stock-in-trade, and the high price obtained, had made quite a stir in the "Fancy," but of that the Professor was sublimely ignorant as he crossed the street in front of a truculent motor-omnibus and stood before the dingy three-storey red-brick house.

He produced the key sent to him by Messrs. Costa & Delay, and opened the door. It was cool after the glare of the burning street, and delightfully silent. He remembered the chorus of crying birds that had greeted his last appearance. The silence now was eloquent.

"Good, good," he said to himself, with a quiet smile, as he noticed the temporary counter built across the front room for cloaks and parcels, "very good indeed."

Then he went upstairs, climbing painfully, for he was still easily exhausted. There was hardly a stick of furniture in the house, nor an inch of carpet on the floor and stairs, but the rooms had been swept and scrubbed; everything was fresh and scrupulously clean, and the tenant to whom he was to sub-let could have no fault to find on that score.

In the first-floor rooms he saw with pleasure the flowers arranged about the boards as he had directed. The air was sweet and perfumed. The windows at the back—the sills deep with jars of roses—opened upon a small bit of green garden, and Parnacute looked out and saw the blue sky and the clouds floating lazily across it.

"Good, very good," he exclaimed again, sitting down on the stairs a moment to recover his breath. The excitement and the heat of the day tired him. And, as he sat, he put his hand to his ear and listened attentively. A sound of birds singing reached him faintly from the upper part of the house.

"Ah!" he said, drawing a deep breath, and colour coining into his cheeks. "Ah! Now I hear them."

The sound of singing came nearer, as on a passing wind. He climbed laboriously to the top floor, and then, after resting again, scrambled up a ladder through an open skylight on to the roof. The moment he put his perspiring face above the tiles a wild chorus of singing birds greeted him with a sound like a whole country-side in spring.

"If only my friend, the park policeman, could see this!" he said aloud, with a delighted chuckle, "and hear it!" He sought a precarious resting-place upon the butt of a chimney-stack, mopping his forehead.

All around him the sea of London roofs and chimneys rolled away in a black sea, but here, like an oasis in a desert, was a roof of limited extent, and not very high compared to others, converted into a perfect garden. Flowers—but why describe them, when he himself did not even know the names? It was enough that his orders had been carried out to his entire satisfaction, and that this little roof was a world of living colour, moving in the wind, scenting the air, welcoming the sunshine.

Everywhere among the pots and boxes of flowers stood the cages. And in the cages the thrushes and blackbirds, the larks and linnets, poured their hearts out with a chorus of song that was more exquisite, he thought, than anything he had ever heard. And there in the corner by the big chimney, carefully shaded from the glare, stood the large cage containing the owls.

"I can almost believe they have guessed my purpose after all," exclaimed the Professor.

For a long time he sat there, leaning against the chimney, oblivious of a blackened collar, listening to the singing, and feasting his eyes upon the garden of flowers all about him. Then the sound of a bell ringing down-stairs roused him suddenly into action, and he climbed with difficulty down again to the hall door.

"Here they come," he thought, greatly excited. "Dear me, I do trust I shall not make any mistakes."

He felt in his pocket for his note-book, and then opened the door into the street.

"Oh, it's only you!" he exclaimed, as his nurse came in with her arms full of parcels.

"Only me," she laughed, "but I've brought the lemonade and the biscuits. The others will be here now any minute. It's after three. There's just time to arrange the glasses and plates. We must expect about fifty according to the letters you got. And mind you don't get over-tired."

"Oh, I'm all right!" he answered.

She ran up-stairs. Before her steps had sounded once on the floor above, a carriage-and-pair stopped at the door, and a footman came up smartly and asked if Professor Parnacute was at home.

"Indeed I am," answered the old man, blushing and laughing at the same time, and then going down himself to the carriage to welcome the little girl and boy who got out. He bowed stiffly and awkwardly to the pretty lady in the victoria, who thanked him for his kindness with a speech he did not hear properly, and then led his callers into the house. They were very shy at first, and hardly knew what to make of it all, but once inside, the boy's sense of adventure was stirred by the sight of the empty shop, and the counter, and the strange array of flowers upon the floor.

He remembered the letter his father had read out from Professor Parnacute a week ago.

"My Lot is No. 7, isn't it, Mr. Professor?" he cried. "I let out a cage of linnets, and get a guinea-pig and a mealy-something-or-other as a present, don't I?"

Mr. Parnacute, shaky and beaming, consulted his note-book hurriedly, and replied that this was "perfectly correct."

"Master Edwin Burton," he read out; "to release—Lot 7. To take away—one guinea-pig, and one mealy rosella."

"I'm Lot 8, please," piped the voice of the little girl, standing with wide-open eyes beside him.

"Oh, are you, my dear?" said he; "yes, yes, I believe you are." He fumbled anew with the note-book. "Here it is," he added, reading aloud again—

"Miss Angelina Burton;" he peered closely in the gloom to decipher the writing; "To release—Lot 8—that's woodlarks, my dear, you know. To take away—one angulated tortoise. Quite correct, yes; quite correct."

He called to the nurse up-stairs to show the children their presents hidden away in boxes among the flowers—their rosella and tortoise—and then went again to the door to receive his other guests, who now began to arrive in a steady stream. To the number of twenty or thirty they came, and not one of them appeared to be much over twelve. And the majority of them left their elders at the door and came in unattended.

The marshalling of this array of youngsters among the birds and flowers was a matter of some difficulty, but here the nurse came to the Professor's assistance with energy and experience, so that his strength was economized and the children were arranged without danger to any one.

And upon that little roof the sight was certainly a unique one. There they all stood, an extraordinary patchwork of colour for the tiles of South-west London—the bright frocks of the girls, the plumage of the birds, the blues and yellows and scarlets of the flowers; while the singing and voices sent up a chorus that brought numerous surprised faces to the windows of the higher buildings about them, and made people stop in the street below and ask themselves with startled faces where in the world these sounds came from this still June afternoon!

"Now!" cried Simon Parnacute, when all lots and owners had been placed carefully side by side. "The moment I give the word of command, open your cages and let the prisoners escape! And point in the direction of the park."

The children stooped and picked up their cages. The voices and the singing in a hundred busy little throats ceased. A hush fell upon the roof and upon the strange gathering. The sun poured blazingly down over everything, and the Professor's face streamed.

"One," he cried, his voice tremulous with excitement, "two, three—and away!"

There was a rattling sound of opening doors and wire bars—and then a sudden burst of half-suppressed, long-drawn "Ahhhhs." At once there followed a rush of fluttering feathers, a rapid vibration of the air, and the small host of prisoners shot out like a cloud into the air, and a moment later with a great whirring of wings had disappeared over the walls beyond the forest of chimneys and were lost to view. Blackbirds, thrushes, linnets and finches were gone in a twinkling, so that the eye could hardly follow them. Only the sea-gulls, puzzled by their sudden freedom, with wings still stiff after their cramped quarters, lingered on the edge of the roof for a few minutes, and looked about them in a dazed fashion, until they, too, realized their liberty and sailed off into the open sky to search for splendours of the sea.

A second hush, deeper even than the first, fell over all for a moment, and then the children with one accord burst into screams of delight and explanation, shouting, for all who cared to listen, the details of how their birds, respectively, had flown; where they had gone; what they thought and looked like; and a hundred other details as to where they would build their nests and the number of eggs they would lay.

And then came the descent for the presents and refreshment. One by one they approached the Professor, holding out the tickets with the number of their "lot" and the description of animal they were to receive and find a home for. The few accompanied by elders came first.

"The owls, I think?" said the pink-faced clergyman who had chaperoned other children besides his own, picking his way across the roof as the crowd tapered off down the skylight. "Two owls," he repeated, with a smile. "In the windy towers of my belfry under the Mendips, I hope—"

"Oh, the very thing, the very place," replied Parnacute, with pleasure, remembering his correspondent. For, of course, the owls had not been released with the other birds.

"And for my little girl you thought, perhaps, a lorikeet—"

"A scaly-breasted lorikeet, papa," she interrupted, with a degree of excitement too intense for smiles, and pronouncing the name as she had learned it—in a single word; "*and* a lizard."

They moved off towards the trap-door, the owl cage under the clergyman's arm. They would receive the lorikeet and lizard downstairs from the nurse on presenting their ticket.

"And remember," added Parnacute slyly, addressing the child, "to comb their feathered trousers with a *very* fine comb!"

The clergyman turned a moment at the skylight as he helped the owls and children to squeeze through.

"I shall have something to say about this in my sermon next Sunday," he said. He smiled as his head disappeared.

"Oh, but, my dear sir—" cried the Professor, tripping over a flower-pot in his pleasure and embarrassment, and just reaching the skylight in time to add, "And, remember, there are cakes and lemonade on the floor below!"

The animals had all been provided with happy homes; the last cab had driven away, and the nurse had gone to find the flower-man. Parnacute had strewn the roof with food, and with moss and hair-material for nesting, in case any of the birds returned. He stood alone and watched the sunset pour its gold over the myriad houses—the cages of the men and women of London town. He felt exhausted; the sky was soothing and pleasant to behold...

He sat down to rest, conscious of a great weakness now that the excitement was over and the reaction had begun to set in. Probably he had exerted himself unduly.

His mind reverted to his first impulsive eccentricity of two months before.

"I knew I should pay for it," he murmured, with a smile, "and I have. But it was worth it."

He stopped abruptly and caught his breath a moment. He was thoroughly over-tired; the excitement of it all had been too much for him. He must get home as quickly as possible to rest. The nurse would be back any minute now.

A sound of wings rapidly beating the air passed overhead, and he looked up and saw a flight of pigeons wheeling by. He fancied, too, that he just caught the notes of a thrush singing far away in the park at the end of the street. He recalled the phrases of that dreadfully haunting list. "Wild singing note," "Can be heard two hundred yards off," "Raving with song." A momentary spasm passed through his frame. Far up in the air the sea-gulls still circled, making their way with all the splendour of real freedom to the sea.

"To-night," he thought, "they will roost on the marshes, or perched upon the lonely cliffs. Good, good, *very* good!"

He got up, stiffly and with difficulty, to watch the pigeons better, and to hear the thrush, and, as he did so, the bell rang down-stairs to admit the nurse and the flower-man.

"Odd," he thought; "I gave her the key!"

He made his way towards the skylight, picking his way with uncertain tread between the flower-boxes; but before he could reach it a head and shoulders suddenly appeared above the opening.

"Odd," he thought again, "that she should have come up so quickly—"

But he did not complete the thought. It was not the nurse at all. A very different figure followed the emerging head and shoulders, and there in front of him on the roof stood—a policeman.

It was *the* policeman.

"Oh," said Parnacute quietly, "it's *you!*" A wild tumult of yearning and happiness caught at his heart and made it impossible to think of anything else to say.

The big blue figure smiled his shining smile.

"One more flight, sir," said the silvery, ringing voice respectfully, "and the last."

The pigeons wheeled past overhead with a sharp whirring of wings. Both men looked up significantly at their vanishing outline over the roofs. A deep silence fell between them. Parnacute was aware that he was smiling and contented.

"I am quite ready, I think," he said in a low tone. "You promised—"

"Yes," returned the other in the voice that was like the ringing of a silver gong, "I promised—without pain."

The Policeman moved softly over to him; he made no sound; the constellations of Orion and the Pleiades shone on his coat-collar. There was another whirring rush as the pigeons swept again overhead and wheeled abruptly, but this time there was no one on the roof to watch them go, and it seemed that their flying wedge, as they flashed away, was larger and darker than before...

And when the nurse returned with the man for the boxes, they came up to the roof and found the body of Simon Parnacute, late Professor of Political Economy, lying face upwards among the flowers. The human cage was empty. Someone had opened the door.

THE END

THE WOLVES OF GOD

and Other Fey Stories

By Algernon Blackwood
and Wilfred Wilson

To the Memory
of
Our Camp-Fires in the Wilderness

THE WOLVES OF GOD

I

As the little steamer entered the bay of Kettletoft in the Orkneys the beach at Sanday appeared so low that the houses almost seemed to be standing in the water; and to the big, dark man leaning over the rail of the upper deck the sight of them came with a pang of mingled pain and pleasure. The scene, to his eyes, had not changed. The houses, the low shore, the flat treeless country beyond, the vast open sky, all looked exactly the same as when he left the island thirty years ago to work for the Hudson Bay Company in distant N. W. Canada. A lad of eighteen then, he was now a man of forty-eight, old for his years, and this was the home-coming he had so often dreamed about in the lonely wilderness of trees where he had spent his life. Yet his grim face wore an anxious rather than a tender expression. The return was perhaps not quite as he had pictured it.

Jim Peace had not done too badly, however, in the Company's service. For an islander, he would be a rich man now; he had not married, he had saved the greater part of his salary, and even in the far-away Post where he had spent so many years there had been occasional opportunities of the kind common to new, wild countries where life and law are in the making. He had not hesitated to take them. None of the big Company Posts, it was true, had come his way, nor had he risen very high in the service; in another two years his turn would have come, yet he had left of his own accord before those two years were up. His decision, judging by the strength in the features, was not due to impulse; the move had been deliberately weighed and calculated; he had renounced his opportunity after full reflection. A man with those steady eyes, with that square jaw and determined mouth, certainly did not act without good reason.

A curious expression now flickered over his weather-hardened face as he saw again his childhood's home, and the return, so often dreamed about, actually took place at last. An uneasy light flashed for a moment in the deep-set grey eyes, but was quickly gone again, and the tanned visage recovered its accustomed look of stern composure. His keen sight took in a dark knot of figures on the landing-pier—his brother, he knew, among them. A wave of home-sickness swept over him. He longed to see his brother again, the old farm, the sweep of open country, the sand-dunes, and the breaking seas. The smell of long-forgotten days came to his nostrils with its sweet, painful pang of youthful memories.

How fine, he thought, to be back there in the old familiar fields of childhood, with sea and sand about him instead of the smother of endless woods that ran a thousand miles without a break. He was glad in particular that no trees were visible, and that rabbits scampering among the dunes were the only wild animals he need ever meet....

Those thirty years in the woods, it seemed, oppressed his mind; the forests, the countless multitudes of trees, had wearied him. His nerves, perhaps, had suffered finally. Snow, frost and sun, stars, and the wind had been his companions during the long days and endless nights in his lonely Post, but chiefly—trees. Trees, trees, trees! On the whole, he had preferred them in stormy weather, though, in another way, their rigid hosts, 'mid the deep silence of still days, had been equally oppressive. In the clear sunlight of a windless day they assumed a waiting, listening, watching aspect that had something spectral in it, but when in motion—well, he preferred a moving animal to one that stood stock-still and stared. Wind, moreover, in a million trees, even the lightest breeze, drowned all other sounds—the howling of the wolves, for instance, in winter, or the ceaseless harsh barking of the husky dogs he so disliked.

Even on this warm September afternoon a slight shiver ran over him as the background of dead years loomed up behind the present scene. He thrust the picture back, deep down inside himself. The self-control, the strong, even violent will that the face betrayed, came into operation instantly. The background was background; it belonged to what was past, and the past was over and done with. It was dead. Jim meant it to stay dead.

The figure waving to him from the pier was his brother. He knew Tom instantly; the years had dealt easily with him in this quiet island; there was no startling, no unkindly change, and a deep emotion, though unexpressed, rose in his heart. It was good to be home again, he realized, as he sat presently in the cart, Tom holding the reins, driving slowly back to the farm at the north end of the island. Everything he found familiar, yet at the same time strange. They passed the school where he used to go as a little bare-legged boy; other boys were now learning their lessons exactly as he used to do. Through the open window he could hear the droning voice of the schoolmaster, who, though invisible, wore the face of Mr. Lovibond, his own teacher.

"Lovibond?" said Tom, in reply to his question. "Oh, he's been dead these twenty years. He went south, you know—Glasgow, I think it was, or Edinburgh. He got typhoid."

Stands of golden plover were to be seen as of old in the fields, or flashing overhead in swift flight with a whir of wings, wheeling and turning together like one huge bird. Down on the empty shore a curlew cried. Its piercing note rose clear above the noisy clamour of the gulls. The sun played softly on the quiet sea, the air was keen but pleasant, the tang of salt mixed sweetly with the clean smells of open country that he knew so well. Nothing of essentials had changed, even the low clouds beyond the healing uplands were the clouds of childhood.

They came presently to the sand-dunes, where rabbits sat at their burrow-mouths, or ran helter-skelter across the road in front of the slow cart.

"They're safe till the colder weather comes and trapping begins," he mentioned. It all came back to him in detail.

"And they know it, too—the canny little beggars," replied Tom. "Any rabbits out where you've been?" he asked casually.

"Not to hurt you," returned his brother shortly.

Nothing seemed changed, although everything seemed different. He looked upon the old, familiar things, but with other eyes. There were, of course, changes, alterations, yet so slight, in a way so odd and curious, that they evaded him; not being of the physical order, they reported to his soul, not to his mind. But his soul, being troubled, sought to deny the changes; to admit them meant to admit a change in himself he had determined to conceal even if he could not entirely deny it.

"Same old place, Tom," came one of his rare remarks. "The years ain't done much to it." He looked into his brother's face a moment squarely, "Nor to you, either, Tom," he added, affection and tenderness just touching his voice and breaking through a natural reserve that was almost taciturnity.

His brother returned the look; and something in that instant passed between the two men, something of understanding that no words had hinted at, much less expressed. The tie was real, they loved each other, they were loyal, true, steadfast fellows. In youth they had known no secrets. The shadow that now passed and vanished left a vague trouble in both hearts.

"The forests," said Tom slowly, "'have made a silent man of you, Jim. You'll miss them here, I'm thinking."

"Maybe," was the curt reply, "but I guess not."

His lips snapped to as though they were of steel and could never open again, while the tone he used made Tom realize that the subject was not one his brother cared to talk about particularly. He was surprised, therefore, when, after a pause, Jim returned to it of his own accord. He was sitting a little sideways as he spoke, taking in the scene with hungry eyes. "It's a queer thing," he observed, "to look round and see nothing but clean empty land, and not a single tree in sight. You see, it don't look natural quite."

Again his brother was struck by the tone of voice, but this time by something else as well he could not name. Jim was excusing himself, explaining. The manner, too, arrested him. And thirty years disappeared as though they had not been, for it was thus Jim acted as a boy when there was something unpleasant he had to say and wished to get it over. The tone, the gesture, the manner, all were there. He was edging up to something he wished to say, yet dared not utter.

"You've had enough of trees then?" Tom said sympathetically, trying to help, "and things?"

The instant the last two words were out he realized that they had been drawn from him instinctively, and that it was the anxiety of deep affection which had prompted them. He had guessed without knowing he had guessed, or rather, without intention or attempt to guess. Jim had a secret. Love's clairvoyance had discovered it, though not yet its hidden terms.

"I have— " began the other, then paused, evidently to choose his words with care. "I've had enough of trees." He was about to speak of something that his brother had unwittingly touched upon in his chance phrase, but instead of finding the words he sought, he gave a sudden start, his breath caught sharply. "What's that?" he exclaimed, jerking his body round so abruptly that Tom automatically pulled the reins. "What is it?"

"A dog barking," Tom answered, much surprised. "A farm dog barking. Why? What did you think it was?" he asked, as he flicked the horse to go on again. "You made me jump," he added, with a laugh. "You're used to huskies, ain't you?"

"It sounded so—not like a dog, I mean," came the slow explanation. "It's long since I heard a sheep-dog bark, I suppose it startled me."

"Oh, it's a dog all right," Tom assured him comfortingly, for his heart told him infallibly the kind of tone to use. And presently, too, he chaired the subject in his blunt, honest fashion, knowing that, also, was the right and kindly thing to do. He pointed out the old farms as they drove along, his brother silent again, sitting stiff and rigid at his side. "And it's good to have you back, Jim, from those outlandish places. There are not too many of the family left now—just you and I, as a matter of fact."

"Just you and I," the other repeated gruffly, but in a sweetened tone that proved he appreciated the ready sympathy and tact. "We'll stick together, Tom, eh? Blood's thicker than water, ain't it? I've learnt that much, anyhow."

The voice had something gentle and appealing in it, something his brother heard now for the first time. An elbow nudged into his side, and Tom knew the gesture was not solely a sign of affection, but grew partly also from the comfort born of physical contact when the heart is anxious. The touch, like the last words, conveyed an appeal for help. Tom was so surprised he couldn't believe it quite.

Scared! Jim scared! The thought puzzled and afflicted him who knew his brother's character inside out, his courage, his presence of mind in danger, his resolution. Jim frightened seemed an impossibility, a contradiction in terms; he was the kind of man who did not know the meaning of fear, who shrank from nothing, whose spirits rose highest when things appeared most hopeless. It must, indeed, be an uncommon, even a terrible danger that could shake such nerves; yet Tom saw the signs and read them clearly. Explain them he could not, nor did he try. All he knew with certainty was that his brother, sitting now beside him in the cart, hid a secret terror in his heart. Sooner or later, in his own good time, he would share it with him.

He ascribed it, this simple Orkney farmer, to those thirty years of loneliness and exile in wild desolate places, without companionship, without the society of women, with only Indians, husky dogs, a few trappers or fur-dealers like himself, but none of the wholesome, natural influences that sweeten life within reach. Thirty years was a long, long time. He began planning schemes to help. Jim must see people as much as possible, and his mind ran quickly over the men and women available. In women the neighbourhood was not rich, but there were several men of the right sort who might be useful, good fellows all. There was John Rossiter, another old Hudson Bay man, who had been factor at Cartwright, Labrador, for many years, and had returned long ago to spend his last days in civilization. There was Sandy McKay, also back from a long spell of rubber-planting in Malay.... Tom was still busy making plans when they reached the old farm and presently sat down to their first meal together since that early breakfast thirty years ago before Jim caught the steamer that bore him off to exile—an exile that now returned him with nerves unstrung and a secret terror hidden in his heart.

"I'll ask no questions," he decided. "Jim will tell me in his own good time. And meanwhile, I'll get him to see as many folks as possible." He meant it too; yet not only for his brother's sake. Jim's terror was so vivid it had touched his own heart too.

"Ah, a man can open his lungs here and breathe!" exclaimed Jim, as the two came out after supper and stood before the house, gazing across the open country. He drew a deep breath as though to prove his assertion, exhaling with slow satisfaction again. "It's good to see a clear horizon and to know there's all that water between—between me and where I've been." He turned his face to watch the plover in the sky, then looked towards the distant shore-line where the sea was just visible in the long evening light. "There can't be too much water for me," he added, half to himself. "I guess they can't cross water—not that much water at any rate."

Tom stared, wondering uneasily what to make of it.

"At the trees again, Jim?" he said laughingly. He had overheard the last words, though spoken low, and thought it best not to ignore them altogether. To be natural was the right way, he believed, natural and cheery. To make a joke of anything unpleasant, he felt, was to make it less serious. "I've never seen a tree come across the Atlantic yet, except as a mast—dead," he added.

"I wasn't thinking of the trees just then," was the blunt reply, "but of—something else. The damned trees are nothing, though I hate the sight of 'em. Not of much account, anyway"—as though he compared them mentally with another thing. He puffed at his pipe, a moment.

"They certainly can't move," put in his brother, "nor swim either."

"Nor another thing," said Jim, his voice thick suddenly, but not with smoke, and his speech confused, though the idea in his mind was certainly clear as daylight. "Things can't hide behind 'em—can they?"

"Not much cover hereabouts, I admit," laughed Tom, though the look in his brother's eyes made his laughter as short as it sounded unnatural.

"That's so," agreed the other. "But what I meant was"—he threw out his chest, looked about him with an air of intense relief, drew in another deep breath, and again exhaled with satisfaction—"if there are no trees, there's no hiding."

It was the expression on the rugged, weathered face that sent the blood in a sudden gulping rush from his brother's heart. He had seen men frightened, seen men afraid before they were actually frightened; he had also seen men stiff with terror in the face both of natural and so-called supernatural things; but never in his life before had he seen the look of unearthly dread that now turned his brother's face as white as chalk and yet put the glow of fire in two haunted burning eyes.

Across the darkening landscape the sound of distant barking had floated to them on the evening wind.

"It's only a farm-dog barking." Yet it was Jim's deep, quiet voice that said it, one hand upon his brother's arm.

"That's all," replied Tom, ashamed that he had betrayed himself, and realizing with a shock of surprise that it was Jim who now played the role of comforter—a startling change in their relations. "Why, what did you think it was?"

He tried hard to speak naturally and easily, but his voice shook. So deep was the brothers' love and intimacy that they could not help but share. Jim lowered his great head. "I thought," he whispered, his grey beard touching the other's cheek, "maybe it was the wolves"—an agony of terror made both voice and body tremble—"the Wolves of God!"

2

The interval of thirty years had been bridged easily enough; it was the secret that left the open gap neither of them cared or dared to cross. Jim's reason for hesitation lay within reach of guesswork, but Tom's silence was more complicated.

With strong, simple men, strangers to affectation or pretence, reserve is a real, almost a sacred thing. Jim offered nothing more; Tom asked no single question. In the latter's mind lay, for one thing, a singular intuitive certainty: that if he knew the truth he would lose his brother. How, why, wherefore, he had no notion; whether by death, or because, having told an awful thing, Jim would hide—physically or mentally—he knew not, nor even asked himself. No subtlety lay in Tom, the Orkney farmer. He merely felt that a knowledge of the truth involved separation which was death.

Day and night, however, that extraordinary phrase which, at its first hearing, had frozen his blood, ran on beating in his mind. With it came always the original, nameless horror that had held him motionless where he stood, his brother's bearded lips against his ear: *The Wolves of God*. In some dim way, he sometimes felt—tried to persuade himself, rather—the horror did not belong to the phrase alone, but was a sympathetic echo of what Jim felt himself. It had entered his own mind and heart. They had always shared in this same strange, intimate way. The deep brotherly tie accounted for it. Of the possible transference of thought and emotion he knew nothing, but this was what he meant perhaps.

At the same time he fought and strove to keep it out, not because it brought uneasy and distressing feelings to him, but because he did not wish to pry, to ascertain, to discover his brother's secret as by some kind of subterfuge that seemed too near to eavesdropping almost. Also, he wished most earnestly to protect him. Meanwhile, in spite of himself, or perhaps because of himself, he watched his brother as a wild animal watches its young. Jim was the only tie he had on earth. He loved him with a brother's love, and Jim, similarly, he knew, loved him. His job was difficult. Love alone could guide him.

He gave openings, but he never questioned:

"Your letter did surprise me, Jim. I was never so delighted in my life. You had still two years to run."

"I'd had enough," was the short reply. "God, man, it was good to get home again!"

This, and the blunt talk that followed their first meeting, was all Tom had to go upon, while those eyes that refused to shut watched ceaselessly always. There was improvement, unless, which never occurred to Tom, it was self-control; there was no more talk of trees and water, the barking of the dogs passed unnoticed, no reference to the loneliness of the backwoods life passed his lips; he spent his days fishing, shooting, helping with the work of the farm, his evenings smoking over a glass—he was more than temperate—and talking over the days of long ago.

The signs of uneasiness still were there, but they were negative, far more suggestive, therefore, than if open and direct. He desired no company, for instance—an unnatural thing, thought Tom, after so many years of loneliness.

It was this and the awkward fact that he had given up two years before his time was finished, renouncing, therefore, a comfortable pension—it was these two big details that stuck with such unkind persistence in his brother's thoughts. Behind both, moreover, ran ever the strange whispered phrase. What the words meant, or whence they were derived, Tom had no possible inkling. Like the wicked refrain of some forbidden song, they haunted him day and night, even his sleep not free from them entirely. All of which, to the simple Orkney farmer, was so new an experience that he knew not how to deal with it at all. Too strong to be flustered, he was at any rate bewildered. And it was for Jim, his brother, he suffered most.

What perplexed him chiefly, however, was the attitude his brother showed towards old John Rossiter. He could almost have imagined that the two men had met and known each other out in Canada, though Rossiter showed him how impossible that was, both in point of time and of geography as well. He had brought them together within the first few days, and Jim, silent, gloomy, morose, even surly, had eyed him like an enemy. Old Rossiter, the milk of human kindness as thick in his veins as cream, had taken no offence. Grizzled veteran of the wilds, he had served his full term with the Company and now enjoyed his well-earned pension. He was full of stories, reminiscences, adventures of every sort and kind; he knew men and values, had seen strange things that only the true wilderness delivers, and he loved nothing better than to tell them over a glass. He talked with Jim so genially and affably that little response was called for luckily, for Jim was glum and unresponsive almost to rudeness. Old Rossiter noticed nothing. What Tom noticed was, chiefly perhaps, his brother's acute uneasiness. Between his desire to help, his attachment to Rossiter, and his keen personal distress, he knew not what to do or say. The situation was becoming too much for him.

The two families, besides—Peace and Rossiter—had been neighbours for generations, had intermarried freely, and were related in various degrees. He was too fond of his brother to feel ashamed, but he was glad when the visit was over and they were out of their host's house. Jim had even declined to drink with him.

"They're good fellows on the island," said Tom on their way home, "but not specially entertaining, perhaps. We all stick together though. You can trust 'em mostly."

"I never was a talker, Tom," came the gruff reply. "You know that." And Tom, understanding more than he understood, accepted the apology and made generous allowances.

"John likes to talk," he helped him. "He appreciates a good listener."

"It's the kind of talk I'm finished with," was the rejoinder. "The Company and their goings-on don't interest me any more. I've had enough."

Tom noticed other things as well with those affectionate eyes of his that did not want to see yet would not close. As the days drew in, for instance, Jim seemed reluctant to leave the house towards evening. Once the full light of day had passed, he kept indoors. He was eager and ready enough to shoot in the early morning, no matter at what hour he had to get up, but he refused point blank to go with his brother to the lake for an evening flight. No excuse was offered; he simply declined to go.

The gap between them thus widened and deepened, while yet in another sense it grew less formidable. Both knew, that is, that a secret lay between them for the first time in their lives, yet both knew also that at the right and proper moment it would be revealed. Jim only waited till the proper moment came. And Tom understood. His deep, simple love was equal to all emergencies. He respected his brother's reserve. The obvious desire of John Rossiter to talk and ask questions, for instance, he resisted staunchly as far as he was able. Only when he could help and protect his brother did he yield a little. The talk was brief, even monosyllabic; neither the old Hudson Bay fellow nor the Orkney farmer ran to many words:

"He ain't right with himself," offered John, taking his pipe out of his mouth and leaning forward. "That's what I don't like to see." He put a skinny hand on Tom's knee, and looked earnestly into his face as he said it.

"Jim!" replied the other. "Jim ill, you mean!" It sounded ridiculous.

"His mind is sick."

"I don't understand," Tom said, though the truth bit like rough-edged steel into the brother's heart.

"His soul, then, if you like that better."

Tom fought with himself a moment, then asked him to be more explicit.

"More'n I can say," rejoined the laconic old backwoodsman. "I don't know myself. The woods heal some men and make others sick."

"Maybe, John, maybe." Tom fought back his resentment. "You've lived, like him, in lonely places. You ought to know." His mouth shut with a snap, as though he had said too much. Loyalty to his suffering brother caught him strongly. Already his heart ached for Jim. He felt angry with Rossiter for his divination, but perceived, too, that the old fellow meant well and was trying to help him. If he lost Jim, he lost the world—his all.

A considerable pause followed, during which both men puffed their pipes with reckless energy. Both, that is, were a bit excited. Yet both had their code, a code they would not exceed for worlds.

"Jim," added Tom presently, making an effort to meet the sympathy half way, "ain't quite up to the mark, I'll admit that."

There was another long pause, while Rossiter kept his eyes on his companion steadily, though without a trace of expression in them—a habit that the woods had taught him.

"Jim," he said at length, with an obvious effort, "is skeered. And it's the soul in him that's skeered."

Tom wavered dreadfully then. He saw that old Rossiter, experienced backwoodsman and taught by the Company as he was, knew where the secret lay, if he did not yet know its exact terms. It was easy enough to put the question, yet he hesitated, because loyalty forbade.

"It's a dirty outfit somewheres," the old man mumbled to himself.

Tom sprang to his feet. "If you talk that way," he exclaimed angrily, "you're no friend of mine—or his." His anger gained upon him as he said it. "Say that again," he cried, "and I'll knock your teeth—"

He sat back, stunned a moment.

"Forgive me, John," he faltered, shamed yet still angry. "It's pain to me, it's pain. Jim," he went on, after a long breath and a pull at his glass, "Jim is scared, I know it." He waited a moment, hunting for the words that he could use without disloyalty. "But it's nothing he's done himself," he said, "nothing to his discredit. I know *that*."

Old Rossiter looked up, a strange light in his eyes.

"No offence," he said quietly.

"Tell me what you know," cried Tom suddenly, standing up again.

The old factor met his eye squarely, steadfastly. He laid his pipe aside.

"D'ye really want to hear?" he asked in a lowered voice. "Because, if you don't—why, say so right now. I'm all for justice," he added, "and always was."

"Tell me," said Tom, his heart in his mouth. "Maybe, if I knew—I might help him." The old man's words woke fear in him. He well knew his passionate, remorseless sense of justice.

"Help him," repeated the other. "For a man skeered in his soul there ain't no help. But—if you want to hear—I'll tell you."

"Tell me," cried Tom. "I *will* help him," while rising anger fought back rising fear.

John took another pull at his glass.

"Jest between you and me like."

"Between you and me," said Tom. "Get on with it."

There was a deep silence in the little room. Only the sound of the sea came in, the wind behind it.

"The Wolves," whispered old Rossiter. "The Wolves of God."

Tom sat still in his chair, as though struck in the face. He shivered. He kept silent and the silence seemed to him long and curious. His heart was throbbing, the blood in his veins played strange tricks. All he remembered was that old Rossiter had gone on talking. The voice, however, sounded far away and distant. It was all unreal, he felt, as he went homewards across the bleak, wind-swept upland, the sound of the sea for ever in his ears....

Yes, old John Rossiter, damned be his soul, had gone on talking. He had said wild, incredible things. Damned be his soul! His teeth should be smashed for that. It was outrageous, it was cowardly, it was not true.

"Jim," he thought, "my brother, Jim!" as he ploughed his way wearily against the wind. "I'll teach him. I'll teach him to spread such wicked tales!" He referred to Rossiter. "God blast these fellows! They come home from their outlandish places and think they can say anything! I'll knock his yellow dog's teeth....!"

While, inside, his heart went quailing, crying for help, afraid.

He tried hard to remember exactly what old John had said. Round Garden Lake—that's where Jim was located in his lonely Post—there was a tribe of Redskins. They were of unusual type. Malefactors among them—thieves, criminals, murderers—were not punished. They were merely turned out by the Tribe to die.

But how?

The Wolves of God took care of them. What were the Wolves of God? A pack of wolves the Redskins held in awe, a sacred pack, a spirit pack—God curse the man! Absurd, outlandish nonsense! Superstitious humbug! A pack of wolves that punished malefactors, killing but never eating them. "Torn but not eaten," the words came back to him, "white men as well as red. They could even cross the sea...."

"He ought to be strung up for telling such wild yarns. By God—I'll teach him!"

"Jim! My brother, Jim! It's monstrous."

But the old man, in his passionate cold justice, had said a yet more terrible thing, a thing that Tom would never forget, as he never could forgive it: "You mustn't keep him here; you must send him away. We cannot have him on the island." And for that, though he could scarcely believe his ears, wondering afterwards whether he heard aright, for that, the proper answer to which was a blow in the mouth, Tom knew that his old friendship and affection had turned to bitter hatred.

"If I don't kill him, for that cursed lie, may God—and Jim—forgive me!"

3

It was a few days later that the storm caught the islands, making them tremble in their sea-born bed. The wind tearing over the treeless expanse was terrible, the lightning lit the skies. No such rain had ever been known. The building shook and trembled. It almost seemed the sea had burst her limits, and the waves poured in. Its fury and the noises that the wind made affected both the brothers, but Jim disliked the uproar most. It made him gloomy, silent, morose. It made him—Tom perceived it at once—uneasy. "Scared in his soul"—the ugly phrase came back to him.

"God save anyone who's out to-night," said Jim anxiously, as the old farm rattled about his head. Whereupon the door opened as of itself. There was no knock. It flew wide, as if the wind had burst it. Two drenched and beaten figures showed in the gap against the lurid sky— old John Rossiter and Sandy. They laid their fowling pieces down and took off their capes; they had been up at the lake for the evening flight and six birds were in the game bag. So suddenly had the storm come up that they had been caught before they could get home.

And, while Tom welcomed them, looked after their creature wants, and made them feel at home as in duty bound, no visit, he felt at the same time, could have been less opportune. Sandy did not matter—Sandy never did matter anywhere, his personality being negligible—but John Rossiter was the last man Tom wished to see just then. He hated the man; hated that sense of implacable justice that he knew was in him; with the slightest excuse he would have turned him out and sent him on to his own home, storm or no storm. But Rossiter provided no excuse; he was all gratitude and easy politeness, more pleasant and friendly to Jim even than to his brother. Tom set out the whisky and sugar, sliced the lemon, put the kettle on, and furnished dry coats while the soaked garments hung up before the roaring fire that Orkney makes customary even when days are warm.

"'It might be the equinoctials," observed Sandy, "if it wasn't late October." He shivered, for the tropics had thinned his blood.

"This ain't no ordinary storm," put in Rossiter, drying his drenched boots. "It reminds me a bit"—he jerked his head to the window that gave seawards, the rush of rain against the panes half drowning his voice—"reminds me a bit of yonder." He looked up, as though to find someone to agree with him, only one such person being in the room.

"Sure, it ain't," agreed Jim at once, but speaking slowly, "no ordinary storm." His voice was quiet as a child's. Tom, stooping over the kettle, felt something cold go trickling down his back. "It's from acrost the Atlantic too."

"All our big storms come from the sea," offered Sandy, saying just what Sandy was expected to say. His lank red hair lay matted on his forehead, making him look like an unhappy collie dog.

"There's no hospitality," Rossiter changed the talk, "like an islander's," as Tom mixed and filled the glasses. "He don't even ask 'Say when?'" He chuckled in his beard and turned to Sandy, well pleased with the compliment to his host. "Now, in Malay," he added dryly, "it's probably different, I guess." And the two men, one from Labrador, the other from the tropics, fell to bantering one another with heavy humour, while Tom made things comfortable and Jim stood silent with his back to the fire. At each blow of the wind that shook the building, a suitable remark was made, generally by Sandy: "Did you hear that now." "Ninety miles an hour at least." "Good thing you build solid in this country!" while Rossiter occasionally, repeated that it was an "uncommon storm" and that "'it reminded" him of the northern tempests he had known "out yonder."

Tom said little, one thought and one thought only in his heart—the wish that the storm would abate and his guests depart. He felt uneasy about Jim. He hated Rossiter. In the kitchen he had steadied himself already with a good stiff drink, and was now half-way through a second; the feeling was in him that he would need their help before the evening was out. Jim, he noticed, had left his glass untouched. His attention, clearly, went to the wind and the outer night; he added little to the conversation.

"Hark!" cried Sandy's shrill voice. "Did you hear that? That wasn't wind, I'll swear." He sat up, looking for all the world like a dog pricking its ears to something no one else could hear.

"The sea coming over the dunes," said Rossiter. "There'll be an awful tide to-night and a terrible sea off the Swarf. Moon at the full, too." He cocked his head sideways to listen. The roaring was tremendous, waves and wind combining with a result that almost shook the ground. Rain hit the glass with incessant volleys like duck shot.

It was then that Jim spoke, having said no word for a long time.

"It's good there's no trees," he mentioned quietly. "I'm glad of that."

"There'd be fearful damage, wouldn't there?" remarked Sandy. "They might fall on the house too."

But it was the tone Jim used that made Rossiter turn stiffly in his chair, looking first at the speaker, then at his brother. Tom caught both glances and saw the hard keen glitter in the eyes. This kind of talk, he decided, had got to stop, yet how to stop it he hardly knew, for his were not subtle methods, and rudeness to his guests ran too strong against the island customs. He refilled the glasses, thinking in his blunt fashion how best to achieve his object, when Sandy helped the situation without knowing it.

"That's my first," he observed, and all burst out laughing. For Sandy's tenth glass was equally his "first," and he absorbed his liquor like a sponge, yet showed no effects of it until the moment when he would suddenly collapse and sink helpless to the ground. The glass in question, however, was only his third, the final moment still far away

"Three in one and one in three," said Rossiter, amid the general laughter, while Sandy, grave as a judge, half emptied it at a single gulp. Good-natured, obtuse as a cart-horse, the tropics, it seemed, had first worn out his nerves, then removed them entirely from his body. "That's Malay theology, I guess," finished Rossiter. And the laugh broke out again. Whereupon, setting his glass down, Sandy offered his usual explanation that the hot lands had thinned his blood, that he felt the cold in these "arctic islands," and that alcohol was a necessity of life with him. Tom, grateful for the unexpected help, encouraged him to talk, and Sandy, accustomed to neglect as a rule, responded readily. Having saved the situation, however, he now unwittingly led it back into the danger zone.

"A night for tales, eh?" he remarked, as the wind came howling with a burst of strangest noises against the house. "Down there in the States," he went on, "they'd say the evil spirits were out. They're a superstitious crowd, the natives. I remember once—" And he told a tale, half foolish, half interesting, of a mysterious track he had seen when following buffalo in the jungle. It ran close to the spoor of a wounded buffalo for miles, a track unlike that of any known animal, and the natives, though unable to name it, regarded it with awe. It was a good sign, a kill was certain. They said it was a spirit track.

"You got your buffalo?" asked Tom.

"Found him two miles away, lying; dead. The mysterious spoor came to an end close beside the carcass. It didn't continue."

"And that reminds me—" began old Rossiter, ignoring Tom's attempt to introduce another subject. He told them of the haunted island at Eagle River, and a tale of the man who would not stay buried on another island off the coast. From that he went on to describe the strange man-beast that hides in the deep forests of Labrador, manifesting but rarely, and dangerous to men who stray too far from camp, men with a passion for wild life over-strong in their blood—the great mythical Wendigo. And while he talked, Tom noticed that Sandy used each pause as a good moment for a drink, but that Jim's glass still remained untouched.

The atmosphere of incredible things, thus, grew in the little room, much as it gathers among the shadows round a forest camp-fire when men who have seen strange places of the world give tongue about them, knowing they will not be laughed at an atmosphere, once established, it is vain to fight against. The ingrained superstition that hides in every mother's son comes up at such times to breathe. It came up now. Sandy, closer by several glasses to the Moment, Tom saw, when he would be suddenly drunk, gave birth again, a tale this time of a Scottish planter who had brutally dismissed a native servant for no other reason than that he disliked him. The man disappeared completely, but the villagers hinted that he would —soon indeed that he had—come back, though "not quite as he went." The planter armed, knowing that vengeance might be violent. A black panther, meanwhile, was seen prowling about the bungalow. One night a noise outside his door on the veranda roused him. Just in time to see the black brute leaping over the railings into the compound, he fired, and the beast fell with a savage growl of pain. Help arrived and more shots were fired into the animal, as it lay, mortally wounded already, lashing its tail upon the grass. The lanterns, however, showed that instead of a panther, it was the servant they had shot to shreds.

Sandy told the story well, a certain odd conviction in his tone and manner, neither of them at all to the liking of his host. Uneasiness and annoyance had been growing in Tom for some time already, his inability to control the situation adding to his anger. Emotion was accumulating in him dangerously; it was directed chiefly against Rossiter, who, though saying nothing definite, somehow deliberately encouraged both talk and atmosphere. Given the conditions, it was natural enough the talk should take the turn it did take, but what made Tom more and more angry was that, if Rossiter had not been present, he could have stopped it easily enough. It was the presence of the old Hudson Bay man that prevented his taking decided action. He was afraid of Rossiter, afraid of putting his back up. That was the truth. His recognition of it made him furious.

"Tell us another, Sandy McKay," said the veteran. "There's a lot in such tales. They're found the world over—men turning into animals and the like."

And Sandy, yet nearer to his moment of collapse, but still showing no effects, obeyed willingly. He noticed nothing; the whisky was good, his tales were appreciated, and that sufficed him. He thanked Tom, who just then refilled his glass, and went on with his tale. But Tom, hatred and fury in his heart, had reached the point where he could no longer contain himself, and Rossiter's last words inflamed him. He went over, under cover of a tremendous clap of wind, to fill the old man's glass. The latter refused, covering the tumbler with his big, lean hand. Tom stood over him a moment, lowering his face. "You keep still," he whispered ferociously, but so that no one else heard it. He glared into his eyes with an intensity that held danger, and Rossiter, without answering, flung back that glare with equal, but with a calmer, anger.

The wind, meanwhile, had a trick of veering, and each time it shifted, Jim shifted his seat too. Apparently, he preferred to face the sound, rather than have his back to it.

"Your turn now for a tale," said Rossiter with purpose, when Sandy finished. He looked across at him, just as Jim, hearing the burst of wind at the walls behind him, was in the act of moving his chair again. The same moment the attack rattled the door and windows facing him. Jim, without answering, stood for a moment, still as death, not knowing which way to turn.

"It's beatin' up from all sides," remarked Rossiter, "like it was goin' round the building."

There was a moment's pause, the four men listening with awe to the roar and power of the terrific wind. Tom listened too, but at the same time watched, wondering vaguely why he didn't cross the room and crash his fist into the old man's chattering mouth. Jim put out his hand and took his glass, but did not raise it to his lips. And a lull came abruptly in the storm, the wind sinking into a moment's dreadful silence. Tom and Rossiter turned their heads in the same instant and stared into each other's eyes. For Tom the instant seemed enormously prolonged. He realized the challenge in the other and that his rudeness had roused it into action. It had become a contest of wills—Justice battling against Love.

Jim's glass had now reached his lips, and the chattering of his teeth against its rim was audible.

But the lull passed quickly and the wind began again, though so gently at first, it had the sound of innumerable swift footsteps treading lightly, of countless hands fingering the doors and windows, but then suddenly with a mighty shout as it swept against the walls, rushed across the roof and descended like a battering-ram against the farther side.

"God, did you hear that?" cried Sandy. "It's trying to get in!" and having said it, he sank in a heap beside his chair, all of a sudden completely drunk. "It's wolves or panthersh," he mumbled in his stupor on the floor, "but whatsh's happened to Malay?" It was the last thing he said before unconsciousness took him, and apparently he was insensible to the kick on the head from a heavy farmer's boot. For Jim's glass had fallen with a crash and the second kick was stopped midway. Tom stood spellbound, unable to move or speak, as he watched his brother suddenly cross the room and open a window into the very teeth of the gale.

"Let be! Let be!" came the voice of Rossiter, an authority in it, a curious gentleness too, both of them new. He had risen, his lips were still moving, but the words that issued from them were inaudible, as the wind and rain leaped with a galloping violence into the room, smashing the glass to atoms and clashing a dozen loose objects helter-skelter on to the floor.

"I saw it!" cried Jim, in a voice that rose above the din and clamour of the elements. He turned and faced the others, but it was at Rossiter he looked. "I saw the leader." He shouted to make himself heard, although the tone was quiet. "A splash of white on his great chest. I saw them all!"

At the words, and at the expression in Jim's eyes, old Rossiter, white to the lips, dropped back into his chair as if a blow had struck him. Tom, petrified, felt his own heart stop. For through the broken window, above yet within the wind, came the sound of a wolf-pack running, howling in deep, full-throated chorus, mad for blood. It passed like a whirlwind and was gone. And, of the three men so close together, one sitting and two standing, Jim alone was in that terrible moment wholly master of himself.

Before the others could move or speak, he turned and looked full into the eyes of each in succession. His speech went back to his wilderness days:

"I done it," he said calmly. "I killed him—and I got ter go."

With a look of mystical horror on his face, he took one stride, flung the door wide, and vanished into the darkness.

So quick were both words and action, that Tom's paralysis passed only as the draught from the broken window banged the door behind him. He seemed to leap across the room, old Rossiter, tears on his cheeks and his lips mumbling foolish words, so close upon his heels that the backward blow of fury Tom aimed at his face caught him only in the neck and sent him reeling sideways to the floor instead of flat upon his back. "Murderer! My brother's death upon you!" he shouted as he tore the door open again and plunged out into the night.

And the odd thing that happened then, the thing that touched old John Rossiter's reason, leaving him from that moment till his death a foolish man of uncertain mind and memory, happened when he and the unconscious, drink-sodden Sandy lay alone together on the stone floor of that farm-house room.

Rossiter, dazed by the blow and his fall, but in full possession of his senses, and the anger gone out of him owing to what he had brought about, this same John Rossiter sat up and saw Sandy also sitting up and staring at him hard. And Sandy was sober as a judge, his eyes and speech both clear, even his face unflushed.

"John Rossiter," he said, "it was not God who appointed you executioner. It was the devil." And his eyes, thought Rossiter, were like the eyes of an angel.

"Sandy McKay," he stammered, his teeth chattering and breath failing him. "Sandy McKay!" It was all the words that he could find. But Sandy, already sunk back into his stupor again, was stretched drunk and incapable upon the farm-house floor, and remained in that condition till the dawn.

Jim's body lay hidden among the dunes for many months and in spite of the most careful and prolonged searching, it was another storm that laid it bare. The sand had covered it. The clothes were gone, and the flesh, torn but not eaten, was naked to the December sun and wind.

CHINESE MAGIC

1

D r. Owen Francis felt a sudden wave of pleasure and admiration
sweep over him as he saw her enter the room. He was in the act
of going out; in fact, he had already said good-bye to his hostess, glad to
make his escape from the chattering throng, when the tall and graceful
young woman glided past him. Her carriage was superb; she had black
eyes with a twinkling happiness in them; her mouth was exquisite.
Round her neck, in spite of the warm afternoon, she wore a soft thing of
fur or feathers; and as she brushed by to shake the hand he had just
shaken himself, the tail of this touched his very cheek. Their eyes met
fair and square. He felt as though her eyes also touched him.

Changing his mind, he lingered another ten minutes, chatting with
various ladies he did not in the least remember, but who remembered
him. He did not, of course, desire to exchange banalities with these other
ladies, yet did so gallantly enough. If they found him absent-minded
they excused him since he was the famous mental specialist whom
everybody was proud to know. And all the time his eyes never left the
tall graceful figure that allured him almost to the point of casting a spell
upon him.

His first impression deepened as he watched. He was aware of excitement, curiosity, longing; there was a touch even of exaltation in him; yet
he took no steps to seek the introduction which was easily enough
procurable. He checked himself, if with an effort. Several times their eyes
met across the crowded room; he dared to believe—he felt instinctively—that his interest was returned. Indeed, it was more than instinct, for
she was certainly aware of his presence, and he even caught her indicating him to a woman she spoke with, and evidently asking who he was.
Once he half bowed, and once, in spite of himself, he went so far as to
smile, and there came, he was sure, a faint, delicious brightening of the
eyes in answer. There was, he fancied, a look of yearning in the face. The
young woman charmed him inexpressibly; the very way she moved delighted him. Yet at last he slipped out of the room without a word, without an introduction, without even knowing her name. He chose his
moment when her back was turned. It was characteristic of him.

For Owen Francis had ever regarded marriage, for himself at least, as a
disaster that could be avoided. He was in love with his work, and his

work was necessary to humanity. Others might perpetuate the race, but he must heal it. He had come to regard love as the bait wherewith Nature lays her trap to fulfill her own ends. A man in love was a man enjoying a delusion, a deluded man. In his case, and he was nearing forty-five, the theory had worked admirably, and the dangerous exception that proved it had as yet not troubled him.

"It's come at last—I do believe," he thought to himself, as he walked home, a new tumultuous emotion in his blood; "the exception, quite possibly, has come at last. I wonder..."

And it seemed he said it to the tall graceful figure by his side, who turned up dark eyes smilingly to meet his own, and whose lips repeated softly his last two words "I wonder..."

The experience, being new to him, was baffling. A part of his nature, long dormant, received the authentic thrill that pertains actually to youth. He was a plan of chaste, abstemious custom. The reaction was vehement. That dormant part of him became obstreperous. He thought of his age, his appearance, his prospects; he looked thirty-eight, he was not unhandsome, his position was secure, even remarkable. That gorgeous young woman—he called her gorgeous—haunted him. Never could he forget that face, those eyes. It was extraordinary—he had left her there unspoken to, unknown, when an introduction would have been the simplest thing in the world.

"But it still is," he replied. And the reflection filled his being with a flood of joy.

He checked himself again. Not so easily is established habit routed. He felt instinctively that, at last, he had met his mate; if he followed it up he was a man in love, a lost man enjoying a delusion, a deluded man. But the way she had looked at him! That air of intuitive invitation which not even the sweetest modesty could conceal! He felt an immense confidence in himself; also he felt oddly sure of her.

The presence of that following figure, already precious, came with him into his house, even into his study at the back where he sat over a number of letters by the open window. The pathetic little London garden showed its pitiful patch. The lilac had faded, but a smell of roses entered. The sun was just behind the buildings opposite, and the garden lay soft and warm in summer shadows.

He read and tossed aside the letters; one only interested him, from Edward Farque, whose journey to China had interrupted a friendship of long standing. Edward Farque's work on Eastern art and philosophy, on Chinese painting and Chinese thought in particular, had made its mark. He was an authority. He was to be back about this time, and his friend smiled with pleasure. "Dear old unpractical dreamer, as I used to call him," he mused. "He's a success, anyhow!" And as he mused, the presence that sat beside him came a little closer, yet at the same time faded. Not that he forgot her—that was impossible—but that just before opening the letter from his friend, he had come to a decision. He had definitely made up his mind to seek acquaintance. The reality replaced the remembered substitute.

"As the newspapers may have warned you," ran the familiar and kinky writing, "I am back in England after what the scribes term my ten years of exile in Cathay. I have taken a little house in Hampstead for six months, and am just settling in. Come to us to-morrow night and let me prove it to you. Come to dinner. We shall have much to say; we both are ten years wiser. You know how glad I shall be to see my old-time critic and disparager, but let me add frankly that I want to ask you a few professional, or, rather, technical, questions. So prepare yourself to come as doctor and as friend. I am writing, as the papers said truthfully, a treatise on Chinese thought. But—don't shy!—it is about Chinese Magic that I want your technical advice [the last two words were substituted for "professional wisdom," which had been crossed out] and the benefit of your vast experience. So come, old friend, come quickly, and come hungry! I'll feed your body as you shall feed my mind. —Yours,

"EDWARD FARQUE."

"P.S.—'The coming of a friend from a far-off land—is not this true joy?'"

Dr. Francis laid down the letter with a pleased anticipatory chuckle, and it was the touch in the final sentence that amused him. In spite of being an authority, Farque was clearly the same fanciful, poetic dreamer as of old. He quoted Confucius as in other days. The firm but kinky writing had not altered either. The only sign of novelty he noticed was the use of scented paper, for a faint and pungent aroma clung to the big quarto sheet.

"A Chinese habit, doubtless," he decided, sniffing it with a puzzled air of disapproval. Yet it had nothing in common with the scented sachets some ladies use too lavishly, so that even the air of the street is polluted by their passing for a dozen yards. He was familiar with every kind of perfumed note-paper used in London, Paris, and Constantinople. This one was difficult. It was delicate and penetrating for all its faintness, pleasurable too. He rather liked it, and while annoyed that he could not name it, he sniffed at the letter several times, as though it were a flower.

"I'll go," he decided at once, and wrote an acceptance then and there. He went out and posted it. He meant to prolong his walk into the Park, taking his chief preoccupation, the face, the eyes, the figure, with him. Already he was composing the note of inquiry to Mrs. Malleson, his hostess of the tea-party, the note whose willing answer should give him the name, the address, the means of introduction he had now determined to secure. He visualized that note of inquiry, seeing it in his mind's eye; only, for some odd reason, he saw the kinky writing of Farque instead of his own more elegant script. Association of ideas and emotions readily explained this. Two new and unexpected interests had entered his life on the same day, and within half an hour of each other. What he could not so readily explain, however, was that two words in his friend's ridiculous letter, and in that kinky writing, stood out sharply from the rest. As he slipped his envelope into the mouth of the red pillar-box they shone vividly in his mind. These two words were "Chinese Magic."

2

It was the warmth of his friend's invitation as much as his own state of inward excitement that decided him suddenly to anticipate his visit by twenty-four hours. It would clear his judgment and help his mind, if he spent the evening at Hampstead rather than alone with his own thoughts. "A dose of China," he thought, with a smile, "will do me good. Edward won't mind. I'll telephone."

He left the Park soon after six o'clock and acted upon his impulse. The connexion was bad, the wire buzzed and popped and crackled; talk was difficult; he did not hear properly. The Professor had not yet come in, apparently. Francis said he would come up anyhow on the chance.

"Velly pleased," said the voice in his ear, as he rang off.

Going into his study, he drafted the note that should result in the introduction that was now, it appeared, the chief object of his life. The way this woman with the black, twinkling eyes obsessed him was—he admitted it with joy—extraordinary. The draft he put in his pocket, intending to re-write it next morning, and all the way up to Hampstead Heath the gracious figure glided silently beside him, the eyes were ever present, his cheek still glowed where the feather boa had touched his skin. Edward Farque remained in the background. In fact, it was on the very door-step, having rung the bell, that Francis realized he must pull himself together. "I've come to see old Farque," he reminded himself, with a smile. "I've got to be interested in him and his, and, probably, for an hour or two, to talk Chinese—" when the door opened noiselessly, and he saw facing him, with a grin of celestial welcome on his yellow face, a Chinaman.

"Oh!" he said, with a start. He had not expected a Chinese servant.

"Velly pleased," the man bowed him in.

Dr. Francis stared round him with astonishment he could not conceal. A great golden idol faced him in the hall, its gleaming visage blazing out of a sort of miniature golden palanquin, with a grin, half dignified, half cruel. Fully double human size, it blocked the way, looking so life-like that it might have moved to meet him without too great a shock to what seemed possible. It rested on a throne with four massive legs, carved, the doctor saw, with serpents, dragons, and mythical monsters generally. Round it on every side were other things in keeping. Name them he could not, describe then he did not try. He summed them up in one word—China: pictures, weapons, cloths and tapestries, bells, gongs, and figures of every sort and kind imaginable.

Being ignorant of Chinese matters, Dr. Francis stood and looked about him in a mental state of some confusion. He had the feeling that he had entered a Chinese temple, for there was a faint smell of incense hanging about the house that was, to say the least, un-English. Nothing English, in fact, was visible at all. The matting on the floor, the swinging curtains of bamboo beads that replaced the customary doors, the silk draperies and pictured cushions, the bronze and ivory, the screens hung with fantastic embroideries, everything was Chinese. Hampstead vanished from his thoughts. The very lamps were in keeping, the ancient lacquered furniture as well. The value of what he saw, an expert could have told him, was considerable.

"You likee?" queried the voice at his side.

He had forgotten the servant. He turned sharply.

"Very much; it's wonderfully done," he said. "Makes you feel at home, John, eh?" he added tactfully, with a smile, and was going to ask how long all this preparation had taken, when a voice sounded on the stairs beyond. It was a voice he knew, a note of hearty welcome in its deep notes.

"The coming of a friend from a far-off land, even from Harley Street— is not this true joy?" he heard, and the next minute was shaking the hand of his old and valued friend. The intimacy between them had always been of the truest.

"I almost expected a pigtail," observed Francis, looking him affectionately up and down, "but, really—why, you've hardly changed at all!"

"Outwardly, not as much, perhaps, as Time expects," was the happy reply, "but inwardly—!" He scanned appreciatively the burly figure of the doctor in his turn. "And I can say the same of you," he declared, still holding his hand tight. "This is a real pleasure, Owen," he went on in his deep voice, "'to see you again is a joy to me. Old friends meeting again—

there's nothing like it in life, I believe, nothing." He gave the hand another squeeze before he let it go. "And we," he added, leading the way into a room across the hall, "neither of us is a fugitive from life. We take what we can, I mean."

The doctor smiled as he noted the un-English turn of language, and together they entered a sitting-room that was, again, more like some inner chamber of a Chinese temple than a back room in a rented Hampstead house.

"I only knew ten minutes ago that you were coming, my dear fellow," the scholar was saying, as his friend gazed round him with increased astonishment, "or I would have prepared more suitably for your reception. I was out till late. All this"—he waved his hand—"surprises you, of course, but the fact is I have been home some days already, and most of what you see was arranged for me in advance of my arrival. Hence its apparent completion. I say 'apparent,' because, actually, it is far from faithfully carried out. Yet to exceed," he added, "is as bad as to fall short."

The doctor watched him while he listened to a somewhat lengthy explanation of the various articles surrounding them. The speaker—he confirmed his first impression—had changed little during the long interval; the same enthusiasm was in him as before, the same fire and dreaminess alternately in the fine grey eyes, the same humour and passion about the mouth, the same free gestures, and the same big voice. Only the lines had deepened on the forehead, and on the fine face the air of thoughtfulness was also deeper. It was Edward Farque as of old, scholar, poet, dreamer and enthusiast, despiser of western civilization, contemptuous of money, generous and upright, a type of value, an individual.

"You've done well, done splendidly, Edward, old man," said his friend presently, after hearing of Chinese wonders that took him somewhat beyond his depth perhaps. "No one is more pleased than I. I've watched your books. You haven't regretted England, I'll be bound?" he asked.

"The philosopher has no country, in any case," was the reply, steadily given, "But out there, I confess, I've found my home." He leaned forward, a deeper earnestness in his tone and expression. And into his face, as he spoke, came a glow of happiness. "My heart," he said, "is in China."

"I see it is, I see it is," put in the other, conscious that he could not honestly share his friend's enthusiasm. "And you're fortunate to be free to live where your treasure is," he added after a moment's pause. "You must be a happy man. Your passion amounts to nostalgia, I suspect. Already yearning to get back there, probably?"

Farque gazed at him for some seconds with shining eyes. "You remember the Persian saying, I'm sure," he said. "'You see a man drink, but you do not see his thirst.' Well," he added, laughing happily, "you may see me off in six months' time, but you will not see my happiness."

While he went on talking, the doctor glanced round the room, marvelling still at the exquisite taste of everything, the neat arrangement, the perfect matching of form and colour. A woman might have done this thing, occurred to him, as the haunting figure shifted deliciously into the foreground of his mind again. The thought of her had been momentarily replaced by all he heard and saw. She now returned, filling him with joy, anticipation and enthusiasm. Presently, when it was his turn to talk, he would tell his friend about this new, unimagined happiness that had burst upon him like a sunrise. Presently, but not just yet. He remembered, too, with a passing twinge of possible boredom to come, that there must be some delay before his own heart could unburden itself in its turn. Farque wanted to ask some professional questions, of course. He had for the moment forgotten that part of the letter in his general interest and astonishment.

"Happiness, yes..." he murmured, aware that his thoughts had wandered, and catching at the last word he remembered hearing. "As you said just now in your own queer way—you haven't changed a bit, let me tell you, in your picturesqueness of quotation, Edward—one must not be fugitive from life; one must seize happiness when and where it offers."

He said it lightly enough, hugging internally his own sweet secret; but he was a little surprised at the earnestness of his friend's rejoinder: "Both of us, I see," came the deep voice, backed by the flash of the far-seeing grey eyes, "have made some progress in the doctrine of life and death." He paused, gazing at the other with sight that was obviously turned inwards upon his own thoughts. "Beauty," he went on presently, his tone even more serious, "has been my lure; yours, Reality...."

"You don't flatter either of us, Edward. That's too exclusive a statement," put in the doctor. He was becoming every minute more and more interested in the workings of his friend's mind. Something about the signs offered eluded his understanding. "Explain yourself, old scholar-poet. I'm a dull, practical mind, remember, and can't keep pace with Chinese subtleties."

"You've left out Beauty," was the quiet rejoinder, "while I left out Reality. That's neither Chinese nor subtle. It is simply true."

"A bit wholesale, isn't it?" laughed Francis. "A big generalization, rather."

A bright light seemed to illuminate the scholar's face. It was as though an inner lamp was suddenly lit. At the same moment the sound of a soft gong floated in from the hall outside, so soft that the actual strokes were not distinguishable in the wave of musical vibration that reached the ear.

Farque rose to lead the way in to dinner.

"What if I—" he whispered, "have combined the two?" And upon his face was a look of joy that reached down into the other's own full heart with its unexpectedness and wonder. It was the last remark in the world he had looked for. He wondered for a moment whether he interpreted it correctly.

"By Jove...!" he exclaimed. "Edward, what d'you mean?"

"You shall hear—after dinner," said Farque, his voice mysterious, his eyes still shining with his inner joy. "I told you I have some questions to ask you—professionally." And they took their seats round an ancient, marvellous table, lit by two swinging lamps of soft green jade, while the Chinese servant waited on them with the silent movements and deft neatness of his imperturbable celestial race.

3

To say that he was bored during the meal were an over-statement of Dr. Francis's mental condition, but to say that he was half-bored seemed the literal truth; for one-half of him, while he ate his steak and savoury and watched Farque manipulating *chou chop suey* and *chou om dong* most cleverly with chop-sticks, was too pre-occupied with his own romance to allow the other half to give its full attention to the conversation.

He had entered the room, however, with a distinct quickening of what may be termed his instinctive and infallible sense of diagnosis. That last remark of his friend's had stimulated him. He was aware of surprise, curiosity, and impatience. Willy-nilly, he began automatically to study him with a profounder interest. Something, he gathered, was not quite as it should be in Edward Farque's mental composition. There was what might be called an elusive emotional disturbance. He began to wonder and to watch.

They talked, naturally, of China and of things Chinese, for the scholar responded to little else, and Francis listened with what sympathy and patience he could muster. Of art and beauty he had hitherto known little, his mind was practical and utilitarian. He now learned that all art was derived from China, where a high, fine, subtle culture had reigned since time immemorial. Older than Egypt was their wisdom. When the western races were eating one another, before Greece was even heard of, the Chinese had reached a level of knowledge and achievement that few realized. Never had they, even in earliest times, been deluded by anthropomorphic conceptions of the Deity, but perceived in everything the expressions of a single whole whose giant activities they reverently worshipped. Their contempt for the western scurry after knowledge, wealth, machinery, was justified, if Farque was worthy of belief. He seemed saturated with Chinese thought, art, philosophy, and his natural bias towards the celestial race had hardened into an attitude to life that had now become ineradicable.

"They deal, as it were, in essences," he declared; "they discern the essence of everything, leaving out the superfluous, the unessential, the trivial. Their pictures alone prove it. Come with me," he concluded, "and see the 'Earthly Paradise,' now in the British Museum. It is like Botticelli, but better than anything Botticelli ever did. It was painted"—he paused for emphasis—"600 years B.C."

The wonder of this quiet, ancient civilization, a sense of its depth, its wisdom, grew upon his listener as the enthusiastic poet described its charm and influence upon himself. He willingly allowed the enchantment of the other's Paradise to steal upon his own awakened heart. There was a good deal Francis might have offered by way of criticism and objection, but he preferred on the whole to keep his own views to himself, and to let his friend wander unhindered through the mazes of his passionate evocation. All men, he well knew, needed a dream to carry them through life's disappointments, a dream that they could enter at will and find peace, contentment, happiness. Farque's dream was China. Why not? It was as good as another, and a man like Farque was entitled to what dream he pleased.

"And their women?" he inquired at last, letting both halves of his mind speak together for the first time.

But he was not prepared for the expression that leaped upon his friend's face at the simple question. Nor for his method of reply. It was no reply, in point of fact. It was simply an attack upon all other types of woman, and upon the white, the English, in particular—their emptiness, their triviality, their want of intuitive imagination, of spiritual grace, of everything, in a word, that should constitute woman a meet companion for man, and a little higher than the angels into the bargain. The doctor listened spellbound. Too humorous to be shocked, he was, at any rate, disturbed by what he heard, displeased a little, too. It threatened too directly his own new tender dream.

Only with the utmost self-restraint did he keep his temper under, and prevent hot words he would have regretted later from tearing his friend's absurd claim into ragged shreds. He was wounded personally as well. Never now could he bring himself to tell his own secret to him. The outburst chilled and disappointed him. But it had another effect—it cooled his judgment. His sense of diagnosis quickened. He divined an *idée fixe*, a mania possibly. His interest deepened abruptly. He watched. He began to look about him with more wary eyes, and a sense of uneasiness, once the anger passed, stirred in his friendly and affectionate heart. They had been sitting alone over their port for some considerable time, the servant having long since left the room. The doctor had sought to change the subject many times without much success, when suddenly Farque changed it for him.

"Now," he announced, "I'll tell you something," and Francis guessed that the professional questions were on the way at last. "We must pity the living, remember, and part with the dead. Have you forgotten old Shan-Yu?"

The forgotten name came back to him, the picturesque East End dealer of many years ago. "The old merchant who taught you your first Chinese? I do recall him dimly, now you mention it. You made quite a friend of him, didn't you? He thought very highly of you—ah, it comes back to me now—he offered something or other very wonderful in his gratitude, unless my memory fails me?"

"His most valuable possession," Farque went on, a strange look deepening on his face, an expression of mysterious rapture, as it were, and one that Francis recognized and swiftly pigeon-holed in his now attentive mind.

"Which was?" he asked sympathetically. "You told me once, but so long ago that really it's slipped my mind. Something magical, wasn't it?" He watched closely for his friend's reply.

Farque lowered his voice to a whisper almost devotional:

"The Perfume of the Garden of Happiness," he murmured, with an expression in his eyes as though the mere recollection gave him joy. "'Burn it,' he told me, 'in a brazier; then inhale. You will enter the Valley of a Thousand Temples wherein lies the Garden of Happiness, and there you will meet your Love. You will have seven years of happiness with your Love before the Waters of Separation flow between you. I give this to you who alone of men here have appreciated the wisdom of my land. Follow my body towards the Sunrise. You, an eastern soul in a barbarian body, will meet your Destiny.'"

The doctor's attention, such is the power of self-interest, quickened amazingly as he heard. His own romance flamed up with power. His friend—it dawned upon him suddenly—loved a. woman.

"Come," said Farque, rising quietly, "we will go into the other room, and I will show you what I have shown to but one other in the world before. You are a doctor," he continued, as he led the way to the silk-covered divan where golden dragons swallowed crimson suns, and wonderful jade horses hovered near. "You understand the mind and nerves. States of consciousness you also can explain, and the effect of drugs is, doubtless, known to you." He swung to the heavy curtains that took the place of door, handed a lacquered box of cigarettes to his friend, and lit one himself. "Perfumes, too," he added, "you probably have studied, with their extraordinary evocative power." He stood in the middle of the room, the green light falling on his interesting and thoughtful face, and for a passing second Francis, watching keenly, observed a change flit over it and vanish. The eyes grew narrow and slid tilted upwards, the skin wore a shade of yellow underneath the green from the lamp of jade, the nose slipped back a little, the cheek-bones forward.

"Perfumes," said the doctor, "no. Of perfumes I know nothing, beyond their interesting effect upon the memory. I cannot help you there. But, you, I suspect," and he looked up with an inviting sympathy that concealed the close observation underneath, "you yourself, I feel sure, can tell me something of value about them?"

"Perhaps," was the calm reply, "perhaps, for I have smelt the perfume of the Garden of Happiness, and I have been in the Valley of a Thousand Temples." He spoke with a glow of joy and reverence almost devotional.

The doctor waited in some suspense, while his friend moved towards an inlaid cabinet across the room. More than broad-minded, he was that much rarer thing, an open-minded man, ready at a moment's notice to discard all preconceived ideas, provided new knowledge that necessitated the holocaust were shown to him. At present, none the less, he held very definite views of his own. "Please ask me any questions you like," he added. "All I know is entirely yours, as always." He was aware of suppressed excitement in his friend that betrayed itself in every word and look and gesture, an excitement intense, and not as yet explained by anything he had seen or heard.

The scholar, meanwhile, had opened a drawer in the cabinet and taken from it a neat little packet tied up with purple silk. He held it, with tender, almost loving care, as he came and sat down on the divan beside his friend.

"This," he said, in a tone, again, of something between reverence and worship, "contains what I have to show you first." He slowly unrolled it, disclosing a yet smaller silken bag within, coloured a deep rich orange. There were two vertical columns of writing on it, painted in Chinese characters. The doctor leaned forward to examine them. His friend translated:

"The Perfume of the Garden of Happiness," he read aloud, tracing the letters of the first column with his finger. "The Destroyer of Honourable Homes," he finished, passing to the second, and then proceeded to unwrap the little silken bag. Before it was actually open, however, and the pale shredded material resembling coloured chaff visible to the eyes, the doctor's nostrils had recognized the strange aroma he had first noticed

about his friend's letter received earlier in the day. The same soft, penetrating odour, sharply piercing, sweet and delicate, rose to his brain. It
stirred at once a deep emotional pleasure in him. Having come to him
first when he was aglow with his own unexpected romance, his mind
and heart full of the woman he had just left, that delicious, torturing
state revived in him quite naturally. The evocative power of perfume
with regard to memory is compelling. A livelier sympathy towards his
friend, and towards what he was about to hear, awoke in him spontaneously.

He did not mention the letter, however. He merely leaned over to smell
the fragrant perfume more easily.

Farque drew back the open packet instantly, at the same time holding
out a warning hand. "Careful," he said gravely, "be careful, my old
friend—unless you desire to share the rapture and the risk that have
been mine. To enjoy its full effect, true, this dust must be burned in a brazier and its smoke inhaled; but even sniffed, as you now would sniff it,
and you are in danger—'"

"Of what?" asked Francis, impressed by the other's extraordinary
intensity of voice and manner.

"Of Heaven; but, possibly, of Heaven before your time."

4

The tale that Farque unfolded then had certainly a strange celestial
flavour, a glory not of this dull world; and as his friend listened, his interest deepened with every minute, while his bewilderment increased. He
watched closely, expert that he was, for clues that might guide his deduc-
tions aright, but for all his keen observation and experience he could
detect no inconsistency, no weakness, nothing that betrayed the smallest mental aberration. The origin and nature of what he already decided
was an *idée fixe,* a mania, evaded him entirely. This evasion piqued and
vexed him; he had heard a thousand tales of similar type before; that this
one in particular should baffle his unusual skill touched his pride. Yet he
faced the position honestly, he confessed himself baffled until the end of
the evening. When he went away, however, he went away satisfied, even
forgetful—because a new problem of yet more poignant interest had
replaced the first.

"It. was after three years out there," said Farque, "that a sense of my
loneliness first came upon me. It came upon me bitterly. My work had
not then been recognized; obstacles and difficulties had increased; I felt
a failure; I had accomplished nothing, And it seemed to me I had misjudged my capacities, taken a wrong direction, and wasted my life

accordingly. For my move to China, remember, was a radical move, and my boats were burnt behind me. This sense of loneliness was really devastating."

Francis, already fidgeting, put up his hand.

"One question, if I may," he said, "and I'll not interrupt again."

"By all means," said the other patiently, "what is it?"

"Were you—we are such old friends"—he apologized—"were you still celibate as ever?"

Farque looked surprised, then smiled. "My habits had not changed," he replied, "I was, as always, celibate."

"Ah!" murmured the doctor, and settled down to listen.

"And I think now," his friend went on, "that it was the lack of companionship that first turned my thoughts towards conscious disappointment. However that may be, it was one evening, as I walked homewards to my little house, that I caught my imagination lingering upon English memories, though chiefly, I admit, upon my old Chinese tutor, the dead Shan-Yu.

"It was dusk, the stars were coming out in the pale evening air, and the orchards, as I passed them, stood like wavering ghosts of unbelievable beauty. The effect of thousands upon thousands of these trees, flooding the twilight of a spring evening with their sea of blossom, is almost unearthly. They seem transparencies, their colour hangs sheets upon the very sky. I crossed a small wooden bridge that joined two of these orchards above a stream, and in the dark water I watched a moment the mingled reflection of stars and flowering branches on the quiet surface. It seemed too exquisite to belong to earth, this fairy garden of stars and blossoms, shining faintly in the crystal depths, and my thought, as I gazed, dived suddenly down the little avenue that memory opened into former days. I remembered Shan-Yu's present, given to me when he died. His very words came back to me: The Garden of Happiness in the Valley of the Thousand Temples, with its promise of love, of seven years of happiness, and the prophecy that I should follow his body towards the Sunrise and meet my destiny.

"This memory I took home with me into my lonely little one-storey house upon the hill. My servants did not sleep there. There was no one near. I sat by the open window with my thoughts, and you may easily guess that before very long I had unearthed the long-forgotten packet from among my things, spread a portion of its contents on a metal tray above a lighted brazier, and was comfortably seated before it, inhaling the light blue smoke with its exquisite and fragrant perfume.

"A light air entered through the window, the distant orchards below me trembled, rose and floated through the dusk, and I found myself, almost at once, in a pavilion of flowers ; a blue river lay shining in the sun before me, as it wandered through a lovely valley where I saw groves of flowering trees among a thousand scattered temples. Drenched in light and colour, the Valley lay dreaming amid a peaceful loveliness that woke what seemed impossible, unrealizable, longings in my heart. I yearned towards its groves and temples, I would bathe my soul in that flood of tender light, and my body in the blue coolness of that winding river. In a thousand temples must I worship. Yet these impossible yearnings instantly were satisfied. I found myself there at once... and the time that passed over my head you may reckon in centuries, if not in ages. I was in the Garden of Happiness and its marvellous perfume banished time and sorrow, there was no end to chill the soul, nor any beginning, which is its foolish counterpart.

"Nor was there loneliness." The speaker clasped his thin hands, and closed his eyes a moment in what was evidently an ecstasy of the sweetest memory man may ever know. A slight trembling ran through his frame, communicating itself to his friend upon the divan beside him— this understanding, listening, sympathetic friend, whose eyes had never once yet withdrawn their attentive gaze from the narrator's face.

"I was not alone," the scholar resumed, opening his eyes again, and smiling out of some deep inner joy. "ShanYu came down the steps of the first temple and took my hand, while the great golden figures in the dim interior turned their splendid shining heads to watch. Then, breathing the soul of his ancient wisdom in my ear, he led me through all the perfumed ways of that enchanted garden, worshipping with me at a hundred deathless shrines, led me, I tell you, to the sound of soft gongs and gentle bells, by fragrant groves and sparkling streams, mid a million gorgeous flowers, until, beneath that unsetting sun, we reached the heart of the Valley, where the source of the river gushed forth beneath the lighted mountains. He stopped and pointed across the narrow waters. I saw the woman—"

"*The* woman," his listener murmured beneath his breath, though Farque seemed unaware of interruption.

"She smiled at me and held her hands out, and while she did so, even before I could express my joy and wonder in response, Shan-Yu, I saw, had crossed the narrow stream and stood beside her. I made to follow then, my heart burning with inexpressible delight. But Shan-Yu held up his hand, as they began to move down the flowered bank together, making a sign that I should keep pace with them, though on my own side.

"Thus, side by side, yet with the blue sparkling stream between us, we followed back along its winding course, through the heart of that enchanted valley, my hands stretched out towards the radiant figure of my Love, and hers stretched out towards me. They did not touch, but our eyes, our smiles, our thoughts, these met and mingled in a sweet union of unimagined bliss, so that the absence of physical contact was unnoticed and laid no injury on our marvellous joy. It was a spirit union, and our kiss a spirit kiss. Therein lay the subtlety and glory of the Chinese wonder, for it was our *essences* that met, and for such union there is no satiety and, equally, no possible end. The Perfume of the Garden of Happiness is an essence. We were in Eternity.

"The stream, meanwhile, widened between us, and as it widened, my Love grew farther from me in space, smaller, less visibly defined, yet ever essentially more perfect, and never once with a sense of distance that made our union less divinely close. Across the widening reaches of blue, sunlit water I still knew her smile, her eyes, the gestures of her radiant being; I saw her exquisite reflection in the stream; and, mid the music of those soft gongs and gentle bells, the voice of Shan-Yu came like a melody to my ears:

"'You have followed me into the sunrise, and have found your destiny. Behold now your Love. In this Valley of a Thousand Temples you have known the Garden of Happiness, and its Perfume your soul now inhales.'

"'I am bathed,' I answered, 'in a happiness divine. It is forever.'

"'The Waters of Separation,' his answer floated like a bell, 'lie widening between you.'

"I moved nearer to the bank, impelled by the pain in his words to take my Love and hold her to my breast.

"'But I would cross to her,' I cried, and saw that, as I moved, Shan-Yu and my Love came likewise closer to the water's edge across the widening river. They both obeyed, I was aware, my slightest wish.

"'Seven years of Happiness you may know,' sang his gentle tones across the brimming flood, 'if you would cross to her. Yet the Destroyer of Honourable Homes lies in the shadows that you must cast outside.'

"I heard his words, I noticed for the first time that in the blaze of this radiant sunshine we cast no shadows on the sea of flowers at our feet, and—I stretched out my arms towards my Love across the river.

"'I accept my destiny,' I cried, 'I will have my seven years of bliss,' and stepped forward into the running flood. As the cool water took my feet, my Love's hands stretched out both to hold me and to bid me stay. There was acceptance in her gesture, but there was warning too.

"I did not falter. I advanced until the water bathed my knees, and my Love, too, came to meet me, the stream already to her waist, while our arms stretched forth above the running flood towards each other.

"The change came suddenly. Shan-Yu first faded behind her advancing figure into air; there stole a chill upon the sunlight; a cool mist rose from the water, hiding the Garden and the hills beyond; our fingers touched, I gazed into her eyes, our lips lay level with the water—and the room was dark and cold about me. The brazier stood extinguished at my side. The dust had burnt out, and no smoke rose. I slowly left my chair and closed the window, for the air was chill."

5

It was difficult at first to return to Hampstead and the details of ordinary life about him. Francis looked round him slowly, freeing himself gradually from the spell his friend's words had laid even upon his analytical temperament. The transition was helped, however, by the details that everywhere met his eye. The Chinese atmosphere remained. More, its effect had gained, if anything. The embroideries of yellow gold, the pictures, the lacquered stools and inlaid cabinets, above all, the exquisite figures in green jade upon the shelf beside him, all this, in the shimmering pale olive light the lamps shed everywhere, helped his puzzled mind to bridge the gulf from the Garden of Happiness into the decorated villa upon Hampstead Heath.

There was silence between the two men for several minutes. Far was it from the doctor's desire to injure his old friend's delightful fantasy. For he called it fantasy, although something in him trembled. He remained, therefore, silent. Truth to tell, perhaps, he knew not exactly what to say.

Farque broke the silence himself. He had not moved since the story ended; he sat motionless, his hands tightly clasped, his eyes alight with the memory of his strange imagined joy, his face rapt and almost luminous, as though he still wandered through the groves of the Enchanted Garden and inhaled the perfume of its perfect happiness in the Valley of the Thousand Temples.

"It was two days later," he went on suddenly in his quiet voice, "only two days afterwards, that I met her."

"You met her? You met the woman of your dream?" Francis's eyes opened very wide.

"In that little harbour town," repeated Farque calmly, "I met her in the flesh. She had just landed in a steamer from up the coast. The details are of no particular interest. She knew me, of course, at once. And, naturally, I knew her."

The doctor's tongue refused to act as he heard. It dawned upon him suddenly that his friend was married. He remembered the woman's touch about the house; he recalled, too, for the first time that the letter of invitation to dinner had said "come to *us*." He was full of a. bewildered astonishment.

The reaction upon himself was odd, perhaps, yet wholly natural. His heart warmed towards his imaginative friend. He could now tell him his own new strange romance. The woman who haunted him crept back into the room and sat between them. He found his tongue.

"You married her, Edward?" he exclaimed.

"She is my wife," was the reply, in a gentle, happy voice.

"A Ch—" he could not bring himself to say the word. "A foreigner?"

" My wife is a Chinese woman," Farque helped him easily, with a delighted smile.

So great was the other's absorption in the actual moment, that he had not heard the step in the passage that his host had heard. The latter stood up suddenly.

"I hear her now," he said. "I'm glad she's come back before you left." He stepped towards the door.

But before he reached it, the door was opened and in came the woman herself. Francis tried to rise, but something had happened to him. His heart missed a beat. Something, it seemed, broke in him. He faced a tall, graceful young English woman with black eyes of sparkling happiness, the woman of his own romance. She still wore the feather boa round her neck. She was no more Chinese than he was.

"My wife," he heard Farque introducing them, as he struggled to his feet, searching feverishly for words of congratulation, normal, everyday words he ought to use, "I'm so pleased, oh, so pleased," Farque was saying—he heard the sound from a distance, his sight was blurred as well—"my two best friends in the world, my English comrade and my Chinese wife." His voice was absolutely sincere with conviction and belief.

"But we have already met," came the woman's delightful voice, her eyes full upon his face with smiling pleasure, "I saw you at Mrs. Malleson's tea only this afternoon."

And Francis remembered suddenly that the Mallesons were old acquaintances of Farque's as well as of himself. "And I even dared to ask who you were," the voice went on, floating from some other space, it seemed, to his ears, "I had you pointed out to me. I had heard of you from Edward, of course. But you vanished before I could be introduced."

The doctor mumbled something or other polite and, he hoped, adequate. But the truth had flashed upon him with remorseless suddenness. She had "heard of" him—the famous mental specialist. Her interest in him was cruelly explained, cruelly both for himself and for his friend. Farque's delusion lay clear before his eyes. An awakening to reality might involve dislocation of the mind. *She,* too, moreover, knew the truth. She was involved as well. And her interest in himself was—consultation.

"Seven years we've been married, just seven years today," Farque was saying thoughtfully, as he looked at them. "Curious, rather, isn't it?"

"Very," said Francis, turning his regard from the black eyes to the grey.

Thus it was that Owen Francis left the house a little later with a mind in a measure satisfied, yet in a measure forgetful too—forgetful of his own deep problem, because another of even greater interest had replaced it.

"Why undeceive him?" ran his thought. "He need never know. It's harmless anyhow—I can tell her that."

But, side by side with this reflection, ran another that was oddly haunting, considering his type of mind: "Destroyer of Honourable Homes," was the form of words it took. And with a sigh he added "Chinese Magic."

RUNNING WOLF

The man who enjoys an adventure outside the general experience of the race, and imparts it to others, must not be surprised if he is taken for either a liar or a fool, as Malcolm Hyde, hotel clerk on a holiday, discovered in due course. Nor is "enjoy" the right word to use in describing his emotions; the word he chose was probably "survive."

When he first set eyes on Medicine Lake he was struck by its still, sparkling beauty, lying there in the vast Canadian backwoods; next, by its extreme loneliness; and, lastly—a good deal later, this—by its combination of beauty, loneliness, and singular atmosphere, due to the fact that it was the scene of his adventure.

"It's fairly stiff with big fish," said Morton of the Montreal Sporting Club. "Spend your holiday there—up Mattawa way, some fifteen miles west of Stony Creek. You'll have it all to yourself except for an old Indian who's got a shack there. Camp on the east side—if you'll take a tip from me." He then talked for half an hour about the wonderful sport; yet he was not otherwise very communicative, and did not suffer questions gladly, Hyde noticed. Nor had he stayed there very long himself. If it was such a paradise as Morton, its discoverer and the most experienced rod in the province, claimed, why had he himself spent only three days there?

"Ran short of grub,'" was the explanation offered; but to another friend he had mentioned briefly, "flies," and to a third, so Hyde learned later, he gave the excuse that his half-breed "took sick," necessitating a quick return to civilization.

Hyde, however, cared little for the explanations; his interest in these came later. "Stiff with fish" was the phrase he liked. He took the Canadian Pacific train to Mattawa, laid in his outfit at Stony Creek, and set off thence for the fifteen-mile canoe-trip without a care in the world.

Travelling light, the portages did not trouble him; the water was swift and easy, the rapids negotiable; everything came his way, as the saying is. Occasionally he saw big fish making for the deeper pools, and was sorely tempted to stop; but he resisted. He pushed on between the immense world of forests that stretched for hundreds of miles, known to deer, bear, moose, and wolf, but strange to any echo of human tread, a deserted and primeval wilderness. The autumn day was calm, the water sang and sparkled, the blue sky hung cloudless over all, ablaze with light. Toward evening he passed an old beaver-dam, rounded a little point, and had his first sight of Medicine Lake. He lifted his dripping paddle; the canoe shot with silent glide into calm water. He gave an exclamation of delight, for the loveliness caught his breath away.

Though primarily a sportsman, he was not insensible to beauty. The lake formed a crescent, perhaps four miles long, its width between a mile and half a mile. The slanting gold of sunset flooded it. No wind stirred its crystal surface. Here it had lain since the redskin's god first made it; here it would lie until he dried it up again. Towering spruce and hemlock trooped to its very edge, majestic cedars leaned down as if to drink, crimson sumachs shone in fiery patches, and maples gleamed orange and red beyond belief. The air was like wine, with the silence of a dream.

It was here the red men formerly "made medicine," with all the wild ritual and tribal ceremony of an ancient day. But it was of Morton, rather than of Indians, that Hyde thought. If this lonely, hidden paradise was really stiff with big fish, he owed a lot to Morton for the information. Peace invaded him, but the excitement of the hunter lay below.

He looked about him with quick, practised eye for a camping-place before the sun sank below the forests and the half-lights came. The Indian's shack, lying in full sunshine on the eastern shore, he found at once; but the trees lay too thick about it for comfort, nor did he wish to be so close to its inhabitant. Upon the opposite side, however, an ideal clearing offered. This lay already in shadow, the huge forest darkening it toward evening; but the open space attracted. He paddled over quickly and examined it. The ground was hard and dry, he found, and a little brook ran tinkling down one side of it into the lake. This outfall, too, would be a good fishing spot. Also it was sheltered. A few low willows marked the mouth.

An experienced camper soon makes up his mind. It was a perfect site, and some charred logs, with traces of former fires, proved that he was not the first to think so. Hyde was delighted. Then, suddenly, disappointment came to tinge his pleasure. His kit was landed, and preparations for putting up the tent were begun, when he recalled a detail that excitement had so far kept in the background of his mind—Morton's advice. But not Morton's only, for the storekeeper at Stony Creek had reinforced it. The big fellow with straggling moustache and stooping shoulders, dressed in shirt and trousers, had handed him out a final sentence with the bacon, flour, condensed milk, and sugar. He had repeated Morton's half-forgotten words:

"Put yer tent on the east shore. I should," he had said at parting.

He remembered Morton, too, apparently. "A shortish fellow, brown as an Indian and fairly smelling of the woods. Travelling with Jake, the halfbreed." That assuredly was Morton. "Didn't stay long, now, did he?" he added in a reflective tone.

"Going Windy Lake way, are yer? Or Ten Mile Water, maybe?" he had first inquired of Hyde.

"Medicine Lake."

"Is that so?" the man said, as though he doubted it for some obscure reason. He pulled at his ragged moustache a moment. "Is that so, now?" he repeated. And the final words followed him down-stream after a considerable pause—the advice about the best shore on which to put his tent.

All this now suddenly flashed back upon Hyde's mind with a tinge of disappointment and annoyance, for when two experienced men agreed, their opinion was not to be lightly disregarded. He wished he had asked the storekeeper for more details. He looked about him, he reflected, he hesitated. His ideal camping-ground lay certainly on the forbidden shore. What in the world, he wondered, could be the objection to it?

But the light was fading; he must decide quickly one way or the other. After staring at his unpacked dunnage and the tent, already half erected, he made up his mind with a muttered expression that consigned both Morton and the storekeeper to less pleasant places. "They must have *some* reason," he growled to himself; "fellows like that usually know what they're talking about. I guess I'd better shift over to the other side—for to-night, at any rate."

He glanced across the water before actually reloading. No smoke rose from the Indian's shack. He had seen no sign of a canoe. The plan, he decided, was away. Reluctantly, then, he left the good camping-ground and paddled across the lake, and half an hour later his tent was up, firewood collected, and two small trout were already caught for supper. But the bigger fish, he knew, lay waiting for him on the other side by the little outfall, and he fell asleep at length on his bed of balsam boughs, annoyed and disappointed, yet wondering how a mere sentence could have persuaded him so easily against his own better judgment. He slept like the dead; the sun was well up before he stirred.

But his morning mood was a very different one. The brilliant light, the peace, the intoxicating air, all this was too exhilarating for the mind to harbour foolish fancies, and he marvelled that he could have been so weak the night before. No hesitation lay in him anywhere. He struck camp immediately after breakfast, paddled back across the strip of shining water, and quickly settled in upon the forbidden shore, as he now called it, with a contemptuous grin. And the more he saw of the spot, the better he liked it. There was plenty of wood, running water to drink, an open space about the tent, and there were no flies. The fishing, moreover, was magnificent. Morton's description was fully justified, and "stiff with big fish" for once was not an exaggeration.

The useless hours of the early afternoon he passed dozing in the sun, or wandering through the underbrush beyond the camp. He found no sign of anything unusual. He bathed in a cool, deep pool; he revelled in the lonely little paradise. Lonely it certainly was, but the loneliness was part of its charm; the stillness, the peace, the isolation of this beautiful backwoods lake delighted him. The silence was divine. He was entirely satisfied.

After a brew of tea, he strolled toward evening along the shore, look-ing for the first sign of a rising fish. A faint ripple on the water, with the lengthening shadows, made good conditions. *Plop* followed *plop*, as the big fellows rose, snatched at their food, and vanished into the depths. He hurried back. Ten minutes later he had taken his rods and was gliding cautiously in the canoe through the quiet water.

So good was the sport, indeed, and so quickly did the big trout pile up in the bottom of the canoe that, despite the growing lateness, he found it hard to tear himself away. "One more," he said, "and then I really will go." He landed that "one more," and was in act of taking it off the hook, when the deep silence of the evening was curiously disturbed. He became abruptly aware that someone watched him. A pair of eyes, it seemed, were fixed upon him from some point in the surrounding shadows.

Thus, at least, he interpreted the odd disturbance in his happy mood; for thus he felt it. The feeling stole over him without the slightest warn-ing. He was not alone. The slippery big trout dropped from his fingers. He sat motionless, and stared about him.

Nothing stirred; the ripple on the lake had died away; there was no wind; the forest lay a single purple mass of shadow; the yellow sky, fast fading, threw reflections that troubled the eye and made distances uncertain. But there was no sound, no movement; he saw no figure any-where. Yet he knew that someone watched him, and a wave of quite unreasoning terror gripped him. The nose of the canoe was against the bank. In a moment, and instinctively, he shoved it off and paddled into deeper water. The watcher, it came to him also instinctively, was quite close to him upon that bank. But where? And who? Was it the Indian?

Here, in deeper water, and some twenty yards from the shore, he paused and strained both sight and hearing to find some possible clue. He felt half ashamed, now that the first strange feeling passed a little. But the certainty remained. Absurd as it was, he felt positive that some-one watched him with concentrated and intent regard. Every fibre in his being told him so; and though he could discover no figure, no new out-line on the shore, he could even have sworn in which clump of willow bushes the hidden person crouched and stared. His attention seemed drawn to that particular clump.

The water dripped slowly from his paddle, now lying across the thwarts. There was no other sound. The canvas of his tent gleamed dimly. A star or two were out. He waited. Nothing happened.

Then, as suddenly as it had come, the feeling passed, and he knew that the person who had been watching him intently had gone. It was as if a current had been turned off; the normal world flowed back; the landscape emptied as if someone had left a room. The disagreeable feeling left him at the same time, so that he instantly turned the canoe in to the shore again, landed, and, paddle in hand, went over to examine the clump of willows he had singled out as the place of concealment. There was no one there, of course, nor any trace of recent human occupancy. No leaves, no branches stirred, nor was a single twig displaced; his keen and practised sight detected no sign of tracks upon the ground. Yet, for all that, he felt positive that a little time ago someone had crouched among these very leaves and watched him. He remained absolutely convinced of it. The watcher, whether Indian, hunter, stray lumberman, or wandering half-breed, had now withdrawn, a search was useless, and dusk was falling. He returned to his little camp, more disturbed perhaps than he cared to acknowledge. He cooked his supper, hung up his catch on a string, so that no prowling animal could get at it during the night, and prepared to make himself comfortable until bedtime. Unconsciously, he built a bigger fire than usual, and found himself peering over his pipe into the deep shadows beyond the firelight, straining his ears to catch the slightest sound. He remained generally on the alert in a way that was new to him.

A man under such conditions and in such a place need not know discomfort until the sense of loneliness strikes him as too vivid a reality. Loneliness in a backwoods camp brings charm, pleasure, and a happy sense of calm until, and unless, it comes too near. It should remain an ingredient only among other conditions; it should not be directly, vividly noticed. Once it has crept within short range, however, it may easily cross the narrow line between comfort and discomfort, and darkness is an undesirable time for the transition. A curious dread may easily follow—the dread lest the loneliness suddenly be disturbed, and the solitary human feel himself open to attack.

For Hyde, now, this transition had been already accomplished; the too intimate sense of his loneliness had shifted abruptly into the worse condition of no longer being quite alone. It was an awkward moment, and the hotel clerk realized his position exactly. He did not quite like it. He sat there, with his back to the blazing logs, a very visible object in the light, while all about him the darkness of the forest lay like an impenetrable wall. He could not see a foot beyond the small circle of his camp-fire; the silence about him was like the silence of the dead. No leaf rustled, no wave lapped; he himself sat motionless as a log.

Then again he became suddenly aware that the person who watched him had returned, and that same intent and concentrated gaze as before was fixed upon him where he lay. There was no warning; he heard no stealthy tread or snapping of dry twigs, yet the owner of those steady eyes was very close to him, probably not a dozen feet away. This sense of proximity was overwhelming.

It is unquestionable that a shiver ran down his spine. This time, moreover, he felt positive that the man crouched just beyond the firelight, the distance he himself could see being nicely calculated, and straight in front of him. For some minutes he sat without stirring a single muscle, yet with each muscle ready and alert, straining his eyes in vain to pierce the darkness, but only succeeding in dazzling his sight with the reflected light. Then, as he shifted his position slowly, cautiously, to obtain another angle of vision, his heart gave two big thumps against his ribs and the hair seemed to rise on his scalp with the sense of cold that shot horribly up his spine. In the darkness facing him he saw two small and greenish circles that were certainly a pair of eyes, yet not the eyes of Indian, hunter, or of any human being. It was a pair of animal eyes that stared so fixedly at him out of the night. And this certainly had an immediate and natural effect upon him.

For, at the menace of those eyes, the fears of millions of long dead hunters since the dawn of time woke in him. Hotel clerk though he was, heredity surged through him in an automatic wave of instinct. His hand groped for a weapon. His fingers fell on the iron head of his small camp axe, and at once he was himself again. Confidence returned; the vague, superstitious dread was gone. This was a bear or wolf that smelt his catch and came to steal it. With beings of that sort, he knew instinctively how to deal, yet admitting, by this very instinct, that his original dread had been of quite another kind.

"I'll damned quick find out what it is," he exclaimed aloud, and snatching a burning brand from the fire, he hurled it with good aim straight at the eyes of the beast before him.

The bit of pitch-pine fell in a shower of sparks that lit the dry grass this side of the animal, flared up a moment, then died quickly down again. But in that instant of bright illumination he saw clearly what his unwelcome visitor was. A big timber wolf sat on its hindquarters, staring steadily at him through the firelight. He saw its legs and shoulders, he saw its hair, he saw also the big hemlock trunks lit up behind it, and the willow scrub on each side. It formed a vivid, clear-cut picture shown in clear detail by the momentary blaze. To his amazement, however, the wolf did not turn and bolt away from the burning log, but withdrew a few yards only, and sat there again on its haunches, staring, staring as before. Heavens, how it stared! He "shoo-ed" it, but without effect; it did not budge. He did not waste another good log on it, for his fear was dissipated now; a timber wolf was a timber wolf, and it might sit there as long as it pleased, provided it did not try to steal his catch. No alarm was in him any more. He knew that wolves were harmless in the summer and autumn, and even when "packed" in the winter, they would attack a man only when suffering desperate hunger. So he lay and watched the beast, threw bits of stick in its direction, even talked to it, wondering only that it never moved. "You can stay there for ever, if you like," he remarked to it aloud, "for you cannot get at my fish, and the rest of the grub I shall take into the tent with me!"

The creature blinked its bright green eyes, but made no move.

Why, then, if his fear was gone, did he think of certain things as he rolled himself in the Hudson Bay blankets before going to sleep? The immobility of the animal was strange, its refusal to turn and bolt was still stranger. Never before had he known a wild creature that was not afraid of fire. Why did it sit and watch him, as with purpose in its dreadful eyes? How had he felt its presence earlier and instantly? A timber wolf, especially a solitary timber wolf, was a timid thing, yet this one feared neither man nor fire. Now, as he lay there wrapped in his blankets inside the cosy tent, it sat outside beneath the stars, beside the fading embers, the wind chilly in its fur, the ground cooling beneath its planted paws, watching him, steadily watching him, perhaps until the dawn.

It was unusual, it was strange. Having neither imagination nor tradition, he called upon no store of racial visions. Matter of fact, a hotel clerk on a fishing holiday, he lay there in his blankets, merely wondering and puzzled. A timber wolf was a timber wolf and nothing more. Yet this timber wolf—the idea haunted him—was different. In a word, the deeper part of his original uneasiness remained. He tossed about, he shivered sometimes in his broken sleep; he did not go out to see, but he woke early and unrefreshed.

Again, with the sunshine and the morning wind, however, the incident of the night before was forgotten, almost unreal. His hunting zeal was uppermost. The tea and fish were delicious, his pipe had never tasted so good, the glory of this lonely lake amid primeval forests went to his head a little; he was a hunter before the Lord, and nothing else. He tried the edge of the lake, and in the excitement of playing a big fish, knew suddenly that it, the wolf, was there. He paused with the rod, exactly as if struck. He looked about him, he looked in a definite direction. The brilliant sunshine made every smallest detail clear and sharp—boulders of granite, burned stems, crimson sumach, pebbles along the shore in neat, separate detail—without revealing where the watcher hid. Then, his sight wandering farther inshore among the tangled undergrowth, he suddenly picked up the familiar, half-expected outline. The wolf was lying behind a granite boulder, so that only the head, the muzzle, and the eyes were visible. It merged in its background. Had he not known it was a wolf, he could never have separated it from the landscape. The eyes shone in the sunlight.

There it lay. He looked straight at it. Their eyes, in fact, actually met full and square. "Great Scott!" he exclaimed aloud, "why, it's like looking at a human being!" From that moment, unwittingly, he established a singular personal relation with the beast. And what followed confirmed this undesirable impression, for the animal rose instantly and came down in leisurely fashion to the shore, where it stood looking back at him. It stood and stared into his eyes like some great wild dog, so that he was aware of a new and almost incredible sensation—that it courted recognition.

"Well! well!" he exclaimed again, relieving his feelings by addressing it aloud, "if this doesn't beat everything I ever saw! What d'you want, anyway?"

He examined it now more carefully. He had never seen a wolf so big before; it was a tremendous beast, a nasty customer to tackle, he reflected, if it ever came to that. It stood there absolutely fearless and full of confidence. In the clear sunlight he took in every detail of it—a huge, shaggy, lean-flanked timber wolf, its wicked eyes staring straight into his own, almost with a kind of purpose in them. He saw its great jaws, its teeth, and its tongue, hung out, dropping saliva a little. And yet the idea of its savagery, its fierceness, was very little in him.

He was amazed and puzzled beyond belief. He wished the Indian would come back. He did not understand this strange behaviour in an animal. Its eyes, the odd expression in them, gave him a queer, unusual, difficult feeling. Had his nerves gone wrong, he almost wondered.

The beast stood on the shore and looked at him. He wished for the first time that he had brought a rifle. With a resounding smack he brought his paddle down flat upon the water, using all his strength, till the echoes rang as from a pistol-shot that was audible from one end of the lake to the other. The wolf never stirred. He shouted, but the beast remained unmoved. He blinked his eyes, speaking as to a dog, a domestic animal, a creature accustomed to human ways. It blinked its eyes in return.

At length, increasing his distance from the shore, he continued fishing, and the excitement of the marvellous sport held his attention—his surface attention, at any rate. At times he almost forgot the attendant beast; yet whenever he looked up, he saw it there. And worse; when he slowly paddled home again, he observed it trotting along the shore as though to keep him company. Crossing a little bay, he spurted, hoping to reach the other point before his undesired and undesirable attendant. Instantly the brute broke into that rapid, tireless lope that, except on ice, can run down anything on four legs in the woods. When he reached the distant point, the wolf was waiting for him. He raised his paddle from the water, pausing a moment for reflection; for this very close attention— there were dusk and night yet to come—he certainly did not relish. His camp was near; he had to land; he felt uncomfortable even in the sunshine of broad day, when, to his keen relief, about half a mile from the tent, he saw the creature suddenly stop and sit down in the open. He waited a moment, then paddled on. It did not follow. There was no attempt to move; it merely sat and watched him. After a few hundred yards, he looked back. It was still sitting where he left it. And the absurd, yet significant, feeling came to him that the beast divined his thought, his anxiety, his dread, and was now showing him, as well as it could, that it entertained no hostile feeling and did not meditate attack.

He turned the canoe toward the shore; he landed; he cooked his supper in the dusk; the animal made no sign. Not far away it certainly lay and watched, but it did not advance. And to Hyde, observant now in a new way, came one sharp, vivid reminder of the strange atmosphere into which his commonplace personality had strayed: he suddenly recalled that his relations with the beast, already established, had progressed distinctly a stage further. This startled him, yet without the accompanying alarm he must certainly have felt twenty-four hours before. He had an understanding with the wolf. He was aware of friendly thoughts toward it. He even went so far as to set out a few big fish on the spot where he had first seen it sitting the previous night. "If he comes," he thought, "he is welcome to them. I've got plenty, anyway." He thought of it now as "he."

Yet the wolf made no appearance until he was in the act of entering his tent a good deal later. It was close on ten o'clock, whereas nine was his hour, and late at that, for turning in. He had, therefore, unconsciously been waiting for him. Then, as he was closing the flap, he saw the eyes close to where he had placed the fish. He waited, hiding himself, and expecting to hear sounds of munching jaws; but all was silence. Only the eyes glowed steadily out of the background of pitch darkness. He closed the flap. He had no slightest fear. In ten minutes he was sound asleep.

He could not have slept very long, for when he woke up he could see the shine of a faint red light through the canvas, and the fire had not died down completely. He rose and cautiously peeped out. The air was very cold; he saw his breath. But he also saw the wolf, for it had come in, and was sitting by the dying embers, not two yards away from where he crouched behind the flap. And this time, at these very close quarters, there was something in the attitude of the big wild thing that caught his attention with a vivid thrill of startled surprise and a sudden shock of cold that held him spellbound. He stared, unable to believe his eyes; for the wolf's attitude conveyed to him something familiar that at first he was unable to explain. Its pose reached him in the terms of another thing with which he was entirely at home. What was it? Did his senses betray him? Was he still asleep and dreaming?

Then, suddenly, with a start of uncanny recognition, he knew. Its attitude was that of a dog. Having found the clue, his mind then made an awful leap. For it was, after all, no dog its appearance aped, but something nearer to himself, and more familiar still. Good heavens! It sat there with the pose, the attitude, the gesture in repose of something almost human. And then, with a second shock of biting wonder, it came to him like a revelation. The wolf sat beside that camp-fire as a man might sit.

Before he could weigh his extraordinary discovery, before he could examine it in detail or with care, the animal, sitting in this ghastly fashion, seemed to feel his eyes fixed on it. It slowly turned and looked him in the face, and for the first time Hyde felt a full-blooded, superstitious fear flood through his entire being. He seemed transfixed with that nameless terror that is said to attack human beings who suddenly face the dead, finding themselves bereft of speech and movement. This moment of paralysis certainly occurred. Its passing, however, was as singular as its advent. For almost at once he was aware of something beyond and above this mockery of human attitude and pose, something that ran along unaccustomed nerves and reached his feeling, even perhaps his heart. The revulsion was extraordinary, its result still more extraordinary and unexpected. Yet the fact remains. He was aware of another thing that had the effect of stilling his terror as soon as it was born. He was aware of appeal, silent, half expressed, yet vastly pathetic. He saw in the savage eyes a beseeching, even a yearning, expression that changed his mood as by magic from dread to natural sympathy. The great grey brute, symbol of cruel ferocity, sat there beside his dying fire and appealed for help.

This gulf betwixt animal and human seemed in that instant bridged. It was, of course, incredible. Hyde, sleep still possibly clinging to his inner being with the shades and half shapes of dream yet about his soul, acknowledged, how he knew not, the amazing fact. He found himself nodding to the brute in half consent, and instantly, without more ado, the lean grey shape rose like a wraith and trotted off swiftly, but with stealthy tread, into the background of the night.

When Hyde woke in the morning his first impression was that he must have dreamed the entire incident. His practical nature asserted itself. There was a bite in the fresh autumn air; the bright sun allowed no half lights anywhere; he felt brisk in mind and body. Reviewing what had happened, he came to the conclusion that it was utterly vain to speculate; no possible explanation of the animal's behaviour occurred to him; he was dealing with something entirely outside his experience. His fear, however, had completely left him. The odd sense of friendliness remained. The beast had a definite purpose, and he himself was included in that purpose. His sympathy held good.

But with the sympathy there was also an intense curiosity. "If it shows itself again," he told himself, "I'll go up close and find out what it wants." The fish laid out the night before had not been touched.

It must have been a full hour after breakfast when he next saw the brute; it was standing on the edge of the clearing, looking at him in the way now become familiar. Hyde immediately picked up his axe and advanced toward it boldly, keeping his eyes fixed straight upon its own. There was nervousness in him, but kept well under; nothing betrayed it; step by step he drew nearer until some ten yards separated them. The wolf had not stirred a muscle as yet. Its jaws hung open, its eyes observed him intently; it allowed him to approach without a sign of what its mood might be. Then, with these ten yards between them, it turned abruptly and moved slowly off, looking back first over one shoulder and then over the other, exactly as a dog might do, to see if he was following.

A singular journey it was they then made together, animal and man. The trees surrounded them at once, for they left the lake behind them, entering the tangled bush beyond. The beast, Hyde noticed, obviously picked the easiest track for him to follow; for obstacles that meant nothing to the four-legged expert, yet were difficult for a man, were carefully avoided with an almost uncanny skill, while yet the general direction was accurately kept. Occasionally there were windfalls to be surmounted; but though the wolf bounded over these with case, it was always waiting for the man on the other side after he had laboriously climbed over. Deeper and deeper into the heart of the lonely forest they penetrated in this singular fashion, cutting across the arc of the lake's crescent, it seemed to Hyde; for after two miles or so, he recognized the big rocky bluff that overhung the water at its northern end. This outstanding bluff he had seen from his camp, one side of it falling sheer into the water; it was probably the spot, he imagined, where the Indians held their medicine-making ceremonies, for it stood out in isolated fashion, and its top formed a private plateau not easy of access. And it was here, close to a big spruce at the foot of the bluff upon the forest side, that the wolf stopped suddenly and for the first time since its appearance gave audible expression to its feelings. It sat down on its haunches, lifted its muzzle with open jaws, and gave vent to a subdued and long-drawn howl that was more like the wail of a dog than the fierce barking cry associated with a wolf.

By this time Hyde had lost not only fear, but caution too; nor, oddly enough, did this warning howl revive a sign of unwelcome emotion in him. In that curious sound he detected the same message that the eyes conveyed—appeal for help. He paused, nevertheless, a little startled, and while the wolf sat waiting for him, he looked about him quickly. There was young timber here; it had once been a small clearing, evidently. Axe and fire had done their work, but there was evidence to an experienced eye that it was Indians and not white men who had once been busy here. Some part of the medicine ritual, doubtless, took place in the little clearing, thought the man, as he advanced again towards his patient leader. The end of their queer journey, he felt, was close at hand.

He had not taken two steps before the animal got up and moved very slowly in the direction of some low bushes that formed a clump just beyond. It entered these, first looking back to make sure that its companion watched. The bushes hid it; a moment later it emerged again. Twice it performed this pantomime, each time, as it reappeared, standing still and staring at the man with as distinct an expression of appeal in the eyes as an animal may compass, probably. Its excitement, meanwhile, certainly increased, and this excitement was, with equal certainty, communicated to the man. Hyde made up his mind quickly. Gripping his axe tightly, and ready to use it at the first hint of malice, he moved slowly nearer to the bushes, wondering with something of a tremor what would happen.

If he expected to be startled, his expectation was at once fulfilled; but it was the behaviour of the beast that made him jump. It positively frisked about him like a happy dog. It frisked for joy. Its excitement was intense, yet from its open mouth no sound was audible. With a sudden leap, then, it bounded past him into the clump of bushes, against whose very edge he stood, and began scraping vigorously at the ground. Hyde stood and stared, amazement and interest now banishing all his nervousness, even when the beast, in its violent scraping, actually touched his body with its own. He had, perhaps, the feeling that he was in a dream, one of those fantastic dreams in which things may happen without involving an adequate surprise; for otherwise the manner of scraping and scratching at the ground must have seemed an impossible phenomenon. No wolf, no dog certainly, used its paws in the way those paws were working. Hyde had the odd, distressing sensation that it was hands, not paws, he watched. And yet, somehow, the natural, adequate surprise he should have felt was absent. The strange action seemed not entirely unnatural. In his heart some deep hidden spring of sympathy and pity stirred instead. He was aware of pathos.

The wolf stopped in its task and looked up into his face. Hyde acted without hesitation then. Afterwards he was wholly at a loss to explain his own conduct. It seemed he knew what to do, divined what was asked, expected of him. Between his mind and the dumb desire yearning through the savage animal there was intelligent and intelligible communication. He cut a stake and sharpened it, for the stones would blunt his axe-edge. He entered the clump of bushes to complete the digging his four-legged companion had begun. And while he worked, though he did not forget the close proximity of the wolf, he paid no attention to it; often his back was turned as he stooped over the laborious clearing away of the hard earth; no uneasiness or sense of danger was in him any more. The wolf sat outside the clump and watched the operations. Its concentrated attention, its patience, its intense eagerness, the gentleness and docility of the grey, fierce, and probably hungry brute, its obvious pleasure and satisfaction, too, at having won the human to its mysterious purpose—these were colours in the strange picture that Hyde thought of later when dealing with the human herd in his hotel again. At the moment he was aware chiefly of pathos and affection. The whole business was, of course, not to be believed, but that discovery came later, too, when telling it to others.

The digging continued for fully half an hour before his labour was rewarded by the discovery of a small whitish object. He picked it up and examined it—the finger-bone of a man. Other discoveries then followed quickly and in quantity. The *cache* was laid bare. He collected nearly the complete skeleton. The skull, however, he found last, and might not have found at all but for the guidance of his strangely alert companion. It lay some few yards away from the central hole now dug, and the wolf stood nuzzling the ground with its nose before Hyde understood that he was meant to dig exactly in that spot for it. Between the beast's very paws his stake struck hard upon it. He scraped the earth from the bone and examined it carefully. It was perfect, save for the fact that some wild animal had gnawed it, the teeth-marks being still plainly visible. Close beside it lay the rusty iron head of a tomahawk. This and the smallness of the bones confirmed him in his judgment that it was the skeleton not of a white man, but of an Indian.

During the excitement of the discovery of the bones one by one, and finally of the skull, but, more especially, during the period of intense interest while Hyde was examining them, he had paid little, if any, attention to the wolf. He was aware that it sat and watched him, never moving its keen eyes for a single moment from the actual operations, but of sign or movement it made none at all. He knew that it was pleased and satisfied, he knew also that he had now fulfilled its purpose in a great measure. The further intuition that now came to him, derived, he felt positive, from his companion's dumb desire, was perhaps the cream of the entire experience to him. Gathering the bones together in his coat, he carried them, together with the tomahawk, to the foot of the big spruce where the animal had first stopped. His leg actually touched the creature's muzzle as he passed. It turned its head to watch, but did not follow, nor did it move a muscle while he prepared the platform of boughs upon which he then laid the poor worn bones of an Indian who had been killed, doubtless, in sudden attack or ambush, and to whose remains had been denied the last grace of proper tribal burial. He wrapped the bones in bark; he laid the tomahawk beside the skull; he lit the circular fire round the pyre, and the blue smoke rose upward into the clear bright sunshine of the Canadian autumn morning till it was lost among the mighty trees far overhead.

In the moment before actually lighting the little fire he had turned to note what his companion did. It sat five yards away, he saw, gazing intently, and one of its front paws was raised a little from the ground. It made no sign of any kind. He finished the work, becoming so absorbed in it that he had eyes for nothing but the tending and guarding of his careful ceremonial fire. It was only when the platform of boughs collapsed, laying their charred burden gently on the fragrant earth among the soft wood ashes, that he turned again, as though to show the wolf what he had done, and seek, perhaps, some look of satisfaction in its curiously expressive eyes. But the place he searched was empty. The wolf had gone.

He did not see it again; it gave no sign of its presence anywhere; he was not watched. He fished as before, wandered through the bush about his camp, sat smoking round his fire after dark, and slept peacefully in his cosy little tent. He was not disturbed. No howl was ever audible in the distant forest, no twig snapped beneath a stealthy tread, he saw no eyes. The wolf that behaved like a man had gone for ever.

It was the day before he left that Hyde, noticing smoke rising from the shack across the lake, paddled over to exchange a word or two with the Indian, who had evidently now returned. The Redskin came down to meet him as he landed, but it was soon plain that he spoke very little

English. He emitted the familiar grunts at first; then bit by bit Hyde stirred his limited vocabulary into action. The net result, however, was slight enough, though it was certainly direct:

"You camp there?" the man asked, pointing to the other side.

"Yes."

"Wolf come?"

"Yes."

"You see wolf?"

"Yes."

The Indian stared at him fixedly a moment, a keen, wondering look upon his coppery, creased face.

"You 'fraid wolf?" he asked after a moment's pause.

"No," replied Hyde, truthfully. He knew it was useless to ask questions of his own, though he was eager for information. The other would have told him nothing. It was sheer luck that the man had touched on the subject at all, and Hyde realized that his own best rôle was merely to answer, but to ask no questions. Then, suddenly, the Indian became comparatively voluble. There was awe in his voice and manner.

"Him no wolf. Him big medicine wolf. Him spirit wolf."

Whereupon he drank the tea the other had brewed for him, closed his lips tightly, and said no more. His outline was discernible on the shore, rigid and motionless, an hour later, when Hyde's canoe turned the corner of the lake three miles away, and landed to make the portages up the first rapid of his homeward stream.

It was Morton who, after some persuasion, supplied further details of what he called the legend. Some hundred years before, the tribe that lived in the territory beyond the lake began their annual medicine-making ceremonies on the big rocky bluff at the northern end; but no medicine could be made. The spirits, declared the chief medicine man, would not answer. They were offended. An investigation followed. It was discovered that a young brave had recently killed a wolf, a thing strictly forbidden, since the wolf was the totem animal of the tribe. To make matters worse, the name of the guilty man was Running Wolf. The offence being unpardonable, the man was cursed and driven from the tribe:

"Go out. Wander alone among the woods, and if we see you we slay you. Your bones shall be scattered in the forest, and your spirit shall not enter the Happy Hunting Grounds till one of another race shall find and bury them."

"Which meant," explained Morton laconically, his only comment on the story, "probably for ever."

FIRST HATE

They had been shooting all day; the weather had been perfect and the powder straight, so that when they assembled in the smoking-room after dinner they were well pleased with themselves. From discussing the day's sport and the weather outlook, the conversation drifted to other, though still cognate, fields. Lawson, the crack shot of the party, mentioned the instinctive recognition all animals feel for their natural enemies, and gave several instances in which he had tested it— tame rats with a ferret, birds with a snake, and so forth.

"Even after being domesticated for generations," he said, "they recognize their natural enemy at once by instinct, an enemy they can never even have seen before. It's infallible. They know instantly."

"Undoubtedly," said a voice from the corner chair; "and so do we."

The speaker was Ericssen, their host, a great hunter before the Lord, generally uncommunicative but a good listener, leaving the talk to others. For this latter reason, as well as for a certain note of challenge in his voice, his abrupt statement gained attention.

"What do you mean exactly by 'so do we'?" asked three men together, after waiting some seconds to see whether he meant to elaborate, which he evidently did not.

"We belong to the animal kingdom, of course," put in a fourth, for behind the challenge there obviously lay a story, though a story that might be difficult to drag out of him. It was.

Ericssen, who had leaned forward a moment so that his strong, humorous face was in clear light, now sank back again into his chair, his expression concealed by the red lampshade at his side. The light played tricks, obliterating the humorous, almost tender lines, while emphasizing the strength of the jaw and nose. The red glare lent to the whole a rather grim expression.

Lawson, man of authority among them, broke the little pause.

"You're dead right," he observed, "but how do you know it?"—for John Ericssen never made a positive statement without a good reason for it. That good reason, he felt sure, involved a personal proof, but a story Ericssen would never tell before a general audience. He would tell it later, however, when the others had left. "There's such a thing as instinctive antipathy, of course," he added, with a laugh, looking around him. "That's what you mean probably."

"I meant exactly what I said," replied the host bluntly. "There's first love. There's first hate, too."

"Hate's a strong word," remarked Lawson.

"So is love," put in another.

"Hate's strongest," said Ericssen grimly. "In the animal kingdom, at least," he added suggestively, and then kept his lips closed, except to sip his liquor, for the rest of the evening—until the party at length broke up, leaving Lawson and one other man, both old trusted friends of many years' standing.

"It's not a tale I'd tell to everybody," he began, when they were alone. "It's true, for one thing; for another, you see, some of those good fellows"—he indicated the empty chairs with an expressive nod of his great head—"some of 'em knew him. You both knew him too, probably."

"The man you hated," said the understanding Lawson.

"And who hated me," came the quiet confirmation. "My other reason," he went on, "for keeping quiet was that the tale involves my wife."

The two listeners said nothing, but each remembered the curiously long courtship that had been the prelude to his marriage. No engagement had been announced, the pair were devoted to one another, there was no known rival on either side; yet the courtship continued without coming to its expected conclusion. Many stories were afloat in consequence. It was a social mystery that intrigued the gossips.

"I may tell you two," Ericssen continued, "'the reason my wife refused for so long to marry me. It is hard to believe, perhaps, but it is true. Another man wished to make her his wife, and she would not consent to marry me until that other man was dead. Quixotic, absurd, unreasonable? If you like. I'll tell you what she said." He looked up with a significant expression in his face which proved that he, at least, did not now judge her reason foolish. "'Because it would be murder,' she told me. 'Another man who wants to marry me would kill you.' "

"She had some proof for the assertion, no doubt?" suggested Lawson.

"None whatever," was the reply. "Merely her woman's instinct. Moreover, I did not know who the other man was, nor would she ever tell me."

"Otherwise you might have murdered him instead?" said Baynes, the second listener.

"I did," said Ericssen grimly. "But without knowing he was the man." He sipped his whisky and relit his pipe. The others waited.

"Our marriage took place two months later—just after Hazel's disappearance."

"Hazel?" exclaimed Lawson and Baynes in a single breath. "Hazel! Member of the Hunters!" His mysterious disappearance had been a nine days' wonder some ten years ago. It had never been explained. They had all been members of the Hunters' Club together.

"That's the chap," Ericssen said. "Now I'll tell you the tale, if you care to hear it." They settled back in their chairs to listen, and Ericssen, who had evidently never told the affair to another living soul except his own wife, doubtless, seemed glad this time to tell it to two men.

"It began some dozen years ago when my brother Jack and I came home from a shooting trip in China. I've often told you about our adventures there, and you see the heads hanging up here in the smoking-room—some of 'em." He glanced round proudly at the walls. "We were glad to be in town again after two years' roughing it, and we looked forward to our first good dinner at the club, to make up for the rotten cooking we had endured so long. We had ordered that dinner in anticipatory detail many a time together. Well, we had it and enjoyed it up to a point—the point of the *entrée,* to be exact.

"Up to that point it was delicious, and we let ourselves go, I can tell you. We had ordered the very wine we had planned months before when we were snow-bound and half starving in the mountains." He smacked his lips as he mentioned it. "I was just starting on a beautifully cooked grouse," he went on, "when a figure went by our table, and Jack looked up and nodded. The two exchanged a brief word of greeting and explanation, and the other man passed on. Evidently they knew each other just enough to make a word or two necessary, but enough.

"'Who's that?' I asked.

"'A new member, named Hazel,' Jack told me. 'A great shot.' He knew him slightly, he explained; he had once been a client of his—Jack was a barrister, you remember—and had defended him in some financial case or other. Rather an unpleasant case, he added. Jack did not 'care about' the fellow, he told me, as he went on with his tender wing of grouse."

Ericssen paused to relight his pipe a moment.

"Not care about him!" he continued. "It didn't surprise me, for my own feeling, the instant I set eyes on the fellow, was one of violent, instinctive dislike that amounted to loathing. Loathing! No. I'll give it the right word—hatred. I simply couldn't help myself; I hated the man from the very first go off. A wave of repulsion swept over me as I followed him down the room a moment with my eyes, till he took his seat at a distant table and was out of sight. Ugh! He was a big, fat-faced man, with an eye-glass glued into one of his pale-blue cod-like eyes—out of condition, ugly as a toad, with a smug expression of intense self-satisfaction on his jowl that made me long to—

"I leave it to you to guess what I would have liked to do to him. But the instinctive loathing he inspired in me had another aspect, too. Jack had not introduced us during the momentary pause beside our table, but as

I looked up I caught the fellow's eye on mine—he was glaring at me instead of at Jack, to whom he was talking—with an expression of malignant dislike, as keen evidently as my own. That's the other aspect I meant. He hated me as violently as I hated him. We were instinctive enemies, just as the rat and ferret are instinctive enemies. Each recognized a mortal foe. It was a case—I swear it—of whoever got first chance."

"Bad as that!" exclaimed Baynes. "I knew him by sight. He wasn't pretty, I'll admit."

"I knew him to nod to," Lawson mentioned. "I never heard anything particular against him." He shrugged his shoulders.

Ericssen went on. "'It was not his character or qualities I hated," he said. "I didn't even know them. That's the whole point. There's no reason you fellows should have disliked him. My hatred—our mutual hatred—was instinctive, as instinctive as first love. A man knows his natural mate; also he knows his natural enemy. I did, at any rate, both with him and with my wife. Given the chance, Hazel would have done me in; just as surely, given the chance, I would have done him in. No blame to either of us, what's more, in my opinion."

"I've felt dislike, but never hatred like that," Baynes mentioned. "I came across it in a book once, though. The writer did not mention the instinctive fear of the human animal for its natural enemy, or anything of that sort. He thought it was a continuance of a bitter feud begun in an earlier existence. He called it memory."

"Possibly," said Ericssen briefly. "My mind is not speculative. But I'm glad you spoke of fear. I left that out. The truth is, I feared the fellow, too, in a way; and had we ever met face to face in some wild country without witnesses I should have felt justified in drawing on him at sight, and he would have felt the same. Murder? If you like. I should call it self-defence. Anyhow, the fellow polluted the room for me. He spoilt the enjoyment of that dinner we had ordered months before in China."

"But you saw him again, of course, later?"

"Lots of times. Not that night, because we went on to a theatre. But in the club we were always running across one another—in the houses of friends at lunch or dinner; at race meetings; all over the place; in fact, I even had some trouble to avoid being introduced to him. And every time we met our eyes betrayed us. He felt in his heart what I felt in mine. Ugh! He was as loathsome to me as leprosy, and as dangerous. Odd, isn't it? The most intense feeling, except love, I've ever known. I remember"—he laughed gruffly—"I used to feel quite sorry for him. If he felt what I felt, and I'm convinced he did, he must have suffered. His one object—to get me out of the way for good—was so impossible. Then

Fate played a hand in the game. I'll tell you how.

"My brother died a year or two later, and I went abroad to try and forget it. I went salmon fishing in Canada. But, though the sport was good, it was not like the old times with Jack. The camp never felt the same without him. I missed him badly. But I forgot Hazel for the time; hating did not seem worth while, somehow.

"When the best of the fishing was over on the Atlantic side, I took a run back to Vancouver and fished there for a bit. I went up the Campbell River, which was not so crowded then as it is now, and had some rattling sport. Then I grew tired of the rod and decided to go after wapiti for a change. I came back to Victoria and learned what I could about the best places, and decided finally to go up the west coast of the island. By luck I happened to pick up a good guide, who was in the town at the moment on business, and we started off together in one of the little Canadian Pacific Railway boats that ply along that coast.

"Outfitting two days later at a small place the steamer stopped at, the guide said we needed another man to help pack our kit over portages, and so forth, but the only fellow available was a Siwash of whom he disapproved. My guide would not have him at any price; he was lazy, a drunkard, a liar, and even worse, for on one occasion he came back without the sportsman he had taken up country on a shooting trip, and his story was not convincing, to say the least. These disappearances are always awkward, of course, as you both know. We preferred, anyhow, to go without the Siwash, and off we started.

"At first our luck was bad. I saw many wapiti, but no good heads; only after a fortnight's hunting did I manage to get a decent head, though even that was not so good as I should have liked.

"We were then near the head waters of a little river that ran down into the Inlet; heavy rains had made the river rise; running downstream was a risky job, what with old log-jams shifting and new ones forming; and, after many narrow escapes, we upset one afternoon and had the misfortune to lose a lot of our kit, amongst it most of our cartridges. We could only muster a few between us. The guide had a dozen; I had two—just enough, we considered, to take us out all right. Still, it was an infernal nuisance. We camped at once to dry out our soaked things in front of a big fire, and while this laundry work was going on, the guide suggested my filling in the time by taking a look at the next little valley, which ran parallel to ours. He had seen some good heads over there a few weeks ago. Possibly I might come upon the herd. I started at once, taking my two cartridges with me.

"It was the devil of a job getting over the divide, for it was a badly bushed-up place, and where there were no bushes there were boulders and fallen trees, and the going was slow and tiring. But I got across at last and came out upon another stream at the bottom of the new valley. Signs of wapiti were plentiful, though I never came up with a single beast all the afternoon. Blacktail deer were everywhere, but the wapiti remained invisible. Providence, or whatever you like to call that which there is no escaping in our lives, made me save my two cartridges."

Ericssen stopped a minute then. It was not to light his pipe or sip his whisky. Nor was it because the remainder of his story failed in the recollection of any vivid detail. He paused a moment to think.

"Tell us the lot," pleaded Lawson. "Don't leave out anything."

Ericssen looked up. His friend's remark had helped him to make up his mind apparently. He *had* hesitated about something or other, but the hesitation passed. He glanced at both his listeners.

"Right," he said. "I'll tell you everything. I'm not imaginative, as you know, and my amount of superstition, I should judge, is microscopic." He took a longer breath, then lowered his voice a trifle. "Anyhow," he went on, "it's true, so I don't see why I should feel shy about admitting it—but as I stood there in that lonely valley, where only the noises of wind and water were audible, and no human being, except my guide, some miles away, was within reach, a curious feeling came over me I find difficult to describe. I felt"—obviously he made an effort to get the word out—"I felt creepy."

"You," murmured Lawson, with an incredulous smile—"you creepy?" he repeated under his breath.

"I felt creepy and afraid," continued the other, with conviction. "I had the sensation of being seen by someone—as if someone, I mean, was watching me. It was so unlikely that anyone was near me in that God-forsaken bit of wilderness, that I simply couldn't believe it at first. But the feeling persisted. I felt absolutely positive somebody was not far away among the red maples, behind a boulder, across the little stream, perhaps, somewhere, at any rate, so near that I was plainly visible to him. It was not an animal. It was human. Also, it was hostile.

"I was in danger.

"You may laugh, both of you, but I assure you the feeling was so positive that I crouched down instinctively to hide myself behind a rock. My first thought, that the guide had followed me for some reason or other, I at once discarded. It was not the guide. It was an enemy.

"No, no, I thought of no one in particular. No name, no face occurred to me. Merely that an enemy was on my trail, that he saw me, and I did not see him, and that he was near enough to me to—well, to take instant action. This deep instinctive feeling of danger, of fear, of anything you like to call it, was simply overwhelming.

"Another curious detail I must also mention. About half an hour before, having given up all hope of seeing wapiti, I had decided to kill a blacktail deer for meat. A good shot offered itself, not thirty yards away. I aimed. But just as I was going to pull the trigger a. queer emotion touched me, and I lowered the rifle. It was exactly as though a voice said, 'Don't!' I heard no voice, mind you; it was an emotion only, a feeling, a sudden inexplicable change of mind—a warning, if you like. I didn't fire, anyhow.

"But now, as I crouched behind that rock, I remembered this curious little incident, and was glad I had not used up my last two cartridges. More than that I cannot tell you. Things of that kind are new to me. They're difficult enough to tell, let alone to explain. But they were *real*.

"I crouched there, wondering what on earth was happening to me, and, feeling a bit of a fool, if you want to know, when suddenly, over the top of the boulder, I saw something moving. It was a man's hat. I peered cautiously. Some sixty yards away the bushes parted, and two men came out on to the river's bank, and I knew them both. One was the Siwash I had seen at the store. The other was Hazel. Before I had time to think I cocked my rifle."

"Hazel. Good Lord!" exclaimed the listeners.

"For a moment I was too surprised to do anything but cock that rifle. I waited for what puzzled me was that, after all, Hazel had *not* seen me. It was only the feeling of his beastly proximity that had made me feel I was seen and watched by him. There was something else, too, that made me pause before—er—doing anything. Two other things, in fact. One was that I was so intensely interested in watching the fellow's actions. Obviously he had the same uneasy sensation that I had. He shared with me the nasty feeling that danger was about. His rifle, I saw, was cocked and ready; he kept looking behind him, over his shoulder, peering this way and that, and sometimes addressing a remark to the Siwash at his side. I caught the laughter of the latter. The Siwash evidently did not think there was danger anywhere. It was, of course, unlikely enough—"

"And the other thing that stopped you?" urged Lawson, impatiently interrupting.

Ericssen turned with a look of grins homour on his face.

"Some confounded or perverted sense of chivalry in me, I suppose," he said, "that made it impossible to shoot him down in cold blood, or, rather, without letting him have a chance. For my blood, as a matter of fact, was far from cold at the moment. Perhaps, too, I wanted the added satisfaction of letting him know who fired the shot that was to end his vile existence."

He laughed again. "It was rat and ferret in the human kingdom," he went on, "but I wanted my rat to have a chance, I suppose. Anyhow, though I had a perfect shot in front of me at easy distance, I did not fire. Instead I got up, holding my cocked rifle ready, finger on trigger, and came out of my hiding place. I called to him. 'Hazel, you beast! So there you are—at last!'"

"He turned, but turned away from me, offering his horrid back. The direction of the voice he misjudged. He pointed down stream, and the Siwash turned to look. Neither of them had seen me yet. There was a big logjam below them. The roar of the water in their ears concealed my footsteps. I was, perhaps, twenty paces from them when Hazel, with a jerk of his whole body, abruptly turned clean round and faced me. We stared into each ocher's eyes.

"The amazement on his face changed instantly to hatred and resolve. He acted with incredible rapidity. I think the unexpected suddenness of his turn made me lose a precious second or two. Anyhow he was ahead of me. He flung his rifle to his shoulder. 'You devil!' I heard his voice. 'I've got you at last!' His rifle cracked, for he let drive the same instant. The hair stirred just above my ear.

"He had missed!

"Before he could draw back his bolt for another shot I had acted.

"'You're not fit to live!' I shouted, as my bullet crashed into his temple. I had the satisfaction, too, of knowing that he heard my words. I saw the swift expression of frustrated loathing in his eyes.

He fell like an ox, his face splashing in the stream. I shoved the body out. I saw it sucked beneath the logjam instantly. It disappeared. There could be no inquest on him, I reflected comfortably. Hazel was gone—gone from this earth, from my life, our mutual hatred over at last."

The speaker paused a moment. "Odd," he continued presently—"very odd indeed." He turned to the others. "I felt quite sorry for him suddenly. I suppose," he added, "the philosophers are right when they gas about hate being very close to love."

His friends contributed no remark.

"Then I came away," he resumed shortly. "My wife—well, you know the rest, don't you? I told her the whole thing. She—she said nothing. But she married me, you see."

There was a moment's silence. Baynes was the first to break it. "But— the Siwash?" he asked. "The witness?"

Lawson turned upon him with something of contemptuous impatience.

"He told you he had *two* cartridges."

Ericssen, smiling grimly, said nothing at all.

THE TARN OF SACRIFICE

John Holt, a vague excitement in him, stood at the door of the little inn, listening to the landlord's directions as to the best way of reaching Scarsdale. He was on a walking tour through the Lake District, exploring the smaller dales that lie away from the beaten track and are accessible only on foot.

The landlord, a hard-featured north countryman, half innkeeper, half sheep farmer, pointed up the valley. His deep voice had a friendly burr in it.

"You go straight on till you reach the head," he said, "then take to the fell. Follow the 'sheep-trod' past the Crag. Directly you're over the top you'll strike the road."

"A road up there!" exclaimed his customer incredulously.

"Aye," was the steady reply. "The old Roman Road. The same road," he added, "the savages came down when they burst through the Wall and burnt everything right up to Lancaster—"

"They were held—weren't they—at Lancaster?" asked the other, yet not knowing quite why he asked it.

"I don't rightly know," came the answer slowly. "Some say they were. But the old town has been that built over since, it's hard to tell." He paused a moment. "At Ambleside," he went on presently, "you can still see the marks of the burning, and at the little fort on the way to Ravenglass."

Holt strained his eyes into the sunlit distance, for he would soon have to walk that road and he was anxious to be off. But the landlord was communicative and interesting. "You can't miss it," he told him. "It runs straight as a spear along the fell top till it meets the Wall. You must hold to it for about eight miles. Then you'll come to the Standing Stone on the left of the track—"

"The Standing Stone, yes?" broke in the other a little eagerly.

"You'll see the Stone right enough. It was where the Romans came. Then bear to the left down another 'trod' that comes into the road there. They say it was the war-trail of the folk that set up the Stone."

"And what did they use the Stone for?" Holt inquired, more as though he asked it of himself than of his companion.

The old man paused to reflect. He spoke at length.

"I mind an old fellow who seemed to know about such things called it a Sighting Stone. He reckoned the sun shone over it at dawn on the longest day right on to the little holm in Blood Tarn. He said they held sacrifices in a stone circle there." He stopped a moment to puff at his black pipe. "Maybe he was right. I have seen stones lying about that may well be that."

The man was pleased and willing to talk to so good a listener. Either he had not noticed the curious gesture the other made, or he read it as a sign of eagerness to start. The sun was warm, but a sharp wind from the bare hills went between them with a sighing sound. Holt buttoned his coat about him. "An odd name for a mountain lake—Blood Tarn," he remarked, watching the landlord's face expectantly.

"Aye, but a good one," was the measured reply. "When I was a boy the old folk had a tale that the savages flung three Roman captives from that crag into the water. There's a book been written about it; they say it was a sacrifice, but most likely they were tired of dragging them along, I say. Anyway, that's what the writer said. One, I mind, now you ask me, was a priest of some heathen temple that stood near the Wall, and the other two were his daughter and her lover." He guffawed. At least he made a strange noise in his throat. Evidently, thought Holt, he was sceptical yet superstitious. "It's just an old tale handed down, whatever the learned folk may say," the old man added.

"A lonely place," began Holt, aware that a fleeting touch of awe was added suddenly to his interest.

"Aye " said the other, "and a bad spot too. Every year the Crag takes its toll of sheep, and sometimes a man goes over in the mist. It's right beside the track and very slippery. Ninety foot of a drop before you hit the water. Best keep round the tarn and leave the Crag alone if there's any mist about. Fishing? Yes, there's some quite fair trout in the tarn, but it's not much fished. Happen one of the shepherd lads from Tyson's farm may give it a turn with an 'otter,'" he went on, "once in a while, but he won't stay for the evening. He'll clear out before sunset."

"Ah! Superstitious, I suppose?"

"It's a gloomy, chancy spot—and with the dusk falling," agreed the innkeeper eventually. "None of our folk care to be caught up there with night coming on. Most handy for a shepherd, too—but Tyson can't get a man to hide there." He paused again, then added significantly: "Strangers don't seem to mind it though. It's only our own folk—"

"Strangers!" repeated the other sharply, as though he had been waiting all along for this special bit of information. "You don't mean to say there are people living up there?" A curious thrill ran over him.

"Aye," replied the landlord, "but they're daft folk—a man and his daughter. They come every spring. It's early in the year yet, but I mind Jim Backhouse, one of Tyson's men, talking about them last week." He stopped to think. "So they've come back," he went on decidedly. "They get milk from the farm."

"And what on earth are they doing up there?" Holt asked.

He asked many other questions as well, but the answers were poor, the information not forthcoming. The landlord would talk for hours about the Crag, the tarn, the legends and the Romans, but concerning the two strangers he was uncommunicative. Either he knew little, or he did not want to discuss them; Holt felt it was probably the former. They were educated town-folk, he gathered with difficulty, rich apparently, and they spent their time wandering about the fell, or fishing. The man was often seen upon the Crag, his girl beside him, bare-legged, dressed as a peasant. "Happen they come for their health, happen the father is a learned man studying the Wall"—exact information was not forthcoming.

The landlord "minded his own business," and inhabitants were too few and far between for gossip. All Holt could extract amounted to this: the couple had been in a motor accident some years before, and as a result they came every spring to spend a month or two in absolute solitude, away from cities and the excitement of modern life. They troubled no one and no one troubled them.

"Perhaps I may see them as I go by the tarn," remarked the walker finally, making ready to go. He gave up questioning in despair. The morning hours were passing.

"Happen you may," was the reply, "for your track goes past their door and leads straight down to Scarsdale. The other way over the Crag saves half a mile, but it's rough going along the scree." He stopped dead. Then he added, in reply to Holt's good-bye: "In my opinion it's not worth it," yet what he meant exactly by "it" was not quite clear.

The walker shouldered his knapsack. Instinctively he gave the little hitch to settle it on his shoulders—much as he used to give to his pack in France. The pain that shot through him as he did so was another reminder of France. The bullet he had stopped on the Somme still made its presence felt at times.... Yet he knew, as he walked off briskly, that he was one of the lucky ones. How many of his old pals would never walk again, condemned to hobble on crutches for the rest of their lives! How many, again, would never even hobble! More terrible still, he remembered, were the blind.... The dead, it seemed to him, had been more fortunate....

He swung up the narrowing valley at a good pace and was soon climbing the fell. It proved far steeper than it had appeared from the door of the inn, and he was glad enough to reach the top and fling himself down on the coarse springy turf to admire the view below.

The spring day was delicious. It stirred his blood. The world beneath looked young and stainless. Emotion rose through him in a wave of optimistic happiness. The bare hills were half hidden by a soft blue haze that made them look bigger, vaster, less earthly than they really were. He saw silver streaks in the valleys that he knew were distant streams and lakes. Birds soared between. The dazzling air seemed painted with exhilarating light and colour. The very clouds were floating gossamer that he could touch. There were bees and dragon-flies and fluttering thistledown. Heat vibrated. His body, his physical sensations, so-called, retired into almost nothing. He felt himself, like his surroundings, made of air and sunlight. A delicious sense of resignation poured upon him. He, too, like his surroundings, was composed of air and sunshine, of insect wings, of soft, fluttering vibrations that the gorgeous spring day produced.... It seemed that he renounced the heavy dues of bodily life, and enjoyed the delights, momentarily at any rate, of a more ethereal consciousness.

Near at hand, the hills were covered with the faded gold of last year's bracken, which ran down in a brimming flood till it was lost in the fresh green of the familiar woods below. Far in the hazy distance swam the sea of ash and hazel. The silver birch sprinkled that lower world with fairy light.

Yes, it was all natural enough. He could see the road quite clearly now, only a hundred yards away from where he lay. How straight it ran along the top of the hill! The landlord's expression recurred to him : "Straight as a spear." Somehow, the phrase seemed to describe exactly the Romans and all their works.... The Romans, yes, and all their works....

He became aware of a sudden sympathy with these long dead conquerors of the world. With them, he felt sure, there had been no useless, foolish talk. They had known no empty words, no bandying of foolish phrases. "War to end war," and "Regeneration of the race"—no hypocritical nonsense of that sort had troubled their minds and purposes. They had not attempted to cover up the horrible in words. With them had been no childish, vain pretence. They had gone straight to their ends.

Other thoughts, too, stole over him, as he sat gazing down upon the track of that ancient road; strange thoughts, not wholly welcome. New, yet old, emotions rose in a tide upon him. He began to wonder.... Had he, after all, become brutalized by the War? He knew quite well that the little "Christianity" he inherited had soon fallen from him like a garment in France. In his attitude to Life and Death he had become, frankly, pagan. He now realized, abruptly, another thing as well: in reality he had never been a "Christian" at any time. Given to him with his mother's milk, he had never accepted, felt at home with Christian dogmas. To him they had always been an alien creed. Christianity met none of his requirements....

But what were his "requirements"? He found it difficult to answer.

Something, at any rate, different and more primitive, he thought....

Even up here, alone on the mountain-top, it was hard to be absolutely frank with himself. With a kind of savage, honest determination, he bent himself to the task. It became suddenly important for him. He must know exactly where he stood. It seemed he had reached a turning point in his life. The war, in the objective world, had been one such turning point; now he had reached another in the subjective life, and it was more important than the first.

As he lay there in the pleasant sunshine, his thoughts went back to the fighting. A friend, he recalled, had divided people into those who enjoyed the war and those who didn't. He was obliged to admit that he had been one of the former—he had thoroughly enjoyed it. Brought up from a youth as an engineer, he had taken to a soldier's life as a duck takes to water. There had been plenty of misery, discomfort, wretchedness; but there had been compensations that, for him, outweighed them. The fierce excitement, the primitive, naked passions, the wild fury, the reckless indifference to pain and death, with the loss of the normal, cautious, pettifogging little daily self all these involved, had satisfied him. Even the actual killing....

He started. A slight shudder ran down his back as the cool wind from the open moorlands came sighing across the soft spring sunshine. Sitting up straight, he looked behind him a moment, as with an effort to turn away from something he disliked and dreaded because it was, he know, too strong for him. But the same instant he turned round again. He faced the vile and dreadful thing in himself he had hitherto sought to deny, evade. Pretence fell away. He could not disguise from himself, that he had thoroughly enjoyed the killing; or, at any rate, had not been shocked by it as by an unnatural and ghastly duty. The shooting and bombing he performed with an effort, always, but the rarer moments when he had been able to use the bayonet... the joy of feeling the steel go home...

He started again, hiding his face a moment in his hands, but he did not try to evade the hideous memories that surged. At times, he knew, he had gone quite mad with the lust of slaughter; he had gone on long after he should have stopped. Once an officer had pulled him up sharply for it, but the next instant had been killed by a bullet. He thought he had gone on killing, but he did not know. It was all a red mist before his eyes and he could only remember the sticky feeling of the blood on his hands when he gripped his rifle....

And now, at this moment of painful honesty with himself, he realized that his creed, whatever it was, must cover all that; it must provide some sort of a philosophy for it; must neither apologize nor ignore it. The heaven that it promised must be a man's heaven. The Christian heaven made no appeal to him, he could not believe in it. The ritual must be simple and direct. He felt that in some dim way he understood why those old people had thrown their captives from the Crag. The sacrifice of an animal victim that could be eaten afterwards with due ceremonial did not shock him. Such methods seemed simple, natural, effective. Yet would it not have been better—the horrid thought rose unbidden in his inmost mind—better to have cut their throats with a flint knife... slowly?

Horror-stricken, he sprang to his feet. These terrible thoughts he could not recognize as his own. Had he slept a moment in the sunlight, dreaming them? Was it some hideous nightmare flash that touched him as he dozed a second? Something of fear and awe stole over him. He stared round for some minutes into the emptiness of the desolate landscape, then hurriedly ran down to the road, hoping to exorcize the strange sudden horror by vigorous movement. Yet when he reached the track he knew that he had not succeeded. The awful pictures were gone perhaps, but the mood remained. It was as though some new attitude began to take definite form and harden within him.

He walked on, trying to pretend to himself that he was some forgotten legionary marching up with his fellows to defend the Wall. Half unconsciously he fell into the steady tramping pace of his old regiment: the words of the ribald songs they had sung going to the front came pouring into his mind. Steadily and almost mechanically he swung along till he saw the Stone as a black speck on the left of the track, and the instant he saw it there rose in him the feeling that he stood upon the edge of an adventure that he feared yet longed for. He approached the great granite monolith with a curious thrill of anticipatory excitement, born he knew not whence.

But, of course, there was nothing. Common sense, still operating strongly, had warned him there would be, could be, nothing. In the waste the great Stone stood upright, solitary, forbidding, as it had stood for thousands of years. It dominated the landscape somewhat ominously. The sheep and cattle had used it as a rubbing-stone, and bits of hair and wool clung to its rough, weather-eaten edges; the feet of generations had worn a cup-shaped hollow at its base. The wind sighed round it plaintively. Its bulk glistened as it took the sun.

A short mile away the Blood Tarn was now plainly visible; he could see the little holm lying in a direct line with the Stone, while, overhanging the water as a dark shadow on one side, rose the cliff-like rock they called "the Crag." Of the house the landlord had mentioned, however, he could see no trace, as he relieved his shoulders of the knapsack and sat down to enjoy his lunch. The tarn, he reflected, was certainly a gloomy place; he could understand that the simple superstitious shepherds did not dare to live there, for even on this bright spring day it wore a dismal and forbidding look. With failing light, when the Crag sprawled its big lengthening shadow across the water, he could well imagine they would give it the widest possible berth. He strolled down to the shore after lunch, smoking his pipe lazily—then suddenly stood still. At the far end, hidden hitherto by a fold in the ground, he saw the little house, a faint column of blue smoke rising from the chimney, and at the same moment a woman came out of the low door and began to walk towards the tarn. She had seen him, she was moving evidently in his direction; a few minutes later she stopped and stood waiting on the path—waiting, he well knew, for him.

And his earlier mood, the mood he dreaded yet had forced himself to recognize, came back upon him with sudden redoubled power. As in some vivid dream that dominates and paralyses the will, or as in the first stages of an imposed hypnotic spell, all question, hesitation, refusal sank away. He felt a pleasurable resignation steal upon him with soft, numbing effect. Denial and criticism ceased to operate, and common sense died with them. He yielded his being automatically to the deeps of an adventure he did not understand. He began to walk towards the woman.

It was, he saw as he drew nearer, the figure of a young girl, nineteen or twenty years of age, who stood there motionless with her eyes fixed steadily on his own. She looked as wild and picturesque as the scene that framed her. Thick black hair hung loose over her back and shoulders; about her head was bound a green ribbon: her clothes consisted of a jersey and a very short skirt which showed her bare legs browned by exposure to the sun and wind.. A pair of rough sandals covered her feet. Whether the face was beautiful or not he could not tell; he only knew that it attracted him immensely and with a strength of appeal that he at once felt curiously irresistible. She remained motionless against the boulder, staring fixedly at him till he was close before her. Then she spoke:

"I am glad that you have come at last," she said in a clear, strong voice that yet was soft and even tender. "We have been expecting you."

"You have been expecting me!" he repeated, astonished beyond words, yet finding the language natural, right and true. A stream of sweet feeling invaded him, his heart beat faster, he felt happy and at home in some extraordinary way he could not understand yet did not question.

"Of course," she answered, looking straight into his eyes with welcome unashamed. Her next words thrilled him to the core of his being. "I have made the room ready for you."

Quick upon her own, however, flashed back the landlord's words, while common sense made a last faint effort in his thought. He was the victim of some absurd mistake evidently. The lonely life, the forbidding surrounding, the associations of the desolate hills had affected her mind. He remembered the accident.

"I am afraid," he offered, lamely enough, "there is some mistake. I am not the friend you were expecting. I—" He stopped. A thin slight sound as of distant laughter seemed to echo behind the unconvincing words.

"There is no mistake," the girl answered firmly, with a quiet smile, moving a step nearer to him, so that he caught the subtle perfume of her vigorous youth. "I saw you clearly in the Mystery Stone. I recognized you at once."

"The Mystery Stone," he heard himself saying, bewilderment increasing, a sense of wild happiness growing with it.

Laughing, she took his hand in hers. "Come," she said, drawing him along with her, "come home with me. My father will be waiting for us; he will tell you everything, and better far than I can."

He went with her, feeling that he was made of sunlight and that he walked on air, for at her touch his own hand responded as with a sudden fierceness of pleasure that he failed utterly to understand, yet did not question for an instant. Wildly, absurdly, madly it flashed across his mind: "This is the woman I shall marry—my woman. I am her man."

They walked in silence for a little, for no words of any sort offered themselves to his mind, nor did the girl attempt to speak. The total absence of embarrassment between them occurred to him once or twice as curious, though the very idea of embarrassment then disappeared entirely. It all seemed natural and unforced, the sudden intercourse as familiar and effortless as though they had known one another always.

"The Mystery Stone," he heard himself saying presently, as the idea rose again to the surface of his mind. "I should like to know more about it. Tell me, dear."

"I bought it with the other things," she replied softly.

"What other things?"

She turned and looked up into his face with a slight expression of surprise; their shoulders touched as they swung along; her hair blew in the wind across his coat. "The bronze collar," she answered in the low voice that pleased him so, "and this ornament that I wear in my hair."

He glanced down to examine it. Instead of a ribbon, as he had first supposed, he saw that it was a circlet of bronze, covered with a beautiful green patina and evidently very old. In front, above the forehead, was a small disk bearing an inscription he could not decipher at the moment. He bent down and kissed her hair, the girl smiling with happy contentment, but offering no sign of resistance or annoyance.

"And," she added suddenly, "the dagger."

Holt started visibly. This time there was a thrill in her voice that seemed to pierce down straight into his heart. He said nothing, however. The unexpectedness of the word she used, together with the note in her voice that moved him so strangely, had a disconcerting effect that kept him silent for a time. He did not ask about the dagger. Something prevented his curiosity finding expression in speech, though the word, with the marked accent she placed upon it, had struck into him like the shock of sudden steel itself, causing him an indecipherable emotion of both joy and pain. He asked instead, presently, another question, and a very commonplace one: he asked where she and her father had lived before they came to these lonely hills. And the form of his question—his voice shook a little as he said it—was, again, an effort of his normal self to maintain its already precarious balance.

The effect of his simple query, the girl's reply above all, increased in him the mingled sensations of sweetness and menace, of joy and dread, that half alarmed, half satisfied him. For a, moment she wore a puzzled expression, as though making an effort to remember.

"Down by the sea," she answered slowly, thoughtfully, her voice very low. "Somewhere by a big harbour with great ships coming in and out. It was there we had the break—the shock—an accident that broke us, shattering the dream we share To-day." Her face cleared a little. "We were in a chariot," she went on more easily and rapidly, "and father—my father was injured, so that I went with him to a palace beyond the Wall till he grew well."

"You were in a chariot?" Holt repeated. "Surely not."

"Did I say chariot?" the girl replied. "How foolish of me!" She shook her hair back as though the gesture helped to clear her mind and memory. "That belongs, of course, to the other dream. No, not a chariot; it was a car. But it had wheels like a chariot—the old warchariots. You know."

"Disk-wheels," thought Holt to himself. He did not ask about the palace. He asked instead where she had bought the Mystery Stone, as she called it, and the other things. Her reply bemused and enticed him farther, for he could not unravel it. His whole inner attitude was shifting with uncanny rapidity and completeness. They walked together, he now realized, with linked arms, moving slowly in step, their bodies touching. He felt the blood run hot and almost savage in his veins. He was aware how amazingly precious she was to him, how deeply, absolutely necessary to his life and happiness. Her words went past him in the mountain wind like flying birds.

"My father was fishing," she went on, "and I was on my way to join him, when the old woman called me into her dwelling and showed me the things. She wished to give them to me, but I refused the present and paid for them in gold. I put the fillet on my head to see if it would fit, and took the Mystery Stone in my hand. Then, as I looked deep into the stone, this present dream died all away. It faded out. I saw the older dreams again—*our* dreams."

"The older dreams!" interrupted Holt. "Ours!" But instead of saying the words aloud, they issued from his lips in a quiet whisper, as though control of his voice had passed a little from him. The sweetness in him became more wonderful, unmanageable; his astonishment had vanished; he walked and talked with his old familiar happy Love, the woman he had sought so long and waited for, the woman who was his mate, as he was hers, she who alone could satisfy his inmost soul.

"The old dream," she replied, "the very old—the oldest of all perhaps—when we committed the terrible sacrilege. I saw the High Priest lying dead—whom my father slew—and the other whom *you* destroyed. I saw you prise out the jewel from the image of the god—with your short bloody spear. I saw, too, our flight to the galley through the hot, awful night beneath the stars—and our escape...."

Her voice died away and she fell silent.

"Tell me more," he whispered, drawing her closer against his side. "What had *you* done?" His heart was racing now. Some fighting blood surged uppermost. He felt that he could kill, and the joy of violence and slaughter rose in him.

"Have you forgotten so completely?" she asked very low, as he pressed her more tightly still against his heart. And almost beneath her breath she whispered into his ear, which he bent to catch the little sound: "I had broken my vows with you."

"What else, my lovely one—my best beloved—what more did you see?" he whispered in return, yet wondering why the fierce pain and anger that he felt behind still lay hidden from betrayal.

"Dream after dream, and always we were punished. But the last time was the clearest, for it was here—here where we now walk together in the sunlight and the wind—it was here the savages hurled us from the rock."

A shiver ran through him, making him tremble with an unaccountable touch of cold that communicated itself to her as well. Her arm went instantly about his shoulder, as he stooped and kissed her passionately. "Fasten your coat about you," she said tenderly, but with troubled breath, when he released her, "for this wind is chill although the sun shines brightly. We were glad, you remember, when they stopped to kill us, for we were tired and our feet were cut to pieces by the long, rough journey from the Wall." Then suddenly her voice grew louder again and the smile of happy confidence came back into her eyes. There was the deep earnestness of love in it, of love that cannot end or die. She looked up into his face. "But soon now," she said, "we shall be free. For you have come, and it is nearly finished—this weary little present dream."

"How," he asked, "shall we get free?" A red mist swam momentarily before his eyes.

"My father," she replied at once, "will tell you all. It is quite easy."

"Your father, too, remembers?"

"The moment the collar touches him," she said, "he is a priest again. See! Here he comes forth already to meet us, and to bid you welcome."

Holt looked up, startled. He had hardly noticed, so absorbed had he been in the words that half intoxicated him, the distance they had covered. The cottage was now close at hand, and a tall, powerfully built man, wearing a shepherd's rough clothing, stood a few feet in front of him. His stature, breadth of shoulder and thick black beard made up a striking figure. The dark eyes, with fire in them, gazed straight into his own, and a kindly smile played round the stern and vigorous mouth.

"Greeting, my son," said a deep, booming voice, "for I shall call you my son as I did of old. The bond of the spirit is stronger than that of the flesh, and with us three the tie is indeed of triple strength. You come, too, at an auspicious hour, for the omens are favourable and the time of our liberation is at hand." He took the other's hand in a grip that might have killed an ox and yet was warm with gentle kindliness, while Holt, now caught wholly into the spirit of some deep reality he could not master yet accepted, saw that the wrist was small, the fingers shapely, the gesture itself one of dignity and refinement.

"Greeting, my father," he replied, as naturally as though he said more modern words.

"Come in with me, I pray," pursued the other, leading the way, "and let me show you the poor accommodation we have provided, yet the best that we can offer."

He stooped to pass the threshold, and as Holt stooped likewise the girl took his hand and he knew that his bewitchment was complete. Entering the low doorway, he passed through a kitchen, where only the roughest, scantiest furniture was visible, into another room that was completely bare. A heap of dried bracken had been spread on the floor in one corner to form a bed. Beside it lay two cheap, coloured blankets. There was nothing else.

"Our place is poor," said the man, smiling courteously, but with that dignity and air of welcome which made the hovel seem a palace. "Yet it may serve, perhaps, for the short time that you will need it. Our little dream here is wellnigh over, now that you have come. The long weary pilgrimage at last draws to a close." The girl had left them alone a moment, and the man stepped closer to his guest. His face grew solemn, his voice deeper and more earnest suddenly, the light in his eyes seemed actually to flame with the enthusiasm of a great belief. "Why have you tarried thus so long, and where?" he asked in a lowered tone that vibrated in the little space. "We have sought you with prayer and fasting, and she has spent her nights for you in tears. You lost the way, it must be. The lesser dreams entangled your feet, I see." A touch of sadness entered the voice, the eyes held pity in them. "It is, alas, too easy, I well know," he murmured. "It is too easy."

"I lost the way," the other replied. It seemed suddenly that his heart was filled with fire. "But now," he cried aloud, "now that I have found her, I will never, never let her go again. My feet are steady and my way is sure."

"For ever and ever, my son," boomed the happy, yet almost solemn answer, "she is yours. Our freedom is at hand."

He turned and crossed the little kitchen again, making a sign that his guest should follow him. They stood together by the door, looking out across the tarn in silence. The afternoon sunshine fell in a golden blaze across the bare hills that seemed to smoke with the glory of the fiery light. But the Crag loomed dark in shadow overhead, and the little lake lay deep and black beneath it.

"Acella, Acella!" called the man, the name breaking upon his companion as with a shock of sweet delicious fire that filled his entire being, as the girl came the same instant from behind the cottage. "The Gods call me," said her father. "I go now to the hill. Protect our guest and comfort him in my absence."

Without another word, he strode away up the hillside and presently was visible standing on the summit of the Crag, his aims stretched out above his head to heaven, his great head thrown back, his bearded face turned upwards. An impressive, even a majestic figure he looked, as his bulk and stature rose in dark silhouette against the brilliant evening sky. Holt stood motionless, watching him for several minutes, his heart swelling in his breast, his pulses thumping before some great nameless pressure that rose from the depths of his being. That inner attitude which seemed a new and yet more satisfying attitude to life than he had known hitherto, had crystallized. Define it he could not, he only knew that he accepted it as natural. It satisfied him. The sight of that dignified, gaunt figure worshipping upon the hill-top enflamed him....

"I have brought the stone," a voice interrupted his reflections, and turning, he saw the girl beside him. She held out for his inspection a dark square object that looked to him at first like a black stone lying against the brown skin of her hand. "The Mystery Stone," the girl added, as their faces bent down together to examine it. "It is there I see the dreams I told you of."

He took it from her and found that it was heavy, composed apparently of something like black quartz, with a brilliant polished surface that revealed clear depths within. Once, evidently, it had been set in a stand or frame, for the marks where it had been attached still showed, and it was obviously of great age. He felt confused, the mind in him troubled yet excited, as he gazed. The effect upon him was as though a wind rose suddenly and passed across his inmost subjective life, setting its entire contents in rushing motion.

"And here," the girl said, "is the dagger."

He took from her the short bronze weapon, feeling at once instinctively its ragged edge, its keen point, sharp and effective still. The handle had long since rotted away, but the bronze tongue, and the holes where the rivets had been, remained, and, as he touched it, the confusion and trouble in his mind increased to a kind of turmoil, in which violence, linked to something tameless, wild and almost savage, was the dominating emotion. He turned to seize the girl and crush her to him in a passionate embrace, but she held away, throwing back her lovely head, her eyes shining, her lips parted, yet one hand stretched out to stop him.

"First look into it with me," she said quietly. "Let us see together."

She sat down on the turf beside the cottage door, and Holt, obeying, took his place beside her. She remained very still for some minutes, covering the stone with both hands as though to warm it. Her lips moved. She seemed to be repeating some kind of invocation beneath her breath, though no actual words were audible. Presently her hands parted. They sat together gazing at the polished surface. They looked within.

"There comes a white mist in the heart of the stone," the girl whispered. "It will soon open. The pictures will then grow. Look!" she exclaimed after a brief pause, "they are forming now."

"I see only mist," her companion murmured, gazing intently. "Only mist I see."

She took his hand and instantly the mist parted. He found himself

peering into another landscape which opened before his eyes as though
it were a photograph. Hills covered with heather stretched away on
every side.

"Hills, I see," he whispered. "The ancient hills—"

"Watch closely," she replied, holding his hand firmly.

At first the landscape was devoid of any sign of life; then suddenly it
surged and swarmed with moving figures. Torrents of men poured over
the hill-crests and down their heathery sides in columns. He could see
them clearly—great hairy men, clad in skins, with thick shields on their
left arms or slung over their backs, and short stabbing spears in their
hands. Thousands upon thousands poured over in an endless stream. In
the distance he could see other columns sweeping in a turning movement. A few of the men rode rough ponies and seemed to be directing
the march, and these, he knew, were the chiefs....

The scene grew dimmer, faded, died away completely. Another took its
place:

By the faint light he knew that it was dawn. The undulating country,
less hilly than before, was still wild and uncultivated. A great wall, with
towers at intervals, stretched away till it was lost in shadowy distance.
On the nearest of these towers he saw a sentinel clad in armour, gazing
out across the rolling country. The armour gleamed faintly in the pale
glimmering light, as the man suddenly snatched up a bugle and blew
upon it. From a brazier burning beside him he next seized a brand and
fired a great heap of brushwood. The smoke rose in a dense column into
the air almost immediately, and from all directions, with incredible
rapidity, figures came pouring up to man the wall. Hurriedly they strung
their bows, and laid spare arrows close beside them on the coping. The
light grew brighter. The whole country was alive with savages; like the
waves of the sea they came rolling in enormous numbers. For several
minutes the wall held. Then, in an impetuous, fearful torrent, they
poured over....

It faded, died away, was gone again, and a moment later yet another
took its place

But this time the landscape was familiar, and he recognized the tarn.
He saw the savages upon the ledge that flanked the dominating Crag;
they had three captives with them. He saw two men. The other was a
woman. But the woman had fallen exhausted to the ground, and a chief
on a rough pony rode back to see what had delayed the march. Glancing
at the captives, he made a fierce gesture with his arm towards the water
far below. Instantly the woman was jerked cruelly to her feet and forced
onwards till the summit of the Crag was reached. A man snatched something from her hand. A second later she was hurled over the brink.

The two men were next dragged on to the dizzy spot where she had stood. Dead with fatigue, bleeding from numerous wounds, yet at this awful moment they straightened themselves, casting contemptuous glances at the fierce savages surrounding them. They were Romans and would die like Romans. Holt saw their faces clearly for the first time. He sprang up with a cry of anguished fury.

"The second man!" he exclaimed. "You saw the second man!"

The girl, releasing his hand, turned her eyes slowly up to his, so that he met the flame of her ancient and undying love shining like stars upon him out of the night of time.

"Ever since that moment," she said in a low voice that trembled, "I have been looking, waiting for you—"

He took her in his arms and smothered her words with kisses, holding her fiercely to him as though he would never let her go. "I, too," he said, his whole being burning with his love, "I have been looking, waiting for you. Now I have found you. We have found each other....!"

The dusk fell slowly, imperceptibly. As twilight slowly draped the gaunt hills, blotting out familiar details, so the strong dream, veil upon veil, drew closer over the soul of the wanderer, obliterating finally the last reminder of To-day. The little wind had dropped and the desolate moors lay silent, but for the hum of distant water falling to its valley bed. His life, too, and the life of the girl, he knew, were similarly falling, falling into some deep shadowed bed where rest would come at last. No details troubled him, he asked himself no questions. A profound sense of happy peace numbed every nerve and stilled his beating heart.

He felt no fear, no anxiety, no hint of alarm or uneasiness vexed his singular contentment. He realized one thing only—that the girl lay in his arms, he held her fast, her breath mingled with his own. They had found each other. What else mattered?

From time to time, as the daylight faded and the sun went down behind the moors, she spoke. She uttered words he vaguely heard, listening though with a certain curious effort, before he closed the thing she said with kisses. Even the fierceness of his blood was gone. The world lay still, life almost ceased to flow. Lapped in the deeps of his great love, he was redeemed, perhaps, of violence and savagery....

"Three dark birds," she whispered, "pass across the sky... they fall beyond the ridge. The omens are favourable. A hawk now follows them, cleaving the sky with pointed wings."

"A hawk," he murmured. "The badge of my old Legion."

"My father will perform the sacrifice," he heard again, though it seemed a long interval had passed, and the man's figure was now invisible on the Crag amid the gathering darkness. "Already he prepares the fire. Look, the sacred island is alight. He has the black cock ready for the knife."

Holt roused himself with difficulty, lifting his face from the garden of her hair. A faint light, he saw, gleamed fitfully on the holm within the tarn. Her father, then, had descended from the Crag, and had lit the sacrificial fire upon the stones. But what did the doings of the father matter now to him?

"The dark bird," he repeated dully, "the black victim the Gods of the Underworld alone accept. It is good, Acella, it is good!" He was about to sink back again, taking her against his breast as before, when she resisted and sat up suddenly.

"It is time," she said aloud. "The hour has come. My father climbs, and we must join him on the summit. Come!"

She took his hand and raised him to his feet, and together they began the rough ascent towards the Crag. As they passed along the shore of the Tarn of Blood, he saw the fire reflected in the ink-black waters; he made out, too, though dimly, a rough circle of big stones, with a larger flagstone lying in the centre. Three small fires of bracken and wood, placed in a triangle with its apex towards the Standing Stone on the distant hill, burned briskly, the crackling material sending out sparks that pierced the columns of thick smoke. And in this smoke, peering, shifting, appearing and disappearing, it seemed he saw great faces moving. The flickering light and twirling smoke made clear sight difficult. His bliss, his lethargy were very deep. They left the tarn below them and hand in hand began to climb the final slope.

Whether the physical effort of climbing disturbed the deep pressure of the mood that numbed his senses, or whether the cold draught of wind they met upon the ridge restored some vital detail of To-day, Holt does not know. Something, at any rate, in him wavered suddenly, as though a centre of gravity had shifted slightly. There was a perceptible alteration in the balance of thought and feeling that had held invariable now for many hours. It seemed to him that something heavy lifted, or rather, began to lift—a weight, a shadow, something oppressive that obstructed light. A ray of light, as it were, struggled through the thick darkness that enveloped him. To him, as he paused on the ridge to recover his breath, came this vague suggestion of faint light breaking across the blackness. It was objective.

"See," said the girl in a low voice, "the moon is rising. It lights the sacred island. The blood-red waters turn to silver."

He saw, indeed, that a huge three-quarter moon now drove with almost visible movement above the distant line of hills; the little tarn gleamed as with silvery armour; the glow of the sacrificial fires showed red across it. He looked down with a shudder into the sheer depth that opened at his feet, then turned to look at his companion. He started and shrank back. Her face, lit by the moon and by the fire, shone pale as death; her black hair framed it with a terrible suggestiveness; the eyes, though brilliant as ever, had a film upon them. She stood in an attitude of both ecstasy and resignation, and one outstretched arm pointed towards the summit where her father stood.

Her lips parted, a marvellous smile broke over her features, her voice was suddenly unfamiliar: "He wears the collar," she uttered. "Come. Our time is here at last, and we are ready. See, he waits for us!"

There rose for the first time struggle and opposition in him; he resisted the pressure of her hand that had seized his own and drew him forcibly along. Whence came the resistance and the opposition he could not tell, but though he followed her, he was aware that the refusal in him strengthened. The weight of darkness that oppressed him shifted a little more, an inner light increased. The same moment they reached the summit and stood beside—the priest. There was a curious sound of fluttering. The figure, he saw, was naked, save for a rough blanket tied loosely about the waist.

"The hour has come at last," cried his deep booming voice that woke echoes from the dark hills about them. "We are alone now with our Gods." And he broke then into a monotonous rhythmic chanting that rose and fell upon the wind, yet in a tongue that sounded strange; his erect figure swayed slightly with its cadences, his black beard swept his naked chest; and his face, turned skywards, shone in the mingled light of moon above and fire below, yet with an added light as well that burned within him rather than without. He was a weird, magnificent figure, a priest of ancient rites invoking his deathless deities upon the unchanging hills.

But upon Holt, too, as he stared in awed amazement, an inner light had broken suddenly. It came as with a dazzling blaze that at first paralysed thought and action. His mind cleared, but too abruptly for movement, either of tongue or hand, to be possible. Then, abruptly, the inner darkness rolled away completely. The light in the wild eyes of the great chanting, swaying figure, he now knew was the light of mania.

The faint fluttering sound increased, and the voice of the girl was oddly mingled with it. The priest had ceased his invocation. Holt, aware that he stood alone, saw the girl go past him carrying a big black bird that struggled with vainly beating wings.

"Behold the sacrifice," she said, as she knelt before her father and held up the victim. "May the Gods accept it as presently They shall accept us too!"

The great figure stooped and took the offering, and with one blow of the knife he held, its head was severed from its body. The blood spattered on the white face of the kneeling girl. Holt was aware for the first time that she, too, was now unclothed; but for a loose blanket, her white body gleamed against the dark heather in the moonlight. At the same moment she rose to her feet, stood upright, turned towards him so that he saw the dark hair streaming across her naked shoulders, and, with a face of ecstasy, yet ever that strange film upon her eyes, her voice came to him on the wind:

"Farewell, yet not farewell! We shall meet, all three, in the underworld. The Gods accept us!"

Turning her face away, she stepped towards the ominous figure behind, and bared her ivory neck and breast to the knife. The eyes of the maniac were upon her own; she was as helpless and obedient as a lamb before his spell.

Then Holt's horrible paralysis, if only just in time, was lifted. The priest had raised his arm, the bronze knife with its ragged edge gleamed in the air, with the other hand he had already gathered up the thick dark hair, so that the neck lay bare and open to the final blow. But it was two other details, Holt thinks, that set his muscles suddenly free, enabling him to act with the swift judgment which, being wholly unexpected, disconcerted both maniac and victim and frustrated the awful culmination. The dark spots of blood upon the face he loved, and the sudden final fluttering of the dead bird's wings upon the ground—these two things, life actually touching death, released the held-back springs.

He leaped forward. He received the blow upon his left arm and hand. It was his right fist that sent the High Priest to earth with a blow that, luckily, felled him in the direction away from the dreadful brink, and it was his right arm and hand, he became aware some time afterwards only, that were chiefly of use in carrying the fainting girl and her unconscious father back to the shelter of the cottage, and to the best help and comfort he could provide....

It was several years afterwards, in a very different setting, that he found himself spelling out slowly to a little boy the lettering cut into a circlet of bronze the child found on his study table. To the child he told a fairy tale, then dismissed him to play with his mother in the garden. But, when alone, he rubbed away the verdigris with great care, for the circlet was thin and frail with age, as he examined again the little picture of a tripod from which smoke issued, incised neatly in the metal. Below it, almost as sharp as when the Roman craftsman cut it first, was the name Acella. He touched the letters tenderly with his left hand, from which two fingers were missing, then placed it in a drawer of his desk and turned the key.

"That curious name," said a low voice behind his chair. His wife had come in and was looking over his shoulder. "You love it, and I dread it." She sat on the desk beside him, her eyes troubled. "It was the name father used to call me in his illness."

Her husband looked at her with passionate tenderness, but said no word.

"And this," she went on, taking the broken hand in both her own, "is the price you paid to me for his life. I often wonder what strange good deity brought you upon the lonely moor that night, and just in the very nick of time. You remember...?"

"The deity who helps true lovers, of course," he said with a smile, evading the question. The deeper memory, he knew, had closed absolutely in her since the moment of the attempted double crime. He kissed her, murmuring to himself as he did so, but too low for her to hear, "Acella; *My* Acella...!"

THE VALLEY
OF THE BEASTS

1

As they emerged suddenly from the dense forest the Indian halted, and Grimwood, his employer, stood beside him, gazing into the beautiful wooded valley that lay spread below them in the blaze of a golden sunset. Both men leaned upon their rifles, caught by the enchantment of the unexpected scene.

"We camp here," said Tooshalli abruptly, after a careful survey. "Tomorrow we make a plan."

He spoke excellent English. The note of decision, almost of authority, in his voice was noticeable, but Grimwood set it down to the natural excitement of the moment. Every track they had followed during the last two days, but one track in particular as well, had headed straight for this remote and hidden valley, and the sport promised to be unusual.

"That's so," he replied, in the tone of one giving an order. "You can make camp ready at once." And he sat down on a fallen hemlock to take off his moccasin boots and grease his feet that ached from the arduous day now drawing to a close. Though under ordinary circumstances he would have pushed on for another hour or two, he was not averse to a night here, for exhaustion had come upon him during the last bit of rough going, his eye and muscles were no longer steady, and it was doubtful if he could have shot straight enough to kill. He did not mean to miss a second time.

With his Canadian friend, Iredale, the latter's half-breed, and his own Indian, Tooshalli, the party had set out three weeks ago to find the "wonderful big moose" the Indians reported were travelling in the Snow River country. They soon found that the tale was true; tracks were abundant; they saw fine animals nearly every day, but though carrying good heads, the hunters expected better still and left them alone. Pushing up the river to a chain of small lakes near its source, they then separated into two parties, each with its nine-foot bark canoe, and packed in for three days after the yet bigger animals the Indians agreed would be found in the deeper woods beyond. Excitement was keen, expectation keener still. The day before they separated, Iredale shot the biggest moose of his life, and its head, bigger even than the grand Alaskan heads, hangs in his house to-day. Grimwood's hunting blood was fairly up. His blood was of the fiery, not to say ferocious, quality. It almost seemed he liked killing for its own sake.

Four days after the party broke into two he came upon a gigantic track, whose measurements and length of stride keyed every nerve he possessed to its highest tension.

Tooshalli examined the tracks for some minutes with care. "It is the biggest moose in the world," he said at length, a new expression on his inscrutable red visage.

Following it all that day, they yet got no sight of the big fellow that seemed to be frequenting a little marshy dip of country, too small to be called valley, where willow and undergrowth abounded. He had not yet scented his pursuers. They were after him again at dawn. Towards the evening of the second day Grimwood caught a sudden glimpse of the monster among a thick clump of willows, and the sight of the magnificent head that easily beat all records set his heart beating like a hammer with excitement. He aimed and fired. But the moose, instead of crashing, went thundering away through the further scrub and disappeared, the sound of his plunging canter presently dying away. Grimwood had missed, even if he had wounded.

They camped, and all next day, leaving the canoe behind, they followed the huge track, but though finding signs of blood, these were not plentiful, and the shot had evidently only grazed the animal. The travelling was of the hardest. Towards evening, utterly exhausted, the spoor led them to the ridge they now stood upon, gazing down into the enchanting valley that opened at their feet. The giant moose had gone down into this valley. He would consider himself safe there. Grimwood agreed with the Indian's judgment. They would camp for the night and continue at dawn the wild hunt after "the biggest moose in the world."

Supper was over, the small fire used for cooking dying down, when Grimwood became first aware that the Indian was not behaving quite as usual. What particular detail drew his attention is hard to say. He was a slow-witted, heavy man, full-blooded, unobservant; a fact had to hurt him through his comfort, through his pleasure, before he noticed it. Yet anyone else must have observed the changed mood of the Redskin long ago. Tooshalli had made the fire, fried the bacon, served the tea, and was arranging the blankets, his own and his employer's, before the latter remarked upon his—silence. Tooshalli had not uttered a word for over an hour and a half, since he had first set eyes upon the new valley, to be exact. And his employer now noticed the unaccustomed silence, because after food he liked to listen to wood talk and hunting lore.

"Tired out, aren't you?" said big Grimwood, looking into the dark face across the firelight. He resented the absence of conversation, now that he noticed it. He was over-weary himself, he felt more irritable than usual, though his temper was always vile.

"Lost your tongue, eh? he went on with a growl, as the Indian returned his stare with solemn, expressionless face. That dark inscrutable look got on his nerves a bit. "Speak up, man!'" he exclaimed sharply. "What's it all about?"

The Englishman had at last realized that there was something to "speak up" about. The discovery, in his present state, annoyed him further. Tooshalli stared gravely, but made no reply. The silence was prolonged almost into minutes. Presently the head turned sideways, as though the man listened. The other watched him very closely, anger growing in him.

But it was the way the Redskin turned his head, keeping his body rigid, that gave the jerk to Grimwood's nerves, providing him with a sensation he had never known in his life before—it gave him what is generally called "the goose-flesh." It seemed to jangle his entire system, yet at the same time made him cautious. He did not like it, this combination of emotions puzzled him.

"Say something, I tell you," he repeated in a harsher tone, raising his voice. He sat up, drawing his great body closer to the fire. "Say something, damn it!"

His voice fell dead against the surrounding trees, making the silence of the forest unpleasantly noticeable. Very still the great woods stood about them; there was no wind, no stir of branches; only the crackle of a snapping twig was audible from time to time, as the night-life moved unwarily sometimes watching the humans round their little fire. The October air had a frosty touch that nipped.

The Redskin did not answer. No muscle of his neck nor of his stiffened body moved. He seemed all ears.

"Well?" repeated the Englishman, lowering his voice this time instinctively. "What d'you hear, God damn it!" The touch of odd nervousness that made his anger grow betrayed itself in his language.

Tooshalli slowly turned his head back again to its normal position, the body rigid as before.

"I hear nothing, Mr. Grimwood," he said, gazing with quiet dignity into his employer's eyes.

This was too much for the other, a man of savage temper at the best of times. He was the type of Englishman who held strong views as to the right way of treating "inferior" races.

"That's a lie, Tooshalli, and I won't have you lie to me. Now what was it? Tell me at once!"

"I hear nothing," repeated the other. "I only think."

"And what is it you're pleased to think?" Impatience made a nasty expression round the mouth.

"I go not," was the abrupt reply, unalterable decision in the voice.

The man's rejoinder was so unexpected that Grimwood found nothing to say at first. For a moment he did not take its meaning; his mind, always slow, was confused by impatience, also by what he considered the foolishness of the little scene. Then in a flash he understood; but he also understood the immovable obstinacy of the race he had to deal with. Tooshalli was informing him that he refused to go into the valley where the big moose had vanished. And his astonishment was so great at first that he merely sat and stared. No words came to him.

"It is—" said the Indian, but used a native term.

"What's that mean?" Grimwood found his tongue, but his quiet tone was ominous.

"Mr. Grimwood, it mean the 'Valley of the Beasts,'" was the reply in a tone quieter still.

The Englishman made a great, a genuine effort at self-control. He was dealing, he forced himself to remember, with a superstitious Redskin. He knew the stubbornness of the type. If the man left him his sport was irretrievably spoilt, for he could not hunt in this wilderness alone, and even if he got the coveted head, he could never, never get it out alone. His native selfishness seconded his effort. Persuasion, if only he could keep back his rising anger, was his role to play.

"The Valley of the Beasts," he said, a smile on his lips rather than in his darkening eyes; "but that's just what we want. It's beasts we're after, isn't it?" His voice had a false cheery ring that could not have deceived a child. "But what d'you mean, anyhow—the Valley of the Beasts?" He asked it with a dull attempt at sympathy.

"It belong to Ishtot, Mr. Grimwood." The man looked him full in the face, no flinching in the eyes.

"My—our—big moose is there," said the other, who recognized the name of the Indian Hunting God, and understanding better, felt confident he would soon persuade his man. Tooshalli, he remembered, too, was nominally a Christian. "We'll follow him at dawn and get the biggest head the world has ever seen. You will be famous," he added, his temper better in hand again. "Your tribe will honour you. And the white hunters will pay you much money."

"He go there to save himself. I go not."

The other's anger revived with a leap at this stupid obstinacy. But, in spite of it, he noticed the odd choice of words. He began to realize that nothing now would move the man. At the same time he also realized that violence on his part must prove worse than useless. Yet violence was natural to his "dominant" type. "That brute Grimwood" was the way most men spoke of him.

"Back at the settlement you're a Christian, remember," he tried, in his clumsy way, another line. "And disobedience means hell-fire. You know that!"

"I a Christian—at the post," was the reply, "but out here the Red God rule. Ishtot keep that valley for himself. No Indian hunt there." It was as though a granite boulder spoke.

The savage temper of the Englishman, enforced by the long difficult suppression, rose wickedly into sudden flame. He stood up, kicking his blankets aside. He strode across the dying fire to the Indian's side. Tooshalli also rose. They faced each other, two humans alone in the wilderness, watched by countless invisible forest eyes.

Tooshalli stood motionless, yet as though he expected violence from the foolish, ignorant white-face. "You go alone, Mr. Grimwood." There was no fear in him.

Grimwood choked with rage. His words came forth with difficulty, though he roared them into the silence of the forest:

"'I pay you, don't I? You'll do what *I* say, not what *you* say!" His voice woke the echoes.

The Indian, arms hanging by his side, gave the old reply.

"I go not," he repeated firmly.

It stung the other into uncontrollable fury.

The beast then came uppermost; it came out. "You've said that once too often, Tooshalli!" and he struck him brutally in the face. The Indian fell, rose to his knees again, collapsed sideways beside the fire, then struggled back into a sitting position. He never once took his eyes from the white man's face.

Beside himself with anger, Grimwood stood over him. "Is that enough? Will you obey me now?" he shouted.

"I go not," came the thick reply, blood streaming from his mouth. The eyes had no flinching in them. "That valley Ishtot keep. Ishtot see us now. *He see you.*" The last words he uttered with strange, almost uncanny emphasis.

Grimwood, arm raised, fist clenched, about to repeat his terrible assault, paused suddenly. His arm sank to his side. What exactly stopped him he could never say. For one thing, he feared his own anger, feared that if he let himself go he would not stop till he had killed—committed murder. He knew his own fearful temper and stood afraid of it. Yet it was not only that. The calm firmness of the Redskin, his courage under pain, and something in the fixed and burning eyes arrested him. Was it also something in the words he had used—"Ishtot see you"—that stung him into a queer caution midway in his violence?

He could not say. He, only knew that a momentary sense of awe came over him. He became unpleasantly aware of the enveloping forest, so still, listening in a kind of impenetrable, remorseless silence. This lonely wilderness, looking silently upon what might easily prove murder, laid a faint, inexplicable chill upon his raging blood. The hand dropped slowly to his side again, the fist unclenched itself, his breath came more evenly.

"Look you here," he said, adopting without knowing it the local way of speech. "I ain't a bad man, though your going-on do make a man damned tired. I'll give you another chance." His voice was sullen, but a new note in it surprised even himself. "I'll do that. You can have the night to think it over, Tooshalli—see? Talk it over with your—"

He did not finish the sentence. Somehow the name of the Redskin God refused to pass his lips. He turned away, flung himself into his blankets, and in less than ten minutes, exhausted as much by his anger as by the day's hard going, he was sound asleep.

The Indian, crouching beside the dying fire, had said nothing.

Night held the woods, the sky was thick with stars, the life of the forest went about its business quietly, with that wondrous skill which millions of years have perfected. The Redskin, so close to this skill that he instinctively used and borrowed from it, was silent, alert and wise, his outline as inconspicuous as though he merged, like his four-footed teachers, into the mass of the surrounding bush.

He moved perhaps, yet nothing knew he moved. His wisdom, derived from that eternal, ancient mother who from infinite experience makes no mistakes, did not fail him. His soft tread made no sound; his breathing, as his weight, was calculated. The stars observed him, but they did not tell; the light air knew his whereabouts, yet without betrayal....

The chill dawn gleamed at length between the trees, lighting the pale ashes of an extinguished fire, also of a bulky, obvious form beneath a blanket. The form moved clumsily. The cold was penetrating.

And that bulky form now moved because a dream had come to trouble it. A dark figure stole across its confused field of vision. The form started, but it did not wake. The figure spoke: "Take this," it whispered, handing a little stick, curiously carved. "It is the totem of great Ishtot. In the valley all memory of the White Gods will leave you. Call upon Ishtot.... Call on Him if you dare"; and the dark figure glided away out of the dream and out of all remembrance....

2

The first thing Grimwood noticed when he woke was that Tooshalli was not there. No fire burned, no tea was ready. He felt exceedingly annoyed. He glared about him, then got up with a curse to make the fire. His mind seemed confused and troubled. At first he only realized one thing clearly—his guide had left him in the night.

It was very cold. He lit the wood with difficulty and made his tea, and the actual world came gradually back to him. The Red Indian had gone; perhaps the blow, perhaps the superstitious terror, perhaps both, had driven him away. He was alone, that was the outstanding fact. For anything beyond outstanding facts, Grimwood felt little interest. Imaginative speculation was beyond his compass. Close to the brute creation, it seemed, his nature lay.

It was while packing his blankets—he did it automatically, a dull, vicious resentment in him—that his fingers struck a bit of wood that he was about to throw away when its unusual shape caught his attention suddenly. His odd dream came back then. But was it a dream? The bit of wood was undoubtedly a totem stick.

He examined it. He paid it more attention than he meant to, wished to. Yes, it was unquestionably a totem stick. The dream, then, was not a dream. Tooshalli had quit, but, following with Redskin faithfulness some code of his own, had left him the means of safety. He chuckled sourly, but thrust the stick inside his belt. "One never knows," he mumbled to himself.

He faced the situation squarely. He was alone in the wilderness. His capable, experienced woodsman had deserted him. The situation was serious. What should he do? A weakling would certainly retrace his steps, following the track they had made, afraid to be left alone in this vast hinterland of pathless forest. But Grimwood was of another build. Alarmed he might be, but he would not give in. He had the defects of his own qualities. The brutality of his nature argued force. He was determined and a sportsman. He would go on. And ten minutes after breakfast, having first made a *cache* of what provisions were left over, he was on his way—down across the ridge and into the mysterious valley, the Valley of the Beasts.

It looked, in the morning sunlight, entrancing. The trees closed in behind him, but he did not notice. It led him on....

He followed the track of the gigantic moose he meant to kill, and the sweet, delicious sunshine helped him. The air was like wine, the seductive spoor of the great beast, with here and there a faint splash of blood on leaves or ground, lay forever just before his eyes. He found the valley, though the actual word did not occur to him, enticing; more and more he noticed the beauty, the desolate grandeur of the mighty spruce and hemlock, the splendour of the granite bluffs which in places rose above the forest and caught the sun.... The valley was deeper, vaster than he had imagined. He felt safe, at home in it, though, again these actual terms did not occur to him.... Here he could hide for ever and find peace.... He became aware of a new quality in the deep loneliness. The scenery for the first time in his life appealed to him, and the form of the appeal was curious—he felt the comfort of it.

For a man of his habit, this was odd, yet the new sensations stole over him so gently, their approach so gradual, that they were first recognized by his consciousness indirectly. They had already established themselves in him before he noticed them; and the indirectness took this form—that the passion of the chase gave place to an interest in the valley itself. The lust of the hunt, the fierce desire to find and kill, the keen wish, in a word, to see his quarry within range, to aim, to fire, to witness the natural consummation of the long expedition—these had all become measurably less, while the effect of the valley upon him had increased in strength. There was a welcome about it that he did not understand.

The change was singular, yet, oddly enough, it did not occur to him as singular; it was unnatural, yet it did not strike him so. To a dull mind of his unobservant, unanalytical type, a change had to be marked and dramatic before he noticed it; something in the nature of a shock must accompany it for him to recognize it had happened. And there had been no shock. The spoor of the great moose was much cleaner, now that he caught up with the animal that made it; the blood more frequent; he had noticed the spot where it had rested, its huge body leaving a marked imprint on the soft ground; where it had reached up to eat the leaves of saplings here and there was also visible; he had come undoubtedly very near to it, and any minute now might see its great bulk within range of an easy shot. Yet his ardour had somehow lessened.

He first realized this change in himself when it suddenly occurred to him that the animal itself had grown less cautious. It must scent him easily now, since a moose, its sight being indifferent, depends chiefly for its safety upon its unusually keen sense of smell, and the wind came from behind him. This now struck him as decidedly uncommon: the moose itself was obviously careless of his close approach. It felt no fear.

It was this inexplicable alteration in the animal's behaviour that made him recognize, at last, the alteration in his own. He had followed it now for a couple of hours and had descended some eight hundred to a thousand feet; the trees were thinner and more sparsely placed; there were open, park-like places where silver birch, sumach and maple splashed their blazing colours; and a crystal stream, broken by many waterfalls, foamed past towards the bed of the great valley, yet another thousand feet below. By a quiet pool against some over-arching rocks, the moose had evidently paused to drink, paused at its leisure, moreover. Grimwood, rising from a close examination of the direction the creature had taken after drinking—the hoof-marks were fresh and very distinct in the marshy ground about the pool—looked suddenly straight into the great creature's eyes. It was not twenty yards from where he stood, yet he had been standing on that spot for at least ten minutes, caught by the wonder and loneliness of the scene. The moose, therefore, had been close beside him all this time. It had been calmly drinking, undisturbed by his presence, unafraid.

The shock came now, the shock that woke his heavy nature into realization. For some seconds, probably for minutes, he stood rooted to the ground, motionless, hardly breathing. He stared as though he saw a vision. The animal's head was lowered, but turned obliquely somewhat, so that the eyes, placed sideways in its great head, could see him properly; its immense proboscis hung as though stuffed upon an English wall; he saw the forefeet planted wide apart, the slope of the enormous shoulders dropping back towards the fine hind-quarters and lean flanks. It was a magnificent bull. The horns and head justified his wildest expectations, they were superb, a record specimen, and a phrase—where had he heard it?—ran vaguely, as from far distance, through his mind: "the biggest moose in the world."

There was the extraordinary fact, however, that he did not shoot; nor feel the wish to shoot. The familiar instinct, so strong hitherto in his blood, made no sign; the desire to kill apparently had left him. To raise his rifle, aim and fire had become suddenly an absolute impossibility.

He did not move. The animal and the human stared into each other's eyes for a length of time whose interval he could not measure. Then came a soft noise close beside him: the rifle had slipped from his grasp and fallen with a thud into the mossy earth at his feet. And the moose, for the first time now, was moving. With slow, easy stride, its great weight causing a squelching sound as the feet drew out of the moist ground, it came towards him, the bulk of the shoulders giving it an appearance of swaying like a ship at sea. It reached his side, it almost touched him, the magnificent head bent low, the spread of the gigantic horns lay beneath his very eyes. He could have patted, stroked it. He saw, with a touch of pity, that blood trickled from a sore in its left shoulder, matting the thick hair. It sniffed the fallen rifle.

Then, lifting its head and shoulders again, it sniffed the air, this time with an audible sound that shook from Grimwood's mind the last possibility that he witnessed a vision or dreamed a dream. One moment it gazed into his face, its big brown eyes shining and unafraid, then turned abruptly, and swung away at a speed ever rapidly increasing across the park-like spaces till it was lost finally among the dark tangle of undergrowth beyond. And the Englishman's muscles turned to paper, his paralysis passed, his legs refused to support his weight, and he sank heavily to the ground....

3

It seems he slept, slept long and heavily; he sat up, stretched himself, yawned and rubbed his eyes. The sun had moved across the sky, for the shadows, he saw, now ran from west to east, and they were long shadows. He had slept evidently for hours, and evening was drawing in. He was aware that he felt hungry. In his pouch-like pockets, he had dried meat, sugar, matches, tea, and the little billy that never left him. He would make a fire, boil some tea and eat.

But he took no steps to carry out his purpose, he felt disinclined to move, he sat thinking, thinking.... What was he thinking about? He did not know, he could not say exactly; it was more like fugitive pictures that passed across his mind. Who, and where, was he? This was the Valley of the Beasts, that he knew; he felt sure of nothing else. How long had he been here, and where had he come from, and why? The questions did not linger for their answers, almost as though his interest in them was merely automatic. He felt happy, peaceful, unafraid.

He looked about him, and the spell of this virgin forest came upon him like a charm; only the sound of falling water, the murmur of wind sighing among innumerable branches, broke the enveloping silence. Overhead, beyond the crests of the towering trees, a cloudless evening sky was paling into transparent orange, opal, mother of pearl. He saw buzzards soaring lazily. A scarlet tanager flashed by. Soon would the owls begin to call and the darkness fall like a sweet black veil and hide all detail, while the stars sparkled in their countless thousands....

A glint of something that shone upon the ground caught his eye—a smooth, polished strip of rounded metal: his rifle. And he started to his feet impulsively, yet not knowing exactly what he meant to do. At the sight of the weapon, something had leaped to life in him, then faded out, died down, and was gone again.

"I'm—I'm—" he began muttering to himself, but could not finish what he was about to say. His name had disappeared completely. "I'm in the Valley of the Beasts," he repeated in place of what he sought but could not find.

This fact, that he was in the Valley of the Beasts, seemed the only positive item of knowledge that he had. About the name something known and familiar clung, though the sequence that led up to it he could not trace. Presently, nevertheless, he rose to his feet, advanced a few steps, stooped and picked up the shining metal thing, his rifle. He examined it a moment, a feeling of dread and loathing rising in him, a sensation of almost horror that made him tremble, then, with a convulsive movement that betrayed an intense reaction of some sort he could not comprehend, he flung the thing far from him into the foaming torrent. He saw the splash it made, he also saw that same instant a large grizzly bear swing heavily along the bank not a dozen yards from where he stood. It, too, heard the splash, for it started, turned, paused a second, then changed its direction and came towards him. It came up close. Its fur brushed his body. It examined him leisurely, as the moose had done, sniffed, half rose upon its terrible hind legs, opened its mouth so that red tongue and gleaming teeth were plainly visible, then flopped back upon all fours again with a deep growling that yet had no anger in it, and swung off at a quick trot back to the bank of the torrent. He had felt its hot breath upon his face, but he had felt no fear. The monster was puzzled but not hostile. It disappeared.

"They know not—" he sought for the word "man," but could not find it. "They have never been hunted."

The words ran through his mind, if perhaps he was not entirely certain of their meaning; they rose, as it were, automatically; a familiar sound lay in them somewhere. At the same time there rose feelings in him that were equally, though in another way, familiar and quite natural, feelings he had once known intimately but long since laid aside.

What were they? What was their origin? They seemed distant as the stars, yet were actually in his body, in his blood and nerves, part and parcel of his flesh. Long, long ago.... Oh, how long, how long?

Thinking was difficult; feeling was what he most easily and naturally managed. He could not think for long; feeling rose up and drowned the effort quickly.

That huge and awful bear—not a nerve, not a muscle quivered in him as its acrid smell rose to his nostrils, its fur brushed down his legs. Yet he was aware that somewhere there was danger, though not here. Somewhere there was attack, hostility, wicked and calculated plans against him—as against that splendid, roaming animal that had sniffed, examined, then gone its own way, satisfied. Yes, active attack, hostility and careful, cruel plans against his safety, but—not here. Here he was safe, secure, at peace; here he was happy; here he could roam at will, no eye cast sideways into forest depths, no ear pricked high to catch sounds not explained, no nostrils quivering to scent alarm. He felt this, but he did not think it. He felt hungry, thirsty too.

Something prompted him now at last to act. His billy lay at his feet, and he picked it up; the matches—he carried them in a metal case whose screw top kept out all moisture—were in his hand. Gathering a few dry twigs, he stooped to light them, then suddenly drew back with the first touch of fear he had yet known.

Fire! What *was* fire? The idea was repugnant to him, it was impossible, he was afraid of fire. He flung the metal case after the rifle and saw it gleam in the last says of sunset, then sink with a little splash beneath the water. Glancing down at his billy, he realized next that he could not make use of it either, nor of the dark dry dusty stuff he had meant to boil in water. He felt no repugnance, certainly no fear, in connexion with these things, only he could not handle them, he did not need them, he had forgotten, yes, "forgotten," what they meant exactly. This strange forgetfulness was increasing in him rapidly, becoming more and more complete with every minute. Yet his thirst must be quenched.

The next moment he found himself at the water's edge; he stooped to fill his billy; paused, hesitated, examined the rushing water, then abruptly moved a few feet higher up the stream, leaving the metal can behind him. His handling of it had been oddly clumsy, his gestures awkward, even unnatural. He now flung himself down with an easy, simple motion of his entire body, lowered his face to a quiet pool he had found, and drank his fill of the cool, refreshing liquid. But, though unaware of the fact, he did not drink. He lapped.

Then, crouching where he was, he ate the meat and sugar from his pockets, lapped more water, moved back a short distance again into the dry ground beneath the trees, but moved this time without rising to his feet, curled his body into a comfortable position and closed his eyes again to sleep... No single question now raised its head in him. He felt contentment, satisfaction only....

He stirred, shook himself, opened half an eye and saw, as he had felt already in slumber, that he was not alone. In the park-like spaces in front of him, as in the shadowed fringe of the trees at his back, there was sound and movement, the sound of stealthy feet, the movement of innumerable dark bodies. There was the pad and tread of animals, the stir of backs, of smooth and shaggy beasts, in countless numbers. Upon this host fell the light of a half moon sailing high in a cloudless sky; the gleam of stars, sparkling in the clear night air like diamonds, shone reflected in hundreds of ever-shifting eyes, most of then but a few feet above the ground. The whole valley was alive.

He sat upon his haunches, staring, staring, but staring in wonder, not

in fear, though the foremost of the great host were so near that he could
have stretched an arm and touched them. It was an ever-moving, ever-
shifting throng he gazed at, spell-bound, in the pale light of moon and
stars, now fading slowly towards the approaching dawn. And the smell
of the forest itself was not sweeter to him in that moment than the mingled perfume, raw, pungent, acrid, of this furry host of beautiful wild animals that moved like a sea, with a strange murmuring, too, like sea, as
the myriad feet and bodies passed to and fro together. Nor was the gleam
of the starry, phosphorescent eyes less pleasantly friendly than those
happy lamps that light home-lost wanderers to cosy rooms and safety.
Through the wild army, in a word, poured to him the deep comfort of
the entire valley, a comfort which held both the sweetness of invitation
and the welcome of some magical home-coming.

No thoughts came to him, but feeling rose in a tide of wonder and
acceptance. He was in his rightful place. His nature had come home.
There was this dim, vague consciousness in him that after long, futile
straying in another place where uncongenial conditions had forced him
to be unnatural and therefore terrible, he had returned at last where he
belonged. Here, in the Valley of the Beasts, he had found peace, security
and happiness. He would be—he was at last—himself.

It was a marvellous, even a magical, scene he watched, his nerves at
highest tension yet quite steady, his senses exquisitely alert, yet no
uneasiness in the full, accurate reports they furnished. Strong as some
deep flood-tide, yet dim, as with untold time and distance, rose over him
the spell of long-forgotten memory of a state where he was content and
happy, where he was natural. The outlines, as it were, of mighty, primitive pictures, flashed before him, yet were gone again before the detail
was filled in.

He watched the great army of the animals, they were all about him
now; he crouched upon his haunches in the centre of an ever-moving
circle of wild forest life. Great timber wolves he saw pass to and fro, lop-
ing past him with long stride and graceful swing, their red tongues
lolling out; they swarmed in hundreds. Behind, yet mingling freely with
them, rolled the huge grizzlies, not clumsy as their uncouth bodies
promised, but swiftly, lightly, easily, their half tumbling gait masking
agility and speed. They gambolled, sometimes they rose and stood half
upright, they were comely in their mass and power, they rolled past him
so close that he could touch them. And the black bear and the brown
went with them, bears beyond counting, monsters and little ones, a
splendid multitude. Beyond them, yet only a little further back, where
the park-like spaces made free movement easier, rose a sea of horns and
antlers like a miniature forest in the silvery moonlight. The immense

tribe of deer gathered in vast throngs beneath the starlit sky. Moose and caribou, he saw, the mighty wapiti, and the smaller deer in their crowding thousands. He heard the sound of meeting horns, the tread of innumerable hoofs, the occasional pawing of the ground as the bigger creatures maneuvered for more space about them. A wolf, he saw, was licking gently at the shoulder of a great bull-moose that had been injured. And the tide receded, advanced again, once more receded, rising and falling like a living sea whose waves were animal shapes, the inhabitants of the Valley of the Beasts.

Beneath the quiet moonlight they swayed to and fro before him. They watched him, knew him, recognized him. They made him welcome.

He was aware, moreover, of a world of smaller life that formed an under-sea, as it were, numerous under-currents rather, running in and out between the great upright legs of the larger creatures. These, though he could not see them clearly, covered the earth, he was aware, in enormous numbers, darting hither and thither, now hiding, now reappearing, too intent upon their busy purposes to pay him attention like their huger comrades, yet ever and anon tumbling against his back, cannoning from his sides, scampering across his legs even, then gone again with a scattering sound of rapid little feet, and rushing back into the general host beyond. And with this smaller world also he felt at home.

How long he sat gazing, happy in himself, secure, satisfied, contented, natural, he could not say, but it was long enough for the desire to mingle with what he saw, to know closer contact, to become one with them all—long enough for this deep blind desire to assert itself, so that at length he began to move from his mossy seat towards them, to move, moreover, as they moved, and not upright on two feet.

The moon was lower now, just sinking behind a towering cedar whose ragged crest broke its light, into silvery spray. The stars were a little paler too. A line of faint red was visible beyond the heights at the valley's eastern end.

He paused and looked about him, as he advanced slowly, aware that the host already made an opening in their ranks and that the bear even nosed the earth in front, as though to show the way that was easiest for him to follow. Then, suddenly, a lynx leaped past him into the low branches of a hemlock, and he lifted his head to admire its perfect poise. He saw in the same instant the arrival of the birds, the army of the eagles, hawks and buzzards, birds of prey—the awakening flight that just precedes the dawn. He saw the flocks and streaming lines, hiding the whitening stars a moment as they passed with a prodigious whirr of wings. There came the hooting of an owl from the tree immediately overhead where the lynx now crouched, but not maliciously, along its branch.

He started. He half rose to an upright position. He knew not why he did so, knew not exactly why he started. But in the attempt to find his new, and, as it now seemed, his unaccustomed balance, one hand fell against his side and came in contact with a hard straight thing that projected awkwardly from his clothing. He pulled it out, feeling it all over with his fingers. It was a little stick. He raised it nearer to his eyes, examined it in the light of dawn now growing swiftly, remembered, or half remembered what it was—and stood stock still.

"The totem stick," he mumbled to himself, yet audibly, finding his speech, and finding another thing—a glint of peering memory—for the first time since entering the valley.

A shock like fire ran through his body; he straightened himself, aware that a moment before he had been crawling upon his hands and knees; it seemed that something broke in his brain, lifting a veil, flinging a shutter free. And Memory peered dreadfully through the widening gap.

"I'm—I'm Grimwood," his voice uttered, though below his breath. "Tooshalli's left me. I'm alone....!"

He was aware of a sudden change in the animals surrounding him. A big, grey wolf sat three feet away, glaring into his face; at its side an enormous grizzly swayed itself from one foot to the other; behind it, as if looking over its shoulder, loomed a gigantic wapiti, its horns merged in the shadows of the drooping cedar boughs. But the northern dawn was nearer, the sun already close to the horizon. He saw details with sharp distinctness now. The great bear rose, balancing a moment on its massive hind-quarters, then took a step towards him, its front paws spread like arms. Its wicked head lolled horribly, as a huge bull-moose, lowering its horns as if about to charge, came up with a couple of long strides and joined it. A sudden excitement ran quivering over the entire host; the distant ranks moved in a new, unpleasant way; a thousand heads were lifted, ears were pricked, a forest of ugly muzzles pointed up to the wind.

And the Englishman, beside himself suddenly with a sense of ultimate terror that saw no possible escape, stiffened and stood rigid. The horror of his position petrified him. Motionless and silent he faced the awful army of his enemies, while the white light of breaking day added fresh ghastliness to the scene which was the setting for his cruel death in the Valley of the Beasts.

Above him crouched the hideous lynx, ready to spring the instant he sought safety in the tree; above it again, he was aware of a thousand talons of steel, fierce hooked beaks of iron, and the angry beating of prodigious livings.

He reeled, for the grizzly touched his body with its outstretched paw; the wolf crouched just before its deadly spring; in another second he would have been torn to pieces, crushed, devoured, when terror, operating naturally as ever, released the muscles of his throat and tongue. He shouted with what he believed was his last breath on earth. He called aloud in his frenzy. It was a prayer to whatever gods there be, it was an anguished cry for help to heaven.

"Ishtot! Great Ishtot, help me!" his voice rang out, while his hand still clutched the forgotten totem stick.

And the Red Heaven heard him.

Grimwood that same instant was aware of a presence that, but for his terror of the beasts, must have frightened him into sheer unconsciousness. A gigantic Red Indian stood before him. Yet, while the figure rose close in front of him, causing the birds to settle and the wild animals to crouch quietly where they stood, it rose also from a great distance, for it seemed to fill the entire valley with its influence, its power, its amazing majesty. In some way, moreover, that he could not understand, its vast appearance included the actual valley itself with all its trees, its running streams, its open spaces and its rocky bluffs. These marked its outline, as it were, the outline of a superhuman shape. There was a mighty bow, there was a quiver of enormous arrows, there was this Redskin figure to whom they belonged.

Yet the appearance, the outline, the face and figure too—these *were* the valley; and when the voice became audible, it was the valley itself that uttered the appalling words. It was the voice of trees and wind, and of running, falling water that woke the echoes in the Valley of the Beasts, as, in that same moment, the sun topped the ridge and filled the scene, the outline of the majestic figure too, with a flood of dazzling light:

"You have shed blood in this my valley.... *I will not save...*"

The figure melted away into the sunlit forest, merging with the newborn day. But Grimwood saw close against his face the shining teeth, hot fetid breath passed over his cheeks, a power enveloped his whole body as though a mountain crushed him. He closed his eyes. He fell. A sharp, crackling sound passed through his brain, but already unconscious, he did not hear it.

His eyes opened again, and the first thing they took in was—fire. He shrank back instinctively.

"It's all right, old man. We'll bring you round. Nothing to be frightened about." He saw the face of Iredale looking down into his own. Behind Iredale stood Tooshalli. His face was swollen. Grimwood remembered the blow. The big man began to cry.

"Painful still, is it?" Iredale said sympathetically. "Here, swallow a little more of this. It'll set you right in no time."

Grimwood gulped down the spirit. He made a violent effort to control himself, but was unable to keep the tears back. He felt no pain. It was his heart that ached, though why or wherefore, he had no idea.

"I'm all to pieces," he mumbled, ashamed yet somehow not ashamed. "My nerves are rotten. What's happened?" There was as yet no memory in him.

"You've been hugged by a bear, old man. But no bones broken. Tooshalli saved you. He fired in the nick of time—a brave shot, for he might easily have hit you instead of the brute."

"The other brute," whispered Grimwood, as the whisky worked in him and memory came slowly back.

"Where are we?" he asked presently, looking about him.

He saw a lake, canoes drawn up on the shore, two tents, and figures moving. Iredale explained matters briefly, then left him to sleep a bit. Tooshalli, it appeared, travelling without rest, had reached Iredale's camping ground twenty-four hours after leaving his employer. He found it deserted, Iredale and his Indian being on the hunt. When they returned at nightfall, he had explained his presence in his brief native fashion: "He struck me and I quit. He hunt now alone in Ishtot's Valley of the Beasts. He is dead, I think. I come to tell you."

Iredale and his guide, with Tooshalli as leader, started off then and there, but Grimwood had covered a considerable distance, though leaving an easy track to follow. It was the moose tracks and the blood that chiefly guided them. They came up with him suddenly enough—in the grip of an enormous bear.

It was Tooshalli that fired.

The Indian lives now in easy circumstances, all his needs cared for, while Grimwood, his benefactor but no longer his employer, has given up hunting. He is a quiet, easy-tempered, almost gentle sort of fellow, and people wonder rather why he hasn't married. "Just the fellow to make a good father," is what they say; "so kind, good-natured and affectionate." Among his pipes, in a glass case over the mantelpiece, hangs a totem stick. He declares it saved his soul, but what he means by the expression he has never quite explained.

THE CALL

The incident—story it never was, perhaps—began tamely, almost meanly; it ended upon a note of strange, unearthly wonder that has haunted him ever since. In Headley's memory, at any rate, it stands out as the loveliest, the most amazing thing he ever witnessed. Other emotions, too, contributed to the vividness of the picture. That he had felt jealousy towards his old pal, Arthur Deane, shocked him in the first place; it seemed impossible until it actually happened. But that the jealousy was proved afterwards to have been without a cause shocked him still more. He felt ashamed and miserable.

For him, the actual incident began when he received a note from Mrs. Blondin asking him to the Priory for a week-end, or for longer, if he could manage it.

Captain Arthur Deane, she mentioned, was staying with her at the moment, and a warm welcome awaited him. Iris she did not mention— Iris Manning, the interesting and beautiful girl for whom it was well known he had a considerable weakness. He found a good-sized house party; there was fishing in the little Sussex river, tennis, golf not far away, while two motor cars brought the remoter country across the downs into easy reach. Also there was a bit of duck shooting for those who cared to wake at 3 a.m. and paddle up-stream to the marshes where the birds were feeding.

"Have you brought your gun?" was the first thing Arthur said to him when he arrived. "Like a fool, I left mine in town."

"I hope you haven't," put in Miss Manning; "because if you have I must get up one fine morning at three o'clock." She laughed merrily, and there was an undernote of excitement in the laugh.

Captain Headley showed his surprise. "That you were a Diana had escaped my notice, I'm ashamed to say," he replied lightly. "Yet I've known you some years, haven't I?" He looked straight at her, and the soft yet searching eye, turning from his friend, met his own securely. She was appraising him, for the hundreth time, and he, for the hundreth time, was thinking how pretty she was, and wondering how long the prettiness would last after marriage.

"I'm not," he heard her answer. "That's just it. But I've promised."

"Rather!" said Arthur gallantly. "And I shall hold you to it," he added still more gallantly—too gallantly, Headley thought. "I couldn't possibly get up at cockcrow without a very special inducement, could I, now? You know me, Dick!"

"Well, anyhow, I've brought my gun," Headley replied evasively, "so you've no excuse, either of you. You'll have to go." And while they were laughing and chattering about it, Mrs. Blondin clinched the matter for them. Provisions were hard to come by; the larder really needed a brace or two of birds; it was the least they could do in return for what she called amusingly her "Armistice hospitality."

"So I expect you to get up at three," she chaffed them, "and return with your Victory birds."

It was from this preliminary skirmish over the tea-table on the lawn five minutes after his arrival that Dick Headley realized easily enough the little game in progress. As a man of experience, just on the wrong side of forty, it was not difficult to see the cards each held. He sighed. Had he guessed an intrigue was on foot he would not have come, yet he might have known that wherever his hostess was, there were the vultures gathered together.

Matchmaker by choice and instinct, Mrs. Blondin could not help herself. True to her name, she was always balancing on matrimonial tightropes—for others.

Her cards, at any rate, were obvious enough; she had laid them on the table for him. He easily read her hand. The next twenty-four hours confirmed this reading. Having made up her mind that Iris and Arthur were destined for each other, she had grown impatient; they had been ten days together, yet Iris was still free. They were good friends only. With calculation, she, therefore, took a step that must bring things further. She invited Dick Headley, whose weakness for the girl was common knowledge. The card was indicated; she played it. Arthur must come to the point or see another man carry her off. This, at least, she planned, little dreaming that the dark King of Spades would interfere.

Miss Manning's hand also was fairly obvious, for both men were extremely eligible *partis*. She was getting on; one or other was to become her husband before the party broke up. This, in crude language, was certainly in her cards, though, being a nice and charming girl, she might camouflage it cleverly to herself and others. Her eyes, on each man in turn when the shooting expedition was being discussed, revealed her part in the little intrigue clearly enough. It was all, thus far, as commonplace as could be.

But there were two more hands Headley had to read—his own and his friend's; and these, he admitted honestly, were not so easy. To take his own first. It was true he was fond of the girl and had often tried to make up his mind to ask her. Without being conceited, he had good reason to believe his affection was returned and that she would accept him. There was no ecstatic love on either side, for he was no longer a boy of twenty, nor was she unscathed by tempestuous love affairs that had scorched the first bloom from her face and heart. But they understood one another; they were an honest couple; she was tired of flirting; both wanted to marry and settle down. Unless a better man turned up she probably would say "Yes" without humbug or delay. It was this last reflection that brought him to the final hand he had to read.

Here he was puzzled. Arthur Deane's rôle in the teacup strategy, for the first time since they had known one another, seemed strange, uncertain. Why? Because, though paying no attention to the girl openly, he met her clandestinely, unknown to the rest of the house-party, and above all without telling his intimate pal—at three o'clock in the morning.

The house-party was in full swing, with a touch of that wild, reckless gaiety which followed the end of the war: "Let us be happy before a worse thing comes upon us," was in many hearts. After a crowded day they danced till early in the morning, while doubtful weather prevented the early shooting expedition after duck. The third night Headley contrived to disappear early to bed. He lay there thinking. He was puzzled over his friend's rôle, over the clandestine meeting in particular. It was the morning before, waking very early, he had been drawn to the window by an unusual sound—the cry of a bird. Was it a bird? In all his experience he had never heard such a curious, half-singing call before. He listened a moment, thinking it must have been a dream, yet with the odd cry still ringing in his ears. It was repeated close beneath his open window, a long, low-pitched cry with three distinct following notes in it.

He sat up in bed and listened hard. No bird that he knew could make such sounds. But it was not repeated a third time, and out of sheer curiosity he went to the window and looked out. Dawn was creeping over the distant downs; he saw their outline in the grey pearly light; he saw the lawn below, stretching down to the little river at the bottom, where a curtain of faint mist hung in the air. And on this lawn he also saw Arthur Deane—with Iris Manning.

Of course, he reflected, they were going after the duck. He turned to look at his watch; it was three o'clock. The same glance, however, showed him his gun standing in the corner. So they were going without a gun. A sharp pang of unexpected jealousy shot through him. He was just going to shout out something or other, wishing them good luck, or asking if they had found another gun, perhaps, when a cold touch crept down his spine. The same instant his heart contracted. Deane had followed the girl into the summer-house, which stood on the right. It was *not* the shooting expedition at all. Arthur was meeting her for another purpose. The blood flowed back, filling his head. He felt an eavesdropper, a sneak, a detective; but, for all that., he felt also jealous. And his jealousy seemed chiefly because Arthur had not told him.

Of this, then, he lay thinking in bed on the third night. The following day he had said nothing, but had crossed the corridor and put the gun in his friend's room. Arthur, for his part, had said nothing either. For the first time in their long, long friendship, there lay a secret between them. To Headley the unexpected revelation came with pain.

For something like a quarter of a century these two had been bosom friends; they had camped together, been in the army together, taken their pleasure together, each the full confidant of the other in all the things that go to make up men's lives. Above all, Headley had been the one and only recipient of Arthur's unhappy love story. He knew the girl, knew his friend's deep passion, and also knew his terrible pain when she was lost at sea. Arthur was burnt out, finished, out of the running, so far as marriage was concerned. He was not a man to love a second time. It was a great and poignant tragedy. Headley, as confidant, knew all. But more than that—Arthur, on his side, knew his friend's weakness for Iris Manning, knew that a marriage was still possible and likely between them. They were true as steel to one another, and each man, oddly enough, had once saved the other's life, thus adding to the strength of a great natural tie.

Yet now one of them, feigning innocence by day, even indifference, secretly met his friend's girl by night, and kept the matter to himself. It seemed incredible. With his own eyes Headley had seen him on the lawn, passing in the faint grey light through the mist into the summerhouse, where the girl had just preceded him. He had not seen her face, but he had seen the skirt sweep round the corner of the wooden pillar. He had not waited to see them come out again.

So he now lay wondering what rôle his old friend was playing in this little intrigue that their hostess, Mrs. Blondin, helped to stage. And, oddly enough, one minor detail stayed in his mind with a curious vividness. As naturalist, hunter, nature-lover, the cry of that strange bird, with its three mournful notes, perplexed him exceedingly.

A knock came at his door, and the door pushed open before he had time to answer. Deane himself came in.

"Wise man," he exclaimed in an easy tone, "'got off to bed. Iris was asking where you were." He sat down on the edge of the mattress, where Headley was lying with a cigarette and an open book he had not read. The old sense of intimacy and comradeship rose in the latter's heart. Doubt and suspicion faded. He prized his great friendship. He met the familiar eyes. "Impossible," he said to himself, "absolutely impossible! He's not playing a game; he's not a rotter!" He pushed over his cigarette case, and Arthur lighted one.

"Done in," he remarked shortly, with the first puff. "Can't stand it any more. I'm off to town to-morrow."

Headley stared in amazement. "Fed up already?" he asked. "Why, I rather like it. It's quite amusing. What's wrong, old man""

"This match-making," said Deane bluntly. "Always throwing that girl at my head. If it's not the duck-shooting stunt at 3 a.m., it's something else. She doesn't care for me and I don't care for her. Besides—"

He stopped, and the expression of his face changed suddenly. A sad, quiet look of tender yearning came into his clear brown eyes.

"*You* know, Dick," he went on in a low, half-reverent tone. "I don't want to marry. I never can."

Dick's heart stirred within him. "'Mary," he said, understandingly.

The other nodded, as though the memories were still too much for him. "I'm still miserably lonely for her," he said. "Can't help it simply. I feel utterly lost without her. Her memory to me is everything." He looked deep into his pal's eyes. "I'm married to that," he added very firmly.

They pulled their cigarettes a moment in silence. They belonged to the male type that conceals emotion behind schoolboy language.

"It's hard luck," said Headley gently, "rotten luck, old man, I understand." Arthur's head nodded several times in succession as he smoked. He made no remark for some minutes. Then presently he said, as though it had no particular importance—for thus old friends show frankness to each other—"Besides, anyhow, it's you the girl's dying for, not me. She's blind as a bat, old Blondin. Even when I'm with her—thrust with her by that old matchmaker for my sins—it's you she talks about. All the talk leads up to you and yours. She's devilish fond of you." He paused a moment and looked searchingly into his friend's face. "I say, old man— are you—I mean, do you mean business there? Because—excuse me interfering—but you'd better be careful. She's a good sort, you know, after all."

"Yes, Arthur, I do like her a bit," Dick told him frankly. "But I can't make up my mind quite. You see, it's like this—"

And they talked the matter over as old friends will, until finally Arthur chucked his cigarette into the grate and got up to go. "Dead to the world," he said, with a yawn. "I'm off to bed. Give you a chance, too," he added with a laugh. It was after midnight.

The other turned, as though something had suddenly occurred to him.

"By the bye, Arthur," he said abruptly, "what bird makes this sound? I

heard it the other morning. Most extraordinary cry. You know everything that flies. What is it?" And, to the best of his ability, he imitated
the strange three-note cry he had heard in the dawn two mornings
before.

To his amazement and keen distress, his friend, with a sound like a stifled groan, sat down upon the bed without a word. He seemed startled.
His face was white. He stared. He passed a hand, as in pain, across his
forehead.

"Do it again," he whispered, in a hushed, nervous voice. "Once again—
for me."

And Headley, looking at him, repeated the queer notes, a sudden revulsion of feeling rising through him. "He's fooling me after all," ran in his
heart, "my old, old pal—"

There was silence for a full minute. Then Arthur, stammering a bit,
said lamely, a certain hush in his voice still: "Where in the world did you
hear that—and *when?*"

Dick Headley sat up in bed. He was not going to lose this friendship,
which, to him, was more than the love of woman. He must help. His pal
was in distress and difficulty. There were circumstances, he realized, that
might be too strong for the best man in the world—sometimes. No, by
God, he would play the game and help him out!

"Arthur, old chap," he said affectionately, almost tenderly. "I heard it
two mornings ago—on the lawn below my window here. It woke me up.
I—I went to look. Three in the morning, about."

Arthur amazed him then. He first took another cigarette and lit it
steadily. He looked round the room vaguely, avoiding, it seemed, the
other's eyes. Then he turned, pain in his face, and gazed straight at him.

"You saw—nothing?" he asked in a louder voice, but a voice that had
something very real and true in it. It reminded Headley of the voice he
heard when he was fainting from exhaustion, and Arthur had said, "Take
it, I tell you. I'm all right," and had passed over the flask, though his own
throat and sight and heart were black with thirst. It was a voice that had
command in it, a voice that did not lie because it could not—yet did lie
and could lie—when occasion warranted.

Headley knew a second's awful struggle.

"Nothing," he answered quietly, after his little pause. "Why?"

For perhaps two minutes his friend hid his face. Then he looked up.

"Only," he whispered, "because that was our secret lover's cry. It seems
so strange you heard it and not I. I've felt her so close of late—Mary!"

The white face held very steady, the firm lips did not tremble, but it
was evident that the heart knew anguish that was deep and poignant.
"We used it to call each other—in the old days. It was our private call.

No one else in the world knew it but Mary and myself."

Dick Headley was flabbergasted. He had no time to think, however.

"It's odd you should hear it and not I," his friend repeated. He looked hurt, bewildered, wounded. Then suddenly his face brightened. "I know," he cried suddenly. "You and I are pretty good pals. There's a tie between us and all that. Why, it's tel—telepathy, or whatever they call it. That's what it is."

He got up abruptly. Dick could think of nothing to say but to repeat the other's words. "Of course, of course. That's it," he said, "telepathy." He stared—anywhere but at his pal.

"Night, night!" he heard from the door, and before he could do more than reply in similar vein Arthur was gone.

He lay for a long time, thinking, thinking. He found it all very strange. Arthur in this emotional state was new to him. He turned it over and over. Well, he had known good men behave queerly when wrought up. That recognition of the bird's cry was strange, of course, but—he knew the cry of a bird when he heard it, though he might not know the actual bird. That was no human whistle. Arthur was—inventing. No, that was not possible. He was worked up, then, over something, a bit hysterical perhaps. It had happened before, though in a milder way, when his heart attacks came on. They affected his nerves and head a little, it seemed. He was a deep sort, Dick remembered. Thought turned and twisted in him, offering various solutions, some absurd, some likely. He was a nervous, high-strung fellow underneath, Arthur was. He remembered that. Also he remembered, anxiously again, that his heart was not quite sound, though what that had to do with the present tangle he did not see.

Yet it was hardly likely that he would bring in Mary as an invention, an excuse—Mary, the most sacred memory in his life, the deepest, truest, best. He had sworn, anyhow, that Iris Manning meant nothing to him.

Through all his speculations, behind every thought, ran this horrid working jealousy. It poisoned him. It twisted truth. It moved like a wicked snake through mind and heart. Arthur, gripped by his new, absorbing love for Iris Manning, lied. He couldn't believe it, he didn't believe it, he wouldn't believe it—yet jealousy persisted in keeping the idea alive in him. It was a dreadful thought. He fell asleep on it.

But his sleep was uneasy with feverish, unpleasant dreams that rambled on in fragments without coming to conclusion. Then, suddenly, the cry of the strange bird came into his dream. He started, turned over, woke up. The cry still continued. It was not a dream. He jumped out of bed.

The room was grey with early morning, the air fresh and a little chill.

The cry came floating over the lawn as before. He looked out, pain clutching at his heart. Two figures stood below, a man and a girl, and the man was Arthur Deane. Yet the light was so dim, the morning being overcast, that had he not expected to see his friend, he would scarcely have recognized the familiar form in that shadowy outline that stood close beside the girl. Nor could he, perhaps, have recognized Iris Manning. Their backs were to him. They moved away, disappearing again into the little summer-house, and this time—he saw it beyond question—the two were hand in hand. Vague and uncertain as the figures were in the early twilight, he was sure of that.

The first disagreeable sensation of surprise, disgust, anger that sickened him turned quickly, however, into one of another kind altogether. A curious feeling of superstitious dread crept over him, and a shiver ran again along his nerves.

"Hallo, Arthur!" he called from the window. There was no answer. His voice was certainly audible in the summer-house. But no one came. He repeated the call a little louder, waited in vain for thirty seconds, then came, the same moment, to a decision that even surprised himself, for the truth was he could no longer bear the suspense of waiting. He must see his friend at once and have it out with him. He turned and went deliberately down the corridor to Deane's bedroom. He would wait there for his return and know the truth from his own lips. But also another thought had come—the gun. He had quite forgotten it—the safety-catch was out of order. He had not warned him.

He found the door closed but not locked; opening it cautiously, he went in.

But the unexpectedness of what he saw gave him a genuine shock. He could hardly suppress a cry. Everything in the room was neat and orderly, no sign of disturbance anywhere, and it was not empty. There, in bed, before his very eyes, was Arthur. The clothes were turned back a little; he saw the pyjamas open at the throat; he lay sound asleep, deeply, peacefully asleep.

So surprised, indeed, was Headley that, after staring a moment, almost unable to believe his sight, he then put out a hand and touched him gently, cautiously on the forehead. But Arthur did not stir or wake; his breathing remained deep and regular. He lay sleeping like a baby.

Headley glanced round the room, noticed the gun in the corner where he himself had put it the day before, and then went out, closing the door behind him softly.

Arthur Deane, however, did not leave for London as he had intended, because he felt unwell and kept to his room upstairs. It was only a slight attack, apparently, but he must lie quiet. There was no need to send for a doctor; he knew just what to do; these passing attacks were common enough. He would be up and about again very shortly. Headley kept him company, saying no single word of what had happened. He read aloud to him, chatted and cheered him up. He had no other visitors. Within twenty-four hours he was himself once more. He and his friend had planned to leave the following day.

But Headley, that last night in the house, felt an odd uneasiness and could not sleep. All night long he sat up reading, looking out of the window, smoking in a chair where he could see the stars and hear the wind and watch the huge shadow of the downs. The house lay very still as the hours passed. He dozed once or twice. Why did he sit up in this unnecessary way? Why did he leave his door ajar so that the slightest sound of another door opening, or of steps passing along the corridor, must reach him? Was he anxious for his friend? Was he suspicious? What was his motive, what his secret purpose?

Headley did not know, and could not even explain it to himself. He felt uneasy, that was all he knew. Not for worlds would he have let himself go to sleep or lose full consciousness that night. It was very odd; he could not understand himself. He merely obeyed a strange, deep instinct that bade him wait and watch. His nerves were jumpy; in his heart lay some unexplicable anxiety that was pain.

The dawn came slowly; the stars faded one by one; the line of the downs showed their grand bare curves against the sky; cool and cloudless the September morning broke above the little Sussex pleasure house. He sat and watched the east grow bright. The early wind brought a scent of marshes and the sea into his room. Then suddenly it brought a sound as well—the haunting cry of the bird with its three following notes. And this time there came an answer.

Headley knew then why he had sat up. A wave of emotion swept him as he heard—an emotion he could not attempt to explain. Dread, wonder, longing seized him. For some seconds he could not leave his chair because he did not dare to. The low-pitched cries of call and answer rang in his ears like some unearthly music. With an effort he started up, went to the window and looked out.

This time the light was sharp and clear. No mist hung in the air. He saw the crimsoning sky reflected like a band of shining metal in the reach of river beyond the lawn. He saw dew on the grass, a sheet of pallid silver. He saw the summer-house, empty of any passing figures. For this time the two figures stood plainly in view before his eyes upon the lawn. They stood there, hand in hand, sharply defined, unmistakable in form and outline, their faces, moreover, turned upwards to the window where he stood, staring down in pain and amazement at them—at Arthur Deane and *Mary*.

They looked into his eyes. He tried to call, but no sound left his throat. They began to move across the dew-soaked lawn. They went, he saw, with a floating, undulating motion towards the river shining in the dawn. Their feet left no marks upon the grass. They reached the bank, but did not pause in their going. They rose a little, floating like silent birds across the river. Turning in mid-stream, they smiled towards him, waved their hands with a gesture of farewell, then, rising still higher into the opal dawn, their figures passed into the distance slowly, melting away against the sunlit marshes and the shadowing downs beyond. They disappeared.

Headley never quite remembers actually leaving the window, crossing the room, or going down the passage. Perhaps he went at once, perhaps he stood gazing into the air above the downs for a considerable time, unable to tear himself away. He was in some marvellous dream, it seemed. The next thing he remembers, at any rate, was that he was standing beside his friend's bed, trying, in his distraught anguish of heart, to call him from that sleep which, on earth, knows no awakening.

EGYPTIAN SORCERY

1

Sanfield paused as he was about to leave the Underground station at Victoria, and cursed the weather. When he left the City it was fine; now it was pouring with rain, and he had neither overcoat nor umbrella. Not a taxi was discoverable in the dripping gloom. He would get soaked before he reached his rooms in Sloane Street.

He stood for some minutes, thinking how vile London was in February, and how depressing life was in general. He stood also, in that moment, though he knew it not, upon the edge of a singular adventure. Looking back upon it in later years, he often remembered this particularly wretched moment of a pouring wet February evening, when everything seemed wrong, and Fate had loaded the dice against him, even in the matter of weather and umbrellas.

Fate, however, without betraying her presence, was watching him through the rain and murk; and Fate, that night, had strange, mysterious eyes. Fantastic cards lay up her sleeve. The rain, his weariness and depression, his physical fatigue especially, seemed the conditions she required before she played these curious cards. Something new and wonderful fluttered close. Romance flashed by him across the driving rain and touched his cheek. He was too exasperated to be aware of it.

Things had gone badly that day at the office, where he was junior partner in a small firm of engineers. Threatened trouble at the works had come to a head. A strike seemed imminent. To add to his annoyance, a new client, whose custom was of supreme importance, had just complained bitterly of the delay in the delivery of his machinery. The senior partners had left the matter in Sanfield's hands; he had not succeeded. The angry customer swore he would hold the firm to its contract. They could deliver or pay up—whichever suited them. The junior partner had made a mess of things.

The final words on the telephone still rang in his ears as he stood sheltering under the arcade, watching the downpour, and wondering whether he should make a dash for it or wait on the chance of its clearing up—when a further blow was dealt him as the rain-soaked poster of an evening paper caught his eye: "Riots in Egypt. Heavy Fall in Egyptian Securities," he read with blank dismay. Buying a paper he turned feverishly to the City article—to find his worst fears confirmed. Delta

Lands, in which nearly all his small capital was invested, had declined a quarter on the news, and would evidently decline further still. The riots were going on in the towns nearest to their property. Banks had been looted, crops destroyed; the trouble was deep-seated.

So grave was the situation that mere weather seemed suddenly of no account at all. He walked home doggedly in the drenching rain, paying less attention to it than if it had been Scotch mist. The water streamed from his hat, dripped clown his back and neck, splashed him with mud and grime from head to foot. He was soaked to the skin. He hardly noticed it. His capital had depreciated by half, at least, and possibly was altogether lost; his position at the office was insecure. How could mere weather matter?

Sitting, eventually, before his fire in dry clothes, after an apology for a dinner he had no heart to eat, he reviewed the situation. He faced a possible total loss of his private capital. Next, the position of his firm caused him grave uneasiness, since, apart from his own mishandling of the new customer, the threatened strike might ruin it completely; a long strain on its limited finances was out of the question. George Sanfield certainly saw things at their worst. He was now thirty-five. A fresh start—the mere idea of it made him shudder—occurred as a possibility in the near future. Vitality, indeed, was at a low ebb, it seemed. Mental depression, great physical fatigue, weariness of life in general made his spirits droop alarmingly, so that almost he felt tired of living. His tie with existence, at any rate, just then was dangerously weak.

Thought turned next to the man on whose advice he had staked his all in Delta Lands. Morris had important Egyptian interests in various big companies and enterprises along the Nile. He had first come to the firm with a letter of introduction upon some business matter, which the junior partner had handled so successfully that acquaintance thus formed had ripened into a more personal tie. The two men had much in common: their temperaments were suited; understanding grew between them; they felt at home and comfortable with one another. They became friends; they felt a mutual confidence. When Morris paid his rare visits to England, they spent much time together; and it was on one of these occasions that the matter of the Egyptian shares was mentioned, Morris urgently advising their purchase.

Sanfield explained his own position clearly enough, but his friend was so confident and optimistic that the purchase eventually had been made. There had been, moreover, Sanfield now remembered, the flavour of a peculiarly intimate and personal kind about the deal. He had remarked it, with a touch of surprise, at the moment, though really it seemed natural enough. Morris was very earnest, holding his friend's interest at heart; he was affectionate almost.

"I'd like to do you this good turn, old man," he said. "I have the strong feeling, somehow, that I owe you this, though heaven alone knows why!" After a pause he added, half shyly: "It may be one of those old memories we hear about nowadays cropping up out of some previous life together." Before the other could reply, he went on to explain that only three men were in the parent syndicate, the shares being unobtainable. "I'll set some of my own aside for you—four thousand or so, if you like."

They laughed together; Sanfield thanked him warmly; the deal was carried out. But the recipient of the favour had wondered a little at the sudden increase of intimacy even while he liked it and responded.

Had he been a fool, he now asked himself, to swallow the advice, putting all his eggs into a single basket? He knew very little about Morris after all.... Yet, while reflection showed him that the advice was honest, and the present riots no fault of the adviser's, he found his thoughts turning in a steady stream towards the man. The affairs of the firm took second place. It was Morris, with his deep-set eyes, his curious ways, his dark skin burnt brick-red by a fierce Eastern sun; it was Morris, looking almost like an Egyptian, who stood before him as he sat thinking gloomily over his dying fire.

He longed to talk with him, to ask him questions, to seek advice. He saw him very vividly against the screen of thought; Morris stood beside him now, gazing out across the limitless expanse of tawny sand. He had in his eyes the "distance" that sailors share with men whose life has been spent amid great trackless wastes. Morris, moreover, now he came to think of it, seemed always a little out of place in England. He had few relatives and, apparently, no friends; he was always intensely pleased when the time came to return to his beloved Nile. He had once mentioned casually a sister who kept house for him when duty detained him in Cairo, but, even here, he was something of an Oriental, rarely speaking of his women folk. Egypt, however, plainly drew him like a magnet. Resistance involved disturbance in his being, even ill-health. Egypt was "home" to him, and his friend, though he had never been there, felt himself its potent spell.

Another curious trait Sanfield remembered, too—his friend's childish superstition; his belief, or half-belief, in magic and the supernatural. Sanfield, amused, had ascribed it to the long sojourn in a land where anything unusual is at once ascribed to spiritual agencies. Morris owed his entire fortune, if his tale could be believed, to the magical apparition of an unearthly kind in some lonely *wadi* among the Bedouins. A sand-diviner had influenced another successful speculation.... He was a picturesque figure, whichever way one took him: yet a successful business man into the bargain.

These reflections and memories, on the other hand, brought small comfort to the man who had tempted Fate by following his advice. It was only a little strange how Morris now dominated his thoughts, directing them towards himself. Morris was in Egypt at the moment.

He went to bed at length, filled with uneasy misgivings, but for a long time he could not sleep. He tossed restlessly, his mind still running on the subject of his long reflections. He ached with tiredness. He dropped off at last. Then came a nightmare dream, in which the firm's works were sold for nearly nothing to an old Arab sheikh who wished to pay for them—in goats. He woke up in a cold perspiration. He had uneasy thoughts. His fancy was travelling. He could not rest.

To distract his mind, he turned on the light and tried to read, and, eventually, towards morning, fell into a sleep of sheer exhaustion. And his final thought—he knew not exactly why—was a sentence Morris had made use of long ago: "I feel I owe you a good turn; I'd like to do something for you...."

This was the memory in his mind as he slipped off into unconsciousness.

But what happens when the mind is unconscious and the tired body lies submerged in deep sleep, no man, they say, can really tell.

2

The next thing he knew he was walking along a sun-baked street in some foreign town that was familiar, although, at first, its name escaped him. Colour, softness, and warmth pervaded it; there was sparkle and lightness in the exhilarating air; it was an Eastern town.

Though early morning, a number of people were already stirring; strings of camels passed him, loaded with clover, bales of merchandise, and firewood. Gracefully-draped women went by silently, carrying water jars of blunt clay upon their heads. Rude wooden shutters were being taken down in the bazaars; the smoke of cooking-fires rose in the blue spirals through the quiet air. He felt strangely at home and happy. The light, the radiance stirred him. He passed a mosque from which the worshippers came pouring in a stream of colour.

Yet, though an Eastern town, it was not wholly Oriental, for he saw that many of the buildings were of semi-European design, and that the natives sometimes wore European dress, except for the fez upon the head. Among them were Europeans, too. Staring into the faces of the passers-by he found, to his vexation, that he could not focus sight as usual, and that the nearer he approached, the less clearly he discerned the features. The faces, upon close attention, at once grew shadowy, merged into each other, or, in some odd fashion, melted into the dazzling sunshine that was their background. All his attempts in this direction failed; impatience seized him; of surprise, however, he was not conscious. Yet this mingled vagueness and intensity seemed perfectly natural.

Filled with a stirring curiosity, he made a strong effort to concentrate his attention, only to discover that this vagueness, this difficulty of focus, lay in his own being, too. He wandered on, unaware exactly where he was going, yet not much perturbed, since there was an objective in view, he knew, and this objective *must* eventually be reached. Its nature, however, for the moment entirely eluded him.

The sense of familiarity, meanwhile, increased; he had been in this town before, although not quite within recoverable memory. It seemed, perhaps, the general atmosphere, rather than the actual streets, he knew; a certain perfume in the air, a tang of indefinable sweetness, a vitality in the radiant sunshine. The dark faces that he could not focus, he yet knew; the flowing garments of blue and red and yellow, the softly-slippered feet, the slouching camels, the burning human eyes that faded ere he fully caught them—the entire picture in this blazing sunlight lay half-hidden, half-revealed. And an extraordinary sense of happiness and well-being flooded him as he walked; he felt at home; comfort and bliss stole over him. Almost he knew his way about. This was a place he loved and knew.

The complete silence, moreover, did not strike him as peculiar until, suddenly, it was broken in a startling fashion. He heard his own name spoken. It sounded close beside his ear.

"George Sanfield!" The voice was familiar. Morris called him. He realized then the truth. He was, of course, in Cairo.

Yet, instead of turning to discover the speaker at his side, he hurried forward, as though he knew that the voice had come through distance. His consciousness cleared and lightened; he felt more alive; his eyes now focused the passers-by without difficulty. He was there to find Morris, and Morris was directing him. All was explained and natural again. He hastened. But, even while he hastened, he knew that his personal desire to speak with his friend about Egyptian shares and Delta Lands was not his single object. Behind it, further in among as yet unstirring shadows, lay another deeper purpose. Yet he did not trouble about it, nor make a conscious effort at discovery. Morris was doing him that "good turn I feel I owe you." This conviction filled him overwhelmingly. The question of how and why did not once occur to him. A strange, great happiness rose in him.

Upon the outskirts of the town now, he found himself approaching a large building in the European style, with wide verandas and a cultivated garden filled with palm trees. A well-kept drive of yellow sand led to its chief entrance, and the man in khaki drill and ridingbreeches walking along this drive, not ten yards in front of him, was—Morris. He overtook him, but his cry of welcome recognition was not answered. Morris, walking with bowed head and stooping shoulders, seemed intensely preoccupied; he had not heard the call.

"Here I am, old fellow!'" exclaimed his friend, holding out a hand. "I've come, you see...!" then paused aghast before the altered face. Morris paid no attention. He walked straight on as though he had not heard. It was the distraught and anguished expression on the drawn and haggard features that impressed the other most. The silence he took without surprise.

It was the pain and suffering in his friend that occupied him. The dark rims beneath heavy eyes, the evidence of sleepless nights, of long anxiety and ceaseless dread, afflicted him with their too-plain story. The man was overwhelmed with some great sorrow. Sanfield forgot his personal trouble; this larger, deeper grief usurped its place entirely.

"Morris! Morris!" he cried yet more eagerly than before. "I've come, you see. Tell me what's the matter. I believe—that I can—help you...!"

The other turned, looking past him through the air. He made no answer. The eyes went through him. He walked straight on, and Sanfield walked at his side in silence. Through the large door they passed together, Morris paying as little attention to him as though he were not there, and in the small chamber they now entered, evidently a waiting-room, an Egyptian servant approached, uttered some inaudible words, and then withdrew, leaving them alone together.

It seemed that time leaped forward, yet stood still; the passage of minutes, that is to say, was irregular, almost fanciful. Whether the interval was long or short, however, Morris spent it pacing up and down the little room, his hands thrust deep into his pockets, his mind oblivious of all else but his absorbing anxiety and grief. To his friend, who watched him by the wall with intense desire to help, he paid no attention. The latter's spoken words went by him, entirely unnoticed; he gave no sign of seeing him; his eyes, as he paced up and down, muttering inaudibly to himself, were fixed every few seconds on an inner door. Beyond that door, Sanfield now divined, lay someone who hesitated on the narrow frontier between life and death.

It opened suddenly and a man, in overall and rubber gloves, came out, his face grave yet with faint signs of hope about it—a doctor, clearly, straight from the operating table. Morris, standing rigid in his tracks, listened to something spoken, for the lips were in movement, though no words were audible. The operation, Sanfield divined, had been successful, though danger was still present. The two men passed out, then, into the hall and climbed a wide staircase to the floor above, Sanfield following noiselessly, though so close that he could touch them. Entering a large, airy room where French windows, carefully shaded with green blinds opened on to a veranda, they approached a bed. Two nurses bent over it. The occupant was at first invisible.

Events had moved with curious rapidity. All this had happened, it seemed, in a single moment, yet with the irregular effect already mentioned which made Sanfield feel it might, equally, have lasted hours. But, as he stood behind Morris and the surgeon at the bed, the deeps in him opened suddenly, and he trembled under a shock of intense emotion that he could not understand. As with a stroke of lightning some heavenly fire set his heart aflame with yearning. The very soul in him broke loose with passionate longing that *must* find satisfaction. It came to him in a single instant with the certain knowledge of an unconquerable conviction. Hidden, yet ever waiting, among the broken centuries, there now leaped upon him this flash of memory—the memory of some sweet and ancient love Time might veil yet could not kill.

He ran forward, past the surgeon and the nurses, past Morris who bent above the bed with a face ghastly from anxiety. He gazed down upon the fair girl lying there, her unbound hair streaming over the pillow. He saw, and he remembered. And an uncontrollable cry of recognition left his lips....

The irregularity of the passing minutes became so marked then, that he might well have passed outside their measure altogether, beyond what men call Time; duration, interval, both escaped. Alone and free with his eternal love, he was safe from all confinement, free, it seemed, either of time or space. His friend, however, was vaguely with him during the amazing instant. He felt acutely aware of the need each had, respectively, for the other, born of a heritage the Past had hidden overlong. Each, it was clear, could do the other a good turn.... Sanfield, though unable to describe or disentangle later, knew, while it lasted, this joy of full, delicious understanding....

The strange, swift instant of recognition passed and disappeared. The cry, Sanfield realized, on coming back to the Present, had been soundless and inaudible as before. No one observed him; no one stirred. The girl, on that bed beside the opened windows, lay evidently dying. Her breath came in gasps, her chest heaved convulsively, each attempt at recovery was slower and more painful than the one before. She was unconscious. Sometimes her breathing seemed to stop. It grew weaker, as the pulse grew fainter. And Sanfield, transfixed as with paralysis, stood watching, waiting, an intolerable yearning in his heart to help. It seemed to him that he waited with a purpose.

This purpose suddenly became clear. He knew why he waited. There was help to be given. He was the one to give it.

The girl's vitality and ebbing nerves, her entire physical organism now fading so quickly towards that final extinction which meant death—could these but be stimulated by a new tide of life, the danger-point now fast approaching might be passed, and recovery must follow. This impetus, he knew suddenly, he could supply. How, he could not tell. It flashed upon him from beyond the stars, as from ancient store of long-forgotten, long-neglected knowledge. It was enough that he felt confident and sure. His soul burned within him; the strength of an ancient and unconquerable love rose through his being. He would try.

The doctor, he saw, was in the act of giving his last aid in the form of a hypodermic injection, Morris and the nurses looking on. Sanfield observed the sharp quick rally, only too faint, too slight; he saw the collapse that followed. The doctor, shrugging his shoulders, turned with a look that could not express itself in words, and Morris, burying his face in his hands, knelt by the bed, shaken with convulsive sobbing. It was the end.

In which moment, precisely, the strange paralysis that had bound Sanfield momentarily, was lifted from his being, and an impelling force, obeying his immense desire, invaded him. He knew how to act. His will, taught long ago, yet long-forgotten, was set free.

"You have come back to me at last," he cried in his anguish and his power, though the voice was, as ever, inaudible and soundless, "*I shall not let you go!*...

Drawn forward nearer and nearer to the bed, he leaned down, as if to kiss the pale lips and streaming hair. But his knowledge operated better than he knew. In the tremendous grip of that power which spins the stars and suns, while drawing souls into manifestation upon a dozen planets, he raced, he dived, he plunged, helpless, yet driven by the creative stress of love and sacrifice towards some eternal purpose. Caught in what seemed a vortex of amazing force, he sank away, as a straw is caught and sunk within the suction of a mighty whirlpool. His memory of Morris, of the doctor, of the girl herself, passed utterly. His entire personality became merged, lost, obliterated. He was aware of nothing; not even aware of nothingness. He lost consciousness....

3

The reappearance was as sudden as the obliteration. He emerged. There had been interval, duration, time. He was not aware of them. A spasm of blinding pain shot through him. He opened his eyes. His whole body was a single devouring pain. He felt cramped, confined, uncomfortable. He must escape. He thrashed about. Someone seized his arm and held it. With a snarl he easily wrenched it free.

He was in bed. How had he come to this? An accident? He saw the faces of nurse and doctor bending over him, eager, amazed, surprised, a trifle frightened. Vague memories floated to him. Who was he? Where had he come from? And where was... where was... someone... who was dearer to him than life itself? He looked about him: the room, the faces, the French windows, the veranda, all seemed only half familiar. He looked, he searched for... someone... but in vain....

A spasm of violent pain burned through his body like a fire, and he shut his eyes. He groaned. A voice sounded just above him: "Take this, dear. Try and swallow a little. It will relieve you. Your brother will be back in a moment. You are much better already."

He looked up at the nurse; he drank what she gave him.

"My brother!" he murmured. "I don't understand. I have no brother." Thirst came over him; he drained the glass. The nurse, wearing a startled look, moved away. He watched her go. He pointed at her with his hand, meaning to say something that he instantly forgot—as he saw his own bare arm. Its dreadful thinness shocked him. He must have been ill for months. The arm, wasted almost to nothing, showed the bone. He sank back exhausted, the sleeping draught began to take effect. The nurse returned quietly to a chair beside the bed, from which she watched him without ceasing as the long minutes passed....

He found it difficult to collect his thoughts, to keep them in his mind when caught. There floated before him a series of odd scenes like coloured pictures in an endless flow. He was unable to catch them. Morris was with him always. They were doing quite absurd, impossible things. They rode together across the desert in the dawn, they wandered through old massive temples, they saw the sun set behind mud villages mid wavering palms, they drifted down a river in a sailing boat of quaint design. It had an enormous single sail. Together they visited tombs cut in the solid rock, hot airless corridors, and huge, dim, vaulted chambers underground. There was an icy wind by night, fierce burning sun by day. They watched vast troops of stars pass down a stupendous sky.... They knew delight and tasted wonder. Strange memories touched them....

"Nurse!" he called aloud, returning to himself again, and remembering that he must speak with his friend about something—he failed to recall exactly what. "Please ask Mr. Morris to come to me."

"At once, dear. He's only in the next room waiting for you to wake." She went out quickly, and he heard her voice in the passage. It sank to a whisper as she came back with Morris, yet every syllable reached him distinctly:

"....and pay no attention if she wanders a little; just ignore it. She's turned the corner, thank God, and that's the chief thing." Each word he heard with wonder and perplexity, with increasing irritability too.

"I'm a hell of a wreck," he said, as Morris came, beaming, to the bedside. "Have I been ill long? It's frightfully decent of you to come, old man."

But Morris, staggered at this greeting, stopped abruptly, half turning to the nurse for guidance. He seemed unable to find words. Sanfield was extremely annoyed; he showed his feeling. "I'm *not* balmy, you old ass!" he shouted. "I'm all right again, though very weak. But I wanted to ask you—oh, I remember now—I wanted to ask you about my—er—*Deltas.*"

"My poor dear Maggie," stammered Morris, fumbling with his voice. "Don't worry about your few shares, darling. Deltas are all right—it's *you we*—"

"Why, the devil, do you call me Maggie?" snapped the other viciously. "And 'darling'!" He felt furious, exasperated. "Have *you* gone balmy, or have I? What in the world are you two up to?" His fury tired him. He lay back upon his pillows, fuming. Morris took a chair beside the bed; he put a hand gently on his wasted arm.

"My darling girl," he said, in what was intended to be a soothing voice, though it stirred the sick man again to fury beyond expression, "you must really keep quiet for a bit. You've had a very severe operation"—his voice shook a little—"but, thank God, you've pulled through and are now on the way to recovery. You are my sister Maggie. It will all come back to you when you're rested—"

"Maggie, indeed!" interrupted the other, trying to sit up again, but too weak to compass it. "Your sister! You bally idiot! Don't you know me? I wish to God the nurse wouldn't 'dear' me in that senseless way. And you, with your atrocious 'darling.' I'm not your precious sister Magpie. I'm—I'm George San—"

But even as he said it, there passed over him some dim lost fragment of a wild, delicious memory he could not seize. Intense pleasure lay in it, could he but recover it. He knew a sweet, forgotten joy. His broken, troubled mind lay searching frantically but without success. It dazzled him.

It shook him with an indescribable emotion—of joy, of wonder, of deep sweet confusion. A rapt happiness rose in him, yet pain, like a black awful shutter, closed in upon the happiness at once. He remembered a girl. But he remembered, too, that he had seen her die. Who was she? Had he lost her... again...!

"My dear fellow," he faltered in a weaker voice to Morris, "my brain's in a whirl. I'm sorry. I suppose I've had some blasted concussion—haven't I?"

But the man beside his bed, he saw, was startled. An extraordinary look came into his face, though he tried to hide it with a smile.

"My shares!" cried Sanfield, with a half scream. "Four thousand of them!"

Whereupon Morris blanched. "George Sanfield!" he muttered, half to himself, half to the nurse who hurried up. "That voice! The very number too!" He looked white and terrified, as if he had seen a ghost. A whispered colloquy ensued between him and the nurse. It was inaudible.

"Now, dearest Maggie," he said at length, making evidently a tremendous effort, "do try and lie quiet for a bit. Don't bother about George Sanfield, my London friend. His shares are quite safe. You've heard me speak of him. It's all right, my darling, quite all right. Oh, believe me! I'm your brother."

"Maggie...!" whispered the man to himself upon the bed, whereupon Morris stooped, and, to his intense horror, kissed him on the cheek. But his horror seemed merged at once in another personality that surged through and over his entire being, drowning memory and recognition hopelessly. "Darling," he murmured. He realized that he was mad, of course. It seemed he fainted....

The momentary unconsciousness soon passed, at any rate. He opened his eyes again. He saw a palm tree out of the window. He knew positively he was *not* mad, whatever else he might be. Dead perhaps? He felt the sheets, the mattress, the skin upon his face. No, he was alive all right. The dull pains where the tight bandages oppressed him were also real. He was among substantial, earthly things. The nurse, he noticed, regarded him anxiously. She was a pleasant-looking young woman. He smiled; and, with an expression of affectionate, even tender pleasure, she smiled back at him.

"You feel better now, a little stronger," she said softly. "You've had a sleep, Miss Margaret." She said "Miss Margaret" with a conscious effort. It was better, perhaps, than "dear"; but his anger rose at once. He was too tired, however, to express his feelings. There stole over him, besides, the afflicting consciousness of an alien personality that was familiar, and yet not his. It strove to dominate him. Only by a great effort could he continue to think his own thoughts. This other being kept trying to intrude, to oust him, to take full possession. It resented his presence with a kind of violence.

He sighed. So strong was the feeling of another personality trying to foist itself upon his own, upon his mind, his body, even upon his very face, that he turned instinctively to the nurse, though unaware exactly what he meant to ask her for.

"My hand-glass, please," he heard himself saying—with horror. The phrase was not his own. Glass or mirror were the words *he* would have used.

A moment later he was staring with acute and ghastly terror at a reflection that was not his own. It was the face of the dead girl he saw within the silver-handled, woman's hand-glass he held up.

* * * * *

The dream with its amazing, vivid detail haunted him for days, even coming between him and his work. It seemed far more real, more vivid than the commonplace events of life that followed. The occurrences of the day were pale compared to its overpowering intensity. And a cable, received the very next afternoon, increased this sense of actual truth—of something that had really happened.

"Hold shares writing Morris."

Its brevity added a convincing touch. He was aware of Egypt even in Throgmorton Street. Yet it was the face of the dead, or dying, girl that chiefly haunted him. She remained in his thoughts, alive and sweet and exquisite. Without her he felt incomplete, his life a failure. He thought of nothing else.

The affairs at the office, meanwhile, went well; unexpected success attended them; there was no strike; the angry customer was pacified. And when the promised letter came from Morris, Sanfield's hands trembled so violently that he could hardly tear it open. Nor could he read it calmly. The assurance about his precious shares scarcely interested him. It was the final paragraph that set his heart beating against his ribs as though a hammer lay inside him:

"....I've had great trouble and anxiety, though, thank God, the danger is over now. I forget if I ever mentioned my sister, Margaret, to you. She keeps house for me in Cairo, when I'm there. She is my only tie in life. Well, a severe operation she had to undergo, all but finished her. To tell you the truth, she very nearly died, for the doctor gave her up. You'll smile when I tell you that odd things happened—at the very last moment. I can't explain it, nor can the doctor. It rather terrified me. But at the very moment when we thought her gone, something revived in her. She became full of unexpected life and vigor. She was even violent— whereas, a moment before, she had not the strength to speak, much less to move. It was rather wonderful, but it was terrible too.

"You don't believe in these things, I know, but I must tell you, because, when she recovered consciousness, she began to babble about yourself, using your name, though she has rarely, if ever, heard it, and even speaking—you won't believe this, of course!—of your shares in Deltas, giving the *exact* number that you hold. When you write, please tell me if you were very anxious about these? Also, whether your thoughts were directed particularly to me? I thought a good deal about you, knowing you might be uneasy, but my mind was pretty full, as you will understand, of her operation at the time. The climax, when all this happened, was about 11 a. m. on February 13th.

"Don't fail to tell me this, as I'm particularly interested in what you may have to say.

"And, now, I want to ask a great favor of you. The doctor forbids Margaret to stay here during the hot weather, so I'm sending her home to some cousins in Yorkshire, as soon as she is fit to travel. It would be most awfully kind—I know how women bore you—if you could manage to meet the boat and help her on her way through London. I'll let you know dates and particulars later, when I hear that you will do this for me...."

Sanfield hardly read the remainder of the letter, which dealt with shares and business matters. But a month later he stood on the dock-pier at Tilbury, watching the approach of the tender from the *Egyptian Mail.*

He saw it make fast; he saw the stream of passengers pour down the gangway; and he saw among them the tall, fair woman of his dream. With a beating heart he went to meet her....

THE DECOY

It belonged to the category of unlovely houses about which an ugly superstition clings, one reason being, perhaps, its inability to inspire interest in itself without assistance. It seemed too ordinary to possess individuality, much less to exert an influence. Solid and ungainly, its huge bulk dwarfing the park timber, its best claim to notice was a negative one—it was unpretentious.

From the little hill its expressionless windows stared across the Kentish Weald, indifferent to weather, dreary in winter, bleak in spring, unblessed in summer. Some colossal hand had tossed it down, then let it starve to death, a country mansion that might well strain the adjectives of advertisers and find inheritors with difficulty. Its soul had fled, said some; it had committed suicide, thought others; and it was an inheritor, before he killed himself in the library, who thought this latter, yielding, apparently, to an hereditary taint in the family. For two other inheritors followed suit, with an interval of twenty years between them, and there was no clear reason to explain the three disasters. Only the first owner, indeed, lived permanently in the house, the others using it in the summer months and then deserting it with relief. Hence, when John Burley, present inheritor, assumed possession, he entered a house about which clung an ugly superstition, based, nevertheless, upon a series of undeniably ugly facts.

This century deals harshly with superstitious folk, deeming them fools or charlatans; but John Burley, robust, contemptuous of half lights, did not deal harshly with them, because he did not deal with them at all. He was hardly aware of their existence. He ignored them as he ignored, say, the Esquimaux, poets, and other human aspects that did not touch his scheme of life. A successful business man, he concentrated on what was real; he dealt with business people. His philanthropy, on a big scale, was also real; yet, though he would have denied it vehemently, he had his superstition as well. No man exists without some taint of superstition in his blood; the racial heritage is too rich to be escaped entirely. Burley's took this form—that unless he gave his tithe to the poor he would not prosper. This ugly mansion, he decided, would make an ideal Convalescent Home.

"Only cowards or lunatics kill themselves," he declared flatly, when his use of the house was criticized. "I'm neither one nor t'other." He let out his gusty, boisterous laugh. In his invigorating atmosphere such weakness seemed contemptible, just as superstition in his presence seemed feeblest ignorance. Even its picturesqueness faded. "I can't conceive," he boomed, "can't even imagine to myself," he added emphatically, "the state of mind in which a. man can think of suicide, much less do it." He threw his chest out with a challenging air. "I tell you, Nancy, it's either cowardice or mania. And I've no use for either."

Yet he was easy-going and good-humoured in his denunciation. He admitted his limitations with a hearty laugh his wife called noisy. Thus he made allowances for the fairy fears of sailorfolk, and had even been known to mention haunted ships his companies owned. But he did so in the terms of tonnage and £ s. d. His scope was big; details were made for clerks.

His consent to pass a night in the mansion was the consent of a practical business man and philanthropist who dealt condescendingly with foolish human nature. It was based on the common-sense of tonnage and £ s. d. The local newspapers had revived the silly story of the suicides, calling attention to the effect of the superstition upon the fortunes of the house, and so, possibly, upon the fortunes of its present owner. But the mansion, otherwise a white elephant, was precisely ideal for his purpose, and so trivial a matter as spending a night in it should not stand in the way. "We must take people as we find them, Nancy."

His young wife had her motive, of course, in making the proposal, and, if she was amused by what she called "spook-hunting," he saw no reason to refuse her the indulgence. He loved her, and took her as he found her—late in life. To allay the superstitions of prospective staff and patients and supporters, all, in fact, whose goodwill was necessary to success, he faced this boredom of a night in the building before its opening was announced. "You see, John, if you, the owner, do this, it will nip damaging talk in the bud. If anything went wrong later it would only be put down to this suicide idea, this haunting influence. The Home will have a bad name from the start. There'll be endless trouble. It will be a failure."

"You think my spending a night there will stop the nonsense?" he inquired.

"According to the old legend it breaks the spell," she replied. "That's the condition, anyhow."

"But somebody's sure to die there sooner or later," he objected. "We can't prevent that."

"We can prevent people whispering that they died unnaturally." She explained the working of the public mind.

"I see," he replied, his lip curling, yet quick to gauge the truth of what she told him about collective instinct.

"Unless *you* take poison in the hall," she added laughingly, "or elect to hang yourself with your braces from the hat peg."

"I'll do it," he agreed, after a moment's thought. "I'll sit up with you. It will be like a honeymoon over again, you and I on the spree—eh?" He was even interested now; the boyish side of him was touched perhaps; but his enthusiasm was less when she explained that three was a better number than two on such an expedition.

"I've often done it before, John. We were always three."

"Who?" he asked bluntly. He looked wonderingly at her, but she answered that if anything went wrong a party of three provided a better margin for help. It was sufficiently obvious. He listened and agreed. "I'll get young Mortimer," he suggested. "Will he do?"

She hesitated. "Well—he's cheery; he'll be interested, too. Yes, he's as good as another." She seemed indifferent.

"And he'll make the time pass with his stories," added her husband.

So Captain Mortimer, late officer on a T.B.D., a "cheery lad," afraid of nothing, cousin of Mrs. Burley, and now filling a good post in the company's London offices, was engaged as third hand in the expedition. But Captain Mortimer was young and ardent, and Mrs. Burley was young and pretty and ill-mated, and John Burley was a neglectful, and self-satisfied husband.

Fate laid the trap with cunning, and John Burley, blind-eyed, careless of detail, floundered into it. He also floundered out again, though in a fashion none could have expected of him.

The night agreed upon eventually was as near to the shortest in the year as John Burley could contrive—June 18th—when the sun set at 8:18 and rose about a quarter to four. There would be barely three hours of true darkness. "You're the expert," he admitted, as she explained that sitting through the actual darkness only was required, not necessarily from sunset to sunrise. "We'll do the thing properly. Mortimer's not very keen, he had a dance or something," he added, noticing the look of annoyance that flashed swiftly in her eyes; "but he got out of it. He's coming." The pouting expression of the spoilt woman amused him. "Oh, no, he didn't need much persuading really," he assured her. "Some girl or other, of course. He's young, remember." To which no comment was forthcoming, though the implied comparison made her flush.

They motored from South Audley Street after an early tea, in due course passing Sevenoaks and entering the Kentish Weald; and, in order that the necessary advertisement should be given, the chauffeur, warned strictly to keep their purpose quiet, was to put up at the country inn and fetch them an hour after sunrise; they would breakfast in London. "He'll tell everybody," said his practical and cynical master; "the local newspaper will have it all next day. A few hours' discomfort is worth while if it ends the nonsense. We'll read and smoke, and Mortimer shall tell us yarns about the sea." He went with the driver into the house to super-intend the arrangement of the room, the lights, the hampers of food, and so forth, leaving the pair upon the lawn.

"Four hours isn't much, but it's something," whispered Mortimer, alone with her for the first time since they started. "It's simply ripping of you to have got me in. You look divine to-night. You're the most wonderful woman in the world." His blue eyes shone with the hungry desire he mistook for love. He looked as if he had blown in from the sea, for his skin was tanned and his light hair bleached a little by the sun. He took her hand, drawing her out of the slanting sunlight towards the rhodo-dendrons.

"I didn't, you silly boy. It was John suggested your coming." She released her hand with an affected effort. "Besides, you overdid it—pre-tending you had a dance."

"You could have objected," he said eagerly, "and didn't. Oh, you're too lovely, you're delicious!" He kissed her suddenly with passion. There was a tiny struggle, in which she yielded too easily, he thought.

"Harry, you're an idiot!" she cried breathlessly, when he let her go. "I really don't know how you dare! And John's your friend. Besides, you know"—she glanced round quickly—"it isn't safe here." Her eyes shone happily, her cheeks were flaming. She looked what she was, a pretty, young, lustful animal, false to ideals, true to selfish passion only. "Lucki-ly," she added, "he trusts me too fully to think anything."

The young man, worship in his eyes, laughed gaily. "There's no harm in a kiss," he said. "You're a child to him, he never thinks of you as a woman. Anyhow, his head's full of ships and kings and sealing-wax," he comforted her, while respecting her sudden instinct which warned him not to touch her again, "and he never sees anything. Why, even at ten yards—"

From twenty yards away a big voice interrupted him, as John Burley came round a corner of the house and across the lawn towards then. The chauffeur, he announced, had left the hampers in the room on the first floor and gone back to the inn. "Let's take a walk round," he added, join-ing them, "and see the garden. Five minutes before sunset we'll go in and feed." He laughed. "We must do the thing faithfully, you know, mustn't we, Nancy? Dark to dark, remember. Come on, Mortimer"—he took the young man's arm—"a last look round before we go in and hang our-selves from adjoining hooks in the matron's room!" He reached out his free hand towards his wife.

"Oh, hush, John!" she said quickly. "I don't like—especially now the dusk is coining." She shivered, as though it were a genuine little shiver, pursing her lips deliciously as she did so; whereupon he drew her forcibly to him, saying he was sorry, and kissed her exactly where she had been kissed two minutes before, while young Mortimer looked on. "We'll take care of you between us," he said. Behind a broad back the pair exchanged a swift but meaning glance, for there was that in his tone which enjoined wariness, and perhaps after all he was not so blind as he appeared. They had their code, these two. "All's well," was signalled; "but another time be more careful!"

There still remained some minutes' sunlight before the huge red ball of fire would sink behind the wooded hills, and the trio, talking idly, a flutter of excitement in two hearts certainly, walked among the roses. It was a perfect evening, windless, perfumed, warm. Headless shadows preceded them gigantically across the lawn as they moved, and one side of the great building lay already dark; bats were flitting, moths darted to and fro above the azalea and rhododendron clumps. The talk turned chiefly on the uses of the mansion as a Convalescent Home, its probable running cost, suitable staff, and so forth.

"Come along," John Burley said presently, breaking off and turning abruptly, "we must be inside, actually inside, before the sun's gone. We must fulfil the conditions faithfully," he repeated, as though fond of the phrase. He was in earnest over everything in life, big or little, once he set his hand to it.

They entered, this incongruous trio of ghost-hunters, no one of them really intent upon the business in hand, and went slowly upstairs to the great room where the hampers lay. Already in the hall it was dark enough for three electric torches to flash usefully and help their steps as they moved with caution, lighting one corner after another. The air inside was chill and damp. "Like an unused museum," said Mortimer. "I can smell the specimens." They looked about them, sniffing. "That's humanity," declared his host, employer, friend, "with cement and white-wash to flavour it"; and all three laughed as Mrs. Barley said she wished they had picked some roses and brought them in. Her husband was again in front on the broad staircase, Mortimer just behind him, when she called out. "I don't like being last," she exclaimed. "It's so black behind me in the hall. I'll come between you two," and the sailor took her outstretched hand, squeezing it, as he passed her up. "There's a figure, remember," she said hurriedly, turning to gain her husband's attention, as when she touched wood at home. "A figure is seen; that's part of the story. The figure of a man." She gave a tiny shiver of pleasurable, half-imagined alarm as she took his arm.

"I hope we shall see it," he mentioned prosaically.

"I hope we shan't," she replied with emphasis. "It's only seen before—

something happens." Her husband said nothing, while Mortimer remarked facetiously that it would be a pity if they had their trouble for nothing. "Something can hardly happen to all three of us," he said lightly, as they entered a large room where the paperhangers had conveniently left a rough table of bare planks. Mrs. Burley, busy with her own thoughts, began to unpack the sandwiches and wine. Her husband strolled over to the window. He seemed restless.

"So this," his deep voice startled her, "is where one of us"—he looked round him—"is to—"

"John!" She stopped him sharply, with impatience. "Several times already I've begged you." Her voice rang rather shrill and querulous in the empty room, a new note in it. She was beginning to feel the atmosphere of the place, perhaps. On the sunny lawn it had not touched her, but now, with the fall of night, she was aware of it, as shadow called to shadow and the kingdom of darkness gathered power. Like a great whispering gallery, the whole house listened.

"Upon my word, Nancy," he said with contrition, as he came and sat down beside her, "I quite forgot again. Only I cannot take it seriously. It's so utterly unthinkable to me that a man—"

"But why evoke the idea at all?" she insisted in a lowered voice, that snapped despite its faintness. "Men, after all, don't do such things for nothing."

"We don't know everything in the universe, do we?" Mortimer put in, trying clumsily to support her. "All I know just now is that I'm famished and this veal and ham pie is delicious." He was very busy with his knife and fork. His foot rested lightly on her own beneath the table; he could not keep his eyes off her face; he was continually passing new edibles to her.

"No," agreed John Burley, "not everything. You're right there."

She kicked the younger man gently, flashing a warning with her eyes as well, while her husband, emptying his glass, his head thrown back, looked straight at them over the rim, apparently seeing nothing. They smoked their cigarettes round the table, Burley lighting a big cigar. "Tell us about the figure, Nancy?" he inquired. "At least there's no harm in that. It's new to me. I hadn't heard about a figure." And she did so willingly, turning her chair sideways from the dangerous, reckless feet. Mortimer could now no longer touch her. "I know very little," she confessed; "only what the paper said. It's a man.... And he changes."

"How changes?" asked her husband. "Clothes, you mean, or what?"

Mrs. Burley laughed, as though she was glad to laugh, Then she answered: "According to the story, he shows himself each time to the man—"

"The man who—?"

"Yes, yes, of course. He appears to the man who dies—as himself."

"H'm," grunted her husband, naturally puzzled. He stared at her.

"Each time the chap saw his own double"—Mortimer came this time usefully to the rescue—"before he did it."

Considerable explanation followed, involving much psychic jargon from Mrs. Burley, which fascinated and impressed the sailor, who thought her as wonderful as she was lovely, showing it in his eyes for all to see. John Burley's attention wandered. He moved over to the window, leaving them to finish the discussion between them; he took no part in it, made no comment even, merely listening idly and watching them with an air of absent-mindedness through the cloud of cigar smoke round his head. He moved from window to window, ensconcing himself in turn in each deep embrasure, examining the fastenings, measuring the thickness of the stonework with his handkerchief. He seemed restless, bored, obviously out of place in this ridiculous expedition. On his big massive face lay a quiet, resigned expression his wife had never seen before. She noticed it now as, the discussion ended, the pair tidied away the debris of dinner, lit the spirit lamp for coffee and laid out a supper which would be very welcome with the dawn. A draught passed through the room, making the papers flutter on the table. Mortimer turned down the smoking lamps with care.

"Wind's getting up a bit—from the south," observed Burley from his niche, closing one-half of the casement window as he said it. To do this, he turned his back a moment, fumbling for several seconds with the latch, while Mortimer, noting it, seized his sudden opportunity with the foolish abandon of his age and temperament. Neither he nor his victim perceived that, against the outside darkness, the interior of the room was plainly reflected in the window-pane. One reckless, the other terrified, they snatched the fearful joy, which might, after all, have been lengthened by another full half-minute, for the head they feared, followed by the shoulders, pushed through the side of the casement still open, and remained outside, taking in the night.

"A grand air," said his deep voice, as the head drew in again. "I'd like to be at sea a night like this." He left the casement open and came across the room towards them. "Now," he said cheerfully, arranging a seat for himself, "let's get comfortable for the night. Mortimer, we expect stories from you without ceasing, until dawn or the ghost arrives. Horrible stories of chains and headless men, remember. Make it a night we shan't forget in a hurry." He produced his gust of laughter.

They arranged their chairs, with other chairs to put their feet on, and Mortimer contrived a footstool by means of a hamper for the smallest feet; the air grew thick with tobacco smoke; eyes flashed and answered, watched perhaps as well; ears listened and perhaps grew wise; occasionally, as a window shook, they started and looked round; there were sounds about the house from time to time, when the entering wind, using broken or open windows, set loose objects rattling.

But Mrs. Burley vetoed horrible stories with decision. A big, empty mansion, lonely in the country, and even with the comfort of John Burley and a lover in it, has its atmosphere. Furnished rooms are far less ghostly. This atmosphere now came creeping everywhere, through spacious halls and sighing corridors, silent, invisible, but all-pervading, John Burley alone impervious to it, unaware of its soft attack upon the nerves. It entered possibly with the summer night wind, but possibly it was always there.... And Mrs. Burley looked often at her husband, sitting near her at an angle; the light fell on his fine strong face; she felt that, though apparently so calm and quiet, he was really very restless; something about him was a little different; she could not define it; his mouth seemed set as with an effort; he looked, she thought curiously to herself, patient and very dignified; he was rather a dear after all. Why did she think the face inscrutable? Her thoughts wandered vaguely, unease, discomfort among them somewhere, while the heated blood—she had taken her share of wine—seethed in her.

Burley turned to the sailor for more stories. "Sea and wind in them," he asked. "No horrors, remember!" and Mortimer told a tale about the shortage of rooms at a Welsh seaside place where spare rooms fetched. fabulous prices, and one man alone refused to let—a retired captain of a South Seas trader, very poor, a bit crazy apparently. He had two furnished rooms in his house worth twenty guineas a week. The rooms faced south; he kept them full of flowers; but he would not let. An explanation of his unworldly obstinacy was not forthcoming until Mortimer—they fished together—gained his confidence. "The South Wind lives in them," the old fellow told him. "I keep them free for her."

"For *her?*"

"It was on the South Wind my love came to me," said the other softly; "and it was on the South Wind that she left—"

It was an odd tale to tell in such company, but he told it well.

"Beautiful," thought Mrs. Burley. Aloud she said a quiet, "Thank you. By 'left,' I suppose he meant she died or ran away?"

John Burley looked up with a certain surprise. "We ask for a story," he said, "and you give us a poem." He laughed. "You're in love, Mortimer," he informed him, "and with my wife probably."

"Of course I am, sir," replied the, young man gallantly. "A sailor's heart, you know," while the face of the woman turned pink, then white. She knew her husband more intimately than Mortimer did, and there was something in his tone, his eyes, his words, she did not like. Harry was an idiot to choose such a tale. An irritated annoyance stirred in her, close upon dislike. "Anyhow, it's better than horrors," she said hurriedly.

"Well," put in her husband, letting forth a minor gust of laughter, "it's possible, at any rate. Though one's as crazy as the other." His meaning was not wholly clear. "If a man really loved," he added in his blunt fashion, "and was tricked by her, I could almost conceive his—"

"Oh, don't preach, John, for Heaven's sake. You're so dull in the pulpit." But the interruption only served to emphasize the sentence which, otherwise, might have been passed over.

"Could conceive his finding life so worthless," persisted the other, "that—" He hesitated. "But there, now, I promised I wouldn't," he went on, laughing good-humouredly. Then, suddenly, as though in spite of himself, driven it seemed: "'Still, under such conditions, he might show his contempt for human nature and for life by—"

It was a tiny stifled scream that stopped him this time.

"John, I hate, I loathe you, when you talk like that. And you've broken your word again." She was more than petulant; a nervous anger sounded in her voice. It was the way he had said it, looking from them towards the window, that made her quiver. She felt him suddenly as a man; she felt afraid of him.

Her husband made no reply; he rose and looked at his watch, leaning sideways towards the lamp, so that the expression of his face was shaded. "Two o'clock," he remarked. "I think I'll take a turn through the house. I may find a workman asleep or something. Anyhow, the light will soon come now." He laughed; the expression of his face, his tone of voice, relieved her momentarily. He went out. They heard his heavy tread echoing down the carpetless long corridor.

Mortimer began at once. "Did he mean anything?" he asked breathlessly. "He doesn't love you the least little bit, anyhow. He never did. I do. You're wasted on him. You belong to me." The words poured out. He covered her face with kisses. "Oh. I didn't mean *that*," he caught between the kisses.

The sailor released her, staring. "What then?" he whispered. "Do you think he saw us on the lawn?" He paused a moment, as she made no reply. The steps were audible in the distance still. "I know!" he exclaimed suddenly. "It's the blessed house he feels. That's what it is. He doesn't like it."

A wind sighed through the room, making the papers flutter; something rattled; and Mrs. Burley started. A loose end of rope swinging from the paperhanger's ladder caught her eye. She shivered slightly.

"He's different," she replied in a low voice, nestling very close again, "and so restless. Didn't you notice what he said just now—that under certain conditions he could understand a man"—she hesitated—"doing it," she concluded, a sudden drop in her voice. "Harry," she looked full into his eyes, "that's not like him. He didn't say that for nothing."

"Nonsense! He's bored to tears, that's all. And the house is getting on your nerves, too." He kissed her tenderly. Then, as she responded, he drew her nearer still and held her passionately, mumbling incoherent words, among which "nothing to be afraid of" was distinguishable. Meanwhile, the steps were coming nearer. She pushed him away. "You must behave yourself. I insist. You shall, Harry," then buried herself in his arms, her face hidden against his neck—only to disentangle herself the next instant and stand clear of him. "I hate you, Harry," she exclaimed sharply, a look of angry annoyance flashing across her face. "And I *hate* myself. Why do you treat me—?" She broke off as the steps came closer, patted her hair straight, and stalked over to the open window.

"I believe after all you're only playing with me," he said viciously. He stared in surprised disappointment, watching her. "It's him you really love," he added jealously. He looked and spoke like a petulant spoilt boy.

She did not turn her head. "He's always been fair to me, kind and generous. He never blames me for anything. Give me a cigarette and don't play the stage hero. My nerves are on edge, to tell you the truth." Her voice jarred harshly, and as he lit her cigarette be noticed that her lips were trembling; his own hand trembled too. He was still holding the match, standing beside her at the window-sill, when the steps crossed the threshold and John Burley came into the room. He went straight up to the table and turned the lamp down. "It was smoking," he remarked. "Didn't you see?"

"I'm sorry, sir," and Mortimer sprang forward, too late to help him. "It was the draught as you pushed the door open." The big man said, "Ah!" and drew a chair over, facing them. "It's just *the* very house," he told them. "I've been through every room on this floor. It will make a splendid Home, with very little alteration, too." He turned round in his creaking wicker chair and looked up at his wife, who sat swinging her legs and smoking in the window embrasure. "Lives will be saved inside these old walls. It's a good investment," he went on, talking rather to himself it seemed. "People will die here, too—"

"Hark!" Mrs. Burley interrupted him. "That noise—what is it?" A faint thudding sound in the corridor or in the adjoining room was audible, making all three look round quickly, listening for a repetition, which did not come. The papers fluttered on the table, the lamps smoked an instant.

"Wind," observed Burley calmly, "our little friend, the South Wind.

Something blown over again, that's all." But, curiously, the three of them stood up. "I'll go and see," he continued. "Doors and windows are all open to let the paint dry." Yet he did not move; he stood there watching a white moth that dashed round and round the lamp, flopping heavily now and again upon the bare deal table.

"Let me go, sir," put in Mortimer eagerly. He was glad of the chance; for the first time he, too, felt uncomfortable. But there was another who, apparently, suffered a discomfort greater than his own and was accordingly even more glad to get away. "I'll go," Mrs. Burley announced, with decision. "I'd like to. I haven't been out of this room since we came. I'm not an atom afraid."

It was strange that for a moment she did not make a move either; it seemed as if she waited for something. For perhaps fifteen seconds no one stirred or spoke. She knew by the look in her lover's eyes that he had now become aware of the slight, indefinite change in her husband's manner, and was alarmed by it. The fear in him woke her contempt; she suddenly despised the youth, and was conscious of a new, strange yearning towards her husband; against her worked nameless pressures, troubling her being. There was an alteration in the room, she thought; something had come in. The trio stood listening to the gentle wind outside, waiting for the sound to be repeated; two careless, passionate young lovers and a man stood waiting, listening, watching in that room; yet it seemed there were five persons altogether and not three, for two guilty consciences stood apart and separate from their owners. John Burley broke the silence.

"Yes, you go, Nancy. Nothing to be afraid of—there. It's only wind." He spoke as though he meant it.

Mortimer bit his lips. "I'll come with you," he said instantly. He was confused. "Let's all three go. I don't think we ought to be separated." But Mrs. Burley was already at the door. "I insist," she said, with a forced laugh. "I'll call if I'm frightened," while her husband, saying nothing, watched her from the table.

"Take this," said the sailor, flashing his electric torch as he went over to her. "Two are better than one." He saw her figure exquisitely silhouetted against the black corridor beyond; it was clear she wanted to go; any nervousness in her was mastered by a stronger emotion still; she was glad to be out of their presence for a bit. He had hoped to snatch a word of explanation in the corridor, but her manner stopped him. Something else stopped him, too.

"First door on the left," he called out, his voice echoing down the empty length. "That's the room where the noise came from. Shout if you want us."

He watched her moving away, the light held steadily in front of her, but she made no answer, and he turned back to see John Burley lighting his cigar at the lamp chimney, his face thrust forward as he did so. He stood a second, watching him, as the lips sucked hard at the cigar to make it draw; the strength of the features was emphasized to sternness. He had meant to stand by the door and listen for the least sound from the adjoining room, but now found his whole attention focused on the face above the lamp. In that minute he realized that Burley had wished—had meant—his wife to go. In that minute also he forgot his love, his shameless, selfish little mistress, his worthless, caddish little self. For John Burley looked up. He straightened slowly, puffing hard and quickly to make sure his cigar was lit, and faced him. Mortimer moved forward into the room, self-conscious, embarrassed, cold.

"Of course it was only wind," he said lightly, his one desire being to fill the interval while they were alone with commonplaces. He did not wish the other to speak. "Dawn wind, probably." He glanced at his wrist-watch. "It's half-past two already, and the sun gets up at a quarter to four. It's light by now, I expect. The shortest night is never quite dark." He rambled on confusedly, for the other's steady, silent stare embarrassed him. A faint sound of Mrs. Burley moving in the next room made him stop a moment. He turned instinctively to the door, eager for an excuse to go.

"That's nothing," said Burley, speaking at last and in a firm quiet voice. "Only my wife, glad to be alone—my young and pretty wife. She's all right. I know her better than you do. Come in and shut the door."

Mortimer obeyed. He closed the door and came close to the table, facing the other, who at once continued.

"If I thought," he said, in that quiet deep voice, "that you two were serious"—he uttered his words very slowly, with emphasis, with intense severity—"do you know what I should do? I will tell you, Mortimer. I should like one of us two—you or myself—to remain in this house, dead."

His teeth gripped his cigar tightly; his hands were clenched; he went on through a half-closed mouth. His eyes blazed steadily.

"I trust her so absolutely—understand me?—that my belief in women, in human beings, would go. And with it the desire to live. Understand me?"

Each word to the young careless fool was a blow in the face, yet it was the softest blow, the flash of a big deep heart, that hurt the most. A dozen answers—denial, explanation, confession, taking all guilt upon himself—crowded his mind, only to be dismissed. He stood motionless and silent, staring hard into the other's eyes. No word passed his lips; there was no time in any case. It was in this position that Mrs. Burley, entering at that moment, found them. She saw her husband's face; the other man stood with his back to her. She came in with a little nervous laugh. "A bell-rope swinging in the wind and hitting a sheet of metal before the fireplace," she informed them. And all three laughed together then, though each laugh had a different sound. "But I hate this house," she added. "I wish we had never come."

"The moment there's light in the sky," remarked her husband quietly, "we can leave. That's the contract; let's see it through. Another half-hour will do it. Sit down, Nancy, and have a bite of something." He got up and placed a chair for her. "I think I'll take another look round." He moved slowly to the door. "I may go out on to the lawn a bit and see what the sky is doing."

It did not take half a minute to say the words, yet to Mortimer it seemed as though the voice would never end. His mind was confused and troubled. He loathed himself, he loathed the woman through whom he had got into this awkward mess.

The situation had suddenly become extremely painful; he had never imagined such a thing; the man he had thought blind had after all seen everything—known it all along, watched them, waited. And the woman, he was now certain, loved her husband; she had fooled him, Mortimer, all along, amusing herself.

"I'll come with you, sir. Do let me," he said suddenly. Mrs. Burley stood pale and uncertain between them. She looked scared. What has happened, she was clearly wondering.

"No, no, Harry"—he called him "Harry" for the first time—"I'll be back in five minutes at most. My wife mustn't be alone either." And he went out.

The young man waited till the footsteps sounded some distance down the corridor, then turned, but he did not move forward; for the first time he let pass unused what he called "an opportunity." His passion had left him; his love, as he once thought it, was gone. He looked at the pretty woman near him, wondering blankly what he had ever seen there to attract him so wildly. He wished to Heaven he was out of it all. He wished he were dead. John Burley's words suddenly appalled him.

One thing he saw plainly—she was frightened. This opened his lips.

"What's the matter?" he asked, and his hushed voice shirked the familiar Christian name. "Did you see anything?" He nodded his head in the direction of the adjoining room. It was the sound of his own voice addressing her coldly that made him abruptly see himself as he really was, but it was her reply, honestly given, in a faint even voice, that told him she saw her own self too with similar clarity. God, he thought, how revealing a tone, a single word can be!

"I saw—nothing. Only I feel uneasy—dear." That "dear" was a call for help.

"Look here," he cried, so loud that she held up a warning finger, "I'm—I've been a damned fool, a cad! I'm most frightfully ashamed. I'll do any-thing—*anything* to get it right." He felt cold, naked, his worthlessness laid bare; she felt, he knew, the same. Each revolted suddenly from the other. Yet he knew not quite how or wherefore this great change had thus abruptly come about, especially on her side. He felt that a bigger, deeper emotion than he could understand was working on them, mak-ing mere physical relationships seem empty, trivial, cheap and vulgar. His cold increased in face of this utter ignorance.

"Uneasy?" he repeated, perhaps hardly knowing exactly why he said it. "Good Lord, but he can take care of himself—"

"Oh, *he* is a man," she interrupted; "yes."

Steps were heard, firm, heavy steps, coming back along the corridor. It seemed to Mortimer that he had listened to this sound of steps all night, and would listen to them till he died. He crossed to the lamp and lit a cigarette, carefully this time, turning the wick down afterwards. Mrs. Burley also rose, moving over towards the door, away from him. They lis-tened a moment to these firm and heavy steps, the tread of a man, John Burley. A man... and a philanderer, flashed across Mortimer's brain like fire, contrasting the two with fierce contempt for himself. The tread became less audible. There was distance in it. It had turned in some-where.

"There!" she exclaimed in a hushed tone. "He's gone in."

"Nonsense! It passed us. He's going out on to the lawn."

The pair listened breathlessly for a moment, when the sound of steps came distinctly from the adjoining room, walking across the boards, apparently towards the window.

"There!" she repeated. "He did go in." Silence of perhaps a minute fol-lowed, in which they heard each other's breathing. "I don't like his being alone—in there," Mrs. Burley said in a thin faltering voice, and moved as though to go out. Her hand was already on the knob of the door, when Mortimer stopped her with a violent gesture.

"Don't! For God's sake, don't!" he cried, before she could turn it. He darted forward. As he laid a hand upon her arm a thud was audible through the wall. It was a heavy sound, and this time there was no wind to cause it.

"It's only that loose swinging thing," he whispered. thickly, a dreadful confusion blotting out clear thought and speech.

"There was no loose swaying thing at all," she said in a failing voice, then reeled and swayed against him. "I invented that. There was nothing." As he caught her, staring helplessly, it seemed to him that a face with lifted lids rushed up at him. He saw two terrified eyes in a patch of ghastly white. Her whisper followed, as she sank into his arms. "It's John. He's—"

At which instant, with terror at its climax, the sound of steps suddenly became audible once more—the firm and heavy tread of John Burley coming out again into the corridor. Such was their amazement and relief that they neither moved nor spoke. The steps drew nearer. The pair seemed petrified; Mortimer did not remove his arms, nor did Mrs. Burley attempt to release herself. They stared at the door and waited. It was pushed wider the next second, and John Burley stood beside them. He was so close he almost touched them—there in each other's arms.

"Jack, dear!" cried his wife, with a searching tenderness that made her voice seem strange.

He gazed a second at each in turn. "I'm going out on to the lawn for a moment," he said quietly. There was no expression on his face; he did not smile, he did not frown; he showed no feeling, no emotion—just looked into their eyes, and then withdrew round the edge of the door before either could utter a word in answer. The door swung to behind him. He was gone.

"He's going to the lawn. He said so." It was Mortimer speaking, but his voice shook and stammered. Mrs. Burley had released herself. She stood now by the table, silent, gazing with fixed eyes at nothing, her lips parted, her expression vacant. Again she was aware of an alteration in the room; something had gone out.... He watched her a second, uncertain what to say or do. It was the face of a drowned person, occurred to him. Something intangible, yet almost visible stood between them in that narrow space. Something had ended, there before his eyes, definitely ended. The barrier between them rose higher, denser. Through this barrier her words came to him with an odd whispering remoteness.

"Harry.... You saw? You noticed?"

"What d'you mean?" he said gruffly. He tried to feel angry, contemptuous, but his breath caught absurdly.

"Harry—he was different. The eyes, the hair, the"—her face grew like death—"the twist in his face—"

"What on earth are you saying? Pull yourself together." He saw that she was trembling down the whole length of her body, as she leaned against the table for support. His own legs shook. He stared hard at her.

"Altered, Harry... altered." Her horrified whisper came at him like a knife. For it was true. He, too, had noticed something about the husband's appearance that was not quite normal. Yet, even while they talked, they heard him going down the carpetless stairs; the sounds ceased as he crossed the hall; then came the noise of the front door banging, the reverberation even shaking the room a little where they stood.

Mortimer went over to her side. He walked unevenly.

"My dear! For God's sake—this is sheer nonsense. Don't let yourself go like this. I'll put it straight with him—it's all my fault." He saw by her face that she did not understand his words; he was saying the wrong thing altogether; her mind was utterly elsewhere. "He's all right," he went on hurriedly. "He's out on the lawn now—"

He broke off at the sight of her. The horror that fastened on her brain plastered her face with deathly whiteness.

"That was not John at all!" she cried, a wail of misery and terror in her voice. She rushed to the window and he followed. To his immense relief a figure moving below was plainly visible. It was John Burley. They saw him in the faint grey of the dawn, as he crossed the lawn, going away from the house. He disappeared.

"There you are! See?" whispered Mortimer reassuringly. "He'll be back in—" when a sound in the adjoining room, heavier, louder than before, cut appallingly across his words, and Mrs. Burley, with that wailing scream, fell back into his arms. He caught her only just in time, for she stiffened into ice, daft with the uncomprehended terror of it all, and helpless as a child.

"Darling, my darling—oh, God!" He bent, kissing her face wildly. He was utterly distraught.

"Harry! Jack—oh, oh!" she wailed in her anguish. "It took on his likeness. It deceived us... to give him time. He's done it."

She sat up suddenly. "Go," she said, pointing to the room beyond, then sank fainting, a dead weight in his arms.

He carried her unconscious body to a chair, then entering the adjoining room he flashed his torch upon the body of her husband hanging from a bracket in the wall. He cut it down five minutes too late.

THE MAN WHO
FOUND OUT
(A NIGHT-MARE)

1

Professor Mark Ebor, the scientist, led a double life, and the only persons who knew it were his assistant, Dr. Laidlaw, and his publishers. But a double life need not always be a bad one, and, as Dr. Laidlaw and the gratified publishers well knew, the parallel lives of this particular man were equally good, and indefinitely produced would certainly have ended in a heaven somewhere that can suitably contain such strangely opposite characteristics as his remarkable personality combined.

For Mark Ebor, F.R.S., etc., etc., was that unique combination hardly ever met with in actual life, a man of science and a mystic.

As the first, his name stood in the gallery of the great, and as the second—but there came the mystery! For under the pseudonym of "Pilgrim" (the author of that brilliant series of books that appealed to so many), his identity was as well concealed as that of the anonymous writer of the weather reports in a daily newspaper. Thousands read the sanguine, optimistic, stimulating little books that issued annually from the pen of "Pilgrim," and thousands bore their daily burdens better for having read; while the Press generally agreed that the author, besides being an incorrigible enthusiast and optimist, was also—a woman; but no one ever succeeded in penetrating the veil of anonymity and discovering that "Pilgrim" and the biologist were one and the same person.

Mark Ebor, as Dr. Laidlaw knew him in his laboratory, was one man; but Mark Ebor, as he sometimes saw him after work was over, with rapt eyes and ecstatic face, discussing the possibilities of "union with God" and the future of the human race, was quite another.

"I have always held, as you know," he was saying one evening as he sat in the little study beyond the laboratory with his assistant and intimate, "that Vision should play a large part in the life of the awakened man—not to be regarded as infallible, of course, but to be observed and made use of as a guide-post to possibilities—"

"I am aware of your peculiar views, sir," the young doctor put in deferentially, yet with a certain impatience.

"'For Visions come from a region of the consciousness where observation and experiment are out of the question," pursued the other with enthusiasm, not noticing the interruption, "'and, while they should be checked by reason afterwards, they should not be laughed at or ignored. All inspiration, I hold, is of the nature of interior Vision, and all our best knowledge has come—such is my confirmed belief—as a sudden revelation to the brain prepared to receive it—"

"Prepared by hard work first, by concentration, by the closest possible study of ordinary phenomena," Dr. Laidlaw allowed himself to observe.

"Perhaps," sighed the other; "but by a process, none the less, of spiritual illumination. The best match in the world will not light a candle unless the wick be first suitably prepared."

It was Laidlaw's turn to sigh. He knew so well the impossibility of arguing with his chief when he was in the regions of the mystic, but at the same time the respect he felt for his tremendous attainments was so sincere that he always listened with attention and deference, wondering how far the great man would go and to what end this curious combination of logic and "illumination" would eventually lead him.

"Only last night," continued the elder man, a sort of light coming into his rugged features, "the vision came to me again—the one that has haunted me at intervals ever since my youth, and that will not be denied."

Dr. Laidlaw fidgeted in his chair.

"About the Tablets of the Gods, you mean—and that they lie somewhere hidden in the sands," he said patiently. A sudden gleam of interest came into his face as he turned to catch the professor's reply.

"And that I am to be the one to find them, to decipher them, and to give the great knowledge to the world—"'

"Who will not believe," laughed Laidlaw shortly, yet interested in spite of his thinly-veiled contempt.

"Because even the keenest minds, in the right sense of the word, are hopelessly—unscientific," replied the other gently, his face positively aglow with the memory of his vision. "Yet what is more likely," he continued after a moment's pause, peering into space with rapt eyes that saw things too wonderful for exact language to describe, "than that there should have been given to man in the first ages of the world some record of the purpose and problem that had been set him to solve? In a word," he cried, fixing his shining eyes upon the face of his perplexed assistant, "that God's messengers in the far-off ages should have given to His creatures some full statement of the secret of the world, of the secret of the soul, of the meaning of life and death—the explanation of our being here, and to what great end we are destined in the ultimate fullness of things?"

Dr. Laidlaw sat speechless. These outbursts of mystical enthusiasm he had witnessed before. With any other man he would not have listened to a single sentence, but to Professor Ebor, man of knowledge and profound investigator, he listened with respect, because he regarded this condition as temporary and pathological, and in some sense a reaction from the intense strain of the prolonged mental concentration of many days.

He smiled, with something between sympathy and resignation as he met the other's rapt gaze.

"But you have said, sir, at other times, that you consider the ultimate secrets to be screened from all possible—"

"The *ultimate* secrets, yes," came the unperturbed reply; "but that there lies buried somewhere an indestructible record of the secret meaning of life, originally known to men in the days of their pristine innocence, I am convinced. And, by this strange vision so often vouchsafed to me, I am equally sure that one day it shall be given to me to announce to a weary world this glorious and terrific message."

And he continued at great length and in glowing language to describe the species of vivid dream that had come to him at intervals since earliest childhood, showing in detail how he discovered these very Tablets of the Gods, and proclaimed their splendid contents—whose precise nature was always, however, withheld from him in the vision—to a patient and suffering humanity.

"The *Scrutator*, sir, well described 'Pilgrim' as the Apostle of Hope," said the young doctor gently, when he had finished; "and now, if that reviewer could hear you speak and realize from what strange depths comes your simple faith—"

The professor held up his hand, and the smile of a little child broke over his face like sunshine in the morning.

"Half the good my books do would be instantly destroyed," he said sadly; "they would say that I wrote with my tongue in my cheek. But wait," he added significantly; "wait till I find these Tablets of the Gods! Wait till I hold the solutions of the old world-problems in my hands! Wait till the light of this new revelation breaks upon confused humanity, and it wakes to find its bravest hopes justified! Ah, then, my dear Laidlaw—"

He broke off suddenly; but the doctor, cleverly guessing the thought in his mind, caught him up immediately.

"Perhaps this very summer," he said, trying hard to make the suggestion keep pace with honesty; "in your explorations in Assyria—your digging in the remote civilization of what was once Chaldea, you may find—what you dream of—"

The professor held up his hand, and the smile of a fine old face.

"Perhaps," he murmured softly, "perhaps!"

And the young doctor, thanking the gods of science that his leader's aberrations were of so harmless a character, went home strong in the certitude of his knowledge of externals, proud that he was able to refer his visions to self-suggestion, and wondering complaisantly whether in his old age he might not after all suffer himself from visitations of the very kind that afflicted his respected chief.

And as he got into bed and thought again of his master's rugged face, and finely shaped head, and the deep lines traced by years of work and self-discipline, he turned over on his pillow and fell asleep with a sigh that was half of wonder, half of regret.

2

It was in February, nine months later, when Dr. Laidlaw made his way to Charing Cross to meet his chief after his long absence of travel and exploration. The vision about the so-called Tablets of the Gods had meanwhile passed almost entirely from his memory.

There were few people in the train, for the stream of traffic was now running the other way, and he had no difficulty in finding the man he had cone to meet. The shock of white hair beneath the low-crowned felt hat was alone enough to distinguish him by easily.

"Here I am at last!" exclaimed the professor, somewhat wearily, clasping his friend's hand as he listened to the young doctor's warm greetings and questions. "Here I am—a little older, and *much* dirtier than when you last saw me!" He glanced down laughingly at his travel-stained garments.

"And *much* wiser," said Laidlaw, with a smile, as he bustled about the platform for porters and gave his chief the latest scientific news.

At last they came down to practical considerations. "And your luggage—where is that? You must have tons of it, I suppose?" said Laidlaw.

"Hardly anything," Professor Ebor answered. "Nothing, in fact, but what you see."

"Nothing but this hand-bag?" laughed the other, thinking he was joking.

"And a small portmanteau in the van," was the quiet reply. "I have no other luggage."

"You have no other luggage?" repeated Laidlaw, turning sharply to see if he were in earnest.

"Why should I need more?" the professor added simply.

Something in the man's face, or voice, or manner—the doctor hardly knew which—suddenly struck him as strange. There was a change in him, a change so profound—so little on the surface, that is—that at first he had not become aware of it. For a moment it was as though an utterly alien personality stood before him in that noisy, bustling throng. Here, in all the homely, friendly turmoil of a Charing Cross crowd, a curious feeling of cold passed over his heart, touching his life with icy finger, so that he actually trembled and felt afraid.

He looked up quickly at his friend, his mind working with startled and unwelcome thoughts.

"Only this?" he repeated, indicating the bag. "But where's all the stuff you went away with? And—have you brought nothing home—no treasures?"

"This is all I have," the other said briefly. The pale smile that went with the words caused the doctor a second indescribable sensation of uneasiness. Something was very wrong, something was very queer; he wondered now that he had not noticed it sooner.

"The rest follows, of course, by slow freight," he added tactfully, and as naturally as possible. "But come, sir, you must be tired and in want of food after your long journey. I'll get a taxi at once, and we can see about the other luggage afterwards."

It seemed to him he hardly knew quite what he was saying; the change in his friend had come upon him so suddenly and now grew upon him more and more distressingly. Yet he could not make out exactly in what it consisted. A terrible suspicion began to take shape in his mind, troubling him dreadfully.

"I am neither very tired, nor in need of food, thank you," the professor said quietly. "And this is all I have. There is no luggage to follow. I have brought home nothing—nothing but what you see."

His words conveyed finality. They got into a taxi, tipped the porter, who had been staring in amazement at the venerable figure of the scientist, and were conveyed slowly and noisily to the house in the north of London where the laboratory was, the scene of their labours of years.

And the whole way Professor Ebor uttered no word, nor did Dr. Laidlaw find the courage to ask a single question.

It was only late that night, before he took his departure, as the two men were standing before the fire in the study—that study where they had discussed so many problems of vital and absorbing interest—that Dr. Laidlaw at last found strength to come to the point with direct questions. The professor had been giving him a superficial and desultory account of his travels, of his journeys by camel, of his encampments among the mountains and in the desert, and of his explorations among the buried temples, and, deeper, into the waste of the pre-historic sands, when suddenly the doctor came to the desired point with a kind of nervous rush, almost like a frightened boy.

"And you found—" he began stammering, looking hard at the other's dreadfully altered face, from which every line of hope and cheerfulness seemed to have been obliterated as a sponge wipes markings from a slate—"you found—"

"I found," replied the other, in a solemn voice, and it was the voice of the mystic rather than the man of science—"I found what I went to seek. The vision never once failed me. It led me straight to the place like a star in the heavens. I found—the Tablets of the Gods."

Dr. Laidlaw caught his breath, and steadied himself on the back of a chair. The words fell like particles of ice upon his heart. For the first time the professor had uttered the well-known phrase without the glow of light and wonder in his face that always accompanied it.

"You have—brought them?" he faltered.

"I have brought then home," said the other, in a voice with a ring like iron; "and I have—deciphered them."

Profound despair, the bloom of outer darkness, the dead sound of a hopeless soul freezing in the utter cold of space seemed to fill in the pauses between the brief sentences. A silence followed, during which Dr. Laidlaw saw nothing but the white face before him alternately fade and return. And it was like the face of a dead man.

"They are, alas, indestructible," he heard the voice continue, with its even, metallic ring.

"Indestructible," Laidlaw repeated mechanically, hardly knowing what he was saying.

Again a silence of several minutes passed, during which, with a creeping cold about his heart, he stood and stared into the eyes of the man he had known and loved so long—aye, and worshipped, too; the man who had first opened his own eyes when they were blind, and had led him to the gates of knowledge, and no little distance along the difficult path beyond; the man who, in another direction, had passed on the strength of his faith into the hearts of thousands by his books.

"I may see them?" he asked at last, in a low voice he hardly recognized as his own. "You will let me know—their message?"

Professor Ebor kept his eyes fixedly upon his assistant's face as he answered, with a smile that was more like the grin of death than a living human smile.

"When I am gone," he whispered; "when I have passed away. Then you shall find them and read the translation I have made. And then, too, in your turn, you must try, with the latest resources of science at your disposal to aid you, to compass their utter destruction." He paused a moment, and his face grew pale as the face of a corpse. "Until that time," he added presently, without looking up, "I must ask you not to refer to the subject again—and to keep my confidence meanwhile—*ab—so—lute—ly.*"

3

A year passed slowly by, and at the end of it Dr. Laidlaw had found it necessary to sever his working connexion with his friend and one-time leader. Professor Ebor was no longer the same man. The light had gone out of his life; the laboratory was closed; he no longer put pen to paper or applied his mind to a single problem. In the short space of a few months he had passed from a hale and hearty man of late middle life to the condition of old age—a man collapsed and on the edge of dissolution. Death, it was plain, lay waiting for him in the shadows of any day—and he knew it.

To describe faithfully the nature of this profound alteration in his character and temperament is not easy, but Dr. Laidlaw summed it up to himself in three words: *Loss of hope.* The splendid mental powers remained indeed undimmed, but the incentive to use them—to use them for the help of others—had gone. The character still held to its fine and unselfish habits of years, but the far goal to which they had been the leading strings had faded away. The desire for knowledge—knowledge for its own sake—had died, and the passionate hope which hitherto had animated with tireless energy the heart and brain of this splendidly equipped intellect had suffered total eclipse. The central fires had gone out. Nothing was worth doing, thinking, working for. There *was* nothing to work for any longer!

The professor's first step was to recall as many of his books as possible; his second to close his laboratory and stop all research. He gave no explanation, he invited no questions. His whole personality crumbled away, so to speak, till his daily life became a mere mechanical process of clothing the body, feeding the body, keeping it in good health so as to avoid physical discomfort, and, above all, doing nothing that could interfere with sleep. The professor did everything he could to lengthen the hours of sleep, and therefore of forgetfulness.

It was all clear enough to Dr. Laidlaw. A weaker man, he knew, would have sought to lose himself in one form or another of sensual indulgence—sleeping-draughts, drink, the first pleasures that came to hand. Self-destruction would have been the method of a little bolder type; and deliberate evil-doing, poisoning with his awful knowledge all he could, the means of still another kind of man. Mark Ebor was none of these. He held himself under fine control, facing silently and without complaint the terrible facts he honestly believed himself to have been unfortunate enough to discover. Even to his intimate friend and assistant, Dr. Laidlaw, he vouchsafed no word of true explanation or lament. He went straight forward to the end, knowing well that the end was not very far away.

And death came very quietly one day to him, as he was sifting in the arm-chair of the study, directly facing the doors of the laboratory—the doors that no longer opened. Dr. Laidlaw, by happy chance, was with him at the time, and just able to reach his side in response to the sudden painful efforts for breath; just in tune, too, to catch the murmured words that fell from the pallid lips like a message from the other side of the grave.

"Read them, if you must; and, if you can—destroy. But"—his voice sank so low that Dr. Laidlaw only just caught the dying syllables—"but—never, never—give them to the world."

And like a grey bundle of dust loosely gathered up in an old garment the professor sank back into his chair and expired.

But this was only the death of the body. His spirit had died two years before.

4

The estate of the dead man was small and uncomplicated, and Dr. Laidlaw, as sole executor and residuary legatee, had no difficulty in settling it up. A month after the funeral he was sitting alone in his upstairs library, the last sad duties completed, and his mind full of poignant memories and regrets for the loss of a friend he had revered and loved, and to whom his debt was so incalculably great. The last two years, indeed, had been for him terrible. To watch the swift decay of the greatest combination of heart and brain he had ever known, and to realize he was powerless to help, was a source of profound grief to him that would remain to the end of his days.

At the same time an insatiable curiosity possessed him. The study of dementia was, of course, outside his special province as a specialist, but he knew enough of it to understand how small a matter might be the actual cause of how great an illusion, and he had been devoured from the very beginning by a ceaseless and increasing anxiety to know what the professor had found in the sands of "Chaldea," what these precious Tablets of the Gods might be, and particularly—for this was the real cause that had sapped the man's sanity and hope—what the inscription was that he had believed to have deciphered thereon.

The curious feature of it all to his own mind was, that whereas his friend had dreamed of finding a message of glorious hope and comfort, he had apparently found (so far as he had found anything intelligible at all, and not invented the whole thing in his dementia) that the secret of the world, and the meaning of life and death, was of so terrible a nature that it robbed the heart of courage and the soul of hope. What, then, could be the contents of the little brown parcel the professor had bequeathed to him with his pregnant dying sentences?

Actually his hand was trembling as he turned to the writing-table and began slowly to unfasten a small old-fashioned desk on which the small gilt initials "M.E." stood forth as a melancholy memento. He put the key into the lock and half turned it. Then, suddenly, he stopped and looked about him. Was that a sound at the back of the room? It was just as though someone had laughed and then tried to smother the laugh with a cough. A slight shiver ran over him as he stood listening.

"This is absurd," he said aloud; "too absurd for belief—that I should be so nervous! It's the effect of curiosity unduly prolonged." He smiled a little sadly and his eyes wandered to the blue summer sky and the plane trees swaying in the wind below his window. "It's the reaction," he continued. "The curiosity of two years to be quenched in a single moment! The nervous tension, of course, must be considerable."

He turned back to the brown desk and opened it without further delay. His hand was firm now, and he took out the paper parcel that lay inside without a tremor. It was heavy. A moment later there lay on the table before him a couple of weather-worn plaques of grey stone—they looked like stone, although they felt like metal—on which he saw markings of a curious character that might have been the mere tracings of natural forces through the ages, or, equally well, the half-obliterated hieroglyphics cut upon their surface in past centuries by the more or less untutored hand of a common scribe.

He lifted each stone in turn and examined it carefully. It seemed to him that a faint glow of heat passed from the substance into his skin, and he put them down again suddenly, as with a gesture of uneasiness.

"A very clever, or a very imaginative man," he said to himself, "who could squeeze the secrets of life and death from such broken lines as those!"

Then he turned to a yellow envelope lying beside them in the desk, with the single word on the outside in the writing of the professor—the word *Translation*.

"Now," he thought, taking it up with a sudden violence to conceal his nervousness, "now for the great solution. Now to learn the meaning of the words, and why mankind was made, and why discipline is worth while, and sacrifice and pain the true law of advancement."

There was the shadow of a sneer in his voice, and yet something in him shivered at the same time. He held the envelope as though weighing it in his hand, his mind pondering many things. Then curiosity won the day, and he suddenly tore it open with the gesture of an actor who tears open a letter on the stage, knowing there is no real writing inside at all.

A page of finely written script in the late scientist's handwriting lay before him. He read it through from beginning to end, missing no word, uttering each syllable distinctly under his breath as he read.

The pallor of his face grew ghastly as he neared the end. He began to shake all over as with ague. His breath came heavily in gasps. He still gripped the sheet of paper, however, and deliberately, as by an intense effort of will, read it through a second time from beginning to end. And this time, as the last syllable dropped from his lips, the whole face of the man flamed with a sadden and terrible anger. His skin became deep, deep red, and he clenched his teeth. With all the strength of his vigorous soul he was struggling to keep control of himself.

For perhaps five minutes he stood there beside the table without stirring a muscle. He might have been carved out of stone. His eyes were shut, and only the heaving of the chest betrayed the fact that he was a living being. Then, with a strange quietness, he lit a match and applied it to the sheet of paper he held in his hand. The ashes fell slowly about him, piece by piece, and he blew them from the window-sill into the air, his eyes following them as they floated away on the summer wind that breathed so warmly over the world.

He turned back slowly into the room. Although his actions and movements were absolutely steady and controlled, it was clear that he was on the edge of violent action. A hurricane might burst upon the still room any moment. His muscles were tense and rigid. Then, suddenly, he whitened, collapsed, and sank backwards into a chair, like a tumbled bundle of inert matter. He had fainted.

In less than half an hour he recovered consciousness and sat up. As before, he made no sound. Not a syllable passed his lips. He rose quietly and looked about the room.

Then he did a curious thing.

Taking a heavy stick from the rack in the corner he approached the mantlepiece, and with a heavy shattering blow he smashed the clock to pieces. The glass fell in shivering atoms.

"Cease your lying voice for ever," he said, in a curiously still, even tone. "There is no such thing as *time!*"

He took the watch from his pocket, swung it round several times by the long gold chain, smashed it into smithereens against the wall with a single blow, and then walked into his laboratory next door, and hung its broken body on the bones of the skeleton in the corner of the room.

"Let one damned mockery hang upon another," he said smiling oddly. "Delusions, both of you, and cruel as false!"

He slowly moved back to the front room. He stopped opposite the bookcase where stood in a row the "Scriptures of the World," choicely bound and exquisitely printed, the late professor's most treasured possession, and next to them several books signed "Pilgrim."

One by one he took them from the shelf and hurled them through the open window.

"A devil's dreams! A devil's foolish dreams!" he cried, with a vicious laugh.

Presently he stopped from sheer exhaustion. He turned his eyes slowly to the wall opposite, where hung a weird array of Eastern swords and daggers, scimitars and spears, the collections of many journeys. He crossed the room and ran his finger along the edge. His mind seemed to waver.

"No," he muttered presently; "not that way. There are easier and better ways than that."

He took his hat and passed downstairs into the street.

5

It was five o'clock, and the June sun lay hot upon the pavement. He felt the metal door-knob burn the palm of his hand.

"Ah, Laidlaw, this is well met," cried a voice at his elbow; "I was in the act of coming to see you. I've a case that will interest you, and besides, I remembered that you flavoured your tea with orange leaves!—and I admit—"

It was Alexis Stephen, the great hypnotic doctor.

"I've had no tea to-day," Laidlaw said, in a dazed manner, after staring for a moment as though the other had struck him in the face. A new idea had entered his mind.

"What's the matter?" asked Dr. Stephen quickly. "Something's wrong with you. It's this sudden heat, or overwork. Come, man, let's go inside."

A sudden light broke upon the face of the younger man, the light of a heaven-sent inspiration. He looked into his friend's face, and told a direct lie.

"Odd," he said, "I myself was just coming to see you. I have something of great importance to test your confidence with. But in *your* house, please," as Stephen urged him towards his own door—"in your house. It's only round the corner, and I—I cannot go back there—to my rooms—till I have told you."

"I'm your patient—for the moment," he added stammeringly as soon as they were seated in the privacy of the hypnotist's sanctum, "and I want—er—"

"My dear Laidlaw," interrupted the other, in that soothing voice of command which had suggested to many a suffering soul that the cure for its pain lay in the powers of its own reawakened will, "I am always at your service, as you know. You have only to tell me what I can do for you, and I will do it." He showed every desire to help him out. His manner was indescribably tactful and direct.

Dr. Laidlaw looked up into his face.

"I surrender my will to you," he said, already calmed by the other's healing presence, "and I want you to treat me hypnotically—and at once. I want you to suggest to me"—his voice became very tense—"that I shall forget—forget till I die everything that has occurred to me during the last two hours; till I die, mind," he added, with solemn emphasis, "till I die."

He floundered and stammered like a frightened boy. Alexis Stephen looked at him fixedly without speaking.

"And further," Laidlaw continued, "I want you to ask me no questions. I wish to forget for ever something I have recently discovered—something so terrible and yet so obvious that I can hardly understand why it is not patent to every mind in the world—for I have had a moment of absolute *clear vision*—of merciless clairvoyance. But I want no one else in the whole world to know what it is—least of all, old friend, yourself."

He talked in utter confusion, and hardly knew what he was saying. But the pain on his face and the anguish in his voice were an instant passport to the other's heart.

"Nothing is easier," replied Dr. Stephen, after a hesitation so slight that the other probably did not even notice it. "'Come into my other room where we shall not be disturbed. I can heal you. Your memory of the last two hours shall be wiped out as though it had never been. You can trust me absolutely."

"I know I can," Laidlaw said simply, as he followed him in.

6

An hour later they passed back into the front room again. The sun was already behind the houses opposite, and the shadows began to gather.

"I went off easily?"' Laidlaw asked.

"You were a little obstinate at first. But though you came in like a lion, you went out like a lamb. I let you sleep a bit afterwards."

Dr. Stephen kept his eyes rather steadily upon his friend's face.

"What were you doing by the fire before you came here?" he asked, pausing, in a casual tone, as he lit a cigarette and handed the case to his patient.

"I? Let me see. Oh, I know; I was worrying my way through poor old Ebor's papers and things. I'm his executor, you know. Then I got weary and came out for a whiff of air." He spoke lightly and with perfect naturalness. Obviously he was telling the truth. "I prefer specimens to papers," he laughed cheerily.

"I know, I know," said Dr. Stephen, holding a lighted match for the cigarette. His face wore an expression of content. The experiment had been a complete success. The memory of the last two hours was wiped out utterly. Laidlaw was already chatting gaily and easily about a dozen other things that interested him. Together they went out into the street, and at his door Dr. Stephen left him with a joke and a wry face that made his friend laugh heartily.

"Don't dine on the professor's old papers by mistake," he cried, as he vanished down the street.

Dr. Laidlaw went up to his study at the top of the house. Half way down he met his housekeeper, Mrs. Fewings. She was flustered and excited, and her face was very red and perspiring.

"There've been burglars here," she cried excitedly, "'or something funny! All your things is just any'ow, sir. I found everything all about everywhere!" She was very confused. In this orderly and very precise establishment it was unusual to find a thing out of place.

"Oh, my specimens!" cried the doctor, dashing up the rest of the stairs at top speed. "Have they been touched or—"

He flew to the door of the laboratory. Mrs. Fewings panted up heavily behind him.

"The labatry ain't been touched," she explained, breathlessly, "but they smashed the libry clock and they've 'ung your gold watch, sir, on the skelinton's hands. And the books that weren't no value they flung out er the window just like so much rubbish. They must have been wild drunk, Dr. Laidlaw, sir!"

The young scientist made a harried examination of the rooms. Nothing of value was missing. He began to wonder what kind of burglars they were. He looked up sharply at Mrs. Fewings standing in the doorway. For a moment he seemed to cast about in his mind for something.

"Odd," he said at length. "I only left here an hour ago and everything was all right then."

"Was it, sir? Yes, sir." She glanced. sharply at him. Her room looked out upon the courtyard, and she must have seen the books come crashing down, and also have heard her master leave the house a few minutes later.

"And what's this rubbish the brutes have left?" he cried, taking up two slabs of worn gray stone, on the writing-table. "Bath brick, or something, I do declare."

He looked very sharply again at the confused and troubled house-keeper.

"Throw them on the dust heap, Mrs. Fewings, and—and let me know if anything is missing in the house, and I will notify the police this evening."

When she left the room he went into the laboratory and took his watch off the skeleton's fingers. His face wore a troubled expression, but after a moment's thought it cleared again. His memory was a complete blank.

"I suppose I left it on the writing-table when I went out to take the air," he said. And there was no one present to contradict him.

He crossed to the window and blew carelessly some ashes of burned paper from the sill, and stood watching them as they floated away lazily over the tops of the trees.

THE EMPTY SLEEVE

1

The Gilmer brothers were a couple of fussy and persnickety old bachelors of a rather retiring, not to say timid, disposition. There was grey in the pointed beard of John, the elder, and if any hair had remained to William it would also certainly have been of the same shade. They had private means. Their main interest in life was the collection of violins, for which they had the instinctive *flair* of true connoisseurs. Neither John nor William, however, could play a single note. They could only pluck the open strings. The production of tone, so necessary before purchase, was done vicariously for them by another.

The only objection they had to the big building in which they occupied the roomy top floor was that Morgan, liftman and caretaker, insisted on wearing a billycock with his uniform after six o'clock in the evening, with a result disastrous to the beauty of the universe. For "Mr. Morgan," as they called him between themselves, had a round and pasty face on the top of a round and conical body. In view, however, of the man's other rare qualities—including his devotion to themselves—this objection was not serious.

He had another peculiarity that amused them. On being found fault with, he explained nothing, but merely repeated the words of the complaint.

"Water in the bath wasn't really hot this morning, Morgan!"

"Water in the bath not reely 'ot, wasn't it, sire?"

Or, from William, who was something of a faddist:

"My jar of sour milk came up late yesterday, Morgan!"

"Your jar sour milk come up late, sir, yesterday?"

Since, however, the statement of a complaint invariably resulted in its remedy, the brothers had learned to look for no further explanation. Next morning the bath *was* hot, the sour milk *was* "brortup" punctually. The uniform and billycock hat, though, remained an eyesore and source of oppression.

On this particular night John Gilmer, the elder, returning from a Masonic rehearsal, stepped into the lift and found Mr. Morgan with his hand ready on the iron rope.

"Fog's very thick outside," said Mr. John pleasantly; and the lift was a third of the way up before Morgan had completed his customary repetition: "Fog very thick outside, yes, sir." And Gilmer then asked casually if his brother were alone, and received the reply that Mr. Hyman had called and had not yet gone away.

Now this Mr. Hyman was a Hebrew, and, like themselves, a connoisseur in violins, but, unlike themselves, who only kept their specimens to look at, he was a skilful and exquisite player. He was the only person they ever permitted to handle their pedigree instruments, to take them from the glass cases where they reposed in silent splendour, and to draw the sound out of their wondrous painted hearts of golden varnish. The brothers loathed to see his fingers touch them, yet loved to hear their singing voices in the room, for the latter confirmed their sound judgment as collectors, and made them certain their money had been well spent. Hyman, however, made no attempt to conceal his contempt and hatred for the mere collector. The atmosphere of the room fairly pulsed with these opposing forces of silent emotion when Hyman played and the Gilmers, alternately writhing and admiring, listened. The occasions, however, were not frequent. The Hebrew only came by invitation, and both brothers made a point of being in. It was a very formal proceeding—something of a sacred rite almost.

John Gilmer, therefore, was considerably surprised by the information Morgan had supplied. For one thing, Hyman, he had understood, was away on the Continent.

"Still in there, you say?" he repeated, after a moment's reflection.

"Still in there, Mr. John, sir." Then, concealing his surprise from the liftman, he fell back upon his usual mild habit of complaining about the billycock hat and the uniform.

"You really should try and remember, Morgan," he said, though kindly. "That hat does *not* go well with that uniform!"

Morgan's pasty countenance betrayed no vestige of expression. "At don't go well with the yewniform, sir," he repeated, hanging up the disreputable bowler and replacing it with a gold-braided cap from the peg. "No, sir, it don't, do it?" he added cryptically, smiling at the transformation thus effected.

And the lift then halted with an abrupt jerk at the top floor. By somebody's carelessness the landing was in darkness, and, to make things worse, Morgan, clumsily pulling the iron rope, happened to knock the billycock from its peg so that his sleeve, as he stooped to catch it, struck the switch and plunged the scene in a moment's complete obscurity.

And it was then, in the act of stepping out before the light was turned on again, that John Gilmer stumbled against something that shot along the landing past the open door. First he thought it must be a child, then a man, then—an animal. Its movement was rapid yet stealthy. Starting backwards instinctively to allow it room to pass, Gilmer collided in the darkness with Morgan, and Morgan incontinently screamed. There was a moment of stupid confusion. The heavy framework of the lift shook a little, as though something had stepped into it and then as quickly jumped out again. A rushing sound followed that resembled footsteps, yet at the same time was more like gliding—someone in soft slippers or stockinged feet, greatly hurrying. Then came silence again. Morgan sprang to the landing and turned up the electric light. Mr. Gilmer, at the same moment, did likewise to the switch in the lift. Light flooded the scene. Nothing was visible.

"Dog or cat, or something, I suppose, wasn't it?" exclaimed Gilmer, following the man out and looking round with bewildered amazement upon a deserted landing. He knew quite well, even while he spoke, that the words were foolish.

"Dog or cat, yes, sir, or—something," echoed Morgan, his eyes narrowed to pin-points, then growing large, but his face stolid.

"The light should have been on." Mr. Gilmer spoke with a touch of severity. The little occurrence had curiously disturbed his equanimity. He felt annoyed, upset, uneasy.

For a perceptible pause the liftman made no reply, and his employer, looking up, saw that, besides being flustered, he was white about the jaws. His voice, when he spoke, was without its normal assurance. This time he did not merely repeat. He explained.

"The light *was* on, sir, when last *I* come up!" he said, with emphasis, obviously speaking the truth. "Only a moment ago," he added.

Mr. Gilmer, for some reason, felt disinclined to press for explanations. He decided to ignore the matter.

Then the lift plunged down again into the depths like a diving-bell into water; and John Gilmer, pausing a moment first to reflect, let himself in softly with his latchkey, and, after hanging up hat and coat in the hall, entered the big sitting-room he and his brother shared in common.

The December fog that covered London like a dirty blanket had penetrated, he saw, into the room. The objects in it were half shrouded in the familiar yellowish haze.

2

In dressing-gown and slippers, William Gilmer, almost invisible in his armchair by the gas-stove across the room, spoke at once. Through the thick atmosphere his face gleamed, showing an extinguished pipe hanging from his lips. His tone of voice conveyed emotion, an emotion he sought to suppress, of a quality, however, not easy to define.

"Hyman's been here," he announced abruptly. "You must have met him. He's this very instant gone out."

It was quite easy to see that something had happened, for "scenes" leave disturbance behind them in the atmosphere. But John made no immediate reference to this. He replied that he had seen no one—which was strictly true—and his brother thereupon, sitting bolt upright in the chair, turned quickly and faced him. His skin, in the foggy air, seemed paler than before.

"That's odd," he said nervously.

"What's odd?" asked John.

"That you didn't see—anything. You ought to have run into one another on the doorstep." His eyes went peering about the room. He was distinctly ill at ease. "You're positive you saw no one? Did Morgan take him down before you came? Did Morgan see him?" He asked several questions at once.

"On the contrary, Morgan told me he was still here with you. Hyman probably walked down, and didn't take the lift at all," he replied. "That accounts for neither of us seeing him." He decided to say nothing about the occurrence in the lift, for his brother's nerves, he saw plainly, were on edge.

William then stood up out of his chair, and the skin of his face changed its hue, for whereas a moment ago it was merely pale, it had now altered to a tint that lay somewhere between white and a livid grey. The man was fighting internal terror. For a moment these two brothers of middle age looked each other straight in the eye. Then John spoke:

"What's wrong, Billy?" he asked quietly. "Something's upset you. What brought Hyman in this way—unexpectedly? I thought he was still in Germany."

The brothers, affectionate and sympathetic, understood one another perfectly. They had no secrets. Yet for several minutes the younger one made no reply. It seemed difficult to choose his words apparently.

"Hyman played, I suppose—on the fiddles?" John helped him, wondering uneasily what was coming. He did not care much for the individual in question, though his talent was of such great use to them.

The other nodded in the affirmative, then plunged into rapid speech, talking under his breath as though he feared someone might overhear. Glancing over his shoulder down the foggy room, he drew his brother close.

"Hyman came," he began, "unexpectedly. He hadn't written, and I hadn't asked him. You hadn't either, I suppose?"

John shook his head.

"When I came in from the dining-room I found him in the passage.

The servant was taking away the dishes, and he had let himself in while the front door was ajar. Pretty cool, wasn't it?"

"He's an original," said John, shrugging his shoulders. "And you welcomed him?" he asked.

"I asked him in, of course. He explained he had something glorious for me to hear. Silenski had played it in the afternoon, and he had bought the music since. But Silenski's 'Strad' hadn't the power—it's thin on the upper strings, you remember, unequal, patchy—and he said no instrument in the world could do it justice but our 'Joseph'—the small Guarnerius, you know, which he swears is the most perfect in the world."

"And what was it? Did he play it?" asked John, growing more uneasy as he grew more interested. With relief he glanced round and saw the matchless little instrument lying there safe and sound in its glass case near the door.

"He played it—divinely: a Zigeuner Lullaby, a fine, passionate, rushing bit of inspiration, oddly misnamed 'lullaby.' And, fancy, the fellow had memorized it already! He walked about the room on tiptoe while he played it, complaining of the light—"

"Complaining of the light?"

"Said the thing was crepuscular, and needed dusk for its full effect. I turned the lights out one by one, till finally there was only the glow of the gas logs. He insisted. You know that way he has with him? And then he got over me in another matter: insisted on using some special strings he had brought with him, and put them on, too, himself—thicker than the A and E *we* use."

For though neither Gilmer could produce a note, it was their pride that they kept their precious instruments in perfect condition for playing, choosing the exact thickness and quality of strings that suited the temperament of each violin; and the little Guarnerius in question always "sang" best, they held, with thin strings.

"Infernal insolence," exclaimed the listening brother, wondering what was coming next. "Played it well, though, didn't he, this Lullaby thing?" he added, seeing that William hesitated. As he spoke he went nearer, sitting down close beside him in a leather chair.

"Magnificent! Pure fire of genius!" was the reply with enthusiasm, the voice at the same time dropping lower. "Staccato like a silver hammer; harmonics like flutes, clear, soft, ringing; and the tone—well, the G string was a baritone, and the upper registers creamy and mellow as a boy's voice. John," he added, "that Guarnerius is the very pick of the period and"—again he hesitated—"Hyman loves it. He'd give his soul to have it."

The more John heard, the more uncomfortable it made him. He had always disliked this gifted Hebrew, for in his secret heart he knew that he had always feared and distrusted him. Sometimes he had felt half afraid of him; the man's very forcible personality was too insistent to be pleasant. His type was of the dark and sinister kind, and he possessed a violent will that rarely failed of accomplishing its desire.

"Wish I'd heard the fellow play," he said at length, ignoring his brother's last remark, and going on to speak of the most matter-of-fact details he could think of. "Did he use the Dodd bow, or the Tourte? That Dodd I picked up last month, you know, is the most perfectly balanced I have ever—"

He stopped abruptly, for William had suddenly got upon his feet and was standing there, searching the room with his eyes. A chill ran down John's spine as he watched him.

"What is it, Billy?" he asked sharply. "Hear anything?"

William continued to peer about him through the thick air.

"Oh, nothing, probably," he said, an odd catch in his voice; "only— I keep feeling as if there was somebody listening. Do you think, perhaps"—he glanced over his shoulder—"there is someone at the door? I wish—I wish you'd have a look, John."

John obeyed, though without great eagerness. Crossing the room slowly, he opened the door, then switched on the light. The passage leading past the bathroom towards the bedrooms beyond was empty. The coats hung motionless from their pegs.

"No one, of course," he said, as he closed the door and came back to the stove. He left the light burning in the passage. It was curious the way both brothers had this impression that they were not alone, though only one of them spoke of it.

"Used the Dodd or the Tourte, Billy—which?" continued John in the most natural voice he could assume.

But at that very same instant the water started to his eyes. His brother, he saw, was close upon the thing he really had to tell. But he had stuck fast.

3

By a great effort John Gilmer composed himself and remained in his chair. With detailed elaboration he lit a cigarette, staring hard at his brother over the flaring match while he did so. There he sat in his dressing-gown and slippers by the fireplace, eyes downcast, fingers playing idly with the red tassel. The electric light cast heavy shadows across the face. In a flash then, since emotion may sometimes express itself in attitude even better than in speech, the elder brother understood that Billy was about to tell him an unutterable thing.

By instinct he moved over to his side so that the same view of the room confronted him.

"Out with it, old man," he said, with an effort to be natural. "Tell me what you saw."

Billy shuffled slowly round and the two sat side by side, facing the fog-draped chamber.

"It was like this," he began softly, "only I was standing instead of sitting, looking over to that door as you and I do now. Hyman moved to and fro in the faint glow of the gas logs against the far wall, playing that 'crepuscular' thing in his most inspired sort of way, so that the music seemed to issue from himself rather than from the shining bit of wood under his chin, when—I noticed something coming over me that was"—he hesitated, searching for words—"that wasn't *all* due to the music," he finished abruptly.

"His personality put a bit of hypnotism on you, eh?"

William shrugged his shoulders.

"The air was thickish with fog and the light was dim, cast upwards upon him from the stove," he continued. "I admit all that. But there wasn't light enough to throw shadows, you see, and—"

"Hyman looked queer?" the other helped him quickly.

Billy nodded his head without turning.

"Changed there before my very eyes"—he whispered it—"turned animal—"

"Animal?" John felt his hair rising.

"That's the only way I can put it. His face and hands and body turned otherwise than usual. I lost the sound of his feet. When the bow-hand or the fingers on the strings passed into the light, they were"—he uttered a soft, shuddering little laugh—"furry, oddly divided, the fingers massed together. And he paced stealthily. I thought every instant the fiddle would drop with a crash and he would spring at me across the room."

"My dear chap—"

"He moved with those big, lithe, striding steps one sees"—John held his breath in the little pause, listening keenly—"one sees those big brutes make in the cages when their desire is aflame for food or escape, or—or fierce, passionate desire for anything they want, with their whole nature—"

"The big felines!" John whistled softly.

"And every minute getting nearer and nearer to the door, as though he meant to make a sudden rush for it and get out."

"With the violin! Of course you stopped him?"

"In the end. But for a long time, I swear to you, I found it difficult to know what to do, even to move. I couldn't get my voice for words of any kind; it was like a spell."

"It *was* a spell," suggested John firmly.

"Then, as he moved, still playing," continued the other, "he seemed to grow smaller; to shrink down below the line of the gas. I thought I should lose sight of him altogether. I turned the light up suddenly. There he was over by the door—crouching."

"Playing on his knees, you mean?"

William closed his eyes in an effort to visualize it again.

"Crouching," he repeated, at length, "close to the floor. At least, I think so. It all happened so quickly, and I felt so bewildered, it was hard to see straight. But at first I could have sworn he was half his natural size. I called to him, I think I swore at him—I forget exactly, but I know he straightened up at once and stood before me down there in the light"—he pointed across the room to the door—"eyes gleaming, face white as chalk, perspiring like midsummer, and gradually filling out, straightening up, whatever you like to call it, to his natural size and appearance again. It was the most horrid thing I've ever seen."

"As an—animal, you saw him still?"

"No; human again. Only much smaller."

"What did he say?"

Billy reflected a moment.

"Nothing that I can remember," he replied. "You see, it was all over in a few seconds. In the full light, I felt so foolish, and nonplussed at first. To see him normal again baffled me. And, before I could collect myself, he had let himself out into the passage, and I heard the front door slam. A minute later—the same second almost, it seemed—you came in. I only remember grabbing the violin and getting it back safely under the glass case. The strings were still vibrating."

The account was over. John asked no further questions. Nor did he say a single word about the lift, Morgan, or the extinguished light on the landing. There fell a longish silence between the two men; and then, while they helped themselves to a generous supply of whisky-and-soda before going to bed, John looked up and spoke:

"If you agree, Billy," he said quietly, "I think I might write and suggest to Hyman that we shall no longer have need for his services."

And Billy, acquiescing, added a sentence that expressed something of the singular dread lying but half concealed in the atmosphere of the room, if not in their minds as well:

"Putting it, however, in a way that need not offend him."

"Of course. There's no need to be rude, is there?"

Accordingly, next morning the letter was written; and John, saying nothing to his brother, took it round himself by hand to the Hebrew's rooms near Euston. The answer he dreaded was forthcoming: "Mr. Hyman's still away abroad," he was told. "But we're forwarding letters; yes. Or I can give you 'is address if you'll prefer it." The letter went, therefore, to the number in Königstrasse, Munich, thus obtained.

Then, on his way back from the insurance company where he went to increase the sum that protected the small Guarnerius from loss by fire, accident, or theft, John Gilmer called at the offices of certain musical agents and ascertained that Silenski, the violinist, was performing at the time in Munich. It was only some days later, though, by diligent inquiry, he made certain that at a concert on a certain date the famous virtuoso had played a Zigeuner Lullaby of his own composition—the very date, it turned out, on which he himself had been to the Masonic rehearsal at Mark Masons' Hall.

John, however, said nothing of these discoveries to his brother William.

4

It was about a week later when a reply to the letter cane from Munich—a letter couched in somewhat offensive terms, though it contained neither words nor phrases that could actually be found fault with. Isidore Hyman was hurt and angry. On his return to London a month or so later, he proposed to call and talk the matter over. The offensive part of the letter lay, perhaps, in his definite assumption that he could persuade the brothers to resume the old relations. John, however, wrote a brief reply to the effect that they had decided to buy no new fiddles; their collection being complete, there would be no occasion for them to invite his services as a performer. This was final. No answer came, and the matter seemed to drop. Never for one moment, though, did it leave the consciousness of John Gilmer. Hyman had said that he would come, and come assuredly he would. He secretly gave Morgan instructions that he and his brother for the future were always "out" when the Hebrew presented himself.

"He must have gone back to Germany, you see, almost at once after his visit here that night," observed William—John, however, making no reply.

One night towards the middle of January the two brothers came home together from a concert in Queen's Hall, and sat up later than usual in their sitting-room discussing over their whisky and tobacco the merits of the pieces and performers. It must have been past one o'clock when they turned out the lights in the passage and retired to bed. The air was still and frosty; moonlight over the roofs—one of those sharp and dry winter nights that now seem to visit London rarely.

"Like the old-fashioned days when we were boys," remarked William, pausing a moment by the passage window and looking out across the miles of silvery, sparkling roofs.

"Yes," added John; "the ponds freezing hard in the fields, rime on the nursery windows, and the sound of a horse's hoofs coming down the road in the distance, eh?" They smiled at the memory, then said good night, and separated. Their rooms were at opposite ends of the corridor; in between were the bathroom, dining-room, and sitting-room. It was a long, straggling flat. Half an hour later both brothers were sound asleep, the flat silent, only a dull murmur rising from the great city outside, and the moon sinking slowly to the level of the chimneys.

Perhaps two hours passed, perhaps three, when John Gilmer, sitting up in bed with a start, wide-awake and frightened, knew that someone was moving about in one of the three rooms that lay between him and his brother. He had absolutely no idea why he should have been frightened, for there was no dream or nightmare-memory that he brought over from unconsciousness, and yet he realized plainly that the fear he felt was by no means a foolish and unreasoning fear. It had a cause and a reason. Also—which made it worse—it was fully warranted. Something in his sleep, forgotten in the instant of waking, had happened that set every nerve in his body on the watch. He was positive only of two things— first, that it was the entrance of this person, moving so quietly there in the flat, that sent the chills down his spine; and, secondly, that this person was *not* his brother William.

John Gilmer was a timid man. The sight of a burglar, his eyes black-masked, suddenly confronting him in the passage, would most likely have deprived him of all power of decision—until the burglar had either shot him or escaped. But on this occasion some instinct told him that it was no burglar, and that the acute distress he experienced was not due to any message of ordinary physical fear. The thing that had gained access to his flat while he slept had first come—he felt sure of it—into his room, and had passed very close to his own bed, before going on. It had then doubtless gone to his brother's room, visiting them both stealthily to make sure they slept. And its mere passage through his room had been enough to wake him and set these drops of cold perspiration upon his skin. For it was—he felt it in every fibre of his body—something hostile.

The thought that it might at that very moment be in the room of his brother, however, brought him to his feet on the cold floor, and set him moving with all the determination he could summon towards the door. He looked cautiously down an utterly dark passage; then crept on tiptoe along it. On the wall were old-fashioned weapons that had belonged to his father; and feeling a curved, sheathless sword that had come from some Turkish campaign of years gone by, his fingers closed tightly round it, and lifted it silently from the three hooks whereon it lay. He passed the doors of the bathroom and dining-room, making instinctively for the big sitting-room where the violins were kept in their glass cases. The cold nipped him. His eyes smarted with the effort to see in the darkness. Outside the closed door he hesitated.

Putting his ear to the crack, he listened. From within came a faint sound of someone moving. The same instant there rose the sharp, delicate "ping" of a violin-string being plucked; and John Gilmer, with nerves that shook like the vibrations of that very string, opened the door wide with a fling and turned on the light at the same moment. The plucked string still echoed faintly in the air.

The sensation that met him on the threshold was the well-known one that things had been going on in the room which his unexpected arrival had that instant put a stop to. A second earlier and he would have discovered it all in the act. The atmosphere still held the feeling of rushing, silent movement with which the things had raced back to their normal, motionless positions. The immobility of the furniture was a mere attitude hurriedly assumed, and the moment his back was turned the whole business, whatever it might be, would begin again. With this presentment of the room, however—a purely imaginative one—came another, swiftly on its heels.

For one of the objects, less swift than the rest, had not quite regained its "attitude" of repose. It still moved. Below the window curtains on the right, not far from the shelf that bore the violins in their glass cases, he made it out, slowly gliding along the floor. Then, even as his eye caught it, it came to rest.

And, while the cold perspiration broke out all over him afresh, he knew that this still moving item was the cause both of his waking and of his terror. This was the disturbance whose presence he had divined in the flat without actual hearing, and whose passage through his room, while he yet slept, had touched every nerve in his body as with ice. Clutching his Turkish sword tightly, he drew back with the utmost caution against the wall and watched, for the singular impression came to him that the movement was not that of a human being crouching, but rather of something that pertained to the animal world. He remembered, flash-like, the movements of reptiles, the stealth of the larger felines, the undulating glide of great snakes. For the moment, however, it did not move, and they faced one another.

The other side of the room was but dimly lighted, and the noise he made clicking up another electric lamp brought the thing flying forward again—towards himself. At such a moment it seemed absurd to think of so small a detail, but he remembered his bare feet, and, genuinely frightened, he leaped upon a chair and swished with his sword through the air about him. From this better point of view, with the increased light to aid him, he then saw two things—first, that the glass case usually covering the Guarnerius violin had been shifted; and, secondly, that the moving object was slowly elongating itself into an upright position. Semi-erect, yet most oddly, too, like a creature on its hind legs, it was coming swiftly towards him. It was making for the door—and escape.

The confusion of ghostly fear was somehow upon him so that he was too bewildered to see clearly, but he had sufficient self-control, it seemed, to recover a certain power of action; for the moment the advancing figure was near enough for him to strike, that curved scimitar flashed and whirred about him, with such misdirected violence, however, that he not only failed to strike it even once, but at the same time lost his balance and fell forward from the chair whereon he perched—straight into it.

And then came the most curious thing of all, for as he dropped, the figure also dropped, stooped low down, crouched, dwindled amazingly in size, and rushed past him close to the ground like an animal on all fours. John Gilmer screamed, for he could no longer contain himself. Stumbling over the chair as he turned to follow, cutting and slashing wildly with his sword, he saw halfway down the darkened corridor beyond the scuttling outline of, apparently, an enormous—cat!

The door into the outer landing was somehow ajar, and the next second the beast was out, but not before the steel had fallen with a crashing blow upon the front disappearing leg, almost severing it from the body.

It was dreadful. Turning up the lights as he went, he ran after it to the outer landing. But the thing he followed was already well away, and he heard, on the floor below him, the same oddly gliding, slithering, stealthy sound, yet hurrying, that he had heard weeks before when something had passed him in the lift and Morgan, in his terror, had likewise cried aloud.

For a time he stood there on that dark landing, listening, thinking, trembling; then turned into the flat and shut the door. In the sitting-room he carefully replaced the glass case over the treasured violin, puzzled to the point of foolishness, and strangely routed in his mind. For the violin itself, he saw, had been dragged several inches from its cushioned bed of plush.

Next morning, however, he made no allusion to the occurrence of the night. His brother apparently had not been disturbed.

5

The only thing that called for explanation—an explanation not fully forthcoming—was the curious aspect of Mr. Morgan's countenance. The fact that this individual gave notice to the owners of the building, and at the end of the month left for a new post, was, of course, known to both brothers; whereas the story he told in explanation of his face was known only to the one who questioned him about it—John. And John, for reasons best known to himself, did not pass it on to the other. Also, for reasons best known to himself, he did not cross-question the liftman about those singular marks, or report the matter to the police.

Mr. Morgan's pasty visage was badly scratched, and there were red lines running from the cheek into the neck that had the appearance of having been produced by sharp points viciously applied—claws. He had been disturbed by a noise in the hall, he said, about three in the morning, a scuffle had ensued in the darkness, but the intruder had got. clear away....

"A cat or something of the kind, no doubt," suggested John Gilmer at the end of the brief recital. And Morgan replied in his usual way: "A cat, or something of the kind, Mr. John, no doubt."

All the same, he had not cared to risk a second encounter, but had departed to wear his billycock and uniform in a building less haunted.

Hyman, meanwhile, made no attempt to call and talk over his dismissal. The reason for this was only apparent, however, several months later when, quite by chance, coming along Piccadilly in an omnibus, the brothers found themselves seated opposite to a man with a thick black beard and blue glasses. William Gilmer hastily rang the bell and got out, saying something half intelligible about feeling faint. John followed him.

"Did you see who it was?" he whispered to his brother the moment they were safely on the pavement. John nodded.

"Hyman, in spectacles. He's grown a beard, too."

"Yes, but did you also notice—"

"What?"

"He had an empty sleeve."

"An empty sleeve?"

"Yes," said William; "he's lost an arm."

There was a long pause before John spoke. At the door of their club the elder brother added:

"Poor devil! He'll never again play on"—then, suddenly changing the preposition—"*with* a pedigree violin!"

And that night in the flat, after William had gone to bed, he looked up a curious old volume he had once picked up on a second-hand bookstall, and read therein quaint descriptions of how the "desire-body of a violent man'" may assume animal shape, operate on concrete matter even at a distance; and, further, how a wound inflicted thereon can reproduce itself upon its physical counterpart by means of the mysterious so-called phenomenon of "re-percussion."

WIRELESS CONFUSION

"Good night, Uncle," whispered the child, as she climbed on to his knee and gave him a resounding kiss. "It's time for me to disappop into bed—at least, so mother says."

"Disappop, then," he replied, returning her kiss, "although I doubt...." He hesitated. He remembered the word was her father's invention, descriptive of the way rabbits pop into their holes and disappear, and the way *good* children should leave the room the instant bed-time was announced. The father—his twin brother—seemed to enter the room and stand beside them. "Then give me another kiss, and disappop!" he said quickly. The child obeyed the first part of his injunction, but had not obeyed the second when the queer thing happened. She had not left his knee; he was still holding her at the full stretch of both arms; he was staring into her laughing eyes, when she suddenly went far away into an extraordinary distance. She retired. Minute, tiny, but still in perfect proportion and clear as before, she was withdrawn in space till she was small as a doll. He saw his own hands holding her, and they too were minute. Down this long corridor of space, as it were, he saw her diminutive figure.

"Uncle!" she cried, yet her voice was loud as before, "but what a funny face! You're pretending you've seen a ghost"—and she was gone from his knee and from the room, the door closing quietly behind her. He saw her cross the floor, a tiny figure. Then, just as she reached the door, she became of normal size again, as if she crossed a line.

He felt dizzy. The loud voice close to his ear issuing from a diminutive figure half a mile away had a distressing effect upon him. He knew a curious qualm as he sat there in the dark. He heard the wind walking round the house, trying the doors and windows. He was troubled by a memory he could not seize.

Yet the emotion instantly resolved itself into one of personal anxiety: something had gone wrong with his eyes. Sight, his most precious possession as an artist, was of course affected. He was conscious of a little trembling in him, as he at once began trying his sight at various objects—his hands, the high ceiling, the trees dim in the twilight on the lawn outside. He opened a book and read half a dozen lines, at changing distances; finally he stared carefully at the second hand of his watch. "Right as a trivet!" he exclaimed aloud. He emitted a long sigh; he was immensely relieved. "Nothing wrong with my eyes."

He thought about the actual occurrence a great deal—he felt as puzzled as any other normal person must have felt. While he held the child actually in his arms, gripping her with both hands, he had seen her suddenly half a mile away. "'Half a mile!" he repeated under his breath, "why it was even more, it was easily a mile." It had been exactly as though he suddenly looked at her down the wrong end of a powerful telescope. It had really happened; he could not explain it; there was no more to be said.

This was the first time it happened to him.

At the theatre, a week later, when the phenomenon was repeated, the stage he was watching fixedly at the moment went far away, as though he saw it from a long way off. The distance, so far as he could judge, was the same as before, about a mile. It was an Eastern scene, realistically costumed and produced, that without an instant's warning withdrew. The entire stage went with it, although he did not actually see it go. He did not see movement, that is. It was suddenly remote, while yet the actors' voices, the orchestra, the general hubbub retained their normal volume. He experienced again the distressing dizziness; he closed his eyes, covering them with his hand, then rubbing the eyeballs slightly; and when he looked up the next minute, the world was as it should be, as it had been, at any rate. Unwilling to experience a repetition of the thing in a public place, however, and fortunately being alone, he left the theatre at the end of the act.

Twice this happened to him, once with an individual, his brother's child, and once with a landscape, an Eastern stage scene. Both occurrences were within the week, during which time he had been considering a visit to the oculist, though without putting his decision into execution. He was the kind of man that dreaded doctors, dentists, oculists, always postponing, always finding reasons for delay. He found reasons now, the chief among them being an unwelcome one—that it was perhaps a brain specialist, rather than an oculist, he ought to consult. This particular notion hung unpleasantly about his mind, when, the day after the theatre visit, the thing recurred, but with a startling difference.

While idly watching a blue-bottle fly that climbed the window-pane with remorseless industry, only to slip down again at the very instant when escape into the open air was within its reach, the fly grew abruptly into gigantic proportions, became blurred and indistinct as it did so, covered the entire pane with its furry, dark, ugly mass, and frightened him so that he stepped back with a cry and nearly lost his balance altogether. He collapsed into a chair. He listened with closed eyes. The metallic buzzing was audible, a small, exasperating sound, ordinarily unable to stir any emotion beyond a mild annoyance. Yet it was terrible;

that so huge an insect should make so faint a sound seemed to him terrible.

At length he cautiously opened his eyes. The fly was of normal size once more. He hastily flicked it out of the window.

An hour later he was talking with the famous oculist in Harley Street... about the advisability of starting reading-glasses. He found it difficult to relate the rest. A curious shyness restrained him.

"Your optic nerves might belong to a man of twenty," was the verdict. "Both are perfect. But at your age it is wise to save the sight as much as possible. There is a slight astigmatism.... " And a prescription for the glasses was written out. It was only when paying the fee, and as a means of drawing attention from the awkward moment, that his story found expression. It seemed to come out in spite of himself. He made light of it even then, telling it without conviction. It seemed foolish suddenly as he told it. "How very odd," observed the oculist vaguely, "dear me, yes, curious indeed. But that's nothing. H'm, h'm!" Either it was no concern of his, or he deemed it negligible.... His only other confidant was a friend of psychological tendencies who was interested and eager to explain. It is on the instant plausible explanation of anything and everything that the reputation of such folk depends; this one was true to type: "A spontaneous invention, my dear fellow—a pictorial rendering of your thought. You are a painter, aren't you? Well, this is merely a rendering in picture-form of"—he paused for effect, the other hung upon his words—"of the odd expression 'disappop.'"

"Ah!" exclaimed the painter.

"You see everything pictorially, of course, don't you?"

"Yes—as a rule."

"There you have it. Your painter's psychology saw the child 'disappopping.' That's all."

"And the fly?" but the fly was easily explained, since it was merely the process reversed. "Once a process has established itself in your mind, you see, it may act in either direction. When a madman says 'I'm afraid Smith will do me an injury,' it means, 'I will do an injury to Smith.'" And he repeated with finality, "That's it."

The explanations were not very satisfactory, the illustration even tactless, but then the problem had not been stated quite fully. Neither to the oculist nor to the other had all the facts been given. The same shyness had been a restraining influence in both cases; a detail had been omitted, and this detail was that he connected the occurrences somehow with his brother whom the war had taken.

The phenomenon made one more appearance—the last—before its character, its field of action rather, altered. He was reading a book when the print became now large, now small; it blurred, grew remote and tiny, then so huge that a single word, a letter even, filled the whole page. He felt as if someone were playing optical tricks with the mechanism of his eyes, trying first one, then another focus.

More curious still, the meaning of the words themselves became uncertain; he did not understand them any more; the sentences lost their meaning, as though he read a strange language, or a language little known. The flash came then—someone was using his eyes—someone else was looking through them.

No, it was not his brother. The idea was preposterous in any ease. Yet he shivered again, as when he heard the walking wind, for an uncanny conviction came over him that it was someone who did not understand eyes but was manipulating their mechanism experimentally. With the conviction came also this: that, while not his brother, it was someone connected with his brother.

Here, moreover, was an explanation of sorts, for if the supernatural existed—he had never troubled his head about it—he could accept this odd business as a manifestation, and leave it at that. He did so, and his mind was eased. This was his attitude: "The supernatural *may* exist. Why not? We cannot know. But we can watch." His eyes and brain, at any rate, were proved in good condition.

He watched. No change of focus, no magnifying or diminishing, came again. For some weeks he noticed nothing unusual of any kind, except that his mind often filled now with Eastern pictures. Their sudden irruption caught his attention, but no more than that; they were sometimes blurred and sometimes vivid; he had never been in the East; he attributed them to his constant thinking of his brother, missing in Mesopotamia these six months. Photographs in magazines and newspapers explained the rest. Yet the persistence of the pictures puzzled him: tents beneath hot cloudless skies, palms, a stretch of desert, dry watercourses, camels, a mosque, a minaret—typical snatches of this kind flashed into his mind with a sense of faint familiarity often. He knew, again, the return of a fugitive memory he could not seize.... He kept a note of the dates, all of them subsequent to the day he read his brother's fate in the official Roll of Honour: "Believed missing; now killed." Only when the original phenomenon returned, but in its altered form, did he stop the practice. The change then affected his life too fundamentally to trouble about mere dates and pictures.

For the phenomenon, shifting its field of action, abruptly became mental, and the singular change of focus took place now in his mind. Events magnified or contracted themselves out of all relation with their intrinsic values, sense of proportion went hopelessly astray. Love, hate and fear experienced sudden intensification, or abrupt dwindling into nothing; the familiar everyday emotions, commonplace daily acts, suffered exaggerated enlargement, or reduction into insignificance, that threatened the stability of his personality. Fortunately, as stated, they were of brief duration; to examine them in detail were to touch the painful absurdities of incipient mania almost; that a lost collar stud could block his exasperated mind for hours, filling an entire day with emotion, while a deep affection of long standing could ebb towards complete collapse suddenly without apparent cause...!

It was the unexpected suddenness of Turkey's spectacular defeat that closed the painful symptoms. The Armistice saw them go. He knew a quick relief he was unable to explain. The telegram that his brother was alive and safe came *after* his recovery of mental balance. It was a shock. But the phenomena had ceased before the shock.

It was in the light of his brother's story that he reviewed the puzzling phenomena described. The story was not more curious than many another, perhaps, yet the details were queer enough. That a wounded Turk to whom he gave water should have remembered gratitude was likely enough, for all travellers know that these men are kindly gentlemen at times; but that this Mohammedan peasant should have been later a member of a prisoner's escort and have provided the means of escape and concealment—weeks in a dry watercourse and months in a hut outside the town—seemed an incredible stroke of good fortune. "He brought me food and water three times a week. I had no money to give him, so I gave him my Zeiss glasses. I taught him a bit of English too. But he liked the glasses best. He was never tired of playing with 'em—making big and little, as he called it. He learned precious little English...."

"My pair, weren't they?" interrupted his brother. "My old climbing glasses."

"Your present to me when I went out, yes. So really you helped me to save my life. I told the old Turk that. I was always thinking about you."

"And the Turk?"

"No doubt.... Through *my* mind, that is. At any rate, he asked a lot of questions about you. I showed him your photo. He died, poor chap—at least they told me so. Probably they shot him."

CONFESSION

The fog swirled slowly round him, driven by a heavy movement of its own, for of course there was no wind. It hung in poisonous thick coils and loops; it rose and sank; no light penetrated it directly from street lamp or motor-car, though here and there some big shop-window shed a glimmering patch upon its ever-shifting curtain.

O'Reilly's eyes ached and smarted with the incessant effort to see a foot beyond his face. The optic nerve grew tired, and sight, accordingly, less accurate. He coughed as he shuffled forward cautiously through the choking gloom. Only the stifled rumble of crawling traffic persuaded him he was in a crowded city at all—this, and the vague outlines of groping figures, hugely magnified, emerging suddenly and disappearing again, as they fumbled along inch by inch towards uncertain destinations.

The figures, however were human beings; they were real. That much he knew. He heard their muffled voices, now close, now distant, strangely smothered always. He also heard the tapping of innumerable sticks, feeling for iron railings or the kerb. These phantom outlines represented living people. He was not alone.

It was the dread of finding himself *quite* alone that haunted him, for he was still unable to cross an open space without assistance. He had the physical strength, it was the mind that failed him. Midway the panic terror might descend upon him, he would shake all over, his will dissolve, he would shriek for help, run wildly—into the traffic probably—or, as they called it in his North Ontario home, "throw a fit" in the street before advancing wheels. He was not yet entirely cured, although under ordinary conditions he was safe enough, as Dr. Henry had assured him.

When he left Regent's Park by Tube an hour ago the air was clear, the November sun shone brightly, the pale blue sky was cloudless, and the assumption that he could manage the journey across London Town alone was justified. The following day he was to leave for Brighton for the week of final convalescence: this little preliminary test of his powers on a bright November afternoon was all to the good. Doctor Henry furnished minute instructions: "You change at Piccadilly Circus—without leaving the underground station, mind—and get out at South Kensington. You know the address of your V.A.D. friend. Have your cup of tea with her, then come back the same way to Regent's Park. Come back before dark—say six o'clock at latest. It's better." He had described exactly what turns to take after leaving the station, so many to the right, so many to the left; it was a little confusing, but the distance was short. "You can always ask. You can't possibly go wrong."

The unexpected fog, however, now blurred these instructions in a confused jumble in his mind. The failure of outer sight reacted upon memory. The V.A.D. besides had warned him her address was "not easy to find the first time. The house lies in a backwater. But with your 'backwoods' instincts you'll probably manage it better than any Londoner!" She, too, had not calculated upon the fog.

When O'Reilly cane up the stairs at South Kensington Station, he emerged into such murky darkness that he thought he was still underground. An impenetrable world lay round him. Only a raw bite in the damp atmosphere told him he stood beneath an open sky. For some little time he stood and stared—a Canadian soldier, his home among clear brilliant spaces, now face to face for the first time in his life with that thing he had so often read about—a bad London fog. With keenest interest and surprise he "enjoyed" the novel spectacle for perhaps ten minutes, watching the people arrive and vanish, and wondering why the station lights stopped dead the instant they touched the street—then, with a sense of adventure—it cost an effort—he left the covered building and plunged into the opaque sea beyond.

Repeating to himself the directions he had received—first to the right, second to the left, once more to the left, and so forth—he checked each turn, assuring himself it was impossible to go wrong. He made correct if slow progress, until someone blundered into him with an abrupt and startling question: "Is this right, do you know, for South Kensington Station?"

It was the suddenness that startled him; one moment there was no one, the next they were face to face, another, and the stranger had vanished into the gloom with a courteous word of grateful thanks. But the little shock of interruption had put memory out of gear. Had he already turned twice to the right, or had he not? O'Reilly realized sharply he had forgotten his memorized instructions. He stood still, making strenuous efforts at recovery, but each effort left him more uncertain than before. Five minutes later he was lost as hopelessly as any townsman who leaves his tent in the backwoods without blazing the trees to ensure finding his way back again.

Even the sense of direction, so strong in him among his native forests, was completely gone. There were no stars, there was no wind, no smell, no sound of running water. There was nothing anywhere to guide him, nothing but occasional dim outlines, groping, shuffling, emerging and disappearing in the eddying fog, but rarely coming within actual speaking, much less touching, distance. He was lost utterly; more, he was alone.

Yet not *quite* alone—the thing he dreaded most. There were figures still in his immediate neighborhood. They emerged, vanished, reappeared, dissolved. No, he was not quite alone. He saw these thickenings of the fog, he heard their voices, the tapping of their cautious sticks, their shuffling feet as well. They were real. They moved, it seemed, about him in a circle, never coming very close.

"But they're real," he said to himself aloud, betraying the weak point in his armour. "They're human beings right enough. I'm positive of that."

He had never argued with Dr. Henry—he wanted to get well; he had obeyed implicitly, believing everything the doctor told him—up to a point. But he had always had his own idea about these "figures," because, among them, were often enough his own pals from the Somme, Gallipoli, the Mespot horror, too. And he ought to know his own pals when he saw them! At the same time he knew quite well he had been "shocked," his being dislocated; half dissolved as it were, his system pushed into some lopsided condition that meant inaccurate registration. True. He grasped that perfectly. But, in that shock and dislocation, had he not possibly picked up another gear? Were there not gaps and broken edges, pieces that no longer dovetailed, fitted as usual, interstices, in a word? Yes, that was the word—interstices. Cracks, so to speak, between his perception of the outside world and his inner interpretation of these? Between memory and recognition? Between the various states of consciousness that usually dovetailed so neatly that the joints were normally imperceptible?

His state, he well knew, was abnormal, but were his symptoms on that account unreal? Could not these "interstices" be used by—others? When he saw his "figures," he used to ask himself: "Are not these the real ones, and the others—the human beings—unreal?"

This question now revived in him with a new intensity. Were these figures in the fog real or unreal? The man who had asked the way to the station, was he not, after all, a shadow merely?

By the use of his cane and foot and what of sight was left to him he knew that he was on an island. A lamppost stood up solid and straight beside him, shedding its faint patch of glimmering light. Yet there were railings, however, that puzzled him, for his stick hit the metal rods distinctly in a series. And there should be no railings round an island. Yet he had most certainly crossed a dreadful open space to get where he was. His confusion and bewilderment increased with dangerous rapidity. Panic was not far away.

He was no longer on an omnibus route. A rare taxi crawled past occasionally, a whitish patch at the window indicating an anxious human face; now and again came a van or cart, the driver holding a lantern as he led the stumbling horse. These comforted him, rare though they were. But it was the figures that drew his attention most. He was quite sure they were real. They were human beings like himself.

For all that, he decided he might as well be positive on the point. He tried one accordingly—a big man who rose suddenly before him out of the very earth.

"Can you give me the trail to Morley Place?" he asked.

But his question was drowned by the other's simultaneous inquiry in a voice much louder than his own.

"I say, is this right for the Tube station, d'you know? I'm utterly lost. I want South Ken."

And by the time O'Reilly had pointed the direction whence he himself had just come, the man was gone again, obliterated, swallowed up, not so much as his footsteps audible, almost as if—it seemed again—he never had been there at all.

This left an acute unpleasantness in him, a sense of bewilderment greater than before. He waited five minutes, not daring to move a step, then tried another figure, a woman this time who, luckily, knew the immediate neighbourhood intimately. She gave him elaborate instructions in the kindest possible way, then vanished with incredible swiftness and ease into the sea of gloom beyond. The instantaneous way she vanished was disheartening, upsetting; it was so uncannily abrupt and sudden. Yet she comforted him. Morley Place, according to her version, was not two hundred yards from where he stood. He felt his way forward, step by step, using his cane, crossing a giddy open space kicking the kerb with each boot alternately, coughing and choking all the time as he did so.

"They were real, I guess, anyway," he said aloud. "'They were both real enough all right. And it may lift a bit soon!" He was making a great effort to hold himself in hand. He was already fighting, that is. He realized this perfectly. The only point was—the reality of the figures. "It may lift now any minute," he repeated louder. In spite of the cold, his skin was sweating profusely.

But, of course, it did not lift. The figures, too, became fewer. No carts were audible. He had followed the woman's directions carefully, but now found himself in some by-way, evidently, where pedestrians at the best of times were rare. There was dull silence all about him. His foot lost the kerb, his cane swept the empty air, striking nothing solid, and panic rose upon him with its shuddering, icy grip. He was alone, he knew himself alone, worse still—he was in another open space.

It took him fifteen minutes to cross that open space, most of the way upon his hands and knees, oblivious of the icy slime that stained his trousers, froze his fingers, intent only upon feeling solid support against his back and spine again. It was an endless period. The moment of collapse was close, the shriek already rising in his throat, the shaking of the whole body uncontrollable, when—his outstretched fingers struck a friendly kerb, and he saw a glimmering patch of diffused radiance overhead. With a great, quick effort he stood upright, and an instant later his stick rattled along an area railing. He leaned against it, breathless, panting, his heart beating painfully while the street lamp gave him the further comfort of its feeble gleam, the actual flame, however, invisible. He looked this way and that; the pavement was deserted. He was engulfed in the dark silence of the fog.

But Morley Place, he knew, must be very close by now. He thought of the friendly little V.A.D. he had known in France, of a warm bright fire, a cup of tea and a cigarette. One more effort, he reflected, and all these would be his. He pluckily groped his way forward again, crawling slowly by the area railings. If things got really bad again, he would ring a bell and ask for help, much as he shrank from the idea. Provided he had no more open spaces to cross, provided he saw no more figures emerging and vanishing like creatures born of the fog and dwelling within it as within their native element—it was the figures he now dreaded more than anything else, more even than the loneliness—provided the panic sense—

A faint darkening of the fog beneath the next lamp caught his eye and made him start. He stopped. It was not a figure this time, it. was the shadow of the pole grotesquely magnified. No, it moved. It moved towards him. A flame of fire followed by ice flowed through him. It was a figure—close against his face. It was a woman.

The doctor's advice came suddenly back to him, the counsel that had cured him of a hundred phantoms:

"Do not ignore them. Treat them as real. Speak and go with them. You will soon prove their unreality then. And they will leave you...."

He made a brave, tremendous effort. He was shaking. One hand clutched the damp and icy area railing.

"Lost your way like myself, haven't you, ma'am?" he said in a voice that trembled. "Do you know where we are at all? Morley Place *I'm* looking for—"

He stopped dead. The woman moved nearer and for the first time he saw her face clearly. Its ghastly pallor, the bright, frightened eyes that stared with a kind of dazed bewilderment into his own, the beauty above all, arrested his speech midway. The woman was young, her tall figure wrapped in a dark fur coat.

"Can I help you?" he asked impulsively, forgetting his own terror for the moment. He was more than startled. Her air of distress and pain stirred a peculiar anguish in him. For a moment she made no answer, thrusting her white face closer as if examining him, so close, indeed, that he controlled with difficulty his instinct to shrink back a little.

"Where am I?" she asked at length, searching his eyes intently. "I'm lost—I've lost myself. I can't find my way back." Her voice was low, a curious wailing in it that touched his pity oddly. He felt his own distress merging in one that was greater.

"Same here," he replied more confidently. "I'm terrified of being alone, too. I've had shell-shock, you know. Let's go together. We'll find a way together—"

"Who are you!" the woman murmured, still staring at him with her big bright eyes, their distress, however, no whit lessened. She gazed at him as though aware suddenly of his presence.

He told her briefly. "And I'm going to tea with a V.A.D. friend in Morley Place. What's your address? Do you know the name of the street?"

She appeared not to hear him, or not to understand exactly; it was as if she was not listening again.

"I came out so suddenly, so unexpectedly," he heard the low voice with pain in every syllable; "I can't find my home again. Just when I was expecting him too—" She looked about her with a distraught expression that made O'Reilly long to carry her in his arms to safety then and there. "He may be there now—waiting for me at this very moment—and I can't get back." And so sad was her voice that only by an effort did O'Reilly prevent himself putting out his hand to touch her. More and more he forgot himself in his desire to help her. Her beauty, the wonder of her strange bright eyes in the pallid face, made an immense appeal. He became calmer. This woman was real enough. He asked again the address, the street and number, the distance she thought it was. "Have you any idea of the direction, ma'am, any idea at all? We'll go together and—"

She suddenly cut him short. She turned her head as if to listen, so that he saw her profile a moment, the outline of the slender neck, a glimpse of jewels just below the fur.

"Hark! I hear him calling! I remember...!" And she was gone from his side into the swirling fog.

Without an instant's hesitation O'Reilly followed her, not only because he wished to help, but because he dared not be left alone. The presence of this strange, lost woman comforted him; he must not lose sight of her, whatever happened. He had to run, she went so rapidly, ever just in front, moving with confidence and certainty, turning right and left, crossing the street, but never stopping, never hesitating, her companion always at her heels in breathless haste, and with a growing terror that he might lose her any minute. The way she found her direction through the dense fog was marvellous enough, but O'Reilly's only thought was to keep her in sight, lest his own panic redescend upon him with its inevitable collapse in the dark and lonely street. It was a wild and panting pursuit, and he kept her in view with difficulty, a dim fleeting outline always a few yards ahead of him. She did not once turn her head, she uttered no sound, no cry; she hurried forward with unfaltering instinct. Nor did the chase occur to him once as singular; she was his safety, and that was all he realized.

One thing, however, he remembered afterwards, though at the actual time he no more than registered the detail, paying no attention to it—a definite perfume she left upon the atmosphere, one, moreover, that he knew, although he could not find its name as he ran. It was associated vaguely, for him, with something unpleasant, something disagreeable. He connected it with misery and pain. It gave him a feeling of uneasiness. More than that he did not notice at the moment, nor could he remember—he certainly did not try—where he had known this particular scent before.

Then suddenly the woman stopped, opened a gate and passed into a small private garden—so suddenly that O'Reilly, close upon her heels, only just avoided tumbling into her. "You've found it?" he cried. "May I come in a moment with you? Perhaps you'll let me telephone to the doctor."

She turned instantly. Her face close against his own, was livid.

"Doctor!" she repeated in an awful whisper. The word meant terror to her. O'Reilly stood amazed. For a second or two neither of them moved. The woman seemed petrified.

"Dr. Henry, you know," he stammered, finding his tongue again. "I'm in his care. He's in Harley Street."

Her face cleared as suddenly as it had darkened, though the original expression of bewilderment and pain still hung in her great eyes. But the terror left them, as though she suddenly forgot some association that had revived it.

"My home," she murmured. "My home is somewhere here. I'm near it. I must get back—in time—for him. I must. He's coming to me." And with these extraordinary words she turned, walked up the narrow path, and stood upon the porch of a two-storey house before her companion had recovered from his astonishment sufficiently to move or utter a syllable in reply. The front door, he saw, was ajar. It had been left open.

For five seconds, perhaps for ten, he hesitated; it was the fear that the door would close and shut him out that brought the decision to his will and muscles. He ran up the steps and followed the woman into a dark hall where she had already preceded him, and amid whose blackness she now had finally vanished. He closed the door, not knowing exactly why he did so, and knew at once by an instinctive feeling that the house he now found himself in with this unknown woman was empty and unoccupied. In a house, however, he felt safe. It was the open streets that were his danger. He stood waiting, listening a moment before he spoke; and he heard the woman moving down the passage from door to door, repeating to herself in her low voice of unhappy wailing some words he could not understand:

"Where is it? Oh, where is it? I must get back...."

O'Reilly then found himself abruptly stricken with dumbness, as though, with these strange words, a haunting terror came up and breathed against him in the darkness.

"Is she after all a figure?" ran in letters of fire across his numbed brain. "Is she unreal—or real?"

Seeking relief in action of some kind, he put out a hand automatically, feeling along the wall for an electric switch, and though he found it by some miraculous chance, no answering glow responded to the click.

And the woman's voice from the darkness: "Ah! Ah! At last I've found it. I'm home again—at last...!" He heard a door open and close upstairs. He was on the ground-floor now—alone. Complete silence followed.

In the conflict of various emotions—fear for himself lest his panic should return, fear for the woman who had led him into this empty house and now deserted him upon some mysterious errand of her own that made him think of madness—in this conflict, that held him a moment spellbound, there was a yet bigger ingredient demanding instant explanation, but an explanation that he could not find. Was the woman real or was she unreal? Was she a human being or a "figure"? The horror of doubt obsessed him with an acute uneasiness that betrayed itself in a return of that unwelcome inner trembling he knew was dangerous.

What saved him from a *crise* that must have had most dangerous results for his mind and nervous system generally, seems to have been the outstanding fact that he felt more for the woman than for himself. His sympathy and pity had been deeply moved; her voice, her beauty, her anguish and bewilderment, all uncommon, inexplicable, mysterious, formed together a claim that drove self into the background. Added to this was the detail that she had left him, gone to another floor without a word, and now, behind a closed door in a room upstairs, found herself face to face at last with the unknown object of her frantic search—with "it," whatever "it" might be. Real or unreal, figure or human being, the overmastering impulse of his being was that he must go to her.

It was this clear impulse that gave him decision and energy to do what he then did. He struck a match, he found a stump of candle, he made his way by means of this flickering light along the passage and up the carpetless stairs. He moved cautiously, stealthily, though not knowing why he did so. The house, he now saw, was indeed untenanted; dust-sheets covered the piled-up furniture; he glimpsed through doors ajar, pictures were screened upon the walls, brackets draped to look like hooded heads. He went on slowly, steadily, moving on tiptoe as though conscious of being watched, noting the well of darkness in the hall below, the grotesque shadows that his movements cast on walls and ceiling. The silence was unpleasant, yet, remembering that the woman was "expecting" someone, he did not wish it broken. He reached the landing and stood still. Closed doors on both sides of a corridor met his sight, as he shaded the candle to examine the scene. Behind which of these doors, he asked himself, was the woman, figure or human being, now alone with "it"?

There was nothing to guide him, but an instinct that he must not delay sent him forward again upon his search. He tried a door on the right—an empty room, with the furniture hidden by dust-sheets, and the mattress rolled up on the bed. He tried a second door, leaving the first one open behind him, and it was, similarly, an empty bedroom. Coming out into the corridor again he stood a moment waiting, then called aloud in a low voice that yet woke echoes unpleasantly in the hall below: "Where are you? I want to help—which room are you in?"

There was no answer; he was almost glad he heard no sound, for he knew quite well that he was waiting really for another sound—the steps of him who was "expected." And the idea of meeting with this unknown third sent a shudder through him, as though related to an interview he dreaded with his whole heart, and must at all costs avoid. Waiting another moment or two, he noted that his candle-stump was burning low, then crossed the landing with a feeling, at once of hesitation and determination, towards a door opposite to him. He opened it; he did not halt on the threshold. Holding the candle at arm's length, he went boldly in.

And instantly his nostrils told him he was right at last, for a whiff of the strange perfume, though this time much stronger than before, greeted him, sending a new quiver along his nerves. He knew now why it was associated with unpleasantness, with pain, with misery, for he recognized it—the odour of a hospital. In this room a powerful anæsthetic had been used—and recently.

Simultaneously with smell, sight brought its message too. On the large double bed behind the door on his right lay, to his amazement, the woman in the dark fur coat. He saw the jewels on the slender neck; but the eyes he did not see, for they were closed—closed, too, he grasped at once, in death. The body lay stretched at full length, quite motionless. He approached. A dark thin streak that came from the parted lips and passed downwards over the chin, losing itself then in the fur collar, was a trickle of blood. It was hardly dry. It glistened.

Strange it was perhaps that, while imaginary fears had the power to paralyse him, mind and body, this sight of something real had the effect of restoring confidence. The sight of blood and death, amid conditions often ghastly and even monstrous, was no new thing to him. He went up quietly, and with steady hand he felt the woman's cheek, the warmth of recent life still in its softness. The final cold had not yet mastered this empty form whose beauty, in its perfect stillness, had taken on the new strange sweetness of an unearthly bloom. Pallid, silent, untenanted, it lay before him, lit by the flicker of his guttering candle. He lifted the fur coat to feel for the unbeating heart. A couple of hours ago at most, he judged, this heart was working busily, the breath came through those parted lips, the eyes were shining in full beauty. His hand encountered a hard knob—the head of a long steel hat-pin driven through the heart up to its hilt.

He knew then which was the figure—which was the real and which the unreal. He knew also what had been meant by "it."

But before he could think or reflect what action he must take, before he could straighten himself even from his bent position over the body on the bed, there sounded through the empty house below the loud clang of the front door being closed. And instantly rushed over him that other fear he had so long forgotten—fear for himself. The panic of his own shaken nerves descended with irresistible onslaught. He turned, extinguishing the candle in the violent trembling of his hand, and tore headlong from the room.

The following ten minutes seemed a nightmare in which he was not master of himself and knew not exactly what he did. All he realized was that steps already sounded on the stairs, coming quickly nearer. The flicker of an electric torch played. on the banisters, whose shadows ran swiftly sideways along the wall as the hand that held the light ascended. He thought in a frenzied second of police, of his presence in the house, of the murdered woman. It was a sinister combination. Whatever happened, he must escape without being so much as even seen. His heart raced madly. He darted across the landing into the room opposite, whose door he had luckily left open. And by some incredible chance, apparently, he was neither seen nor heard by the man who, a moment later, reached the landing, entered the room where the body of the woman lay, and closed the door carefully behind him.

Shaking, scarcely daring to breathe lest his breath be audible, O'Reilly, in the grip of his own personal terror, remnant of his uncured shock of war, had no thought of what duty might demand or not demand of him. He thought only of himself. He realized one clear issue—that he must get out of the house without being heard or seen. Who the new-comer was he did not know, beyond an uncanny assurance that it was *not* him whom the woman had "expected," but the murderer himself, and that it was the murderer, in his turn, who was expecting this third person. In that room with death at his elbow, a death he had himself brought about but an hour or two ago, the murderer now hid in waiting for his second victim. And the door was closed.

Yet any minute it might open again, cutting off retreat.

O'Reilly crept out, stole across the landing, reached the head of the stairs, and began, with the utmost caution, the perilous descent. Each time the bare boards creaked beneath his weight, no matter how stealthily this weight was adjusted, his heart missed a beat. He tested each step before he pressed upon it, distributing as much of his weight as he dared upon the banisters. It was a little more than half-way down that, to his horror, his foot caught in a projecting carpet tack; he slipped on the polished wood, and only saved himself from falling headlong by a wild clutch at the railing, making an uproar that seemed to him like the explosion of a hand-grenade in the forgotten trenches. His nerves gave way then, and panic seized him. In the silence that followed the resounding echoes he heard the bedroom door opening on the floor above.

Concealment was now useless. It was impossible, too. He took the last flight of stairs in a series of leaps, four steps at a time, reached the hall, flew across it, and opened the front door, just as his pursuer, electric torch in hand, covered half the stairs behind him. Slamming the door, he plunged headlong into the welcome, all-obscuring fog outside.

The fog had now no terrors for him, he welcomed its concealing mantle; nor did it matter in which direction he ran so long as he put distance between him and the house of death. The pursuer had, of course, not followed him into the street. He crossed open spaces without a tremor. He ran in a circle nevertheless, though without being aware he did so. No people were about, no single groping shadow passed him; no boom of traffic reached his ears, when he paused for breath at length against an area railing. Then for the first time he made the discovery that he had no hat. He remembered now. In examining the body, partly out of respect, partly perhaps unconsciously, he had taken it off and laid it—on the very bed.

It was there, a tell-tale bit of damning evidence, in the house of death. And a series of probable consequences flashed through his mind like lightning. It was a new hat fortunately; more fortunate still, he had not yet written name or initials in it; but the maker's mark was there for all to read, and the police would go immediately to the shop where he had bought it only two days before. Would the shop-people remember his appearance? Would his visit, the date, the conversation be recalled? He thought it was unlikely; he resembled dozens of men; he had no outstanding peculiarity. He tried to think, but his mind was confused and troubled, his heart was beating dreadfully, he felt desperately ill. He sought vainly for some story to account for his being out in the fog and far from home without a hat. No single idea presented itself.

He clung to the icy railings, hardly able to keep upright, collapse very near—when suddenly a figure emerged from the fog, paused a moment to stare at him, put out a hand and caught him, and then spoke:

"You're ill, my dear sir," said a man's kindly voice. "Can I be of any assistance? Come, let me help you." He had seen at once that it was not a case of drunkenness. "Come, take my arm, won't you? I'm a physician. Luckily, too, you are just outside my very house. Come in." And he half dragged, half pushed O'Reilly, now bordering on collapse, up the steps and opened the door with his latch-key.

"Felt ill suddenly—lost in the fog... terrified, but be all right soon, thanks awfully—" the Canadian stammered his gratitude, but already feeling better. He sank into a chair in the hall, while the other put down a paper parcel he had been carrying, and led him presently into a comfortable room; a fire burned brightly; the electric lamps were pleasantly shaded; a decanter of whisky and a siphon stood on a small table beside a big arm-chair; and before O'Reilly could find another word to say the other had poured him out a glass and bade him sip it slowly, without troubling to talk till he felt better.

"That will revive you. Better drink it slowly. You should never have been out a night like this. If you've far to go, better let me put you up—"

"Very kind, very kind, indeed," mumbled O'Reilly, recovering rapidly in the comfort of a presence he already liked and felt even drawn to.

"No trouble at all," returned the doctor. "I've been at the front, you know. I can see what your trouble is—shell-shock, I'll be bound."

The Canadian, much impressed by the other's quick diagnosis, noted also his tact and kindness. He had made no reference to the absence of a hat, for instance.

"Quite true," he said. "I'm with Dr. Henry, in Harley Street," and he added a few words about his case. The whisky worked its effect, he revived more and more, feeling better every minute. The other handed him a cigarette; they began to talk about his symptoms and recovery; confidence returned in a measure, though he still felt badly frightened. The doctor's manner and personality did much to help, for there was strength and gentleness in the face, though the features showed unusual determination, softened occasionally by a sudden hint as of suffering in the bright, compelling eyes. It was the face, thought O'Reilly, of a man who had seen much and probably been through hell, but of a man who was simple, good, sincere. Yet not a man to trifle with; behind his gentleness lay something very stern. This effect of character and personality woke the other's respect in addition to his gratitude. His sympathy was stirred.

"You encourage me to make another guess," the man was saying, after a successful reading of the impromptu patient's state, "that you have had, namely, a severe shock quite recently, and"—he hesitated for the merest fraction of a second—"that it would be a relief to you," he went on, the skilful suggestion in the voice unnoticed by his companion, "it would be wise as well, if you could unburden yourself to—someone—who would understand." He looked at O'Reilly with a kindly and very pleasant smile. "Am I not right, perhaps?" he asked in his gentle tone.

"Someone who would understand," repeated the Canadian. "That's my trouble exactly. You've hit it. It's all so incredible."

The other smiled. "The more incredible," he suggested, "the greater your need for expression. Suppression, as you may know, is dangerous in cases like this. You think you have hidden it, but it bides its time and comes up later, causing a lot of trouble. Confession, you know"—he emphasized the word—"confession is good for the soul!"

"You're dead right," agreed the other.

"Now if you can, bring yourself to tell it to someone who will listen and believe—to myself, for instance. I am a doctor, familiar with such things. I shall regard all you say as a professional confidence, of course; and, as we are strangers, my belief or disbelief is of no particular consequence. I may tell you in advance of your story, however—I think I can promise it—that I shall believe all you have to say."

O'Reilly told his story without more ado, for the suggestion of the skilled physician had found easy soil to work in. During the recital his host's eyes never once left his own. He moved no single muscle of his body. His interest seemed intense.

"A bit tall, isn't it?" said the Canadian, when his tale was finished. "And the question is—" he continued with a threat of volubility which the other checked instantly.

"Strange, yes, but incredible, no," the doctor interrupted. "I see no reason to disbelieve a single detail of what you have just told me. Things equally remarkable, equally incredible, happen in all large towns, as I know from personal experience. I could give you instances." He paused a moment, but his companion, staring into his eyes with interest and curiosity, made no comment. "Some years ago, in fact," continued the other, "I knew of a very similar case—strangely similar."

"Really! I should be immensely interested—"

"So similar that it seems almost a coincidence. You may find it hard, in your turn, to credit it." He paused again, while O'Reilly sat forward in his chair to listen. "Yes," pursued the doctor slowly, "I think everyone connected with it is now dead. There is no reason why I should not tell it, for one confidence deserves another, you know. It happened during the Boer War—as long ago as that," he added with emphasis. "It is really a very commonplace story in one way, though very dreadful in another, but a man who has served at the front will understand and—I'm sure—will sympathize."

"I'm sure of that," offered the other readily.

"A colleague of mine, now dead, as I mentioned—a surgeon, with a big practice, married a young and charming girl. They lived happily together for several years. His wealth made her very comfortable. His consulting-room, I must tell you, was some distance from his house—just as this might be—so that she was never bothered with any of his cases. Then came the war. Like many others, though much over age, he volunteered. He gave up his lucrative practice and went to South Africa. His income, of course, stopped; the big house was closed; his wife found her life of enjoyment considerably curtailed. This she considered a great hardship, it seems. She felt a bitter grievance against him. Devoid of imagination, without any power of sacrifice, a selfish type, she was yet a beautiful, attractive woman—and young. The inevitable lover came upon the scene to console her. They planned to run away together. He was rich. Japan they thought would suit them. Only, by some ill luck, the husband got wind of it and arrived in London just in the nick of time."

"Well rid of her," put in O'Reilly, "I think."

The doctor waited a moment. He sipped his glass. Then his eyes fixed upon his companion's face somewhat sternly.

"Well rid of her, yes," he continued, "only he determined to make that riddance final. He decided to kill her—and her lover. You see, he loved her."

O'Reilly made no comment. In his own country this method with a faithless woman was not unknown. His interest was very concentrated. But he was thinking, too, as he listened, thinking hard.

"He planned the time and place with care," resumed the other in a lower voice, as though he might possibly be overheard. "They met, he knew, in the big house, now closed, the house where he and his young wife had passed such happy years during their prosperity. The plan failed, however, in an important detail—the woman came at the appointed hour, but without her lover. She found death waiting for her—it was a painless death. Then her lover, who was to arrive half an hour later, did not come at all. The door had been left open for him purposely. The house was dark, its rooms shut up, deserted; there was no caretaker even. It was a foggy night, just like this."

"And the other?" asked O'Reilly in a failing voice. "The lover—"

"A man did come in," the doctor went on calmly, "but it was not the lover. It was a stranger."

"A stranger?" the other whispered. "And the surgeon—where was he all this time?"

"Waiting outside to see him enter—concealed in the fog. He saw the man go in. Five minutes later he followed, meaning to complete his vengeance, his act of justice, whatever you like to call it. But the man who had come in was a stranger—he came in by chance—just as you might have done—to shelter from the fog—or—"

O'Reilly, though with a great effort, rose abruptly to his feet. He had an appalling feeling that the man facing him was mad. He had a keen desire to get outside, fog or no fog, to leave this room, to escape from the calm accents of this insistent voice. The effect of the whisky was still in his blood. He felt no lack of confidence. But words came to him with difficulty.

"I think I'd better be pushing off now, doctor," he said clumsily. "But I feel I must thank you very much for all your kindness and help." He turned and looked hard into the keen eyes facing him. "Your friend," he asked in a whisper, "the surgeon—I hope—I mean, was he ever caught?"

"No," was the grave reply, the doctor standing up in front of him, "he was never caught." O'Reilly waited a moment before he made another remark. "Well," he said at length, but in a louder tone than before, "I think—I'm glad." He went to the door without shaking hands.

"You have no hat," mentioned the voice behind him. "If you'll wait a moment I'll get you one of mine. You need not trouble to return it." And the doctor passed him, going into the hall. There was a sound of tearing paper, O'Reilly left the house a moment later with a hat upon his head, but it was not till he reached the Tube station half an hour afterwards that he realized it was his own.

THE LANE THAT RAN EAST AND WEST

1

The curving strip of lane, fading into invisibility east and west, had always symbolized life to her. In some minds life pictures itself a straight line, uphill, downhill, flat, as the case may be; in hers it had been, since childhood, this sweep of country lane that ran past her cottage door. In thick white summer dust, she invariably visualized it, blue and yellow flowers along its untidy banks of green. It flowed, it glided, sometimes it rushed. Without a sound it ran along past the nut trees and the branches where honeysuckle and wild roses shone. With every year now its silent speed increased.

From either end she imagined, as a child, that she looked over into outer space—from the eastern end into the infinity before birth, from the western into the infinity that follows death. It was to her of real importance.

From the veranda the entire stretch was visible, not more than five hundred yards at most; from the platform in her mind, whence she viewed existence, she saw her own life, similarly, as a white curve of flowering lane, arising she knew not whence, gliding whither she could not tell. At eighteen she had paraphrased the quatrain with a smile upon her red lips, her chin tilted, her strong grey eyes rather wistful with yearning—

> Into this little lane, and why not knowing,
> Nor whence, like water willy-nilly flowing,
> And out again—like dust along the waste,
> I know not whither, willy-nilly blowing.

At thirty she now repeated it, the smile still there, but the lips not quite so red, the chin a trifle firmer, the grey eyes stronger, clearer, but charged with a more wistful and a deeper yearning.

It was her turn of mind, imaginative, introspective, querulous perhaps, that made the bit of running lane significant. Food with the butcher's and baker's carts came to her from its eastern, its arriving end, as she called it; news with the postman, adventure with rare callers. Youth, hope, excitement, all these came from the sunrise. Thence came likewise spring and summer, flowers, butterflies, the swallows. The fairies, in her childhood, had come that way too, their silver feet and gossamer wings brightening the summer dawns; and it was but a year ago that Dick Messenger, his car stirring a cloud of thick white dust, had also come into her life from the space beyond the sunrise.

She sat thinking about him now—how he had suddenly appeared out of nothing that warm June morning, asked her permission about some engineering business on the neighbouring big estate over the hill, given her a dog-rose and a bit of fern-leaf, and eventually gone away with her promise when he left. Out of the eastern end he appeared; into the western end he vanished.

For there was this departing end as well, where the lane curved out of sight into the space behind the yellow sunset. In this direction went all that left her life. Her parents, each in turn, had taken that way to the churchyard. Spring, summer, the fading butterflies, the restless swallows, all left her round that western curve. Later the fairies followed them, her dreams one by one, the vanishing years as well—and now her youth, swifter, ever swifter, into the region where the sun dipped nightly among pale rising stars, leaving her brief strip of life colder, more and more unlit.

Just beyond this end she imagined shadows.

She saw Dick's car whirling towards her, whirling away again, making for distant Mexico, where his treasure lay. In the interval he had found that treasure and realized it. He was now coming back again. He had landed in England yesterday.

Seated in her deck-chair on the veranda, she watched the sun sink to the level of the hazel trees. The last swallows already flashed their dark wings against the fading gold. Over that western end to-morrow or the next day, amid a cloud of whirling white dust, would emerge, again out of nothingness, the noisy car that brought Dick Messenger back to her, back from the Mexican expedition that ensured his great new riches, back into her heart and life. In the other direction she would depart a week or so later, her life in his keeping, and his in hers... and the feet of their children, in due course, would run up and down the mysterious lane in search of flowers, butterflies, excitement, in search of life.

She wondered... and as the light faded her wondering grew deeper. Questions that had lain dormant for twelve months became audible suddenly. Would Dick be satisfied with this humble cottage which meant so much to her that she felt she could never, never leave it? Would not his money, his new position, demand palaces elsewhere? He was ambitious. Could his ambitions set an altar of sacrifice to his love? And she—could she, on the other hand, walk happy and satisfied along the western curve, leaving her lane finally behind her, lost, untravelled, forgotten? Could she face this sacrifice for him? Was he, in a word, *the* man whose appearance out of the sunrise she had been watching and waiting for all these hurrying, swift years?

She wondered. Now that the decisive moment was so near, unhappy doubts assailed her. Her wondering grew deeper, spread, enveloped, penetrated her being like a gathering darkness. And the sun sank lower, dusk crept along the hedgerows, the flowers closed their little burning eyes. Shadows passed hand in hand along the familiar bend that was so short, so soon travelled over and left behind that a mistake must ruin all its sweetest joy. To wander down it with a companion to whom its flowers, its butterflies, its shadows brought no full message, must turn it chill, dark, lonely, colourless... Her thoughts slipped on thus into a soft inner reverie born of that scented twilight hour of honeysuckle and wild roses, born too of her deep self-questioning, of wonder, of yearning unsatisfied.

The lane, meanwhile, produced its customary few figures, moving homewards through the dusk. She knew them well, these familiar figures of the countryside, had known them from childhood onwards—labourers, hedgers, ditchers and the like, with whom now, even in her reverie, she exchanged the usual friendly greetings across the wicket-gate. This time, however, she gave but her mind to them, her heart absorbed with its own personal and immediate problem.

Melancey had come and gone; old Averill, carrying his hedger's sickle-knife, had followed; and she was vaguely looking for Hezekiah Purdy, bent with years and rheumatism, his tea-pail always rattling, his shuffling feet making a sorry dust, when the figure she did not quite recognize came into view, emerging unexpectedly from the sunride end. Was it Purdy? Yes—no—yet, if not, who was it? Of course it must be Purdy. Yet while the others, being homeward bound, came naturally from west to east, with this new figure it was otherwise, so that he was half-way down the curve before she fully realized him. Out of the eastern end the man drew nearer, a stranger therefore; out of the unknown regions where the sun rose, and where no shadows were, he moved towards her down the deserted lane, perhaps a trespasser, an intruder possibly, but certainly an unfamiliar figure.

Without particular attention or interest, she watched him drift nearer down her little semi-private lane of dream, passing leisurely from east to west, the mere fact that he was there establishing an intimacy that remained at first unsuspected. It was her eye that watched him, not her mind. What was he doing here, where going, whither come, she wondered vaguely, the lane both his background and his starting-point? A little by-way, after all, this haunted lane. The real world, she knew, swept down the big high-road beyond, unconscious of the humble folk its unimportant tributary served. Suddenly the burden of the years assailed her. Had she, then, missed life by living here?

Then, with a little shock, her heart contracted as she became aware of two eyes fixed upon her in the dusk. The stranger had already reached the wicket-gate and now stood leaning against it, staring at her over its spiked wooden top. It was certainly not old Purdy. The blood rushed back into her heart again as she returned the gaze. He was watching her with a curious intentness, with an odd sense of authority almost, with something that persuaded her instantly of a definite purpose in his being there. He was waiting for her—expecting her to come down and speak with him, as she had spoken with the others. Of this, her little habit, he made use, she felt. Shyly, half-nervously, she left her deck-chair and went slowly down the short gravel path between the flowers, noticing meanwhile that his clothes were ragged, his hair unkempt, his face worn and ravaged as by want and suffering, yet that his eyes were curiously young. His eyes, indeed, were full brown smiling eyes, and it was the surprise of his youth that impressed her chiefly. That he could be tramp or trespasser left her. She felt no fear.

She wished him "Good evening" in her calm, quiet voice, adding with sympathy, "And who are you, I wonder? You want to ask me something?" It flashed across her that his shabby clothing was somehow a disguise. Over his shoulder hung a faded sack. "I can do something for you?" she pursued inquiringly, as was her kindly custom. "If you are hungry, thirsty, or—"

It was the expression of vigour leaping into the deep eyes that stopped her. "If you need clothes," she had been going to add. She was not frightened, but suddenly she paused, gripped by a wonder she could not understand.

And his first words justified her wonder. "I have something for you," he said, his voice faint, a kind of stillness in it as though it came through distance. Also, though this she did not notice, it was an educated voice, and it was the absence of surprise that made this detail too natural to claim attention. She had expected it. "Something to give you. I have brought it for you," the man concluded.

"Yes," she replied, aware, again without comprehension, that her courage and her patience were both summoned to support her. "Yes," she repeated more faintly, as though this was all natural, inevitable, expected. She saw that the sack was now lifted from his shoulder and that his hand plunged into it, as it hung apparently loose and empty against the gate. His eyes, however, never for one instant left her own. Alarm, she was able to remind herself, she did not feel. She only recognized that this ragged figure laid something upon her spirit she could not fathom, yet was compelled to face.

His next words startled her. She drew, if unconsciously, upon her courage:

"A dream."

The voice was deep, yet still with the faintness as of distance in it. His hand, she saw, was moving slowly from the empty sack. A strange attraction, mingled with pity, with yearning too, stirred deeply in her. The face, it seemed, turned soft, the eyes glowed with some inner fire of feeling. Her heart now beat unevenly.

"Something—to—sell to me," she faltered, aware that his glowing eyes upon her made her tremble. The same instant she was ashamed of the words, knowing they were uttered by a portion of her that resisted, and this was not the language he deserved.

He smiled, and she knew her resistance a vain make-believe he pierced too easily, though he let it pass in silence.

"There is, I mean, a price—for every dream," she tried to save herself, conscious delightfully that her heart was smiling in return.

The dusk enveloped them, the corncrakes were calling from the fields, the scent of honeysuckle and wild roses lay round her in a warm wave of air, yet at the same time she felt as if her naked soul stood side be side with this figure in the infinitude of space beyond the sunrise end. The golden stars hung calm and motionless above them. "That price"—his answer fell like a summons she had actually expected—"you pay to another, not to me." The voice grew fainter, farther away, dropping through empty space behind her, "All dreams are but a single dream. You pay that price to—"

Her interruption slipped spontaneously from her lips, its inevitable truth a prophecy:

"To myself!"

He smiled again, but this time he did not answer. His hand, instead, now moved across the gate towards her.

And before she quite realized what had happened, she was holding a little object he had passed across to her. She had taken it, obeying, it seemed, an inner compulsion and authority which were inevitable, foreordained. Lowering her face she examined it in the dusk—a small green leaf of fern—fingered it with tender caution as it lay in her palm, gazed for some seconds closely at the tiny thing.... When she looked up again the stranger, the seller of dreams, as she now imagined him, had moved some yards away from the gate, and was moving still, a leisurely quiet tread that stirred no dust, a shadowy outline soft with dusk and starlight, moving towards the sunrise end, whence he had first appeared.

Her heart gave a sudden leap, as once again the burden of the years assailed her. Her words seemed driven out: "Who are you? Before you go—your name! What is your name?"

His voice, now faint with distance as he melted from sight against the dark fringe of hazel trees, reached her but indistinctly, though its meaning was somehow clear:

"The dream," she heard like a breath of wind against her ear, "shall bring its own name with it. I wait..." Both sound and figure trailed off into the unknown space beyond the eastern end, and, leaning against the wicket-gate as usual, the white dust settling about his heavy boots, the tea-pail but just ceased from rattling, was—old Purdy.

Unless the mind can fix the reality of an event in the actual instant of its happening, judgment soon dwindles into a confusion between memory and argument. Five minutes later, when old Purdy had gone has way again, she found herself already wondering, reflecting, questioning. Yearning had perhaps conjured with emotion to fashion both voice and figure out of imagination, out of this perfumed dusk, out of the troubled heart's desire. Confusion in time had further helped to metamorphose old Purdy into some legendary shape that had stolen upon her mood of reverie from the shadows of her beloved lane.... Yet the dream she had accepted from a stranger hand, a little fern leaf, remained at any rate to shape a delightful certainty her brain might criticize while her heart believed. The fern leaf assuredly was real. A fairy gift! Those who eat of this fern-seed, she remembered as she sank into sleep that night, shall see the fairies! And, indeed, a few hours later she walked in dream along the familiar curve between the hedges, her own childhood taking her by the hand as she played with the flowers, the butterflies, the glad swallows beckoning while they flashed. Without the smallest sense of surprise or unexpectedness, too, she met at the eastern end—two figures. They stood, as she with her childhood stood, hand in hand, the seller of dreams and her lover, waiting since time began, she realized, waiting with some great unuttered question on their lips. Neither addressed her, neither spoke a word. Dick looked at her, ambition, hard and restless, shining in his eyes; in the eyes of the other—dark, gentle, piercing, but extraordinarily young for all the ragged hair about the face, the shabby clothes, the ravaged and unkempt appearance—a brightness as of the coming dawn.

A choice, she understood, was offered to her; there was a decision she must make. She realized, as though some great wind blew it into her from outer space, another, a new standard to which her judgment must inevitably conform, or admit the purpose of her life evaded finally. The same moment she knew what her decision was. No hesitation touched her. Calm, yet trembling, her courage and her patience faced the decision and accepted it. The hands then instantly fell apart, unclasped. One figure turned and vanished down the lane towards the departing end, but with the other, now hand in hand, she rose floating, gliding without effort, a strange bliss in her heart, to meet the sunrise.

"He has awakened... so he cannot stay," she heard, like a breath of wind that whispered into her ear. "I, who bring you this dream—I wait."

She did not wake at once when the dream was ended, but slept on long beyond her accustomed hour, missing thereby Melancey, Averill, old Purdy as they passed the wicket-gate in the early hours. She woke, however, with a new clear knowledge of herself, of her mind and heart, to all of which in simple truth to her own soul she must conform. The fern-seed she placed in a locket attached to a fine gold chain about her neck. During the long, lonely, expectant yet unsatisfied years that followed she wore it day and night.

2

She had the curious feeling that she remained young. Others grew older, but not she. She watched her contemporaries slowly give the signs, while she herself held stationary. Even those younger than herself went past her, growing older in the ordinary way, whereas her heart, her mind, even her appearance, she felt certain, hardly aged at all. In a room full of people she felt pity often as she read the signs in their faces knowing her own unchanged. Their eyes were burning out but hers burned on. It was neither vanity nor delusion, but an inner conviction she could not alter.

The age she held to was the year she had received the fern-seed from old Purdy, or rather, from an imaginary figure her reverie had set momentarily in old Purdy's place. That figure of her reverie, the dream that followed, the subsequent confession to Dick Messenger, meeting his own half-way—these marked the year when she stopped growing older. To that year she seemed chained, gazing into the sunrise end—waiting, ever waiting.

Whether in her absent-minded reverie she had actually plucked the bit of fern herself, or whether, after all, old Purely had handed it to her, was not a point that troubled her. It was in her locket about her neck still, day and night. The seller of dreams was an established imaginative reality in her life. Her heart assured her she would meet him again one day.

She waited. It was very curious, it was rather pathetic. Men came and went, she saw her chances pass; her answer was invariably "No."

The break came suddenly, and with devastating effect. As she was dressing carefully for the party, full of excited anticipation like some young girl still, she saw looking out upon her from the long mirror a face of plain middle-age. A blackness rose about her. It seemed the mirror shattered. The long, long dream, at any rate, fell in a thousand broken pieces at her feet. It was perhaps the ball dress, perhaps the flowers in her hair; it may have been the low-cut gown that betrayed the neck and throat, or the one brilliant jewel that proved her eyes now dimmed beside it—but most probably it was the tell-tale hands, whose ageing no artifice ever can conceal. The middle-aged woman, at any rate, rushed from the glass and claimed her.

It was a long time, too, before the signs of tears had been carefully obliterated again, and the battle with herself—to go or not to go—was decided by clear courage. She would not send a hurried excuse of illness, but would take the place where she now belonged. She saw herself, a fading figure, more than half-way now towards the sunset end, within sight even of the shadowed emptiness that lay beyond the sun's dipping edge. She had lingered overlong, expecting a dream to confirm a dream; she had been oblivious of the truth that the lane went rushing just the same. It was now too late. The speed increased. She had waited, waited for nothing. The seller of dreams was a myth. No man could need her as she now was.

Yet the chief ingredient in her decision was, oddly enough, itself a sign of youth. A party, a ball, is ever an adventure. Fate, with her destined eyes aglow, may be bidden too, waiting among the throng, waiting for that very one who hesitates whether to go or not to go. Who knows what the evening may bring forth? It was this anticipation, faintly beckoning, its voice the merest echo of her shadowy youth, that tipped the scales between an evening of sleepless regrets at home and hours of neglected loneliness, watching the young fulfil the happy night. This and her courage weighed the balance down against the afflicting weariness of her sudden disillusion.

Therefore she went, her aunt, in whose house she was a visitor, accompanying her. They arrived late, walking under the awning alone into the great mansion. Music, flowers, lovely dresses, and bright happy faces filled the air about them. The dancing feet, the flashing eyes, the swing of the music, the throng of graceful figures expressed one word—pleasure. Pleasure, of course, meant youth. Beneath the calm summer stars youth realized itself prodigally, reckless of years to follow. Under the same calm stars, some fifty miles away in Kent, her stretch of deserted lane flowed peacefully, never pausing, passing relentlessly out into unknown space beyond the edge of the world. A girl and a middle-aged woman bravely watched both scenes.

"Dreadfully overcrowded," remarked her prosaic aunt. "When I was a young thing there was more taste—always room to dance, at any rate."

"It is a rabble rather," replied the middle-aged woman, while the girl added, "but I enjoy it." She had enjoyed one duty-dance with an elderly man to whom her aunt had introduced her. She now sat watching the rabble whirl and laugh. Her friend, behind unabashed lorgnettes, made occasional comments.

"There's Mabel. Look at her frock, will you—the naked back. The way he holds her, too!"

She looked at Mabel Messenger, exactly her own age, wife of the successful engineer, yet bearing herself almost like a girl.

"*He's* away in Mexico, as usual," went on her aunt, "with somebody else, also as usual."

"I don't envy her," mentioned the middle-aged woman, while the girl added, "but she did well for herself, anyhow."

"It's a mistake to wait too long," was a suggestion she did not comment on.

The host's brother came up and carried off her aunt. She was left alone. An old gentleman dropped into the vacated chair. Only in the centre of the brilliantly lit room was there dancing now; people stood and talked in animated throngs, every seat along the walls, every chair and sofa in alcove corners occupied. The landing outside the great flung doors was packed; some, going on elsewhere, were already leaving, but others arriving late still poured up the staircase. Her loneliness remained unnoticed; with many other women, similarly stationed behind the whirling, moving dancers, she sat looking on, an artificial smile of enjoyment upon her face, but the eyes empty and unlit.

Two pictures she watched simultaneously—the gay ballroom and the lane that ran east and west.

Midnight was past and supper over, though she had not noticed it. Her aunt had disappeared finally, it seemed. The two pictures filled her mind, absorbed her. What she was feeling was not clear, for there was confusion in her between the two scenes somewhere—as though the brilliant ballroom lay set against the dark background of the lane beneath the quiet stars. The contrast struck her. How calm and lovely the night lane seemed against this feverish gaiety, this heat, this artificial perfume, these exaggerated clothes. Like a small, rapid cinema-picture the dazzling ballroom passed along the dark throat of the deserted lane. A patch of light, alive with whirling animalculæ, it shone a moment against the velvet background of the midnight country-side. It grew smaller and smaller. It vanished over the edge of the departing end. It was gone.

Night and the stars enveloped her, and her eyes became accustomed to the change, so that she saw the sandy strip of lane, the hazel bushes, the dim outline of the cottage. Her naked soul, it seemed again, stood facing an infinitude. Yet the scent of roses, of dew-soaked grass came to her. A blackbird was whistling in the hedge. The eastern end showed itself now more plainly. The tops of the trees defined themselves. There came a glimmer in the sky, an early swallow flashed past against a streak of pale sweet gold. Old Purdy, his tea-pail faintly rattling, a stir of thick white dust about his feet, came slowly round the curve. It was the sunrise.

A deep, passionate thrill ran through her body from head to feet. There was a clap beside her—in the air it seemed—as though the wings of the early swallow had flashed past her very ear, or the approaching sunrise called aloud. She turned her head—along the brightening lane, but also across the gay ballroom. Old Purdy, straightening up his bent shoulders, was gazing over the wicket-gate into her eyes.

Something quivered. A shimmer ran fluttering before her sight. She trembled. Over the crowd of intervening heads, as over the spiked top of the little gate, a man was gazing at her.

Old Purdy, however, did not fade, nor did his outline wholly pass. There was this confusion between two pictures. Yet this man who gazed at her was in the London ballroom. He was so tall and straight. The same moment her aunt's face appeared below his shoulder, only just visible, and he turned his head, but did not turn his eyes, to listen to her. Both looked her way; they moved, threading their way towards her. It meant an introduction coming. He had asked for it.

She did not catch his name, so quickly, yet so easily and naturally the little formalities were managed, and she was dancing. The same sweet, dim confusion was about her. His touch, his voice, his eyes combined extraordinarily in a sense of complete possession to which she yielded utterly. The two pictures, moreover, still held their place. Behind the glaring lights ran the pale sweet gold of a country dawn; woven like a silver thread among the strings she heard the blackbirds whistling; in the stale, heated air lay the subtle freshness of a summer sunrise. Their dancing feet bore them along in a flowing motion that curved from east to west.

They danced without speaking; one rhythm took them; like a single person they glided over the smooth, perfect floor, and, more and more to her, it was as if the floor flowed with them, bearing them along. Such dancing she had never known. The strange sweetness of the confusion that half-entranced her increased—almost as though she lay upon her partner's arms and that he bore her through the air. Both the sense of weight and the touch of her feet on solid ground were gone delightfully. The London room grew hazy, too; the other figures faded; the ceiling, half transparent, let through a filtering glimmer of the dawn. Her thoughts—surely he shared them with her—went out floating beneath this brightening sky. There was a sound of wakening birds, a smell of flowers.

They had danced perhaps five minutes when both stopped abruptly as with one accord.

"Shall we sit it out—if you've no objection?" he suggested in the very instant that the same thought occurred to her. "The conservatory, among the flowers," he added, leading her to the corner among scented blooms and plants, exactly as she herself desired. There were leaves and ferns about them in the warm air. The light was dim. A streak of gold in the sky showed through the glass. But for one other couple they were alone.

"I have something to say to you," he began. "You must have thought it curious—I've been staring at you so. The whole evening I've been watching you."

"I—hadn't noticed," she said truthfully, her voice, as it were, not quite her own. "I've not been dancing—only once, that is."

But her heart was dancing as she said it. For the first time she became aware of her partner more distinctly—of his deep, resonant voice, his soldierly tall figure, his deferential, almost protective manner. She turned suddenly and looked into his face. The clear, rather penetrating eyes reminded her of someone she had known.

At the same instant he used her thought, turning it in his own direction. "I can't remember, for the life of me," he said quietly, "where I have seen you before. Your face is familiar to me, oddly familiar—years ago—in my first youth somewhere."

It was as though he broke something to her gently—something he was sure of and knew positively, that yet might shock and startle her.

The blood rushed from her heart as she quickly turned her gaze away. The wave of deep feeling that rose with a sensation of glowing warmth troubled her voice. "I find in you, too, a faint resemblance to—someone I have met," she murmured. Without meaning it she let slip the added words, "when I was a girl."

She felt him start, but he saved the situation, making it ordinary again by obtaining her permission to smoke, then slowly lighting his cigarette before he spoke.

"You must forgive me," he put in with a smile, "but your name, when you were kind enough to let me be introduced, escaped me. I did not catch it."

She told him her surname, but he asked in his persuasive yet somehow masterful way for the Christian name as well. He turned round instantly as she gave it, staring hard at her with meaning, with an examining intentness, with open curiosity. There was a question on his lips, but she interrupted, delaying it by a question of her own. Without looking at him she knew and feared his question. Her voice just concealed a trembling that was in her throat.

"My aunt," she agreed lightly, "is incorrigible. Do you know I didn't catch yours either? Oh—I meant your surname," she added, confusion gaining upon her when he mentioned his first name only.

He became suddenly more earnest, his voice deepened, his whole manner took on the guise of deliberate intention backed by some profound emotion that he could no longer hide. The music, which had momentarily ceased, began again, and a couple, who had been sitting out diagonally across from them, rose and went out. They were now quite alone. The sky was brighter.

"I must tell you," he went on in a way that compelled her to look up and meet his intent gaze. "You really must allow me. I feel sure somehow you'll understand. At any rate," he added like a boy, "you won't laugh."

She believes she gave the permission and assurance. Memory fails her a little here, for as she returned his gaze, it seemed a curious change came stealing over him, yet at first so imperceptibly, so vaguely, that she could not say when it began, nor how it happened.

"Yes," she murmured, "please—" The change defined itself. She stopped dead.

"I know now where I've seen you before. I remember." His voice vibrated like a wind in big trees. It enveloped her.

"Yes," she repeated in a whisper, for the hammering of her heart made both a louder tone or further words impossible. She knew not what he was going to say, yet at the same time she knew with accuracy. Her eyes gazed helplessly into his. The change absorbed her. Within his outline she watched another outline grow. Behind the immaculate evening clothes a ragged, unkempt figure rose. A worn, ravaged face with young burning eyes peered through his own. "Please, please," she whispered again very faintly. He took her hand in his.

His voice came from very far away, yet drawing nearer, and the scene about them faded, vanished. The lane that curved east and west now stretched behind him, and she sat gazing towards the sunrise end, as years ago when the girl passed into the woman first.

"I knew—a friend of yours—Dick Messenger," he was saying in this distant voice that yet was close beside her, "knew him at school, at Cambridge, and later in Mexico. We worked in the same mines together, only he was contractor and I was—in difficulties. That made no difference. He—he told me about a girl—of his love and admiration, an admiration that remained, but a love that had already faded."

She saw only the ragged outline within the well-groomed figure of the man who spoke. The young eyes that gazed so piercingly into hers belonged to him, the seller of her dream of years before. It was to this ragged stranger in her lane she made her answer

"I, too, now remember," she said softly. "Please go on."

"He gave me his confidence, asking me where his duty lay, and I told him that the real love comes once only; it knows no doubt, no fading. I told him this—"

"We both discovered it in time," she said to herself, so low it was scarcely audible, yet not resisting as he laid his other hand upon the one he already held.

"I also told him there was only one true dream," the voice continued, the inner face drawing nearer to the outer that contained it. "I asked him, and he told me—everything. I knew all about this girl. Her picture, too, he showed me."

The voice broke off. The flood of love and pity, of sympathy and understanding that rose in her like a power long suppressed, threatened tears, yet happy, yearning tears like those of a girl, which only the quick, strong pressure of his hands prevented.

"The—little painting—yes, I know it," she faltered.

"It saved me," he said simply. "It changed my life. From that moment I began—living decently again—living for an ideal." Without knowing that she did so, the pressure of her hand upon his own came instantly. "He—he gave it to me," the voice went on, "to keep. He said he could neither keep it himself nor destroy it. It was the day before he sailed. I remember it as yesterday. I said I must give him something in return, or it would cut friendship. But I had nothing in the world to give. We were in the hills. I picked a leaf of fern instead. 'Fernseed,' I told him, 'it will make you see the fairies and find your true dream.' I remember his laugh to this day—a sad, uneasy laugh. 'I shall give it to her,' he told me, 'when I give her my difficult explanation.' But I said, 'Give it with my love, and tell her that I wait.' He looked at me with surprise, incredulous. Then he said slowly, 'Why not? If—if only you hadn't let yourself go to pieces like this!'"

An immensity of clear emotion she could not understand passed over her in a wave. Involuntarily she moved closer against him. With her eyes unflinchingly upon his own, she whispered: "You were hungry, thirsty, you had no clothes.... You waited!"

"You're reading my thoughts, as I knew one day you would." It seemed as if their minds, their bodies too, were one, as he said the words. "You, too—you waited." His voice was low.

There came a glow between them as of hidden fire; their faces shone; there was a brightening as of dawn upon their skins, within their eyes, lighting their very hair. Out of this happy sky his voice floated to her with the blackbird's song:

"And that night I dreamed of you. I dreamed I met you in an English country lane."

"We did," she murmured, as though it were quite natural.

"I dreamed I gave you the fern leaf—across a wicket-gate—and in front of a little house that was our home. In my dream—I handed to you—a dream—"

"You did." And as she whispered it the two figures merged into one before her very eyes. "See," she added softly, "I have it still. It is in my locket at this moment, for I have worn it day and night through all these years of waiting." She began fumbling at her chain.

He smiled. "Such things," he said gently, "are beyond me rather. I have found you. That's all that matters. That"—he smiled again—"is real at any rate."

"A vision," she murmured, half to herself and half to him, "I can understand. A dream, though wonderful, is a dream. But the little fern you gave me," drawing the fine gold chain from her bosom, "the actual leaf I have worn all these years in my locket!"

He smiled as she held the locket out to him, her fingers feeling for the little spring. He shook his head, but so slightly she did not notice it.

"I will prove it to you," she said. "I must. Look!" she cried, as with trembling hand she pressed the hidden catch. "There! There!"

With heads close together they bent over. The tiny lid flew open. And as he took her for one quick instant in his arms the sun flashed his first golden shaft upon them, covering them with light. But her exclamation of incredulous surprise he smothered with a kiss. For inside the little locket there lay—nothing. It was quite empty.

"VENGEANCE IS MINE"

I

An active, vigorous man in Holy orders, yet compelled by heart trouble to resign a living in Kent before full middle age, he had found suitable work with the Red Cross in France; and it rather pleased a strain of innocent vanity in him that Rouen, whence he derived his Norman blood, should be the scene of his activities.

He was a gentle-minded soul, a man deeply read and thoughtful, but goodness perhaps his out-standing quality, believing no evil of others. He had been slow, for instance, at first to credit the German atrocities, until the evidence had compelled him to face the appalling facts. With acceptance, then, he had experienced a revulsion which other gentle minds have probably also experienced—a burning desire, namely, that the perpetrators should be fitly punished.

This primitive instinct of revenge—he called it a lust—he sternly repressed; it involved a descent to lower levels of conduct irreconcilable with the progress of the race he so passionately believed in. Revenge pertained to savage days. But, though he hid away the instinct in his heart, afraid of its clamour and persistency, it revived from time to time, as fresh horrors made it bleed anew. It remained alive, unsatisfied; while, with its analysis, his mind strove unconsciously. That an intellectual nation should deliberately include frightfulness as a chief item in its creed perplexed him horribly; it seemed to him conscious spiritual evil openly affirmed. Some genuine worship of Odin, Wotan, Moloch lay still embedded in the German outlook, and beneath the veneer of their pretentious culture. He often wondered, too, what effect the recognition of these horrors must have upon gentle minds in other men, and especially upon imaginative minds. How did they deal with the fact that this appalling thing existed in human nature in the twentieth century? Its survival, indeed, caused his belief in civilization as a whole to waver. Was progress, his pet ideal and cherished faith, after all a mockery? Had human nature not advanced...?

His work in the great hospitals and convalescent camps beyond the town was tiring; he found little time for recreation, much less for rest; a light dinner and bed by ten o'clock was the usual way of spending his evenings. He had no social intercourse, for everyone else was as busy as himself. The enforced solitude, not quite wholesome, was unavoidable.

He found no outlet for his thoughts. Firsthand acquaintance with suffering, physical and mental, was no new thing to him, but this close familiarity, day by clay, with maimed and broken humanity preyed considerably on his mind, while the fortitude and cheerfulness shown by the victims deepened the impression of respectful, yearning wonder made upon him. They were so young, so fine and careless, these lads whom the German lust for power had robbed of limbs, and eyes, of mind, of life itself. The sense of horror grew in him with cumulative but unrelieved effect.

With the lengthening of the days in February, and especially when March saw the welcome change to summer time, the natural desire for open air asserted itself. Instead of retiring early to his dingy bedroom, he would stroll out after dinner through the ancient streets. When the air was not too chilly, he would prolong these outings, starting at sunset, and coming home beneath the bright mysterious stars. He knew at length every turn and winding of the old-world alleys, every gable, every tower and spire, from the *Vieux Marché*, where Joan of Arc was burnt, to the busy quays, thronged now with soldiers from half a dozen countries. He wandered on past grey gateways of crumbling stone that marked the former banks of the old tidal river. An English army, five centuries ago, had camped here among reeds and swamps, besieging the Norman capital, where now they brought in supplies of men and material upon modern docks, a mighty invasion of a very different kind. Imaginative reflection was his constant mood.

But it was the haunted streets that touched him most, stirring some chord his ancestry had planted in him. The forest of spires thronged the air with strange stone flowers, silvered by moonlight as though white fire streamed from branch and petal; the old church towers soared; the cathedral touched the stars. After dark the modern note, paramount in the daylight, seemed hushed; with sunset it underwent a definite nightchange. Although the darkened streets kept alive in him the menace of fire and death, the crowding soldiers, dipped to the face in shadow, seemed somehow negligible; the leaning roofs and gables hid them in a purple sea of mist that blurred their modern garb, steel weapons, and the like. Shadows themselves, they entered the being of the town, their feet moved silently; there was a hush and murmur; the brooding buildings absorbed them easily.

Ancient and modern, that is, unable successfully to mingle, let fall grotesque, incongruous shadows on his thoughts. The spirit of mediæval days stole over him, exercising its inevitable sway upon a temperament already predisposed to welcome it. Witchcraft and wonder, pagan superstition and speculation, combined with an ancestral tendency to weave a spell, half of acceptance, half of shrinking, about his imaginative soul in which poetry and logic seemed otherwise fairly balanced. Too weary for critical judgment to discern clear outlines, his mind, during these magical twilight walks, became the playground of opposing forces, some power of dreaming, it seems, too easily in the ascendant. The soul of ancient Rouen, stealing beside his footsteps in the dusk, put forth a shadowy hand and touched him.

This shadowy spell he denied as far as in him lay, though the resistance offered by reason to instinct lacked true driving power. The dice were loaded otherwise in such a soul. His own blood harked back unconsciously to the days when men were tortured, broken on the wheel, walled up alive, and burnt for small offences. This shadowy hand stirred faint ancestral memories in him, part instinct, part desire. The next step, by which he saw a similar attitude flowering full blown in the German frightfulness, was too easily made to be rejected. The German horrors made him believe that this ignorant cruelty of olden days threatened the world now in a modern, organized shape that proved its survival in the human heart. Shuddering, he fought against the natural desire for adequate punishment, but forgot that repressed emotions sooner or later must assert themselves. Essentially irrepressible, they may force an outlet in distorted fashion. He hardly recognized, perhaps, their actual claim, yet it was audible occasionally. For, owing to his loneliness, the natural outlet, in talk and intercourse, was denied.

Then, with the softer winds, he yearned for country air. The sweet spring days had come; morning and evening were divine; above the town the orchards were in bloom. Birds blew their tiny bugles on the hills. The midday sun began to burn.

It was the time of the final violence, when the German hordes flung like driven cattle against the Western line where free men fought for liberty. Fate hovered dreadfully in the balance that spring of 1918; Amiens was threatened, and if Amiens fell, Rouen must be evacuated. The town, already full, became now over-full. On his way home one evening he passed the station, crowded with homeless new arrivals. "Got the wind up, it seems, in Amiens!" cried a cheery voice, as an officer he knew went by him hurriedly. And as he heard it the mood of the spring became of a sudden uppermost. He reached a decision. The German horror came abruptly closer. This further overcrowding of the narrow streets was more than he could face.

It was a small, personal decision merely, but he *must* get out among woods and fields, among flowers and wholesome, growing things, taste simple, innocent life again. The following evening he would pack his haversack with food and tramp the four miles to the great *Forêt Verte*—

delicious name!—and spend the night with trees and stars, breathing his full of sweetness, calm and peace. He was too accustomed to the thunder of the guns to he disturbed by it. The song of a thrush, the whistle of a blackbird, would easily drown that. He made his plan accordingly.

The next two nights, however, a warm soft rain was falling; only on the third evening could he put his little plan into execution. Anticipatory enjoyment, meanwhile, lightened his heart; he did his daily work more competently, the spell of the ancient city weakened somewhat. The shadowy hand withdrew.

2

Meanwhile, a curious adventure intervened.

His good and simple heart, disciplined these many years in the way a man should walk, received upon its imaginative side, a stimulus that, in his ease, amounted to a shock. That a strange and comely woman should make eyes at him disturbed his equilibrium considerably; that he should enjoy the attack, though without at first responding openly—even without full comprehension of its meaning—disturbed it even more. It was, moreover, no ordinary attack.

He saw her first the night after his decision when, in a mood of disappointment due to the rain, he came down to his lonely dinner. The room, he saw, was crowded with new arrivals, from Amiens, doubtless, where they had "the wind up." The wealthier civilians had fled for safety to Rouen. These interested and, in a measure, stimulated him. He looked at them sympathetically, wondering what dear home-life they had so hurriedly relinquished at the near thunder of the enemy guns, and, in so doing, he noticed, sitting alone at a small table just in front of his own— yet with her back to him—a woman.

She drew his attention instantly. The first glance told him that she was young and well-to-do; the second, that she was unusual. What precisely made her unusual he could not say, although he at once began to study her intently. Dignity, atmosphere, personality, he perceived beyond all question. She sat there with an air. The becoming little hat with its challenging feather slightly tilted, the set of the shoulder, the neat waist and slender outline; possibly, too, the hair about the neck, and the faint perfume that was wafted towards him as the serving girl swept past, combined in the persuasion. Yet he felt it as more than a persuasion. She attracted him with a subtle vehemence he had never felt before. The instant he set eyes upon her his blood ran faster. The thought rose passionately in him, almost the words that phrased it: "I wish I knew her."

This sudden flash of response his whole being certainly gave—to the back of an unknown woman. It was both vehement and instinctive. He lay stress upon its instinctive character; he was aware of it before reason told him why. That it was "in response" he also noted, for although he had not seen her face and she assuredly had made no sign, he felt that attraction which involves also invitation. So vehement, moreover, was this response in him that he felt shy and ashamed the same instant, for it almost seemed he had expressed his thought in audible words. He flushed, and the flush ran through his body; he was conscious of heated blood as in a youth of twenty-five, and when a man past forty knows this touch of fever he may also know, though he may not recognize it, that the danger signal which means possible abandon has been lit. Moreover, as though to prove his instinct justified, it was at this very instant that the woman turned and stared at him deliberately. She looked into his eyes, and he looked into hers. He knew a moment's keen distress, a sharpest possible discomfort, that after all he *had* expressed his desire audibly. Yet, though he blushed, he did not lower his eyes. The embarrassment passed instantly, replaced by a thrill of strangest pleasure and satisfaction. He knew a tinge of inexplicable dismay as well. He felt for a second helpless before what seemed a challenge in her eyes. The eyes were too compelling. They mastered him.

In order to meet his gaze she had to make a full turn in her chair, for her table was placed directly in front of his own. She did so without concealment. It was no mere attempt to see what lay behind by making a half-turn and pretending to look elsewhere; no corner of the eye business; but a full, straight, direct, significant stare. She looked into his soul as though she called him, he looked into hers as though he answered. Sitting there like a statue, motionless, without a bow, without a smile, he returned her intense regard unflinchingly and yet unwillingly. He made no sign. He shivered again.... It was perhaps ten seconds before she turned away with an air as if she had delivered her message and received his answer, but in those ten seconds a series of singular ideas crowded his mind, leaving an impression that ten years could never efface. The face and eyes produced a kind of intoxication in him. There was almost recognition, as though she said "Ah, there you are! I was waiting; you'll have to come, of course. You must!" And just before she turned away she smiled.

He felt confused and helpless.

The face he described as unusual; familiar, too, as with the atmosphere of some long forgotten dream, and if beauty perhaps was absent, character and individuality were supreme. Implacable resolution was stamped upon the features, which yet were sweet and womanly, stirring an emotion in him that he could not name and certainly did not recognize. The eyes, slanting a little upwards, were full of fire, the mouth voluptuous but very firm, the chin and jaw most delicately modelled, yet with a masculine strength that told of inflexible resolve. The resolution, as a whole, was the most relentless he had ever seen upon a human countenance. It dominated him. "How vain to resist the will," he thought, "that lies behind!" He was conscious of enslavement; she conveyed a message that he must obey, admitting compliance with her unknown purpose.

That some extraordinary wordless exchange was registered thus between them seemed very clear; and it was just at this moment, as if to signify her satisfaction, that she smiled. At his feeling of willing compliance with some purpose in her mind., the smile appeared. It was faint, so faint indeed that the eyes betrayed it rather than the mouth and lips; but it was there; he saw it and he thrilled again to this added touch of wonder and enchantment. Yet, strangest of all, he maintains that with the smile there fluttered over the resolute face a sudden arresting tenderness, as though some wild flower lit a granite surface with its melting loveliness. He was aware in the clear strong eyes of unshed tears, of sympathy, of selfsacrifice he called maternal, of clinging love. It was this tenderness, as of a soft and gracious mother, and this implacable resolution, as of a stern, relentless man, that left upon his receptive soul the strange impression of sweetness yet of domination.

The brief ten seconds were over. She turned away as deliberately as she had turned to look. He found himself trembling with confused emotions he could not disentangle, could not even name; for, with the subtle intoxication of compliance in his soul lay also a vigorous protest that included refusal, even a violent refusal given with horror. This unknown woman, without actual speech or definite gesture, had lit a flame in him that linked on far away and out of sight with the magic of the ancient city's mediæval spell. Both, he decided, were undesirable, both to be resisted.

He was quite decided about this. She pertained to forgotten yet unburied things, her modern aspect a mere disguise, a disguise that some deep unsatisfied instinct in him pierced with ease.

He found himself equally decided, too, upon another thing which, in spite of his momentary confusion, stood out clearly: the magic of the city, the enchantment of the woman, both attacked a constitutional weakness in his blood, a line of least resistance. It wore no physical aspect, breathed no hint of ordinary romance; the mere male and female, moral or immoral touch was wholly absent; yet passion lurked there, tumultuous if hidden, and a tract of consciousness, long untravelled, was lit by sudden ominous flares. His character, his temperament, his calling in life as a former clergyman and now a Red Cross worker, being what they were, he stood on the brink of an adventure not dangerous alone but containing a challenge of fundamental kind that involved his very soul.

No further thrill, however, awaited him immediately. He left his table before she did, having intercepted no slightest hint of desired acquaintanceship or intercourse. He, naturally, made no advances; she, equally, made no smallest sign. Her face remained hidden, he caught no flash of eyes, no gesture, no hint of possible invitation. He went upstairs to his dingy room, and in due course fell asleep. The next day he saw her not, her place in the dining-room was empty; but in the late evening of the following day, as the soft spring sunshine found him prepared for his postponed expedition, he met her suddenly on the stairs. He was going down with haversack and in walking kit to an early dinner, when he saw her coming up; she was perhaps a dozen steps below him; they must meet. A wave of confused, embarrassed pleasure swept him. He realized that this was no chance meeting. She meant to speak to him.

Violent attraction and an equally violent repulsion seized him. There was no escape, nor, had escape been possible, would he have attempted it. He went down four steps, she mounted four towards him; then he took one and she took one. They met. For a moment they stood level, while he shrank against the wall to let her pass. He had the feeling that but for the support of that wall he must have lost his balance and fallen into her, for the sunlight from the landing window caught her face and lit it, and she was younger, he saw, than he had thought, and far more comely. Her atmosphere enveloped him, the sense of attraction and repulsion became intense. She moved past him with the slightest possible bow of recognition; then, having passed, she turned.

She stood a little higher than himself, a step at most, and she thus looked down at him. Her eyes blazed into his. She smiled, and he was aware again of the domination and the sweetness. The perfume of her near presence drowned him; his head swam. "We count upon you," she said in a low firm voice, as though giving a command; "I know... we may. We do." And, before he knew what he was saying, trembling a little between deep pleasure and a contrary impulse that sought to choke the utterance, he heard his own voice answering. "You can count upon me...." And she was already half-way up the next flight of stairs ere he could move a muscle, or attempt to thread a meaning into the singular exchange.

Yet meaning, he well knew, there was.

She was gone; her footsteps overhead had died away. He stood there trembling like a boy of twenty, yet also like a man of forty in whom fires, long dreaded, now blazed sullenly. She had opened the furnace door, the draught rushed through. He felt again the old unwelcome spell; he saw the twisted streets 'mid leaning gables and shadowy towers of a day forgotten; he heard the ominous murmurs of a crowd that thirsted for wheel and scaffold and fire; and, aware of vengeance, sweet and terrible, aware, too, that he welcomed it, his heart was troubled and afraid.

In a brief second the impression came and went; following it swiftly, the sweetness of the woman swept him he forgot his shrinking in a rush of wild delicious pleasure. The intoxication in him deepened. She had recognized him! She had bowed and even smiled; she had spoken, assuming familiarity, intimacy, including him in her secret purposes! It was this sweet intimacy cleverly injected, that overcame the repulsion he acknowledged, winning complete obedience to the unknown meaning of her words. This meaning, for the moment, lay in darkness; yet it was a portion of his own self, he felt, that concealed it of set purpose. He kept it hid, he looked deliberately another way; for, if he faced it with full recognition, he knew that he must resist it to the death. He allowed himself to ask vague questions—then let her dominating spell confuse the answers so that he did not hear them. The challenge to his soul, that is, he evaded.

What is commonly called sex lay only slightly in his troubled emotions; her purpose had nothing that kept step with chance acquaintanceship. There lay meaning, indeed, in her smile and voice, but these were no handmaids to a vulgar intrigue in a foreign hotel. Her will breathed cleaner air; her purpose aimed at some graver, mightier climax than the mere subjection of an elderly victim like himself. That will, that purpose, he felt certain, were implacable as death, the resolve in those bold eyes was not a common one. For, in some strange way, he divined the strong maternity in her; the maternal instinct was deeply, even predominantly, involved; he felt positive that a divine tenderness, deeply outraged, was a chief ingredient too. In some way, then, she needed him, yet not she alone, for the pronoun "we" was used, and there were others with her; in some way, equally, a part of him was already her and their accomplice, an unresisting slave, a willing co-conspirator.

He knew one other thing, and it was this that he kept concealed so carefully from himself. His recognition of it was sub-conscious possibly, but for that very reason true: her purpose was consistent with the satisfaction at last of a deep instinct in him that clamoured to know gratification. It was for these odd, mingled reasons that he stood trembling when she left him on the stairs, and finally went down to his hurried meal with a heart that knew wonder, anticipation, and delight, but also dread.

3

The table in front of him remained unoccupied; his dinner finished, he went out hastily.

As he passed through the crowded streets, his chief desire was to be quickly free of the old mulled buildings and airless alleys with their clinging atmosphere of other days. He longed for the sweet taste of the heights, the smells of the forest whither he was bound. This *Forêt Verte*, he knew, rolled for leagues towards the north, empty of houses as of human beings; it was the home of deer and birds and rabbits, of wild boar too. There would be spring flowers among the brushwood, anemones, celandine, oxslip, daffodils. The vapours of the town oppressed him, the warm and heavy moisture stifled; he wanted space and the sight of clean simple things that would stimulate his mind with lighter thoughts.

He soon passed the Rampe, skirted the ugly villas of modern Bihorel and, rising now with every step, entered the *Route Neuve*. He went unduly fast; he was already above the Cathedral spire; below him the Seine meandered round the chalky hills, laden with war-barges, and across a dip, still pink in the afterglow, rose the blunt Down of Bonsecours with its anti-aircraft batteries. Poetry and violent fact crashed everywhere; he longed to top the hill and leave these unhappy reminders of death behind him. In front the sweet woods already beckoned through the twilight. He hastened. Yet while he deliberately fixed his imagination on promised peace and beauty, an undercurrent ran sullenly in his mind, busy with quite other thoughts. The unknown woman and her singular words, the following mystery of the ancient city, the soft, beating wonder of the two together, these worked their incalculable magic persistently about him. Repression merely added to their power. His mind was a prey to some shadowy, remote anxiety that, intangible, invisible, yet knocked with ghostly fingers upon some door of ancient memory.... He watched the moon rise above the eastern ridge, in the west the afterglow of sunset still hung red. But these did not hold his attention as they normally must have done. Attention seemed elsewhere. The undercurrent bore him down a siding, into a backwater, as it were, that clamoured for discharge.

He thought suddenly, then, of weather, what he called "German weather"—that combination of natural conditions which so oddly favoured the enemy always. It had often occurred to him as strange; on sea and land, mist, rain and wind, the fog and drying sun worked ever on *their* side. The coincidence was odd, to say the least. And now this glimpse of rising moon and sunset sky reminded him unpleasantly of the subject. Legends of pagan weather-gods passed through his mind like hurrying shadows. These shadows multiplied, changed form, vanished and returned. They came and went with incoherence, a straggling stream, rushing from one point to another, maneuvering for position, but all rolled, unguided by his will. The physical exercise filled his brain with blood, and thought danced undirected, picture upon picture driving by, so that soon he slipped from German weather and pagan gods to the witchcraft of past centuries, of its alleged association with the natural powers of the elements, and thus, eventually, to his cherished beliefs that humanity had advanced.

Such remnants of primitive days were grotesque superstition, of course. But had humanity advanced? Had the individual progressed after all? Civilization, was it not the merest artificial growth? And the old perplexity rushed through his mind again—the German barbarity and blood-lust, the savagery, the undoubted sadic impulses, the frightfulness taught with cool calculation by their highest minds, approved by their professors, endorsed by their clergy, applauded by their women even—all the unwelcome, undesired thoughts came flocking back upon him, escorted by the trooping shadows. They lay, these questions, still unsolved within him; it was the undercurrent, flowing more swiftly now, that bore them to the surface. It had acquired momentum; it was leading somewhere.

They were a thoughtful, intellectual race, these Germans; their music, literature, philosophy, their science—how reconcile the opposing qualities? He had read that their herd-instinct was unusually developed, though betraying the characteristics of a low wild savage type—the lupine. It might be true. Fear and danger wakened this collective instinct into terrific activity, making them blind and humourless; they fought best, like wolves, in contact; they howled and whined and boasted loudly all together to inspire terror; their Hymn of Hate was but an elaboration of the wolf's fierce bark, giving them herd-courage; and a savage discipline was necessary to their lupine type.

These reflections thronged his mind as the blood coursed in his veins with the rapid climbing; yet one and all, the beauty of the evening, the magic of the hidden town, the thoughts of German horror, German weather, German gods, all these, even the odd detail that they revived a pagan practice by hammering nails into effigies and idols—all led finally to one blazing centre that nothing could dislodge nor anything conceal; a woman's voice and eyes. To these he knew quite well, was due the undesired intensification of the very mood, the very emotions, the very thoughts he had come out on purpose to escape.

"It is the night of the vernal equinox," occurred to him suddenly, sharp as a whispered voice beside him. He had no notion whence the idea was born. It had no particular meaning, so far as he remembered.

"It had *then*..." said the voice imperiously, rising, it seemed, directly out of the under-current in his soul.

It startled him. He increased his pace. He walked very quickly, whistling softly as he went.

The dusk had fallen when at length he topped the long, slow hill, and left the last of the atrocious straggling villas well behind him. The ancient city lay far below in murky haze and smoke, but tinged now with the silver of the growing moon.

4

He stood now on the open plateau. He was on the heights at last.

The night air met him freshly in the face, so that he forgot the fatigue of the long climb uphill, taken too fast somewhat for his years. He drew a deep draught into his lungs and stepped out briskly.

Far in the upper sky light flaky clouds raced through the reddened air, but the wind kept to these higher strata, and the world about him lay very still. Few lights showed in the farms and cottages, for this was the direct route of the Gothas, and nothing that could help the German hawks to find the river was visible.

His mind cleared pleasantly; this keen sweet air held no mystery; he put his best foot foremost, whistling still, but a little more loudly than before. Among the orchards he saw the daisies glimmer. Also, he heard the guns, a thudding concussion in the direction of the coveted Amiens, where, some sixty miles as the crow flies, they roared their terror into the calm evening skies. He cursed the sound, in the town below it was not audible. Thought jumped then to the men who fired them, and so to the prisoners who worked on the roads outside the hospitals and camps he visited daily. He passed them every morning and night, and the N.C.O. invariably saluted his Red Cross uniform, a salute he returned, when he could not avoid it, with embarrassment.

One man in particular stood out clearly in this memory; he had exchanged glances with him, noted the expression of his face, the number of his gang printed on coat and trousers—"82." The fellow had somehow managed to establish a relationship; he would look up and smile or frown; if the news, from his point of view, was good, he smiled; if it was bad, he scowled; once, insolently enough—when the Germans had taken Albert, Péronne, Bapaume—he grinned.

Something about the sullen, close-cropped face, typically Prussian, made the other shudder. It was the visage of an animal, neither evil nor malignant, even good-natured sometimes when it smiled, yet of an animal that could be fierce with the lust of happiness, ferocious with delight. The sullen savagery of a human wolf lay in it somewhere. He pictured its owner impervious to shame, to normal human instinct as civilized people know these. Doubtless he read his own feelings into it. He could imagine the man doing anything and everything, regarding chivalry and sporting instinct as proof of fear or weakness. He could picture this member of the wolf-pack killing a woman or a child, mutilating, cutting off little hands even, with the conscientious conviction that it was right and sensible to destroy *any* individual of an enemy tribe. It was, to him, an atrocious and inhuman face.

It now cropped up with unpleasant vividness, as he listened to the distant guns and thought of Amiens with its back against the wall, its inhabitants flying—

Ah! Amiens...! He again saw the woman staring into his obedient eyes across the narrow space between the tables. He smelt the delicious perfume of her dress and person on the stairs. He heard her commanding voice, her very words: "We count on you.... I know we can... we do." And her background was of twisted streets, dark alley-ways and leaning gables....

He hurried, whistling loudly an air that he invented suddenly, using his stick like a golf club at every loose stone his feet encountered, making as much noise as possible. He told himself he was a parson and a Red Cross worker. He looked up and saw that the stars were out. The pace made him warm, and he shifted his haversack to the other shoulder. The moon, he observed, now cast his shadow for a long distance on the sandy road.

After another mile, while the air grew sharper and twilight surrendered finally to the moon, the road began to curve and dip, the cottages lay farther out in the dim fields, the farms and barns occurred at longer intervals. A dog barked now and again; he saw cows lying down for the night beneath shadowy fruit-trees. And then the scent in the air changed slightly, and a darkening of the near horizon warned him that the forest had come close.

This was an event. Its influence breathed already a new perfume: the shadows from its myriad trees stole out and touched him. Ten minutes later he reached its actual frontier cutting across the plateau like a line of sentries at attention. He slowed down a little. Here, within sight and touch of his long-desired objective, he hesitated. It stretched, he knew from the map, for many leagues to the north, uninhabited, lonely, the home of peace and silence; there were flowers there, and cool sweet spaces where the moonlight fell. Yet here, within scent and touch of it, he slowed down a moment to draw breath. A forest on the map is one thing; visible before the eyes when night has fallen, it is another. It is real.

The wind, not noticeable hitherto, now murmured towards him from the serried trees that seemed to manufacture darkness out of nothing. This murmur hummed about him. It enveloped him. Piercing it, another sound that was not the guns just reached him, but so distant that he hardly noticed it. He looked back. Dusk suddenly merged in night. He stopped.

"How practical the French are, he said to himself—aloud—as he looked at the road running straight as a ruled line into the heart of the trees. "They waste no energy, no space, no time. Admirable!"

It pierced the forest like a lance, tapering to a faint point in the misty distance. The trees ate its undeviating straightness as though they would smother it from sight, as though its rigid outline marred their mystery. He admired the practical makers of the road, yet sided, too, with the poetry of the trees. He stood there staring, waiting, dawdling.... About him, save for this murmur of the wind, was silence. Nothing living stirred. The world lay extraordinarily still. That other distant sound had died away.

He lit his pipe, glad that the match blew out and the damp tobacco needed several matches before the pipe drew properly. His puttees hurt him a little, he stooped to loosen them. His haversack swung round in front as he straightened up again, he shifted it laboriously to the other shoulder. A tiny stone in his right boot caused irritation. Its removal took a considerable time, for he had to sit down, and a log was not at once forthcoming. Moreover, the laces gave him trouble, and his fingers had grown thick with heat and the knots were difficult to tie....

"There!" He said it aloud, standing up again. "Now at last, I'm ready!" Then added a mild imprecation, for his pipe had gone out while he stooped over the recalcitrant boot, and it had to be lighted once again. "Ah!" he gasped finally with a sigh as, facing the forest for the third time, he shuffled his tunic straight, altered his haversack once more, changed his stick from the right hand to the left—and faced the foolish truth without further pretence.

He mopped his forehead carefully, as though at the same time trying to mop away from his mind a faint anxiety, a very faint uneasiness, that gathered there. Was someone standing near him? Had somebody come close? He listened intently. It was the blood singing in his ears, of course, that curious distant noise. For, truth to tell, the loneliness bit just below the surface of what he found enjoyable. It seemed to him that somebody was coming, someone he could not see, so that he looked back over his shoulder once again, glanced quickly right and left, then peered down the long opening cut through the woods in front—when there came suddenly a roar and a blaze of dazzling light from behind, so instantaneously that he barely had time to obey the instinct of self-preservation and step aside. He actually leapt. Pressed against the hedge, he saw a motor-car rush past him like a whirlwind, flooding the sandy road with fire; a second followed it; and, to his complete amazement, then, a third.

They were powerful, private cars, so-called. This struck him instantly. Two other things he noticed, as they dived down the throat of the long white road—they showed no tail-lights. This made him wonder. And, secondly, the drivers, clearly seen, were women. They were not even in uniform—which made him wonder even more. The occupants, too, were women. He caught the outline of toque and feather—or was it flowers?—against the closed windows in the moonlight as the procession rushed past him.

He felt bewildered and astonished. Private motors were rare, and military regulations exceedingly strict; the danger of spies dressed in French uniform was constant; cars armed with machine guns, he knew, patrolled the countryside in all directions. Shaken and alarmed, he thought of favoured persons fleeing stealthily by night, of treachery, disguise and swift surprise; he thought of various things as he stood peering down the road for ten minutes after all sight and sound of the cars had died away. But no solution of the mystery occurred to him. Down the white throat the motors vanished. His pipe had gone out; he lit it, and puffed furiously.

His thoughts, at any rate, took temporarily a new direction now. The road was not as lonely as he had imagined. A natural reaction set in at once, and this proof of practical, modern life banished the shadows from his mind effectually. He started off once more, oblivious of his former hesitation. He even felt a trifle shamed and foolish, pretending that the vanished mood had not existed. The tobacco had been damp. His boot had really hurt him.

Yet bewilderment and surprise stayed with him. The swiftness of the incident was disconcerting; the cars arrived and vanished with such extraordinary rapidity; their noisy irruption into this peaceful spot seemed incongruous; they roared, blazed, rushed and disappeared; silence resumed its former sway.

But the silence persisted, whereas the noise was gone.

This touch of the incongruous remained with him as he now went ever deeper into the heart of the quiet forest. This odd incongruity of dreams remained.

5

The keen air stole from the woods, cooling his body and his mind; anemones gleamed faintly among the brushwood, lit by the pallid moonlight. There were beauty, calm and silence, the slow breathing of the earth beneath the comforting sweet stars. War, in this haunt of ancient peace, seemed an incredible anachronism. His thoughts turned to gentle happy hopes of a day when the lion and the lamb would yet lie down together, and a little child would lead them without fear. His soul dwelt with peaceful longings and calm desires.

He walked on steadily, until the inflexible straightness of the endless road began to afflict him, and he longed for a turning to the right or left. He looked eagerly about him for a woodland path. Time mattered little; he could wait for the sunrise and walk home "beneath the young grey dawn"; he had food and matches, he could light a fire, and sleep— No!— after all, he would not light a fire, perhaps; he might be accused of signalling to hostile aircraft, or a *garde forestière* might catch him. He would not bother with a fire. The night was warm, he could enjoy himself and pass the time quite happily without artificial heat; probably he would need no sleep at all.... And just then he noticed an opening on his right, where a seductive pathway led in among the trees. The moon, now higher in the sky, lit this woodland trail enticingly; it seemed the very opening he had looked for, and with a thrill of pleasure he at once turned down it; leaving the ugly road behind him with relief.

The sound of his footsteps hushed instantly on the leaves and moss; the silence became noticeable; an unusual stillness followed; it seemed that something in his mind was also hushed. His feet moved stealthily, as though anxious to conceal his presence from surprise. His steps dragged purposely; their rustling through the thick dead leaves, perhaps, was pleasant to him. He was not sure.

The path opened presently into a clearing where the moonlight made a pool of silver, the surrounding brushwood fell away; and in the centre a gigantic outline rose. It was, he saw, a beech tree that dwarfed the surrounding forest by its grandeur. Its bulk loomed very splendid against the sky, a faint rustle just audible in its myriad tiny leaves. Dipped in the moonlight, it had such majesty of proportion, such symmetry, that he stopped in admiration. It was, he saw, a multiple tree, five stems springing with attempted spirals out of an enormous trunk; it was immense; it had a presence, the space framed it to perfection. The clearing, evidently, was a favourite resting place for summer picknickers, a playground, probably, for city children on holiday afternoons; woodcutters, too, had been here recently, for he noticed piled brushwood ready to be carted. It indicated admirably, he felt, the limits of his night expedition. Here he would rest awhile, eat his late supper, sleep perhaps round a small— No! again—a fire he need *not* make; a spark might easily set the woods ablaze, it was against both forest and military regulations. This idea of a fire, otherwise so natural, was distasteful, even repugnant, to him. He wondered a little why it recurred. He noticed this time, moreover, something unpleasant connected with the suggestion of a fire, something that made him shrink; almost a ghostly dread lay hidden in it.

This startled him. A dozen excellent reasons, supplied by his brain, warned him that a fire was unwise; but the true reason, supplied by another part of him, concealed itself with care, as though afraid that reason might detect its nature and fix the label on. Disliking this reminder of his earlier mood, he moved forward into the clearing, swinging his stick aggressively and whistling. He approached the tree, where a dozen thick roots dipped into the earth. Admiring, looking up and down, he paced slowly round its prodigious girth, then stood absolutely still. His heart stopped abruptly, his blood became congealed. He saw something that filled him with a sudden emptiness of terror. On this western side the shadow lay very black; it was between the thick limbs, half stem, half root, where the dark hollows gave easy hiding-places, that he was positive he detected movement. A portion of the trunk had moved.

He stood stock still and stared—not three feet from the trunk—when there came a second movement. Concealed in the shadows there crouched a living form. The movement defined itself immediately. Half reclining, half standing, a living being pressed itself close against the tree, yet fitting so neatly into the wide scooped hollows, that it was scarcely distinguishable from its ebony background. But for the chance movement he must have passed it undetected. Equally, his outstretched fingers might have touched it. The blood rushed from his heart, as he saw this second movement.

Detaching itself from the obscure background, the figure rose and stood before him. It swayed a little, then stepped out into the patch of moonlight on his left. Three feet lay between them. The figure then bent over. A pallid face with burning eyes thrust forward and peered straight into his own.

The human being was a woman. The same instant he recognized the eyes that had stared him out of countenance in the dining-room two nights ago. He was petrified. She stared him out of countenance now.

And, as she did so, the under-current he had tried to ignore so long swept to the surface in a tumultuous flood, obliterating his normal self. Something elaborately built up in his soul by years of artificial training collapsed like a house of cards, and he knew himself undone.

"They've got me...!" flashed dreadfully through his mind. It was, again, like a message delivered in a dream where the significance of acts performed and language uttered, concealed at the moment, is revealed much later only.

"After all—they've got me...!"

6

The dialogue that followed seemed strange to him only when looking back upon it. The element of surprise again was negligible if not wholly absent, but the incongruity of dreams, almost of nightmare, became more marked. Though the affair was unlikely, it was far from incredible. So completely were this man and woman involved in some purpose common to them both that their talk, their meeting, their instinctive sympathy at the time, seemed natural. The same stream bore them irresistibly towards the same far sea. Only, as yet, this common purpose remained concealed. Nor could he define the violent emotions that troubled him. Their exact description was in him, but so deep that he could not draw it up. Moonlight lay upon his thought, merging clear outlines.

Divided against himself, the cleavage left no authoritative self in control; his desire to take an immediate decision resulted in a confused struggle, where shame and pleasure, attraction and revulsion mingled painfully. Incongruous details tumbled helter-skelter about his mind: for no obvious reason, he remembered again his Red Cross uniform, his former holy calling, his nationality too; he was a servant of mercy, a teacher of the love of God; he was an English gentleman. Against which rose other details, as in opposition, holding just beyond the reach of words, yet rising, he recognized well enough, from the bed-rock of the human animal, whereon a few centuries have imposed the thin crust of refinement men call civilization. He was aware of joy and loathing.

In the first few seconds he knew the clash of a dreadful fundamental struggle, while the spell of this woman's strange enchantment poured over him, seeking the reconciliation he himself could not achieve. Yet the reconciliation *she* sought meant victory or defeat; no compromise lay in it. Something imperious emanating from her already dominated the warring elements towards a coherent whole. He stood before her, quivering with emotions he dared not name. Her great womanhood he recognized, acknowledging obedience to her undisclosed intentions. And this idea of coming surrender terrified him. Whence came, too, that queenly touch about her that made him feel he should have sunk upon his knees?

The conflict resulted in a curious compromise. He raised his hand; he saluted; he found very ordinary words.

"You passed me only a short time ago," he stammered, "in the motors. There were others with you—"

"Knowing that you would find us and come after. We count on your presence and your willing help." Her voice was firm as with unalterable conviction. It was persuasive too. He nodded, as though acquiescence seemed the only course.

"We need your sympathy; we must have your power too."

He bowed again. "My power!" Something exulted in him. But he murmured only. It was natural, he felt; he gave consent without a question.

Strange words he both understood and did not understand. Her voice, low and silvery, was that of a gentle, cultured woman, but command rang through it with a clang of metal, terrible behind the sweetness. She moved a little closer, standing erect before him in the moonlight, her figure borrowing something of the great tree's majesty behind her. It was incongruous, this gentle and yet sinister air she wore. Whence came, in this calm peaceful spot, the suggestion of a wild and savage background to her? Why were there tumult and oppression in his heart, pain, horror, tenderness and mercy, mixed beyond disentanglement? Why did he think already, but helplessly, of escape, yet at the same time burn to stay? Whence came again, too, a certain queenly touch he felt in her?

"The gods have brought you," broke across his turmoil in a half whisper whose breath almost touched his face. "You belong to us."

The deeps rose in him. Seduced by the sweetness and the power, the warring divisions in his being drew together. His under-self more and more obtained the mastery she willed. Then something in the French she used flickered across his mind with a faint reminder of normal things again.

"Belgian—" he began, and then stopped short, as her instant rejoinder broke in upon his halting speech and petrified him. In her voice sang that triumphant tenderness that only the feminine powers of the Universe may compass: it seemed the sky sang with her, the mating birds, wild flowers, the south wind and the running streams. All these, even the silver birches, lent their fluid, feminine undertones to the two pregnant words with which she interrupted him and completed his own unfinished sentence:

"—and mother."

With the dreadful calm of an absolute assurance, she stood and watched him.

His understanding already showed signs of clearing. She stretched her hands out with a passionate appeal, a yearning gesture, the eloquence of which should explain all that remained unspoken. He saw their grace and symmetry, exquisite in the moonlight, then watched them fold together in an attitude of prayer. Beautiful mother hands they were; hands made to smooth the pillows of the world, to comfort, bless, caress, hands that little children everywhere must lean upon and love—perfect symbol of protective, self-forgetful motherhood.

This tenderness he noted; he noted next—the strength. In the folded hands he divined the expression of another great world-power, fulfilling the implacable resolution of the mouth and eyes. He was aware of relentless purpose, more—of merciless revenge, as by a protective motherhood outraged beyond endurance. Moreover, the gesture held appeal; these hands, so close that their actual perfume reached him, sought his own in help. The power in himself as man, as male, as father—this was required of him in the fulfillment of the unknown purpose to which this woman summoned him. His understanding cleared still more.

The couple faced one another, staring fixedly beneath the giant beech that overarched them. In the dark of his eyes, he knew, lay growing terror. He shivered, and the shiver passed down his spine, making his whole body tremble. There stirred in him all excitement he loathed, yet welcomed, as the primitive male in him, answering the summons, reared up with instinctive, dreadful glee to shatter the bars that civilization had so confidently set upon its freedom. A primal emotion of his underbeing, ancient lust that had too long gone hungry and unfed, leaped towards some possible satisfaction. It was incredible; it was, of course, a dream. But judgment wavered; increasing terror ate his will away. Violence and sweetness, relief and degradation, fought in his soul, as he trembled before a power that now slowly mastered him. This glee and loathing formed their ghastly partnership. He could have strangled the woman where she stood. Equally, he could have knelt and kissed her feet.

The vehemence of the conflict paralysed him.

"A mother's hands..." he murmured at length, the words escaping like bubbles that rose to the surface of a seething cauldron and then burst.

And the woman smiled as though she read his mind and saw his little trembling. The smile crept down from the eyes towards the mouth; he saw her lips part slightly; he saw her teeth.

But her reply once more transfixed him. Two syllables she uttered in a voice of iron:

"Louvain."

The sound acted upon him like a Word of Power in some Eastern fairy tale. It knit the present to a past that he now recognized could never die.

Humanity had *not* advanced. The hidden source of his secret joy began to glow. For this woman focused in him passions that life had hitherto denied, pretending they were atrophied, and the primitive male, the naked savage rose up, with glee in its lustful eyes and blood upon its lips. Acquired civilization, a pitiful mockery, split through its thin veneer and fled.

"Belgian... Louvain... Mother . ." he whispered, yet astonished at the volume of sound that now left his mouth. His voice had a sudden fullness. It seemed a cave-man roared the words.

She touched his hand, and he knew a sudden intensification of life within him; immense energy poured through his veins; a mediæval spirit used his eyes; great pagan instincts strained and urged against his heart, against his very muscles. He longed for action.

And he cried aloud: "I am with you, with you to the end!"

Her spell had vivified beyond all possible resistance that primitive consciousness which is ever the bed-rock of the human animal.

A racial memory, inset against the forest scenery, flashed suddenly through the depths laid bare. Below a sinking moon dark figures flew in streaming lines and groups; tormented cries went down the wind; he saw torn, blasted trees that swayed and rocked; there was a leaping fire, a gleaming knife, an altar. He saw a sacrifice.

It flashed away and vanished. In its place the woman stood, with shining eyes fixed on his face, one arm outstretched, one hand upon his flesh. She shifted slightly, and her cloak swung open. He saw clinging skins wound closely about her figure; leaves, flowers and trailing green hung from her shoulders, fluttering down the lines of her triumphant physical beauty. There was a perfume of wild roses, incense, ivy bloom, whose subtle intoxication drowned his senses. He saw a sparkling girdle round the waist, a knife thrust through it tight against the hip. And his secret joy, the glee, the pleasure of some unlawful and unholy lust leaped through his blood towards the abandonment of satisfaction.

The moon revealed a glimpse, no more. An instant he saw her thus, half savage and half sweet, symbol of primitive justice entering the present through the door of vanished centuries.

The cloak swung back again, the outstretched hand withdrew, but from a world he knew had altered.

To-day sank out of sight. The moon shone pale with terror and delight on Yesterday.

7

Across this altered world a faint new sound now reached his ears, as though a human wail of anguished terror trembled and changed into the cry of some captured helpless animal. He thought of a wolf apart from the comfort of its pack, savage yet abject. The despair of a last appeal was in the sound. It floated past, it died away. The woman moved closer suddenly.

"All is prepared," she said, in the same low, silvery voice; "we must not tarry. The equinox is come, the tide of power flows. The sacrifice is here; we hold him fast. We only awaited you." Her shining eyes were raised to his. "Your soul is with us now?" she whispered.

"My soul is with you."

"And midnight," she continued, "is at hand. We use, of course, their methods. Henceforth the gods—their old-world gods—shall work on our side. They demand a sacrifice, and justice has provided one."

His understanding cleared still more then; the last veil of confusion was drawing from his mind. The old, old names went thundering through his consciousness—Odin, Wotan, Moloch—accessible ever to invocation and worship of the rightful kind. It seemed as natural as though he read in his pulpit the prayer for rain, or gave out the hymn for those at sea. That was merely an empty form, whereas this was real. Sea, storm and earthquake, all natural activities, lay under the direction of those elemental powers called the gods. Names changed, the principle remained.

"Their weather shall be ours," he cried, with sudden passion, as a memory of unhallowed usages he had thought erased from life burned in him; while, stranger still, resentment stirred—revolt—against the system, against the very deity he had worshipped hitherto. For these had never once interfered to help the cause of right; their feebleness was now laid bare before his eyes. And a two-fold lust rose in him. "Vengeance is ours!" he cried in a louder voice, through which this sudden loathing of the cross poured hatred. "Vengeance and justice! Now bind the victim! Bring on the sacrifice!"

"He is already bound." And as the woman moved a little, the curious erection behind her caught his eye—the piled brushwood he had imagined was the work of woodmen, picnickers, or playing children. He realized its true meaning.

It now delighted and appalled him. Awe deepened in him, a wind of ice passed over him. Civilization made one more fluttering effort. He gasped, he shivered; he tried to speak. But no words came. A thin cry, as of a frightened child, escaped him.

"It is the only way," the woman whispered softly. "We steal from them the power of their own deities." Her head flung back with a marvellous gesture of grace and power; she stood before him a figure of perfect womanhood, gentle and tender, yet at the same time alive and cruel with the passions of an ignorant and savage past. Her folded hands were clasped, her face turned heavenwards. "I am a mother," she added, with amazing passion, her eyes glistening in the moonlight with unshed tears. "To all"—she glanced towards the forest, her voice rising to a wild and poignant cry—"all, all of us are mothers!"

It was then the final clearing of his understanding happened, and he realized his own part in what would follow. Yet before the realization he felt himself not merely ineffective, but powerless. The struggling forces in him were so evenly matched that paralysis of the will resulted. His dry lips contrived merely a few words of confused and feeble protest.

"Me!" he faltered. "My help—?"

"Justice," she answered; and though softly uttered, it was as though the mediæval towers clanged their bells. That secret, ghastly joy again rose in him; admiration, wonder, desire followed instantly. A fugitive memory of Joan of Arc flashed by, as with armoured wings, upon the moonlight. Some power similarly heroic, some purpose similarly inflexible, emanated from this woman, the savour of whose physical enchantment, whose very breath, rose to his brain like incense. Again he shuddered. The spasm of secret pleasure shocked him. He sighed. He felt alert, yet stunned.

Her words went down the wind between them:

"You are so weak, you English," he heard her terrible whisper, "so nobly forgiving, so fine, yet so forgetful. You refuse the weapon *they* place within your hands." Her face thrust closer, the great eyes blazed upon him. "If we would save the children"—the voice rose and fell like wind—"we must worship where they worship, we must sacrifice to their savage deities...."

The stream of her words flowed over him with this nightmare magic that seemed natural, without surprise. He listened, he trembled, and again he sighed. Yet in his blood there was sudden roaring.

"....Louvain... the hands of little children... we have the proof," he heard, oddly intermingled with another set of words that clamoured vainly in his brain for utterance; "the diary in his own handwriting, his gloating pleasure... the little, innocent hands...."

"Justice is mine!" rang through some fading region of his now fainting soul, but found no audible utterance.

"....Mist, rain and wind... the gods of German Weather.... We all... are mothers...."

"I will repay," came forth in actual words, yet so low he hardly heard the sound. But the woman heard.

"*We!*" she cried fiercely, "*we* will repay!"...

"God!" The voice seemed torn from his throat. "Oh God—*my* God!"

"*Our* gods," she said steadily in that tone of iron, "are near. The sacrifice is ready. And *you*—servant of mercy, priest of a younger deity, and English—you bring the power that makes it effectual. The circuit is complete."

It was perhaps the tears in her appealing eyes, perhaps it was her words, her voice, the wonder of her presence; all combined possibly in the spell that finally then struck down his will as with a single blow that paralysed his last resistance. The monstrous, half-legendary spirit of a primitive day recaptured him completely; he yielded to the spell of this tender, cruel woman, mother and avenging angel, whom horror and suffering had flung back upon the practices of uncivilized centuries. A common desire, a common lust and purpose, degraded both of them. They understood one another. Dropping back into a gulf of savage worship that set up idols in the place of God, they prayed to Odin and his awful Crew...

It was again the touch of her hand that galvanized him. She raised him; he had been kneeling in slavish wonder and admiration at her feet. He leaped to do the bidding, however terrible, of this woman who was priestess, queen indeed, of a long-forgotten orgy.

"Vengeance at last!" he cried, in an exultant voice that no longer frightened him. "Now light the fire! Bring on the sacrifice!"

There was a rustling among the nearer branches, the forest stirred; the leaves of last year brushed against advancing feet. Yet before he could turn to see, before even the last words had wholly left his lips, the woman, whose hand still touched his fingers, suddenly tossed her cloak aside, and flinging her bare arms about his neck, drew him with impetuous passion towards her face and kissed him, as with delighted fury of exultant passion, full upon the mouth. Her body, in its clinging skins, pressed close against his own; her heat poured into him. She held him fiercely, savagely, and her burning kiss consumed his modern soul away with the fire of a primal day.

"The gods have given you to us," she cried, releasing him. "Your soul is ours!"

She turned—they turned together—to look for one upon whose last hour the moon now shed her horrid silver.

8

This silvery moonlight fell upon the scene.

Incongruously he remembered the flowers that soon would know the cuckoo's call; the soft mysterious stars shone down; the woods lay silent underneath the sky.

An amazing fantasy of dream shot here and there. "I am a man, an Englishman, a padre!" ran twisting through his mind, as though *she* whispered them to emphasize the ghastly contrast of reality. A memory of his own Kentish village with its Sunday school fled past, his dream of the Lion and the Lamb close after it. He saw children playing on the green.... He saw their happy little hands....

Justice, punishment, revenge—he could not disentangle them. No longer did he wish to. The tide of violence was at his lips, quenching an ancient thirst. He drank. It seemed he could drink forever. These tender pictures only sweetened horror. That kiss had burned his modern soul away.

The woman waved her hand; there swept from the underbrush a score of figures dressed like herself in skins, with leaves and flowers entwined among their flying hair. He was surrounded in a moment. Upon each face he noted the same tenderness and terrible resolve that their commander wore. They pressed about him, dancing with enchanting grace, yet with full-blooded abandon, across the chequered light and shadow. It was the brimming energy of their movements that swept him off his feet, waking the desire for fierce rhythmical expression. His own muscles leaped and ached; for this energy, it seemed, poured into him from the tossing arms and legs, the shimmering bodies whence hair and skins flung loose, setting the very air awhirl. It flowed over into inanimate objects even, so that the trees waved their branches although no wind stirred—hair, skins and hands, rushing leaves and flying fingers touched his face, his neck, his arms and shoulders, catching him away into this orgy of an ancient, sacrificial ritual. Faces with shining eyes peered into his, then sped away; grew in a cloud upon the moonlight; sank back in shadow; reappeared, touched him, whispered, vanished. Silvery limbs gleamed everywhere. Chanting rose in a wave, to fall away again into forest rustlings; there were smiles that flashed, then fainted into moonlight, red lips and gleaming teeth that shone, then faded out. The secret glade, picked from the heart of the forest by the moon, became a torrent of tumultuous life, a whirlpool of passionate emotions Time had not killed.

But it was the eyes that mastered him, for in their yearning, mating so incongruously with the savage grace—in the eyes shone ever tears. He was aware of gentle women, of womanhood, of accumulated feminine power that nothing could withstand, but of feminine power in majesty, its essential protective tenderness roused, as by tribal instinct, into a collective fury of implacable revenge. He was, above all, aware of motherhood—of mothers. And the man, the male, the father in him rose like a storm to meet it.

From the torrent of voices certain sentences emerged; sometimes chanted, sometimes driven into his whirling mind as though big whispers thrust them down his ears. "You are with us to the end," he caught. "We have the proof. And punishment is ours!"

It merged in wind, others took its place:

"We hold him fast. The old gods wait and listen."

The body of rushing whispers flowed like a storm-wind past.

A lovely face, fluttering close against his own, paused an instant, and starry eyes gazed into his with a passion of gratitude, dimming a moment their stern fury with a mother's tenderness: "For the little ones... it is necessary, it is the only way.... Our own children...." The face went out in a gust of blackness, as the chorus rose with a new note of awe and reverence, and a score of throats uttered in unison a single cry: "The raven! The White Horses! His signs! Great Odin hears!"

He saw the great dark bird flap slowly across the clearing, and melt against the shadow of the giant beech; he heard its hoarse, croaking note; the crowds of heads bowed low before its passage. The White Horses he did not see; only a sound as of considerable masses of air regularly displaced was audible far overhead. But the veiled light, as though great thunder-clouds had risen, he saw distinctly. The sky above the clearing where he stood, panting and dishevelled, was blocked by a mass that owned unusual outline. These clouds now topped the forest, hiding the moon and stars. The flowers went out like nightlights blown. The wind rose slowly, then with sudden violence. There was a roaring in the tree-tops. The branches tossed and shook.

"The White Horses!" cried the voices, in a frenzy of adoration. "He is here!"

It came swiftly, this collective mass; it was both apt and terrible. There was an immense footstep. It was there.

Then panic seized him, he felt an answering tumult in himself, the Past surged through him like a sea at flood. Some inner sight, peering across the wreckage of To-day, perceived an outline that in its size dwarfed mountains, a pair of monstrous shoulders, a face that rolled through a full quarter of the heavens. Above the ruin of civilization, now fulfilled in the microcosm of his own being, the menacing shadow of a forgotten deity peered down upon the earth, yet upon one detail of it chiefly—the human group that had been wildly dancing, but that now chanted in solemn conclave about a forest altar.

For some minutes a dead silence reigned; the pouring winds left emptiness in which no leaf stirred; there was a hush, a stillness that could be felt. The kneeling figures stretched forth a level sea of arms towards the altar; from the lowered heads the hair hung down in torrents, against which the naked flesh shone white; the skins upon the rows of backs gleamed yellow. The obscurity deepened overhead. It was the time of adoration. He knelt as well, arms similarly outstretched, while the lust of vengeance burned within him.

Then came, across the stillness, the stirring of big wings, a rustling as the great bird settled in the higher branches of the beech. The ominous note broke through the silence; and with one accord the shining backs were straightened. The company rose, swayed, parting into groups and lines. Two score voices resumed the solemn chant. The throng of pallid faces passed to and fro like great fire-flies that shone and vanished. He, too, heard his own voice in unison, while his feet, as with instinctive knowledge, trod the same measure that the others trod.

Out of this tumult and clearly audible above the chorus and the rustling feet rang out suddenly, in a sweetly fluting tone, the leader's voice:

"'The Fire! But first the hands!"

A rush of figures set instantly towards a thicket where the underbrush stood densest. Skins, trailing flowers, bare waving arms and tossing hair swept past on a burst of perfume. It was as though the trees themselves sped by. And the torrent of voices shook the very air in answer

"The Fire! But first-the hands!"

Across this roaring volume pierced then, once again, that wailing sound which seemed both human and nonhuman—the anguished cry as of some lonely wolf in metamorphosis, apart from the collective safety of the pack, abjectly terrified, feeling the teeth of the final trap, and knowing the helpless feet within the steel. There was a crash of rending boughs and tearing branches. There was a tumult in the thicket, though of brief duration—then silence.

He stood watching, listening, overmastered by a diabolical sensation of expectancy he knew to be atrocious. Turning in the direction of the cry, his straining eyes seemed filled with blood; in his temples the pulses throbbed and hammered audibly. The next second he stiffened into a stone-like rigidity, as a figure, struggling violently yet half collapsed, was borne hurriedly past by a score of eager arms that swept it towards the beech tree, and then proceeded to fasten it in an upright position against the trunk. It was a man bound tight with thongs, adorned with leaves and flowers and trailing green. The face was hidden, for the head sagged forward on the breast, but he saw the arms forced flat against the giant trunk, held helpless beyond all possible escape; he saw the knife, poised and aimed by slender, graceful fingers above the victim's wrists laid bare; he saw the—hands.

"An eye for an eye," he heard, "a tooth for a tooth!" It rose in awful chorus. Yet this time, although the words roared close about him, they seemed farther away, as if wind brought them through the crowding trees from far off.

"Light the fire! Prepare the sacrifice!" came on a following wind; and, while strange distance held the voices as before, a new faint sound now audible was very close. There was a crackling. Some ten feet beyond the tree a column of thick smoke rose in the air; he was aware of heat not meant for modern purposes; of yellow light that was not the light of stars.

The figure writhed, and the face swung suddenly sideways. Glaring with panic hopelessness past the judge and past the hanging knife, the eyes found his own. There was a pause of perhaps five seconds, but in these five seconds centuries rolled by. The priest of To-day looked down into the well of time. For five hundred years he gazed into those twin eyeballs, glazed with the abject terror of a last appeal. They recognized one another.

The centuries dragged appallingly. The drama of civilization, in a sluggish stream, went slowly by, halting, meandering, losing itself, then reappearing. Sharpest pains, as of a thousand knives, accompanied its dreadful, endless lethargy. Its million hesitations made him suffer a million deaths of agony. Terror, despair and anger, all futile and without effect upon its progress, destroyed a thousand times his soul, which yet some hope—a towering, indestructible hope—a thousand times renewed. This despair and hope alternately broke his being, ever to fashion it anew. His torture seemed not of this world. Yet hope survived. The sluggish stream moved onward, forward....

There came an instant of sharpest, dislocating torture. The yellow light grew slightly brighter. He saw the eyelids flicker.

It was at this moment he realized abruptly that he stood alone, apart from the others, unnoticed apparently, perhaps forgotten; his feet held steady; his voice no longer sang. And at this discovery a quivering shock ran through his being, as though the will were suddenly loosened into a new activity, yet an activity that halted between two terrifying alternatives.

It was as though the flicker of those eyelids loosed a spring.

Two instincts, clashing in his being, fought furiously for the mastery.

One, ancient as this sacrifice, savage as the legendary figure brooding in the heavens above him, battled fiercely with another, acquired more recently in human evolution, that had not yet crystallized into permanence. He saw a child, playing in a Kentish orchard with toys and flowers the little innocent hands made living... he saw a lowly manger, figures kneeling round it, and one star shining overhead in piercing and prophetic beauty.

Thought was impossible; he saw these symbols only, as the two contrary instincts, alternately hidden and revealed, fought for permanent possession of his soul. Each strove to dominate him; it seemed that violent blows were struck that wounded physically; he was bruised, he ached, he gasped for breath; his body swayed, held upright only, it seemed, by the awful appeal in the fixed and staring eyes.

The challenge had come at last to final action; the conqueror, he well knew, would remain an integral portion of his character, his soul.

It was the old, old battle, waged eternally in every human heart, in every tribe, in every race, in every period, the essential principle indeed, behind the great world-war. In the stress and confusion of the fight, as the eyes of the victim, savage in victory, abject in defeat—the appealing eyes of that animal face against the tree stared with their awful blaze into his own, this flashed clearly over him. It was the battle between might and right, between love and hate, forgiveness and vengeance, Christ and the Devil. He heard the menacing thunder of "an eye for an eye, a tooth for a tooth," then above its angry volume rose suddenly another small silvery voice that pierced with sweetness:—"Vengeance is mine, I will repay..." sang through him as with unimaginable hope.

Something became incandescent in him then. He realized a singular merging of powers in absolute opposition to each other. It was as though they harmonized. Yet it was through this small, silvery voice the apparent magic came. The words, of course, were his own in memory, but they rose from his modern soul, now reawakening.

He started painfully. He noted again that he stood apart, alone, perhaps forgotten of the others. The woman, leading a dancing throng about the blazing brushwood, was far from him. Her mind, too sure of his compliance, had momentarily left him. The chain was weakened. The circuit knew a break.

But this sudden realization was not of spontaneous origin. His heart had not produced it of its own accord. The unholy tumult of the orgy held him too slavishly in its awful sway for the tiny point of his modern soul to have pierced it thus unaided. The light flashed to him from an outside, natural source of simple loveliness—the singing of a bird. From the distance, faint and exquisite, there had reached him the silvery notes of a happy thrush, awake in the night, and telling its joy over and over again to itself. The innocent beauty of its song came through the forest and fell into his soul...

The eyes, he became aware, had shifted, focusing now upon an object nearer to them. The knife was moving. There was a convulsive wriggle of the body, the head dropped loosely forward, no cry was audible. But, at the same moment, the inner battle ceased and an unexpected climax came. Did the soul of the bully faint with fear? Did the spirit leave him at the actual touch of earthly vengeance? The watcher never knew. In that appalling moment when the knife was about to begin the mission that the fire would complete, the roar of inner battle ended abruptly, and that small silvery voice drew the words of invincible power from his reawakening soul. "Ye do it also unto me..." pealed o'er the forest.

He reeled. He acted instantaneously. Yet before he had dashed the knife from the hand of the executioner, scattered the pile of blazing wood, plunged through the astonished worshippers with a violence of strength that amazed even himself; before he had torn the thongs apart and loosened the fainting victim from the tree; before he had uttered a single word or cry, though it seemed to him he roared with a voice of thousands—he witnessed a sight that came surely from the Heaven of his earliest childhood days, from that Heaven whose God is love and whose forgiveness was taught him at his mother's knee.

With superhuman rapidity it passed before him and was gone. Yet it was no earthly figure that emerged from the forest, ran with this incredible swiftness past the startled throng, and reached the tree. He saw the shape; the same instant it was there; wrapped in light, as though a flame from the sacrificial fire flashed past him over the ground. It was of an incandescent brightness, yet brightest of all were the little outstretched hands. These were of purest gold, of a brilliance incredibly shining.

It was no earthly child that stretched forth these arms of generous forgiveness and took the bewildered prisoner by the hand just as the knife descended and touched the helpless wrists. The thongs were already loosened, and the victim, fallen to his knees, looked wildly this way and that for a way of possible escape, when the shining hands were laid upon his own. The murderer rose. Another instant and the throng must have been upon him, tearing him limb from limb. But the radiant little face looked down into his own; she raised him to his feet; with superhuman swiftness she led him through the infuriated concourse as though he had become invisible, guiding him safely past the furies into the cover of the trees. Close before his eyes, this happened; he saw the waft of golden brilliance, he heard the final gulp of it, as wind took the dazzling of its fiery appearance into space. They were gone....

9

He stood watching the disappearing motor-cars, wondering uneasily who the occupants were and what their business, whither and why did they hurry so swiftly through the night? He was still trying to light his pipe, but the damp tobacco would not burn.

The air stole out of the forest, cooling his body and his mind; he saw the anemones gleam; there was only peace and calm about him, the earth lay waiting for the sweet, mysterious stars. The moon was higher; he looked up; a late bird sang. Three strips of cloud, spaced far apart, were the footsteps of the South Wind, as she flew to bring more birds from Africa. His thoughts turned to gentle, happy hopes of a day when the lion and the lamb should lie down together, and a little child should lead them. War, in this haunt of ancient peace, seemed an incredible anachronism.

He did not go farther; he did not enter the forest; he turned back along the quiet road he had come, ate his food on a farmer's gate, and over a pipe sat dreaming of his sure belief that humanity had advanced. He went home to his hotel soon after midnight. He slept well, and next day walked back the four miles from the hospitals, instead of using the car. Another hospital searcher walked with him. They discussed the news.

"The weather's better anyhow," said his companion. "In our favour at last!"

"That's something," he agreed, as they passed a gang of prisoners and crossed the road to avoid saluting.

"Been another escape, I hear," the other mentioned. "He won't get far. How on earth do they manage it? The M.O. had a yarn that he was helped by a motor-car. I wonder what they'll do to him."

"Oh, nothing much. Bread and water and extra work, I suppose?"

The other laughed. "I'm not so sure," he said lightly. "Humanity hasn't advanced very much in that kind of thing."

A fugitive memory flashed for an instant through the other's brain as he listened. He had an odd feeling for a second that he had heard this conversation before somewhere. A ghostly sense of familiarity brushed his mind, then vanished. At dinner that night the table in front of him was unoccupied. He did not, however, notice that it was unoccupied.

THE END

The Best in Mystery & Noir Fiction Past & Present

1-933586-26-5 **Benjamin Appel** Sweet Money Girl / Life and Death of a Tough Guy $21.95
1-933586-03-6 **Malcolm Braly** Shake Him Till He Rattles / It's Cold Out There $19.95
1-933586-10-9 **Gil Brewer** Wild to Possess / A Taste for Sin $19.95
1-933586-20-6 **Gil Brewer** A Devil for O'Shaugnessy / The Three-Way Split $14.95
1-933586-24-9 **W. R. Burnett** It's Always Four O'Clock / Iron Man $19.95
1-933586-31-1 **Catherine Butzen** Thief of Midnight $15.95
1-933586-38-9 **James Hadley Chase** Come Easy--Go Easy / In a Vain Shadow $19.95
0-9667848-0-4 **Storm Constantine** Oracle Lips (limited hb) $45.00
1-933586-30-3 **Jada M. Davis** One for Hell $19.95
1-933586-43-5 **Bruce Elliot** One is a Lonely Number /
                Elliott Chaze Black Wings Has My Angel $19.95
1-933586-34-6 **Don Elliott** Gang Girl / Sex Bum $19.95
1-933586-12-5 **A. S. Fleischman** Look Behind You Lady / The Venetian Blonde $19.95
1-933568-28-1 **A. S. Fleischman** Danger in Paradise / Malay Woman $19.95
1-933586-35-4 **Orrie Hitt** The Cheaters / Dial "M" for Man $19.95
0-9667848-7-1 **Elisabeth Sanxay Holding** Lady Killer / Miasma $19.95
0-9667848-9-8 **Elisabeth Sanxay Holding** The Death Wish / Net of Cobwebs $19.95
0-9749438-5-1 **Elisabeth Sanxay Holding** Strange Crime in Bermuda / Too Many Bottles $19.95
1-933586-16-8 **Elisabeth Sanxay Holding** The Old Battle Ax / Dark Power $19.95
1-933586-17-6 **Russell James** Underground / Collected Stories $14.95
0-9749438-8-6 **Day Keene** Framed in Guilt / My Flesh is Sweet $19.95
1-933586-33-8 **Day Keene** Dead Dolls Don't Talk / Hunt the Killer / Too Hot to Hold $23.95
1-933586-21-4 **Mercedes Lambert** Dogtown / Soultown $14.95
1-933586-14-1 **Dan Marlowe/Fletcher Flora/Charles Runyon** Trio of Gold Medals $15.95
1-933586-07-9 **Ed by McCarthy & Gorman** Invasion of the Body Snatchers: A Tribute $19.95
1-933586-09-5 **Margaret Millar** An Air That Kills / Do Evil in Return $19.95
1-933586-23-0 **Wade Miller** The Killer / Devil on Two Sticks $17.95
1-933586-27-3 **E. Phillips Oppenheim** The Amazing Judgment / Mr. Laxworthy's Adventures $19.95
0-9749438-3-5 **Vin Packer** Something in the Shadows / Intimate Victims $19.95
1-933586-05-2 **Vin Packer** Whisper His Sin / The Evil Friendship $19.95
1-933586-18-4 **Richard Powell** A Shot in the Dark / Shell Game $14.95
1-933586-19-2 **Bill Pronzini** Snowbound / Games $14.95
0-9667848-8-x **Peter Rabe** The Box / Journey Into Terror $21.95
0-9749438-4-3 **Peter Rabe** Murder Me for Nickels / Benny Muscles In $19.95
1-933586-00-1 **Peter Rabe** Blood on the Desert / A House in Naples $21.95
1-933586-11-7 **Peter Rabe** My Lovely Executioner / Agreement to Kill $19.95
1-933586-22-2 **Peter Rabe** Anatomy of a Killer / A Shroud for Jesso $14.95
1-933586-32-x **Peter Rabe** The Silent Wall / The Return of Marvin Palaver $19.95
0-9749438-2-7 **Douglas Sanderson** Pure Sweet Hell / Catch a Fallen Starlet $19.95
1-933586-06-0 **Douglas Sanderson** The Deadly Dames / A Dum-Dum for the President $19.95
1-933586-29-X **Charlie Stella** Johnny Porno $15.95
1-933586-39-7 **Charlie Stella** Rough Riders $15.95
1-933586-08-7 **Harry Whittington** A Night for Screaming / Any Woman He Wanted $19.95
1-933586-25-7 **Harry Whittington** To Find Cora / Like Mink Like Murder / Body and Passion $23.95
1-933586-36-2 **Harry Whittington** Rapture Alley / Winter Girl / Strictly for the Boys $23.95

STARK HOUSE PRESS
www.StarkHousePress.com

18816943R00249

Made in the USA
San Bernardino, CA
31 January 2015